TO OUTLIVE ETERNITY

AND OTHER STORIES

TO OUTLIVE ETERNITY

AND OTHER STORIES

POUL ANDERSON

A Baen Book

Baen Publishing Enterprises
P.O. Box 1403
Riverdale, NY 10471
www.baen.com

ISBN 10: 1-4165-2113-5
ISBN 13: 978-1-4165-2113-6

Cover art by Bob Eggleton

First Baen printing, March 2007

Distributed by Simon & Schuster
1230 Avenue of the Americas
New York, NY 10020

Library of Congress Cataloging-in-Publication Data: t/k

Printed in the United States of America

10 9 8 7 6 5 4 3 2 1

CONTENTS

TO OUTLIVE ETERNITY

✳ I ✳

Leonora Christine was in the tenth year of her journey when grief came upon her.

An outside watcher, quiescent with respect to the stars, might have seen the thing before she did; for at her speed she must need to run half blind. Even without better instrumental capabilities, he would have known of the disaster a few weeks ahead. But he would have had no way to cry his warning, and it could not have helped her.

And there was no watcher anyhow: only night, bestrewn with multitudinous cold points that were suns, the frosty cataract of the Milky Way and the rare phantom glimmer of a nebula or a sister galaxy. Nine light-years from Sol, the ship was ilimitably alone.

An automatic alarm roused Captain Telander. As he struggled upward from sleep, First Mate Lindgren's voice followed: *"Kors i Herrens namn!"* The horror in it jerked him fully awake. He didn't stop to use the intercom; he left his cabin and ran toward the command bridge. Nor would he have stopped to dress. They didn't trouble much with uniforms, and some of the people aboard were ceasing to trouble with clothes.

But as it happened, he was clad. Lulled by the sameness of nine and a half years—even in ship's time, more than one year—he had been reading a microtaped novel and had dozed off in his chair. And then jaws of the universe snapped shut.

The corridor throbbed faintly around him, an endless pulse of driving energies. Ventilators gusted fresh air in his face, and it was subtly scented with clover. Murals hid metal and plastic with scenes of forest around a sunlit lake. The deck covering was green and springy as grass. But always the ship whispered and shivered, always one remembered the deeps outside.

Lars Telander flung himself up the companionway and into the bridge compartment. Ingrid Lindgren stood near the viewscope. It was not what counted; however massive and sophisticated, it was almost a toy. What truth could tell was in the instruments which glittered across the entire forward bulkhead. But her eyes would not leave it.

The captain brushed past her. The warning which had caused him to be summoned was still blazoned on a screen linked to the primary computer. He read. The breath sucked in between his teeth. As he stood, a slot opened with a click and extruded a printout. He snatched it. His gaze whipped across letters and figures. Quantification—decimal-point detail, after more data had come in and more calculation had been done—the basic Mene, Mene stood unchanged on the screen.

He stabbed the general alarm button. Sirens wailed; echoes went ringing down the corridors. On the intercom he ordered all hands not on duty to report to commons with the passengers. After a moment, harshly, he added that channels would be open so that those people standing watch could also get the news.

"But what are we going to do?" Lindgren cried.

"Very little, I fear." The captain went to the viewscope. "Is anything visible in this?"

"Barely. I think. Fourth quadrant." She clenched her fists and turned from him.

He took for granted that she meant the eyepiece for dead ahead and peered into that. At high magnification, space leaped at him. The scene was somewhat blurred and distorted. Optical circuits did not compensate perfectly for the aberration and Doppler effect experienced when one crowded the speed of light. But he saw starpoints, diamond, amethyst, ruby, topaz, emerald, a Fafnir's hoard. Near the center burned the one called Beta Virginis, whither they were bound, thirty-three years after they said farewell to Earth. It should have looked very like the sun of home, but something of spectral shift remained to tinge it ice blue. And, yes, on the verge of human vision

. . . that wisp? That smoky cloudlet, perhaps to wipe out this ship and these fifty human lives?

Noise broke in on his concentration, shouts, footfalls, the sounds of fear. He straightened. "I had better go aft," he said without tone. Lindgren moved to join him. "No, keep the bridge."

"Why?" Her temper stretched thin and broke. "Regulations?"

"Yes," he nodded. "You have not yet been relieved." A smile of sorts touched his lean face. "Unless you believe in God, regulations are now the only comfort we have."

✳ II ✳

There was no space to spare in space. Every cubic centimeter inside the hull must work. But human beings intelligent and sensitive enough to adventure out here would have gone crazy without some room and privacy. Thus each of the twenty-five cabins could be divided into two cubicles if the pair who occupied it chose. And commons was more than a place for meals and meetings. The largest section was ball court and gymnasium. Offside rooms held tiny bowers, gardens, hobby shops, a swimming pool. Along one bulkhead stood three dream booths.

In this moment, however, none of these things had any more meaning than did drapes or murals or the bright casual clothes of the gathered people. They had not taken time to set out chairs. Everyone stood. Every eye locked onto Telander as he mounted the dais. Nobody stirred save to breathe, but sweat glistened on faces and could be smelled. The murmur of the ship seemed somehow to have grown louder.

The captain hesitated for a moment. They were from so many nations, those men and women—Europe, Asia, America, Africa, Luna. Of course they all knew Swedish; like every other extrasolar expedition, this one went in a Control Authority ship. But some did not know it well. For scientists, particularly, English and Russian remained the chief international tongues. Since Telander happened to be more at ease in the former, he sighed and fell back on it.

"Ladies and gentlemen, I have just gotten grave news. Let me say immediately that our prospects of survival are not in the least hopeless, as far as can be judged from present data and computations. But we are in trouble. The risk was not unforeseen, but by its nature is one that cannot be provided against, at any rate in the present rather early stage of Bussard drive technology—"

"Get to the point, God damn it!" Telander couldn't see who shouted out of the pack, but knew that voice: Williams, the short, cocky North American chemist.

"Quiet, you," said Constable Reymont. Unlike most of them, who stood with male and female hands clutched together, he was alone, a little apart from the rest: a stocky, dark, hard-featured man with a scar seaming his brow. He wore a drab gray coverall and had pinned on his badge of authority.

"You can't—" Someone must have nudged Williams, for he spluttered into silence.

Telander's gaunt body shifted nervously from foot to foot. "Instruments have . . . have detected an obstacle. A small nebula. Extremely small, a mere clot of dust and gas, probably less than a thousand million kilometers across. It is traveling at an abnormal velocity. Perhaps it is the remnant of a larger thing cast out by a supernova, a remnant still held together by hydromagnetic forces. Or perhaps it is a proto-star. I do not know. The fact is, we are going to strike it. In about twenty-four hours, ship's time. What will happen then, I do not know either. With luck, we can ride out the impact and not suffer serious damage. Otherwise . . . well, we knew this journey would have its hazards."

He heard indrawn breaths, like his own on the bridge, and saw eyes go white-rimmed, mouths mutter, fingers trace signs in the air. Quickly, he went on: "We cannot do much to prepare. A little, ah, battening down, yes; but in general, the ship is as taut as possible already. When the moment approaches, most of you will be ordered into shock harness, and everyone will wear space armor. But—the meeting is now open for discussion." Williams's hand rocketed past the shoulder of tall M'Botu.

"Yes?"

One could imagine the red-faced indignation. "Sir! An unmanned probe did make the trip to Beta Virginis first, did it not? It did radio back an assurance that this route was free of danger.

Did it not? Well, then, who is responsible for our blundering into this muck?"

Voices lifted toward a babble. "Quiet!" Charles Reymont called. He didn't speak loud, but he pushed the sound from his lungs in such a way that it struck home. Several resentful glances were cast at him, but the talkers came to order.

"I thought I had explained," Telander said. "The cloud is small, nonluminous, undetectable at any great distance. It has a high velocity. Thus, even if the robot carrier had taken our identical path, the nebulina would have been well offside at the time—more than fifty years ago, remember. Furthermore, we can be quite certain the robot did not go exactly as we are going. Quite apart from the relative motions of the stars, the distance between Sol and Beta Virginis is thirty-two light-years. That is greater than our poor minds can picture. The slightest variation in the curves taken from star to star means a difference of many astronomical units in the middle."

"This thing couldn't have been foreseen," Reymont added. "The odds were against our running into it. But somebody has to draw the long odds now and then."

Telander stiffened. "I did not recognize you, Constable," he said.

Reymont flushed. "Captain, I was trying to expedite matters, so some clotbrains won't keep you there explaining the obvious till we smash."

"No insults to shipmates, Constable. And kindly wait to be recognized before you speak."

"I beg the captain's pardon." Reymont folded his arms and blanked his features.

Telander said with care: "Please do not be afraid to ask questions, however elementary they may seem. You are all supposed to be educated in the theory, at least, of interstellar cosmonautics. But I, whose profession this is, know how strange the paradoxes are, how hard to keep straight in one's mind. Best if everyone understands, as well as may be, exactly what we face . . . Professor Glassgold?"

The molecular biologist lowered her hand and said timidly, almost too low to hear: "Can't we—I mean—nebular objects like that, they are hard vacuums by ordinary standards. Aren't they? And we, we are not only traveling just under the speed of light . . . we are gaining more speed every second. And so more mass. Our mass right now, as far as the rest of the universe is concerned, must be, well, several hundred thousand tons. Which is enormous for a spaceship, even this big a spaceship, isn't it? So why can we not smash right on through? Why should we notice a bit of dust and gas?"

"A good point," Telander said, "and if we are lucky, that is more or less what will happen. Not entirely, though. Remember, we *are* going unbelievably fast, so fast that we can actually use the hydrogen of space for fuel and exhaust. So if we run into a concentration of matter perhaps a hundred times as dense, at this speed, *ja*, we must hope that our forcefields can handle it, and the material components endure the stresses. Engineering extrapolations suggest we will not suffer grave damage. But those are mere extrapolations. There has been no chance as yet to test them. We are, after all, in a pioneering era . . . Dr. Iwamoto?"

"*S-s-sst!* I presume we have no possibility of avoidances? One day ship's time is maybe one month cosmic time, so? We have not time to go around this nebu—nebulina?"

"No, I fear not. We perceive ourselves as accelerating at a steady five gravities. At least, our instruments do, if not our bodies." Telander paused. His mouth twisted. "Excuse me. I maunder. But I want to make certain that everyone is quite clear about the facts. In terms of the outside universe, our acceleration is not constant, but steadily decreasing. Therefore we cannot change course fast. Even a full vector normal to our velocity would not get us far enough aside before the encounter. Ah, Engineer Fedoroff?"

"Might it help if we decelerated? We must keep one or another mode operative at all times, to be sure, but I should think that deceleration now would soften the collision."

"The computer has not made any recommendations yet. Probably the information is insufficient. In any event, the difference would be slight, a few hundred kilometers per second, out of almost three hundred thousand. No, regardless of what we do, we have no choice except to—ah—"

"Bull through," Reymont murmured. Telander heard and cast him a look of annoyance. Reymont didn't seem to mind.

As discussion progressed, though he grew increasingly tense, his eyes flickered from one speaker to the next and the lines between lips and nostrils deepened in his face. When at last Telander said, "Dismissed," the constable pushed almost brutally through the uncertain milling of the rest and plucked the captain's sleeve.

"I think we had better hold a private talk, sir." His Swedish, like his English, was fluent, but marred by a choppy accent. He had been born and raised in the turbulent sublevels of Polyugorsk and somehow made his way to Mars (Telander was sure the means had been devious), where he fought with the Zebras during the troubles. Later he went homeward as far as Luna, joined the Rescue Corps and soon rose to colonel's rank. Telander knew Reymont had done much to organize the police branch of his service along more efficient lines than before, but nonetheless doubted the Authority's wisdom in offering him a berth on this expedition.

The captain said with a chill, "Now is hardly the time to deny anyone access to information, Constable."

"Oh, call our working by ourselves politeness, not to antagonize people," Reymont answered impatiently.

Telander shrugged. "Come with me to the bridge, then. I have no time for special conferences."

Williams and a couple of others seemed to feel differently, but Reymont drove them off with a glare and a bark. Telander must perforce smile a bit as he left the commons. "You do have your uses," he confessed.

"As a parliamentary hatchet man? I think . . . I am afraid . . . there will be more call on me than that," Reymont said.

"Well, conceivably at Beta Virginis. Dubious, though. The robot sent back no indication of intelligent life on the one seemingly Earthlike planet. At most, we might encounter a few savages armed with spears—who would probably not be hostile to us. The dangers are subtler."

Reymont flushed as before. "I'm sorry," Telander added in haste. "I was thinking aloud. No intention of talking to you like a three-year-old. Of course you know all this. I am not entirely convinced by your claim that a degree of military-type discipline may be essential to surviving hazards like possible diseases. But we shall see. Certainly a specialist in rescue and disaster control is going to be welcome."

"You maunder again, Captain," Reymont said. "You're pretty

badly shaken by what we're driving into. I believe our chances are not quite as good as you pretended. Right?"

Telander looked around. The corridor was empty, but still he lowered his voice. "I simply don't know. No Bussard ship has been tested under conditions like those ahead of us. Obviously! We will either get through in reasonable shape or we will die, a quick clean death. I saw no reason to make worse what hours remain for our people, by dwelling on that last."

Reymont scowled. "You overlook a third possibility. We may survive, but in *bad* shape."

"How the devil could we?"

"Hard to say. Perhaps we'll take such a buffeting that people are killed. Key personnel, whom we can ill afford to lose—not that fifty is any great number against a world. In such case, however . . ." Reymont brooded a while. Footsteps thudded beneath the mumble of energies. "They reacted well, on the whole," he said. "They were picked for courage and coolness. In a few instances, though, the picking was not very successful. Suppose we do find ourselves, let's say, disabled. What then? How long will morale last, or sanity itself? I want to be prepared to maintain discipline."

"In that connection," Telander said, cold once more, "please remember that you act under my orders and subject to the articles of the expedition."

"Damnation!" Reymont exploded. "What do you take me for? Some would-be Mao? I'm requesting your authority to deputize a few trustworthy men and *make* them quietly ready for emergencies. I'll issue them weapons, but stunner type. If nothing goes wrong—or if something does but everybody behaves himself—what have we lost?"

"Trust in each other," Telander said.

They had come to the bridge. Reymont entered with his companion, arguing further. Telander made a chopping gesture to shut him up and strode toward the computer. "Anything new?" he asked.

"Yes. The instruments have begun to draw a density map," Lindgren said. She had started on seeing Reymont and now spoke mechanically, not looking at him. Under the short fair hair her face went red and then white. "It is recommended—" She pointed to the screen and the latest printout.

Telander studied them. "Hm. To pass through a less dense region, we should generate a lateral vector by using the Number Three and Four decelerators in conjunction with the entire accelerator system . . . A procedure with dangers of its own. This calls for discussion." He flipped the intercom controls and spoke briefly to the chief engineer and the navigation officer. "In the plotting room. On the double!"

He turned to go. "Captain—" Reymont attempted.

"Not now," Telander said, already on his way.

"But—"

"The answer is no." Telander vanished out the door.

Reymont stood a moment, head lowered and shoulders hunched as if to charge. But he had nowhere to go. Ingrid Lindgren regarded him for a time that shivered—a minute or more, ship's chronology, which was half an hour in the lives of the stars and planets—before she said, quite softly: "What did you want of him?"

"Oh." Reymont turned about. "His order to recruit a small police reserve. He gave me something stupid about my not trusting my fellows."

Their eyes locked. "And not letting them alone in what may be their final hours," she said.

"I know. There's little for them to do, they think, except wait. So they'll spend the time . . . talking; reading favorite poems; eating favorite foods, with maybe a wine ration for this occasion; playing music, opera and ballet and theater tapes, or in some cases, something livelier, maybe bawdier; making love. Especially making love." Reymont spat out his words.

"Is that so bad?" she asked. "If we must go out, shouldn't we do so in a civilized, decent, life-loving way?"

"By being a trifle less civilized, *et cetera*, we might increase our chance of not going out," Reymont snapped.

She bridled. "Are you that afraid to die?"

Reymont shrugged. "No. But I like to live."

"I wonder. You know why I left you. Not your crudeness by itself. You can't help your background. But your unwillingness to do anything about overcoming it. Your caveman jealousy, for instance."

"I do have a poor man's primitive morality," he said. "Frankly, having seen what education and culture make people into, I'm less and less interested in acquiring them."

The spirit gave way in her. Her eyes blurred, she reached out to touch him and said, "Oh, Carl, are we going to fight the same old fight over again, now on perhaps our last day alive?" He stood rigid. She went on, fast: "I admired you. I wanted you to be my life's partner, the father of my children—on Beta Three if we find we really can settle there; on Earth if we have to return. But we're so alone, here between the stars! We have to take what comfort we can, and give it, or we may not survive."

"Unless we can control our own emotions," he said.

"Do you think there was any emotion . . . anything but friendship, and pity, and—and a wish to make sure he did *not* fall seriously in love with me—with Harry? Why, he's hardly more than a boy! And the articles say, in so many words, we can't have formal marriages en route, because we're already too constricted and deprived in every other way—"

"So you and I terminated a relationship which had become unsatisfactory," Reymont said.

"You've found plenty of others since!" she flared.

"For a week or two. So have you. No matter. As you have said, we're both free individuals. Why should I carry a grudge, just because it turned out to be impossible to keep a social relationship with you? I certainly don't want to spoil your fun after you go off watch."

Knuckles stood white on her fists. "What will you be doing?"

"Since I wasn't given authority to deputize," Reymont said, "I'll have to ask for volunteers."

"You can't!"

"I wasn't actually forbidden. I'll only ask a few men, in private, who are likely to agree. Are you going to tell the captain?"

She turned from him. "No," she said. "Please go away."

His boots clacked off down the companion.

✳ III ✳

The ship drove on.

She was not small. This hull must house fifty human beings, with every life-support apparatus required in the ultimate hostility which is outer space. It must carry closed-ecology food, air, and waste-disposal systems, tools, machinery, supplies, spare parts, instruments, references, a pair of auxiliary craft capable of ferrying to and from a planetary surface. For the expedition was not merely going for a look: not at such cost in resources, labor, skill, dreams and years.

At a minimum, these people would spend half a decade in the Beta Virginis System, learning what little they could. But if the third planet where the robot probe was now in orbit, from which it beamed its signals to an Earth that received them a generation later . . . if that planet really was habitable, the expedition never would come home, not even the professional spacemen. They would live out their lives, and belike their children and grandchildren would too, exploring its manifold mysteries and flashing their discoveries to the hungry minds on Earth. For any planet is a *world* infinitely complex, infinitely varied. And this world seemed to be so homelike that the strangenesses it must hold would be yet the more vivid.

The folk of *Leonora Christine* were quite frank in their hope that they could indeed establish a true scientific base. They often speculated that their descendants might have no desire whatsoever to go back: that Beta Three might evolve from base to colony to New Earth to jumping-off place for the next starward leap. For there was no other way by which man could travel far in the galaxy.

Consider: A single light-year is an inconceivable abyss. Denumerable, but inconceivable. At an ordinary speed—say, a good pace for a car in megalopolitan traffic, two kilometers per minute—one would need almost nine million years to cross it. And in Sol's neighborhood, the stars averaged some nine light-years apart. Beta Virginis was thirty-two distant.

Nevertheless, such spaces could be conquered. A ship accelerating continuously at one gravity would have traveled half a light-year in less than one year of time. And she would be moving very near the ultimate velocity, 300,000 kilometers per second. Thereafter she could, so to speak, coast along at one light-year per year: until, within half a light-year of journey's end, she began her deceleration.

But that is an incomplete picture. It takes no account of relativity. Precisely because there is an absolute limiting speed (at which light travels in vacuo; likewise neutrinos) there is an interdependence of space, time, mass, and energy. The tau factor enters the equations.

An outside observer, "at rest," measures the mass of the spaceship. The result he gets is the mass that the ship would have, measured when she was not moving with respect to him, divided by tau. Thus, the faster the ship moves, the more massive she is, as regards the universe at large. She gets this extra mass from the sheer kinetic energy of motion: $e = mc^2$.

Furthermore, if the "stationary" observer could compare the ship's clocks with his own, he would notice a difference. The interlude between two events (such as the birth and the death of a man) measured aboard the ship where they take place, is equal to the interlude which the outsider measures—also divided by tau. One might say that time moves proportionately slower on a starship.

Lengths, however, shrink; the outsider sees the ship shortened in the direction of motion by the factor tau.

But measurements made on shipboard are every bit as valid as those made outside. To a crewman, looking forth at the universe, the stars are compressed and have gained in mass; the distances between them have shriveled; they shine, they evolve at a strangely increase rate. *He* has not changed, not with respect to himself. How could he?

Yet the picture is more complicated even than this. One must bear in mind that the ship has, in fact, been accelerated and will be decelerated in relation to the general background of the cosmos. This takes the whole problem out of special and into general relativity. The ship-star situation is not really symmetrical. When velocities match once again and reunion takes place, the star will have passed through a longer time than the ship did.

So to reach other suns in a reasonable portion of your life expectancy—Accelerate continuously, right up to the interstellar midpoint, when you make turnover and start slowing down *again*. You are limited by the speed of light, which you can never quite reach. But you are not limited in how close you can approach that speed. And thus you have no limit on your tau factor.

Practical problems arise. Where is the mass-energy to do this coming from? It would be useful to run tau down to 1/100. You could cross a light-century in a single year of your own experience. (Though of course you could never regain the century which had passed in the outside universe, during which your friends grew old and died.) But this would also, inevitably, involve a hundredfold increase of mass. Each ton of ship that left the Solar System must become a hundred tons. The thought of carrying enough fuel along from the start is ludicrous.

But who says we must do so? Fuel and reaction mass are there in space! It is pervaded with hydrogen. True, the concentration is not great by ordinary standards—about one atom per cubic centimeter in the galactic vicinity of Sol. But this makes thirty billion atoms per second, striking every square centimeter of the ship's cross-section, when she approaches light speed. The energies are unthinkable. Megaroentgens per hour of hard radiation would be released by impact; and more than a thousand r within an hour are fatal. No material shielding would help. Even supposing it impossibly thick to start with, it would soon be eroded away.

However, in the days of *Leonora Christine* non-material means were available: magnetohydrodynamic fields, whose pulses reached forth across millions of kilometers to seize atoms by their dipoles and control their streaming. These fields did not serve passively, as mere armor. They fed the gas into a ramjet system—if that phrase may be used for the starlike violence of an ongoing thermonuclear reaction, and for the hurricane of plasma cast aft to push the ship nearer and nearer ultimate c.

The forces involved were not just enormous; of necessity, they were precise. They were, indeed, so precise that they could be used within the hull as well as outside. They could operate on the asymmetries of atoms and molecules to produce an acceleration uniform with that of the basic field-generator complex itself. Rather, that uniformity was minus one terrestrial gravity. In effect, weight remained constant aboard, no matter how high the rate at which the ship gained speed.

This cushioning was only possible at relativistic velocities. While tau was small, atoms were insufficiently massive, skittish. But as they approached c, they grew heavier—not to themselves, of course, but to everything else—and so the interplay of fields between ship and universe could establish a stable configuration.

Thus the flight pattern was: A year at one gee, to get near light speed. Switchover to cushioned, high-acceleration mode. The bulk of the journey would be covered in a few months of crew time. At the end, another year must pass while the ship braked to interplanetary velocities and closed in on her goal.

And so, because velocity was never constant, the "twin paradox" did not arise. Tau was no static multiplying factor; it was dynamic; its work on mass, space and time could be observed as a fundamental thing, creating a forever different relationship between men and the universe through which they traveled.

The ship was not small. Yet she was the barest glint of metal, in that vast immaterial web of forces which surrounded and permeated her. She herself no longer generated them. She had initiated the process, when she reached minimum ram-jet speed; but now it was too huge, too swift, it could only be created and sustained by itself. The primary reactor, the venturi tubes, the entire system which thrust her, was not contained in the hull. Most of it was not material at all, but a resultant of cosmic-scale forces. The ship's control devices, under computer direction, were not remotely analogous to autopilots. They were more like catalysts, which judiciously used could affect the course of those appalling reactions, could build them up, in time slow them down and snuff them out—but not fast.

A month of cosmic time, a day of interior time, was too little to swerve around the suddenly perceived nebular pit. Only a few things could be done. Then nothing remained except to wait and see if she survived.

She struck.

It was too swiftly changing a pattern of assault too great. The delicate dance of energies which balanced out acceleration pressures could not be continued. The computer directed a circuit to break, shutting off that particular system, before positive feedback wrecked it.

Spacesuited, strapped into safety cocoons, alone with whatever memory could be kept of a farewell handclasp or kiss, the folk of *Leonora Christine* felt weight shift and change. A troll sat on each chest and choked each throat, darkness went raggedly before eyes. Sweat started forth, hearts slugged, pulses brawled. That noise was answered by the ship, a metal *groan*, a rip and a crash. She was not meant to endure stresses like these. Her safety factors were small; mass was too precious for anything else. And she rammed hydrogen atoms swollen to the heaviness of silicon or phosphorus, dust particles bloated into meteoroids. Velocity had flattened the cloud longitudinally; it was thin—she tore through in seconds. But by that same token, the nebulina was no longer a cloud to her. It was a well-nigh solid wall.

Her outside force-screens absorbed the battering, flung matter aside in turbulent streams, protected the hull from everything except slowdown drag. But reaction was inevitable, on the fields themselves and thus on the devices which, borne outside, produced and controlled them. Frameworks crumpled. Electronic elements fused. Cryogenic liquids boiled from shattered containers.

So one of the thermonuclear fires went out.

The stars saw the event differently. They saw a tenuous murky mist struck by an object incredibly swift and dense. Hydromagnetic forces snatched at atoms, whirled them about, ionized them, battered them together. The object was encompassed in a meteor blaze. During the hour or so of its passage, it drilled a tunnel through the nebulina. That tunnel was wider than the drill, because a shock wave spread outward—and outward and outward and outward, destroying what stability there had been, casting substance forth in gouts and tatters.

A sun and planets had been in embryo here. Now they would never form.

The invader passed. It had not lost much speed. Accelerating once more, it dwindled away toward remoter stars.

✴ IV ✴

Reymont struggled back to consciousness. He could not have been darkened long. Could he? Noise had ceased. Was he deafened? Had the air puffed through some hole into space? Were the screens down, had gamma-colored death already sleeted through him?

No. When he listened, he made out the familiar low beat of energies. Perhaps it even penetrated him a bit louder than formerly. Perhaps the deck's subliminal shiver had quickened a trifle. The hull structure must be loosened by what it had undergone. Yet a fluoropanel shone steadily in his vision. The shadow of his cocoon frame was cast on a bulkhead and had the soft edges which be-tokened ample air. Weight had returned to a single gee. "To hell with melodrama," he heard himself say. His voice sounded far-off, a stranger's. "We got work."

He fumbled with his harness. Muscles throbbed and ached. A trickle of blood ran over his mouth, tasting salty. Or was it sweat? *Nichevo.* He was functional. He crawled free, opened his helmet, sniffed—slight smell of scorch and ozone, nothing serious—and gusted one deep sigh before shedding his spacesuit.

His cabin half was a mess. The brackets holding his meager personal belongings on their shelves had given way and let everything smash across the deck. He found his stunner beneath his regular bunk and strapped it on before sliding aside the panel which cut off the other section.

Chi-yuen Ai-ling's slight form lay inert. Reymont unlatched her faceplate and listened carefully. Her breathing was normal, no wheeze or gurgle to suggest injured lungs. Probably she had just fainted. He left her. Others might need help worse. No strong sentiment was between him and her anyway. After breaking up with Ingrid Lindgren and playing the field a bit, he'd moved in with Chi-yuen on a basis of mutual convenience. She didn't want to appear standoffish, but her consuming interest was in developing some ideas about planetology which the probe data from their goal had suggested to her. A steady relationship with one man kept the rest from making well-intentioned advances. Similarly, he wanted to retire from close human contacts without being obvious about it. Nobody had to know that the panel across this cabin was usually drawn shut.

Ivan Fedoroff was already out in the corridor. "How goes it?" Reymont hailed.

"I am on my way to see," the engineer flung back and ran.

"But—" Reymont cut off his words and pushed into Johann Freiwald's section. The machinist sat slumped on his bunk. "*Raus mit dir,*" Reymont said. "And don't forget your gun."

"I have a headache like carpenters in my skull," Freiwald protested.

"You offered to help me. I thought you were a man."

✳ ✳ ✳

Freiwald cast Reymont a resentful glance, but got into motion. They were busy for the next hour. *Leonora Christine*'s crew was busier yet, inspecting, measuring, conferring low-voiced and apart. But that, at least, gave them little time to feel pain or let terror grow. The scientist majority had no such anodyne. From the fact that they were alive and the ship apparently working as before, they might have drawn cheer . . . only why didn't Captain Telander announce anything? Reymont bullied them into commons, started some making coffee and others attending to the most badly bruised. At last he went alone to the command bridge.

The door was closed. He knocked. Fedoroff's voice boomed, "No admittance. Please wait for the captain to address you."

"This is the constable," Reymont said.

"Well? Haven't you anything better to do than meddle?" Lindgren called.

"I've assembled your passengers," Reymont said. "They're getting over being stunned. They're beginning to realize something isn't quite right. Not knowing what, in their present condition, will crack them open. Maybe we won't be able to glue the pieces back together."

"Go tell them an announcement will be made very soon," Telander said without steadiness.

"You tell them. The intercom's working, isn't it? Tell them you're making exact evaluations of damage, so you can lay out a program for repair as soon as possible. But first let me in to help find words for announcing the disaster."

The door flew wide. Fedoroff grabbed Reymont's arm and tried to pull him through. Reymont yanked free, an expert movement. His other hand smacked stingingly edge-on across the engineer's wrist. "Don't do that," he said. "Not ever." He stepped into the bridge and closed the door himself.

Fedoroff growled and doubled his fists. Lindgren hurried to him and laid a hand on his shoulder. "No, Ivan," she begged. "Please." The Russian subsided, stiffly. They glowered at him in the thrumming stillness: captain, mate, engineer, second engineer, navigation officer, biosystems chief. He looked past them. The console had suffered, some panels twisted, some meters torn loose. "Is that the trouble?" he asked, pointing.

"No," said Boudreau, the navigator. "Instruments can be replaced."

Reymont sought the viewscope. The compensator circuits were also dead. He put his head into the hood of the electronic periscope.

A hemispheric simulacrum sprang from the darkness at him: uncompensated, the view he would actually have seen from outside on the hull. At light speed, aberration distorted the sky. The stars were crowded forward, streaming thinly amidships; and because of Doppler effect they shone steel blue, violet, X-ray. Aft the patterns approached what had once been familiar—but not very closely, and those stars were reddened, like dying embers, as if time were snuffing them out. Reymont shuddered a little and drew his head back into the comforting smallness of the bridge.

"Well?" he said.

"The decelerator system—" Telander swallowed. "We cannot stop."

Reymont's face went altogether expressionless. "Go on," he said.

Fedoroff spoke. His words came flat with fury. "You will recall, I hope, we had activated the decelerators, two of them anyhow, but they belong to an integrated system. Which has to be a separate system from the accelerators, since to slow down we do not push gas through a ram jet but reverse its vector."

Reymont did not stir at the insult. Lindgren caught her breath. After a moment Fedoroff sagged.

"Well," he said tiredly, "the accelerators were operating too. I imagine, on that account, their field strength protected them. But the decelerators—out. Wrecked."

"How?"

"We can only determine that the thermonuclear core is extinguished. In the nature of the case, the decelerators must have been subject to greater stress than the accelerators. I suppose that those forces, reacting through the hydromagnetic fields, broke apart the material assembly which they contain. That assembly, you know, generates and maintains the magnetic bottle which itself contains the ongoing atomic reactions." Fedoroff looked at the deck. "No doubt we could repair the system if we could get at it," he muttered. "But no one can go near the reaction which powers the accelerator and live long enough to do any work. Nor could any remote-control robot we might build. Too much radiation for its circuits. And, of course, we cannot shut off the accelerator. That would mean shutting off the whole set of forcefields which it maintains. Hydrogen bombardment would kill everyone aboard within a minute."

"We have no directional control whatsoever?" Reymont asked, still without tone.

"Yes, yes, we do that. The accelerator pattern can be varied," Boudreau said. "It has four Venturis, and we can damp down some— get a sidewise as well as forward vector—but don't you see, on any path we take, we must continue accelerating or we die."

"Accelerating forever," Telander said.

"At least, though," Lindgren whispered, "we can stay in the galaxy. Swing around and around its heart." Her gaze went to the viewscope, and they knew what she thought of: behind that curtain of blue stars, blackness, intergalactic void, an ultimate aloneness. "At least . . . we can grow old . . . with suns around us. Even if we can't ever touch a planet again."

Telander's features writhed. He cried, "How do I tell our people?"

"We have no hope," Reymont said. It was hardly a question.

"None," Fedoroff said.

"Oh, we can live out our lives," said Pereira. "The biosystems have triple protection. They are intact. We could actually increase their productivity. Do not fear hunger or thirst or suffocation. But I would not advise that we have children."

Lindgren said out of nightmare, staring at a bulkhead as if she could see through: "When the last of us dies—We must put in an automatic cutoff. The ship must not keep on running after our deaths. Let the radiation do what it will, let cosmic friction break her to bits and let the bits drift off into those millions of light-years . . . yonder."

"Why?" asked Reymont like a machine.

"Isn't it obvious? If we throw ourselves into a circular path . . . consuming hydrogen in our accelerator, always traveling faster, running tau down and down as the thousands of years pass . . . we get more massive. We could end by consuming the galaxy."

Telander laughed, a harsh little noise in his throat. "No. Not that," he said. "I have seen calculations. They were made in the early stages of discussing Bussard ships. Someone worried about one getting out of control. But it isn't serious. A spacecraft, any human work, is too insignificant. Tau would have to become something like, well, shall we say ten to the minus twentieth power, before the ship's mass was equal to that of a very small star. And the odds are always astronomical against her colliding with anything more important than a nebula. Besides, the universe won't last so long. No, we are going to die. But the cosmos is safe from us."

"How long can we live?" Lindgren breathed. She cut Pereira off. "I don't mean in ship's time. If you say we can manage to die of old age, I believe you. But I think in a year or two we will stop eating, or cut our throats, or agree to turn the accelerator off, or something."

"Not if I can help it," Reymont snapped.

She gave him a dreary look. "Do you mean you would continue— not just cut off from man, from living Earth, but from the whole universe?"

He regarded her steadily in return. One hand rested on his gun butt. "Don't you have that much guts?" he asked.

"But fifty years inside this flying hell!" she nearly screamed. "How many will that be outside?"

"Easy," Fedoroff said and took her by the shoulders. She clung to him and snatched after air.

Boudreau said, carefully dry: "The time relationship appears to be somewhat academic to us, *n'est-ce pas?* And it depends in any case on what course we take. If we let ourselves continue straight out into space, naturally we will enter a much thinner interstellar medium. The rate of decrease of tau will be proportionately smaller than here, and get smaller as we move beyond this entire group of galaxies. On the other hand, if we stay within our own galaxy, if we try for a cyclical path taking us through the denser hydrogen concentrations, we could soon get a very small tau. We might see billions of years go by. That could be quite fascinating." His smile was forced. "And we have each other. A goodly company. I am with the constable. There are better ways to live, but also worse."

Lindgren hid her face against Fedoroff's breast. He held her with one arm, patted her awkwardly with the other hand. After a while (an hour or so in the history of the stars) she looked up again.

"I'm sorry," she gulped. "You're right. We do have each other." Her glance went from one to the next, ending at Reymont.

"But, but how shall I tell them?" Telander groaned.

"I suggest you do not," Reymont said. "Let the mate break the news."

"What?" Lindgren asked.

"You are a *simpático* person," he said. "I remember."

She moved from Fedoroff's loosened grasp, a step toward Reymont. Abruptly the constable tautened. He stood for a second as if blind, before he whirled from her and confronted the navigator.

"Quick!" he exclaimed. "Do you know—"

"If you think I should—" Lindgren had begun to say.

"Not now," he interrupted, "Boudreau, come here! We have some figuring to do."

❋V❋

The silence went on and on.

Ingrid Lindgren stared from the dais where she stood with Lars Telander, down at her people. They looked back at her. And not a one in that chamber could find words.

Hers had been well chosen. The truth was less savage in her voice than in any man's. But when she came to her planned midpoint—"We have lost Earth, lost Beta Three, lost the mankind we belonged to. We have left to us courage, love and, yes, hope"—she could not continue. She stood with lip caught between teeth, fingers twisted together, and the slow tears ran from her eyes.

Telander bestirred himself. "Ah . . . if you will be so good," he tried, "Kindly listen. A means does not exist . . ." The ship jeered at him in her tone of distant lightnings.

Glassgold broke. She did not weep loudly, but her very struggle to stop made the sound more dreadful. M'Botu, beside her, attempted consolation. He, though, had clamped such stoicism on himself that he might as well have been a robot. Iwamoto withdrew a little from them both, from them all, one could see how he pulled his soul into some nirvana with a lock on its door. Williams shook his fists at the overhead and raved. Another voice, female, started to keen. A woman considered the man with whom she had been keeping company, said, "You, for my whole life?" and stalked from him. He tried to follow her and bumped into a crewman who snarled and offered to fight if he didn't apologize. A seething went through the entire human mass.

"Listen to me," Telander called. "Please listen."

Reymont shook loose the arm which Chi-yuen Ai-ling clutched, in the first row, and jumped onto the dais. "You'll never bring them around that way," he warned *sotto voce*. "You've always worked with disciplined professionals. Let me handle these civilians." He turned on them. "Quiet, there!" Echoes bounced around his roar. "Shut your hatches. Act like adults for once. We haven't the personnel to change your diapers for you."

Williams yelped with resentment. M'Botu growled, rather more meaningfully. Reymont drew his stunner. "Hold your places!" He dropped his vocal volume, but everyone heard him as if he stood beside. "The first one to move gets knocked out. Afterward we'll court-martial him. I'm the constable of this expedition, and I intend to maintain order and effective cooperation." He grinned into their faces. "If you feel I exceed my authority, you're welcome to file a complaint with the appropriate bureau in Stockholm. But for now, you'll listen!"

He tongue-lashed them until their adrenals seemed to be active again. It didn't take long.

"Very well," he finished and turned mild. "We'll say no more about this. I realize you've had a shock which none of you were prepared psychologically to meet. But we've nevertheless got a problem. And it has a solution, too, of sorts, if we can work together. I repeat: if."

Lindgren had swallowed her weeping. "I think I was supposed to—" she said. He shook his head at her and went on:

"We can't repair the decelerators because we can't turn off the accelerators. The reason is, as the mate has explained, we must keep its forcefields for shielding against interstellar gas. So it looks as if we're bottled in this hull. Which was never intended to house us for more than a few years, ship's time. Well, I don't like the prospect either. But I did get an idea. A possibility of escape, if we have the nerve and determination. Navigator Boudreau checked the figures for me. We have a chance of success."

"Get to the point, will you?" yelled Williams.

"I'm glad to see some spirit," Reymont said. "It'll have to be kept under control, though or we are finished. But, to make this as short as possible—afterward Captain Telander and the specialist officers can explain details—the idea is this."

His flat delivery might have been used to describe a new method of bookkeeping. "If we can leave the galaxy, get out where gas is virtually nonexistent in space, we can safely turn off the fields. Then we can go outside of the hull and repair the decelerators. Now astronomical data are not as precise as one might like, but we do know that even in nearby intergalactic space, the medium is too dense. Much thinner than here, of course, but still so thick, in terms of atoms struck per second, as to kill us without protection.

"However, galaxies generally occur in clusters. Our galaxy, the Magellanic Clouds, M31 in Andromeda, and thirteen others, large and small, make one such group. The space it occupies is about six million light-years across. Beyond them is an enormously greater distance to the next galactic family. And in that stretch, we hope, the gas is thin enough for us not to need shielding."

Reymont lifted both hands. He had holstered his gun. "Wait, wait!" he managed to laugh. "Don't bother. I already know what you're trying to say. Ten or twenty million light-years, however far we must go, is impossible. We haven't the tau for it. A ratio of fifty, or a hundred, or a thousand, does us no good whatsoever. Agreed. But remember, we have no limit on our tau. Especially if we widen our scoop fields and, also, pass through parts of this galaxy where gas is denser than here. Both of these we can do. The exact parameters we've been using were determined by our course to Beta Virginis; but the ship is not restricted to them. We could go as high as ten gee, maybe higher.

"So. A rough estimate indicates that if we swing partway around this galaxy and then plunge straight inward through its middle and out the other side—we'd have to make that partial circuit anyway; we can't turn on a ten-*öre* coin at our speed!—we can pick up the necessary tau. Remember, it'll decrease constantly. Our transmit time to Beta would have been much less than we figured on if we hadn't meant to stop there: if, instead of making turnover at midpassage, we had simply kept cramming on the speed. Navigator Boudreau estimates—estimates, mind you; we'll have to gather data as we go; but a good, informed guess—he thinks we can finish with this galaxy and head out beyond it in a little over one year."

"How long cosmic time?" challenged from the gathering.

"Does that matter?" Reymont retorted. "You know the dimensions. The galactic disk is about 100,000 light-years in diameter. At present we're some 30,000 light-years from the center. A quarter million years altogether? Who can tell? It'll depend on what course we take, which in turn will depend on what long-range observation can show us." He stabbed a finger at them. "*I* know. You wonder, what if we hit a cloud such as got us into this miserable situation. Well, I have two answers for that. First, we have to take some chances. But second, as our tau gets smaller and smaller, we'll be able to use regions which are denser and denser. We'll have too much mass to be affected as we were this time. Do you see? The more we have, the more we can get. We may well leave the galaxy with an universe tau on the order of a hundred million. If so, by ship's time we'll be outside of this entire galactic cluster in days!"

"And how do we get back?" Glassgold called—but alert and interested.

"We don't," Reymont admitted. "We keep on till we find another galactic cluster. There we reverse process, decelerate. We'll be helped somewhat by the fact of recession. The other groups are already moving away from ours, you know. We won't have quite so much relative velocity to kill. But eventually we'll be inside a single galaxy. Our tau will be up to something reasonable. We can start looking for a planet where we can live.

"Yes, yes, yes!" he barked into their babble, impatient again. "Millions of years in the future. Millions of light-years from here. The human race most likely extinct . . . in this part of the universe. But can't we start over, in another space and time? Or would you rather sit in this metal shell, feeling sorry for yourselves, till you grow senile and die childless? Unless you can't stand the gaff, and blow out the brains you flatter yourselves you have. I'm for going on, as long as strength lasts. Will anyone who feels differently be so good as to get out of the way?"

He stalked from the dais. "Ah . . . Navigation Officer Boudreau," Telander said into the rising noise. "Will you come here? Ladies and gentlemen, this meeting is now open for questions—"

Chi-yuen Ai-ling caught Reymont's hand. He glanced down at her. "You were marvelous," she exclaimed.

His mouth tightened. He looked from her, from Lindgren, across the group, to the enclosing bulkheads. "Thanks," he replied curtly. "Wasn't anything."

"Oh, but it was. You gave us back hope." She lowered her gaze and colored. "I am honored to share a cabin with you."

He didn't seem to hear. "Anybody could have presented a shiny new idea," he said. "They'll grasp at anything, right now. I only expedited matters. When they accept the program, that's when the real trouble begins."

✳ VI ✳

Forcefields shifted about. They were not mere static tubes and screens. What formed them was the incessant interplay of electromagnetic pulses, whose generation, propagation and heterodyning must be under control at every nanosecond, from the quantum level to the cosmic. As exterior conditions—matter density, radiation, impinging field strengths, gravitational space-curvature—changed, instant by instant, their reaction on the ship's immaterial web was registered; data were fed into the computers; handling a thousand simultaneous Fourier series as the smallest of their tasks, these machines sent back their answers; the generating and controlling devices, swimming aft of the hull in a vortex of their own output, made their supple adjustments. Into this homeostasis, this tightrope walk across the chance of improper response—which would mean distortion and collapse of the fields, nova-like destruction of the ship—entered a human command. It became part of the data. A starboard intake was widened, a port intake throttled back; but carefully, carefully. *Leonora Christine* swung around onto her new course.

The stars saw the ponderous movement of a steadily larger mass, taking months and years before the deviation from its original track was significant. Not that the object they saw was slow. It was a planet-sized shell of incandescence, where atoms were seized by its outermost force-fringes and excited into thermal, fluorescent, synchrotron radiation. And it came barely behind the wave front which announced its march. But the galaxy was vast. The ship's luminosity was soon lost across light-years.

The ship's passage crawled through abysses which seemingly had no end.

In her own time, though, the story was another. She moved through a universe ever more strange—more rapidly aging, more massive, more compressed. Thus the rate at which she could gulp down hydrogen, burn some of it to energy and hurl the rest off in a billion-kilometer jetflame . . . that rate kept increasing for her. Each minute, as counted by her clocks, took a larger fraction off her tau than the last minute had added to it.

Inboard, nothing changed. Air and metal still carried the deep beat of acceleration, whose net internal thrust still stood at an even one gravity. The interior powerplant continued to give light, electricity, thermostatic control.

And the biosystems reclaimed oxygen and water, processed waste, produced food, maintained human life. Entropy increased. People grew older at the ancient rate of sixty seconds per minute, sixty minutes per hour.

But those hours were always less related to the hours and years which passed outside. Loneliness closed on the ship like fingers.

✷VII✷

Reymont paused for a moment at the entrance to commons. The main room lay big and quiet. At first it had been in constant use, an almost hysterical crowding together. But lately, aside from meals, the tendency was for scientists and crewfolk to form little cliques, or retreat into solitariness. Not many ball games went on in the gym any more; the hobby shops were often deserted. No serious quarrels had developed. It was just a matter of confessing by one's actions that one was weary to death of the same faces and the same conversations, and therefore meant to spend most of the time apart—reading, watching taped shows, writing, thinking, sleeping as much as possible. Offsetting this tendency in some was a change in the sexual habits of others. Reymont wasn't sure whether that betokened a breakdown or a groping toward a new pattern better suited to present conditions. Maybe both. At any rate, most relationships had become transient, though some groups stayed more or less together as wholes and went in for a good deal of experimentation.

He didn't care one way or another about that. He wished they'd all pull themselves together, get more exercise and do less brooding. But he couldn't persuade many. His inflexible enforcement of certain basic rules had pretty well isolated him socially.

Apropos which—yes. He strode across the deck. A light above each of the three dream booths said it was occupied. He fished a master key from his pocket and opened the lids, one by one. Two he closed again. But at the third he swore. The stretched-out body, the face under the somnohelmet, belonged to Emma Glassgold.

For a moment he stood looking down at the little woman. Peace dwelt in her smile. But skin was loose and unhealthily colored. The EEG screens behind the helmet said she was in a soothed condition. So she could be roused fast without danger. Reymont snapped down the override switch on the timer. The oscilloscopic trace of the hypnotic pulses that had been fed into her brain flattened and darkened.

She stirred. "*Shalom, Moshe,*" he heard her whisper. There was nobody aboard named Moshe.

He slid the helmet off, uncovering her eyes. She squeezed them tighter shut, knuckled them, and tried to turn around in the box.

"Come on," Reymont said. "Wake up." He gave her a shake.

She blinked at him. The breath snapped into her. She sat straight. He could almost see the dream fade away behind those eyes. "Come on," he repeated, offering his hand to assist. "Climb out of that damned coffin."

"*Ach,* no, no," she slurred. "You . . . I was with my Moshe."

"I'm sorry, but—"

She crumpled into sobbing. Reymont slapped the booth, a cracking across every other noise. "All right," he said, "I'll make that a direct order. Out! And report to Dr. Winblad."

"What the devil's going on here?"

Reymont turned. Norbert Williams must have heard him and

come in from the pool, because the chemist was nude and wet. He was also furious. "So now you're bullying women," he said in a thickened tone. "Not even big women. Get away from here."

Reymont stood where he was. "We have regulations about the use of dream booths," he said. "If someone hasn't the self-discipline to observe them, I have to compel."

"Yah! Snooping around, watching us, shoving your nose up everybody's privacy—God, I'm not going to put up with it any longer!"

"Don't," Glassgold pleaded. "Don't fight." She seemed to shrink into herself. "I will go."

"Like hell you will," the North American answered. "Stay. Insist on your rights." His features burned crimson. "I've had a bellyful of this little tin Jesus, and now's the time to do something about him."

Reymont said, spacing his words: "The regulations limiting use of the booths weren't written for fun, Williams. Too much sleep, too much artificial stimulation of dreams, is bad. It becomes addictive. The end result can be insanity."

"Listen." The chemist made an obvious effort to curb his own wrath. "People aren't identical. *You* may think we can be chopped and trimmed to fit your pattern—you and your dragooning us into calisthenics, your arranging work details that any child could see aren't for anything except to keep us busy a few hours per day, your smashing the still that Pedro Rodrigues built—your whole petty dictatorship, ever since the voyage began, worse and worse since we veered off on this Flying Dutchman chase—" He swallowed. "Listen," he said. "Those regulations. Like here. They're written to make sure nobody gets too much dream time. Of course. But how do you know that some of us are getting enough? We've all got to spend some time in the booths. You also, Constable Iron Man. You also. The ship's too sterile an environment. It's a sensory-deprivation place. We've got to have substitutes."

"Certainly—" Reymont interrupted.

"Now how can you tell how much substitute anyone else may need? You don't have the sensitivity God gave a cockroach. Do you know one mucking thing about Emma's background? I do. I know she's a fine, courageous woman . . . perfectly well able to judge her own necessities, and guide herself . . . she doesn't need you to run her life for her." Williams pointed. "There's the door. Use it."

"Norbert, don't," Glassgold shivered. She climbed from the box and tried to come between the men. Reymont eased her to one side and answered Williams:

"If exceptions are to be made, the ship's doctor is the one to determine them. Not you. She has to see Dr. Winblad anyway, after this. She can ask him for a medical authorization."

"I know how far she'll get with him. That bastard won't even issue tranquilizers."

"We've a long trip ahead of us. Unforeseeable stresses to undergo. If we start getting dependent on pacifiers—"

"Did you ever think, without some such help, we'll go crazy and die? We'll decide for ourselves, thank you. Now go away, I said!"

Glassgold sought once more to intervene. Reymont had to seize her by the arms to move her.

"*Get your hands off her, you swine!*" Williams charged in with both fists flailing.

Reymont released Glassgold and drifted back, to where more room for maneuvering was available. Williams yelped and followed. Reymont guarded himself against the inexpert blows until, after a minute, he sprang close. A karate flurry, two chops, a gush from emptied lungs, and Williams went to the deck. He huddled retching. Blood dripped from his nose.

Glassgold shrieked and ran to him. She knelt, pulled him close, glared up at Reymont. "Aren't you brave?" she spat.

The constable spread his palms. "Was I supposed to let him hit me?"

"You c-c-could have left."

"No. My duty is to maintain order on board. Until Captain Telander relieves me from that, I'll continue to do so."

"Very well," Glassgold said between her teeth. "We are going to the captain at once. I am lodging a formal complaint against you."

Reymont shook his head. "It was explained and agreed on," he answered, "that the skipper mustn't be bothered with our ordinary troubles and bickerings. Not under these new circumstances, when we're bound into the absolute unknown. He has to think of the ship."

Williams groaned his way back toward full consciousness.

"But we will go to First Mate Lindgren," Reymont said. "I have to file charges against both of you."

Glassgold compressed her lips. "As you wish," she said.

"Not Lin'gren," Williams mouthed. "Lin'gren an' him, they was—"

"No longer," Glassgold said. "She couldn't stand any more of him, even before the disaster. She will be fair." She rose, helped Williams up, supported him the whole way to officer country.

Several people saw them pass and started to ask what had happened. Reymont glowered them into silence. The looks they returned him were sullen. At the first intercom callbox, he dialed Lindgren's cabin and requested her to come to the interview room.

It was minuscule but soundproof, a place for confidential hearings and necessary humiliations. Lindgren seated herself behind the desk. She had donned a uniform for the occasion. The fluoropanels spilled light onto her frost-blonde hair; the voice in which she asked Reymont to commence was equally cold.

He gave a short, flat account of what had happened. "I charge Professor Glassgold with violation of a rule on personal hygiene," he finished, "and Mr. Williams with assault."

"Mutiny?" Lindgren inquired. Williams looked dismayed.

"No, madam. Assault will suffice," Reymont said. To the chemist: "Consider yourself lucky. We can't psychologically afford a full-dress trial, which a charge of mutiny would bring. Not unless you keep on with this kind of behavior."

"That will do, Constable," Lindgren snapped. "Professor Glassgold, please give me your version of what happened."

Anger still upbore the biologist. "I plead guilty to the violation as alleged," she said without a waver, "but I am also pleading guilty and asking for a full review of my case—of everybody's case—as provided by the articles. Not Dr. Winblad's judgment alone; a board of ship's officers and my colleagues. As for the fight, Norbert was intolerably provoked, and he was made the victim of sheer viciousness."

"Your statement, Mr. Williams?"

"I don't know how I stand under your damn reg—" The North American checked himself. "Pardon, ma'am," he said, a little thickly still through his puffed lips. "I never did memorize space law. I thought common sense and good will would see us through.

Reymont may be technically in the right, but I've had about as much of his brazen-headed interference as I can tolerate."

"Then, Professor Glassgold, Mr. Williams, are you willing to abide by my judgment? You are entitled to a regular trial if you so desire."

Williams managed a lopsided grin. "Matters are bad enough already, ma'am. I suppose this has to go in the log, but maybe it does-n't have to go in everyone's ears."

"Oh, yes," Glassgold whispered. She caught Williams' hand.

Reymont opened his mouth. "You are under my authority, Constable," Lindgren intercepted him. "You may, of course, appeal to Captain Telander."

"No, madam," Reymont clipped.

"Very well." Lindgren leaned back. A smile thawed her features. "I suggest that accusations on every side of the case be dropped . . . or, more accurately, never *be* filed. Let's sit down—go ahead, use that bench—let's talk this problem out as among human beings who are all in, shall I say, the same boat."

"Him too?" Williams jerked a thumb toward Reymont.

"We must have law and discipline, you know," Lindgren said mildly. "Without them, we die. Perhaps Constable Reymont gets over-zealous. Or perhaps not. He is, though, the only police and military specialist we have. If you dissent from him—well, that's what I am here for. Do sit down. I'll ring for coffee. We might make a raid on our cigarette ration, too."

"If the mate pleases," Reymont said, "I'll excuse myself."

"No, we have things to say to you also," Glassgold declared.

Reymont kept his eyes on Lindgren's. It was as if sparks flew between. "As you explained, madam," he said, "my business is to uphold the rules of the ship. No more, no less. This has become something else: a personal counselling session. I suggest the lady and gentleman will talk more freely without me."

"I believe you are right, Constable," the mate nodded. "Dismissed."

He sketched a salute and left. On his way down the corridor, Freiwald greeted him with an approximation of cordiality. But then, Freiwald was one of his half-dozen deputies.

He entered his cabin. The partition was drawn aside. Chi-yuen

Ai-ling sat on his bunk rather than her own. She wore something light and frilly, which made her look like a little girl, a sad one. "Hello," she said tonelessly. "You have thunder in your face. What happened?"

Reymont joined her and related it.

"Well," she sighed, "can you blame them so much?"

"No. I suppose not. Though—I don't know. They're supposed to be the best Earth could offer. Intelligence, education, stable personality, good health, dedication. And they know they'd likely never come home again. At a minimum, they'd come back to an Earth older than the one they left by the better part of a century." Reymont ran a hand through his wirebrush hair. "So things have changed," he said. "We're off to an unknown destiny, maybe to death, certainly to complete isolation. But is this so different from what we were planning on from the start? Should it make people go to pieces?"

"Yes," Chi-yuen said. "It does."

"You too. I've noticed." He gave her a ferocious look. "You were busy at first, your theoretical work, your programming the studies you meant to carry out in the Beta Virginis System. And when the trouble hit us, you rallied as well as anyone."

A ghostly smile crossed her lips. "You inspired me," she said.

"Since then, however . . . more and more, you sit doing nothing. I think you and I had the beginnings of, uh, real friendship; but you don't often make any meaningful contact with me of late, nor with anyone else. No more work. No more big daydreams. Not even much crying into your pillow after lights out . . . oh, yes, I'd lie awake and hear you. Why, Ai-ling? What's happening to you? To most of our people?"

"I suppose we have not quite your raw will to survive at any cost," she said, almost under her breath.

"I'd consider some prices for life too high myself. But here—We have what we need to exist. A certain amount of comfort as well. An adventure like nothing we'd dreamed of. What's wrong?"

"Do you know what the year is on Earth?" she countered.

"No. I was the one who suggested to Captain Telander he order that particular clock removed. You may as well know that now. Too morbid an attitude was developing around it."

"Most of us can make our own estimates anyway. At present, I believe it is about 10,000 Anno Domini at home. Give or take some centuries. And, oh, yes, I recognize that for a nonsense statement. I understand about the concept of simultaneity breaking down under relativistic conditions. But still that date does have a meaning. We are absolute exiles. Already. Irrevocably. What has happened on Earth? What is happening throughout the galaxy? What have men done? What are they becoming? We will never share in it. We cannot."

She had spoken in a level, almost indifferent voice. He tried to break her apathy with sharpness: "What of that? If we'd gone to Beta Three and stayed, we'd have had a thread of radio contact, words a generation old before we heard them. Nothing else. And our own deaths would have closed us off from the universe. The common fate of man. Why should we whine because ours takes an unexpected shape?"

She regarded him for a space before she said, "You don't really want an answer for yourself. You want to provoke one from me."

Startled, he said, "Well . . . yes."

"You understand people a great deal better than you let on. Your business, I suppose. You tell me what our trouble is."

"Loss of purpose," he said at once. "The crewfolk aren't in such bad condition yet. They have their jobs to keep them occupied. But most of those aboard are scientists. They'd signed their lives over to the Beta Virginis expedition. You, for example, intended to study planetology there. So you had that to look forward to; and meanwhile you had your preparations to play with. Now you have no idea what will happen. You know just that it'll be something altogether different from what you expected. That it may be death—because we are taking some frightful risks—and you can do nothing to help, only sit passive and be carried. Naturally your morale cracks."

"What do you suggest I do, Charles?"

"Well, why not continue your theoretical work? Try to generalize it. Eventually we'll be looking for a planet to settle on. Your specialty will be very much needed."

"You know what the odds are against our ever finding a home. We are going to keep on this devil's chase until we die."

"Damnation, we can improve the odds!"

"How?"

"That's one of the things you ought to be working on."

She smiled again, a little more alive. "Do you know, Charles," she said, "you make me want to. If for no other reason than to make you stop flogging at me. Is that why you are so hard on people?"

He considered her. She had borne up thus far better than most. Maybe she would gain fresh courage from, well, sharing with him. And every glint of will and hope was to be nurtured. "Can you keep a trade secret?" he asked.

Her glance actually sparkled. "You should know me that well by now." One bare foot rubbed across his thigh.

He patted it and grinned. "An old principle," he said. "Works in military and para-military organizations. I've been applying it here. The human animal wants a father-mother image but, at the same time, resents being disciplined. You can get stability like this: The ultimate authority-source is kept remote, godlike, practically unapproachable. Your immediate superior is a mean son of a bitch who makes you toe the mark and whom you therefore hate. But *his* superior is as kind and sympathetic as rank allows. Do you follow me?"

She laid a finger to her chin. "No, not really."

"Well, in the present case—oh, you'll never know how carefully I maneuvered, those first few months after we hit the nebulina, to help things work out this way—Captain Telander has been isolated, along with those officers most concerned with the actual operation of the ship. He doesn't realize that. He agreed to my argument that he shouldn't be distracted by ordinary business, because his whole attention must go to getting us safely through the galaxy's clouds and clusters. But this has removed him from the informal, intimate basis on which we operated before. He dines separately, with Boudreau and Fedoroff. He takes his recreation and exercise alone in the cabin we've enlarged for him. When he needs a woman, he requests her most politely to visit him, and never asks the same one twice. And so on and so on.

"I can't claim credit for the whole development. Much of it is natural, almost inevitable evolution. The logic of our problem brought it about, given some nursing by me. The end result, however, is that our good gray friend Lars Telander has been transformed into the Old Man."

Chi-yuen half smiled, half sighed. "Poor Old Man! Why?"

"I told you," Reymont said. "Psychological necessity. The average person aboard has to feel that his life is in competent hands. Of course, no one believes consciously that the captain is infallible. But there's an unconscious need for such an aura. Therefore, we have now established things so that the captain's human-level judgment never is put to the test."

"Lindgren is the surrogate there?" Chi-yuen looked closely at Reymont.

He nodded. "I'm the traditional top sergeant. Hard, harsh, demanding, overbearing, inconsiderate, brutal. Not so bad as to provoke a petition for my removal. But enough to irritate, to be unpopular. That's good for the others, you know. It's healthier to be mad at me than to brood on personal woes . . . as you, my dear, have been doing.

"Now Lindgren smooths things out. As first mate, she sustains my power. But she also overrides it from time to time. She exercises her rank to bend regulations in favor of need. As a result, she adds benignity to the attributes of Ultimate Authority."

Reymont shrugged. "Thus far, the system's worked," he finished. "It's beginning to break down. We'll have to add a new factor."

Chi-yuen gazed at him so long that he shifted uncomfortably on the bunk. At last she asked, "Did you plan this with Ingrid?"

"Eh?" he said, surprised. "Oh, no. Certainly not. Her role demands that she *not* be a Machiavelli type who plays the part deliberately."

"You know her so well . . . from old acquaintance?"

"Yes." He reddened. "What of that? These days we have to keep aloof from each other. For obvious reasons."

"I think you find ways to continue rebuffing her, Charles."

"M-m-m . . . damnation, leave me alone. What I want to do is help you get back some real will to live."

"So that I, in turn, can help you keep going?"

"Well, uh, yes. I'm no superman. It's been too long since anyone held my hand."

"Are you saying that because you mean it, or because it serves your purpose?" Chi-yuen tossed back her dark locks. "Never mind. Don't answer. We will help each other, what little we can. Afterward, if we survive—we will settle that when we have survived."

His dark, scarred features softened. "You have for a fact begun to think in survival terms *again*," he said. "Good. Thanks."

She chuckled. Her arms went about his neck. "Come here, you."

✳ VIII ✳

The speed of light can be approached, but no body possessing rest mass can quite attain it. Smaller and smaller grew the increments of velocity by which *Leonora Christine* neared that impossible ultimate. Thus it might have seemed that the universe which her crew observed could not be distorted further. Aberration could, at most, displace a star 45°; Doppler effect might infinitely redden the light from astern, but could only double the frequency of light ahead.

But there was no limit on inverse tau, and that was the measure of change in perceived space and experienced time. Accordingly, there was no limit to the violet shift either; and the cosmos fore and aft could shrink toward a zero thickness wherein all the galaxies were crowded.

Thus, as she made her great swing partly around the Milky Way and turned for a plunge straight through its heart, *Leonora Christine*'s periscope revealed a weird demesne. The nearer stars streamed past, faster and faster, until at last the human eye could see them marching across the field of view; because by that time, many years passed outside while a minute or two ticked away inside the ship. That field was no longer black. It was a shimmering purple, which deepened and brightened as the months went by; because the interaction of forcefields and interstellar medium—eventually, interstellar magnetism—was releasing quanta. The farther stars were coalescing into two globes, fiery blue ahead, ember crimson aft. But gradually those globes shrank toward points, and dimmed; because well-nigh the whole of their radiation had been shifted out of the visible spectrum, toward gamma rays and long radio waves.

The viewscope had been repaired, but was increasingly less able to compensate, to show the sky as a stationary observer would have seen it. The circuits simply could not distinguish individual stars any longer, at more than a few parsecs' remove. The electronicians took the instrument apart and rebuilt it to step up lowered and step down heightened frequencies, lest men fly altogether sightless.

That project, and certain other remodelings, provided a useful outlet for those able to help. Such people began to emerge from their shells. Nonetheless, Reymont found a need to hale the astronomer Elof Nilsson to the interview room.

Ingrid Lindgren sat behind her desk, once more uniformed. She had lost weight, and dark circles lay beneath her eyes. The cabin thrummed louder than normal, and occasionally a shiver went through ribs and deck. Here, in the immense clouds which surrounded the clear space at the galaxy's core, *Leonora Christine* moved according to an eerie sort of aerodynamics. Her inverse tau was now so enormous that density did not trouble her, rather she swallowed matter still more greedily than before. But she flew as if through a wind blowing between the sun clusters.

"So you accuse Dr. Nilsson of spreading disaffection, Constable?" Lindgren's tone was weary. "The articles provide for free speech."

"We are scientists," the astronomer said waspishly. "We have not only the right but the obligation to state what is true." He was a short, rather ugly man who had not gotten along ideally with his fellows even before the crisis came. Since then he had let a scraggly beard grow and seldom bathed. His clothes were begrimed.

Reymont shifted on the bench. Both men were seated at Lindgren's urging. "You don't have the right to spread horror stories," he said. "Didn't you notice what you were doing to Jane Sadler, for instance, when you talked the way you did at mess?"

"I merely brought out into the open what everybody has known from the start," Nilsson rasped. "They hadn't the courage to discuss it in detail. I do."

"They hadn't the meanness to discuss it," Reymont answered. "You do."

"No personalities," Lindgren said. "Tell me what the matter was." She had lately been taking her meals alone in the cabin she shared with the naturalist Olga Sobieski. In fact, she was not seen much off duty.

"You know," Nilsson said. "We've raised the subject before."

She couldn't quite suppress dislike in the look she gave him. "What subject? We've talked about many."

"Talked, yes, like reasonable people," Reymont said. "Not lectured a tableful of shipmates, most of them feeling low already."

"Please, Constable. Proceed, Dr. Nilsson."

The astronomer puffed himself up. "An elementary thing," he said. "I cannot understand why the rest of you have been such idiots as not to give it serious consideration before. You blandly assume we will come to rest in some other galaxy and find a habitable planet. But will you tell me how? Think of the requirements. Mass, temperature, irradiation, atmosphere, hydrosphere, biosphere . . . the best estimate is that one per cent of the stars have planets which are any approximation to Earth."

"Oh," Lindgren said. "Yes, everybody knows—"

Nilsson was not to be deprived of his platform. Perhaps he didn't bother to hear her. He ticked points off on his fingers. "If one per cent of the stars are suitable, do you realize how many we will have to examine in order to have an even chance of finding what we need? It is conceivable that we will be lucky and come upon our New Earth at the very first star we try. But the odds against this are a hundred to one. Thus we will have to try many. Now the examination of each involves almost a year of deceleration. To depart from it and search elsewhere requires another year of acceleration. Those are years of ship's time, remember, because nearly the whole period is spent at velocities which are small compared to light's and which, thus, involve a negligible tau factor. Hence we must allow two of our years per star, as a minimum. The fifty-fifty chance of which I spoke—and mind you, that is only a fifty-fifty chance—the odds are as good that we will not find New Earth in the first seventy-five stars as they are that we will—this chance requires a hundred or a hundred and fifty years of search. We will not live so long. Therefore our whole endeavor, the risks we take in this fantastic dive straight through the galaxy and out into intergalactic space, it is all futile. *Quod erat demonstrandum.*"

"Among your many detestable characteristics, Nilsson," Reymont drawled, "is your habit of droning the obvious through your nose."

"Madam!" the astronomer gasped. "I protest! I shall file charges of personal abuse!"

"Cut back," Lindgren said. "Both of you. I must admit your conduct offers provocation, Dr. Nilsson. On the other hand, Constable, you should remember that Dr. Nilsson is one of the most distinguished men in his profession that Earth has . . . Earth had. He deserves respect."

"Not the way he behaves," Reymont said. "Or smells."

"Be polite, Constable, or I'll charge you myself," Lindgren said. She drew breath. "You don't seem to make allowance for humanness. We are adrift in space and time; the Earth we knew is a hundred thousand years in its grave; we are rushing nearly blind through a crowded part of space; we may at any minute strike something that will destroy us; at best, we must look forward to months, probably years in a cramped and barren environment. Don't you expect people to react to that?"

"Yes, madam, I do," Reymont said. "I don't, however, expect them to behave so as to make matters worse."

"There is some truth in that," Lindgren admitted.

Nilsson squirmed and looked sulky. "I was just trying to spare them disappointment at the end of this flight," he muttered.

"Are you quite certain you weren't indulging your ego—? Never mind. Your standpoint is legitimate." Lindgren signed.

"No, it isn't," Reymont said. "He gets his one per cent by counting every star. Obviously we aren't going to bother with red dwarfs— the vast majority—or blue giants or anything outside a fairly narrow spectral range. Which reduces the field of search by a whopping factor."

"Make the factor ten," Nilsson said. "I don't really believe that, but let's grant we have a ten per cent probability of finding New Earth at any one of the Sol-type stars we try. That nevertheless requires us to hunt among five or more to get our even chance. A dozen years? The youngest among us will be past his youth. Some will be getting old. The loss of so many reproductive years means a corresponding loss of heredity; and our gene pool is small, indeed minimal, to start with. You must agree on the impossibility of having children while we are in space. If nothing else, we are too crowded. Yet if we wait one or two decades to start having them, we can't beget enough. Few will be grown to self-sufficiency by the time their parents start getting helpless with advancing years. And in any case, the human stock will certainly die out in a few generations. I know something about genetic drift, you see."

He looked smug. "I didn't wish to hurt your feelings," he said. "My desire was to be of service, by showing your concept of a bold pioneer community, planting humankind afresh in a new galaxy . . . showing that chatter for the romantic fantasy which it is."

"Have you an alternative?" Lindgren asked.

Nilsson's mouth twisted, an uncontrollable tic. "Nothing but realism," he said. "Acceptance of the fact that we will never leave this ship. Adjustment of our behavior to that fact."

"You understand, I suppose," Reymont said, "that for half the people aboard, the logical thing to do once they've decided you're right is to commit suicide."

"That may well be," Nilsson said.

"Do you hate life so much yourself?" Lindgren asked.

Nilsson jerked on the bench. He gobbled. Reymont made haste to say:

"I didn't haul you in here only to scold you. I want to know why you haven't any ideas for improving our chances."

"What ideas?"

"That's what I'm asking you. You're the observational astronomer. As I recall, you were in charge of programs back home which located something like fifty other planetary systems. You actually identified individual planets across all those light-years. Why can't you do the same for this ship?"

"Ridiculous!" Nilsson pounced. "I see that I must explain the matter in kindergarten terms. Will you bear with me, Mate Lindgren? Listen carefully, Constable. True, a very large spaceborne instrument can pick out an object the size of Jupiter at a distance of several parsecs. This is provided the object gets sufficient illumination, but not so much that it is lost in the glare of its sun. Also true, by mathematical analysis of perturbation data gathered over a period of years, some idea can be obtained about companion planets which are too small to photograph directly. Ambiguities in the equations can, to a degree, be resolved by close interferometric study of flare-type phenomena on the star; planets do exercise a certain small influence upon such cycles.

"But." His finger prodded Reymont's chest. "But you do not realize how uncertain those results are. Journalists were fond of trumpeting that yet another Earthlike world had been discovered. The fact always was, however, that this was one possible interpretation of our data. Only one among several possible size and orbit distributions. And subject to a gross probable error. All this, mind you, with the largest, finest instruments which could be orbited. Instruments such as we certainly do not have with us here.

"No, even at home, the sole way to get detailed information about extrasolar planets was to send a probe or a manned expedition there. In our case, the sole way is to decelerate for a close look. And thereafter, I am certain, to go on. Because you must be aware that a planet which otherwise seems ideal could be lifeless, or could have a native biochemistry useless or deadly to us.

"I implore you, Constable, to learn a little science, a little logic, perhaps just a touch of realism. Eh?" Nilsson ended with a crow of triumph.

"Doctor—" Lindgren began.

Reymont smiled crookedly. "Don't worry, madam," he said. "No fight will start. His words don't diminish *me*." He regarded the other man with care. "Believe it or not, I knew very well what you've told us. I also know you are, or were, an able fellow. That you made some innovations, some new gadgets and systems of your own, which were responsible for a lot of discoveries. Well, why not put your brain to work on the problem we have here?"

"Will you be so good as to condescend to suggest a procedure?" Nilsson fleered.

"I'm no scientist, nor much of a technician," Reymont said. "But a few things look obvious to me. Let's suppose we have entered our target galaxy. We've shed the ultra-low tau we needed to get there, but we still have one of . . . oh, whatever is convenient. Ten to the minus third, perhaps? Well, that gives you a mighty long baseline and cosmic-time period to make your observations. In the course of some weeks or months, ship's time, you can collect more data on a given star than you had on any of Sol's neighbors. I should think you could find ways to use relativity effects to give you information that wasn't available at home. And, naturally, you'll be observing a large number of Sol-type stars simultaneously. So you're bound to find some which you can prove—prove with such exact figures that there's no reasonable doubt—have planets with masses and orbits about like Earth's."

"But even then," Lindgren said hesitantly, "the question of atmosphere, biosphere, that remains. We still need to take a close-range look."

"Yes, yes," Reymont agreed. "But must we stop to take it? Suppose, instead, we lay out a course which brings us hard by the most promising suns, one after the next—while we continue to travel near light-speed. In cosmic time, we'll have hours or days to make studies of any planet that interests us. Spectroscopic, thermoscopic, photographic, magnetic, write your own list of clues. We can get a good idea of conditions on the surface. Biological conditions, too. We could look for things like thermodynamic disequilibrium, chlorophy 11 reflection spectra, polarization by microbe populations based on 1-amino acids . . . yes, I think we can get an excellent idea of whether that planet is suitable. At high tau, we can examine any number in a short stretch of our own time. Our instruments will have to be automated, in fact; we ourselves couldn't work fast enough. Then, when we do find the right world, we can brake, make turnaround and come back. That will take a couple of years, I admit. But they'll be endurable years. Because we'll know, with very high certainty, that we have a home waiting for us!"

Color mounted in Lindgren's cheeks. Her eyes looked less dull. He had not seen so much life in her for months. "By God," she breathed, "why didn't you speak of this before?"

"I was too busy to think beyond the next day," Reymont said. "Why didn't you, though, Dr. Nilsson?"

"Because the whole thing is absurd," the astronomer said. "You presuppose instrumentation we do not have—"

"Well, can't we build it? We do have tools, precision equipment, construction supplies. Maybe we can't put together an enormous telescope, a mirror a few molecules thick, around the hull, once we're safe in intergalactic space. I'm not sure we can't, but let's assume so. Is that the only way? How about electronic amplification, for instance?"

"You talk of instruments which don't exist. Especially those with which you want to analyze a planet's biochemistry as you zip past at light speed. No such thing—such sensitivity and range—no such thing has ever been constructed."

"Well?" Reymont said.

Nilsson and Lindgren stared at him. Silence thrummed.

"Well, why can't we develop what we need?" Reymont asked in a puzzled voice. "Here's a whole shipful of some of the most talented, highly trained, imaginative people our civilization produced. They include almost any scientific specialty you care to name; but they're used to interdisciplinary work as well. Suppose, for instance, Emma Glassgold and Norbert Williams got together to work out the specifications for a life-analyzing instrument. They'd consult others as needed. Eventually they'd employ physicists, electronicians and such for the actual building and debugging. Meanwhile, you, Dr. Nilsson, have been in charge of a team making gadgets for long-range planetography. In fact, you're the logical man to head up the instrumentation program."

His enthusiasm waxed. The hardness fell from him. He said, eager as a boy: "Why, this is precisely what we've needed! A fascinating, vital sort of job that demands everything everybody can give. And those whose specialties aren't called for, they'll be necessary too. They'll be assistants, manual workers—I suppose we'll have to remodel a lot of the ship's interior to accommodate the bigger instruments—Ingrid, it's a way not just to save our lives but our minds! Our souls!"

He sprang to his feet. She did too. Their hands reached out and clasped.

Suddenly they grew aware of Nilsson.

He sat less than dwarfish, hunched, shivering, altogether collapsed.

Lindgren went to him in alarm. "What's the matter?" she exclaimed.

He stared at the deck. "Impossible," he mumbled. "Impossible."

"No. Surely not," she said urgently. "I mean, you wouldn't have to discover any new laws of nature or anything like that, would you? It seems to be only a question of applying known principles."

"In unheard-of ways." Nilsson hid his face. "God better me, I haven't the brains any more."

Lindgren and Reymont exchanged a look above his bent back. She shaped words, unspoken. Once he had taught her the Rescue Corps emergency trick of lip-reading, and they had practiced it as a game they shared, a thing that made them more private and more one. *Can we succeed without him?*

I doubt it. He is in fact the best man to organize that kind of project. At least, lacking him, we have a much poorer chance.

Lindgren sat down beside Nilsson. She laid an arm across his shoulders. "What's the matter?" she asked most softly.

"I have no hope," he snuffled. "Nothing to live for."

"Oh, but you do."

"What? You know Rosana . . . deserted me . . . months ago. No other woman—Why should I care? What's left for me?"

Reymont's lips formed, *Now he's begun pitying himself.* Lindgren frowned and shook her head.

"No, you're wrong, Elof," she murmured. "We do care for you. Would we ask for your help now if we didn't honor you?"

"My mind." He sat straight and glared at her out of swimming eyes. "You want my mind, yes. My advice. My knowledge and skill. To save yourselves. But do you want me? Do you think of me as, as, as a human being? No! Dirty old Nilsson. One is barely polite to him. *But* when he starts to talk, one finds the earliest possible excuse to leave. One does not invite him to one's parties. Most certainly never to one's cabin. At most, if desperate, one asks him to be a fourth for bridge or to lead an instrument development effort. Well, what do you expect him to do? Thank you?"

"But that isn't true!"

"Oh, I'm not as childish as some," he said. "I'd help you if I could. But my mind is blank, I tell you. I haven't had an original thought since the disaster. Call it fear of death paralyzing me. Call it a sort of impotence. I don't care what you call it. Because you don't care either. No one has offered me friendship, comfort, anything. I have been left alone in the dark and the cold. Do you wonder that my mind has frozen?"

Lindgren looked away, so that none but Reymont could see what expressions chased across her features. When she faced Nilsson again, she was calm.

"I can't say how sorry I am," she told him. "You are a little to blame yourself, Elof. You acted so . . . so self-sufficient . . . we assumed you didn't want to be bothered. The way Olga Sobieski, for instance, doesn't want to. That's why she moved in with me. When you moved in with Hussein Sadek—"

"He keeps the panel closed between our halves," Nilsson shrilled.

"He never opens it. But I often hear, off-watch, first one girl in there, then another."

"Well, but now we understand," Lindgren said. She smiled. "And to be quite honest, Elof, I've grown a little tired of my own current existence."

Nilsson made a strangled noise.

"I believe we have some personal business to discuss," Lindgren said. She was pale again, but continued to smile. "Do you mind, Constable?"

"No," said Reymont. "Of course not." He left the cabin.

✷ IX ✷

Leonora Christine stormed through the galactic nucleus in 20,000 years. To those aboard, the time was measured in hours. They were hours of tension, while the hull shook and groaned from stress, and the outside view was of little more than a blinding blazing fog: because here the concentration of interstellar matter was great indeed. The chance of striking a sun was not negligible; lurking in a dust cloud, it could be upon the ship before any course alteration was possible. (No one knew what would happen to the star. It might go nova. But certainly the vessel herself would be destroyed, too swiftly for her crew to realize they were dead.) On the other hand, this was the region where tau plunged to values that could merely be estimated, not measured with precision, most surely not comprehended.

There was a respite while she crossed the region of clear space at the very center, like passing through the eye of a hurricane. Foxe-Jameson, the astrophysicist, came near weeping. "Too bloody awful! The answers to a million questions, right here, and I've not a single instrument adapted for the conditions!"

His shipmates grinned. "And where would you publish?" someone asked. Renascent hope was often expressing itself in a kind of gallows humor.

But there was no joking when Boudreau called a conference with Telander and Reymont. That was soon after the ship had emerged from the dust clouds on the far side of the nucleus—by then, her jets used dust as readily as gas—and headed out through a spiral arm. The viewscope showed a red fireball dwindling behind, a gathering darkness ahead. People off duty celebrated in commons with music, dance, a liquor ration. They had run the cosmic shoals and not been wrecked. Laughter, stamping, lilt of an accordion drifted faintly to the bridge.

"It's like this," the navigator said. "Nilsson's project is showing results already, you know; and we also have my standard observational gear, together with some stuff intended for research from a Beta Virginis base. I prepared to take my readings before we entered the galactic core. Now that we're out, I have taken them."

Captain Telander's gaunted visage grew tight, as if readying for a new blow. "What result?" he asked.

"What readings?" Reymont added. "I mean, what specifically were you studying?"

"Matter density in space ahead of us," Boudreau said. "Within this galaxy, between galaxies, between galactic clusters. Given our present tau, the frequency shift of the neutral-hydrogen radio spectrum, I can get results of unprecedented accuracy."

"Oh, yes. That. What have you found out?"

Boudreau braced himself. "The gas concentration drops off more slowly than we thought," he said. "With the tau we will probably have by the time we leave this galaxy . . . thirty million light-years out, as nearly as I can determine, we still will not dare turn off the force-fields."

Telander closed his eyes. Reymont nodded, jerkily. "We've discussed the possibility of that being the case," he said, word by word. The scar stood livid on his brow. "That even halfway between two clusters, we won't be able to make our repair. But you act as if you had some proposal."

"The one we talked about, you and I," Boudreau said to the captain.

Reymont waited.

Boudreau told him in a dispassionate voice: "The astronomers had learned before we left home, a cluster or family of galaxies like our local group is not the highest form in which matter is organized. Such groups of one or two dozen galaxies do, in turn, tend to occur in larger associations. Superfamilies, so to speak—"

Reymont made a rusty chuckle. "Call them clans," he suggested.

"Eh? Why . . . well. All right. A clan is composed of several families. Now the average distance between members of a family is, oh, perhaps a million light-years. The average distance between one family and the next is greater, as one would expect: on the order of fifty million light-years. Our plan was to leave this family and go to the nearest attainable one beyond. Both would have belonged to the same clan."

"Instead, we'll have to leave the entire clan," Reymont said.

"Yes, I am afraid so."

"How far is it to the next one?"

"I don't know. I didn't take journals along. They would be a little obsolete by now, eh?"

"Be careful," Telander warned.

Boudreau gulped. "I beg the captain's pardon. That was a rather dangerous joke." He went back to lecturing tone: "I don't believe anyone was sure. Probably less than five hundred million light-years, though. Otherwise the hierarchical structure of the galaxies would have been easier for astronomers to identify than it was. Surely, between such clans, space is so close to an absolute vacuum that we won't need protection."

"Can we navigate there?" Reymont demanded.

Sweat glistened on Boudreau's cheeks. "You see the risk," he said. "We will be bound into the totally unknown. Accurate sightings and placements will be unobtainable. We shall need such a tau—"

"A minute," Reymont said. "Let me outline the situation in my layman's language, to make sure I understand you." He paused, rubbing his chin with a sandpapery sound (under the distant music), frowning, until his thoughts were collected.

"We must get—not only into interfamily but interclan space," he said. "We must do this in a reasonable shipboard time. Therefore we must run tau down to a value of a billionth or less. Can we do this at all? Evidently so, or you wouldn't talk as you've done. I imagine the method is to set ourselves a course within this family such that we will pass through the nuclei of at least one other galaxy. And then go likewise through the next family—through as many individual galaxies as possible, always accelerating.

"Once the entire clan is behind us, we should be able to make our repair. But then we'll need a similar period of deceleration. And because our tau will be so great and space so utterly empty, we'll be unable to steer. Not enough material will be there for the jets to work on, nor enough navigational data to guide us. We'll just have to hope that we'll pass through another clan.   •

"We should do that. Eventually. By sheer statistics. But we may go so far first that the expansion of the universe will be working against us. We may be out yonder a long while indeed."

"Correct," Telander said. "You do understand."

"—But me and my true love will never meet again,
On the bonnie, bonnie banks of Loch Lomond."

"Well," Reymont said, "there doesn't appear to be any virtue in caution. In fact, for us it's become a vice."

"What do you mean?" Boudreau asked.

Reymont shrugged. "We need more than the tau for crossing space to the next clan. We need the tau for a hunt which may take us past any number of clans, through billions of light-years, until we find one we can enter. I trust you can plot us a course within this first clan that will give us that kind of tau. Don't worry about collisions with anything. We can't afford such worries. Just steer us through the densest dust and gas you can find."

"You . . . are taking this . . . rather coolly," Telander said.

"What am I supposed to do? Burst into tears?"

"That's why I thought you should also hear the news first," Boudreau said. "You may know how to break it to the others."

Reymont considered both men for a moment that stretched. "I'm not the captain, you know," he said softly.

Telander's smile was a spasm. "In certain respects, Constable, you are—"

Reymont turned, went to the instrument console, stood before those goblin eyes with head bent and thumbs hooked in belt. "Well," he said. "If you really want me to take charge."

"I think you had better."

"Well, in that case. They're good people. Morale is bound upward again, now that they see some genuine accomplishment of their own. I think they'll be able to realize, not just intellectually but emotionally, that there is no human difference between a million and a billion, or ten billion, light-years. The exile is still the same."

"But the time involved—" Telander said.

"Yes. That." Reymont looked at them again. "I don't know how much more of our own lifespans we can devote to this voyage. Not very much. The conditions are too unnatural. So we absolutely have to raise tau as high as may be, no matter what the hazard. Not simply to make the trip itself short enough for us to endure. But for the psychological need to do our utmost, at all times."

"How is that?"

"Don't you see? It's our way of fighting back at the universe. *Vogue la galère.* Go for broke. Full steam ahead and damn the torpedoes. I think, if I can put the matter to our people in such terms, they'll rally. For a while, anyhow."

"The wee birdies sing and the flowers of spring,
And in sunshine the waters are sleeping—"

Dark.

The absolute night.

Instruments, straining magnification, reconverting wavelengths, identified some glimmer in that pit. Human senses found nothing, nothing.

"We're dead." Fedoroff's voice echoed in helmets and earplugs.

"I feel alive," Reymont said.

"What else is death but the final cutting off? No sun, no stars, no sound, no weight, no shadow—" Fedoroff's breath was ragged, to clear over a radio which no longer carried the surf noise of cosmic interference. His head was invisible against empty space. The lamp at his waist threw a dull puddle of light onto the hull, that was reflected and lost in horrible distances.

"Keep moving," Reymont ordered.

"Why are you out with this work party, Constable?" said another man's voice. "What do you know about it?"

"I know we'd better get the job done. Which seems to be more than you knotheads do."

"What's the hurry?" Fedoroff gibed. "We have eternity. We're dead, remember."

"We will indeed be dead if we're caught, force-shields down, in anything like a real concentration of matter," Reymont answered. "One atom per cubic meter—or less—could kill us. And with our tau, the nearest galactic clan is only days away."

"So?"

"So are you absolutely certain, Engineer Fedoroff, that we won't strike an embryo galaxy, family, clan . . . some enormous hydrogen cloud, still dark, still falling in on itself . . . at any instant?"

"At any megayear, you mean," Fedoroff said. But he started aft from the main personnel lock. His gang followed.

It was, in truth, a flitting of ghosts. One had thought of space as black. But now one remembered that it had been full of stars. Any shape was silhouetted against suns, clusters, constellations, nebulae, sister galaxies; oh, the universe was pervaded with light! The *inner* universe. Here was worse than a dark background. Here was no background. None whatsoever. The squat, unhuman forms of men in space armor, the long curve of the hull, were seen as gleams, disconnected and fugitive, With acceleration ended, weight was ended also. Not even the slight differential-gravity of being in orbit existed. A man moved as if in an infinite dream of swimming, flying, falling. And yet . . . he remembered that this weightless body of his bore the mass of a mountain. Was there a real heaviness in his floating; or had the constants of inertia subtly changed, out here where the metric of space-time was flattened to nearly a straight line; or was it an illusion, spawned in the tomb of stillness which engulfed him? What was illusion? What was reality? Was reality?

Roped together, clinging with frantic magnetism to the ship's iron (curious, the horror one felt of getting somehow pitched loose—extinction would be the same as if that had happened in the lost little spaceways of the Solar System—but the thought of blazing across megayears as a stellar-scale meteorite was peculiarly lonely), the engineer detail made their way along the hull and the spidery framework which trailed it. Now that the accelerator system had been shut down, those ribs were all which held the generators together. They seemed terribly frail.

"Suppose we can't fix the decelerators," came a voice. "Do we go on? What happens to us? I mean, won't the laws be different, out on the edge of the universe? Won't we turn into something not human?"

"Space is finite," Reymont barked into the blackness. "'The edge of the universe' is a meaningless noise. And let's start by supposing that we can fix this stupid machine."

He heard a few oaths and grinned the faintest bit. When they halted and began to secure themselves individually to the framework that surrounded their task site, Fedoroff took the chance to lay his helmet against Reymont's and talk in private by conduction.

"Thanks, Constable," he said.

"What for?"

"Being such a prosaic bastard."

"Well, we have a prosaic job of repair to do. We may have come a long way, we may by now have outlived the race that produced us, but we haven't changed from a variety of proboscis monkey. Why take ourselves so mucking seriously?"

"Hm. I see why the Old Man said you should come along. All right, let's have a look at the problem here."

✳ XI ✳

Reymont opened the door to his cabin. Weariness made him careless. Bracing himself a trifle too hard against the bulkhead, he let go the handle and drifted free.

For a moment he cartwheeled in midair. Then he bumped into the opposite side of the corridor, pushed and darted back across. Once inside the cabin, he grasped a stanchion before shutting the door behind him.

At this hour, he had expected Chi-yuen to be asleep. But she floated a few centimeters off her bunk, a single line anchoring her amidst currents. As he entered, she returned her book to a drawer with a quickness that showed she hadn't really been paying attention to it.

"Not you, too?" Reymont asked. His question seemed loud. They had been so long accustomed to the engine pulse as well as the gravity of acceleration that free fall brimmed the ship with silence.

"What?" Her smile was tentative and troubled. She had had scant contact with him lately. There was too much for him to do under these changed conditions, organizing, ordering, cajoling, arranging, planning. He would come here to snatch what sleep he might.

"Have you also become unable to rest in zero gee?" he said.

"No. That is, I can. A strange, light sort of sleep, filled with dreams, but I seem fairly refreshed afterward."

"Good," he sighed. "Two more cases have developed."

"Insomniac, do you mean?"

"Yes. Verging on nervous collapse. Every time they do drift off, you know, they wake again screaming. Nightmares. I'm not sure whether weightlessness alone does it to them, or if that's only the last bit of breaking stress. Neither is Dr. Winblad. I was just conferring with him. He wanted my opinion on what to do, now that he's running short of psycho-drugs."

"What did you suggest?"

Reymont grimaced. "I told him who I thought unconditionally had to have them, and who might survive a while without."

"The trouble isn't simply the psychological effect, you realize," Chi-yuen said. "It is the exhaustion. Pure physical exhaustion, from trying to do things in a gravityless environment."

"Of course." Reymont began unfastening his coverall, one leg hooked around a stanchion to hold him in place. "Quite unnecessary. The regular spacemen know how to handle themselves. I do. A few others. We don't get worn out, trying to coordinate our muscles. It's those groundlubber scientists who do."

"How much longer, Charles?"

"In free fall? I don't know. We appear to be bearing down on a galactic clan. Our forcefields have already been reactivated, as a precaution. Because we *might* enter a sufficient gas density at any moment for the jets to work. But we can't be sure. Detailed observation is plain impossible, with the tau we now have."

"But what is the maximum time before we enter that clan and start to have weight again?"

"Less than a week, ship's clocks. Can't estimate closer."

She sighed relief. "We can stand that. And then . . . then we will be making for our new home."

"Hope so," Reymont grunted. He stored his clothes, shivered a little and took out a pair of pajamas.

Chi-yuen started. "What do you mean by that? Don't you know?"

"Look, Ai-ling," he said in an exhausted tone, "we've come two or three billion light-years from Earth. As far in time. We have no charts. No standard of measurement. Our tau is a number to guess at. We take spectrograms of entire galactic families, and assuming they are 'normal'—whatever that is!—we calculate tau from the frequency shift. But the probable error is huge. There are factors like absorption which simply aren't in our handbooks. Quite possibly some of the constants of physics are different enough out here to affect our results. How in hell's flaming name do you expect anyone to bring in an exact answer?"

"I'm sorry—"

"This has been explained to everyone," Reymont said. "Repeatedly. Are the officers to blame if passengers won't listen to their reports? Some of you are going to pieces. Some of you have barricaded yourselves with apathy, or religion, or sex, or whatever comes to hand, till nothing registers on your memories. Most of you—well, it *was* healthy to work on Nilsson's R & D, but that's become a defense reaction in its own right. Another way of focusing your attention so as to exclude the big bad universe. And now, when free fall prevents you carrying on, you too crawl into your nice hidey-holes." His voice lifted in anger. "Go ahead. Do what you want. The whole wretched lot of you. Only don't come and peck at me any longer. D' you hear?"

He yanked on the pajamas and started to climb into his bunk. Chi-yuen unbuckled her lifeline, pushed across to him, embraced him.

"Oh, darling," she whispered. "I'm sorry. You are so tired, are you not?"

"Been hard on us all," he said lethargically.

"Most on you." Her fingers traced the cheekbones standing out under taut skin, the deep lines, the sunken and bloodshot eyes. "Why don't you rest?"

"I'd like to."

She maneuvered his mass into a stretched-out position, clipped on his leash, and drew herself close. Her hair floated across his face, smelling of summers on Earth. "Do," she said. "You can." For you, isn't it good not to have weight?"

"M-m-m, yes. Ai-ling, you know Tetsuo Iwasaki pretty well. Do you think he can manage without tranquilizers? Sven Winblad and I weren't sure—"

"Hush." Her palm covered his mouth. "None of that."

"But—"

"No. I won't have it. The ship isn't going to fall apart if you get one decent night's sleep."

"Well . . . well . . . maybe not."

"Close your eyes. Let me stroke your face—so. Isn't that better already? Now think of nice things."

"Like what?"

"Have you forgotten? Think of home. No. Best not that, I suppose. Think of the home we are going to find. Blue sky. Warm bright sun, light falling through leaves, dappling the shade, blinking on a river; and the river flows, flows, flows, singing you to sleep—"

"Um-m-m."

She kissed him very lightly. "Our own house. A garden. Strange colorful flowers. Oh, but we will plant seeds from Earth too, roses, honeysuckle, rosemary for remembrance. Our children."

He stirred. The fret returned to him. "Wait a minute, we can't make personal commitments. Not yet. You might not want, uh, any given man. I'm fond of you, of course, but—"

She brushed his eyes shut again before he saw the pain on her. "We are daydreaming, Charles," she laughed low. "Do stop being so solemn and literal-minded. Just think about children, everyone's children, playing in a garden. Think about the river. Forests. Mountains. Birdsong. Peace."

He tightened an arm around her waist. "You're a good person," he murmured.

"So are you. A good person who needs to be cuddled. Would you like me to sing you to sleep?"

"Yes." His words were already becoming indistinct. "Please. I like Chinese cradle songs."

She continued smoothing his forehead while she drew breath.

The intercom circuit clicked shut. "Constable," said Telander's voice, "are you there?"

Reymont jerked awake. "Don't," Chi-yuen begged. "Yes," Reymont said, "here I am."

"Would you come to the bridge? And don't alert anyone."

"Aye, aye. Right away." Reymont unbuckled his lifeline and pulled the pajama top over his head.

"They could not give you five minutes, could they?" she said bitterly.

"Must be serious," he rapped. "You'll keep this confidential till you hear from me." In a few motions he had donned coverall and shoes again and was on his way.

Telander and, surprisingly, Nilsson awaited him. The captain looked as if he had been struck in the belly. The astronomer was excited but had not lost his recent air of confidence and self-control He clutched a bescribbled sheet of paper. "Navigation difficulty, eh?" Reymont deduced. "Where's Boudreau?"

"This doesn't concern him immediately," Nilsson said. "I have been making my own observations with some of the new instruments. I have reached a, ah, disappointing conclusion."

Reymont wrapped fingers around a grip and hung in the stillness, regarding them. The fluorolight cast the hollows of his face into shadow. The gray streaks which had lately appeared in his hair seemed vivid by contrast. "We can't make that galactic clan ahead of us after all," he said.

"That's right." Telander drooped.

"No, not strictly right," Nilsson declared fussily. "We will pass through. In fact, we will pass through not just the general region, but a fair number of galaxies within the families that comprise the clan."

"You can distinguish so much detail already?" Reymont wondered. "Boudreau can't."

"I told you I have some of the equipment working," Nilsson said. "The precision seems even greater than hoped for when, ah, we instigated the project. Yes, I have a reasonably good map of the part of the clan which we might traverse. I have now finished making certain computations on that basis."

"Go on," Reymont said. "Once we get in where the jets have some matter to work on, why can't we brake?"

"We can. Of course we can. But our inverse tau is enormous. Remember, we acquired it by passing through the densest attainable portions of several galaxies, en route to interclan space. It was necessary. I do not dispute the wisdom of the decision. But the result is that this particular clan, at least, does not have enough material in it—not enough, I mean, within that conoidal volume which includes all our possible paths intersecting that clan, from this point we are now at—not enough for us to lose our entire velocity. We will emerge on the other side of the clan—after an estimated six months of ship's time under deceleration, mind you—with a tau that is still ten to the minus third or fourth. This, you can see, will make it quite impossible to reach another clan before we die of old age. Especially in view of the fact which we are currently experiencing, that no significant acceleration is possible between clans."

The pompous voice cut off, the beady eyes looked expectant. Reymont met that gaze rather than Telander's sick, gutted stare. "Why am I being told this, and not Lindgren?" he asked.

A tenderness made Nilsson, briefly, another man. "She works so very hard. What can she do here? I thought I had best let her sleep."

"Well, what can *I* do?"

"Give me . . . us . . . your advice," Telander said.

"But sir, you're the captain!"

"We've been over this ground before, Carl. I can, well, yes, I suppose I can make the decisions, issue the commands, order the routines, which will take us crashing on through space, more or less safely." Telander extended his hands. They trembled like autumn leaves. "More than that I can no longer do, Carl. I have not the strength left. You must tell our shipmates."

"Tell them we've failed?" Reymont grated. "Tell them, in spite of everything, we're damned to fly on till we go crazy and die? You don't want much of me, *do* you, Captain?"

"The news may not be that bad," Nilsson said.

Reymont snatched at him, missed and hung with the breath raw in his throat. "We have some hope?"

The little man spoke with a briskness that turned his pedantry into a sort of bugle call:

"Perhaps. I have no data yet. The distances are too vast. We can-

not choose another galactic clan as being accessible to us, and aim for
it. We would see it with too great an inaccuracy, and across too many
millions of years of time. But I do believe we can base a hope on sheer
statistics. Someplace, eventually, we could meet the right configuration. Either a large clan through whose galaxy-densest portions we
can lay a course; or else two or three clans, rather close to each other,
more or less in a straight line, so that we can pass through them in
succession. Do you see? If we could come upon something like that,
we would be in good shape. We would be able to brake ourselves in
a mere few years of ship's time."

"What are the odds?" Reymont's words rattled.

Nilsson shook his head. "I cannot say. But perhaps not too bad.
This is a big and varied cosmos. If we continue sufficiently long, I
should imagine we have a fair probability of encountering what we
need."

"How long is sufficiently long?" Reymont lifted a hand. "Stop.
Don't bother answering. It's on the order of billions of years. Tens of
billions, maybe. That means we need a lower tau yet. A tau so low
that we can actually circumnavigate the universe . . . in months,
maybe in weeks. And that, in turn, means we can't start braking as
we enter this clan up ahead. No. We accelerate again. After we've
passed through—well, no doubt we'll have a shorter period of ship's
time in free fall than this one was, until we strike another clan.
Probably there, too, we'll find it advisable to accelerate, running tau
still higher. We'll do so at every chance we get, from now till we see
a journey's end we can make use of. Right?"

Telander shuddered. "Right," he said. "Can any of us endure it?"

"We'll have to," Reymont said. Now, once more, he spoke in the
voice of command. "I'll figure out a tactful way to announce your
news. I'll have the few men I can trust ready . . . no, not for violence.
Ready with leadership, steadiness, encouragement. And we'll embark
on a training program for free fall. No reason why it has to cause this
much trouble. We'll teach every one of those groundlubbers how to
handle himself in zero gee. How to sleep. By God, how to hope!" He
smote his palms together with a pistol noise.

"Don't forget, we can depend on some of the women too,"
Nilsson said.

"Yes. Of course. Like Ingrid Lindgren."

"Like her indeed," Nilsson said gravely. "You know what she has done for me."

"M-hm. She is quite a girl, isn't she? I'm afraid you will have to go rouse her, Elof. We've got to get our cadre together—the unbreakables; the people who understand people—we must plan this thing. Start suggesting some names."

✳ XII ✳

"Oh, please," Jane Sadler had begged. "Come help him."

"You can't?" Reymont asked.

She shook her head. "I've tried. But I think I make matters worse. In his present condition. I being a woman." She flushed. "Know what I mean?"

"Well, I'm no psychologist," Reymont said. "But I'll see what I can do."

He left the bower where she had caught him in a private moment. The dwarfed trees, tumbling vines, grass and flowers made a place of healing for him. But he had noticed that comparatively few others went into that room any longer. Did it remind them of too much?

A zero-gee handball game bounced from corner to corner of the gymnasium. They were spacemen who played, though, and grimly rather than gleefully. Most of the civilians came here for little except their compulsory exercises and—in a sporadic, uninterested fashion—their meals. No one hailed Reymont as he went by.

Further down the main corridor, a door stood open on a workshop. A lathe hummed within, a cutting torch glowed blue, several men were gathered around a bench discussing something. That was good. The instrument project continued. But it did so terminally, as mere refinement. Most of the labor was finished; cargo had been shifted. Number Two hold converted to an observatory, its haywire tangle neatened. There wasn't any work left for the bulk of Nilsson's team. There wasn't anything left except to abide.

Abruptly the ship quivered.

Weight grabbed at Reymont. He barely avoided falling to the deck. A metal noise toned through the hull, like a basso profundo gong. It was soon over. Free flight resumed. *Leonora Christine* had gone through another galaxy.

Such passages were becoming more frequent by the day. Would they never meet the right configuration to stop?

Well, of course you had to employ your force screens, either accelerating or decelerating. And you dared not decelerate till you were quite sure. But each spate of acceleration made the required conditions for coming to a halt that much more tight. So you went on. And inverse tau grew.

Reymont knocked on the cabin door he wanted. Hearing no reply, he tried it. Locked. But Sadler's adjoining door wasn't. He entered her cabin half and slid back the panel.

Johann Freiwald floated against his bunk. The husky shape was curled into an imitation of a fetus. But the eyes held awareness.

Reymont grasped a stanchion, encountered that stare, and said noncommittally, "I wondered why you weren't around, Hansi. Now I hear you aren't feeling well. Anything I can do for you?"

Freiwald grunted.

"Well, you can do a lot for me," Reymont said. "I need you pretty badly. You're a deputy. One of the half dozen who's stood by me—policeman, counselor, work-party boss, idea man—through this whole thing. You can't be spared yet."

Freiwald spoke as if with difficulty. "I shall have to be spared."

"Why? What's the matter?"

"I can't go on any more. That's all. I can't."

"Why not?" Reymont asked. "What jobs we have left to do aren't hard, physically. Anyhow, you're tough. Weightlessness never bothered you. You're a trained engineer, a pragmatist, a cheerful earthy soul. Not one of those self-appointed delicates who have to be coddled because their tender souls can't bear a long voyage." He sneered. "Or are you one?"

Freiwald stirred. His cheeks reddened a little. "I am a man," he said. "Not a robot. Eventually I start thinking."

"My friend, do you imagine we would have survived this far if the officers, at least, did not spend every waking hour thinking?"

"I don't mean your damned measurements, computations, course adjustments, equipment modifications. That's nothing but the instinct to stay alive. A lobster trying to climb out of a kettle has as much dignity. I ask myself, though, why? What are we doing? What does it mean?"

"*Et tu, Brute.*" Reymont sighed.

Freiwald twisted about so that his gaze was straight into the constable's. "Because you are so insensitive . . . Do you know what year this is?"

"No. Neither do you. We have no way of determining it. And if you wonder what the year is on Earth, that's meaningless. Under these conditions, we have no simultaneity with—"

"Be quiet! I know that whole quacking. We have come many billion light-years. We are rounding the curve of space. If we came back, this instant, to the Solar System, we would not find anything. The sun died long ago. It swelled and brightened till Earth was devoured; it became a variable, guttering like a candle in the wind; it sank away to a white dwarf, an ember, an ash. The human race is dead!"

"Not necessarily," Reymont said.

"Then it's become something we could not comprehend. We are ghosts." Freiwald's lips trembled. He bit them till blood ran. "We hunt on and on, senselessly, meaninglessly—" Again acceleration thundered through the ship. "There," he whispered. His eyes were wide, white-rimmed, as if with fear. "We passed through yet another galaxy. Another good part of a million years. To us, seconds."

"Oh, not quite that," Reymont said. "Our tau can't be that low. We probably quartered a spiral arm."

"Destroying how many worlds? Don't tell me. I know the figures. We are not as massive as a star. But our energy—I think we could pass through the very heart of a sun and not notice."

"Perhaps."

"That's part of our hell. That we've become a menace to—to—"

"Don't say it. Don't think it. Because it isn't true. We're interacting with dust and gas, nothing else. We do transit many galaxies, because galaxies lie comparatively close to each other in terms of their own size. Within a family, the members are about ten diameters apart, or even less. Individual stars within any single galaxy, though, that's another situation entirely. Their diameters are such tiny fractions of a light-year. In a nucleus, the most crowded part . . . well, the separation of two stars is still like the separation of two men, one at either end of a continent. A big continent. Asia, say."

Freiwald looked away. "There is no more Asia," he said. "No more anything."

"There's us," Reymont said. "We're alive, we're real, we have hope. What more do you want? Some grandiose philosophical significance? Forget it. That's a luxury. Our descendants will invent it, along with tedious epics about our heroism. We just have the sweat, tears, blood—" his grin flashed—"in short, the unglamorous bodily secretions. And what's so bad about that? Your trouble is, you think a combination of acrophobia, sensory deprivation and nervous strain is a metaphysical crisis. Myself, I don't look down on our lobster-like instinct to survive. I'm glad we have one."

Freiwald floated motionless.

Reymont clapped his shoulder. "I'm not belittling your difficulties," he said. "It *is* hard to keep going. Our worst enemy is despair; and it wrestles every one of us to the deck, every now and then."

"Not you," Freiwald said.

"Oh, yes," Reymont said. "Me too. I get my feet back, though. So will you."

"Well—" Freiwald scowled. "Maybe."

Reymont reached under his tunic and extracted a small flat flask. "Rank has its privileges," he smiled. "Here."

"What?"

"Scotch. The genuine article, not that witch's brew the Scandinavians think is an imitation. I prescribe a hearty dose for you, and for myself, as far as that goes. I'd enjoy a relaxed talk. Haven't had any such for longer than I can remember."

They had been at it for some while, and life was coming back in Freiwald's manner, when the intercom said with Ingrid Lindgren's voice: "Is Constable Reymont there?"

"Uh, yes," Freiwald said.

"Sadler told me so," the mate said. "Could you come to the bridge?"

"Urgent?" Reymont asked.

"Not really, I guess. The latest navigational sights seem to indicate a—a changing region of space. We may have to modify our cruising plan. I thought you might like to discuss it."

"All right," Reymont said.

"Me too," the other man said. He looked at the flask, shook his head sadly and offered it back.

"No, you may as well finish it, "Reymont said. "Not alone, however. That's bad, drinking alone. I'll tell Sadler."

"Well, now." Freiwald genuinely laughed. "That's kind of you."

Emerging, closing the door behind him, Reymont glanced up and down the corridor. No one else was in sight. Then he sagged, eyes covered, body shaking. After a minute he drew a breath and started for the bridge.

Norbert Williams happened to come the other way. "Hello," the chemist said.

"You're looking cheerier than most," Reymont remarked.

"Well, yes, I guess I am. Emma and I, we got talking, and we may have hit on yet another way to tell at a distance whether a planet has our type of life. A plankton-type population, you see, ought to impart certain thermal radiation characteristics to ocean surfaces; and given Doppler effect, making those frequencies something we can properly analyze—"

"Good. Do go ahead and work on it. And if you should co-opt a few others, that'd be a help."

"Sure, we've already thought of that."

"And would you pass the word, wherever she is, Sadler ought to go to her cabin? Her boy friend's waiting with a surprise."

Williams's guffaw followed Reymont on down the corridor.

But the companionway to the bridge was empty and still; and Lindgren stood watch alone. Her hands strained around the grips at the base of the viewscope. When she turned about at his entry, he saw that her face was quite without color.

He closed the door. "What's wrong?" he asked hushedly.

"You didn't let on to anyone?"

"No, of course not, when the business had to be grim. What is it?" She tried to speak and could not.

"Is anyone else due at this meeting?" Reymont asked.

She shook her head. He went to her, anchored himself with a leg wrapped around a rail, and received her in his arms. "No," she said against his breast. "Elof and . . . Auguste Boudreau . . . they told me.

They asked me to tell . . . the Old Man. They don't dare. Don't know how. I don't either." Her fingers clutched at him until the nails bit through his tunic. "Carl, what shall we do?"

He ruffled her hair, staring across her head, feeling her tension. Again the ship boomed and leaped; and soon again. The notes that rang through her were noticeably higher pitched than before. The draft from a ventilator felt cold. The metal around seemed to shrink inward.

"Go on," he said at last. "Tell me, *alskling*."

"The universe—the whole universe—it's dying."

He made a noise in his gullet. Otherwise he waited.

At length she was able to pull far enough back from him that they could look into each other's eyes. She said in a slurred, hurried voice:

"Maybe the universe has a shorter lifespan than was thought. Or maybe we have traveled longer, in cosmic time, than we knew. Fifty, a hundred billion years. I don't know. I just know what the others told me. What they have been observing. The galaxies we see are growing dimmer. As if, one by one, the stars are going out. And no new stars being formed. No new galaxies. The men weren't sure. The observations are so hard to make. But they began to wonder. And then they started checking Doppler shifts more carefully. Especially of late, when we seem to pass through so many galaxies. They found that what they observed could not be explained by any tau that we can possibly have. Another factor had to be involved. The galaxies are getting more crowded. Space isn't expanding any longer. Its reached its limit and is collapsing inward again. Elof says the collapse will go on. And on. To the end."

"We?" he asked.

"Who knows? Except that we can't stop. We could, I mean. But by the time we did, nothing would be left . . . except blackness, burned-out suns, absolute zero, death, death. Nothing."

"We don't want that," he said stupidly.

"No. What do we want? I think—Carl, shouldn't we say good-by? All of us, to each other? A last party, with wine and candle-light. And afterward go to our cabins. You and I to ours. And say good night. We have morphine for everyone. And oh, Carl, we're all so tired. It will be so good to sleep."

Reymont drew her close to him again.

"Did you ever read *Moby Dick*?" she whispered. "That's us. We've pursued the White Whale to the end of time. And now . . . that question. *What is man, that he should outlive his God?*"

Reymont put her from him, gently and went to the viewscope. Looking forth, he saw, for a moment, a galaxy pass. It must be only some ten-thousands of parsecs distant, for he saw it across the dark very large and clear. The form was chaotic. Whatever structure it had once had was disintegrated. No individual suns could be seen; those would have had to be giants, therefore young, and no young stars existed any more. The galaxy was a dull vague red, deepening at the fringes to the hue of clotted blood.

It drifted away from his sight. The ship went through another, storm-shaken by it, but of that one nothing was visible—nothing at all.

Reymont returned himself to the command bridge. Teeth gleamed in his visage. "No!" he said.

✳ XIII ✳

From the dais of commons, he and she looked upon their assembled shipmates.

The gathering was seated, safety-harnessed into chairs whose leg-bolts had been secured at the proper places to the gym deck. Anything else would have been dangerous. Not that weightlessness prevailed yet. Between the tau which atoms now had with respect to *Leonora Christine*, and the compression of lengths in her own measurement because of that tau, and the dwindling radius of the cosmos itself, her ram jets drove her at a goodly fraction of one gee across the outermost deeps of interclan space. But oftener and oftener came spurts of higher acceleration as she passed through galaxies. They were too fast for the interior fields to compensate. They felt like the buffeting of waves; and each time the noise that sang in the hull was more shrill and windy.

Four dozen bodies hurled against each other could have meant broken bones or worse. But two people, trained and alert, could keep their feet with the help of a handrail. And it was needful that they do so. In this hour, folk must have before their gaze a man and a woman who stood together unbowed.

Ingrid Lindgren completed her relation. "—that is what is happening. We will not be able to stop before the death of the universe."

The muteness into which she had spoken seemed to deepen. A few women wept, a few men shaped oaths or prayers, but none was above a whisper. In the front row, Captain Telander bent his head and closed his eyes. The ship lurched in another squall. Sound passed by, throbbing, groaning, whistling.

Lindgren's hand briefly clasped Reymont's. "Now the constable has something to tell you," she said.

He trod a little forward. Sunken and bloodshot, his eyes appeared to regard them in ferocity. His tunic was wolf-gray, and besides his badge he wore his gun, the ultimate emblem. He said, quietly but with none of the mate's compassion:

"I know you think this is the end. We've tried and failed, and you think you should be left alone to make your peace with yourselves or your God. Well, I don't say you shouldn't do that. I have no idea what is going to happen to us. I don't believe anyone can predict any more. Nature is becoming too alien to our whole past experience of it. In honesty, I agree that our chances do look extremely poor.

"But I don't think they are zero, either. I think we have a duty— to the race that begot us, to the children we might yet bring forth ourselves—a duty to keep trying, right to the finish. For most of you, that won't involve more than continuing to live, continuing to stay sane. I'm well aware that that could be as hard a task as human beings ever undertook. The crew and the scientists who have relevant specialties will, in addition, have to carry on the work of the ship. Which may turn out to be pretty difficult.

"So make your peace. Interior peace. That's the only kind which ever existed anyway. The exterior fight goes on. I propose we wage it with no thought of surrender."

His words rang aloud: "I propose we go on to the next cycle of the cosmos."

That snatched them to alertness. Above a collective gasp and inarticulate cries, a few stridencies could be made out: "No! Lunacy!"— "Good man!"—"Impossible!"—"Blasphemy!"

Reymont drew his gun and fired. The shot shocked them into abrupt quiet.

He grinned into their faces. "Blank cartridge," he said. "Better than a gavel. We'll discuss this in orderly fashion. Captain Telander, will you preside?"

"No," said the Old Man faintly. "You. Please."

"Very well. Comments . . . ah, probably Navigator Boudreau should speak first."

The officer said, in an almost indignant voice: "The universe took somewhere between fifty and a hundred billion years to complete its expansion. It won't collapse in less time. Do you seriously believe we can acquire such a tau that we will outlive the cycle?"

"We can try," Reymont said. The ship trembled and bellied. "We gained a few more per cent right there. As matter gets denser, we naturally accelerate faster. Space itself is being pulled into a tighter and tighter curve. We couldn't circumnavigate the universe before, because it didn't last that long, in the form we knew it. But we should be able to circle the shrinking universe again and again. I'm no expert on theoretical cosmology, but I did check with Professor Chidambaran who knows more about the subject than anyone else aboard, and he agrees. Would you like to explain, sir?"

"Yes," the Indian said, rising. "Time as well as space must be taken into account. The characteristics of the whole continuum will change quite radically. In effect, our present exponential decrease of the tau factor in ship's time should itself increase to a much higher order." He paused. "At a rough estimate, I would say that the time we experience, from now to the ultimate collapse, will be less than three months."

Into the hush that followed, he added, "However, as I told Constable Reymont when he requested me to make this calculation, I do not see how we can survive. Apparently the theory of an oscillating universe is correct. It will be reborn. But first all matter and energy will be collected in a monobloc of ultimate density and temperature. We might pass through a star, at our present velocity, and be unharmed. But we can scarcely pass through the primordial nucleon. My personal suggestion is that we cultivate serenity." He sat down.

"Not a bad idea," Reymont said. "But I don't think that's the sole thing we should do. We should keep flying also. Bear in mind, nobody knows for sure what's going to happen. My guess is that everything will not get squeezed into a single zero-point Something. That's the kind of oversimplification which helps our math along but never does tell a whole story. I think the central core of mass is bound to have an enormous hydrogen envelope, even before the explosion. The outer parts of that envelope may not be too hot, or radiant, or dense for us. Space will be so small, though, that we can circle around and around the monobloc as a kind of satellite. When it blows up and space starts to expand again, we'll naturally spiral out ourselves. I know this is a very sloppy way of phrasing, but it hints at what we can perhaps do . . . Mr. Williams?"

"I never thought of myself as a religious man," the chemist said. It was odd and disturbing to see him so humbled. "But this is too much. We're—well, what are we? Animals. My God—very literally, my God—we can't go on . . . having regular bowel movements . . . while creation happens!"

Beside him, Emma Glassgold looked startled, then angry. Her hand shot aloft.

"Speaking as a believer myself," she said, "I must say that that is sheer nonsense. I'm sorry, Norbert, dear, but it is. God made us the way He wanted us to be. There's nothing shameful about any part of His handiwork. I would like to watch Him fashion new stars and praise Him, as long as He sees fit that I should."

"Good for you!" Ingrid Lindgren called.

"I might add," Reymont said, "I being a man with no poetry in his soul, and I suspect no soul to keep poetry in . . . I might suggest you people look into yourselves and ask what psychological twists make you so unwilling to live through the moment where time begins again. Isn't there, down inside, some identification with—your parents, maybe? You shouldn't see your parents in bed, therefore you shouldn't see a new cosmos begotten. Now that doesn't make sense." He paused. "Of course, what's about to happen is awesome. But so was everything. Always. I never thought stars were more mysterious, or had more magic, than flowers."

Others wanted to talk. Eventually, everyone did. But their sentences threshed wearily around and around the point. It was not to no purpose. They had to unburden themselves. But by the time they could finally adjourn the meeting, Reymont and Lindgren were near a collapse of their own.

They did seize a moment's low-speaking privacy, as the people broke into small groups and the ship roared with the hollow noise of her passage. "I can't move in with you tonight after all," Reymont said. "We'd have to help move personal gear, not to mention explaining to our cabin partners, and I'm so tired I can't. Tomorrow."

"No, not then, either," Ingrid Lindgren answered. "I'm sorry, but I've changed my mind."

Stricken, he exclaimed: "You don't want to?"

"You'll never know how much I want to, darling. But can we risk it? The emotional balance is so fragile. Anything might let chaos loose in anyone of us. Suppose Elof or Ai-ling took it hard that we left . . . left now, when death is so near. The despair, maybe the suicide of a single person could bring the whole ship down in hysteria." She gripped both his hands. "Afterward, of course. When we're safe. I'll never let you go then."

"We may never be safe," he said. "Chances are we won't. I want you back before we die."

"And I want you. But we can't. We mustn't. They depend on you. Absolutely. You're the only man who can lead us through what lies ahead. You've given me enough strength that I can help you a little. But even so . . . Carl, it was never easy to be a king."

She wheeled and walked quickly from him.

✴ XIV ✴

Leonora Christine shouted, shuddered, and leaped.

Space flamed around her, a firestorm, hydrogen kindled to fluorescence by that supernal sun which was forming at the heart of existence, which burned brighter and brighter as the galaxies rained down into it. The gas hid the central travail behind sheets, banners and spears of radiance, aurora, flame, lightning. Forces, unmeasurably vast, tore through and through the atmosphere: electric, magnetic, gravitational, nuclear fields; shock waves bursting across megaparsecs; tides and currents and cataracts. On the fringes of creation, through billion-year cycles which passed as moments, the ship of man flew.

Flew.

There was no other word. As far as humanity was concerned, or the most swiftly computing and reacting of machines, she fought a hurricane—but such a hurricane as had not been known since last the stars were melted together and hammered afresh.

"*Yah-h-h!*" screamed Aeropilot Lenkei, and rode the ship down the trough of a wave whose crest shook loose a foam of supernovae. The haggard men on the steering bridge with him stared into the screen that had been built. What raged in it was not reality—present reality transcended any picturing or understanding—but a representation of exterior forcefields. It burned and roiled and spewed great sparks and globes. It bellowed in the metal of the ship, in flesh and skulls.

"Can't you stand any more?" Reymont shouted from his own seat. "Barrios, relieve him."

The other flyboat man shook his head. He was too stunned, too beaten by the hour of his own previous watch.

"Okay." Reymont unharnessed himself. "I'll try. I've handled a lot of different types of craft." No one heard him through the fury around, but all saw him fight across the pitching, whirling deck, against two full gravities. He took the auxiliary control chair, on the opposite side of Lenkei from Barrios, and laid his mouth close to the pilot's ear. "Phase me in."

Barrios nodded. Together their hands moved across the control board.

They must hold *Leonora Christine* well away from the growing monobloc, whose radiation would surely kill them; at the same time, they must stay where the gas was so dense that tau could continue to decrease for them, turning these final phoenix begayears into hours; and they must keep the ship riding safely through a chaos that, did it ever strike her full on, would rip her into nuclear particles. No computers, no instruments, no precedents might guide them. It must be done on instinct and trained reflex.

Slowly, Reymont entered the pattern, until he could steer alone.

The rhythms of rebirth were wild, but they were there. Ease on starboard . . . vector at nine o'clock low . . . now *push* that thrust! . . . brake a little here . . . don't let her broach . . . swing wide of the flame if you can . . . Thunder brawled. The air was sharp with ozone, and cold.

The screen blanked. An instant later, every fluoropanel in the ship turned simultaneously ultraviolet and infrared, and darkness plunged down. Those who lay harnessed in aloneness, throughout the hull, heard invisible lightnings walk down the corridors. Those on command bridge, pilot bridge, engine room, who manned the ship, felt a heaviness greater than planets—they could not move, nor stop a movement once begun—and then felt a lightness such that their bodies began to break asunder—and this was a change in inertia itself, in every constant of nature as space-time-matter-energy underwent its ultimate convulsion—for a moment infinitesimal and infinite, men, women, ship and death were one.

It passed, so swiftly that they were not certain it had ever been. Light came back and outside vision. The storm grew fiercer. But now through it, seen distorted so that they appeared to be blue-white firedrops that broke into sparks as they flew, now came nascent galaxies.

The monobloc had exploded. Creation had begun.

Reymont went over to deceleration. *Leonora Christine* started slowly to slow; and she flew out into a reborn light.

✳ XV ✳

Boudreau and Nilsson nodded at each other. They chuckled. "Yes, indeed," the astronomer said.

Reymont looked restlessly around the clutter of meters and apparatus which was the observatory. "Yes, what?" he demanded. He jerked one thumb at a screen which offered a visual display. Space swarmed with little dancing incandescences. "I can see for myself. The galaxies are still close together. Most of them are still nothing but clouds of hydrogen. And hydrogen is still quite thick between them. But what of it?"

"Computation on the basis of data," Nilsson said mysteriously.

"We felt you deserved, as well as needed, to hear in confidence, so that you might be the one who makes the announcement."

"Well?"

"Never mind details," Boudreau said. "This result came out of the problem you set us, to find which directions the matter was headed in, and which directions the antimatter. You recall, we were able to do this by tracing the paths of plasma masses through the magnetic fields of the universe as a whole. And so this vessel is safely into the matter half of the plenum.

"Now in the course of making those studies, we collected and processed an astonishing amount of data. And here is what else we have learned. The cosmos is new, in some respects disordered. Things have not yet sorted themselves out. Within a short range of us, as such distances go, are material complexes—galaxies and proto-galaxies—with every possible velocity.

"We can use that fact to our advantage. That is, we can pick whatever clan, family, individual galaxy we want to make our goal—pick in such a way that we can arrive with zero relative speed at any point of its development that we choose. Within fairly wide limits, anyhow. We couldn't get to a galaxy which is more than about ten billion years old by the time we arrived; not unless we wanted to approach it circuitously. Nor can we overhaul any before it is about one billion years old. But otherwise, we can choose what we like.

"And . . . whatever we elect, the maximum shipboard time required to arrive, braked, will be no longer than a few weeks!"

Reymont said an amazed obscenity.

"You see," Nilsson added, "we can select a galaxy whose velocity is almost identical with ours."

"Oh, yes," Reymont muttered. "I can see that much. But I'm not used to having luck in our favor."

"Not luck," Nilsson said. "Given an oscillating universe, this development was inevitable. Or so we perceive by hindsight. We need merely use the fact.

"Best you decide on our goal," he urged. "Now. Those other idiots, they would wrangle for hours, if you put it to a vote. And every hour means untold cosmic time lost, which narrows our choices. If you will tell us what you want, we'll plot an appropriate course, and the ship can start off very shortly with that vector. The expedition will accept any *fait accompli* you hand them, and thank you for it. You know that."

Reymont ran a hand through his hair. It was quite gray, and his tone was always flat with weariness. "What we want is a suitable planet," he said.

"Yes," Nilsson agreed. "May I suggest a planet—a system—of the same approximate age as Earth had? Say, four or five billion years? It seems to take about so long for a fair probability of the kind of biosphere we like having evolved. That is, we could live in a Mesozoic type of environment, I suppose, but we would rather not."

"Seems reasonable," Reymont nodded. "How about metals, though?"

"Ah, yes. We want a planet as rich in heavy elements as Earth was. Not too much less, or an industrialized civilization will be hard to establish. Not too much more, or we could find numerous areas where the soil is metal-poisoned. Since higher elements are formed in the earlier generations of stars, we should look for a galaxy that will be as old, at rendezvous, as ours was."

"No," Reymont said. "Younger."

"Eh?" Boudreau blinked.

"We can probably find a planet like Earth, also with respect to metals, in a young galaxy," Reymont said. "A globular cluster ought to have had plenty of supernovae in its early stages, which ought to have enriched the interstellar medium, so that G-type suns forming later would have about the same composition as Sol. As we enter our target galaxy, let's scout for such a cluster.

"But supposing we end up on a planet less well endowed with iron and uranium than Earth was . . . that won't matter. We have the technology to make do with light alloys and organics. We have hydrogen fusion for power.

"The important thing is that we be just about the first intelligent race alive."

They stared at him.

He smiled one-sidedly. "I'd like us to have our pick of planets, when we get around to interstellar colonization," he said. "And I'd like us to become the—oh, the elders. Not imperialists; that idea's ridiculous; but the people who were there first, and know their way around, and are worth learning from. Never mind what shape the younger races have. Who cares? But let's make this, as early as possible, a human galaxy, in the deepest sense of the word 'human.' Maybe even a human universe.

"I think we've earned that right."

✳ XVI ✳

That *Leonora Christine* took less than a month to find her new home was partly good fortune, but also due forethought.

The new-born atoms had burst outward with a random distribution of velocities. Thus, in the course of mega- and begayears, they formed hydrogen clouds which attained distinct individualities. While they drifted apart, these clouds condensed into sub-clouds— which, under the eons-long action of manifold forces, differentiated themselves into separate families, then separate galaxies, then individual suns.

But inevitably, in the early stages, exceptional situations occurred. Galaxies were as yet near to each other. They still contained anomalous groups. And so they exchanged matter. A large star cluster, for example, might form within one galaxy, but having more than escape velocity, might cross to another (with suns forming in it meanwhile) that could capture it.

Zeroing in on her destination, *Leonora Christine* kept watch for such a cluster: one whose speed she could easily match. And, as she entered its domain, she looked for a star of the right characteristics, spectral and velocital. To nobody's surprise, the nearest one had planets.

She might then, as originally planned, have gone by at high speed, making observations while she passed through the system. But Reymont said otherwise. For this once, let a chance be taken. The odds weren't so bad. Measurements made across light-years with the newest instruments and techniques developed aboard ship gave some reason to believe that a certain child of that yellow sun might offer a good home for men.

If not—a year would have been lost, the year needed to approach light-speed again with respect to the entire galaxy. But if there actually was a planet such as lived in memory, two years would have been gained.

The gamble seemed worthwhile. Given twenty-five fertile couples, an extra two years meant an extra half hundred ancestors for the future race.

Leonora Christine found her world, that very first time.

✳ XVII ✳

On a hill that viewed wide across a beautiful valley, a man stood with his woman.

Here was not New Earth. That would have been too much to expect. The river far below them was tinted gold with tiny life and ran through meadows whose many-fronded growth was blue. Trees looked as if they were feathered, in shades of the same color, and the wind set certain blossoms in them to chiming. It bore scents which were like cinnamon, and iodine, and horses, and nothing for which men had a name. On the opposite side lifted stark palisades, black and red, fanged with crags, where flashed the horns of a glacier.

Yet the air was warm; and humankind could thrive here. Enormous above river and ridges, towered clouds which shone silver in the sun.

Ingrid Lindgren said, "You mustn't leave her, Carl. Not in so final a way."

"What are you talking about?" Reymont retorted. "We can't leave each other. None of us can. Ai-ling understands you're something unique to me. But so is she, in her own way. So are we all, everyone to everyone else. Aren't we? After what we've been through together?"

"Yes. It's only—I never thought to hear such words from you, Carl, darling."

He laughed. "What did you expect?"

"Oh, I don't know. Something harsh and unyielding. Even cruel."

"The time for that is over," he said. "We've got where we were going. Now we have to start fresh."

"Also with each other?" she asked, a little teasingly.

"Yes. Of course. We'll need to take from the past what's good, and forget what was bad. Like . . . well, the whole question of jealously simply isn't relevant. We need to share our genes around as much as possible. Judas! Fifty of us to start a whole intelligent species again! So your worry about someone being hurt, or left out, or any such thing—it doesn't arise. With all the work ahead of us, personalities have no importance whatsoever."

He pulled her to him and chuckled down at her. "Not that we can't tell the universe that Ingrid Lindgren is the loveliest object in it," he said, threw himself down under a tall old tree, and tugged her hand. "Come here. I told you we were going to take a holiday."

Steely scaled, with a skirling along its wings, passed overhead one of those creatures called dragons.

Lindgren joined Reymont, but hesitantly. "I don't know if we should, Carl," she said.

"Why not?" he asked, surprised.

"So much to do."

"Construction, planting, everything's coming along fine. We can well afford to loaf a bit."

"But . . . all right," she said, the words hard and unwillingly brought forth. "Let's face the fact. Kings get no holidays."

"What are you babbling about?" Reymont lounged back against the rough, sweet-scented bole and rumpled her hair, which was bright beneath the young sun. After dark, there would be three moons to shine upon her, and more stars in the sky than men had known before.

"You," she said. "They look to you, the man who saved them, the man who dared survive, they look to you for—"

He interrupted her in the most enjoyable way.

"Carl!" she protested.

"Do you mind?"

"No. Certainly not. On the contrary. But—I mean, your work—"

"My work," he said, "is my share of the community's job. No more and no less. As for any other position: if nominated I will not run; if elected I will not serve,"

She looked at him with a kind of horror. "You can't mean that!"

"I sure as hell can." he answered. For a moment he turned serious again. "Once a crisis is past, once people manage for themselves . . . what better can a king do than lay down his crown?"

Then he laughed and made her laugh with him, and they were merely human. Which was enough.

NO TRUCE WITH KINGS

"Song, Charlie! Give's a song!"

"Yay, Charlie!"

The whole mess was drunk, and the junior officers at the far end of the table were only somewhat noisier than their seniors near the colonel. Rugs and hangings could not much muffle the racket, shouts, stamping boots, thump of fists on oak and clash of cups raised aloft, that rang from wall to stony wall. High up among shadows that hid the rafters they hung from, the regimental banners stirred in a draft, as if to join the chaos. Below, the light of bracketed lanterns and bellowing fireplace winked on trophies and weapons.

Autumn comes early on Echo Summit, and it was storming outside, wind-hoot past the watchtowers and rain-rush in the courtyards, an undertone that walked through the buildings and down all corridors, as if the story were true that the unit's dead came out of the cemetery each September Nineteenth night and tried to join the celebration but had forgotten how. No one let it bother him, here or in the enlisted barracks, except maybe the hex major. The Third Division, the Catamounts, was known as the most riotous gang in the Army of the Pacific States of America, and of its regiments the Rolling Stones who held Fort Nakamura were the wildest.

"Go on, boy! Lead off. You've got the closest thing to a voice in the whole goddamn Sierra," Colonel Mackenzie called. He loosened the collar of his black dress tunic and lounged back, legs asprawl, pipe in one hand and beaker of whisky in the other: a thickset man with blue wrinkle-meshed eyes in a battered face, his cropped hair turned gray but his mustache still arrogantly red.

77

"Charlie is my darlin', my darlin', my darlin'," sang Captain Hulse. He stopped as the noise abated a little. Young Lieutenant Amadeo got up, grinned, and launched into one they well knew.

"I am a Catamountain, I guard a border pass.
And every time I venture out, the cold will freeze m—"

"Colonel, sir. Begging your pardon."
Mackenzie twisted around and looked into the face of Sergeant Irwin. The man's expression shocked him. "Yes?"

"I am a bloody hero, a decorated vet:
The Order of the Purple Shaft, with pineapple clusters yet!"

"Message just come in, sir. Major Speyer asks to see you right away."
Speyer, who didn't like being drunk, had volunteered for duty tonight; otherwise men drew lots for it on a holiday. Remembering the last word from San Francisco, Mackenzie grew chill.
The mess bawled forth the chorus, not noticing when the colonel knocked out his pipe and rose.

"The guns go boom! Hey, tiddley boom!
The rockets vroom, the arrows zoom.
From slug to slug is damn small room.
Get me out of here and back to the good old womb!
(Hey, doodle dee day!)"

All right-thinking Catamounts maintained that they could operate better with the booze sloshing up to their eardrums than any other outfit cold sober. Mackenzie ignored the tingle in his veins; forgot it. He walked a straight line to the door, automatically taking his sidearm off the rack as he passed by. The song pursued him into the hall.

"For maggots in the rations, we hardly ever lack.
You bite into a sandwich and the sandwich bites right back.
The coffee is the finest grade of Sacramento mud.

The ketchup's good in combat, though, for simulating blood.
(Cho-orus!)
> *The drums go bump! Ah-tumpty-tump!*
> *The bugles make like Gabri'l's trump—"*

Lanterns were far apart in the passage. Portraits of former commanders watched the colonel and the sergeant from eyes that were hidden in grotesque darknesses. Footfalls clattered too loudly here.

> *"I've got an arrow in my rump.*
> *Right about and rearward, heroes, on the jump!*
> *(Hey, doodle dee day!)"*

Mackenzie went between a pair of fieldpieces flanking a stairway—they had been captured at Rock Springs during the Wyoming War, a generation ago—and upward. There was more distance between places in this keep than his legs liked at their present age. But it was old, had been added to decade by decade; and it needed to be massive, chiseled and mortared from Sierra granite, for it guarded a key to the nation. More than one army had broken against its revetments, before the Nevada marches were pacified, and more young men than Mackenzie wished to think about had gone from this base to die among angry strangers.

But she's never been attacked from the west. God, or whatever you are, you can spare her that, can't you?

The command office was lonesome at this hour. The room where Sergeant Irwin had his desk lay so silent: no clerks pushing pens, no messengers going in or out, no wives making a splash of color with their dresses as they waited to see the colonel about some problem down in the Village. When he opened the door to the inner room, though, Mackenzie heard the wind shriek around the angle of the wall. Rain slashed at the black windowpane and ran down in streams which the lanterns turned molten.

"Here the colonel is, sir," Irwin said in an uneven voice. He gulped and closed the door behind Mackenzie.

Speyer stood by the commander's desk. It was a beat-up old object with little upon it: an inkwell, a letter basket, an interphone, a photograph of Nora, faded in these dozen years since her death. The major was a tall and gaunt man, hooknosed, going bald on top. His uniform always looked unpressed, somehow. But he had the sharpest brain in the Cats, Mackenzie thought; and Christ, how could any man read as many books as Phil did! Officially he was the adjutant, in practice the chief adviser.

"Well?" Mackenzie said. The alcohol did not seem to numb him, rather make him too acutely aware of things: how the lanterns smelled hot (when would they get a big enough generator to run electric lights?), and the floor was hard under his feet, and a crack went through the plaster of the north wall, and the stove wasn't driving out much of the chill. He forced bravado, stuck thumbs in belt and rocked back on his heels. "Well, Phil, what's wrong now?"

"Wire from Frisco," Speyer said. He had been folding and unfolding a piece of paper, which he handed over.

"Huh? Why not a radio call?"

"Telegram's less likely to be intercepted. This one's in code, at that. Irwin decoded it for me."

"What the hell kind of nonsense is this?"

"Have a look, Jimbo, and you'll find out. It's for you, anyway. Direct from GHQ."

Mackenzie focused on Irwin's scrawl. The usual formalities of an order; then:

You are hereby notified that the Pacific States Senate has passed a bill of impeachment against Owen Brodsky, formerly Judge of the Pacific States of America, and deprived him of office. As of 2000 hours this date, former Vice Humphrey Fallon is Judge of the PSA in accordance with the Law of Succession. The existence of dissident elements constituting a public danger has made it necessary for Judge Fallon to put the entire nation under martial law, effective at 2100 hours this date. You are therefore issued the following instructions:

1. The above intelligence is to be held strictly confidential until an official proclamation is made. No person who has received knowledge in the course of transmitting this message shall divulge same to any other person whatsoever. Violators of this section and anyone thereby receiving information shall be placed immediately in solitary confinement to await court-martial.

2. You will sequestrate all arms and ammunition except for ten percent of available stock, and keep same under heavy guard.

3. You will keep all men in the Fort Nakamura area until you are relieved. Your relief is Colonel Simon Hollis, who will start from San Francisco tomorrow morning with one battalion. They are expected to arrive at Fort Nakamura in five days, at which time you will surrender your command to him. Colonel Hollis will designate those officers and enlisted men who are to be replaced by members of his battalion, which will be integrated into the regiment. You will lead the men replaced back to San Francisco and report to Brigadier General Mendoza at New Fort Baker. To avoid provocations, these men will be disarmed except for officers' sidearms.

4. For your private information, Captain Thomas Danielis has been appointed senior aide to Colonel Hollis.

5. You are again reminded that the Pacific States of America are under martial law because of a national emergency. Complete loyalty to the legal government is required. Any mutinous talk must be severely punished. Anyone giving aid or comfort to the Brodsky faction is guilty of treason and will be dealt with accordingly.

Gerald O'Donnell, Gen. APSA, CINC

Thunder went off in the mountains like artillery. It was a while before Mackenzie stirred, and then merely to lay the paper on his desk. He could only summon feeling slowly, up into a hollowness that filled his skin.

"They dared," Speyer said without tone. "They really did."

"Huh?" Mackenzie swiveled eyes around to the major's face. Speyer didn't meet that stare. He was concentrating his own gaze on his hands, which were now rolling a cigarette. But the words jerked from him, harsh and quick:

"I can guess what happened. The warhawks have been hollering for impeachment ever since Brodsky compromised the border dispute with West Canada. And Fallon, yeah, he's got ambitions of his own. But his partisans are a minority and he knows it. Electing him Vice helped soothe the warhawks some, but he'd never make Judge the regular way, because Brodsky isn't going to die of old age before Fallon does, and anyhow more than fifty percent of the Senate are sober, satisfied bossmen who don't agree that the PSA has a divine mandate to reunify the continent. I don't see how an impeachment could get through an honestly convened Senate. More likely they'd vote out Fallon."

"But a Senate had been called," Mackenzie said. The words sounded to him like someone else talking. "The newscasts told us."

"Sure. Called for yesterday 'to debate ratification of the treaty with West Canada.' But the bossmen are scattered up and down the country, each at his own Station. They have to *get* to San Francisco. A couple of arranged delays—hell, if a bridge just happened to be blown on the Boise railroad, a round dozen of Brodsky's staunchest supporters wouldn't arrive on time—so the Senate has a quorum, all right, but every one of Fallon's supporters are there, and so many of the rest are missing that the warhawks have a clear majority. Then they meet on a holiday, when no cityman is paying attention. Presto, impeachment and a new Judge!" Speyer finished his cigarette and stuck it between his lips while he fumbled for a match. A muscle twitched in his jaw.

"You sure?" Mackenzie mumbled. He thought dimly that this moment was like one time he'd visited Puget City and been invited for a sail on the Guardian's yacht, and a fog had closed in. Everything was cold and blind, with nothing you could catch in your hands.

"Of course I'm not sure!" Speyer snarled. "Nobody will be sure till it's too late." The matchbox shook in his grasp.

"They, uh, they got a new Cinc too, I noticed."

"Uh-huh. They'd want to replace everybody they can't trust, as fast as possible, and De Barros was a Brodsky appointee." The match flared with a hellish *scrit*. Speyer inhaled till his cheeks collapsed. "You and me included, naturally. The regiment reduced to minimum armament so that nobody will get ideas about resistance when the new colonel arrives. You'll note he's coming with a battalion at his heels just the same, just in case. Otherwise he could take a plane and be here tomorrow."

"Why not a train?" Mackenzie caught a whiff of smoke and felt for his pipe. The bowl was hot in his tunic pocket.

"Probably all rolling stock has to head north. Get troops among the bossmen there to forestall a revolt. The valleys are safe enough, peaceful ranchers and Esper colonies. None of them'll pot-shot

Fallonite soldiers marching to garrison Echo and Donner outposts."
A dreadful scorn weighted Speyer's words.

"What are we going to do?"

"I assume Fallon's take-over followed legal forms; that there was
a quorum," Speyer said. "Nobody will ever agree whether it was really Constitutional. . . . I've been reading this damned message over
and over since Irwin decoded it. There's a lot between the lines. I
think Brodsky's at large, for instance. If he were under arrest this
would've said as much, and there'd have been less worry about rebellion. Maybe some of his household troops smuggled him away in
time. He'll be hunted like a jackrabbit, of course."

Mackenzie took out his pipe but forgot he had done so. "Tom's
coming with our replacements," he said thinly.

"Yeah. Your son-in-law. That was a smart touch, wasn't it? A kind
of hostage for your good behavior, but also a backhand promise that
you and yours won't suffer if you report in as ordered. Tom's a good
kid. He'll stand by his own."

"This is his regiment too," Mackenzie said. He squared his shoulders. "He wanted to fight West Canada, sure. Young and . . . and a lot
of Pacificans did get killed in the Idaho Panhandle during the skir-
mishes. Women and kids among 'em."

"Well," Speyer said, "you're the colonel, Jimbo. What should we
do?"

"Oh, Jesus, I don't know. I'm nothing but a soldier." The pipestem
broke in Mackenzie's fingers. "But we're not some bossman's personal militia here. We swore to support the Constitution."

"*I* can't see where Brodsky's yielding some of our claims in Idaho
is grounds for impeachment. I think he was right."

"Well—"

"A *coup d'état* by any other name would stink as bad. You may
not be much of a student of current events, Jimbo, but you know as
well as I do what Fallon's Judgeship will mean. War with West
Canada is almost the least of it. Fallon also stands for a strong central
government. He'll find ways to grind down the old bossman families.
A lot of their heads and scions will die in the front lines; that stunt
goes back to David and Uriah. Others will be accused of collusion
with the Brodsky people—not altogether falsely—and impoverished
by fines. Esper communities will get nice big land grants, so their

economic competition can bankrupt still other estates. Later wars will keep bossmen away for years at a time, unable to supervise their own affairs, which will therefore go to the devil. And thus we march toward the glorious goal of Reunification."

"If Esper Central favors him, what can we do? I've heard enough about psi blasts. I can't ask my men to face them."

"You could ask your men to face the Hellbomb itself, Jimbo, and they would. A Mackenzie has commanded the Rolling Stones for over fifty years."

"Yes. I thought Tom, someday—"

"We've watched this brewing for a long time. Remember the talk we had about it last week?"

"Uh-huh."

"I might also remind you that the Constitution was written explicitly 'to confirm the separate regions in their ancient liberties.'"

"Let me alone!" Mackenzie shouted. "I don't know what's right or wrong, I tell you! Let me alone!"

Speyer fell silent, watching him through a screen of foul smoke. Mackenzie walked back and forth a while, boots slamming the floor like drumbeats. Finally he threw the broken pipe across the room so it shattered.

"Okay." He must ram each word past the tension in his throat. "Irwin's a good man who can keep his lip buttoned. Send him out to cut the telegraph line a few miles downhill. Make it look as if the storm did it. The wire breaks often enough, heaven knows. Officially, then, we never got GHQ's message. That gives us a few days to contact Sierra Command HQ. I won't go against General Cruikshank . . . but I'm pretty sure which way he'll go if he sees a chance. Tomorrow we prepare for action. It'll be no trick to throw back Hollis' battalion, and they'll need a while to bring some real strength against us. Before then the first snow should be along, and we'll be shut off for the winter. Only we can use skis and snowshoes, ourselves, to keep in touch with the other units and organize something. By spring—we'll see what happens."

"Thanks, Jimbo." The wind almost drowned Speyer's words.

"I'd . . . I'd better go tell Laura."

"Yeah." Speyer squeezed Mackenzie's shoulder. There were tears in the major's eyes.

Mackenzie went out with parade-ground steps, ignoring Irwin: down the hall, down a stairway at its other end, past guarded doors where he returned salutes without really noticing, and so to his own quarters in the south wing.

His daughter had gone to sleep already. He took a lantern off its hook in his bleak little parlor, and entered her room. She had come back here while her husband was in San Francisco.

For a moment Mackenzie couldn't quite remember why he had sent Tom there. He passed a hand over his stubbly scalp, as if to squeeze something out . . . oh, yes, ostensibly to arrange for a new issue of uniforms; actually to get the boy out of the way until the political crisis had blown over. Tom was too honest for his own good, an admirer of Fallon and the Esper movement. His outspokenness had led to friction with his brother officers. They were mostly of bossman stock or from well-to-do protectee families. The existing social order had been good to them. But Tom Danielis began as a fisher lad in a poverty-stricken village on the Mendocino coast. In spare moments he'd learned the three R's from a local Esper; once literate, he joined the Army and earned a commission by sheer guts and brains. He had never forgotten that the Espers helped the poor and that Fallon promised to help the Espers. . . . Then, too, battle, glory, Reunification, Federal Democracy, those were heady dreams when you were young.

Laura's room was little changed since she left it to get married last year. And she had only been seventeen then. Objects survived which had belonged to a small person with pigtails and starched frocks—a teddy bear loved to shapelessness, a doll house her father had built, her mother's picture drawn by a corporal who stopped a bullet at Salt Lake. Oh, God, how much she had come to look like her mother.

Dark hair streamed over a pillow turned gold by the light. Mackenzie shook her as gently as he was able. She awoke instantly, and he saw the terror within her.

"Dad! Anything about Tom?"

"He's okay." Mackenzie set the lantern on the floor and himself on the edge of the bed. Her fingers were cold where they caught at his hand.

"He isn't," she said. "I know you too well."

"He's not been hurt yet. I hope he won't be."

Mackenzie braced himself. Because she was a soldier's daughter, he told her the truth in a few words; but he was not strong enough to look at her while he did. When he had finished, he sat dully listening to the rain.

"You're going to revolt," she whispered.

"I'm going to consult with SCHQ and follow my commanding officer's orders," Mackenzie said.

"You know what they'll be . . . once he knows you'll back him."

Mackenzie shrugged. His head had begun to ache. Hangover started already? He'd need a good deal more booze before he could sleep tonight. No, no time for sleep—yes, there would be. Tomorrow would do to assemble the regiment in the courtyard and address them from the breech of Black Hepzibah, as a Mackenzie of the Rolling Stones always addressed his men, and—. He found himself ludicrously recalling a day when he and Nora and this girl here had gone rowing on Lake Tahoe. The water was the color of Nora's eyes, green and blue and with sunlight flimmering across the surface, but so clear you could see the rocks on the bottom; and Laura's own little bottom had stuck straight in the air as she trailed her hands astern.

She sat thinking for a space before saying flatly: "I suppose you can't be talked out of it." He shook his head. "Well, can I leave tomorrow early, then?"

"Yes. I'll get you a coach."

"T-t-to hell with that. I'm better in the saddle than you are."

"Okay. A couple of men to escort you, though." Mackenzie drew a long breath. "Maybe you can persuade Tom—"

"No. I can't. Please don't ask me to, Dad."

He gave her the last gift he could: "I wouldn't want you to stay. That'd be shirking your own duty. Tell Tom I still think he's the right man for you. Goodnight, duck." It came out too fast, but he dared not delay. When she began to cry he must unfold her arms from his neck and depart the room.

"But I had not expected so much killing!"

"Nor I . . . at this stage of things. There will be more yet, I am afraid, before the immediate purpose is achieved."

"You told me—"

"I told you our hopes, Mwyr. You know as well as I that the Great Science is only exact on the broadest scale of history. Individual events are subject to statistical fluctuation."

"That is an easy way, is it not, to describe sentient beings dying in the mud?"

"You are new here. Theory is one thing, adjustment to practical necessities is another. Do you think it does not hurt me to see that happen which I myself have helped plan?"

"Oh, I know, I know. Which makes it no easier to live with my guilt."

"To live with your responsibilities, you mean."

"Your phrase."

"No, this is not semantic trickery. The distinction is real. You have read reports and seen films, but I was here with the first expedition. And here I have been for more than two centuries. Their agony is no abstraction to me."

"But it was different when we first discovered them. The aftermath of their nuclear wars was still so horribly present. That was when they needed us—the poor starveling anarchs—and we, we did nothing but observe."

"Now you are hysterical. Could we come in blindly, ignorant of every last fact about them, and expect to be anything but one more disruptive element? An element whose effects we ourselves would not have been able to predict. That would have been criminal indeed, like a surgeon who started to operate as soon as he met the patient, without so much as taking a case history. We had to let them go their own way while we studied in secret. You have no idea how desperately hard we worked to gain information and understanding. That work goes on. It was only seventy years ago that we felt enough assurance to introduce the first new factor into this one selected society. As we continue to learn more, the plan will be adjusted. It may take us a thousand years to complete our mission."

"But meanwhile they have pulled themselves back out of the wreckage. They are finding their own answers to their problems. What right have we to—"

"I begin to wonder, Mwyr, what right you have to claim even the title of apprentice psychodynamician. Consider what their 'answers'

actually amount to. Most of the planet is still in a state of barbarism. This continent has come farthest toward recovery, because of having the widest distribution of technical skills and equipment before the destruction. But what social structure has evolved? A jumble of quarrelsome successor states. A feudalism where the balance of political, military, and economic power lies with a landed aristocracy, of all archaic things. A score of languages and subcultures developing along their own incompatible lines. A blind technology worship inherited from the ancestral society that, unchecked, will lead them in the end back to a machine civilization as demoniac as the one that tore itself apart three centuries ago. Are you distressed that a few hundred men have been killed because our agents promoted a revolution which did not come off quite so smoothly as we hoped? Well, you have the word of the Great Science itself that, without our guidance, the totaled misery of this race through the next five thousand years would outweigh by three orders of magnitude whatever pain we are forced to inflict."

"—Yes. Of course. I realize I am being emotional. It is difficult not to be at first, I suppose."

"You should be thankful that your initial exposure to the hard necessities of the plan was so mild. There is worse to come."

"So I have been told."

"In abstract terms. But consider the reality. A government ambitious to restore the old nation will act aggressively, thus embroiling itself in prolonged wars with powerful neighbors. Both directly and indirectly, through the operation of economic factors they are too naive to control, the aristocrats and freeholders will be eroded away by those wars. Anomic democracy will replace their system, first dominated by a corrupt capitalism and later by sheer force of whoever holds the central government. But there will be no place for the vast displaced proletariat, the one-time landowners and the foreigners incorporated by conquest. They will offer fertile soil to any demagogue. The empire will undergo endless upheaval, civil strife, despotism, decay, and outside invasion. Oh, we will have much to answer for before we are done!"

"Do you think . . . when we see the final result . . . will the blood wash off us?"

"No. We pay the heaviest price of all."

✳ ✳ ✳

Spring in the high Sierra is cold, wet, snowbanks melting away from forest floor and giant rocks, rivers in spate until their canyons clang, a breeze ruffling puddles in the road. The first green breath across the aspen seems infinitely tender against pine and spruce, which gloom into a brilliant sky. A raven swoops low, gruk, gruk, look out for that damn hawk! But then you cross timber line and the world becomes tumbled blue-gray immensity, with the sun ablaze on what snows remain and the wind sounding hollow in your ears.

Captain Thomas Danielis, Field Artillery, Loyalist Army of the Pacific States, turned his horse aside. He was a dark young man, slender and snub-nosed. Behind him a squad slipped and cursed, dripping mud from feet to helmets, trying to get a gun carrier unstuck. Its alcohol motor was too feeble to do more than spin the wheels. The infantry squelched on past, stoop-shouldered, worn down by altitude and a wet bivouac and pounds of mire on each boot. Their line snaked from around a prowlike crag, up the twisted road and over the ridge ahead. A gust brought the smell of sweat to Danielis.

But they were good joes, he thought. Dirty, dogged, they did their profane best. His own company, at least, was going to get hot food tonight, if he had to cook the quartermaster sergeant.

The horse's hoofs banged on a block of ancient concrete jutting from the muck. If this had been the old days . . . but wishes weren't bullets. Beyond this part of the range lay lands mostly desert, claimed by the Saints, who were no longer a menace but with whom there was scant commerce. So the mountain highways had never been considered worth repaving, and the railroad ended at Hangtown. Therefore the expeditionary force to the Tahoe area must slog through unpeopled forests and icy uplands, God help the poor bastards.

God help them in Nakamura, too, Danielis thought. His mouth drew taut, he slapped his hands together and spurred the horse with needless violence. Sparks shot from iron shoes as the beast clattered off the road toward the highest point of the ridge. The man's saber banged his leg.

Reining in, he unlimbered his field glasses. From here he could look across a jumbled sweep of mountainscape, where cloud shadows sailed over cliffs and boulders, down into the gloom of a canyon and across to the other side. A few tufts of grass thrust out beneath him, mummy brown, and a marmot wakened early from winter sleep whistled somewhere in the stone confusion. He still couldn't see the castle. Nor had he expected to, as yet. He knew this country . . . how well he did!

There might be a glimpse of hostile activity, though. It had been eerie to march this far with no sign of the enemy, of anyone else whatsoever; to send out patrols in search of rebel units that could not be found; to ride with shoulder muscles tense against the sniper's arrow that never came. Old Jimbo Mackenzie was not one to sit passive behind walls, and the Rolling Stones had not been given their nickname in jest.

If Jimbo is alive. How do I know he is? That buzzard yonder may be the very one which hacked out his eyes.

Danielis bit his lip and made himself look steadily through the glasses. Don't think about Mackenzie, how he outroared and outdrank and outlaughed you and you never minded, how he sat knotting his brows over the chessboard where you could mop him up ten times out of ten and *he* never cared, how proud and happy he stood at the wedding. . . . Nor think about Laura, who tried to keep you from knowing how often she wept at night, who now bore a grandchild beneath her heart and woke alone in the San Francisco house from the evil dreams of pregnancy. one of those dogfaces plodding toward the castle which has killed every army ever sent against it— every one of them has somebody at home and hell rejoices at how many have somebody on the rebel side. Better look for hostile spoor and let it go at that.

Wait! Danielis stiffened. A rider—He focused. *One of our own.* Fallon's army added a blue band to the uniform. *Returning scout.* A tingle went along his spine. He decided to hear the report firsthand. But the fellow was still a mile off, perforce riding slowly over the hugger-mugger terrain. There was no hurry about intercepting him. Danielis continued to survey the land.

A reconnaissance plane appeared, an ungainly dragonfly with sunlight flashing off a propeller head. Its drone bumbled among rock walls, where echoes threw the noise back and forth. Doubtless an auxiliary to the scouts, employing two-way radio communication.

Later the plane would work as a spotter for artillery. There was no use making a bomber of it; Fort Nakamura was proof against anything that today's puny aircraft could drop, and might well shoot the thing down.

A shoe scraped behind Danielis. Horse and man whirled as one. His pistol jumped into his hand.

It lowered. "Oh. Excuse me, Philosopher."

The man in the blue robe nodded. A smile softened his stern face. He must be around sixty years old, hair white and skin lined, but he walked these heights like a wild goat. The Yang and Yin symbol burned gold on his breast.

"You're needlessly on edge, son," he said. A trace of Texas accent stretched out his words. The Espers obeyed the laws wherever they lived, but acknowledged no country their own: nothing less than mankind, perhaps ultimately all life through the space-time universe. Nevertheless, the Pacific States had gained enormously in prestige and influence when the Order's unenterable Central was established in San Francisco at the time when the city was being rebuilt in earnest. There had been no objection—on the contrary—to the Grand Seeker's desire that Philosopher Woodworth accompany the expedition as an observer. Not even from the chaplains; the churches had finally gotten it straight that the Esper teachings were neutral with respect to religion.

Danielis managed a grin. "Can you blame me?"

"No blame. But advice. Your attitude isn't useful. Does nothin' but wear you out. You've been fightin' a battle for weeks before it began."

Danielis remembered the apostle who had visited his home in San Francisco—by invitation, in the hope that Laura might learn some peace. His simile had been still homelier: "You only need to wash one dish at a time." The memory brought a smart to Danielis' eyes, so that he said roughly:

"I might relax if you'd use your powers to tell me what's waiting for us."

"I'm no adept, son. Too much in the material world, I'm afraid. Somebody's got to do the practical work of the Order, and someday I'll get the chance to retire and explore the frontier inside me. But you need to start early, and stick to it a lifetime, to develop your full powers." Woodworth looked across the peaks, seemed almost to merge himself with their loneliness.

Danielis hesitated to break into that meditation. He wondered what practical purpose the Philosopher was serving on this trip. To bring back a report, more accurate than untrained senses and undisciplined emotions could prepare? Yes, that must be it. The Espers might yet decide to take a hand in this war. However reluctantly, Central had allowed the awesome psi powers to be released now and again, when the Order was seriously threatened; and Judge Fallon was a better friend to them than Brodsky or the earlier Senate of Bossmen and House of People's Deputies had been.

The horse stamped and blew out its breath in a snort. Woodworth glanced back at the rider. "If you ask me, though," he said, "I don't reckon you'll find much doin' around here. I was in the Rangers myself, back home, before I saw the Way. This country feels empty."

"If we could know!" Danielis exploded. "They've had the whole winter to do what they liked in the mountains, while the snow kept us out. What scouts we could get in reported a beehive—as late as two weeks ago. What have they planned?"

Woodworth made no reply.

It flooded from Danielis, he couldn't stop, he had to cover the recollection of Laura bidding him good-by on his second expedition against her father, six months after the first one came home in bloody fragments:

"If we had the resources! A few wretched little railroads and motor cars; a handful of aircraft; most of our supply trains drawn by mules—what kind of mobility does that give us? And what really drives me crazy . . . we know how to make what they had in the old days. We've got the books, the information. More, maybe, than the ancestors. I've watched the electrosmith at Fort Nakamura turn out transistor units with enough bandwidth to carry television, no bigger than my fist. I've seen the scientific journals, the research labs, biology, chemistry, astronomy, mathematics. And all useless!"

"Not so," Woodworth answered mildly. "Like my own Order, the community of scholarship's becomin' supranational. Printin' presses, radiophones, telescribes—"

"I say useless. Useless to stop men killing each other because there's no authority strong enough to make them behave. Useless to take a farmer's hands off a horse-drawn plow and put them on the wheel of a tractor. We've got the knowledge, but we can't apply it."

"You do apply it, son, where too much power and industrial plant isn't required. Remember, the world's a lot poorer in natural resources than it was before the Hellbombs. I've seen the Black Lands myself, where the firestorm passed over the Texas oilfields." Woodworth's serenity cracked a little. He turned his eyes back to the peaks.

"There's oil elsewhere," Danielis insisted. "And coal, iron, uranium, everything we need. But the world hasn't got the organization to get at it. Not in any quantity. So we fill the Central Valley with crops that'll yield alcohol, to keep a few motors turning; and we import a dribble of other stuff along an unbelievably inefficient chain of middlemen; and most of it's eaten by the armies." He jerked his head toward that part of the sky which the handmade airplane had crossed. "That's one reason we've got to have Reunification. So we can rebuild."

"And the other?" Woodworth asked softly.

"Democracy—universal suffrage—" Danielis swallowed. "And so fathers and sons won't have to fight each other again."

"Those are better reasons," Woodworth said. "Good enough for the Espers to support. But as for that machinery you want—" He shook his head. "No, you're wrong there. That's no way for men to live."

"Maybe not," Danielis said. "Though my own father wouldn't have been crippled by overwork if he'd had some machines to help him. . . . Oh, I don't know. First things first. Let's get this war over with and argue later." He remembered the scout, now gone from view. "Pardon me, Philosopher, I've got an errand."

The Esper raised his hand in token of peace. Danielis cantered off.

Splashing along the roadside, he saw the man he wanted, halted by Major Jacobsen. The latter, who must have sent him out, sat mounted near the infantry line. The scout was a Klamath Indian, stocky in buckskins, a bow on his shoulder. Arrows were favored over guns by many of the men from the northern districts: cheaper than bullets, no noise, less range but as much firepower as a bolt-action rifle. In the bad old days before the Pacific States had formed their union, archers along forest trails had saved many a town from conquest; they still helped keep that union loose.

"Ah, Captain Danielis," Jacobsen hailed. "You're just in time. Lieutenant Smith was about to report what his detachment found out."

"And the plane," said Smith imperturbably. "What the pilot told us he'd seen from the air gave us the guts to go there and check for ourselves."

"Well?"

"Nobody around."

"What?"

"Fort's been evacuated. So's the settlement. Not a soul."

"But—but—" Jacobsen collected himself. "Go on."

"We studied the signs as best's we could. Looks like noncombatants left some time ago. By sledge and ski, I'd guess, maybe north to some strong point. I suppose the men shifted their own stuff at the same time, gradual-like, what they couldn't carry with 'em at the last. Because the regiment and its support units, even field artillery, pulled out just three-four days ago. Ground's all tore up. They headed downslope, sort of west by northwest, far's we could tell from what we saw."

Jacobsen choked. "Where are they bound?"

A flaw of wind struck Danielis in the face and ruffled the horses' manes. At his back he heard the slow plop and squish of boots, groan of wheels, chuff of motors, rattle of wood and metal, yells and whipcracks of muleskinners. But it seemed very remote. A map grew before him, blotting out the world.

The Loyalist Army had had savage fighting the whole winter, from the Trinity Alps to Puget Sound—for Brodsky had managed to reach Mount Rainier, whose lord had furnished broadcasting facilities, and Rainier was too well fortified to take at once. The bossmen and the autonomous tribes rose in arms, persuaded that a usurper threatened their damned little local privileges. Their protectees fought beside them, if only because no rustic had been taught any higher loyalty than to his patron. West Canada, fearful of what Fallon might do when he got the chance, lent the rebels aid that was scarcely even clandestine.

Nonetheless, the national army was stronger: more matériel, better organization, above everything an ideal of the future. Cinc O'Donnell had outlined a strategy—concentrate the loyal forces at a few points, overwhelm resistance, restore order and establish bases in the region, then proceed to the next place—which worked. The government now controlled the entire coast, with naval units to keep an eye on the Canadians in Vancouver and guard the important Hawaii trade routes; the northern half of Washington almost to the Idaho line; the Columbia Valley; central California as far north as Redding. The remaining rebellious Stations and towns were isolated from each other in mountains, forests, deserts. Bossdom after bossdom fell as the loyalists pressed on, defeating the enemy in detail, cutting him off from supplies and hope. The only real worry had been Cruikshank's Sierra Command, an army in its own right rather than a levy of yokels and citymen, big and tough and expertly led. This expedition against Fort Nakamura was only a small part of what had looked like a difficult campaign.

But now the Rolling Stones had pulled out. Offered no fight whatsoever. Which meant that their brother Catamounts must also have evacuated. You don't give up one anchor of a line you intend to hold. So?

"Down into the valleys," Danielis said; and there sounded in his ears, crazily, the voice of Laura as she used to sing. *Down in the valley, valley so low.*

"Judas!" the major exclaimed. Even the Indian grunted as if he had taken a belly blow. "No, they couldn't. We'd have known."

Hang your head over, hear the wind blow. It hooted across cold rocks.

"There are plenty of forest trails," Danielis said. "Infantry and cavalry could use them, if they're accustomed to such country. And the Cats are. Vehicles, wagons, big guns, that's slower and harder. But they only need to outflank us, then they can get back onto Forty and Fifty—and cut us to pieces if we attempt pursuit. I'm afraid they've got us boxed."

"The eastern slope—" said Jacobsen helplessly.

"What for? Want to occupy a lot of sagebrush? No, we're trapped here till they deploy in the flatlands." Danielis closed a hand on his saddlehorn so that the knuckles went bloodless. "I miss my guess if this isn't Colonel Mackenzie's idea. It's his style, for sure."

"But then they're between us and Frisco! With damn near our whole strength in the north—"

Between me and Laura, Danielis thought.

He said aloud: "I suggest, Major, we get hold of the C.O. at once. And then we better get on the radio." From some well he drew the power to raise his head. The wind lashed his eyes. "This needn't be a disaster. They'll be easier to beat out in the open, actually, once we come to grips."

Roses love sunshine, violets love dew,
Angels in heaven know I love you.

The rains which fill the winter of the California lowlands were about ended. Northward along a highway whose pavement clopped under hoofs, Mackenzie rode through a tremendous greenness. Eucalyptus and live oak, flanking the road, exploded with new leaves. Beyond them on either side stretched a checkerboard of fields and vineyards, intricately hued, until the distant hills on the right and the higher, nearer ones on the left made walls. The freeholder houses that had been scattered across the land a ways back were no longer to be seen. This end of the Napa Valley belonged to the Esper community at St. Helena. Clouds banked like white mountains over the western ridge. The breeze bore to Mackenzie a smell of growth and turned earth.

Behind him it rumbled with men. The Rolling Stones were on the move. The regiment proper kept to the highway, three thousand boots slamming down at once with an earthquake noise, and so did the guns and wagons. There was no immediate danger of attack. But the cavalrymen attached to the force must needs spread out. The sun flashed off their helmets and lance heads.

Mackenzie's attention was directed forward. Amber walls and red tile roofs could be seen among plum trees that were a surf of pink and white blossoms. The community was big, several thousand people. The muscles tightened in his abdomen. "Think we can trust them?" he asked, not for the first time. "We've only got a radio agreement to a parley."

Speyer, riding beside him, nodded. "I expect they'll be honest. Particularly with our boys right outside. Espers believe in non-violence anyway."

"Yeah, but if it did come to fighting—I know there aren't very many adepts so far. The Order hasn't been around long enough for that. But when you get this many Espers together, there's bound to be a few who've gotten somewhere with their damned psionics. I don't want my men blasted, or lifted in the air and dropped, or any such nasty thing."

Speyer threw him a sidelong glance. "Are you scared of them, Jimbo?" he murmured.

"Hell, no!" Mackenzie wondered if he was a liar or not. "But I don't like 'em."

"They do a lot of good. Among the poor, especially."

"Sure, sure. Though any decent bossman looks after his own protectees, and we've got things like churches and hospices as well. I don't see where just being charitable—and they can afford it, with the profits they make on their holdings—I don't see where that gives any right to raise the orphans and pauper kids they take in, the way they do: so's to make the poor tikes unfit for life anywhere outside."

"The object of that, as you well know, is to orient them toward the so-called interior frontier. Which American civilization as a whole is not much interested in. Frankly, quite apart from the remarkable powers some Espers have developed, I often envy them."

"You, Phil?" Mackenzie goggled at his friend.

The lines drew deep in Speyer's face. "This winter I've helped shoot a lot of my fellow countrymen," he said low. "My mother and wife and kids are crowded with the rest of the Village in the Mount Lassen fort, and when we said good-by we knew it was quite possibly permanent. And in the past I've helped shoot a lot of other men who never did me any personal harm." He sighed. "I've often wondered what it's like to know peace, inside as well as outside."

Mackenzie sent Laura and Tom out of his head.

"Of course," Speyer went on, "the fundamental reason you—and I, for that matter—distrust the Espers is that they do represent something alien to us. Something that may eventually choke out the whole concept of life that we grew up with. You know, a couple weeks back in Sacramento I dropped in at the University research lab to see what was going on. Incredible! The ordinary soldier would swear it was witchwork. It was certainly more weird than . . . than simply reading minds or moving objects by thinking at them. But to you or me it's a shiny new marvel. We'll wallow in it.

"Now why's that? Because the lab is scientific. Those men work with chemicals, electronics, subviral particles. That fits into the educated American's world-view. But the mystic unity of creation . . . no, not our cup of tea. The only way we can hope to achieve Oneness is to renounce everything we've ever believed in. At your age or mine, Jimbo, a man is seldom ready to tear down his whole life and start from scratch."

"Maybe so." Mackenzie lost interest. The settlement was quite near now.

He turned around to Captain Hulse, riding a few paces behind. "Here we go," he said. "Give my compliments to Lieutenant Colonel Yamaguchi and tell him he's in charge till we get back. If anything seems suspicious, he's to act at his own discretion."

"Yes, sir." Hulse saluted and wheeled smartly about. There had been no practical need for Mackenzie to repeat what had long been agreed on; but he knew the value of ritual. He clicked his big sorrel gelding into a trot. At his back he heard bugles sound orders and sergeants howl at their platoons.

Speyer kept pace. Mackenzie had insisted on bringing an extra man to the discussion. His own wits were probably no match for a high-level Esper, but Phil's might be.

Not that there's any question of diplomacy or whatever. I hope. To ease himself, he concentrated on what was real and present—hoof-beats, the rise and fall of the saddle beneath him, the horse's muscles rippling between his thighs, the creak and jingle of his saber belt, the clean odor of the animal—and suddenly remembered this was the sort of trick the Espers recommended.

None of their communities was walled, as most towns and every bossman's Station was. The officers turned off the highway and went down a street between colonnaded buildings. Side streets ran off in both directions. The settlement covered no great area, though, being composed of groups that lived together, sodalities or superfamilies or whatever you wanted to call them. Some hostility toward the Order and a great many dirty jokes stemmed from that practice. But Speyer, who should know, said there was no more sexual swapping around than in the outside world. The idea was simply to get away from possessiveness, thee versus me, and to raise children as part of a whole rather than an insular clan.

The kids were out, staring round-eyed from the porticoes, hundreds of them. They looked healthy and, underneath a natural fear of the invaders, happy enough. But pretty solemn, Mackenzie thought; and all in the same blue garb. Adults stood among them, expressionless. Everybody had come in from the fields as the regiment neared. The silence was like barricades. Mackenzie felt sweat begin to trickle down his ribs. When he emerged on the central square, he let out his breath in a near gasp.

A fountain, the basin carved into a lotus, tinkled in the middle of the plaza. Flowering trees stood around it. The square was defined on three sides by massive buildings that must be for storage. On the fourth side rose a smaller temple-like structure with a graceful cupola, obviously headquarters and meeting house. On its lowest step were ranked half a dozen blue-robed men, five of them husky youths. The sixth was middle-aged, the Yang and Yin on his breast. His features, ordinary in themselves, held an implacable calm.

Mackenzie and Speyer drew rein. The colonel flipped a soft salute. "Philosopher Gaines? I'm Mackenzie, here's Major Speyer." He swore at himself for being so awkward about it and wondered what to do with his hands. The young fellows he understood, more or less; they watched him with badly concealed hostility. But he had some trouble meeting Gaines' eyes.

The settlement leader inclined his head. "Welcome, gentlemen. Won't you come in?"

Mackenzie dismounted, hitched his horse to a post and removed his helmet. His worn reddish-brown uniform felt shabbier yet in these surroundings. "Thanks. Uh, I'll have to make this quick."

"To be sure. Follow me, please."

Stiff-backed, the young men trailed after their elders, through an entry chamber and down a short hall. Speyer looked around at the mosaics. "Why, this is lovely," he murmured.

"Thank you," said Gaines. "Here's my office." He opened a door of superbly grained walnut and gestured the visitors through. When he closed it behind himself, the acolytes waited outside.

The room was austere, whitewashed walls enclosing little more than a desk, a shelf of books, and some backless chairs. A window opened on a garden. Gaines sat down. Mackenzie and Speyer followed suit, uncomfortable on this furniture.

"We'd better get right to business," the colonel blurted.

Gaines said nothing. At last Mackenzie must plow ahead:

"Here's the situation. Our force is to occupy Calistoga, with detachments on either side of the hills. That way we'll control both the Napa Valley and the Valley of the Moon . . . from the northern ends, at least. The best place to station our eastern wing is here. We plan to establish a fortified camp in the field yonder. I'm sorry about the damage to your crops, but you'll be compensated once the proper government has been restored. And food, medicine—you understand this army has to requisition such items, but we won't let anybody suffer undue hardship and we'll give receipts. Uh, as a precaution we'll need to quarter a few men in this community, to sort of keep an eye on things. They'll interfere as little as possible. Okay?"

"The charter of the Order guarantees exemption from military requirements," Gaines answered evenly. "In fact, no armed man is supposed to cross the boundary of any land held by an Esper settlement. I cannot be party to a violation of the law, Colonel."

"If you want to split legal hairs, Philosopher," Speyer said, "then I'll remind you that both Fallon and Judge Brodsky have declared martial law. Ordinary rules are suspended."

Gaines smiled. "Since only one government can be legitimate," he said, "the proclamations of the other are necessarily null and void. To a disinterested observer, it would appear that Judge Fallon's title is the stronger, especially when his side controls a large continuous area rather than some scattered bossdoms."

"Not any more, it doesn't," Mackenzie snapped.

Speyer gestured him back. "Perhaps you haven't followed the developments of the last few weeks, Philosopher," he said. "Allow me to recapitulate. The Sierra Command stole a march on the Fallonites and came down out of the mountains. There was almost nothing left in the middle part of California to oppose us, so we took over rapidly. By occupying Sacramento, we control river and rail traffic. Our bases extend south below Bakersfield, with Yosemite and King's Canyon not far away to provide sites for extremely strong positions. When we've consolidated this northern end of our gains, the Fallonite forces around Redding will be trapped between us and the powerful bossmen who still hold out in the Trinity, Shasta, and Lassen regions. The very fact of our being here has forced the enemy to evacuate the Columbia Valley, so that San Francisco may be defended.

It's an open question which side today has the last word in the larger territory."

"What about the army that went into the Sierra against you?" Gaines inquired shrewdly. "Have you contained them?"

Mackenzie scowled. "No. That's no secret. They got out through the Mother Lode country and went around us. They're down in Los Angeles and San Diego now."

"A formidable host. Do you expect to stand them off indefinitely?"

"We're going to make a hell of a good try," Mackenzie said. "Where we are, we've got the advantage of interior communications. And most of the freeholders are glad to slip us word about whatever they observe. We can concentrate at any point the enemy starts to attack."

"Pity that this rich land must also be torn apart by war."

"Yeah. Isn't it?"

"Our strategic objective is obvious enough," Speyer said. "We have cut enemy communications across the middle, except by sea, which is not very satisfactory for troops operating far inland. We deny him access to a good part of his food and manufactured supplies, and most especially to the bulk of his fuel alcohol. The backbone of our own side is the bossdoms, which are almost self-contained economic and social units. Before long they'll be in better shape than the rootless army they face. I think Judge Brodsky will be back in San Francisco before fall."

"If your plans succeed," Gaines said.

"That's our worry." Mackenzie leaned forward, one fist doubled on his knee. "Okay, Philosopher. I know you'd rather see Fallon come out on top, but I expect you've got more sense than to sign up in a lost cause. Will you cooperate with us?"

"The Order takes no part in political affairs, Colonel, except when its own existence is endangered."

"Oh, pipe down. By 'cooperate' I don't mean anything but keeping out from under our feet."

"I am afraid that would still count as cooperation. We cannot have military establishments on our lands."

Mackenzie stared at Gaines' face, which had set into granite lines, and wondered if he had heard aright. "Are you ordering us off?" a stranger asked with his voice.

"Yes," the Philosopher said.

"With our artillery zeroed in on your town?"

"Would you really shell women and children, Colonel?"

O Nora—"We don't need to. Our men can walk right in."

"Against psi blasts? I beg you not to have those poor boys destroyed." Gaines paused, then: "I might also point out that by losing your regiment you imperil your whole cause. You are free to march around our holdings and proceed to Calistoga."

Leaving a Fallonite nest at my back, spang across my communications southward. The teeth grated together in Mackenzie's mouth.

Gaines rose. "The discussion is at an end, gentlemen," he said. "You have one hour to get off our lands."

Mackenzie and Speyer stood up too. "We're not done yet," the major said. Sweat studded his forehead and the long nose. "I want to make some further explanations."

Gaines crossed the room and opened the door. "Show these gentlemen out," he said to the five acolytes.

"No, by God!" Mackenzie shouted. He clapped a hand to his sidearm.

"Inform the adepts," Gaines said.

One of the young men turned. Mackenzie heard the slap-slap of his sandals, running down the hall. Gaines nodded. "I think you had better go," he said.

Speyer grew rigid. His eyes shut. They flew open and he breathed, "*Inform* the adepts?"

Mackenzie saw the stiffness break in Gaines' countenance. There was no time for more than a second's bewilderment. His body acted for him. The gun clanked from his holster simultaneously with Speyer's.

"Get that messenger, Jimbo," the major rapped. "I'll keep these birds covered."

As he plunged forward, Mackenzie found himself worrying about the regimental honor. Was it right to open hostilities when you had come on a parley? But Gaines had cut the talk off himself—

"Stop him!" Gaines yelled.

The four remaining acolytes sprang into motion. Two of them barred the doorway, the other two moved in on either side. "Hold it or I'll shoot!" Speyer cried, and was ignored.

Mackenzie couldn't bring himself to fire on unarmed men. He gave the youngster before him the pistol barrel in his teeth. Bloody-faced, the Esper lurched back. Mackenzie stiff-armed the one coming in from the left. The third tried to fill the doorway. Mackenzie put a foot behind his ankles and pushed. As he went down, Mackenzie kicked him in the temple, hard enough to stun, and jumped over him.

The fourth was on his back. Mackenzie writhed about to face the man. Those arms that hugged him, pinioning his gun, were bear strong. Mackenzie put the butt of his free left hand under the fellow's nose, and pushed. The acolyte must let go. Mackenzie gave him a knee in the stomach, whirled, and ran.

There was not much further commotion behind him. Phil must have them under control. Mackenzie pelted along the hall, into the entry chamber. Where had that goddamn runner gone? He looked out the open entrance, onto the square. Sunlight hurt his eyes. His breath came in painful gulps, there was a stitch in his side, yeah, he was getting old.

Blue robes fluttered from a street. Mackenzie recognized the messenger. The youth pointed at this building. A gabble of his words drifted faintly through Mackenzie's pulse. There were seven or eight men with him—older men, nothing to mark their clothes . . . but Mackenzie knew a high-ranking officer when he saw one. The acolyte was dismissed. Those whom he had summoned crossed the square with long strides.

Terror knotted Mackenzie's bowels. He put it down. A Catamount didn't stampede, even from somebody who could turn him inside out with a look. He could do nothing about the wretchedness that followed, though. *If they clobber me, so much the better, I won't lie awake nights wondering how Laura is.*

The adepts were almost to the steps. Mackenzie trod forth. He swept his revolver in an arc. "Halt!" His voice sounded tiny in the stillness that brooded over the town.

They jarred to a stop and stood there in a group. He saw them enforce a catlike relaxation, and their faces became blank visors. None spoke. Finally Mackenzie was unable to keep silent.

"This place is hereby occupied under the laws of war," he said. "Go back to your quarters."

"What have you done with our leader?" asked a tall man. His voice was even but deeply resonant.

"Read my mind and find out," Mackenzie gibed. *No, you're being childish.* "He's okay, long's he keeps his nose clean. You too. Beat it."

"We do not wish to pervert psionics to violence," said the tall man. "Please do not force us."

"Your chief sent for you before we'd done anything," Mackenzie retorted. "Looks like violence was what he had in mind. On your way."

The Espers exchanged glances. The tall man nodded. His companions walked slowly off. "I would like to see Philosopher Gaines," the tall man said.

"You will pretty soon."

"Am I to understand that he is being held a prisoner?"

"Understand what you like." The other Espers were rounding the corner of the building. "I don't want to shoot. Go on back before I have to."

"An impasse of sorts," the tall man said. "Neither of us wishes to injure one whom he considers defenseless. Allow me to conduct you off these grounds."

Mackenzie wet his lips. Weather had chapped them rough. "If you can put a hex on me, go ahead," he challenged. "Otherwise scram."

"Well, I shall not hinder you from rejoining your men. It seems the easiest way of getting you to leave. But I most solemnly warn that any armed force which tries to enter will be annihilated."

Guess I had better go get the boys, at that. Phil can't mount guard on those guys forever.

The tall man went over to the hitching post. "Which of these horses is yours?" he asked blandly.

Almighty eager to get rid of me, isn't he—Holy hellfire! There must be a rear door!

Mackenzie spun on his heel. The Esper shouted. Mackenzie dashed back through the entry chamber. His boots threw echoes at him. No, not to the left, there's only the office that way. Right . . . around this corner—

A long hall stretched before him. A stairway curved from the middle. The other Espers were already on it.

"Halt!" Mackenzie called. "Stop or I'll shoot!"

The two men in the lead sped onward. The rest turned and headed down again, toward him.

He fired with care, to disable rather than kill. The hall reverberated with the explosions. One after another they dropped, a bullet in leg or hip or shoulder. With such small targets, Mackenzie missed some shots. As the tall man, the last of them, closed in from behind, the hammer clicked on an empty chamber.

Mackenzie drew his saber and gave him the flat of it alongside the head. The Esper lurched. Mackenzie got past and bounded up the stair. It wound like something in a nightmare. He thought his heart was going to go to pieces.

At the end, an iron door opened on a landing. One man was fumbling with the lock. The other blue-robe attacked.

Mackenzie stuck his sword between the Esper's legs. As his opponent stumbled, the colonel threw a left hook to the jaw. The man sagged against the wall. Mackenzie grabbed the robe of the other and hurled him to the floor. "Get out," he rattled.

They pulled themselves together and glared at him. He thrust air with his blade. "From now on I aim to kill," he said.

"Get help, Dave," said the one who had been opening the door. "I'll watch him." The other went unevenly down the stairs. The first man stood out of saber reach. "Do you want to be destroyed?" he asked.

Mackenzie turned the knob at his back, but the door was still locked. "I don't think you can do it," he said. "Not without what's here."

The Esper struggled for self-control. They waited through minutes that stretched. Then a noise began below. The Esper pointed. "We have nothing but agricultural implements," he said, "but you have only that blade. Will you surrender?"

Mackenzie spat on the floor. The Esper went on down.

Presently the attackers came into view. There might be a hundred, judging from the hubbub behind them, but because of the curve Mackenzie could see no more than ten or fifteen—burly fieldhands, their robes tucked high and sharp tools aloft. The landing was too wide for defense. He advanced to the stairway, where they could only come at him two at a time.

A couple of sawtoothed hay knives led the assault. Mackenzie parried one blow and chopped. His edge went into meat and struck bone. Blood ran out, impossibly red, even in the dim light here. The man fell to all fours with a shriek. Mackenzie dodged a cut from the companion. Metal clashed on metal. The weapons locked. Mackenzie's arm was forced back. He looked into a broad suntanned face. The side of his hand smote the young man's larynx. The Esper fell against the one behind and they went down together. It took a while to clear the tangle and resume action.

A pitchfork thrust for the colonel's belly. He managed to grab it with his left hand, divert the tines, and chop at the fingers on the shaft. A scythe gashed his right side. He saw his own blood but wasn't aware of pain. A flesh wound, no more. He swept his saber back and forth. The forefront retreated from its whistling menace. *But God, my knees are like rubber, I can't hold out another five minutes.*

A bugle sounded. There was a spatter of gunfire. The mob on the staircase congealed. Someone screamed.

Hoofs banged across the ground floor. A voice rasped: "Hold everything, there! Drop those weapons and come on down. First man tries anything gets shot."

Mackenzie leaned on his saber and fought for air. He hardly noticed the Espers melt away.

When he felt a little better, he went to one of the small windows and looked out. Horsemen were in the plaza. Not yet in sight, but nearing, he heard infantry.

Speyer arrived, followed by a sergeant of engineers and several privates. The major hurried to Mackenzie. "You okay, Jimbo? You been hurt!"

"A scratch," Mackenzie said. He was getting back his strength, though no sense of victory accompanied it, only the knowledge of aloneness. The injury began to sting. "Not worth a fuss. Look."

"Yes, I suppose you'll live. Okay, men, get that door open."

The engineers took forth their tools and assailed the lock with a vigor that must spring half from fear. "How'd you guys show up so soon?" Mackenzie asked.

"I thought there'd be trouble," Speyer said, "so when I heard shots I jumped through the window and ran around to my horse. That was just before those clodhoppers attacked you; I saw them gathering as

I rode out. Our cavalry got in almost at once, of course, and the dog-faces weren't far behind."

"Any resistance?"

"No, not after we fired a few rounds in the air." Speyer glanced outside. "We're in full possession now."

Mackenzie regarded the door. "Well," he said, "I feel better about our having pulled guns on them in the office. Looks like their adepts really depend on plain old weapons, huh? And Esper communities aren't supposed to have arms. Their charters say so. . . . That was a damn good guess of yours, Phil. How'd you do it?"

"I sort of wondered why the chief had to send a runner to fetch guys that claim to be telepaths. There we go!"

The lock jingled apart. The sergeant opened the door. Mackenzie and Speyer went into the great room under the dome.

They walked around for a long time, wordless, among shapes of metal and less identifiable substances. Nothing was familiar. Mackenzie paused at last before a helix which projected from a transparent cube. Formless darknesses swirled within the box, sparked as if with tiny stars.

"I figured maybe the Espers had found a cache of old-time stuff, from just before the Hellbombs," he said in a muffled voice. "Ultra-secret weapons that never got a chance to be used. But this doesn't look like it. Think so?"

"No," Speyer said. "It doesn't look to me as if these things were made by human beings at all."

"But do you not understand? They occupied a settlement! That proves to the world that Espers are not invulnerable. And to complete the catastrophe, they seized its arsenal."

"Have no fears about that. No untrained person can activate those instruments. The circuits are locked except in the presence of certain encephalic rhythms which result from conditioning. That same conditioning makes it impossible for the so-called adepts to reveal any of their knowledge to the uninitiated, no matter what may be done to them."

"Yes, I know that much. But it is not what I had in mind. What frightens me is the fact that the revelation will spread. Everyone will know the Esper adepts do not plumb unknown depths of the psyche *after all, but merely have access to an advanced physical science. Not only will this lift rebel spirits, but worse, it will cause many, perhaps most of the Order's members to break away in disillusionment."*

"Not at once. News travels slowly under present conditions. Also, Mwyr, you underestimate the ability of the human mind to ignore data which conflict with cherished beliefs."

"But—"

"Well, let us assume the worst. Let us suppose that faith is lost and the Order disintegrates. That will be a serious setback to the plan, but not a fatal one. Psionics was merely one bit of folklore we found potent enough to serve as the motivator of a new orientation toward life. There are others, for example the widespread belief in magic among the less educated classes. We can begin again on a different basis, if we must. The exact form of the creed is not important. It is only scaffolding for the real structure: a communal, anti-materialistic social group, to which more and more people will turn for sheer lack of anything else, as the coming empire breaks up. In the end, the new culture can and will discard whatever superstitions gave it the initial impetus."

"A hundred-year setback, at least."

"True. It would be much more difficult to introduce a radical alien element now, when the autochthonous society has developed strong institutions of its own, than it was in the past. I merely wish to reassure you that the task is not impossible. I do not actually propose to let matters go that far. The Espers can be salvaged."

"How?"

"We must intervene directly."

"Has that been computed as being unavoidable?"

"Yes. The matrix yields an unambiguous answer. I do not like it any better than you. But direct action occurs oftener than we tell neophytes in the schools. The most elegant procedure would of course be to establish such initial conditions in a society that its evolution along desired lines becomes automatic. Furthermore, that would let us close our minds to the distressing fact of our own blood guilt. Unfortunately, the Great Science does not extend down to the details of day-to-day practicality.

"In the present instance, we shall help to smash the reactionaries. The government will then proceed so harshly against its conquered

opponents that many of those who accept the story about what was found at St. Helena will not live to spread the tale. The rest . . . well, they will be discredited by their own defeat. Admittedly, the story will linger for lifetimes, whispered here and there. But what of that? Those who believe in the Way will, as a ride, simply be strengthened in their faith, by the very process of denying such ugly rumors. As more and more persons, common citizens as well as Espers, reject materialism, the legend will seem more and more fantastic. It will seem obvious that certain ancients invented the tale to account for a fact that they in their ignorance were unable to comprehend."

"I see. . . ."

"You are not happy here, are you, Mwyr?"

"I cannot quite say. Everything is so distorted."

"Be glad you were not sent to one of the really alien planets."

"I might almost prefer that. There would be a hostile environment to think about. One could forget how far it is to home."

"Three years' travel."

"You say that so glibly. As if three shipboard years were not equal to fifty in cosmic time. As if we could expect a relief vessel daily, not once in a century. And . . . as if the region that our ships have explored amounts to one chip out of this one galaxy!"

"That region will grow until someday it engulfs the galaxy."

"Yes, yes, yes. I know. Why do you think I chose to become a psychodynamician? Why am I here, learning how to meddle with the destiny of a world where I do not belong? 'To create the union of sentient beings, each member species a step toward life's mastery of the universe.' Brave slogan! But in practice, it seems, only a chosen few races are to be allowed the freedom of that universe."

"Not so, Mwyr. Consider these ones with whom we are, as you say, meddling. Consider what use they made of nuclear energy when they had it. At the rate they are going, they will have it again within a century or two. Not long after that they will be building spaceships. Even granted that time lag attenuates the effects of interstellar contact, those effects are cumulative. So do you wish such a band of carnivores turned loose on the galaxy?

"No, let them become inwardly civilized first; then we shall see if they can be trusted. If not, they will at least be happy on their own planet, in a mode of life designed for them by the Great Science.

Remember, they have an immemorial aspiration toward peace on earth; but that is something they will never achieve by themselves. I do not pretend to be a very good person, Mwyr. Yet this work that we are doing makes me feel not altogether useless in the cosmos."

Promotion was fast that year, casualties being so high. Captain Thomas Danielis was raised to major for his conspicuous part in putting down the revolt of the Los Angeles citymen. Soon after occurred the Battle of Maricopa, when the loyalists failed bloodily to break the stranglehold of the Sierran rebels on the San Joaquin Valley, and he was brevetted lieutenant colonel. The army was ordered northward and moved warily under the coast ranges, half expecting attack from the east. But the Brodskyites seemed too busy consolidating their latest gains. The trouble came from guerrillas and the hedgehog resistance of bossman Stations. After one particularly stiff clash, they stopped near Pinnacles for a breather.

Danielis made his way through camp, where tents stood in tight rows between the guns and men lay about dozing, talking, gambling, staring at the blank blue sky. The air was hot, pungent with cookfire smoke, horses, mules, dung, sweat, boot oil; the green of the hills that lifted around the site was dulling toward summer brown. He was idle until time for the conference the general had called, but restlessness drove him. *By now I'm a father,* he thought, *and I've never seen my kid.*

At that, I'm lucky, he reminded himself. *I've got my life and limbs.* He remembered Jacobsen dying in his arms at Maricopa. You wouldn't have thought the human body could hold so much blood. Though maybe one was no longer human, when the pain was so great that one could do nothing but shriek until the darkness came.

And I used to think war was glamorous. Hunger, thirst, exhaustion, terror, mutilation, death, and forever the sameness, boredom grinding you down to an ox. . . . I've had it. I'm going into business after the war. Economic integration, as the bossman system breaks up, yes, there'll be a lot of ways for a man to get ahead, but decently, without a weapon in his hand—Danielis realized he was repeating thoughts that were months old. What the hell else was there to think about, though?

The large tent where prisoners were interrogated lay near his path. A couple of privates were conducting a man inside. The fellow was blond, burly, and sullen. He wore a sergeant's stripes, but otherwise his only item of uniform was the badge of Warden Echevarry, bossman in this part of the coastal mountains. A lumberjack in peacetime, Danielis guessed from the look of him; a soldier in a private army whenever the interests of Echevarry were threatened; captured in yesterday's engagement.

On impulse, Danielis followed. He got into the tent as Captain Lambert, chubby behind a portable desk, finished the preliminaries, and blinked in the sudden gloom.

"Oh." The intelligence officer started to rise. "Yes, sir?"

"At ease," Danielis said. "Just thought I'd listen in."

"Well, I'll try to put on a good show for you." Lambert reseated himself and looked at the prisoner, who stood with hunched shoulders and widespread legs between his guards. "Now, sergeant, we'd like to know a few things."

"I don't have to say nothing except name, rank, and home town," the man growled. "You got those."

"Um-m-m, that's questionable. You aren't a foreign soldier, you're in rebellion against the government of your own country."

"The hell I am! I'm an Echevarry man."

"So what?"

"So my Judge is whoever Echevarry says. He says Brodsky. That makes you the rebel."

"The law's been changed."

"Your mucking Fallon got no right to change any laws. Especially part of the Constitution. I'm no hillrunner, Captain. I went to school some. And every year our Warden reads his people the Constitution."

"Times have changed since it was drawn," Lambert said. His tone sharpened. "But I'm not going to argue with you. How many riflemen and how many archers in your company?"

Silence.

"We can make things a lot easier for you," Lambert said. "I'm not asking you to do anything treasonable. All I want is to confirm some information I've already got."

The man shook his head angrily.

Lambert gestured. One of the privates stepped behind the captive, took his arm, and twisted a little.

"Echevarry wouldn't do that to me," he said through white lips.

"Of course not," Lambert said. "You're his man."

"Think I wanna be just a number on some list in Frisco? Damn right I'm my bossman's man!"

Lambert gestured again. The private twisted harder.

"Hold on, there," Danielis barked. "Stop that!"

The private let go, looking surprised. The prisoner drew a sobbing breath.

"I'm amazed at you, Captain Lambert," Danielis said. He felt his own face reddening. "If this has been your usual practice, there's going to be a court-martial."

"No, sir," Lambert said in a small voice. "Honest. Only . . . they don't talk. Hardly any of them. What'm I supposed to do?"

"Follow the rules of war."

"With rebels?"

"Take that man away," Danielis ordered. The privates made haste to do so.

"Sorry, sir," Lambert muttered. "I guess . . . I guess I've lost too many buddies. I hate to lose more, simply for lack of information."

"Me too." A compassion rose in Danielis. He sat down on the table edge and began to roll a cigarette. "But you see, we aren't in a regular war. And so, by a curious paradox, we have to follow the conventions more carefully than ever before."

"I don't quite understand, sir."

Danielis finished the cigarette and gave it to Lambert: olive branch or something. He started another for himself. "The rebels aren't rebels by their own lights," he said. "They're being loyal to a tradition that we're trying to curb, eventually to destroy. Let's face it, the average bossman is a fairly good leader. He may be descended from some thug who grabbed power by strong-arm methods during the chaos, but by now his family's integrated itself with the region he rules. He knows it, and its people, inside out. He's there in the flesh, a symbol of the community and its achievements, its folkways and essential independence. If you're in trouble, you don't have to work through some impersonal bureaucracy, you go direct to your bossman. His duties are as clearly defined as your own, and a good deal more demanding, to balance his privileges. He leads you in battle and in the ceremonies that give color and meaning to life. Your fathers and his have worked and played together for two or three hundred years. The land is alive with the memories of them. You and he *belong.*

"Well, that has to be swept away, so we can go on to a higher level. But we won't reach that level by alienating everyone. We're not a conquering army; we're more like the Householder Guard putting down a riot in some city. The opposition is part and parcel of our own society."

Lambert struck a match for him. He inhaled and finished: "On a practical plane, I might also remind you, Captain, that the federal armed forces, Fallonite and Brodskyite together, are none too large. Little more than a cadre, in fact. We're a bunch of younger sons, countrymen who failed, poor citymen, adventurers, people who look to their regiment for that sense of wholeness they've grown up to expect and can't find in civilian life."

"You're too deep for me, sir, I'm afraid," Lambert said.

"Never mind," Danielis sighed. "Just bear in mind, there are a good many more fighting men outside the opposing armies than in. If the bossmen could establish a unified command, that'd be the end of the Fallon government. Luckily, there's too much provincial pride and too much geography between them for this to happen—unless we outrage them beyond endurance. What we want the ordinary freeholder, and even the ordinary bossman, to think, is: 'Well, those Fallonites aren't such bad guys, and if I keep on the right side of them I don't stand to lose much, and should even be able to gain something at the expense of those who fight them to a finish.' You see?"

"Y-yes. I guess so."

"You're a smart fellow, Lambert. You don't have to beat information out of prisoners. Trick it out."

"I'll try, sir."

"Good." Danielis glanced at the watch that had been given him as per tradition, together with a sidearm, when he was first commissioned. (Such items were much too expensive for the common man. They had not been so in the age of mass production; and perhaps in the coming age—) "I have to go. See you around."

He left the tent feeling somewhat more cheerful than before. *No doubt I am a natural-born preacher,* he admitted, *and I never could quite join in the horseplay at mess, and a lot of jokes go completely by me; but if I can get even a few ideas across where they count, that's pleasure enough.* A strain of music came to him, some men and a banjo under a tree, and he found himself whistling along. It was good that this much morale remained, after Maricopa and a northward march whose purpose had not been divulged to anybody.

The conference tent was big enough to be called a pavilion. Two sentries stood at the entrance. Danielis was nearly the last to arrive, and found himself at the end of the table, opposite Brigadier General Perez. Smoke hazed the air and there was a muted buzz of conversation, but faces were taut.

When the blue-robed figure with a Yang and Yin on the breast entered, silence fell like a curtain. Danielis was astonished to recognize Philosopher Woodworth. He'd last seen the man in Los Angeles, and assumed he would stay at the Esper center there. Must have come here by special conveyance, under special orders. . . .

Perez introduced him. Both remained standing, under the eyes of the officers. "I have some important news for you, gentlemen," Perez said most quietly. "You may consider it an honor to be here. It means that in my judgment you can be trusted, first, to keep absolute silence about what you are going to hear, and second, to execute a vital operation of extreme difficulty." Danielis was made shockingly aware that several men were not present whose rank indicated they should be.

"I repeat," Perez said, "any breach of secrecy and the whole plan is ruined. In that case, the war will drag on for months or years. You know how bad our position is. You also know it will grow still worse as our stocks of those supplies the enemy now denies us are consumed. We could even be beaten. I'm not defeatist to say that, only realistic. We could lose the war.

"On the other hand, if this new scheme pans out, we may break the enemy's back this very month."

He paused to let that sink in before continuing:

"The plan was worked out by GHQ in conjunction with Esper Central in San Francisco some weeks ago. It's the reason we are headed north—" He let the gasp subside that ran through the stifling air. "Yes, you know that the Esper Order is neutral in political disputes. But you also know that it defends itself when attacked. And you probably know that an attack was made on it by the rebels. They seized the Napa Valley settlement and have been spreading malicious rumors about the Order since then. Would you like to comment on that, Philosopher Woodworth?"

The man in blue nodded and said coolly: "We've our own ways of findin' out things—intelligence service, you might say—so I can give y'all a report of the facts. St. Helena was assaulted at a time when most of its adepts were away, helpin' a new community get started out in Montana." *How did they travel so fast?* Danielis wondered. *Teleport, or what?* "I don't know, myself, if the enemy knew about that or were just lucky. Anyhow, when the two or three adepts that were left came and warned them off, fightin' broke out and the adepts were killed before they could act." He smiled. "We don't claim to be immortal, except the way every livin' thing is immortal. Nor infallible, either. So now St. Helena's occupied. We don't figure to take any immediate steps about that, because a lot of people in the community might get hurt.

"As for the yarns the enemy command's been handin' out, well, I reckon I'd do the same, if I had a chance like that. Everybody knows an adept can do things that nobody else can. Troops that realize they've done wrong to the Order are goin' to be scared of supernatural revenge. You're educated men here, and know there's nothin' supernatural involved, just a way to use the powers latent in most of us. You also know the Order doesn't believe in revenge. But the ordinary foot soldier doesn't think your way. His officers have got to restore his spirit somehow. So they fake some equipment and tell him that's what the adepts were really usin'—an advanced technology, sure, but only a set of machines that can be put out of action if you're brave, same as any other machine. That's what happened.

"Still, it is a threat to the Order; and we can't let an attack on our people go unpunished, either. So Esper Central has decided to help out your side. The sooner this war's over, the better for everybody."

A sigh gusted around the table, and a few exultant oaths. The hair stirred on Danielis' neck. Perez lifted a hand.

"Not too fast, please," the general said. "The adepts are not going to go around blasting your opponents for you. It was one hell of a tough decision for them to do as much as they agreed to. I, uh, understand that the, uh, personal development of every Esper will be set back many years by this much violence. They're making a big sacrifice.

"By their charter, they can use psionics to defend an establishment against attack. Okay . . . an assault on San Francisco will be construed as one on Central, their world headquarters."

The realization of what was to come was blinding to Danielis. He scarcely heard Perez' carefully dry continuation:

"Let's review the strategic picture. By now the enemy holds more than half of California, all of Oregon and Idaho, and a good deal of Washington. We, this army, we're using the last land access to San Francisco that we've got. The enemy hasn't tried to pinch that off yet, because the troops we pulled out of the north—those that aren't in the field at present—make a strong city garrison that'd sally out. He's collecting too much profit elsewhere to accept the cost.

"Nor can he invest the city with any hope of success. We still hold Puget Sound and the southern California ports. Our ships bring in ample food and munitions. His own sea power is much inferior to ours: chiefly schooners donated by coastal bossmen, operating out of Portland. He might overwhelm an occasional convoy, but he hasn't tried that so far because it isn't worth his trouble; there would be others, more heavily escorted. And of course he can't enter the Bay, with artillery and rocket emplacements on both sides of the Golden Gate. No, about all he can do is maintain some water communication with Hawaii and Alaska.

"Nevertheless, his ultimate object is San Francisco. It has to be— the seat of government and industry, the heart of the nation.

"Well, then, here's the plan. Our army is to engage the Sierra Command and its militia auxiliaries again, striking out of San Jose. That's a perfectly logical maneuver. Successful, it would cut his California forces in two. We know, in fact, that he is already concentrating men in anticipation of precisely such an attempt.

"We aren't going to succeed. We'll give him a good stiff battle and be thrown back. That's the hardest part: to feign a serious defeat, even convincing our own troops, and still maintain good order. We'll have a lot of details to thresh out about that.

"We'll retreat northward, up the Peninsula toward Frisco. The enemy is bound to pursue. It will look like a God-given chance to destroy us and get to the city walls.

"When he is well into the Peninsula, with the ocean on his left and the Bay on his right, we will outflank him and attack from the rear.

The Esper adepts will be there to help. Suddenly he'll be caught, between us and the capital's land defenses. What the adepts don't wipe out, we will. Nothing will remain of the Sierra Command but a few garrisons. The rest of the war will be a mopping-up operation.

"It's a brilliant piece of strategy. Like all such, it's damn difficult to execute. Are you prepared to do the job?"

Danielis didn't raise his voice with the others. He was thinking too hard of Laura.

Northward and to the right there was some fighting. Cannon spoke occasionally, or a drumfire of rifles; smoke lay thin over the grass and the wind-gnarled live oaks which covered those hills. But down along the seacoast was only surf, blowing air, a hiss of sand across the dunes.

Mackenzie rode on the beach, where the footing was easiest and the view widest. Most of his regiment were inland. But that was a wilderness: rough ground, woods, the snags of ancient homes, making travel slow and hard. Once this area had been densely peopled, but the firestorm after the Hellbomb scrubbed it clean and today's reduced population could not make a go on such infertile soil. There didn't even seem to be any foemen near this left wing of the army.

The Rolling Stones had certainly not been given it for that reason. They could have borne the brunt at the center as well as those outfits which actually were there, driving the enemy back toward San Francisco. They had been blooded often enough in this war, when they operated out of Calistoga to help expel the Fallonites from northern California. So thoroughly had that job been done that now only a skeleton force need remain in charge. Nearly the whole Sierra Command had gathered at Modesto, met the northward-moving opposition army that struck at them out of San Jose, and sent it in a shooting retreat. Another day or so, and the white city should appear before their eyes.

And there the enemy will be sure to make a stand, Mackenzie thought, *with the garrison to reinforce him. And his positions will have to be shelled; maybe we'll have to take the place street by street. Laura, kid, will you be alive at the end?*

Of course, maybe it won't happen that way. Maybe my scheme'll work and we'll win easy—What a horrible word "maybe" is! He slapped his hands together with a pistol sound.

Speyer threw him a glance. The major's people were safe; he'd even been able to visit them at Mount Lassen, after the northern campaign was over. "Rough," he said.

"Rough on everybody," Mackenzie said with a thick anger. "This is a filthy war."

Speyer shrugged. "No different from most, except that this time Pacificans are on the receiving as well as the giving end."

"You know damn well I never liked the business, anyplace."

"What man in his right mind does?"

"When I want a sermon I'll ask for one."

"Sorry," said Speyer, and meant it.

"I'm sorry too," said Mackenzie, instantly contrite. "Nerves on edge. Damnation! I could almost wish for some action."

"Wouldn't be surprised if we got some. This whole affair smells wrong to me."

Mackenzie looked around him. On the right the horizon was bounded by hills, beyond which the low but massive San Bruno range lifted. Here and there he spied one of his own squads, afoot or ahorse. Overhead sputtered a plane. But there was plenty of concealment for a redoubt. Hell could erupt at any minute . . . though necessarily a small hell, quickly reduced by howitzer or bayonet, casualties light. (Huh! Every one of those light casualties was a man dead, with women and children to weep for him, or a man staring at the fragment of his arm, or a man with eyes and face gone in a burst of shot, and what kind of unsoldierly thoughts were these?)

Seeking comfort, Mackenzie glanced left. The ocean rolled greenish-gray, glittering far out, rising and breaking in a roar of white combers closer to land. He smelled salt and kelp. A few gulls mewed above dazzling sands. There was no sail or smoke-puff—only emptiness. The convoys from Puget Sound to San Francisco and the lean swift ships of the coastal bossmen were miles beyond the curve of the world.

Which was as it should be. Maybe things were working out okay on the high waters. One could only try, and hope. And . . . it had been his suggestion, James Mackenzie speaking at the conference General Cruikshank held between the battles of Mariposa and San Jose; the same James Mackenzie who had first proposed that the Sierra Command come down out of the mountains, and who had exposed the gigantic fraud of Esperdom, and succeeded in playing down for his men the fact that behind the fraud lay a mystery one hardly dared think about. He would endure in the chronicles, that colonel, they would sing ballads about him for half a thousand years.

Only it didn't feel that way. James Mackenzie knew he was not much more than average bright under the best of conditions, now dull-minded with weariness and terrified of his daughter's fate. For himself he was haunted by the fear of certain crippling wounds. Often he had to drink himself to sleep. He was shaved, because an officer must maintain appearances, but realized very well that if he hadn't had an orderly to do the job for him he would be as shaggy as any buck private. His uniform was faded and threadbare, his body stank and itched, his mouth yearned for tobacco but there had been some trouble in the commissariat and they were lucky to eat. His achievements amounted to patchwork jobs carried out in utter confusion, or to slogging like this and wishing only for an end to the whole mess. One day, win or lose, his body would give out on him—he could feel the machinery wearing to pieces, arthritic twinges, shortness of breath, dozing off in the middle of things—and the termination of himself would be as undignified and lonely as that of every other human slob. Hero? What an all-time laugh!

He yanked his mind back to the immediate situation. Behind him a core of the regiment accompanied the artillery along the beach, a thousand men with motorized gun carriages, caissons, mule-drawn wagons, a few trucks, one precious armored car. They were a dun mass topped with helmets, in loose formation, rifles or bows to hand. The sand deadened their footfalls, so that only the surf and the wind could be heard. But whenever the wind sank, Mackenzie caught the tune of the hex corps: a dozen leathery older men, mostly Indians, carrying the wands of power and whistling together the Song Against Witches. He took no stock in magic himself, yet when that sound came to him the skin crawled along his backbone.

Everything's in good order, he insisted. *We're doing fine.*

Then: *But Phil's right. This is a screwball business. The enemy should have fought through to a southward line of retreat, not let themselves be boxed.*

Captain Hulse galloped close. Sand spurted when he checked his horse. "Patrol report, sir."

"Well?" Mackenzie realized he had almost shouted. "Go ahead."

"Considerable activity observed about five miles northeast. Looks like a troop headed our way."

Mackenzie stiffened. "Haven't you anything more definite than that?"

"Not so far, with the ground so broken."

"Get some aerial reconnaissance there, for Pete's sake!"

"Yes, sir. I'll throw out more scouts, too."

"Carry on here, Phil." Mackenzie headed toward the radio truck. He carried a minicom in his saddlebag, of course, but San Francisco had been continuously jamming on all bands and you needed a powerful set to punch a signal even a few miles. Patrols must communicate by messenger.

He noticed that the firing inland had slacked off. There were decent roads in the interior Peninsula a ways further north, where some resettlement had taken place. The enemy, still in possession of that area, could use them to effect rapid movements.

If they withdrew their center and hit our flanks, where we're weakest—

A voice from field HQ, barely audible through the squeals and buzzes, took his report and gave back what had been seen elsewhere. Large maneuvers right and left, yes, it did seem as if the Fallonites were going to try a breakthrough. Could be a feint, though. The main body of the Sierrans must remain where it was until the situation became clearer. The Rolling Stones must hold out a while on their own.

"Will do." Mackenzie returned to the head of his columns. Speyer nodded grimly at the word.

"Better get prepared, hadn't we?"

"Uh-huh." Mackenzie lost himself in a welter of commands, as officer after officer rode to him. The outlying sections were to be pulled in. The beach was to be defended, with the high ground immediately above.

Men scurried, horses neighed, guns trundled about. The scout plane returned, flying low enough to get a transmission through: yes, definitely an attack on the way; hard to tell how big a force, through the damned tree cover and down in the damned arroyos, but it might well be at brigade strength.

Mackenzie established himself on a hilltop with his staff and runners. A line of artillery stretched beneath him, across the strand. Cavalry waited behind them, lances agleam, an infantry company for support. Otherwise the foot soldiers had faded into the landscape. The sea boomed its own cannonade, and gulls began to gather as if they knew there would be meat before long.

"Think we can hold them?" Speyer asked.

"Sure," Mackenzie said. "If they come down the beach, we'll enfilade them, as well as shooting up their front. If they come higher, well, that's a textbook example of defensible terrain. 'Course, if another troop punches through the lines further inland, we'll be cut off, but that isn't our worry right now."

"They must hope to get around our army and attack our rear."

"Guess so. Not too smart of them, though. We can approach Frisco just as easily fighting backwards as forwards."

"Unless the city garrison makes a sally."

"Even then. Total numerical strengths are about equal, and we've got more ammo and alky. Also a lot of bossman militia for auxiliaries, who're used to disorganized warfare in hilly ground."

"If we do whip them—" Speyer shut his lips together.

"Go on," Mackenzie said.

"Nothing."

"The hell it is. You were about to remind me of the next step: how do we take the city without too high a cost to both sides? Well, I happen to know we've got a hole card to play there, which might help."

Speyer turned pitying eyes away from Mackenzie. Silence fell on the hilltop.

It was an unconscionably long time before the enemy came in view, first a few outriders far down the dunes, then the body of him, pouring from the ridges and gullies and woods. Reports flickered about Mackenzie—a powerful force, nearly twice as big as ours, but with little artillery; by now badly short of fuel, they must depend far more than we on animals to move their equipment. They were evidently going to charge, accept losses in order to get sabers and bayonets among the Rolling Stones' cannon. Mackenzie issued his directions accordingly.

The hostiles formed up, a mile or so distant. Through his field glasses Mackenzie recognized them, red sashes of the Madera Horse, green and gold pennon of the Dagos, fluttering in the iodine wind. He'd campaigned with both outfits in the past. It was treacherous to remember that Ives favored a blunt wedge formation and use the fact against him. . . . One enemy armored car and some fieldpieces, light horse-drawn ones, gleamed wickedly in the sunlight.

Bugles blew shrill. The Fallonite cavalry laid lance in rest and started trotting. They gathered speed as they went, a canter, a gallop, until the earth trembled with them. Then their infantry got going, flanked by its guns. The car rolled along between the first and second line of foot. Oddly, it had no rocket launcher on top or repeater barrels thrust from the fire slits. Those were good troops, Mackenzie thought, advancing in close order with that ripple down the ranks which bespoke veterans. He hated what must happen.

His defense waited immobile on the sand. Fire crackled from the hillsides, where mortar squads and riflemen crouched. A rider toppled, a dogface clutched his belly and went to his knees, their companions behind moved forward to close the lines again. Mackenzie looked to his howitzers. Men stood tensed at sights and lanyards. Let the foe get well in range—There! Yamaguchi, mounted just rearward of the gunners, drew his saber and flashed the blade downward. Cannon bellowed. Fire spurted through smoke, sand gouted up, shrapnel sleeted over the charging force. At once the gun crews fell into the rhythm of reloading, relaying, refiring, the steady three rounds per minute which conserved barrels and broke armies. Horses screamed in their own tangled red guts. But not many had been hit. The Madera cavalry continued in full gallop. Their lead was so close now that Mackenzie's glasses picked out a face, red, freckled, a ranch boy turned trooper, his mouth stretched out of shape as he yelled.

The archers behind the defending cannon let go. Arrows whistled skyward, flight after flight, curved past the gulls and down again. Flame and smoke ran ragged in the wiry hill grass, out of the ragged-leaved live oak copses. Men pitched to the sand, many still hideously astir, like insects that had been stepped on. The fieldpieces on the enemy left flank halted, swiveled about, and spat return fire. Futile . . . but God, their officer had courage! Mackenzie saw the advancing lines waver. An attack by his own horse and foot, down the beach, ought to crumple them. "Get ready to move," he said into his mini-com. He saw his men poise. The cannon belched anew.

The oncoming armored car slowed to a halt. Something within it chattered, loud enough to hear through the explosions.

A blue-white sheet ran over the nearest hill. Mackenzie shut half-blinded eyes. When he opened them again, he saw a grass fire through the crazy patterns of after-image. A Rolling Stone burst from cover, howling, his clothes ablaze. The man hit the sand and rolled over. That part of the beach lifted in one monster wave, crested twenty feet high, and smashed across the hill. The burning soldier vanished in the avalanche that buried his comrades.

"*Psi blast!*" someone screamed, thin and horrible, through chaos and ground-shudder. "The Espers—"

Unbelievably, a bugle sounded and the Sierran cavalry lunged forward. Past their own guns, on against the scattering opposition . . . and horses and riders rose into the air, tumbled in a giant's invisible whirligig, crashed bone-breakingly to earth again. The second rank of lancers broke. Mounts reared, pawed the air, wheeled and fled in every direction.

A terrible deep hum filled the sky. Mackenzie saw the world as if through a haze, as if his brain were being dashed back and forth between the walls of his skull. Another glare ran across the hills, higher this time, burning men alive.

"They'll wipe us out," Speyer called, a dim voice that rose and fell on the air tides. "They'll re-form as we stampede—"

"No!" Mackenzie shouted. "The adepts must be in that car. Come on!"

Most of his horse had recoiled on their own artillery, one squealing, trampling wreck. The infantry stood rigid, but about to bolt. A glance thrown to his right showed Mackenzie how the enemy themselves were in confusion, this had been a terrifying surprise to them too, but as soon as they got over the shock they'd advance and there'd be nothing left to stop them. . . . It was as if another man spurred his mount. The animal fought, foam-flecked with panic. He slugged its head around, brutally, and dug in spurs. They rushed down the hill toward the guns.

He needed all his strength to halt the gelding before the cannon mouths. A man slumped dead by his piece, though there was no mark on him. Mackenzie jumped to the ground. His steed bolted.

He hadn't time to worry about that. Where was help? "Come here!" His yell was lost in the riot. But suddenly another man was beside him, Speyer, snatching up a shell and slamming it into the breach. Mackenzie squinted through the telescope, took a bearing by guess and feel. He could see the Esper car where it squatted among dead and hurt. At this distance it looked too small to have blackened acres.

Speyer helped him lay the howitzer. He jerked the lanyard. The gun roared and sprang. The shell burst a few yards short of target, sand spurted and metal fragments whined.

Speyer had the next one loaded. Mackenzie aimed and fired. Overshot this time, but not by much. The car rocked. Concussion might have hurt the Espers inside; at least, the psi blasts had stopped. But it was necessary to strike before the foe got organized again.

He ran toward his own regimental car. The door gaped, the crew had fled. He threw himself into the driver's seat. Speyer clanged the door shut and stuck his face in the hood of the rocket-launcher periscope. Mackenzie raced the machine forward. The banner on its rooftop snapped in the wind.

Speyer aimed the launcher and pressed the firing button. The missile burned across intervening yards and exploded. The other car lurched on its wheels. A hole opened in its side.

If the boys will only rally and advance— Well, if they don't, I'm done for anyway. Mackenzie squealed to a stop, flung open the door and leaped out. Curled, blackened metal framed his entry. He wriggled through, into murk and stenches.

Two Espers lay there. The driver was dead, a chunk of steel through his breast. The other one, the adept, whimpered among his unhuman instruments. His face was hidden by blood. Mackenzie pitched the corpse on its side and pulled off the robe. He snatched a curving tube of metal and tumbled back out.

Speyer was still in the undamaged car, firing repeaters at those hostiles who ventured near. Mackenzie jumped onto the ladder of the disabled machine, climbed to its roof and stood erect. He waved the blue robe in one hand and the weapon he did not understand in the other. "Come on, you sons!" he shouted, tiny against the sea wind. "We've knocked 'em out for you! Want your breakfast in bed too?"

One bullet buzzed past his ear. Nothing else. Most of the enemy, horse and foot, stayed frozen. In that immense stillness he could not tell if he heard surf or the blood in his own veins.

Then a bugle called. The hex corps whistled triumphantly; their tomtoms thuttered. A ragged line of his infantry began to move toward him. More followed. The cavalry joined them, man by man and unit by unit, on their flanks. Soldiers ran down the smoking hillsides.

Mackenzie sprang to sand again and into his car. "Let's get back," he told Speyer. "We got a battle to finish."

"Shut up!" Tom Danielis said.

Philosopher Woodworth stared at him. Fog swirled and dripped in the forest, hiding the land and the brigade, gray nothingness through which came a muffled noise of men and horses and wheels, an isolated and infinitely weary sound. The air was cold, and clothing hung heavy on the skin.

"Sir," protested Major Lescarbault. The eyes were wide and shocked in his gaunted face.

"I dare tell a ranking Esper to stop quacking about a subject of which he's totally ignorant?" Danielis answered. "Well, it's past time that somebody did."

Woodworth recovered his poise. "All I said, son, was that we should consolidate our adepts and strike the Brodskyite center," he reproved. "What's wrong with that?"

Danielis clenched his fists. "Nothing," he said, "except it invites a worse disaster than you've brought on us yet."

"A setback or two," Lescarbault argued. "They did rout us on the west, but we turned their flank here by the Bay."

"With the net result that their main body pivoted, attacked, and split us in half," Danielis snapped. "The Espers have been scant use since then . . . now the rebels know they need vehicles to transport their weapons, and can be killed. Artillery zeroes in on their positions, or bands of woodsmen hit and run, leaving them dead, or the enemy simply goes around any spot where they're known to be. We haven't got enough adepts!"

"That's why I proposed gettin' them in one group, too big to withstand," Woodworth said.

"And too cumbersome to be of any value," Danielis replied. He felt more than a little sickened, knowing how the Order had cheated him his whole life; yes, he thought, that was the real bitterness, not the fact that the adepts had failed to defeat the rebels—by failing, essentially, to break their spirit—but the fact that the adepts were only someone else's cat's paws and every gentle, earnest soul in every Esper community was only someone's dupe.

Wildly he wanted to return to Laura—there'd been no chance thus far to see her—Laura and the kid, the last honest reality this fog-world had left him. He mastered himself and went on more evenly:

"The adepts, what few of them survive, will of course be helpful in defending San Francisco. An army free to move around in the field can deal with them, one way or another, but your . . . your weapons can repel an assault on the city walls. So that's where I'm going to take them."

Probably the best he could do. There was no word from the northern half of the loyalist army. Doubtless they'd withdrawn to the capital, suffering heavy losses en route. Radio jamming continued, hampering friendly and hostile communications alike. He had to take action, either retreat southward or fight his way through to the city. The latter course seemed wisest. He didn't believe that Laura had much to do with his choice.

"I'm no adept myself," Woodworth said. "I can't call them mind to mind."

"You mean you can't use their equivalent of radio," Danielis said brutally. "Well, you've got an adept in attendance. Have him pass the word."

Woodworth flinched. "I hope," he said, "I hope you understand this came as a surprise to me too."

"Oh, yes, certainly, Philosopher," Lescarbault said unbidden.

Woodworth swallowed. "I still hold with the Way and the Order," he said harshly. "There's nothin' else I can do. Is there? The Grand Seeker has promised a full explanation when this is over." He shook his head. "Okay, son, I'll do what I can."

A certain compassion touched Danielis as the blue robe disappeared into the fog. He rapped his orders the more severely.

Slowly his command got going. He was with the Second Brigade; the rest were strewn over the Peninsula in the fragments into which the rebels had knocked them. He hoped the equally scattered adepts, joining him on his march through the San Bruno range, would guide some of those units to him. But most, wandering demoralized, were sure to surrender to the first rebels they came upon.

He rode near the front, on a muddy road that snaked over the highlands. His helmet was a monstrous weight. The horse stumbled beneath him, exhausted by—how many days?—of march, counter-march, battle, skirmish, thin rations or none, heat and cold and fear, in an empty land. Poor beast, he'd see that it got proper treatment when they reached the city. That all those poor beasts behind him did, after trudging and fighting and trudging again until their eyes were filmed with fatigue.

There'll be chance enough for rest in San Francisco. We're impregnable there, walls and cannon and the Esper machines to landward, the sea that feeds us at our backs. We can recover our strength, regroup our forces, bring fresh troops down from Washington and up from the south by water. The war isn't decided yet . . . God help us.

I wonder if it will ever be.

And then, will Jimbo Mackenzie come to see us, sit by the fire and swap yarns about what we did? Or talk about something else, anything else? If not, that's too high a price for victory.

Maybe not too high a price for what we've learned, though. Strangers on this planet . . . what else could have forged those weapons? The adepts will talk if I myself have to torture them till they do. But Danielis remembered tales muttered in the fisher huts of his boyhood, after dark, when ghosts walked in old men's minds. Before the holocaust there had been legends about the stars, and the legends lived on. He didn't know if he would be able to look again at the night sky without a shiver.

This damned fog—

Hoofs thudded. Danielis half drew his sidearm. But the rider was a scout of his own, who raised a drenched sleeve in salute. "Colonel, an enemy force about ten miles ahead by road. Big."

So we'll have to fight now. "Do they seem aware of us?"

"No, sir. They're proceeding east along the ridge there."

"Probably figure to occupy the Candlestick Park ruins," Danielis

murmured. His body was too tired for excitement. "Good stronghold, that. Very well, Corporal." He turned to Lescarbault and issued
instructions.

The brigade formed itself in the formlessness. Patrols went out.
Information began to flow back, and Danielis sketched a plan that
ought to work. He didn't want to try for a decisive engagement, only
brush the enemy aside and discourage them from pursuit. His men
must be spared, as many as possible, for the city defense and the
eventual counteroffensive.

Lescarbault came back. "Sir! The radio jamming's ended!"

"What?" Danielis blinked, not quite comprehending.

"Yes, sir. I've been using a minicom—" Lescarbault lifted the wrist
on which his tiny transceiver was strapped—"for very short-range
work, passing the battalion commanders their orders. The interference stopped a couple of minutes ago. Clear as daylight."

Danielis pulled the wrist toward his own mouth. "Hello, hello,
radio wagon, this is the C.O. You read me?"

"Yes, sir," said the voice.

"They turned off the jammer in the city for a reason. Get me the
open military band."

"Yes, sir." Pause, while men mumbled and water runneled unseen
in the arroyos. A wraith smoked past Danielis' eyes. Drops coursed
off his helmet and down his collar. The horse's mane hung sodden.

Like the scream of an insect:

"—here at once! Every unit in the field, get to San Francisco at
once! We're under attack by sea!"

Danielis let go Lescarbault's arm. He stared into emptiness while
the voice wailed on and forever on.

"—bombarding Potrero Point. Decks jammed with troops. They
must figure to make a landing there—"

Danielis' mind raced ahead of the words. It was as if Esp were no
lie, as if he scanned the beloved city himself and felt her wounds in
his own flesh. There was no fog around the Gate, of course, or so
detailed a description could not have been given. Well, probably
some streamers of it rolled in under the rusted remnants of the
bridge, themselves like snowbanks against blue-green water and
brilliant sky. But most of the Bay stood open to the sun. On the
opposite shore lifted the Eastbay hills, green with gardens and

agleam with villas; and Marin shouldered heavenward across the strait, looking to the roofs and walls and heights that were San Francisco. The convoy had gone between the coast defenses that could have smashed it, an unusually large convoy and not on time: but still the familiar big-bellied hulls, white sails, occasional fuming stacks, that kept the city fed. There had been an explanation about trouble with commerce raiders; and the fleet was passed on into the Bay, where San Francisco had no walls. Then the gun covers were taken off and the holds vomited armed men.

Yes, they did seize a convoy, those piratical schooners. Used radio jamming of their own; together with ours, that choked off any cry of warning. They threw our supplies overboard and embarked the boss-man militia. Some spy or traitor gave them the recognition signals. Now the capital lies open to them, her garrison stripped, hardly an adept left in Esper Central, the Sierrans thrusting against her southern gates, and Laura without me.

"We're coming!" Danielis yelled. His brigade groaned into speed behind him. They struck with a desperate ferocity that carried them deep into enemy positions and then stranded them in separated groups. It became knife and saber in the fog. But Danielis, because he led the charge, had already taken a grenade on his breast.

East and south, in the harbor district and at the wreck of the Peninsula wall, there was still some fighting. As he rode higher, Mackenzie saw how those parts were dimmed by smoke, which the wind scattered to show rubble that had been houses. The sound of firing drifted to him. But otherwise the city shone untouched, roofs and white walls in a web of streets, church spires raking the sky like masts, Federal House on Nob Hill and the Watchtower on Telegraph Hill as he remembered them from childhood visits. The Bay glittered insolently beautiful.

But he had no time for admiring the view, nor for wondering where Laura huddled. The attack on Twin Peaks must be swift, for surely Esper Central would defend itself.

On the avenue climbing the opposite side of those great humps, Speyer led half the Rolling Stones. (Yamaguchi lay dead on a pock-marked beach.) Mackenzie himself was taking this side. Horses clopped along Portola, between blankly shuttered mansions; guns trundled and creaked, boots knocked on pavement, moccasins slithered, weapons rattled, men breathed heavily and the hex corps whistled against unknown demons. But silence overwhelmed the noise, echoes trapped it and let it die. Mackenzie recollected nightmares when he fled down a corridor which had no end. *Even if they don't cut loose at us,* he thought bleakly, *we've got to seize their place before our nerve gives out.*

Twin Peaks Boulevard turned off Portola and wound steeply to the right. The houses ended; wild grasses alone covered the quasi-sacred hills, up to the tops where stood the buildings forbidden to all but adepts. Those two soaring, iridescent, fountainlike skyscrapers had been raised by night, within a matter of weeks. Something like a moan stirred at Mackenzie's back.

"Bugler, sound the advance. On the double!"

A child's jeering, the notes lifted and were lost. Sweat stung Mackenzie's eyes. If he failed and was killed, that didn't matter too much . . . after everything which had happened . . . but the regiment, the regiment—

Flame shot across the street, the color of hell. There went a hiss and a roar. The pavement lay trenched, molten, smoking and reeking. Mackenzie wrestled his horse to a standstill. *A warning only. But if they had enough adepts to handle us, would they bother trying to scare us off?* "Artillery, open fire!"

The field guns bellowed together, not only howitzers but motorized 75s taken along from Alemany Gate's emplacements. Shells went overhead with a locomotive sound. They burst on the walls above and the racket thundered back down the wind.

Mackenzie tensed himself for an Esper blast, but none came. Had they knocked out the final defensive post in their own first barrage? Smoke cleared from the heights and he saw that the colors which played in the tower were dead and that wounds gaped across loveliness, showing unbelievably thin framework. It was like seeing the bones of a woman murdered by his hand.

Quick, though! He issued a string of commands and led the horse and foot on. The battery stayed where it was, firing and firing with hysterical fury. The dry brown grass started to burn, as red-hot fragments scattered across the slope. Through mushroom bursts, Mackenzie saw the building crumble. Whole sheets of facing broke and fell to earth. The skeleton vibrated, took a direct hit and sang in metal agony, slumped and twisted apart.

What was that which stood within?

There were no separate rooms, no floors, nothing but girders, enigmatic machines, here and there a globe still aglow like a minor sun. The structure had enclosed something nearly as tall as itself, a finned and shining column, almost like a rocket shell but impossibly huge and fair.

Their spaceship, Mackenzie thought in the clamor. *Yes, of course, the ancients had begun making spaceships, and we always figured we would again someday. This, though—!*

The archers lifted a tribal screech. The riflemen and cavalry took it up, crazy, jubilant, the howl of a beast of prey. By Satan, we've whipped the stars themselves! As they burst onto the hillcrest, the shelling stopped, and their yells overrode the wind. Smoke was acrid as blood smell in their nostrils.

A few dead blue-robes could be seen in the debris. Some half-dozen survivors milled toward the ship. A bowman let fly. His arrow glanced off the landing gear but brought the Espers to a halt. Troopers poured over the shards to capture them.

Mackenzie reined in. Something that was not human lay crushed near a machine. Its blood was deep violet color. *When the people have seen this, that's the end of the Order.* He felt no triumph. At St. Helena he had come to appreciate how fundamentally good the believers were.

But this was no moment for regret, or for wondering how harsh the future would be with man taken entirely off the leash. The building on the other peak was still intact. He had to consolidate his position here, then help Phil if need be.

However, the minicom said, "Come on and join me, Jimbo. The fracas is over," before he had completed his task. As he rode alone toward Speyer's place, he saw a Pacific States flag flutter up the mast on that skyscraper's top.

Guards stood awed and nervous at the portal. Mackenzie dismounted and walked inside. The entry chamber was a soaring, shimmering fantasy of colors and arches, through which men moved troll-like. A corporal led him down a hall. Evidently this building had been used for quarters, offices, storage, and less understandable purposes. . . . There was a room whose door had been blown down with dynamite. The fluid abstract murals were stilled, scarred, and sooted. Four ragged troopers pointed guns at the two beings whom Speyer was questioning.

One slumped at something that might answer to a desk. The avian face was buried in seven-fingered hands and the rudimentary wings quivered with sobs. *Are they able to cry, then?* Mackenzie thought, astonished, and had a sudden wish to take the being in his arms and offer what comfort he was able.

The other one stood erect in a robe of woven metal. Great topaz eyes met Speyer's from a seven-foot height, and the voice turned accented English into music.

"—a G-type star some fifty light-years hence. It is barely visible to the naked eye, though not in this hemisphere."

The major's fleshless, bristly countenance jutted forward as if to peck. "When do you expect reinforcements?"

"There will be no other ship for almost a century, and it will only bring personnel. We are isolated by space and time; few can come to work here, to seek to build a bridge of minds across that gulf—"

"Yeah," Speyer nodded prosaically. "The light-speed limit. I thought so. If you're telling the truth."

The being shuddered. "Nothing is left for us but to speak truth, and pray that you will understand and help. Revenge, conquest, any form of mass violence is impossible when so much space and time lies between. Our labor has been done in the mind and heart. It is not too late, even now. The most crucial facts can still be kept hidden— oh, listen to me, for the sake of your unborn!"

Speyer nodded to Mackenzie. "Everything okay?" he said. "We got us a full bag here. About twenty left alive, this fellow the boss-man. Seems like they're the only ones on Earth."

"We guessed there couldn't be many," the colonel said. His tone and his feelings were alike ashen. "When we talked it over, you and me, and tried to figure what our clues meant. They'd have to be few, or they'd've operated more openly."

"Listen, listen," the being pleaded. "We came in love. Our dream was to lead you—to make you lead yourselves—toward peace, fulfill-ment. . . . Oh, yes, we would also gain, gain yet another race with whom we could someday converse as brothers. But there are many races in the universe. It was chiefly for your own tortured sakes that we wished to guide your future."

"That controlled history notion isn't original with you," Speyer grunted. "We've invented it for ourselves now and then on Earth. The last time it led to the Hellbombs. No, thanks!"

"But we *know*! The Great Science predicts with absolute certainty—"

"Predicted this?" Speyer waved a hand at the blackened room.

"There are fluctuations. We are too few to control so many savages in every detail. But do you not wish an end to war, to all your ancient sufferings? I offer you that for your help today."

"You succeeded in starting a pretty nasty war yourselves," Speyer said.

The being twisted its fingers together. "That was an error. The plan remains, the only way to lead your people toward peace. I, who have traveled between suns, will get down before your boots and beg you—"

"Stay put!" Speyer flung back. "If you'd come openly, like honest folk, you'd have found some to listen to you. Maybe enough, even. But no, your do-gooding had to be subtle and crafty. You knew what was right for us. We weren't entitled to any say in the matter. God in heaven, I've never heard anything so arrogant!"

The being lifted its head. "Do you tell children the whole truth?"

"As much as they're ready for."

"Your child-culture is not ready to hear these truths."

"Who qualified you to call us children—besides yourselves?"

"How do you know you are adult?"

"By trying adult jobs and finding out if I can handle them. Sure, we make some ghastly blunders, we humans. But they're our own. And we learn from them. You're the ones who won't learn, you and that damned psychological science you were bragging about, that wants to fit every living mind into the one frame it can understand.

"You wanted to re-establish the centralized state, didn't you? Did you ever stop to think that maybe feudalism is what suits man? Some one place to call our own, and belong to, and be part of; a community with traditions and honor; a chance for the individual to make decisions that count; a bulwark for liberty against the central overlords, who'll always want more and more power; a thousand different ways to live. We've always built supercountries, here on Earth, and we've always knocked them apart again. I think maybe the whole idea is wrong. And maybe this time we'll try something better. Why not a world of little states, too well rooted to dissolve in a nation, too small to do much harm—slowly rising above petty jealousies and spite, but keeping their identities—a thousand separate approaches to our problems. Maybe then we can solve a few of them . . . for ourselves!"

"You will never do so," the being said. "You will be torn in pieces all over again."

"That's what you think. I think otherwise. But whichever is right—and I bet this is too big a universe for either of us to predict— we'll have made a free choice on Earth. I'd rather be dead than domesticated.

"The people are going to learn about you as soon as Judge Brodsky's been reinstated. No, sooner. The regiment will hear today, the city tomorrow, just to make sure no one gets ideas about suppressing the truth again. By the time your next spaceship comes, we'll be ready for it: in our own way, whatever that is."

The being drew a fold of robe about its head. Speyer turned to Mackenzie. His face was wet. "Anything . . . you want to say . . . Jimbo?"

"No," Mackenzie mumbled. "Can't think of anything. Let's get our command organized here. I don't expect we'll have to fight any more, though. It seems to be about ended down there."

"Sure." Speyer drew an uneven breath. "The enemy troops elsewhere are bound to capitulate. They've got nothing left to fight for. We can start patching up pretty soon."

There was a house with a patio whose wall was covered by roses. The street outside had not yet come back to life, so that silence dwelt here under the yellow sunset. A maidservant showed Mackenzie through the back door and departed. He walked toward Laura, who sat on a bench beneath a willow. She watched him approach but did not rise. One hand rested on a cradle.

He stopped and knew not what to say. How thin she was!

Presently she told him, so low he could scarcely hear: "Tom's dead."

"Oh, no." Darkness came and went before his eyes.

"I learned the day before yesterday, when a few of his men straggled home. He was killed in the San Bruno."

Mackenzie did not dare join her, but his legs would not upbear him. He sat down on the flagstones and saw curious patterns in their arrangement. There was nothing else to look at.

Her voice ran on above him, toneless: "Was it worth it? Not only Tom, but so many others, killed for a point of politics?"

"More than that was at stake," he said.

"Yes, I heard on the radio. I still can't understand how it was worth it. I've tried very hard, but I can't."

He had no strength left to defend himself. "Maybe you're right, duck. I wouldn't know."

"I'm not sorry for myself," she said. "I still have Jimmy. But Tom was cheated out of so much."

He realized all at once that there was a baby, and he ought to take his grandchild to him and think thoughts about life going on into the future. But he was too empty.

"Tom wanted him named after you," she said.

Did you, Laura? he wondered. Aloud: "What are you going to do now?"

"I'll find something."

He made himself glance at her. The sunset burned on the willow leaves above and on her face, which was now turned toward the infant he could not see. "Come back to Nakamura," he said.

"No. Anywhere else."

"You always loved the mountains," he groped. "We—"

"No." She met his eyes. "It isn't you, Dad. Never you. But Jimmy is not going to grow up a soldier." She hesitated. "I'm sure some of the Espers will keep going, on a new basis, but with the same goals. I think we should join them. He ought to believe in something different from what killed his father, and work for it to become real. Don't you agree?"

Mackenzie climbed to his feet against Earth's hard pull. "I don't know," he said. "Never was a thinker. . . . Can I see him?"

"Oh, Dad—"

He went over and looked down at the small sleeping form. "If you marry again," he said, "and have a daughter, would you call her for her mother?" He saw Laura's head bend downward and her hands clench. Quickly he said, "I'll go now. I'd like to visit you some more, tomorrow or sometime, if you'll have me."

Then she came to his arms and wept. He stroked her hair and murmured, as he had done when she was a child. "You do want to return to the mountains, don't you? They're your country too, your people, where you belong."

"Y-you'll never know how much I want to."

"Then why not?" he cried.

His daughter straightened herself. "I can't," she said. "Your war is ended. Mine has just begun."

Because he had trained that will, he could only say, "I hope you win it."

"Perhaps in a thousand years—" She could not continue.

Night had fallen when he left her. Power was still out in the city, so the street lamps were dark and the stars stood forth above all roofs. The squad that waited to accompany their colonel to barracks looked wolfish by lantern light. They saluted him and rode at his back, rifles ready for trouble; but there was only the iron sound of horseshoes.

PROGRESS

✳ 1 ✳

"There they are! Aircraft ho-o-o!"

Keanua's bull bellow came faintly down to Ranu from the crow's nest, almost drowned in the slatting and cracking of sails. He could have spoken clearly head-to-head, but best save that for real emergencies. Otherwise, by some accident, the Brahmards might learn about it.

If they don't already know, Ranu thought.

The day was too bright for what was going to happen. Big, wrinkled waves marched past. Their backs were a hundred different blues, from the color of the sky overhead to a royal midnight; their troughs shaded through gray-amber to a clear green. Foam swirled intricately upon them. Further off they became a single restlessness that glittered with sunlight, on out to the horizon. They rushed and rumbled, they smacked against the hulls, which rolled somewhat beneath Ranu's feet, making him aware of the interplay in his leg muscles. The air was mild, but had a strong thrust and saltiness to it.

Ranu wished he could sink into the day. Nothing would happen for minutes yet. He should think only about sunlight warming his skin, wind ruffling his hair, blue shadows upon an amazingly white cloud high up where the air was not so swift. Once the Beneghalis arrived, he might be dead. Keanua, he felt sure, wasn't worrying about that until the time came. But then, Keanua was from Taiiti. Ranu had been born and bred in N'Zealann; his Maurai genes were too mixed with the old fretful Ingliss. It showed on his body also, tall and lean, with narrow face and beaky nose, brown hair and the rarity of blue eyes.

He unslung his binoculars and peered after the airship. A light touch on his arm recalled him. He lowered the glasses and smiled lopsidedly at Alisabeta Kanukauai.

"Still too far to see from here," he told her. "The topmasts get in the way. But don't bother going aloft. She'll be overhead before you could swarm halfway up the shrouds."

The wahine nodded. She was rather short, a trifle on the stocky side, but because she was young her figure looked good in the brief lap-lap. A hibiscus flower from the deck garden adorned her blue-black locks, which were cut off just below the ears like the men's. Sailors couldn't be bothered with glamorous tresses, even on a trimaran as broad and stable as this. On some ships, of course, a woman had no duties beyond housekeeping. But Alisabeta was a cyberneticist. The Lohannaso Shippers' Association, to which she and Ranu were both related by blood, preferred to minimize crews; so everybody doubled as something else.

That was one reason the *Aorangi* had been picked for this task. The fact of Alisabeta's technical training could not be hidden from the Brahmards. Eyes sharpened by suspicion would see a thousand subtle traces in her manner, left by years of mathematical logic, physics, engineering. But such would be quite natural in a Lohannaso girl.

Moreover, if this job went sour, only three lives would have been sacrificed. Some merchant craft had as many as ten kanakas and three wahines aboard.

"I suppose I'd better get back to the radio," said Alisabeta. "They may want to call."

"I doubt that," said Ranu. "If they aren't simply going to attack us from above, they'll board. They told us they would, when we talked before. But yes, I suppose you had better stand by."

His gaze followed her with considerable pleasure. Usually, in the culture of the Sea People, there was something a little unnatural about a career woman, a female to whom her own home and children were merely incidental if she elected to have them at all. But Alisabeta had been as good a cook, as merry a companion, as much alive in a man's arms on moonlit nights, as any seventeen-year-old signed on to see the world before she settled down. And she was a damned interesting talk-friend, too. Her interpretations of the shaky ethno-political situation were so shrewd you might have thought her formally educated in psychodynamics.

I wonder, Ranu said to himself slowly, not for the first time. *Marriage could perhaps work out. It's almost unheard of for a sailor, even a skipper, to have a private woman along. And children. . . . But it has been done, once in a while.*

She vanished behind the carved porch screen of the radio shack, on whose vermin-proofed thatch a bougainvillea twined and flared with color. Ranu jerked his mind back to the present. *Time enough to make personal plans if we get out of this alive.*

The airship hove into view. The shark-shaped gasbag was easily a hundred meters long, the control fins spread out like roc's wings. Propeller noise came softly down through the wind. On the flanks was painted the golden Siva symbol of the Brahmard scientocracy: destruction and rebirth.

Rebirth of what? Well, that's what we're here to learn.

The *Aorangi* was drifting before the wind, but not very fast, with her sails and vanes skewed at such lunatic angles. The aircraft paced her easily, losing altitude until it was hardly above deck level, twenty meters away. Ranu saw turbaned heads and high-collared tunics lining the starboard observation verandah. Keanua, who had scrambled down from the crow's nest, hurried to the port rail and placed himself by one of the cargo-loading king posts. He pulled off his shirt—even a Taiitian needed protection against this tropical sea glare, above the shade of the sails—and waved it to attract attention. Ranu saw a man on the flyer nod and issue instructions.

Keanua worked the emergency handwheels. A boom swung out. A catapult in the bow of the airship fired a grapnel. That gunner was good; the hook engaged the cargo sling on the first try. It had two lines attached, Keanua—a thick man with elaborate tattoos on his flat cheerful face—brought the grapnel inboard and made one cable fast. He carried the other one aft and secured it to a bollard at the next king post. With the help of the airship's stern catapult he repeated this process in reverse. The two craft were linked.

For a minute the Beneghali pilot got careless and let the cables draw taut. The *Aorangi* heeled with the drag on her. Sails thundered overhead. Ranu winced at the thought of the stresses imposed on his masts and yards. Ship timber wasn't exactly cheap, even after centuries of good forest management. (Briefly and stingingly he recalled those forests, rustling leaves, sunflecked shadows, a glade that suddenly opened on an enormous vista of downs and grazing sheep and one white waterfall: his father's home.) The aircraft was far less able to take such treatment, and the pilot made haste to adjust its position.

When the configuration was balanced, with the Beneghali vessel several meters aloft, a dozen men slid down a cable. The first came in a bosun's chair arrangement, but the others just wrapped an arm and a leg around the line. Each free hand carried a weapon.

Ranu crossed the deck to meet them. The leader got out of the chair with dignity. He was not tall, but he held himself straight as a rifle barrel. Trousers, tunic, turban were like snow under the sun. His face was sharp, with tight lips in a grizzled beard. He bowed stiffly. "At your service, Captain," he said in the Beneghali version of Hinji. "Scientist-administrator Indravarman Dhananda makes you welcome to these waters." The tone was flat.

Ranu refrained from offering a handshake in the manner of the Maurai Federation. "Captain Ranu Karelo Makintairu," he said. Like many sailors, he spoke fluent Hinji. His companions had acquired the language in a few weeks' intensive training. They approached, and Ranu introduced them. "Aeromotive engineer Keanua Filipoa Jouberti; cyberneticist Alisabeta Kanukauai."

Dhananda's black eyes darted about. "Are there others?" he asked.

"No," grunted Keanua. "We wouldn't be in this pickle if we had some extra hands."

The bearded, green-uniformed soldiers had quietly moved to command the whole deck. Some stood where they could see no one lurked behind the cabins. They wasted no admiration on grain of wood, screens of Okkaidan shoji, or the strong curve of the roofs. This was an inhumanly businesslike civilization. Ranu noted that besides swords and telescoping pikes, they had two submachine guns.

Yes, he thought with a little chill under his scalp, *Federation Intelligence made no mistake. Something very big indeed is hidden on that island.*

Dhananda ceased studying him. It was obvious that the scantily clad Maurai bore no weapons other than their knives. "You will forgive our seeming distrustfulness, Captain," the Brahmard said. "But the Buruma coast is still infested with pirates."

"I know." Ranu made his features smile. "You see the customary armament emplacements on our deck."

"Er . . . I understand from your radio call that you are in distress."

"Considerable," said Alisabeta. "Our engine is disabled. Three people cannot possibly trim those sails, and resetting the vanes won't help much."

"What about dropping the sails and going on propellers?" asked Dhananda. His coldness returned. In Beneghal, only women for hire—a curious institution the Maurai knew almost nothing about—traveled freely with men.

"The screws run off the same engine, sir," Alisabeta answered, more demurely than before.

"Well, you can let most of the sails fall, can't you, and stop this drift toward the reefs?"

"Not without smashing our superstructure," Ranu told him. "Synthetic or not, that fabric has a lot of total area. It's *heavy*. Worse, it'd be blown around the decks, fouling gear and breaking cabins. Also, we'd still have extremely poor control." He pointed at the steering wheel aft in the pilothouse, now lashed in place. "The whole rudder system on craft of this type is based on sail and vane adjustment. For instance, with the wind abeam like this, we ought to strip the mainmast and raise the *wanaroa*—oh, never mind. It's a specially curve-battened, semitubular sail with vanes on its yard to redirect airflow aloft. These trimarans have shallow draft and skimpy keel. It makes them fast, but requires exact rigging—"

"Mmmm . . . yes, I think I understand." Dhananda tugged his beard and brooded. "What do you need to make you seaworthy again?"

"A dock and a few days to work," said Alisabeta promptly. "With your help, we should be able to make Port Arberta."

"Um-m-m. There are certain difficulties about that. Could you not get a tow on to the mainland from some other vessel?"

"Not in time," said Ranu. He pointed east, where a shadow lay on the horizon. "We'll be aground in a few more hours if something isn't done."

"You know how little trade comes on this route at this season," Alisabeta added. "Yours was the only response to our SOS, except for a ship near the Nicbars." She paused before continuing with what Ranu hoped was not overdone casualness: "That ship promised to inform our Association of our whereabouts. Her captain assumed a Beneghali patrol would help us put into Arberta for repairs."

She was not being altogether untruthful. Ships did lie at Car Nicbar—camouflaged sea and aircraft, waiting. But they were hours distant.

Dhananda was not silent long. Whatever decision the Brahmard had made, it came with a swiftness and firmness that Ranu admired. (Though such qualities were not to be wished for in an enemy, were they?) "Very well," he yielded, rather sourly. "We shall assist you into harbor and see that the necessary work is completed. You can also radio the mainland that you will be late. Where are you bound?"

"Calcut," said Ranu. "Wool, hides, preserved fish, timber, and algal oils."

"You are from N'Zealann, then," Dhananda concluded.

"Yes. Wellantoa registry. Uh, I'm being inhospitable. Can we not offer the honorable scientist refreshment?"

"Later. Let us get started first."

That took an hour or so. The Beneghalis were landlubbers. But they could pull strongly on a line at Keanua's direction. So the plasticloth was lowered, slowly and awkwardly, folded and stowed. A couple of studding sails and jibs were left up, a spanker and flowsail were raised, the vanes were adjusted, and the ship began responding somewhat to her rudder. The aircraft paced alongside, still attached. It was far too lightly built, of wicker and fabric, to serve as a drogue; but it helped modify the wind pattern. With her crabwise motion toward the reefs halted, the *Aorangi* limped landward.

Ranu took Dhananda on a guided tour. Few Hinjan countries carried an ocean-borne trade. Their merchants went overland by camel caravan or sent high-priced perishables by air. The Brahmard had never been aboard one of the great vessels that bound together the Maurai Federation, from Awaii in the west to N'Zealann in the south, and carried the Cross and Stars flag around the planet. He was clearly looking for concealed weapons and spies in the woodwork. But he was also interested in the ship for her own sake.

"I am used to schooners and junks and the like," he said. "This looks radical."

"It's a rather new design," Ranu agreed. "But more are being built. You'll see many in the future."

With most sails down, the deck had taken on an austere appearance. Only the cabins, the hatches and king posts, cleats and bollards and defense installations, the sunpower collectors forward, and Keanua's flower garden broke that wide sweep. The three hulls were hidden beneath it, except where the prows jutted forth, bearing extravagantly carved tiki figureheads. There were three masts. Those fore and aft were more or less conventional; the mainmast was a tripod, wrought to withstand tremendous forces. Dhananda admitted he was bewildered by the variety of yards and lines hanging against the sky.

"We trim exactly, according to wind and current," Ranu explained. "Continuous measurements are taken by automatic instruments. A computer below decks calculates what's necessary, and directs the engine in the work."

"I know aerodynamics and hydrodynamics are thoroughly developed disciplines," the Beneghali said, impressed. "Large modern aircraft couldn't move about on such relatively feeble motors as they have unless they were designed with great care. But I had not appreciated the extent to which the same principles are being applied to marine architecture." He sighed. "That is one basic trouble with the world today, Captain. Miserably slow communications. Yes, one can send a radio signal, or cross the ocean in days if the weather is favorable. But so few people do it. The volume of talk and traffic is so small. An invention like this ship can exist for decades before anyone outside its own country is really aware of it The benefits are denied to more remote people for . . . generations, sometimes."

He seemed to recognize the intensity that had crept into his voice, and broke off.

"Oh, I don't know," said Ranu. "International improvement does go on. Two hundred years ago, say, my ancestors were fooling around with multi-masted hermaphrodite craft, and the Mericans used sails and fan keels on their blimps—with no anticatalyst for the hydrogen! Can you imagine such a firetrap? At the same time, if you'll pardon my saying so, the Hinjan subcontinent was a howling chaos of folk migrations. You couldn't have used even those square-rigger blimps, if someone had offered them to you."

"What has that to do with my remarks?" Dhananda asked, bridling.

"Just that I believe the Maurai government is right in advocating that the world go slow in making changes," said Ranu. He was being deliberately provocative, hoping to get a hint of how far things had gone on South Annaman. But Dhananda only shrugged, the dark face congealed into a mask.

"I would like to see your engine," said the Brahmard.

"This way, then. It's no different in principle from your airship motor, though: just bigger. Runs off dielectric accumulators. Of course, on a surface ship we have room to carry solar collectors and thus recharge our own system."

"I am surprised that you do not dispense with sails and drive the ship with propellers."

"We do, but only in emergencies. After all, sunlight is not a particularly concentrated energy source. We'd soon exhaust our accumulators if we made them move us at anything like a decent speed. Not even the newest type of fuel cells have capacity enough. As for that indirect form of sunpower storage known as organic fuel . . . well, we have the same problem in the Islands as you do on the continents. Oil, wood, peat, and coal are too expensive for commercial use. But we find the wind quite satisfactory. Except, to be sure, when the engine breaks down and we can't handle our sails! Then I could wish I were on a nice old-fashioned schooner, not this big, proud, thirty-knot tripler."

"What happened to your engine, anyhow?"

"A freak accident. A defective rotor, operating at high speed, threw a bearing exactly right to break a winding line. I suppose you know that armatures are usually wound with ceramic tubing impregnated with a conductive solution. This in turn shorted out everything else. The damage is reparable. If we'd had ample sea room, we wouldn't have bothered with that SOS." Ranu tried to laugh. "That's why humans are aboard, you know. Theoretically, our computer could be built to do everything. But in practice, something always happens that requires a brain that can think."

"A computer could be built to do that, too," said Dhananda.

"But could it be built to give a damn?" Ranu muttered in his own language. As he started down a ladder, one of the soldiers came between him and the sun, so that he felt the shadow of a pike across his back.

✳ II ✳

For centuries after the War of Judgment, the Annaman Islands lay deserted. Their natives regressed easily to a savage state, and took the few outside settlers along. The jungle soon reclaimed those towns the Ingliss had built in their own day. But eventually the outside world recovered somewhat. With its mixed Hinji-Tamil-Paki population firmly under the control of the Udayana Raj, Beneghal accumulated sufficient resources to send out an occasional ship for exploration and trade. A garrison was established on South Annaman. Then the Maurai came. Their more efficient vessels soon dominated seaborne traffic. Nonetheless, Beneghal maintained its claim to the islands. The outpost grew into Port Arberta—which, however, remained small and sleepy, seldom visited by foreign craft.

After the Scientistic Revolution in Beneghal put the Brahmards in power, those idealistic oligarchs tried to start an agricultural colony nearby. But the death rate was infamous, and the project was soon discontinued. Since then, as far as the world knew, there had been nothing more important here than a meteorological station.

But the world didn't know much, Ranu reflected.

He and his companions followed the Beneghalis ashore. The wharf lay bare and bleached in the evening light. A few concrete warehouses stood with empty windows. Some primitive fisher boats had obviously lain docked, unused, for months. Beyond the waterfront, palm-thatched huts straggled up from the bay. Ranked trees bespoke a plantation on the other side of the village. Then the jungle began, solid green on the hills, which rose inland in tiers until their ridges gloomed against the purpling east.

How quiet it was! The villagers had come on the run when they sighted the great ship. They stood massed and staring, several hundred of them—native Annamanese or half-breeds, with black skins and tufty hair and large shy eyes, clad in little more than loincloths. The mainland soldiers towered over them; the Maurai were veritable giants. They should have been swarming about, these people, chattering, shouting, giggling, hustling their wares, the potbellied children clamoring for sweets. But they only stared.

Keanua asked bluntly, "What ails these folk? We aren't going to eat them."

"They are afraid of strangers," Dhananda replied. "Slave raiders used to come here."

But that was ended fifty years ago, Ranu thought. *No, any xenophobia they have now is due to rather more recent indoctrination.*

"Besides," the Brahmard went on pointedly, "is it not Maurai doctrine that no culture has the right to meddle with the customs of any other?"

Alisabeta winced. "Yes," she said.

Dhananda made a surface smile. "I am afraid you will find our hospitality somewhat limited here. We haven't many facilities for entertainment."

Ranu looked to his right, past the village, where a steep bluff upheaved itself. On its crest he saw the wooden latticework supporting a radio transmitter—chiefly for the use of the weather observers—and, some new construction, bungalows and hangars around an airstrip. The earth scars were not entirely healed; this was hardly more than two or three years old. "You seem to be expanding," he remarked with purposeful naïveté.

"Yes, yes," said Dhananda. "Our government still hopes to civilize these islands and open them to extensive cultivation. Everyone knows that the Beneghali mainland population is bulging at the seams. But first we must study conditions. Not only the physical environment which defeated our earlier attempt, but the inland tribes. We want to treat them fairly; but what does that mean in their own terms? The old intercultural problem. So we have scientific teams here, making studies."

"I see." As she walked toward a waiting donkey cart, Alisabeta studied the villagers with practical sympathy. Ranu, who had encountered many odd folk around the world, believed he could make the same estimate as she. The little dark people were not undernourished, although their fishers had not put out to sea for a long time. They did not watch the Beneghalis as peasants watch tyrants. Rather, there was unease in the looks they gave the Maurai.

Water lapped in the bay. A gull mewed, cruising about with sunlight golden upon its wings. Otherwise the silence grew enormous. It continued after the donkey trotted off, followed by hundreds of eyes. When the graveled road came up where the airfield was, a number of Beneghalis emerged from the houses to watch. They stood on their verandahs with the same withdrawn suspiciousness as the islanders.

The stillness was broken by a roar. A man came bounding down the steps of the largest house and across the field. He was as tall as Ranu and as broad as Keanua, dressed in kilt and blouse, his hair and moustache lurid yellow against a boiled-lobster complexion. A Merican! Ranu stiffened. He saw Alisabeta's fist clench on her knee. Their driver halted the cart.

"Hoy! Welcome! Dhananda, why in Oktai's name didn't you tell me company was coming?"

The Brahmard looked furious. "We have just gotten here," he answered in a strained voice. "I thought you were—" He broke off.

"At the laboratory for the rest of this week?" the Merican boomed. "Oh yes, so I was, till I heard a foreign ship was approaching the harbor. One of your lads here was talking on the radiophone with our place, asking about our supplies or something. He mentioned it. I overheard. Commandeered an aircraft the first thing. *Why* didn't you let me know? Welcome, you!" He reached a huge paw across the lap of Dhananda, who sat tense, and engulfed Ranu's hand.

"Lorn's the name," he said. "Lorn sunna Browen, of Corado University—and, with all due respect to my good Brahmard colleagues, sick for the sight of a new face. You're Maurai, of course. N'Zealanners, I'd guess. Right?"

He had been a major piece of the jigsaw puzzle that Federation Intelligence had fitted together. Relations between the Sea People and the clans of southwest Merica remained fairly close, however little direct trade went on. After all, missions from Awaii had originally turned those aerial pirates to more peaceable ways. Moreover, despite the slowness and thinness of global communications, an international scientific community did exist. So the Maurai professors had been able to nod confidently and say, yes, that Lorn fellow in

Corado is probably the world's leading astrophysicist, and the Brahmards wouldn't hire him for no reason.

But there was nothing furtive about him, Ranu saw. He was genuinely delighted to have visitors.

The Maurai introduced themselves. Lorn jogged alongside the cart, burbling like a cataract. "What, Dhananda, you were going to put them up in that lousy dâk? Nothing doing! I've got my own place here, and plenty of spare room. No, no, Cap'n Ranu, don't bother about thanks. The pleasure is mine. You can show me around your boat if you want to. I'd be interested in that."

"Certainly," said Alisabeta. She gave him her best smile. "Though isn't that a little out of your field?"

Ranu jerked in alarm. But it was Keanua's growl which sounded in their brains: "*Hoai, there, be careful! We're supposed to be plain merchant seamen, remember? We never heard of this Lorn man.*"

"*I'm sorry!*" Her brown eyes widened in dismay. "*I forgot.*"

"*Amateurs, the bunch of us,*" Ranu groaned. "*Let's hope our happy comrade Dhananda is just as inept. But I'm afraid he isn't.*"

The Brahmard was watching them keenly. "Why, what do you think the honorable Lorn's work is?" he asked.

"Something to do with your geographical research project," said Alisabeta. "What else?" She cocked her head and pursed her lips. "Now, let me see if I can guess. The Mericans are famous for dry farming . . . but this climate is anything except dry. They are also especially good at mining and ore processing. Ah, hah! You've found heavy-metal deposits in the jungle and aren't letting on."

Lorn, who had grown embarrassed under Dhananda's glare, cleared his throat and said with false heartiness: "Well, now, we don't want news to get around too fast, you understand? Spring a surprise on the mercantile world, eh?"

"Best leave the explanations to me, honorable sir." Dhananda's words fell like lumps of stone. The two soldiers accompanying the party in the cart hefted their scabbarded swords. Lorn glowered and clapped a hand to his broad clansman's dagger.

The moment passed. The cart stopped before a long white bungalow. Servants—mainlanders who walked like men better accustomed to uniforms than livery—took the guests' baggage and bowed them in. They were given adjoining bedrooms, comfortably furnished in the ornate upper-class Hinji style. Since he knew his stuff would be searched anyway, Ranu let a valet help him change into a formal shirt and sarong. But he kept his knife. That was against modern custom, when bandits and barbarians were no longer quite so likely to come down the chimney. Nonetheless, Ranu was not going to let this knife out of his possession.

The short tropic twilight was upon them when they gathered on the verandah for drinks. Dhananda sat in a corner, nursing a glass of something nonalcoholic. Ranu supposed the Brahmard—obviously the security chief here—had pulled rank on Lorn and insisted on being invited to eat. The Maurai skipper stretched out in a wicker chair with Keanua on his left, Alisabeta on his right, Lorn confronting them.

Darkness closed in, deep and blue. The sea glimmered below; the land lay black, humping up toward stars that one by one trod brilliantly forth. Yellow candlelight spilled from windows where the dinner table was being set. Bats darted on the fringe of sight. A lizard scuttled in the thatch overhead. From the jungle came sounds of wild pigs grunting, the scream of a startled peacock, numberless insect chirps. Coolness descended layer by layer, scented with jasmine.

Lorn mopped his brow and cheeks. "I wish to God I were back in Corado," he said in his own Ingliss-descended language, which he was gladdened to hear Ranu understood. "This weather gets me. My clan has a lodge on the north rim of the Grann Canyon. Pines and deer and—Oh, well, it's worth a couple of years here. Not just the pay." Briefly, something like holiness touched the heavy features. "The work."

"I beg your pardon," Dhananda interrupted from the shadows, "but no one else knows what you are telling us."

"Oh, sorry. I forgot." The Merican switched to his badly accented Hinji. "I wanted to say, friends, when I finish here I'd like to go home via N'Zealann. It must be about the most interesting place on Earth. Wellantoa's damn near the capital of the planet, or will be one day, eh?"

"Perhaps!" Dhananda snapped.

"No offense," said Lorn. "I don't belong to the Sea People either, you know. But they are the most progressive country going."

"In certain ways," Dhananda conceded. "In others—forgive me, guests, if I call your policies a little antiprogressive. For example, your consistent discouragement of attempts to civilize the world's barbarian societies."

"Not that exactly," defended Ranu. "When they offer a clear threat to their neighbors, of course the Federation is among the first powers to send in the peace enforcers—which, in the long run, means psychodynamic teams, to redirect the energies of the barbarians concerned. A large-scale effort is being mounted at this moment in Sina, as I'm sure you have heard."

"Just like you did with my ancestors, eh?" said Lorn, unabashed.

"Well, yes. But the point is, we don't want to mold anyone else into our own image; nor see them molded into the image of, say, Beneghali factory workers or Meycan peons or Orgonian foresters. So our government does exert pressure on other civilized governments to leave the institutions of backward peoples as much alone as possible."

"Why?" Dhananda leaned forward. His beard jutted aggressively. "It's easy enough for you Maurai. Your population growth is under control. You have your sea ranches, your synthetics plants, your worldwide commerce. Do you think the rest of mankind is better off in poverty, slavery, and ignorance?"

"Of course not," said Alisabeta. "But they'll get over that by themselves, in their own ways. Our trade and our example—I mean all the more advanced countries—such things can help. But they mustn't help too much, or the same thing will happen again that happened before the War of Judgment. I mean . . . what's the Hinji word? We call it cultural pseudo-morphosis."

"A mighty long word for a lady as cute as you," said Lorn sunna Browen: He sipped his gin noisily, leaned over and patted her knee. Ranu gathered that his family had stayed behind when the Brahmards hired him for this job; and in their primness they had not furnished him with a surrogate.

"You know," the Merican went on, "I'm surprised that merchant seamen can talk as academically as you do."

"Not me," grinned Keanua. "I'm strictly a deckhand type."

"I notice you have a bamboo flute tucked in your sarong," Lorn pointed out.

"Well, uh, I do play a little. To while away the watches."

"Indeed," murmured Dhananda. "And your conversation is very well informed, Captain Makintairu."

"Why shouldn't it be?" answered the Maurai, surprised. He thought of the irony if they should suspect he was not really a tramp-ship skipper. Because he was nothing else; he had been nothing else his whole adult life. "I went to school," he said. "We take books along on our voyages. We talk with people in foreign ports. That's all."

"Nevertheless—" Dhananda paused. "It is true," he admitted reflectively, "that Federation citizens in general have the reputation of being rather intellectual. More, even, than would be accounted for by your admirable hundred-percent literacy rate."

"Oh no." Alisabeta laughed. "I assure you, we're the least scholarly race alive. We like to learn, of course, and think and argue. But isn't that simply one of the pleasures in life, among many others? Our technology does give us abundant leisure for that sort of thing."

"Ours doesn't," said Dhananda grimly.

"Too many people, too few resources," Lorn agreed. "You must've been to Calcut before, m' lady. But have you ever seen the slums? And I'll bet you never traveled through the hinterland and watched those poor dusty devils trying to scratch a living from the agrocollectives."

"I did once," said Keanua with compassion.

"Well!" Lorn shook himself, tossed off his drink, and rose. "We've gotten far too serious. I assure you, m' lady, we aren't dry types at Corado University either. I'd like to take you and a couple of crossbows with me into the Rockies after mountain goat. . . . Come, I hear the dinner gong." He took Alisabeta's arm.

Ranu trailed after. *Mustn't overeat,* he thought. *This night looks like the best time to start prowling.*

✳ III ✳

There was no moon. The time for the *Aorangi* had been chosen with that in mind. Ranu woke at midnight, as he had told himself to do. He had the common Maurai knack of sleeping a short time and being refreshed thereby. Sliding off the bed, he stood for minutes looking out and listening. The airstrip reached bare beyond the house, gray under the stars. The windows in one hangar showed light

A sentry tramped past. His forest-green turban and clothes, his dark face, made him another blackness. But a sheen went along his gun barrel. An actual explosive-cartridge rifle. And . . . his beat took him by this house.

Still, he was only one man. He should have been given partners. The Brahmards were as unskilled in secrecy and espionage as the Maurai. When Earth held a mere four or five scientifically-minded nations, with scant and slow traffic between them, serious conflict rarely arose. Even today Beneghal did not maintain a large army. Larger than the Federation's—but Beneghal was a land power and needed protection against barbarians. The Maurai had a near monopoly on naval strength, for a corresponding reason; and it wasn't much of a navy.

Call them, with truth, as horrible as you liked, those centuries during which the human race struggled back from the aftermath of nuclear war had had an innocence that the generations before the Judgment lacked. *I am afraid,* thought Ranu with a sadness that surprised him a bit, *we too are about to lose that particular virginity.*

No time for sentiment. "*Keanua, Alisabeta,*" he called in his head. He felt them come to alertness. "*I'm going out for a look.*"

"*Is that wise?*" The girl's worry fluttered in him. "*If you should be caught—*"

"*My chances are best now. We have them off-balance, arriving so unexpectedly. But I bet Dhananda will double his precautions tomorrow, after he's worried overnight that we may be spies.*"

"*Be careful, then,*" Keanua said. Ranu felt a kinesthetic overtone, as if a hand reached under the pillow for a knife. "*Yell if you run into trouble. I think we might fight our way clear.*"

"*Oh! Stay away from the front entrance,*" Alisabeta warned. "*When Lorn took me out on the verandah after dinner to talk, I noticed a man squatting under the willow tree there. He may just have been an old syce catching a breath of air, but more likely he's an extra watchman.*"

"*Thanks.*" Ranu omitted any flowery Maurai leave-taking. His friends would be in contact. But he felt their feelings like a handclasp about him. Neither had questioned that he must be the one who ventured forth. As captain, he had the honor and obligation to assume extra hazards. Yet Keanua grumbled and fretted, and there was something in the girl's mind, less a statement than a color: she felt closer to him than to any other man.

Briefly, he wished for the physical touch of her. But— The guard was safely past. Ranu glided out the open window.

For a space he lay flat on the verandah. Faint stirrings and voices came to him from the occupied hangar. Candles had been lit in one bungalow. The rest slept, ghostly under the sky. So far nothing was happening in the open. Ranu slithered down into the flowerbed. Too late he discovered it included roses. He bit back a sailor's oath and crouched for minutes more.

All right, better get started. He had no special training in sneakery, but most Maurai learned judo arts in school, and afterward their work and their sports kept them supple. He went like a shadow among shadows, rounding the field until he came to one of the new storehouses.

Covered by the gloom at a small rear door, he drew his knife. A great deal of miniaturized circuitry had been packed into its handle, together with a tiny accumulator cell. The jewel on the pommel was a lens, and when he touched it in the right way a pencil beam of blue light sprang forth. He examined the lock. Not plastic, nor even aluminum bronze: steel. *And* the door was iron reinforced. What was so valuable inside?

From Ranu's viewpoint, a ferrous lock was a lucky break. He turned the knife's inconspicuous controls, probing and grasping with magnetic pulses, resolutely suppressing the notion that every star was staring at him. After a long and sweaty while, he heard tumblers click. He opened the door gently and went through.

His beam flickered about. The interior held mostly shelves, from floor to ceiling, loaded with paperboard cartons. He padded across the room, chose a box on a rear shelf that wouldn't likely be noticed for weeks, and slit the tape. Hm . . . as expected. A dielectric energy accumulator, molecular-distortion type. Standard equipment, employed by half the powered engines in the world.

But so many—in this outpost of loneliness?

His sample was fresh, too. Uncharged. Maurai agents had already seen, from commercial aircraft that "happened" to be blown off course, that there was only one solar-energy collection station on the whole archipelago. Nor did the islands have hydroelectric or tidal generators. Yet obviously these cells had been shipped here to be charged.

Which meant that the thing in the hills had developed much further than Federation Intelligence knew.

"Nan damn it," Ranu whispered. "Shark-toothed Nan damn and devour it."

He stood for a little turning the black cube over and over in his hands. His skin prickled. Then, with a shiver, he repacked the cell and left the storehouse as quietly as he had entered.

Outside he paused. Ought he to do anything else? This one bit of information justified the whole *Aorangi* enterprise. If he tried for more and failed, and his coworkers died with him, the effort would have gone for nothing.

However. . . . Time was hideously short. An alarmed Dhananda would find ways to keep other foreigners off the island—a faked wreck or something to make the harbor unusable—until too late. At least, Ranu must assume so.

He did not agonize over his decision; that was not a Maurai habit. He made it. *Let's have a peek in that lighted hangar, just for luck, before going to bed. Tomorrow I'll try and think of some way to get inland and see the laboratory.*

A cautious half hour later, he stood flattened against a wall and peered through a window. The vaulted interior of the hangar was nearly filled by a pumped-up gasbag. Motors idled, hardly audible, propellers not yet engaged. Several mechanics were making final checks. Two men from the bungalow where candles had been lit—Brahmards themselves, to judge from their white garb and authoritative manner—stood waiting while some junior attendants loaded boxed apparatus into the gondola. Above the whirr, Ranu caught a snatch of talk between them:

"—unsanctified hour. Why *now*, for Vishnu's sake?"

"Those fool newcomers. They might not be distressed mariners, ever think of that? In any case, they mustn't see us handling stuff like this." Four men staggered past bearing a coiled cable. The uninsulated ends shone the red of pure copper. "You don't use that for geographical research, what?"

Ranu felt his hair stir.

Two soldiers embarked with guns. Ranu doubted they were going along merely because of the monetary value of that cable, fabulous though it was.

The scientists followed. The ground crew manned a capstan. Their ancient, wailing chant came like a protest—that human muscles must so strain when a hundred horses snored in the same room. The hangar roof and front wall folded creakily aside.

Ranu went rigid.

He must unconsciously have shot his thought to the other Maurai. "*No!*" Alisabeta cried to him.

Keanua said more slowly: "*That's cannibal recklessness, skipper. You might fall and smear yourself over three degrees of latitude. Or if you should be seen—*"

"*I'll never have a better chance,*" Ranu said. "*We've already invented a dozen different cover stories in case I disappear. So pick one and use it.*"

"*But you,*" Alisabeta begged. "*Alone out there!*"

"*It might be worse for you, if Dhananda should decide to get tough,*" Ranu answered. The Ingliss single-mindedness had come upon him, overriding the easy, indolent Maurai blood. But then that second heritage woke with a shout, for those who first possessed N'Zealann, the canoe men and moa hunters, would have dived laughing into an escapade like this.

He pushed down the glee and related what he had found in the storehouse. "*If you feel any doubt about your own safety, any time, forget me and leave,*" he ordered. "*Intelligence has got to know at least this much. If I'm detected yonder in the hills, I'll try to get away and hide in the jungle.*" The hangar was open, the aircraft slipping its cables, the propellers becoming bright transparent circles as they were engaged. "*Farewell. Good luck.*"

"*Tanaroa be with you,*" Alisabeta called through her tears.

Ranu dashed around the corner. The aircraft rose on a slant, gondola an ebony slab, bag a pale storm cloud. The propellers threw wind in his face. He ran along the vessel's shadow, poised, and sprang.

Almost, he didn't make it. His fingers closed on something, slipped, clamped with the strength of terror. Both hands, now! He was gripping an ironwood bar, part of the mooring gear, his legs adangle over an earth that fell away below him with appalling swiftness. He sucked in a breath and chinned himself, got one knee over the bar, clung there and gasped.

The electric motors purred. A breeze whittered among struts and spars. Otherwise Ranu was alone with his heartbeat. After a while it slowed. He hitched himself to a slightly more comfortable crouch and looked about. The jungle was black, dappled with dark gray, far underneath him. The sea that edged it shimmered in starlight with exactly the same whiteness as the nacelles along the gondola. He heard a friendly creaking of wickerwork, felt a sort of throb as the gasbag expanded in this higher-level air. The constellations wheeled grandly around him.

He had read about jet aircraft that outpaced the sun, before the nuclear war. Once he had seen a representation, on a fragment of ancient cinema film discovered by archeologists and transferred to new acetate; a sound track had been included. He did not understand how anyone could want to sit locked in a howling coffin like that when he might have swum through the air, intimate with the night sky, as Ranu was now doing.

However precariously, his mind added with wryness. He had not been seen, and he probably wasn't affecting the trim enough to make the pilot suspicious. Nevertheless, he had scant time to admire the view. The bar along which he sprawled, the sisal guy on which he leaned one shoulder, dug into his flesh. His muscles were already tiring. If this trip was any slower than he had guessed it would be, he'd tumble to earth.

Or else be too clumsy to spring off unseen and melt into darkness as the aircraft landed.

Or when he turned up missing in the morning, Dhananda might guess the truth and lay a trap for him.

Or anything! Stop your fuss, you idiot. You need all your energy for hanging on.

✷ IV ✷

The Brahmard's tread was light on the verandah, but Alisabeta's nerves were strung so taut that she sensed him and turned about with a small gasp. For a second they regarded each other, unspeaking, the dark, slight, bearded man in his neat whites and the strongly built girl whose skin seemed to glow golden in the shade of a trellised grapevine. Beyond, the airstrip flimmered in midmorning sunlight. Heat hazes wavered on the hangar roofs.

"You have not found him?" she asked at last, without tone.

Dhananda's head shook slowly, as if his turban had become heavy. "No. Not a trace, I came back to ask you if you have any idea where he might have gone."

"I told your deputy my guess. Ranu . . . Captain Makintairu is in the habit of taking a swim before breakfast. He may have gone down to the shore about dawn and—" She hoped he would take her hesitation to mean no more than an unspoken: *Sharks. Rip tides. Cramp.*

But the sable gaze continued to probe her. "It is most improbable that he could have left this area unobserved," Dhananda said. "You have seen our guards. More of them are posted downhill."

"What are you guarding against?" she counterattacked, to divert him. "Are you less popular with the natives than you claim to be?"

He parried her almost contemptuously: "We have reason to think two of the Buruman pirate kings have made alliance and gotten some aircraft. We do have equipment and materials here that would be worth stealing. Now, about Captain Makintairu. I cannot believe he left unseen unless he did so deliberately, taking great trouble about it. Why?"

"I don't know, I tell you!"

"You must admit we are duty bound to consider the possibility that you are not simple merchant mariners."

"What else? Pirates ourselves? Don't be absurd." *I dare you to accuse us of being spies. Because then I will ask what there is here to spy on.*

Only . . . then what will you do?

Dhananda struck the porch railing with a fist. Bitterness spoke: "Your Federation swears so piously it doesn't intervene in the development of other cultures."

"Except when self-defense forces us to," Alisabeta said. "And only a minimum."

He ignored that. "In the name of nonintervention, you are always prepared to refuse some country the sea-ranching equipment that would give it a new start, or bribe somebody else *with* such equipment not to begin a full-fledged merchant service to a third and backward country . . . a service that might bring the backward country up-to-date in less than a generation. You talk about encouraging cultural diversity. You seem seriously to believe it's moral keeping the Okkaidans impoverished fishermen so they'll be satisfied to write haiku and grow dwarf gardens for recreation. And yet—by Kali herself, your agents are everywhere!"

"If you don't want us here," Alisabeta snapped, "deport us and complain to our government."

"I may have to do more than that."

"But I swear—"

"Alisabeta! Keanua!"

Distance-attenuated, Ranu's message still stiffened her where she stood. She felt his tension, and an undertone of hunger and thirst, like a thrum along her own nerves. The verandah faded about her, and she stood in murk and heard a slamming of great pumps. Was there really a red warning light that went flash-flash-flash above a bank of transformers taller than a man?

"Yes, I'm inside," the rapid, blurred voice said in her skull. *"I watched my chance from the jungle edge. When an oxcart came along the trail with a sleepy native driver, I clung to the bottom and was carried through the gates. Food supplies. Evidently the workers here have a contract with some nearby village. The savages bring food and do guard duty. I've seen at least three of them prowling about with blowguns. Anyhow, I'm in. I dropped from the cart and slipped into a side tunnel. Now I'm sneaking around, hoping not to be seen.*

"The place is huge! They must have spent years enlarging a chain of natural caves. Air conduits everywhere—I daresay that's how our signals are getting through; I sense you, but faintly. Forced ventilation, with thermostatic controls. Can you imagine *power expenditure on such a scale? I'm going toward the center of things now for a look. My signal will probably be screened out till I come back near the entrance again."*

"Don't, skipper," Keanua pleaded. *"You've seen plenty. We know for a fact that Intelligence guessed right. That's enough."*

"Not quite," Ranu said. The Maurai rashness flickered along the

edge of his words. "*I want to see if the project is as far advanced as I fear. If not, perhaps the Federation won't have to take emergency measures. I'm afraid we will, though.*"

"*Ranu!*" Alisabeta called. His thought enfolded her. But static exploded, interfering energies that hurt her perceptions. When it lifted, an emptiness was in her head where Ranu had been.

"Are you ill, my lady?" Dhananda barked the question.

She looked dazedly out at the sky, unable to answer. He moved nearer. "What are you doing?" he pressed.

"*Steady, girl,*" Keanua rumbled.

Alisabeta swallowed, squared her shoulders, and faced the Brahmard. "I'm worrying about Captain Makintairu," she said coldly. "Does that satisfy you?"

"No."

"Hoy, there, you!" rang a voice from the front door. Lorn sunna Browen came forth. His kilted form overtopped them both; the light eyes sparked at Dhananda. "What kind of hospitality is this? Is he bothering you, my lady?"

"I am not certain that these people have met the obligations of guests," Dhananda said, his control cracking open.

Lorn put arms akimbo, fists knotted. "Until you can prove that, though, just watch your manners. Eh? As long as I'm here, this is my house, not yours."

"Please," Alisabeta said. She hated fights. Why had she ever volunteered for this job? "I beg you . . . don't."

Dhananda made a jerky bow. "Perhaps I am overzealous," he said without conviction. "If so, I ask your pardon. I shall continue the search for the captain."

"I think—meanwhile—I'll go down to our ship and help Keanua with the repairs," Alisabeta whispered.

"Very well," said Dhananda.

Lorn took her arm. "Mind if I come too? You, uh, you might like to have a little distraction from thinking about your poor friend. And I never have seen an oceangoing craft close by. They flew me here when I was hired."

"I suggest you return to your own work, sir," Dhananda said in a harsh tone.

"When I'm good and ready, I will," Lorn answered airily. "Come,

Miss . . . uh . . . m' lady." He led Alisabeta down the stair and around the strip. Dhananda watched from the portico, motionless.

"You mustn't mind him," Lorn said after a bit. "He's not a bad sort. A nice family man, in fact, pretty good chess player, and a devil on the polo field. But this has been a long grind, and his responsibility has kind of worn him down."

"Oh yes. I understand," Alisabeta said. *But still he frightens me.*

Lorn ran a hand through his thinning yellow mane. "Most Brahmards are pretty decent," he said. "I've come to know them in the time I've been working here. They're recruited young, you know, with psychological tests to weed out those who don't have the . . . the dedication, I guess you'd call it. Oh, sure, naturally they enjoy being a boss caste. But somebody has to be. No Hinjan country has the resources or the elbow room to govern itself as loosely as you Sea People do. The Brahmards want to modernize Beneghal—eventually the world. Get mankind back where it was before the War of Judgment, and go on from there."

"I know," Alisabeta said.

"I don't see why you Maurai are so dead set against that. Don't you realize how many people go to bed hungry every night?"

"Of course, of course we do!" she burst out. It angered her that tears should come so close to the surface of her eyes. "But so they did before the War. Can't anyone else see . . . turning the planet into one huge factory isn't the answer? Have you read any history? Did you ever hear of . . . oh, just to name one movement that called itself progressive . . . the Communists? They too were going to end poverty and famine. They were going to reorganize society along rational lines. Well, we have contemporary records to prove that in Rossaya alone, in the first thirty or forty years it had power, their regime killed twenty million of their own citizens. Starved them, shot them, worked them to death in labor camps. The total deaths, in all the Communist countries, may have gone as high as a hundred million. And this was *before* evangelistic foreign policies brought on nuclear war. How many famines and plagues would it take to wipe out that many human lives? And how much was the life of the survivors worth, under such masters?"

"But the Brahmards aren't like that," he protested. "See for yourself, down in this village. The natives are well taken care of. Nobody abuses them or coerces them. Same thing on the mainland. There's a lot of misery yet in Beneghal—mass starvation going on right now—but it'll be overcome."

"Why haven't the villagers been fishing?" she challenged.

"Eh?" Taken aback, Lorn paused on the downhill path. The sun poured white across them both, made the bay a bowl of molten brass, and seemed to flatten the jungle leafage into one solid listless green. The air was very empty and quiet. But Ranu crept through the belly of a mountain, where machines hammered. . . .

"Well, it hasn't been practical to allow that," said the Merican. "Some of our work is confidential. We can't risk information leaking out. But the Beneghalis have been feeding them. Oktai, it amounts to a holiday for the fishers. They aren't complaining."

Alisabeta decided to change the subject, or even this big bundle of guilelessness might grow suspicious. "So you're a scientist," she said. "How interesting. But what do they need you here for? I mean, they have good scientists of their own."

"I . . . uh . . . I have specialized knowledge which is, uh, applicable," he said. "You know how the sciences and technologies hang together. Your Island biotechs breed new species to concentrate particular metals out of seawater, so naturally they need metallurgic data too. In my own case—uh—" Hastily: "I do want to visit your big observatory in N'Zealann on my way home. I hear they've photographed an ancient artificial satellite, still circling the Earth after all these centuries. I think maybe some of the records our archeologists have dug up in Merica would enable us to identify it. Knowing its original orbit and so forth, we could compute out a lot of information about the solar system."

"Tanaroa, yes!" Despite everything, eagerness jumped in her.

His red face, gleaming with sweat, lifted toward the blank blue sky. "Of course," he murmured, almost to himself, "that's a piddle compared to what we'd learn if we could get back out there in person."

"Build space probes again? Or actual manned ships?"

"Yes. If we had the power, and the industrial plant. By Oktai, but I get sick of this!" Lorn exclaimed. His grip on her arm tightened unconsciously until she winced. "Scraping along on lean ores, tailings, scrap, synthetics, substitutes . . . because the ancients exhausted so much. Exhausted the good mines, most of the fossil fuels, coal, petroleum, uranium . . . then smashed their industry in the War and let the machines corrode away to unrecoverable dust in the dark ages that followed. That's what's holding us back, girl. We know everything our ancestors did and then some. But we haven't got the equipment they had to process materials on the scale they did, and we haven't the natural resources to rebuild that equipment. A vicious circle. We haven't got the capital to make it economically feasible to produce the giant industries that could accumulate the capital."

"I think we're doing quite well," she said, gently disengaging herself. "Sunpower, fuel cells, wind and water, biotechnology, sea ranches and sea farms, efficient agriculture—"

"We could do better, though." His arm swept a violent arc that ended with a finger pointed at the bay. "There! The oceans. Every element in the periodic table is dissolved in them. Billions of tons. But we'll never get more than a minimum out with your fool solar and biological methods. We need energy. Power to evaporate water by the cubic kilometer. Power to synthesize oil by the megabarrel. Power to go to the stars."

The rapture faded. He seemed shaken by his own words, shut his lips as if retreating behind the walrus moustache, and resumed walking. Alisabeta came along in silence. Their feet scrunched in gravel and sent up little puffs of dust. Presently the dock resounded under them; they boarded the *Aorangi,* and went across to the engine-room hatch.

Keanua paused in his labors as they entered. He had opened the aluminum-alloy casing and spread parts out on the deck, where he squatted in a sunbeam from an open porthole. Elsewhere the room was cool and shadowy; wavelets lapped the hull.

"Good day," said the Taiitian. His smile was perfunctory, his thoughts inside the mountain with Ranu.

"Looks as if you're immobilized for a while," Lorn said, lounging back against a flame-grained bulkhead panel.

"Until we find what has happened to our friend, surely," Keanua answered.

"I'm sorry about him," Lorn said. "I hope he comes back soon."

"Well, we can't wait indefinitely for him," Alisabeta made herself say. "If he isn't found by the time the engine is fixed, best we start for

Calcut. Your group will send him on when he does appear, won't you?"

"Sure," said Lorn. "If he's alive. Uh, 'scuse me, my lady.'

"No offense. We don't hold with euphemisms in the Islands."

"It does puzzle the deuce out of me," Keanua grunted. "He's a good swimmer, if he did go for a swim. Of course, he might have taken a walk instead, into the jungle. Are you sure the native tribes are always peaceful?"

"Um—"

"Can you hear me? Can you hear me?"

Ranu's voice was as tiny in Alisabeta's head as the scream of an insect. But they felt the pain that jagged in it. He had been wounded.

"Get out! Get away as fast as you can! I've seen—the thing—it's working! I swear it must be working. Pouring out power ... some kind of chemosynthetic plant beyond—They saw me as I started back. Put a blowgun dart in my thigh. Alarms hooting everywhere. I think I can beat them to the entrance, though, get into the forest—"

Keanua had leaped to his feet. The muscles moved like snakes under his skin. *"Escape, with natives tracking you?"* he snarled.

Ranu's signal strengthened as he came nearer the open air. *"This place has radiophone contact with the town. Dhananda's undoubtedly being notified right now. Get clear, you two!"*

"If ... if we can," Alisabeta faltered. *"But you—"*

"GET UNDER WEIGH, I TELL YOU!"

✳V✳

Lorn stared from one to another of them. "What's wrong?" A hand dropped to his knife. Years at a desk had not much slowed his mountaineer's reflexes.

Alisabeta glanced past him at Keanua. There was no need for words. The Taiitian's grasp closed on Lorn's dagger wrist.

"What the hell—!" The Merican yanked with skill. His arm snapped out between the thumb and fingers holding him, and a sunbeam flared off steel.

Keanua closed in. His left arm batted sideways to deflect the knife.

His right hand, stiffly held, poked at the solar plexus. But Lorn's left palm came chopping down, edge on. A less burly wrist than Keanua's would have broken. As it was, the sailor choked on an oath and went pale around the nostrils. Lorn snatched his opponent's knife from the sheath and threw it out the porthole.

The Merican could then have ripped Keanua's belly. But instead he paused. "What's got into you?" he asked in a high, bewildered voice. "Miss Alisa—" He half looked around for her.

Keanua recovered enough to go after the clansman's dagger. One arm under the wrist for a fulcrum, the other arm applying the leverage of his whole body—Lorn's hand bent down, the fingers were pulled open by their own tendons, the blade tinkled to the deck. "Get it, girl!" Keanua said. He kicked it aside. Lorn had already grappled him.

Alisabeta slipped past their trampling legs to snatch the weapon. Her pulse thuttered in her throat. It was infinitely horrible that the sun should pour so brilliant through the porthole. The chuckle of water on the hull was lost in the rough breath and stamp of feet, back and forth as the fight swayed. Lorn struck with a poleax fist, but Keanua dropped his head and took the blow on his skull. Anguish stabbed through the Merican's knuckles. He let go his adversary. Keanua followed the advantage, seeking a stranglehold. Lorn's foot lashed out, caught the Taiitian in the stomach, sent him lurching away.

No time to gape! Alisabeta ran up the ladder onto the main deck. A few black children stood on the wharf, sucking their thumbs and staring endlessly at the ship. Except for them, Port Arberta seemed asleep. But no, yonder in the heat shimmer . . . dust on the downhill path. . . . She shaded her eyes. A man in white and three soldiers in green; headed this way, surely. Dhananda had been informed that a spy had entered the secret place. Now he was on his way to arrest the spy's indubitable accomplices.

But with only three men?

Wait! He doesn't know about head-to-head. He can't tell that we here know he knows about Ranu. So he plans to capture us by surprise—so we won't destroy evidence or scuttle the ship or something— Yes, he'll come aboard with some story about searching for Ranu, and have his men aim their guns at us when he makes a signal. Not before.

"Ranu, what should I do?"

There was no answer, only—when she concentrated—a sense of pain in the muscles, fire in the lungs, heat and sweat and running. He fled through the jungle with the blowgun men on his trail, unable to think of anything but a biding place.

Alisabeta bit her nails. Lesu Haristi, Son of Tanaroa, what to do, what to do? She had been about to call the advance base on Car Nicbar. A single radio shout, to tell them what had been learned, and then surrender to Dhananda. But that was a desperation measure. It would openly involve the Federation government. Worse, any outsider who happened to be tuned to that band—and considerable radio talk went on these days—might well record and decode and get some inkling of what was here and tell the world. And this would in time start similar kettles boiling elsewhere . . . and the Federation couldn't sit on that many lids, didn't want to, wasn't equipped to— *Stop maundering, you ninny! Make up your mind!*

Alisabeta darted back down into the engine room. Keanua and Lorn rolled on the deck, locked together. She picked a wrench from among the tools and poised it above the Merican's head. His scalp shone pinkly through the yellow hair, a bald spot, and last night he had shown her pictures of his children. . . . No. She couldn't. She threw the wrench aside, pulled off her lap-lap, folded it into a strip, and drew it carefully around Lorn's throat. A twist; he choked and released Keanua; the Taiitian got a grip and throttled him unconscious in thirty seconds.

"Thanks! Don't know . . . if I could have done that . . . alone. Strong's an orca, him." As he talked Keanua deftly bound and gagged the Merican, Lorn stirred, blinked, writhed helplessly, and glared his hurt and anger.

Alisabeta had already slid back a certain panel. The compartment behind held the other engine, the one that was not damaged. She connected it to the gears while she told Keanua what she had seen. "If we work it right, I think we can also capture those other men," she said. "That'll cause confusion, and they'll be useful hostages, am I right?"

"Right. Good girl." Keanua slapped her bottom and grinned. Remembering Beneghali customs, she put the lap-lap on again and went topside.

Dhananda and his guards reached the dock a few minutes later. She waved at them but kept her place by the saloon cabin door. They crossed the gangplank, which boomed under their boots. The Brahmard's countenance was stormy. "Where are the others?" he demanded.

"In there." She nodded at the cabin. "Having a drink. Won't you join us?"

He hesitated. "If you will too, my lady."

"Of course." She went ahead. The room was long, low, and cool, furnished with little more than straw mats and shoji screens. Keanua stepped from behind one of them. He held a repeating blowgun.

"Stay where you are, friends," he ordered around the mouthpiece. "Raise your hands."

A soldier spat a curse and snatched for his submachine gun. Keanua puffed. The feeder mechanism clicked. Three darts buried themselves in the planking at the soldier's feet. "Cyanide," Keanua reminded them. He kept the bamboo tube steady. "Next time I aim to kill."

"What do you think you are doing?' Dhananda breathed. His features had turned almost gray. But he lifted his arms with the others. Alisabeta took their weapons. She cast the guns into a corner as if they were hot to the touch.

"Secure them," Keanua said. He made the prisoners lie down while the girl hogtied them. Afterward he carried each below through a hatch in the saloon deck to a locker where Lorn already lay. As he made Dhananda fast to a shackle bolt he said, "We're going to make a break for it. Would you like to tell your men ashore to let us go without a fight? I'll run a microphone down here for you."

"No," Dhananda said. "You pirate swine."

"Suit yourself. But if we get sunk you'll drown too. Think about that." Keanua went back topside.

Alisabeta stood by the cabin door, straining into a silence that hissed. "I can't hear him at all," she said from the verge of tears. "Is he dead?"

"No time for that now," Keanua said. "We've got to get started. Take the wheel. I think once we're past the headland, we'll pick up a little wind."

She nodded dumbly and went to the pilothouse. Keanua cast off.

Several adult villagers materialized as if by sorcery to watch. The engine pulsed, screws caught the water, the *Aorangi* stood out into the bay. Keanua moved briskly about, preparing the ship's armament. It was standard for a civilian vessel: a catapult throwing bombs of jellied fish oil, two flywheel guns that cast streams of small sharp rocks. Since pirates couldn't get gunpowder, merchantmen saw no reason to pay its staggering cost. One of the Intelligence officers had wanted to supply a rocket launcher, but Ranu had pointed out that it would be hard enough to conceal the extra engine.

Men must be swarming like ants on the hilltop. Alisabeta watched four of them come down on horseback. The dust smoked behind them. They flung open the doors of a boat-house and emerged in a watercraft that zoomed within hailing distance.

A Beneghali officer rose in the stern sheets and bawled through a megaphone—his voice was soon lost on that sun-dazzled expanse—"Ahoy, there! Where are you bound?"

"Your chief's commandeered us to make a search," Keanua shouted back.

"Yes? Where is he? Let me speak to him."

"He's below. Can't come now."

"Stand by to be boarded."

Keanua said rude things. Alisabeta guided the ship out through the channel, scarcely hearing. Partly she was fighting down a sense of sadness and defilement—she had attacked guests—and partly she kept crying for Ranu to answer. Only the gulls did.

The boat darted back to shore. Keanua came aft. "They'll be at us before long," he said bleakly. "I told 'em their own folk would go down with us, and they'd better negotiate instead. Implying we really are pirates, you know. But they wouldn't listen."

"Certainly not," Alisabeta said. "Every hour of haggling is time gained for us. They know that."

Keanua sighed. "Well, so it goes. I'll holler to Nicbar."

"What signal?" Though cipher messages would be too risky, a few codes had been agreed upon: mere standardized impulses, covering preset situations.

"Attack. Come here as fast as they can with everything they've got," Keanua decided.

"Just to save our lives? Oh no!"

The Taiitian shook his head. "To wipe out that damned project in the hills. Else the Brahmards will get the idea, and mount so big a guard from now on that we won't be able to come near without a full-scale war."

He stood quiet awhile. "Two of us on this ship, and a couple hundred of them," he said. "We'll have a tough time staying alive, girl, till the relief expedition gets close enough for a head-to-head." He yawned and stretched, trying to ease his tension. "Of course, I'd rather like to stay alive for my own sake, too."

There was indeed a breeze on the open sea, which freshened slightly as the *Aorangi* moved south. They set the computer to direct sail hoisting and disengaged the screws. The engine would be required at full capacity to power the weapons. After putting the wheel on autopilot, Keanua and Alisabeta helped each other into quilted combat armor and alloy helmets.

Presently the airships came aloft. That was the sole possible form of onslaught, she knew. With their inland mentalities, the Brahmards had stationed no naval units here. There were—one, two, three—a full dozen vessels, big and bright in the sky. They assumed formation and lined out in pursuit

✳ VI ✳

Ranu awoke so fast that for a moment he blinked about him in wonderment: where was he, what had happened? He lay in a hollow beneath a fallen tree, hidden by a cascade of trumpet-flower vines. The sun turned their leaves nearly yellow; the light here behind them was thick and green, the air unspeakably hot. He couldn't be sure how much of the crawling over his body was sweat and how much was ants. His right thigh needled him where the dart had pierced it. A smell of earth and crushed vegetation filled his nostrils, mingled with his own stench. Nothing but his heartbeat and the distant liquid notes of a bulbul interrupted noonday silence.

Oh yes, he recalled wearily. *I got out the main entrance. Stiff-armed a sentry and sprang into the brush. A score of Beneghalis after me . . . shook them, but just plain had to outrun the natives . . . longer*

legs. I hope I covered my trail, once beyond their sight. Must have, or they'd've found me here by now. I've been unconscious for hours. The ship!

Remembrance rammed into him. He sucked a breath between his teeth, nearly jumped from his hiding place, recovered his wits and dug fingers into the mold under his belly. At last he felt able to reach forth head-to-head. *"Alisabeta! Are you there? Can you hear me?"* Her answer was instant. Not words—a gasp, a laugh, a sob, clearer and stronger than he had ever known before; and as their minds embraced, some deeper aspect of self. Suddenly he became her, aboard the ship.

No more land was to be seen, only the ocean, blue close at hand, shining like mica farther out where the sun smote it. The wreckage of an aircraft bobbed a kilometer to starboard, gondola projecting from beneath the flattened bag. The other vessels maneuvered majestically overhead. Their propeller whirr drifted across an empty deck.

The *Aorangi* had taken a beating. Incendiaries could not ignite fireproofed material, but had left scorches everywhere. The cabins were kindling wood. A direct hit with an explosive bomb had shattered the foremast, which lay in a tangle across the smashed sunpower collectors. The after boom trailed overside. What sails were still on the yards hung in rags. A near miss had opened two compartments in the port hull, so that the trimaran was low on that side, the deck crazily tilted.

Three dead men sprawled amidships in a black spatter of clotting blood. Ranu recollected with Alisabeta's horror: when an aircraft sank grapnels into the fore-skysail and soldiers came swarming down ropes, she hosed them with stones. Most had dropped overboard, but those three hit with nauseating sounds. Then Keanua, at the catapult, put four separate fire-shells into the gasbag. Even against modern safety devices, that served to touch off the hydrogen. The aircraft cast loose and drifted slowly seaward. The flames were pale, nearly invisible in the light, but steam puffed high when it ditched. The Maurai, naturally, made no attempt to hinder the rescue operation that followed. Later the Beneghalis had been content with bombing and strafing. Once the defenders were out of action, they could board with no difficulty.

"They aren't pressing the attack as hard as they might," Keanua

reported. "*But then, they hope to spare our prisoners, and don't know we have reinforcements coming. If we can hold out that long—*" He sensed how close was the rapport between Ranu and the girl, and withdrew with an embarrassed apology. Still, Ranu had had time to share the pain of burns and a pellet in his shoulder.

Alisabeta crouched in the starboard slugthrower turret. It was hot and dark and vibrated with the whining flywheel. The piece of sky in her sights was fiery blue, a tatter of sail was blinding white. He felt her fear. Too many bomb splinters, too many concussion blows, had already weakened this plywood shelter. An incendiary landing just outside would not set it afire, but could pull out the oxygen. "*So, so,*" Ranu caressed her. "*I am here now.*" Their hands swung the gun about

The lead airship peeled off the formation and lumbered into view. For the most part the squadron had passed well above missile range and dropped bombs—using crude sights, luckily. But the last several passes had been strafing runs. Keanua thought that was because their explosives were nearly used up. The expenditure of high-energy chemicals had been great, even for an industrialized power like Beneghal. Alisabeta believed they were concerned for the prisoners.

No matter. Here they came!

The airship droned low above the gaunt A of the mainmast. Its shadow swooped before it. So did a pellet storm, rocks thunking, booming, skittering, the deck atremble under their impact. Alisabeta and Ranu got the enemy's forward gun turret, a thick wooden bulge on the gondola, in their sights. They pressed the pedal that engaged the feeder. Their weapon came to life with a howl. Stones flew against the wickerwork above.

From the catapult emplacement, Keanua roared. Alisabeta heard him this far aft. A brief and frightful clatter drowned him out. The airship fell off course, wobbled, veered, and drifted aside. The girl saw the port nacelle blackened and dented. Keanua had scored a direct hit on that engine, disabled it, crippled the flyer.

"*Hurrao!*" Ranu whooped.

Alisabeta leaned her forehead on the gun console. She shivered with exhaustion. "*How long can we go on like this? Our magazines will soon be empty. Our sun cells are almost drained, and no way to recharge them. Don't let me faint, Ranu. Hold me, my dear—*"

"It can't be much longer. Modern military airships can do a hundred kilometers per hour. The base on Car Nicbar isn't more than four hundred kilometers away. Any moment."

This moment!

Again Keanua shouted. Alisabeta dared step out on deck for a clear view, gasped, and leaned against the turret. The Beneghalis, at their altitude, had seen the menace well before now. That last assault on the *Aorangi* was made in desperation. They marshaled themselves for battle.

Still distant, but rapidly swelling, came fifteen lean golden-painted ships. Each had four spendthrift engines to drive it through the sky; each was loaded with bombs and slugs and aerial harpoons. The Beneghalis had spent their ammunition on the *Aorangi*.

As the newcomers approached, Ranu-Alisabeta made out their insignia. Not Maurai, of course; not anything, though the dragons looked rather Sinese. Rumor had long flown about a warlord in Yunnan who had accumulated sufficient force to attempt large-scale banditry. On the other hand, there were always upstart buccaneers from Buruma, Iryan, or from as far as Smalilann—

"Get back under cover," Ranu warned Alisabeta. *"Anything can happen yet."* When she was safe, he sighed. *"Now my own job starts."*

"Ranu, no, you're hurt."

"They'll need a guide. Farewell for now. Tanaroa be with you . . . till I come back."

Gently, he disengaged himself. His thought flashed upward. *"Ranu Makintairu calling. Can you hear me?"*

"Loud and clear." Aruwera Samitu, chief Intelligence officer aboard the flagship, meshed minds and whistled. *"You've had a thin time of it, haven't you?"*

"Well, we've gotten off easier than we had any right to, considering how far the situation has progressed. Listen. Your data fitted into a picture which was perfectly correct, but three or four years obsolete. The Brahmards are not just building an atomic power station here. They've built it. It's operating."

"What!"

"I swear it must be." Swiftly, Ranu sketched what he had seen. *"It can't have been completed very long, or we'd be facing some real opposition. In fact, the research team is probably still busy getting a few*

final bugs out. But essentially the work is complete. As your service deduced, the Beneghalis didn't have the scientific resources to do this themselves, on the basis of ancient data. I'd guess they got pretty far, but couldn't quite make the apparatus go. So they imported Lorn sunna Browen. And he, with his knowledge of nuclear processes in the stars, developed a fresh approach. I can't imagine what. But ... they've done something on this island that the whole ancient world never achieved. Controlled hydrogen fusion."

"Is the plant very big?"

"*Tremendous. But the heart seems to be in one room. A circular chamber lined with tall iron cores. I hardly dare guess how many tons of iron. They must have combed the world.*"

"*They did. That was our first clue. Our own physicists think the reaction must be contained by magnetic fields—But no time for that. The air battle's beginning. I expect we can clear away these chaps within an hour. Can you, then, guide us in?*"

"*Yes. After I've located myself. Good luck.*"

Ranu focused attention back on his immediate surroundings. Let's see, early afternoon, so that direction was west, and he'd escaped along an approximate southeasterly track. Setting his jaws against the pain in his leg, he crawled from the hollow and limped into the canebrakes.

His progress was slow, with many pauses to climb a tree and get the lay of the land. It seemed to him that he was making enough noise to rouse Nan down in watery hell. More than an hour passed before he came on a man-made path, winding between solid walls of brush. Ruts bespoke wagons, which meant it ran from some native village to the caves. By now Ranu's chest was laboring too hard for him to exercise any forester's caution. He set off along the road.

The jungle remained hot and utterly quiet. He felt he could hear anyone else approaching in plenty of time to hide. But the Annamanese caught him unexpectedly.

They leaped from an overhead branch, two dark dwarfs in loincloths, armed with daggers and blowguns. Ranu hardly glimpsed them as they fell. He had no time to think, only to react. His left hand chopped at a skinny neck. He heard a cracking sound. The native dropped like a stone.

The other one squealed and scuttered aside. Ranu drew his knife.

The blowgun rose. Ranu charged. He was dimly aware of the dart as it went past his ear. It wasn't poisoned—the Annamanese left that sort of thing to the civilized nations—but it could have reached his heart. He caught the tube and yanked it away. Fear-widened eyes bulged at him. The savage pulled out his dagger and stabbed. He was not very skillful. Ranu parried the blow, taking only a minor slash on his forearm, and drove his own blade home. The native wailed. Ranu hit again.

Then there was nothing but sunlit thick silence and two bodies that looked still smaller than when they had lived. *Merciful Lesu, did I have to do this?*

Come on, Ranu. Pick up those feet of yours. He closed the staring eyes and continued on his way. When he was near the caverns, he found a hiding place and waited.

Not for long. Such Beneghali aircraft as did not go into the sea fled. They took a stand above Port Arberta, prepared to defend it against slavers. But the Maurai left a guard at hover near the water-ship and cruised on past, inland over the hills. Ranu resumed contact with Aruwera, who relayed instructions to the flagship navigation officer. Presently the raiders circled above the power laboratory.

Soldiers—barbarically painted and clad—went down by para-chute. The fight on the ground was bitter but short. When the last sentry had run into the woods, the Maurai swarmed through the installation.

In the cold fluorescent light that an infinitesimal fraction of its output powered, Aruwera looked upon the fusion reactor with awe. "What a thing!" he kept breathing. "What a *thing!*"

"I hate to destroy it," said his chief scientific aide. "Tanaroa! I'll have bad dreams for the rest of my life. Can't we at least salvage the plans?"

"If we can find them in time to microphotograph," Aruwera said. "Otherwise they'll have to be burned as part of the general vandal-ism. Pirates wouldn't steal blueprints. We've got to wreck everything as if for the sake of the iron and whatever else looks commercially valuable . . . load the loot and be off before the whole Beneghali air force arrives from the mainland. And, yes, send a signal to dismantle the Car Nicbar base. Let's get busy. Where's the main shutoff switch?"

The scientist began tracing circuits fast and knowingly, but with revulsion still in him. "How much did this cost?" he wondered. "How much of this country's wealth are we robbing?"

"Quite a bit," said Ranu. He spat. "I don't care about that, though. Maybe now they can tax their peasants less. What I do care about—" He broke off. Numerous Beneghalis and some Maurai had died today. The military professionals around him would not understand how the memory hurt, of two little black men lying dead in the jungle, hardly bigger than children.

✳ VII ✳

The eighth International Physical Society convention was held in Wellantoa. It was more colorful than previous ones, for several other nations (tribes, clans, alliances, societies, religions, anarchisms . . . whatever the more or less political unit might be in a particular civilization) had now developed to the point of supporting physicists. Robes, drawers, breastplates, togas joined the accustomed sarongs and tunics and kilts. At night, music on a dozen different scales wavered from upper-level windows. Those who belonged to poetically minded cultures struggled to translate each other's compositions, and often took the basic idea into their own repertory. On the professional side, there were a number of outstanding presentations, notably a Maurai computer that used artificial organic tissue and a Brasilean mathematician's generalized theory of turbulence processes.

Lorn sunna Browen was a conspicuous attender. Not that many people asked him about his Thrilling Adventure with the Pirates. That had been years ago, after all, and he'd given short answers from the first. "They kept us on some desert island till the ransom came, then they set us off near Port Arberta after dark. We weren't mistreated. Mainly we were bored." Lorn's work on stellar evolution was more interesting.

However, the big balding man disappeared several times from the convention lodge. He spoke to odd characters down on the waterfront; money went from hand to hand; at last he got a message that brought a curiously grim chuckle from him. Promptly he went into the street and hailed a pedicab.

He got out at a house in the hills above the city. A superb view of groves and gardens sloped down to the harbor, thronged with masts under the afternoon sun. Even in their largest town, the Sea People didn't like to be crowded. This dwelling was typical: whitewashed brick, red tile roof, riotous flowerbeds. A pennant on the flagpole, under the Cross and Stars, showed that a shipmaster lived here.

When he was home. But the hired prowler had said Captain Makintairu was currently at sea. His wife had stayed ashore this trip, having two children in school and a third soon to be born. The Merican dismissed the cab and strode over the path to the door. He knocked.

The door opened. The woman hadn't changed much, he thought: fuller of body, a patch of gray in her hair, but otherwise—He bowed. "Good day, my lady Alisabeta," he said.

"Oh!" Her mouth fell open. She swayed on her feet. He was afraid she was about to faint. The irony left him.

"I'm sorry," he exclaimed. He caught her hands. She leaned on him an instant. "I'm so sorry. I never meant—I mean—"

She took a long breath and straightened. Her laugh was shaky. "You surprised me for fair," she said. "Come in."

He followed her. The room beyond was sunny, quiet, book-lined. She offered him a chair. "W-w-would you like a glass of beer?" She bustled nervously about. "Or I can make some tea. If you'd rather. That is . . . tea. Coffee?"

"Beer is fine, thanks." His Maurai was fairly fluent; any scientist had to know that language. "How've you been?"

"V-very well. And you?"

"All right."

A stillness grew. He stared at his knees, wishing he hadn't come. She put down two glasses of beer on a table beside him, took a chair opposite, and regarded him for a long while. When finally he looked up, he saw she had drawn on some reserve of steadiness deeper than his own. The color had returned to her face. She even smiled.

"I never expected you would find us, you know," she said.

"I wasn't sure I would myself," he mumbled. "Thought I'd try, though, as long as I was here. No harm in trying, I thought. Why didn't you change your name or your home base or something?"

"We considered it. But our mission had been so ultrasecret. And Makintairu is a common N'Zealanner name. We didn't plan to do anything but sink back into the obscurity of plain sailor folk. That's all we ever were, you realize."

"I wasn't sure about that. I thought from the way you handled yourselves—I figured you for special operatives,"

"Oh, heavens, no. Intelligence had decided the truth was less likely to come out if the advance agents were a bona fide merchant crew, that had never been involved in such work before and never would be again. We got some training for the job, but not much, really."

"I guess the standard of the Sea People is just plain high, then," Lorn said. "Must come from generations of taking genetics into consideration when couples want to have kids, eh? That'd never work in my culture, I'm sorry to say. Not the voluntary way you do it, anyhow. We're too damned possessive."

"But we could never do half the things you've accomplished," she replied. "Desert reclamation, for instance. We simply couldn't organize that many people that efficiently for so long a time."

He drank half his beer and fumbled in a breast pocket for a cigar. "Can you satisfy my curiosity on one point?" he asked. "These past years I've wondered and wondered about what happened. I can only figure your bunch must have been in direct contact with each other. Your operation was too well coordinated for anything else. And yet you weren't packing portable radios. Are you telepaths, or what?"

"Goodness, no!" She laughed, more relaxed every minute. "We did have portable radios. Ultraminiaturized sets, surgically implanted, using body heat for power. Hooked directly into the nervous system, and hence using too broad a band for conventional equipment to read. It was rather like telepathy, I'll admit. I missed the sensation when the sets were removed afterward."

"Hm." Somewhat surer of his own self, he lit the cigar and squinted at her through the first smoke. "You're spilling your secrets mighty freely on such short notice, aren't you?"

"The transceivers aren't a secret any longer. That's more my professional interest than yours, and you've been wrapped up in preparations for your convention, so evidently you haven't heard. But the basic techniques were released last year, as if freshly invented.

The psychologists are quite excited about it as a research and therapeutic tool."

"I see. And as for the fact my lab was not raided by corsairs but by an official Federation party—" Lorn's mouth tightened under the moustache. "You're confessing that too, huh?"

"What else can I do, now you've found us? Kill you? There was far too much killing." Her hand stole across the table until it rested on his. The dark eyes softened; he saw a trace of tears. "Lorn," she murmured, "we hated our work."

"I suppose." He sat quiet, looked at his cigar end, drew heavily on the smoke, and looked back at her. "I was nearly as bitter as Dhananda at first . . . bitter as the whole Brahmard caste. The biggest accomplishment of my life, gone. Not even enough notes left to reconstruct the plans. No copies had been sent to the mainland, you see, for security reasons. We were afraid of spies; or someone might've betrayed us out of sheer hysteria, associating nuclear energy with the Judgment. Though, supposing we had saved the blueprints, there'd have been no possibility of rebuilding. Beneghal's treasury was exhausted. People were starving, close to revolt in some districts, this had been so expensive, and nothing ever announced to show for their taxes. Did you stop to think of that? That you were robbing Beneghali peasants who never did you any harm?"

"Often," she said. "But remember, the tax collectors had skinned them first. The cost of that reactor project would have bought them a great deal of happiness and advancement. As witness the past several years, after the Brahmards buckled down to attaining more modest goals."

"But the reactor was working! Unlimited energy. In ten years' time, Beneghal could've been overflowing with every industrial material. The project would have paid off a thousand times over. And you smashed it!"

Lorn sank back in his chair. Slowly, his fist unclenched. "We couldn't prove the job had not been done by pirates," he said without tone. "Certainly Beneghal couldn't declare war on the mighty Maurai Federation without proof enough to bring in a lot of indignant allies. Especially when your government offered such a whopping big help to relieve the famine. . . . But we could suspect. We could feel morally certain. And angry. God, how angry!

"Until—" He sighed. "I don't know. When I came home and got back into the swing of my regular work . . . and bit by bit re-realized what a decent, helpful, ungreedy bunch your people always have been . . . I finally decided you must've had some reason that seemed good to you. I couldn't imagine what, but . . . oh, I don't know. Reckon we have to take some things on faith, or life would get too empty. Don't worry, Alisabeta. I'm not going to make any big public revelation. Wouldn't do any good, anyway. Too much water's gone under that particular dam. Your government might be embarrassed, but no one would care enough to make real trouble. Probably most folks would think I was lying. So I'll keep my mouth shut." He raised blue eyes that looked like a child's, a child who has been struck without knowing what the offense was. "But could you tell me why? What you were scared of?"

"Surely," said Alisabeta. She leaned farther across the table, smiled with great gentleness, and stroked his cheek, just once. "Poor well-meaning man!

"There's no secret about our motives. The only secret is that we did take action. Our arguments have been known for decades—ever since the theoretical possibility of controlled hydrogen fusion began to be seriously discussed. That's why the Brahmards were so furtive about their project. They knew we'd put pressure on to stop them."

"Yes, Dhananda always said you were jealous. Afraid you'd lose your position as the world's top power."

"Well, frankly, that's part of it. By and large, we like the way things are going. We want to stay able to protect what we like. We weren't afraid Beneghal would embark on a career of world conquest or any such stupidity. But given atomic energy, they could manufacture such quantities of war materiel as to be invincible—explosives, motor vehicles, jet planes, yes, nuclear weapons. Once they presented us with a fait accompli like that, we wouldn't be able to do anything about events. Beneghal would take the lead. Our protests could be ignored; eventually, no one anywhere would listen to us. We could only regain leadership by embarking on a similar program. And the War of Judgment proved where a race like that would end!"

"M-m-m . . . yes—"

"Even if we refrained from trying for a nuclear capability, others would not. You understand that's why the Brahmards never have told the world what they were doing. They see as well as us the scramble to duplicate their feat that would immediately follow.

"But there's a subtle and important reason why Beneghal in particular shouldn't be allowed to dominate the scene. The Brahmards are missionaries at heart. They think the entire planet should be converted to their urban-industrial ideal. Whereas we believe—and we have a good deal of psychodynamic science to back us—we believe the many different cultures that grew up in isolation during the dark ages should continue their own evolution. Think, Lorn. The most brilliant eras of history were always when alien societies came into reasonably friendly contact. When Egypt and Crete met in the Eighteenth Dynasty; Phoenician, Persian, Greek in classical times; Nippon and Sina in the Nara period; Byzantium, Asia, and Europe crossbreeding to make the Renaissance—and, yes, our era right now!

"Oh, surely, the Brahmard approach has much to offer. We don't want to suppress it. Neither do we want it to take over the world. But given the power and productivity, the speed and volume of traffic, the resource consumption, the population explosion . . . given everything that your project would have brought about . . . the machine culture would absorb the whole human race again. As it did before the Judgment. Not by conquest, but by being so much stronger materially that everyone would have to imitate it or go under."

Breathless, Alisabeta reached for her glass. Lorn rubbed his chin. "M-m-m . . . maybe," he said. "If industrialism can feed and clothe people better, though, doesn't it deserve to win out?"

"Who says it can?" she argued. "It can feed and clothe more people, yes. But not necessarily better. And are sheer numbers any measure of quality, Lorn? Don't you want to leave some places on Earth where a man can go to be alone?

"And, too, suppose industrialism did begin to spread. Think of the transition period. I told you once about the horrors that are a matter of historical record, when the ancient Communists set out to westernize their countries overnight. That would happen again. Not that the Brahmards would do it; they're good men. But other leaders elsewhere—half barbarian, childishly eager for power and prestige, breaking their home cultures to bits in their impatience—such leaders would arise.

"Of course it's wrong that people go poor and hungry. But that problem has more than one solution. Each civilization can work out its own. We do it in the Islands by exploiting the seas and limiting our population. You do it in Merica by dry farming and continental trade. The Okkaidans do it by making moderation into a way of life. The Sberyaks are developing a fascinating system of reindeer ranches. And on and on. How much we learn from each other!"

"Even from Beneghal," Lorn said dryly.

"Yes," she nodded, quite grave. "Machine techniques especially. Although . . . well, let them do as they please, but no one in the Islands envies them. I really don't think their way—the old way—is anything like the best. Man isn't made for it. If industrialism was so satisfying, why did the industrial world commit suicide?"

"I suppose that's another reason you're afraid of atomic energy," he said. "Atomic war."

She shook her head. "We aren't afraid. We could develop the technology ourselves and keep anyone else from doing so. But we don't want that tight a control on the world. We think Maurai interference should be kept to an absolute minimum."

"Nevertheless," he said, sharp-toned, "you do interfere."

"True," she agreed. "That's another lesson we've gotten from history. The ancients could have saved themselves if they'd had the courage—been hardhearted enough—to act before things snowballed. If the democracies had suppressed every aggressive dictatorship in its infancy; or if they had simply enforced their ideal of an armed world government at the time when they had the strength to do—Well." She glanced down. Her hand left his and went slowly across her abdomen; a redness crept into her cheeks. "No," she said, "I'm sorry people got hurt, that day at Annaman, but I'm not sorry about the end result. I always planned to have children, you see."

Lorn stirred. His cigar had gone out. He relit it. The first puff was as acrid as expected. Sunlight slanted in the windows to glow on the wooden floor, on a batik rug from Smatra and a statuette of strangely disturbing beauty from somewhere in Africa.

"Well," he said, "I told you I've dropped my grudge. I guess you don't figure to hold atomic energy down forever."

"Oh no. Someday, in spite of everything we do, Earth will have grown unified and dull. Then it will again be time to try for the stars."

"So I've heard various of your thinkers claim. Me, though . . . philosophically, I don't like your attitude. I'm resigned to it, sure. Can't have every wish granted in this life. I did get the fun of working on that project, at least. But damn it, Alisabeta, I think you're wrong. If your society can't handle something big and new like the tamed atom, why, by Oktai, you've proved your society isn't worth preserving."

He felt instantly regretful and started to apologize: no offense meant, just a difference of viewpoint and— But she didn't give him a chance to say the words. She raised her head, met his gaze, and smiled like a cat.

"Our society can't handle something new?" she murmured. "Oh, my dear Lorn, what do you think we were doing that day?"

UN-MAN

✹ I ✹

They were gone, their boat whispering into the sky with all six of them aboard. Donner had watched them from his balcony—he had chosen the apartment carefully with a view to such features—as they walked out on the landing flange and entered the shell. Now their place was vacant and it was time for him to get busy.

For a moment hesitation was in him. He had waited many days for this chance, but a man does not willingly enter a potential trap. His eyes strayed to the picture on his desk. The darkly beautiful young woman and the children in her arms seemed to be looking at him, her lips were parted as if she were about to speak. He wanted to press the button that animated the film, but didn't quite dare. Gently, his fingers stroked the glass over her cheek.

"Jeanne," he whispered. "Jeanne, honey."

He got to work. His colorful lounging pajamas were exchanged for a gray outfit that would be inconspicuous against the walls of the building. An ordinary featureless mask, its sheen carefully dulled to non-reflection, covered his face. He clipped a flat box of tools to his belt and painted his fingertips with collodion. Picking up a reel of cord in one hand, he returned to the balcony.

From here, two hundred and thirty-four stories up, he had a wide view of the Illinois plain. As far as he could see, the land rolled green with corn, hazing into a far horizon out of which the great sky lifted. Here and there, a clump of trees had been planted, and the white streak of an old highway crossed the field, but otherwise it was one

183

immensity of growth. The holdings of Midwest Agricultural reached beyond sight.

On either hand, the apartment building lifted sheer from the trees and gardens of its park. Two miles long, a city in its own right, a mountain of walls and windows, the unit dominated the plain, sweeping heavenward in a magnificent arrogance that ended sixty-six stories above Donner's flat. Through the light prairie wind that fluttered his garments, the man could hear a low unending hum, muted pulsing of machines and life—the building—itself like a giant organism.

There were no other humans in sight. The balconies were so designed as to screen the users from view of neighbors on the same level, and anyone in the park would find his upward glance blocked by trees. A few brilliant points of light in the sky were airboats, but that didn't matter.

Donner fastened his reel to the edge of the balcony and took the end of the cord in his fingers. For still another moment he stood, letting the sunlight and wind pour over him, filling his eyes with the reaching plains and the high, white-clouded heaven.

He was a tall man, his apparent height reduced by the width of shoulders and chest, a curious rippling grace in his movements. His naturally yellow hair had been dyed brown and contact lenses made his blue eyes dark, but otherwise there hadn't been much done to his face—the broad forehead, high cheekbones, square jaw, and jutting nose were the same. He smiled wryly behind the blank mask, took a deep breath, and swung himself over the balcony rail.

The cord unwound noiselessly, bearing him down past level after level. There was a risk involved in this daylight burglary—someone might happen to glance around the side wall of a balcony and spot him, and even the custom of privacy would hardly keep them from notifying the unit police. But the six he was after didn't time their simultaneous departures for his convenience.

The looming facade slid past, blurred a little by the speed of his descent. One, two, three—He counted as he went by, and at the eighth story down tugged the cord with his free hand. The reel braked and he hung in midair.

A long and empty way down—He grinned and began to swing himself back and forth, increasing the amplitude of each arc until his soles were touching the unit face. On the way back, he grasped the balcony rail, just beyond the screening side wall, with his free hand. His body jerked to a stop, the impact like a blow in his muscles.

Still clinging to the cord, he pulled himself one-armed past the screen, over the rail, and onto the balcony floor. Under the gray tunic and the sweating skin, his sinews felt as if they were about to crack. He grunted with relief when he stood freely, tied the cord to the rail, and unclipped his tool case.

The needle of his electronic detector flickered. So there was an alarm hooked to the door leading in from the balcony. Donner traced it with care, located a wire, and cut it. Pulling a small torch from his kit, he approached the door. Beyond its transparent plastic, the rooms lay quiet: a conventional arrangement of furniture, but with a waiting quality over it.

Imagination, thought Donner impatiently, and cut the lock from the door. As he entered, the autocleaner sensed his presence and its dust-sucking wind whined to silence.

The man forced the lock of a desk and riffled through the papers within. One or two in code he slipped into his pocket, the rest were uninteresting. There must be more, though. Curse it, this was their regional headquarters!

His metal detector helped him about the apartment, looking for hidden safes. When he found a large mass buried in a wall, he didn't trouble with searching for the button to open it, but cut the plastic facing away. The gang would know their place had been raided, and would want to move. If they took another flat in the same building, Donner's arrangement with the superintendent would come into effect; they'd get a vacancy which had been thoughtfully provided with all the spy apparatus he could install. The man grinned again.

Steel gleamed at him through the scorched and melted wall. It was a good safe, and he hadn't time to diddle with it. He plugged in his electric drill, and the diamond head gnawed a small hole in the lock. With a hypodermic he inserted a few cubic centimeters of levinite, and touched it off by a UHF beam. The lock jangled to ruin, and Donner opened the door.

He had only time to see the stet-gun within, and grasp the terrible fact of its existence. Then it spat three needles into his chest, and he whirled down into darkness.

✳ II ✳

Once or twice he had begun to waken, stirring dimly toward light, and the jab of a needle had thrust him back. Now, as his head slowly cleared, they let him alone. And that was worse.

Donner retched and tried to move. His body sagged against straps that held him fast in his chair. Vision blurred in a huge nauseous ache; the six who stood watching him were a ripple of fever-dream against an unquiet shadow.

"He's coming around," said the thin man unnecessarily.

The heavy-set, gray-haired man in the conservative blue tunic glanced at his timepiece. "Pretty fast, considering how he was dosed. Healthy specimen."

Donner mumbled. The taste of vomit was bitter in his mouth. "Give him some water," said the bearded man.

"Like hell!" The thin man's voice was a snarl. His face was dead white against the shifting, blurring murk of the room, and there was a fever in his eyes. "He doesn't rate it, the—Un-man!"

"Get him some water," said the gray-haired one quietly. The skeletal younger man slouched sulkily over to a chipped basin with an old-fashioned tap and drew a glassful.

Donner swallowed it greedily, letting it quench some of the dry fire in his throat and belly. The bearded man approached with a hypo.

"Stimulant," he explained. "Bring you around faster." It bit into Donner's arm and he felt his heartbeat quicken. His head was still a keen pulsing pain, but his eyes steadied and he looked at the others with returning clarity.

"We weren't altogether careless," said the heavy-set man. "That stet-gun was set to needle anybody who opened the safe without pressing the right button first. And, of course, a radio signal was emitted which brought us back in a hurry. We've kept you unconscious till now."

Donner looked around him. The room was bare, thick with the dust and cobwebs of many years, a few pieces of old-style wooden furniture crouched in ugliness against the cracked plaster walls. There was a single window, its broken glass panes stuffed with rags, dirt so thick on it that he could not be sure if there was daylight outside. But the hour was probably after dark. The only illumination within was from a single fluoro in a stand on the table.

He must be in Chicago, Donner decided through a wave of sickness. One of the vast moldering regions that encompassed the inhabited parts of the dying city—deserted, not worth destroying as yet, the lair of rats and decay. Sooner or later, some agricultural outfit would buy up the nominal title from the government which had condemned the place and raze what had been spared by fire and rot. But it hadn't happened yet, and the empty slum was a good hideaway for anybody.

Donner thought of those miles of ruinous buildings, wrapped in night, looming hollow against a vacant sky—dulled echoes in the cracked and grass-grown streets, the weary creak of a joist, the swift patter of feet and glare of eyes from the thick dark, menace and loneliness for further than he could run.

Alone, alone. He was more alone here than in the outermost reaches of space. He knew starkly that he was going to die.

Jeanne. O Jeanne, my darling.

"You were registered at the unit as Mark Roberts," said the woman crisply. She was thin, almost as thin as the bitter-eyed young man beside her. The face was sharp and hungry, the hair close cropped, the voice harsh with purpose. "But your ID tattoo is a fake—it's a dye that comes off with acid. We got your thumbprint and that number on a check and called the bank central like in an ordinary verification, and the robofile said yes, that was Mark Roberts and the account was all right." She leaned forward, her face straining against the blur of night, and spat it at him. "Who are you really? Only a secret service man could get by with that kind of fake. Whose service are you in?"

"It's obvious, isn't it?" snapped the thin man. "He's not American Security. We know that. So he must be an Un-man."

The way he said the last word made it an ugly, inhuman sound. "*The* Un-man!" he repeated.

"Our great enemy," said the heavy-set one thoughtfully. "*The* Un-man—not just an ordinary operative, with human limitations, but the great and secret one who's made so much trouble for us."

He cocked his gray head and stared at Donner. "It fits what fragmentary descriptions we have," he went on. "But then, the U.N. boys can do a lot with surgery and cosmetics, can't they? And *the* Un-Man has been killed several times. An operator was bagged in Hong Kong only last month which the killer swore must be our enemy—he said nobody else could have led them such a chase."

That was most likely Weinberger, thought Donner. An immense weariness settled on him. They were so few, so desperately few, and one by one the Brothers went down into darkness. He was next, and after him—

"What I can't understand," said a fifth man—Donner recognized him as Colonel Samsey of the American Guard—"is why, if the U. N. Secret Services does have a corps of—uh—supermen, it should bother to disguise them to look all alike. So that we'll think we're dealing with an immortal?" He chuckled grimly. "Surely they don't expect us to be rattled by that!"

"Not supermen," said the gray-haired one. "Enormously able, yes, but the Un-men aren't infallible. As witness this one." He stood before Donner, his legs spread and his hands on his hips. "Suppose you start talking. Tell us about yourself."

"I can tell you about your own selves," answered Donner. His tongue felt thick and dry, but the acceptance of death made him, all at once, immensely steady. "You are Roger Wade, president of Brain Tools, Incorporated, and a prominent supporter of the Americanist Party." To the woman: "You are Marta Jennings, worker for the Party on a full-time basis. Your secretary, Mr. Wade—" his eyes roved to the gaunt young man—"is Rodney Borrow, Exogene Number—"

"*Don't call me that!*" Cursing, Borrow lunged at Donner. He clawed like a woman. When Samsey and the bearded man dragged him away, his face was death-white and he dribbled at the mouth.

"And the experiment was a failure," taunted Donner cruelly.

"Enough!" Wade slapped the prisoner, a ringing open-handed buffet. "We want to know something new, and there isn't much time. You are, of course, immunized against truth drugs—Dr. Lewin's tests have already confirmed that—but I assume you can still feel pain."

After a moment, he added quietly. "We aren't fiends. You know that we're patriots." *Working with the nationalists of a dozen other countries!* thought Donner. "We don't want to hurt or kill unnecessarily."

"But first we want your real identity," said the bearded man, Lewin. "Then your background of information about us, the future plans of your chief, and so on. However, it will be sufficient for now if you answer a few questions pertaining to yourself, residence and so on."

Oh, yes, thought Donner, the weariness like a weight on his soul. *That'll do. Because then they'll find Jeanne and Jimmy, and bring them here, and—*

Lewin wheeled forth a lie detector. "Naturally, we don't want our time wasted by false leads," he said.

"It won't be," replied Donner. "I'm not going to say anything."

Lewin nodded, unsurprised, and brought out another machine. "This one generates low-frequency, low-voltage current," he remarked. "Quite painful. I don't think your will can hold out very long. If it does, we can always try prefrontal lobotomy; you won't have inhibitions then. But we'll give you a chance with this first."

He adjusted the electrodes on Donner's skin. Borrow licked his lips with a dreadful hunger.

Donner tried to smile, but his mouth felt stiff. The sixth man, who looked like a foreigner somehow, went out of the room.

There was a tiny receiver in Donner's skull, behind the right mastoid. It could only pick up messages of a special wave form, but it had its silencing uses too. After all, electric torture is a common form of inquisition, and very hard to bear.

He thought of Jeanne, and of Jimmy, and of the Brotherhood. He wished that the last air he was to breathe weren't stale and dusty.

The current tore him with a convulsive anguish. His muscles jerked against the straps and he cried out. Then the sensitized communicator blew up, releasing a small puff of fluorine.

The image Donner carried into death was that of Jeanne, smiling and bidding him welcome home.

✷ **III** ✷

Barney Rosenberg drove along a dim, rutted trail toward the sheer loom of the escarpment. Around its corner lay Drygulch. But he wasn't hurrying. As he got closer, he eased the throttle of his sandcat and the engine's purr became almost inaudible.

Leaning back in his seat, he looked through the tiny plastiglass cab at the Martian landscape. It was hard to understand that he would never see it again.

Even here, five miles or so from the colony, there was no trace of man save himself and his engine and the blurred track through sand and bush. Men had come to Mars on wings of fire, they had hammered out their cities with a clangorous brawl of life, mined and smelted and begun their ranches, trekked in sandcats and air-suits from the polar bogs to the equatorial scrubwoods—and still they had left no real sign of their passing. Not yet. Here a tin can or broken tool, there a mummified corpse in the wreck of a burst seal-tent, but sand and loneliness drifted over them, night and cold and forgetfulness. Mars was too old and strange for thirty years of man to matter.

The desert stretched away to Rosenberg's left, tumbling in steep drifts of sand from the naked painted hills. Off to the sharply curving horizon the desert marched, an iron barrenness of red and brown and tawny yellow, knife-edged shadows and a weird vicious shimmer of pale sunlight. Here and there a crag lifted, harsh with mineral color, worn by the passing of ages and thin wind to a fluted fantasy. A sandstorm was blowing a few miles off, a scud of dust hissing over stone, stirring the low gray-green brush to a sibilant murmur. On his right the hills rose bare and steep, streaked with blue and green of copper ores, gashed and scored and murmurous with wind. He saw life, the dusty thorn-bushes and the high gaunt cactoids and a flicker of movement as a tiny leaper fled. In one of the precipices, a series of carved, time-blurred steps went up to the ruin of a cliff dwelling abandoned—how long ago?

Overhead the sky was enormous, a reaching immensity of deep greenish blue-violet, incredibly high and cold and remote. The stars glittered faintly in its abyss, the tiny hurtling speck of a moon less bright than they. A shrunken sun stood in a living glory of corona and zodiacal light, the winged disc of royal Egypt lifting over Mars. Near the horizon a thin layer of ice crystals caught the luminescence in a chilly sparkle. There was wind, Rosenberg knew, a whimpering ghost of wind blowing through the bitter remnant of atmosphere, but he couldn't hear it through the heavy plastiglass and somehow he felt that fact as a deeper isolation.

It was a cruel world, this Mars, a world of cold and ruin and soaring scornful emptiness, a world that broke men's hearts and drained their lives from them—rainless, oceanless, heatless, kindless, where the great wheel of the stars swung through a desert of millennia, where the days cried with wind and the nights rang and groaned with frost. It was a world of waste and mystery, a niggard world where a man ate starvation and drank thirst and finally went down in darkness. Men trudged through unending miles, toil and loneliness and quiet creeping fear, sweated and gasped, cursed the planet and wept for the dead and snatched at warmth and life in the drab colony towns. *It's all right when you find yourself talking to the sandbuggers—but when they start talking back, it's time to go home.*

And yet—and yet— The sweep of the polar moors, thin faint swirl of wind, sunlight shattered to a million diamond shards on the hoarfrost cap; the cloven tremendousness of Rasmussen Gorge, a tumbling, sculptured wilderness of fairy stone, uncounted shifting hues of color and fleeting shadow; the high cold night of stars, fantastically brilliant constellations marching over a crystal heaven, a silence so great you thought you could hear God speaking over the universe; the delicate day-flowers of the Syrtis forests, loveliness blooming with the bitter dawn and dying in the swift sunset; traveling and searching, rare triumph and much defeat, but always the quest and the comradeship. Oh, yes, Mars was savage to her lovers, but she gave them of her strange beauty and they would not forget her while they lived.

Maybe Stef was the lucky one, thought Rosenberg. *He died here.*

He guided the sandcat over a razorback ridge. For a moment he paused, looking at the broad valley beyond. He hadn't been to Drygulch for a couple of years; that'd be almost four Earth years, he remembered.

The town, half underground below its domed roof, hadn't changed much outwardly, but the plantations had doubled their area. The genetic engineers were doing good work, adapting terrestrial food plants to Mars and Martian plants to the needs of humans. The colonies were already self-supporting with regard to essentials, as they had to be considering the expense of freight from Earth. But they still hadn't developed a decent meat animal; that part of the diet had to come from yeast-culture factories in the towns and nobody saw a beefsteak on Mars. *But we'll have that too, one of these years.*

A worn-out world, stern and bitter and grudging, but it was being tamed. Already the new generation was being born. There wasn't much fresh immigration from Earth these days, but man was unshakably rooted here. Someday he'd get around to modifying the atmosphere and weather till humans could walk free and unclothed over the rusty hills—but that wouldn't happen till he, Rosenberg, was dead, and in an obscure way he was glad of it.

The cat's supercharging pumps roared, supplementing tanked oxygen with Martian air for the hungry Diesel as the man steered it along the precarious trail. It was terribly thin, that air, but its oxygen was mostly ozone and that helped. Passing a thorium mine, Rosenberg scowled. The existence of fissionables was the main reason for planting colonies here in the first place, but they should be saved for Mars.

Well, I'm not really a Martian any longer. I'll be an Earthman again soon. You have to die on Mars, like Stef, and give your body back to the Martian land, before you altogether belong here.

The trail from the mine became broad and hard-packed enough to be called a road. There was other traffic now, streaming from all corners—a loaded ore-car, a farmer coming in with a truckful of harvested crops, a survey expedition returning with maps and specimens. Rosenberg waved to the drivers. They were of many nationalities, but except for the Pilgrims that didn't matter. Here they were simply humans. He hoped the U.N. would get around to internationalizing the planets soon.

There was a flag on a tall staff outside the town, the Stars and Stripes stiff against an alien sky. It was of metal—it had to be in that murderous corroding atmosphere—and Rosenberg imagined that they had to repaint it pretty often. He steered past it, down a long ramp leading under the dome. He had to wait his turn at the airlock, and wondered when somebody would invent a better system of oxygen conservation. These new experiments in submolar mechanics offered a promising lead.

He left his cat in the underground garage, with word to the attendant that another man, its purchaser, would pick it up later. There was an odd stinging in his eyes and he patted its scarred flanks. Then he took an elevator and a slideway to the housing office and arranged for a room; he had a couple of days before the *Phobos* left. A shower and a change of clothes were sheer luxury and he reveled in them. He didn't feel much desire for the cooperative taverns and pleasure joints, so he called up Doc Fieri instead.

The physician's round face beamed at him in the plate. "Barney, you old sandbugger! When'd you get in?"

"Just now. Can I come up?"

"Yeah, sure. Nothing doing at the office—that is, I've got company, but he won't stay long. Come right on over."

Rosenberg took a remembered route through crowded hallways and elevators till he reached the door he wanted. He knocked: Drygulch's imports and its own manufactories needed other things more urgently than call and recorder circuits. "Come in!" bawled the voice.

Rosenberg entered the cluttered room, a small leathery man with gray-sprinkled hair and a beaky nose, and Fieri pumped his hand enthusiastically. The guest stood rigid in the background, a lean ascetic figure in black—a Pilgrim. Rosenberg stiffened inwardly. He didn't like that sort, Puritan fanatics from the Years of Madness who'd gone to Mars so they could be unhappy in freedom. Rosenberg didn't care what a man's religion was, but nobody on Mars had a right to be so clannish and to deny cooperation as much as New Jerusalem. However, he shook hands politely, relishing the Pilgrim's ill-concealed distaste—they were anti-Semitic too.

"This is Dr. Morton," explained Fieri. "He heard of my research and came around to inquire about it."

"Most interesting," said the stranger. "And most promising, too. It will mean a great deal to Martian colonization."

"And surgery and biological research everywhere," put in Fieri. Pride was bursting from him.

"What is it, Doc?" asked Rosenberg, as expected.

"Suspended animation," said Fieri.

"Hm?"

"Uh-huh. You see, in what little spare time I have, I've puttered around with Martian biochemistry. Fascinating subject, and unearthly in two meanings of the word. We've nothing like it at home—don't need it. Hibernation and estivation approximate it, of course."

"Ummm . . . yes." Rosenberg rubbed his chin. "I know what you mean. Everybody does. The way so many plants and animals needing heat for their metabolisms can curl up and 'sleep' through the nights, or even through the whole winter. Or they can survive prolonged droughts that way." He chuckled. "Comparative matter, of course. Mars is in a state of permanent drought, by Earthly standards."

"And you say, Dr. Fieri, that the natives can do it also?" asked Morton.

"Yes. Even they, with a quite highly developed nervous system, can apparently 'sleep' through such spells of cold or famine. I had to rely on explorers' fragmentary reports for that datum. There are so few natives left, and they're so shy and secretive. But last year I did finally get a look at one in such a condition. It was incredible—respiration was indetectable, the heartbeat almost so, the encephalograph showed only a very slow, steady pulse. But I got blood and tissue samples, and was able to analyze and compare them with secretions from other life forms in suspension."

"I thought even Martians' blood would freeze in a winter night," said Rosenberg.

"It does. The freezing point is much lower than with human blood, but not so low that it can't freeze at all. However, in suspension, there's a whole series of enzymes released. One of them, dissolved in the bloodstream, changes the characteristics of the plasma. When ice crystals form, they're *more* dense than the liquid, therefore cell walls aren't ruptured and the organism survives. Moreover, a slow circulation of oxygen-bearing radicals and nutrient solutions takes place even through the ice, apparently by some process analogous to ion exchange. Not much, but enough to keep the organism alive and undamaged. Heat, a sufficient temperature, causes the breakdown of these secretions and the animal or plant revives. In the case of suspension to escape thirst or famine, the process is somewhat different, of course, though the same basic enzymes are involved."

Fieri laughed triumphantly and slapped a heap of papers on his desk. "Here are my notes. The work isn't complete yet. I'm not quite ready to publish, but it's more or less a matter of detail now." A Nobel Prize glittered in his eye.

Morton skimmed through the manuscript. "*Very* interesting," he murmured. His lean, close-cropped head bent over a structural formula. "The physical chemistry of this material must be weird."

"It is, Morton, it is." Fieri grinned.

"Hmmmm—do you mind if I borrow this to read? As I mentioned earlier, I believe my lab at New Jerusalem could carry out some of these analyses for you."

"That'll be fine. Tell you what, I'll make up a stat of this whole mess for you. I'll have it ready by tomorrow."

"Thank you." Morton smiled, though it seemed to hurt his face. "This will be quite a surprise, I'll warrant. You haven't told anyone else?"

"Oh, I've mentioned it around, of course, but you're the first person who's asked for the technical details. Everybody's too busy with their own work on Mars. But it'll knock their eyes out back on Earth. They've been looking for something like this ever since—since the Sleeping Beauty story—and here's the first way to achieve it."

"I'd like to read this too, Doc," said Rosenberg.

"Are you a biochemist?" asked Morton.

"Well, I know enough biology and chemistry to get by, and I'll have leisure to wade through this before my ship blasts."

"Sure, Barney," said Fieri. "And do me a favor, will you? When you get home, tell old Summers at Cambridge—England, that is— about it. He's their big biochemist, and he always said I was one of his brighter pupils and shouldn't have switched over to medicine. I'm a hell of a modest cuss, huh? But damn it all, it's not everybody who grabs onto something as big as this!"

Morton's pale eyes lifted to Rosenberg's. "So you are returning to Earth?" he asked.

"Yeah. The *Phobos.*" He felt he had to explain, that he didn't want the Pilgrim to think he was running out. "More or less doctor's orders, you understand. My helmet cracked open in a fall last year, and before I could slap a patch on I had a beautiful case of the bends, plus the low pressure and the cold and the ozone raising the very devil with my lungs." Rosenberg shrugged, and his smile was bitter. "I suppose I'm fortunate to be alive. At least I have enough credit saved to retire. But I'm just not strong enough to continue working on Mars, and it's not the sort of place where you can loaf and remain sane."

"I see. It is a shame. When will you be on Earth, then?"

"Couple of months. The *Phobos* goes orbital most of the way—do I look like I could afford an acceleration passage?" Rosenberg turned to Fieri. "Doc, will there be any other old sanders coming home this trip?"

"'Fraid not. You know there are darn few who retire from Mars to Earth. They die first. You're one of the lucky ones."

"A lonesome trip, then. Well, I suppose I'll survive it."

Morton made his excuses and left. Fieri stared after him. "Odd fellow. But then, all these Pilgrims are. They're anti almost everything. He's competent, though, and I'm glad he can tackle some of those analyses for me." He slapped Rosenberg's shoulder. "But forget it, old man! Cheer up and come along with me for a beer. Once you're stretched out on those warm white Florida sands, with blue sky and blue sea and luscious blondes walking by, I guarantee you won't miss Mars."

"Maybe not." Rosenberg looked unhappily at the floor. "It's never been the same since Stef died. I didn't realize how much he'd meant to me till I'd buried him and gone on by myself."

"He meant a lot to everyone, Barney. He was one of those people who seem to fill the world with life, wherever they are. Let's see—he was about sixty when he died, wasn't he? I saw him shortly before, and he could still drink any two men under the table, and all the girls were still adoring him."

"Yeah. He was my best friend, I suppose. We tramped Earth and the planets together for fifteen years." Rosenberg smiled. "Funny thing, friendship. Stef and I didn't even talk much. It wasn't needed. The last five years have been pretty empty without him."

"He died in a cave-in, didn't he?"

"Yes. We were exploring up near the Sawtooths, hunting a uranium lode. Our diggings collapsed, he held that toppling roof up with his shoulders and yelled at me to scramble out—then before he could get clear, it came down and burst his helmet open. I buried him on a hill, under a cairn, looking out over the desert. He was always a friend of high places."

"Mmmmmm—yes— Well, thinking about Stefan Rostomily won't help him or us now. Let's go get that beer, shall we?"

✳ IV ✳

The shrilling within his head brought Robert Naysmith to full awareness with a savage force. His arm jerked, and the brush streaked a yellow line across his canvas.

"Naysmith!" The voice rattled harshly in his skull. "Report to Prior at Frisco Unit. Urgent. Martin Donner has disappeared, presumed dead. You're on his job now. Hop to it, boy."

For a moment Naysmith didn't grasp the name. He'd never met anyone called Donner. Then—yes, that was on the list, Donner was one of the Brotherhood. And dead now.

Dead— He had never seen Martin Donner, and yet he knew the man with an intimacy no two humans had realized before the Brothers came. Sharp in his mind rose the picture of the dead man, smiling a characteristic slow smile, sprawled back in a relaxer with a glass of Scotch in one strong blunt-fingered hand. The Brothers were all partial to Scotch, thought Naysmith with a twisting sadness. And Donner had been a mech-volley fan, and had played good chess, read a lot and sometimes quoted Shakespeare, tinkered with machinery, probably had a small collection of guns—

Dead. Sprawled sightlessly somewhere on the turning planet, his muscles stiff, his body already devouring itself in proteolysis, his brain darkened, withdrawn into the great night, and leaving an irreparable gap in the tight-drawn line of the Brotherhood.

"You might pick up a newscast on your way," said the voice in his head conversationally. "It's hot stuff."

Naysmith's eyes focused on his painting. It was shaping up to be a good one. He had been experimenting with techniques, and this latest caught the wide sunlit dazzle of California beach, the long creaming swell of waves, the hot cloudless sky and the thin harsh grass and the tawny-skinned woman who sprawled on the sand. Why did they have to call him just now?

"Okay, Sofie," he said with resignation. "That's all. I've got to get back."

The sun-browned woman rolled over on one elbow and looked at him. "What the devil?" she asked. "We've only been here three hours. The day's hardly begun."

"It's gone far enough, I'm afraid." Naysmith began putting away his brushes. "Home to civilization."

"But I don't want to!"

"What has that got to do with it?" He folded his easel.

"But why?" she cried, half getting up.

"I have an appointment this afternoon." Naysmith strode down the beach toward the trail. After a moment, Sofie followed.

"You didn't tell me that," she protested.

"You didn't ask me," he said. He added a "Sorry" that was no apology at all.

There weren't many others on the beach, and the parking lot was relatively uncluttered. Naysmith palmed the door of his boat and it opened for him. He slipped on tunic, slacks, and sandals, put a beret rakishly atop his sun-bleached yellow hair, and entered the boat. Sofie followed, not bothering to don her own clothes.

The ovoid shell slipped skyward on murmuring jets. "I'll drop you off at your place," said Naysmith. "Some other time, huh?"

She remained sulkily silent. They had met accidentally a week before, in a bar. Naysmith was officially a cybernetic epistemologist on vacation, Sofie an engineer on the Pacific Colony project, off for a holiday from her job and her free-marriage group. It had been a pleasant interlude, and Naysmith regretted it mildly.

Still—the rising urgent pulse of excitement tensed his body and cleared the last mists of artistic preoccupation from his brain. You lived on a knife edge in the Service, you drew breath and looked at the sun and grasped after the real world with a desperate awareness of little time. None of the Brotherhood were members of the Hedonists, they were all too well-balanced for that, but inevitably they were epicureans.

When you were trained from—well, from birth, even the sharpness of nearing death could be a kind of pleasure. *Besides,* thought Naysmith, *I might be one of the survivors.*

"You are a rat, you know," said Sofie.

"Squeak," said Naysmith. His face—the strange strong face of level fair brows and wide-set blue eyes, broad across the high cheekbones and in the mouth, square-jawed and crag-nosed—split in a grin that laughed with her while it laughed at her. He looked older than his twenty-five years. And she, thought Sofie with sudden tiredness, looked younger than her forty. Her people had been well off even during the Years of Hunger; she'd always been exposed to the best available biomedical techniques, and if she claimed thirty few would call her a liar. But—

Naysmith fiddled with the radio. Presently a voice came out of it; he didn't bother to focus the TV.

". . . the thorough investigation demanded by finance minister Arnold Besser has been promised by President Lopez. In a prepared statement, the President said: "The rest of the ministry, like myself, are frankly inclined to discredit this accusation and believe that the Chinese government is mistaken. However, its serious nature—""

"Lopez, eh? The U.N. President himself," murmured Naysmith. "That means the accusation has been made officially now."

"What accusation?" asked the woman. "I haven't heard a 'cast for a week."

"The Chinese government was going to lodge charges that the assassination of Kwang-ti was done by U.N. secret agents," said Naysmith.

"Why, that's ridiculous!" she gasped. "The *U.N.*?" She shook her dark head. "They haven't the—right. The U.N. agents, I mean. Kwang-ti was a menace, yes, but assassination! I don't believe it."

"Just think what the anti-U.N. factions all over the Solar System, including our own Americanists, are going to make of this," said Naysmith. "Right on top of charges of corruption comes one of murder!"

"Turn it off," she said. "It's too horrible."

"These are horrible times, Sofie."

"I thought they were getting better." She shuddered. "I remember the tail-end of the Years of Hunger, and then the Years of Madness, and the Socialist Depression—people in rags, starving; you could see their bones—and a riot once, and the marching uniforms, and the great craters—No! The U.N.'s like a dam against all that hell. It *can't* break!"

Naysmith put the boat on automatic and comforted her. After all, anyone loyal to the U.N. deserved a little consideration.

Especially in view of the suppressed fact that the Chinese charge was absolutely true.

He dropped the woman off at her house, a small prefab in one of the colonies, and made vague promises about looking her up again. Then he opened the jets fully and. streaked north toward Frisco Unit.

✳ V ✳

There was a lot of traffic around the great building, and his autopilot was kept busy bringing him in. Naysmith slipped a mantle over his tunic and a conventional half-mask over his face, the latter less from politeness than as a disguise. He didn't think he was being watched, but you were never sure. American Security was damnably efficient.

If ever wheels turned within wheels, he thought sardonically, modern American politics did the spinning. The government was officially Labor and pro-U.N., and was gradually being taken over by its sociodynamicists, who were even more in favor of world federation. However, the conservatives of all stripes, from the mildly socialist Republicans to the extreme Americanists, had enough seats in Congress and enough power generally to exert a potent influence. Among other things, the conservative coalition had prevented the abrogation of the Department of Security, and Hessling, its chief, was known to have Americanist leanings. So there were at least a goodly number of S-men out after "foreign agents"—which included Un-men.

Fourre had his own agents in American Security, of course. It was largely due to their efforts that the American Brothers had false IDs and that the whole tremendous fact of the Brotherhood had remained secret. But some day, thought Naysmith, the story would come out—and then the heavens would fall.

So thin a knife edge, so deep an abyss of chaos and ruin—Society was mad, humanity was a race of insane, and the few who strove to build stability were working against shattering odds. *Sofie was right. The U.N. is a dike, holding back a sea of radioactive blood from the lands of men. And I,* thought Naysmith wryly, *seem to be the little boy with his finger in the dike.*

His boat landed on the downward ramp and rolled into the echoing vastness of the unit garage. He didn't quite dare land on Prior's flange. A mechanic tagged the vehicle, gave Naysmith a receipt, and guided him toward an elevator. It was an express, bearing him swiftly past the lower levels of shops, offices, service establishments, and places of education and entertainment, up to the residential stories. Naysmith waited for his stop. No one spoke to anyone else, the custom of privacy had become too ingrained. He was just as glad of that.

On Prior's level, the hundred and seventh, he stepped onto the slideway going east, transferred to a northbound strip at the second corner, and rode half a mile before he came to the alcove he wanted. He got off, the rubbery floor absorbing the very slight shock, and entered the recess. When he pressed the door button, the recorded voice said: "I am sorry, Mr. Prior is not at home. Do you wish to record a message?"

"Shut up and let me in," said Naysmith.

The code sentence activated the door, which opened for him. He stepped into a simply furnished vestibule as the door chimed. Prior's voice came over the intercom: "Naysmith?"

"The same."

"Come on in, then. Living room."

Naysmith hung up his mask and mantle, slipped off his sandals, and went down the hall. The floor was warm and resilient under his bare feet, like living flesh. Beyond another door that swung aside was the living room, also furnished with a bachelor austerity. Prior was a lone wolf by nature, belonging to no clubs and not even the loosest free-marriage group. His official job was semantic analyst for a large trading outfit; it gave him a lot of free time for his U.N. activities, plus a good excuse for traveling anywhere in the Solar System.

Naysmith's eyes flickered over the dark negroid face of his co-worker—Prior was not a Brother, though he knew of the band—and rested on the man who lay in the adjoining relaxer. "Are *you* here, chief?" He whistled. "Then it must be really big."

"Take off your clothes and get some sun-lamp," invited Prior, waving his eternal cigaret at a relaxer. "I'll try to scare up some Scotch for you."

"Why the devil does the Brotherhood always have to drink

Scotch?" grumbled Étienne Fourre. "Your padded expense accounts eat up half my budget. Or drink it up, I should say."

He was squat and square and powerful, and at eighty was still more alive than most boys. Small black eyes glistened in a face that seemed carved from scarred and pitted brown rock; his voice was a bass rumble from the shaggy chest, its English hardly accented. Geriatrics could only account for some of the vitality that lay like a coiled spring in him, for the entire battery of diet, exercise, and chemistry has to be applied from birth to give maximum effect and his youth antedated the science. *But he'll probably outlive us all,* thought Naysmith.

There was something of the fanatic about Étienne Fourre. He was a child of war whose most relentless battle had become one against war itself. As a young man he had been in the French Resistance of World War II. Later he had been high in the Western liaison with the European undergrounds of World War III, entering the occupied and devastated lands himself on his dark missions. He had fought with the liberals against the neo-fascists in the Years of Hunger and with the gendarmerie against the atomists in the Years of Madness and with U.N. troops in the Near East where his spy system had been a major factor in suppressing the Great Jehad. He had accepted the head of the secret service division of the U.N. Inspectorate after the Conference of Rio revised the charter and had proceeded quietly to engineer the coup which overthrew the anti-U.N. government of Argentina. Later his men had put the finger on Kwang-ti's faked revolution in the Republic of Mongolia, thus ending that conquest-from-within scheme; and he was ultimately the one responsible for the Chinese dictator's assassination. The Brotherhood was his idea from the beginning, his child and his instrument.

Such a man, thought Naysmith, would in earlier days have stood behind the stake and lash of an Inquisition, would have marched at Cromwell's side and carried out the Irish massacres, would have helped set up world-wide Communism—a sternly religious man, for all his mordant atheism, a living sword which needed a war. *Thank God he's on our side!*

"All right, what's the story?" asked the Un-man aloud.

"How long since you were on a Service job?" countered Fourre.

"About a year. Schumacher and I were investigating the

Arbeitspartei in Germany. The other German Brothers were tied up in that Austrian business, you remember, and I speak the language well enough to pass for a Rhinelander when I'm in Prussia."

"Yes, I recall. You have been loafing long enough, my friend." Fourre took the glass of wine offered him by Prior, sipped it, and grimaced. "*Merde!* Won't these Californians ever give up trying?" Swinging back to Naysmith: "I am calling in the whole Brotherhood on this. I shall have to get back to Rio fast, the devil is running loose down there with those Chinese charges and I will be lucky to save our collective necks. But I have slipped up to North America to get you people organized and under way. I am pretty damn sure that the leadership of our great unknown enemy is down in Rio—probably with Besser, who is at least involved in it but has taken some very excellent precautions against assassination—and it would do no good to kill him only to have someone else take over. At any rate, the United States is still a most important focus of anti-U.N. activity, and Donner's capture means a rapid deterioration of things here. Prior, who was Donner's contact man, tells me that he was apparently closer to spying out the enemy headquarters for this continent than any other operative. Now that Donner is gone, Prior has recommended you to succeed in his assignment."

"Which was what?"

"I will come to that. Donner was an engineer by training. You are a cybernetic analyst, *hein*?"

"Yes, officially," said Naysmith. "My degrees are in epistemology and communications theory, and my supposed job is basic-theoretical consultant. Troubleshooter in the realm of ideas." He grinned. "When I get stuck, I can always refer the problem to Prior here."

"Ah, so. You are then necessarily something of a linguist too, eh? Good. Understand, I am not choosing you for your specialty, but rather for your un-specialty. You are too old to have had the benefit of Synthesis training. Some of the younger Brothers are getting it, of course—there is a lad in Mexico, Peter Christian, whose call numbers you had better get from Prior in case you need such help."

"Meanwhile, an epistemologist or semanticist is the closest available thing to an integrating synthesist. By your knowledge of language, psychology, and the general sciences, you should be well equipped to fit together whatever information you can obtain and derive a larger picture from them. I don't know." Fourre lit a cigar and puffed ferociously.

"Well, I can start anytime. I'm on extended leave of absence from my nominal job already," said Naysmith. "But what about this Donner? How far had he gotten, what happened to him, and so on?"

"I'll give you the background, because you'll need it," said Prior. "Martin Donner was officially adopted in Canada, and, as I said, received a mechanical engineering degree there. About four years ago we had reason to think the enemy was learning that he wasn't all he seemed, so we transferred him to the States, flanged up an American ID for him and so on. Recently he was put to work investigating the Americanists. His leads were simple: he got a job with Brain Tools, Inc., which is known to be lousy with Party members. He didn't try to infiltrate the Party—we already have men in it, of course, though they haven't gotten very high—but he did snoop around, gather data, and finally put the snatch on a certain man and pumped him full of truth drug." Naysmith didn't ask what had happened to the victim; the struggle was utterly ruthless, with all history at stake. "That gave him news about the midwestern headquarters of the conspiracy, so he went there. It was one of the big units in Illinois. He got himself an apartment and—disappeared. That was almost two weeks ago." Prior shrugged. "He's quite certainly dead by now. If they didn't kill him themselves, he'll have found a way to suicide."

"You can give me the dossier on what Donner learned and communicated to you?" asked Naysmith.

"Yes, of course, though I don't think it'll help you much." Prior looked moodily at his glass. "You'll be pretty much on your own. I needn't add that anything goes, from privacy violation to murder, but that with the Service in such bad odor right now you'd better not leave any evidence. Your first job, though, is to approach Donner's family. You see, he was married."

"Oh?"

"I don't mean free-married, or group-married, or trial-married, or any other version," snapped Prior impatiently. "I mean *married.* Old style. One kid."

"Hmmmm—that's not so good, is it?"

"No. Un-men really have no business marrying that way, and most especially the Brothers don't. However—you see the difficulties, don't you? *If* Donner is still alive, somehow, and the gang traces his ID and grabs the wife and kid, they've got a hold on him that may make him spill all he knows; if by some chance he is still alive. No sane man is infinitely loyal to a cause."

"Well, I suppose you provided Donner with a midwestern ID."

"Sure. Or rather, he used the one we already had set up—name, fingerprints, number, the data registered at Midwest Central. Praise Allah, we've got friends in the registry bureau! But Donner's case is bad. In previous instances where we lost a Brother, we've been able to recover the corpse or were at least sure that it was safely destroyed. Now the enemy has one complete Brother body, ready for finger-printing, retinals, bloodtyping, Bertillon measurements, autopsy, and everything else they can think of. We can expect them to check that set of physical data against every ID office in the country. And when they find the same identification under different names and numbers in each and every file—all hell is going to let out for noon."

"It will take time, of course," said Fourre. "We have put in dupli-cate sets of non-Brother data too, as you know; that will give them extra work to do. Nor can they be sure which set corresponds to Donner's real identity."

In spite of himself, Naysmith grinned again. "Real identity" was an incongruous term as applied to the Brotherhood. However—

"Nevertheless," went on Fourre, "there is going to be an investi-gation in every country on Earth and perhaps the Moon and planets. The Brotherhood is going to have to go underground, in this coun-try at least. And just now when I have to be fighting for my service's continued existence down in Rio!"

They're closing in. We always knew, deep in our brains, that this day would come, and now it is upon us.

"Even assuming Donner is dead, which is more likely," said Prior, "his widow would make a valuable captive for the gang. Probably she knows very little about her husband's Service activities, but she undoubtedly has a vast amount of information buried in her subcon-scious—faces, snatches of overheard conversation, perhaps merely the exact dates Donner was absent on this or that mission. A skilled man could get it out of her, you know—thereby presenting the enemy detectives with any number of leads—some of which would go straight to our most cherished secrets."

"Haven't you tried to spirit her away?" asked Naysmith.

"She won't spirit," said Prior. "We sent an accredited agent to warn her she was in danger and advise her to come away with him. She refused flat. After all, how can she be sure our agent isn't the creature of the enemy? Furthermore, she took some very intelligent precautions, such as consulting the local police, leaving notes in her bankbox to be opened if she disappears without warning, and so on, which have in effect made it impossibly difficult for us to remove her against her will. If nothing else, we couldn't stand the publicity. All we've been able to do is put a couple of men to watching her—and one of these was picked up by the cops the other day and we had hell's own time springing him."

"She's got backbone," said Naysmith.

"Too much," replied Prior. "Well, you know your first assignment. Get her to go off willingly with you, hide her and the kid away somewhere, and then go underground yourself. After that, it's more or less up to you, boy."

"But how'll I persuade her to—"

"Isn't it obvious?" snapped Fourre.

It was. Naysmith grimaced. "What kind of skunk do you take me for?" he protested feebly. "Isn't it enough that I do your murders and robberies for you?"

<h1 style="text-align:center">✴VI✴</h1>

Brigham City, Utah was not officially a colony, having existed long before the postwar resettlements. But it had always been a lovely town, and had converted itself almost entirely to modern layout and architecture. Naysmith had not been there before, but he felt his heart warming to it—*the same as Donner, who is dead now.*

He opened all jets and screamed at his habitual speed low above the crumbling highway. Hills and orchards lay green about him under a high clear heaven, a great oasis lifted from the wastelands by the hands of men. They had come across many-miled emptiness, those men of another day, trudging dustily by their creaking, bumping, battered wagons on the way to the Promised Land. He, today, sat on plastic-foam cushions in a metal shell, howling at a thousand miles an hour till the echoes thundered, but was himself fleeing the persecutors.

Local traffic control took over as he intersected the radio beam. He relaxed as much as possible, puffing a nervous cigaret while the autopilot brought him in. When the boat grounded in a side lane, he slipped a full mask over his head and resumed, manually, driving.

The houses nestled in their screens of lawn and trees, the low half-underground homes of small families. Men and women, some in laboring clothes, were about on the slideways, and there were more children in sight, small bright flashes of color laughing and shouting, than was common elsewhere. The Mormon influence, Naysmith supposed; free-marriage and the rest hadn't ever been very fashionable in Utah. Most of the fruit-raising plantations were still privately owned small-holdings too, using cooperation to compete with the giant government-regulated agricultural combines. But there would nevertheless be a high proportion of men and women here who commuted to outside jobs by airbus—workers on the Pacific Colony project, for instance.

He reviewed Prior's file on Donner, passing the scanty items through his memory. The Brothers were always on call, but outside their own circle they were as jealous of their privacy as anyone else. It had, however, been plain that Jeanne Donner worked at home as a mail-consultant semantic linguist—correcting manuscript of various kinds—and gave an unusual amount of personal attention to her husband and child.

Naysmith felt inwardly cold.

Here was the address. He brought the boat to a silent halt and started up the walk toward the house. Its severe modern lines and curves were softened by a great rush of morning glory, and it lay in the rustling shade of trees, and there was a broad garden behind it. That was undoubtedly Jeanne's work; Donner would have hated gardening.

Instinctively, Naysmith glanced about for Prior's watchman. Nowhere in sight. But then, a good operative wouldn't be. Perhaps that old man, white-bearded and patriarchal, on the slideway; or the delivery boy whipping down the street on his biwheel; or even the little girl skipping rope in the park across the way. She might not be what she seemed: the biological laboratories could do strange things, and Fourre had built up his own secret shops—

The door was in front of him, shaded by a small vine-draped portico. He thumbed the button, and the voice informed him that no one was at home. Which was doubtless a lie, but—*Poor kid! Poor girl, huddled in there against fear, against the night which swallowed her man—waiting for his return, for a dead man's return.* Naysmith shook his head, swallowing a gorge of bitterness, and spoke into the recorder: "Hello, honey, aren't you being sort of inhospitable?"

She must have activated the playback at once, because it was only a moment before the door swung open. Naysmith caught her in his arms as he stepped into the vestibule.

"Marty, Marty, Marty!" She was sobbing and laughing, straining against him, pulling his face down to hers. The long black hair blinded his stinging eyes. "Oh, Marty, take off that blasted mask. It's been so long—"

She was of medium height, lithe and slim in his grasp, the face strong under its elfish lines, the eyes dark and lustrous and very faintly slanted, and the feel and the shaking voice of her made him realize his own loneliness with a sudden desolation. He lifted the mask, letting its helmet-shaped hollowness thud on the floor, and kissed her with hunger. *God damn it,* he thought savagely, Donner *would have to pick the kind I'm a sucker for! But then, he'd be bound to do so, wouldn't he?*

"No time, sweetheart," he said urgently, while she ruffled his hair. "Get some clothes and a mask—Jimmy too, of course. Never mind packing anything. Just call up the police and tell 'em you're leaving of your own accord. We've got to get out of here fast."

She stepped back a pace and looked at him with puzzlement. "What's happened, Marty?" she whispered.

"Fast, I said!" He brushed past her into the living room. "I'll explain later."

She nodded and was gone into one of the bedrooms, bending over a crib and picking up a small sleepy figure. Naysmith lit another cigaret while his eyes prowled the room.

It was a typical prefab house, but Martin Donner, this other self who was now locked in darkness, had left his personality here. None of the mass-produced featureless gimmickry of today's floaters: this was the home of people who had meant to stay. Naysmith thought of the succession of apartments and hotel rooms which had been his life, and the loneliness deepened in him.

Yes—just as it should be. Donner had probably built that stone fireplace himself, not because it was needed but because the flicker of burning logs was good to look on. There was an antique musket hanging above the mantel, which bore a few objects: old marble clock, wrought-brass candlesticks, a flashing bit of Lunar crystal. The desk was a mahogany anachronism among relaxers. There were some animated films on the walls, but there were a couple of reproductions too—a Rembrandt rabbi and a Constable landscape—and a few engravings. There was an expensive console with a wide selection of music wires. The bookshelves held their share of microprint rolls, but there were a lot of old-style volumes too, carefully rebound. Naysmith smiled as his eye fell on the well-thumbed set of Shakespeare.

The Donners had not been live-in-the-past cranks, but they had not been rootless either. Naysmith sighed and recalled his anthropology. Western society had been based on the family as an economic and social unit; the first *raison d'être* had gone out with technology, the second had followed in the last war and the postwar upheavals. Modern life was an impersonal thing. Marriage—permanent marriage—came late when both parties were tired of chasing and was a loose contract at best; the crèche, the school, the public entertainment, made children a shadowy part of the home. And all of this reacted on the human self. From a creature of strong, highly focused emotional life, with a personality made complex by the interaction of environment and ego, Western man was changing to something like the old Samoan aborigines; easy-going, well-adjusted, close friendship and romantic love sliding into limbo. You couldn't say that it was good or bad, one way or the other; but you wondered what it would do to society.

But what could be done about it? You couldn't go back again, you couldn't support today's population with medieval technology even if the population had been willing to try. But that meant accepting the philosophical basis of science, exchanging the cozy medieval cosmos for a bewildering grid of impersonal relationships and abandoning the old cry of man shaking his fist at an empty heaven. *Why?* If you wanted to control population and disease, (and the first, at least, was still a hideously urgent need) you accepted chemical contraceptives and antibiotic tablets and educated people to carry them in their pockets; but then it followed that the traditional relationships between the sexes became something else. Modern technology had no use for the pick-and-shovel laborer or for the routine intellectual; so you were faced with a huge class of people not fit for anything else, and what were you going to do about it? What your great, unbelievably complex civilization-machine needed, what it *had* to have in appalling quantity, was the trained man, trained to the limit of his capacity. But then education had to start early and, being free as long as you could pass exams, be ruthlessly selective. Which meant that your first classes, Ph.D.s at twenty or younger, looked down on the Second schools, who took out their frustration on the Thirds—intellectual snobbishness, social friction, but how to escape it?

And it was, after all, a world of fantastic anachronisms. It had grown too fast and too unevenly. Hindu peasants scratched in their tiny fields and lived in mud huts while each big Chinese collective was getting its own powerplant. Murderers lurked in the slums around Manhattan Crater while a technician could buy a house and furniture for six months' pay. Floating colonies were being established in the oceans, cities rose on Mars and Venus and the Moon, while Congo natives drummed at the rain-clouds. Reconciliation— *how?*

Most people looked at the surface of things. They saw that the great upheavals, the World Wars and the Years of Hunger and the Years of Madness and the economic breakdowns, had been accompanied by the dissolution of traditional social modes, and they thought that the first was the cause of the second. "Give us a chance and we'll bring back the good old days." They couldn't see that those good old days had carried the seeds of death within them, that the change in technology had brought a change in human nature itself which would have deeper effects than any ephemeral transition period. War, depression, the waves of manic perversity, the hungry men and the marching men and the doomed men, were not causes, they were effects—symptoms. The world was changing and you can't go home again.

The psychodynamicists thought they were beginning to understand the process, with their semantic epistemology, games theory, least effort principle, communications theory—maybe so. It was too early to tell. The Scientific Synthesis was still more a dream than an achievement, and there would have to be at least one generation of Synthesis-trained citizens before the effects could be noticed. Meanwhile, the combination of geriatrics and birth control, necessary as both were, was stiffening the population with the inevitable intellectual rigidity of advancing years, just at the moment when original thought was more desperately needed than ever before in history. The powers of chaos were gathering, and those who saw the truth and fought for it were so terribly few. *Are you absolutely sure you're right? Can you really justify your battle?*

"Daddy!"

Naysmith turned and held out his arms to the boy. A two-year-old, a sturdy lad with light hair and his mother's dark eyes, still half misted with sleep, was calling him. *My son—Donner's son, damn it!*

"Hullo, Jimmy." His voice shook a little.

Jeanne picked the child up. She was masked and voluminously cloaked, and her tones were steadier than his. "All right, shall we go?"

Naysmith nodded and went to the front door. He was not quite there when the bell chimed.

"Who's that?" His ragged bark and the leap in his breast told him how strained his nerves were.

"I don't know. I've been staying indoors since—" Jeanne strode swiftly to one of the bay windows and lifted a curtain, peering out. "Two men. Strangers."

Naysmith fitted the mask on his own head and thumbed the playback switch. The voice was hard and sharp. "This is the Federal police. We know you are in, Mrs. Donner. Open at once."

"S-men!" Her whisper shuddered.

Naysmith nodded grimly. "They've tracked you down so soon, eh? Run and see if there are any behind the house."

Her feet pattered across the floor. "Four in the garden," she called.

"All right." Naysmith caught himself just before asking if she could shoot. He pulled the small flat stet-pistol from his tunic and gave it to her as she returned. He'd have to assume her training; the needler was recoilless anyway. "'Once more unto the breach, dear friends—' We're getting out of here. Keep close behind me and shoot at their faces or hands. They may have breastplates under the clothes."

His own magnum automatic was cold and heavy in his hand. It was no gentle sleepy-gas weapon. At short range it would blow a hole in a man big enough to put your arm through, and a splinter from its bursting slug killed by hydrostatic shock. The rapping on the door grew thunderous.

She was all at once as cool as he. "Trouble with the law?" she asked crisply.

"The wrong kind of law," he answered. "We've still got cops on our side, though, if that's any consolation."

They couldn't be agents of Fourre's or they would have given him the code sentence. That meant they were sent by the same power which had murdered Martin Donner. He felt no special compunctions about replying in kind. The trick was to escape.

Naysmith stepped back into the living room and picked up a light table, holding it before his body as a shield against needles. Returning to the hall he crowded himself in front of Jeanne and pressed the door switch.

As the barrier swung open, Naysmith fired, a muted hiss and a dull thump of lead in flesh. That terrible impact sent the S-man off the porch and tumbling to the lawn in blood. His companion shot as if by instinct, a needle thunking into the table. Naysmith gunned him down even as he cried out.

Now—outside—to the boat and fast Sprinting across the grass, Naysmith felt the wicked hum of a missile fan his cheek. Jeanne whirled, encumbered by Jimmy, and sprayed the approaching troop with needles as they burst around the corner of the house.

Naysmith was already at the opening door of his jet. He fired once again while his free hand started the motor.

The S-men were using needles. They wanted the quarry alive. Jeanne stumbled, a dart in her arm, letting Jimmy slide to earth. Naysmith sprang back from the boat. A needle splintered on his mask and he caught a whiff that made his head swoop.

The detectives spread out, approaching from two sides as they ran. Naysmith was shielded on one side by the boat, on the other by Jeanne's unstirring form as he picked her up. He crammed her and the child into the seat and wriggled across them. Slamming the door, he grabbed for the controls.

The whole performance had taken less than a minute. As the jet stood on its tail and screamed illegally skyward, Naysmith realized for the thousandth time that no ordinary human would have been fast enough and sure enough to carry off that escape. The S-men were good but they had simply been outclassed.

They'd check the house, inch by inch and find his recent finger-prints, and those would be the same as the stray ones left here and there throughout the world by certain Un-man operatives—the same as Donner's. It was *the* Un-man, the hated and feared shadow who could strike in a dozen places at once, swifter and deadlier than flesh had a right to be, and who had now risen from his grave to harry them again. He, Naysmith, had just added another chapter to a legend.

Only—the S-men didn't believe in ghosts. They'd look for an answer. And if they found the right answer, that was the end of every dream.

And meanwhile the hunt was after him. Radio beams, license numbers, air-traffic analysis, broadcast alarms, ID files—all the resources of a great and desperate power would be hounding him across the world, and nowhere could he rest.

✳ VII ✳

Jimmy was weeping in fright, and Naysmith comforted him as well as possible while ripping through the sky. It was hard to be gay, laugh with the boy and tickle him and convince him it was all an exciting game, while Jeanne slumped motionless in the seat and the earth blurred below. But terror at such an early age could have devastating psychic effects and had to be allayed at once. *It's all I can do for you, son. The Brotherhood owes you that much, after the dirty trick it played in bringing you into this world as the child of one of us.*

When Jimmy was at ease again, placed in the back seat to watch a television robotshow, Naysmith surveyed his situation. The boat had more legs than the law permitted, which was one good aspect. He had taken it five miles up, well above the lanes of controlled traffic, and was running northward in a circuitous course. His hungry engines gulped oil at a frightening rate; he'd have to stop for a refill two or three times. Fortunately, he had plenty of cash along. The routine identification of a thumbprint check would leave a written invitation to the pursuers, whereas they might never stumble on the isolated fuel stations where he meant to buy.

Jeanne came awake, stirring and gasping. He held her close to him until the spasm of returning consciousness had passed and her eyes were clear again. Then he lit a cigaret for her and one for himself, and leaned back against the cushions.

"I suppose you're wondering what this is all about," he said.

"Uh-huh." Her smile was uncertain. "How much can you tell me?"

"As much as is safe for you to know," he answered. *Damn it, how much does she already know. I can't give myself away yet! She must be aware that her husband is—was—an Un-man, that his nominal job was a camouflage, but the details?*

"Where are we going?" she asked.

"I've got a hiding place for you and the kid, up in the Canadian Rockies. Not too comfortable, I'm afraid, but reasonably safe. If we can get there without being intercepted. It—"

"*We interrupt this program to bring you an urgent announcement. A dangerous criminal is at large in an Airflyte numbered USA-1349-U-7683. Repeat, USA-1349-U-7683. This man is believed to be accompanied by a woman and child. If you see the boat, call the nearest police headquarters or Security office at once. The man is wanted for murder and kidnapping, and is thought to be the agent of a foreign power. Further announcements with complete description will follow as soon as possible.*"

The harsh voice faded and the robotshow came back on. "Man, oh man, oh man," breathed Naysmith. "They don't waste any time, do they?"

Jeanne's face was white, but her only words were: "How about painting this boat's number over?"

"Can't stop for that now or they'd catch us sure." Naysmith

scanned the heavens. "Better strap yourself and Jimmy in, though. If a police boat tracks us, I've got machine guns in this one. We'll blast them."

She fought back the tears with a heart-wrenching gallantry. "Mind explaining a little?"

"I'll have to begin at the beginning," he said cautiously. "To get it all in order, I'll have to tell you a lot of things you already know. But I want to give you the complete pattern. I want to break away from the dirty names like spy and traitor, and show you what we're really trying to do."

"*We?*" She caressed the pronoun. No sane human likes to stand utterly alone.

"Listen," said Naysmith. "I'm an Un-man. But a rather special kind. I'm not in the Inspectorate, allowed by charter and treaty to carry out investigations and report violations of things like disarmament agreements to the council. I'm in the U.N. Secret Service—the *secret* Secret Service—and our standing is only quasi-legal. Officially we're an auxiliary to the Inspectorate; in practice we do a hell of a lot more. The Inspectorate is supposed to tell the U.N. Moon bases where to plant their rocket bombs; the Service tries to make bombardment unnecessary by forestalling hostile action."

"By assassinating Kwang-ti?" she challenged.

"Kwang-ti was a menace. He'd taken China out of the U.N. and was building up her armies. He'd made one attempt to take over Mongolia by sponsoring a phony revolt, and nearly succeeded. I'm not saying that he was knocked off by a Chinese Un-man, in spite of his successor government's charges. I'm just saying it was a good thing he died."

"He did a lot for China."

"Sure. And Hitler did a lot for Germany and Stalin did a lot for Russia, all of which was nullified, along with a lot of innocent people, when those countries went to war. Never forget that the U.N. exists first, last, and all the time to keep the peace. Everything else is secondary."

Jeanne lit another cigaret from the previous one. "Tell me more," she said in a voice that suggested she had known this for a long time.

"Look," said Naysmith, "the enemies the U.N. has faced in the past were as nothing to what endangers it now. Because before the enmity has always been more or less open. In the Second War, the U.N. got started as a military alliance against the fascist powers. In the Third War it became, in effect, a military alliance against its own dissident and excommunicated members. After Rio it existed partly as an instrument of multilateral negotiation but still primarily as an alliance of a great many states, not merely Western, to prevent or suppress wars anywhere in the world. Oh, I don't want to play down its legal and cultural and humanitarian and scientific activities, but the essence of the U.N. was force, men and machines it could call on from all its member states—even against a member of itself, if that nation was found guilty by a majority vote in the Council. It wasn't quite as large of the United States as you think to turn its Lunar bases over to the U.N. It thought it could still control the Council as it had done in the past, but matters didn't work out that way. Which is all to the good. We need a truly international body."

"Anyway, the principle of intervention to stop all wars, invited or not, led to things like the Great Jehad and the Brazil-Argentine affair. Small-scale war fought to prevent large-scale war. Then when the Russian government appealed for help against its nationalist insurgents, and got it, the precedent of active intervention within a country's own boundaries was set—much to the good and much to the distaste of almost every government, including the American. The conservatives were in power here about that time, you remember, trying unsuccessfully to patch up the Socialist Depression, and they nearly walked us out of membership. Not quite, though. And those other international functions, research and trade regulation and so on, have been growing apace."

"You see where this is leading? I've told you many times before—" a safe guess, that—"but I'll tell you again. The U.N. is in the process of becoming a federal world government. Already it has its own Inspectorate, its own small police force, and its Lunar Guard. Slowly, grudgingly, the nations are being induced to disarm—we abolished our own draft ten years or so back, remember? There's a movement afoot to internationalize the planets and the ocean developments, put them under direct U.N. authority. We've had international currency stabilization for a long time now; sooner or later, we'll adopt one money unit for the world. Tariffs are virtually extinct. Oh, I could go on all day."

"Previous proposals to make a world government of the U.N. were voted down. Nations were too short-sighted. But it is nevertheless happening, slowly, piece by piece, so that the final official unification of man will be only a formality. Understand? Of course you do. It's obvious. The trouble is, our enemies have begun to understand it too."

Naysmith lit a cigaret for himself and scowled at the blue cloud swirling from his nostrils. "There are so many who would like to break the U.N. There are nationalists and militarists of every kind, every country, men who would rise to power if the old anarchy returned. The need for power is a physical hunger in that sort. There are big men of industry, finance and politics, who'd like to cut their enterprises loose from regulation. There are labor leaders who want a return of the old strife which means power and profit for them. There are religionists of a dozen sorts who don't like our population-control campaigns and the quiet subversion of anti-contraceptive creeds. There are cranks and fanatics who seek a chance to impose their own beliefs, everyone from Syndics to Neocommunists, Pilgrims to Hedonists. There are those who were hurt by some or other U.N. action; perhaps they lost a son in one of our campaigns, perhaps a new development or policy wiped out their business. They want revenge. Oh, there are a thousand kind of them, and if once the U.N. collapses they'll all be free to go fishing in troubled waters."

"Tell me something new," said Jeanne impatiently.

"I have to lead up to it, darling. I have to explain what this latest threat is. You see, these enemies of ours are getting together. All over the world, they're shelving their many quarrels and uniting into a great secret organization whose one purpose is to weaken and destroy the U.N. You wouldn't think fanatical nationalists of different countries could cooperate? Well, they can, because it's the only way they'll ever have a chance later on to attack each other. The leadership of this organization, which we Un-men somewhat inelegantly refer to as the gang, is brilliant; a lot of big men are members and the whole thing is beautifully set up. Such entities as the Americanist Party have become fronts for the gang. Whole governments are backing them, governments which are reluctant U.N. members only because of public opinion at home and the pressure that can be brought to bear on non-members. Kwang-ti's successors brought China back in, I'm sure, only to ruin us from within. U.N. Councillors are among their creatures, and I know not how many U.N. employees."

Naysmith smiled humorlessly. "Even now, the great bulk of people throughout the world are pro-U.N., looking on it as a deliverer from the hell they've survived. So one way the enemy has to destroy us is by sabotage from inside. Corruption, arrogance, inefficiency, illegal actions—perpetrated by their own agents in the U.N. and becoming matters of public knowledge. You've heard a lot of that, and you'll hear still more in the months to come if this is allowed to go on. Another way is to ferret out some of our darker secrets— secrets which every government necessarily has—and make them known to the right people. All right, let's face it: Kwang-ti *was* assassinated by an Un-man. We thought the job had been passed off as the work of democratic conspirators, but apparently there's been a leak somewhere and the Chinese accusation is shaking the whole frail edifice of international cooperation. The Council will stall as long as possible, but eventually it'll have to disown the Service's action and heads will roll. Valuable heads."

"Now if at the proper moment, with the U.N. badly weakened, whole nations walking out again, public confidence trembling, there should be military revolutions within key nations—and the Moon bases seized by ground troops from a nearby colony—Do you see it? Do you see the return of international anarchy, dictatorship, war— and every Un-man in the Solar System hunted to his death?"

✳ VIII ✳

By a roundabout course avoiding the major towns and colonies, it was many hours even at the air boat's speed to Naysmith's goal. He found his powers of invention somewhat taxed enroute. First he had to give Jeanne a half true account of his whereabouts in the past weeks. Then Jimmy, precociously articulate—as he should be, with both parents well into the genius class—felt disturbed by the gravity of his elders and the imminent redisappearance of a father whom he obviously worshipped, and could only be comforted by Naysmith's long impromptu saga of Crock O'Dile, a green Irish alligator who worked at the Gideon Kleinmein Home for Helpless and Houseless Horses. Finally there were others to contend with, a couple of filling station operators and the clerk in a sporting goods store where he purchased supplies: they had to be convinced in an unobtrusive way that these were dull everyday customers to be forgotten as soon as they were gone. It all seemed to go off easily enough, but Naysmith was cold with the tension of wondering whether any of these people had heard the broadcast alarms. Obviously not, so far. But when they got home and, inevitably, were informed, would they remember well enough?

He zigzagged over Washington, crossing into British Columbia above an empty stretch of forest. There was no official reason for an American to stop, but the border was a logical place for the S-men to watch.

"Will the Canadian police cooperate in hunting us?" asked Jeanne.

"I don't know," said Naysmith. "It depends. You see, American Security, with its broad independent powers, has an anti-U.N. head. On the other hand, the President is pro-U.N. as everybody knows, and Fourre will doubtless see to it that he learns who this wanted criminal is. He can't actually countermand the chase without putting himself in an untenable position, but he can obstruct it in many ways and can perhaps tip off the Canadian government. All on the Q.T., of course."

The boat swung east until it was following the mighty spine of the Rockies, an immensity of stone and forest and snow turning gold with sunset. Naysmith had spent several vacations here, camping and painting, and knew where he was headed. It was after dark when he slanted the boat downward, feeling his way with the radar.

There was an abandoned uranium-hunting base here, one of the shacks still habitable. Naysmith bounced the boat to a halt on the edge of a steep cliff, cut the engines, and yawned hugely. "End of the line," he said.

They climbed out, burdened with equipment, food, and the sleeping child. Naysmith wheeled the vehicle under a tall pine and led the way up a slope. Jeanne drew a lungful of the sharp moonlit air and sighed. "Martin, it's beautiful! Why didn't you ever take me here before?"

He didn't answer. His flashlight picked out the crumbling face of the shack, its bare wood and metal blurred with many years. The door creaked open on darkness. Inside, it was bare, the flooring rotted away to a soft black mould, a few sticks of broken furniture scattered like bones. Taking a purchased ax, he went into the woods after spruce boughs, heaping them under the sleeping bags which Jeanne had laid out. Jimmy whimpered a little in his dreams, but they didn't wake him to eat.

Naysmith's watch showed midnight before the cabin was in order. He strolled out for a final cigaret and Jeanne followed to stand beside him. Her fingers closed about his.

The Moon was nearly full, rising over a peak whose heights were one glitter of snow. Stars wheeled enormously overhead, flashing and flashing in the keen cold air. The forests growing up the slant of this mountain soughed with wind, tall and dark and heady-scented, filled with night and mystery. Down in the gorge there was a river, a long gleam of broken moonlight, the fresh wild noise of its passage drifting up to them. Somewhere an owl hooted.

Jeanne shivered in the chill breeze and crept against Naysmith. He drew his mantle about both of them, holding her close. The little red eye of his cigaret waxed and waned in the dark.

"It's so lovely here," she whispered. "Do you have to go tomorrow?"

"Yes." His answer came harshly out of his throat. "You've supplies enough for a month. If anyone chances by, then you're of course just a camper on vacation. But I doubt they will, this is an isolated spot. If I'm not back within three weeks, though, follow the river down. There's a small colony about fifty miles from here. Or I may send one of our agents to get you. He'll have a password—let's see— 'The crocodiles grow green in Ireland.' Okay?"

Her laugh was muted and wistful.

"I'm sorry to lay such a burden on you, darling," he said contritely.

"It's nothing—except that you'll be away, a hunted man, and I won't know—"She bit her lip. Her face was white in the streaming moon-glow. "This is a terrible world we live in."

"No, Jeanne. It's a—a potentially lovely world. My job is to help keep it that way." He chucked her under the chin, fighting to smile. "Don't let it worry you. Goodnight, sweet princess."

She kissed him with yearning. For an instant Naysmith hung back. *Should I tell her? She's safely away now—she has a right to know I'm not her husband—*

"What's wrong, Marty? You seem so strange."

I don't dare. I can't tell her—not while the enemy is abroad, not while there's a chance of their catching her. And a little longer in her fool's paradise—I can drop out of sight, let someone else give her the news—You crawling coward!

He surrendered. But it was a cruel thing to know, that she was really clasping a dead man to her.

They walked slowly back to the cabin.

Colonel Samsey woke with an animal swiftness and sat up in bed. Sleep drained from him as he saw the tall figure etched black against his open balcony door. He grabbed for the gun under his pillow.

"I wouldn't try that, friend." The voice was soft. Moonlight streamed in to glitter on the pistol in the intruder's hand.

"Who are you?" Samsey gasped it out, hardly aware of the incredible fact yet. Why—he was a hundred and fifty stories up. His front entrance was guarded, and no copter could so silently have put this masked figure on his balcony.

"Out of bed, boy. Fast! Okay, now clasp your hands on top of your head."

Samsey felt the night wind cold on his naked body. It was a helplessness, this standing unclothed and alone, out of his uniform and pistol belt, looking down the muzzle of a stranger's gun. His close-cropped scalp felt stubbly under his palms.

"How did you get in?" he whispered.

Naysmith didn't feel it necessary to explain the process. He had walked from the old highway on which he had landed his jet and used vacuum shoes and gloves to climb the sheer face of Denver Unit. "Better ask why I came," he said.

"All right, blast you! Why? This is a gross violation of privacy, plus menace and—" Samsey closed his mouth with a snap. Legality had plainly gone by the board.

"I want some information." Naysmith seated himself half-way on a table, one leg swinging easily, the gun steady in his right hand while his left fumbled in a belt pouch. "And you, as a high-ranking officer in the American Guard and a well-known associate of Roger Wade, seemed likeliest to have it."

"You're crazy! This is—We're just a patriotic society. You know that. Or should. We—"

"Cram it, Samsey," said Naysmith wearily. "The American Guard has ranks, uniforms, weapons, and drills. Every member belongs to the Americanist Party. You're a private army, Nazi style, and you've done the murders, robberies, and beatings of the Party for the past five years. As soon as the government is able to prove that in court, you'll all go to the Antarctic mines and you know it. Your hope is that your faction can be in power before there's a case against you."

"Libel! We're a patriotic social group—"

"I regret my approach," said Naysmith sardonically. And he did. Direct attack of this sort was not only unlawful, it was crude and of very limited value. But he hadn't much choice. He *had* to get some kind of line on the enemy's plans, and the outlawing of the Brotherhood and the general suspicion cast on the Service meant that standard detective approaches were pretty well eliminated for the time being. Half a loaf— "Nevertheless, I want certain information. The big objective right now is to overthrow the U.N. How do you intend to accomplish that? Specifically, what is your next assignment?"

"You don't expect—"

Samsey recoiled as Naysmith moved. The Un-man's left hand come out of his pouch like a striking snake even as his body hurtled across the floor. The right arm grasped Samsey's biceps, twisting him around in front of the intruder, a knee in his back, while the hypodermic needle plunged into his neck.

Samsey struggled, gasping. The muscles holding him were like steel, cat-lithe, meeting his every wrench with practiced ease. And now the great wave of dizziness came. He lurched and Naysmith supported him, easing him back to the bed.

The hypo had been filled with four cubic centimeters of a neoscopaneurine mixture, very nearly a lethal dose. But it would act fast! Naysmith did not think the colonel had been immunized against such truth drugs. The gang wouldn't trust its lower echelons that much.

Moonlight barred the mindlessly drooling face on the pillow with a streak of icy silver. It was very quiet here, only the man's labored breathing and the sigh of wind blowing the curtains at the balcony door. Naysmith gave his victim a stimulant injection, waited a couple of minutes, and began his interrogation.

Truth drugs have been misnamed. They do not intrinsically force the subject to speak truth; they damp those higher brain centers needed to invent a lie or even to inhibit response. The subject babbles, with a strong tendency to babble on those subjects he has previously been most concerned to keep secret. A skilled psychologist can lead the general direction of the talk.

First, of course, the private nastiness which every human has buried within himself came out, like suppuration from an inflamed wound. Naysmith had been through this before, but he grimaced— Samsey was an especially bad sort. These aggressively manly types often were. Naysmith continued patiently until he got onto more interesting topics.

Samsey didn't know anyone higher in the gang than Wade. Well, that was to be expected. In fact, Naysmith thought scornfully, he, the outsider, knew more about the organization of the enemy than any one member below the very top ranks. But this was a pretty general human characteristic too. A man did his job, for whatever motives of power, profit, or simple existence he might have, and didn't even try to learn where it fitted into the great general pattern. The synthesizing mentality is tragically rare.

But a free society at least permitted its members to learn, and a rational society encouraged them to do so; whereas totalitarianism, from the bossy foreman to the hemispheric dictator, was based on the deliberate suppression of communications. Where there was no feedback, there could be no stability except through the living death of imposed intellectual rigidity.

Back to business! Here came something he had been waiting for, the next task for the American Guard's thugs. The *Phobos* was due in from Mars in a week. Guardsmen were supposed to arrange the death of one Barney Rosenberg, passenger, as soon as possible after his debarkation on Earth. Why? The reason was not given and had not been asked, but a good description of the man was available.

Mars—yes, the Guard was also using a privately owned spaceship to run arms to a secret base in the Thyle II country, where they were picked up by Pilgrims.

So! The Pilgrims were in on the gang. The Service had suspected as much, but here was proof. This might be the biggest break of all, but Naysmith had a hunch that it was incidental. Somehow, the murder of an obscure returnee from Mars impressed him as involving greater issues.

There wasn't more which seemed worth the risk of waiting. Naysmith had a final experiment to try.

Samsey was a rugged specimen, already beginning to pull out of his daze. Nay smith switched on a lamp, its radiance falling across the distorted face below him. The eyes focused blurrily on his sheening mask. Slowly, he lifted it.

"Who am I, Samsey?" he asked quietly.

A sob rattled in the throat. "Donner—but you're dead. We killed you in Chicago. You died, you're dead."

That settled that. Naysmith replaced his mask. Systematically, he repaired the alarms he had annulled for his entry and checked the room for traces of his presence. None. Then he took Samsey's gun from beneath the pillow. Silenced, naturally. He folded the lax fingers about the trigger and blew the colonel's brains out.

They'd suspect it wasn't suicide, of course, but they might not think of a biochemical autopsy before the drugs in the bloodstream had broken down beyond analysis. At least there was one less of them. Naysmith felt no qualms. This was not a routine police operation, it was war.

He went back to the balcony, closing the door behind him. Swinging over the edge as he adjusted his vacuum cups, he started the long climb earthward.

The Service could ordinarily have provided Naysmith with an excellent disguise, but the equipment needed was elaborate and he dared not assume that any of the offices which had it were unwatched by Security. Better rely on masks and the feeble observational powers of most citizens to brazen it out.

Calling Prior from a public communibooth, even using the scrambler, was risky too, but it had to be done. The mails were not to be trusted any more, and communication was an absolute necessity for accomplishment.

The voice was gray with weariness: "Mars, eh? Nice job, Naysmith. What should we do?"

"Get the word to Fourre, of course, for whatever he can make of it. And a coded radio message to our operatives on Mars. They can check this Pilgrim business and also look into Rosenberg's background and associates. Should be a lot of leads there. However, I'll try to snatch Rosenberg myself, with a Brother or two to help me, before the Americanists get him."

"Yeah, you'd better. The Service's hands are pretty well tied just now while the U.N. investigation of the Chinese accusations is going on. Furthermore, we can't be sure of many of our own people. So we, and especially the Brotherhood, will have to act pretty much independently for the time being. Carry on as well as you can. However, I can get your information to Rio and Mars all right."

"Good man. How are things going with you?"

"Don't call me again, Naysmith. I'm being watched, and my own men can't stop a really all-out assassination attempt." Prior chuckled dryly. "If they succeed, we can talk it over in hell."

"To modify what the old *cacique* said about Spaniards in Heaven, if there are nationalists in hell, I'm not sure if I want to go there. Okay, then. And good luck!"

It was only the next day that the newscasts carried word of the murder of one Nathan Prior, semanticist residing at Frisco Unit. It was believed to be the work of foreign agents, and S-men had been assigned to aid the local police.

✷ IX ✷

Most of the Brothers had, of course, been given disguises early in their careers. Plastic surgery had altered the distinctive countenance and the exact height, false fingerprints and retinals had been put in their ID records; each of them had a matching set of transparent plastic "tips" to put on his own fingers when he made a print for any official purpose. These men should temporarily be safe, and there was no justification for calling on their help yet. They were sitting tight and wary, for if the deadly efficiency of Hessling's organization came to suspect them and pull them in, an elementary physical exam would rip the masquerade wide open.

That left perhaps a hundred undisguised Brothers in the United States when word came for them to go underground. Identical physique could be too useful—for example, in furnishing unshakable alibis, or in creating the legend of a superman who was everywhere—to be removed from all. Some of these would be able to assume temporary appearances and move in public for a while. The rest had to cross the border or hide.

The case of Juho Lampi was especially unfortunate. He had made enough of a name as a nucleonic engineer in Finland to be invited to America, and his disguise was only superficial. When Fourre's warning went out on the code circuit, he left his apartment in a hurry. A mechanic at the garage where he hired an airboat recognized the picture that had been flashed over the entire country. Lampi read the man's poorly hidden agitation, slugged him, and stole the boat, but it put the S-men on his trail. It told them, furthermore, that the identical men were not only American.

Lampi had been given the name and address of a woman in Iowa. The Brothers were organized into cells of half a dozen each, with its own rendezvous and contacts, and this was to be Lampi's while he was in the States. He went there after dark and got a room. Somewhat later, Naysmith showed up. Naysmith, being more nearly a full-time operative, knew where several cells had their meeting places. He collected Lampi and decided not to wait for anyone else. The *Phobos* was coming to Earth in a matter of hours. Naysmith had gone to Iowa in a self-driven boat hired from a careless office in Colorado; now, through the woman running the house, the two men rented another and flew back to Robinson field.

"I have my own boat—repainted, new number, and so on—parked near here," said Naysmith. "We'll take off in it. If we get away."

"And then what?" asked Lampi. His English was good, marked with only a trace of accent. The Brothers were natural linguists.

"I don't know. I just don't know." Naysmith looked moodily about him. "We're being hunted as few have ever been hunted." He murmured half to himself:

> "*I heard myself proclaim'd;*
> *And by the happy hollow of a tree*
> *Escap'd the hunt. No port is free; no place,*
> *That guard and most unusual vigilance*
> *Does not attend my taking.*"

✹ ✹ ✹

They were sitting in the Moonjumper bar and restaurant adjacent to the spaceport. They had chosen a booth near the door, and the transparent wall on this side opened onto the field. Its great pale expanse of concrete stretched under glaring floodlights out toward darkness, a gigantic loom of buildings on three sides of it. Coveralled mechanics were busy around a series of landing cradles. A uniformed policeman strolled by, speaking idly with a technician. Or was it so casual? The technie looked solemn.

"Oh, well," said Lampi. "To get onto a more cheerful subject, have you seen Warschawski's latest exhibition?"

"What's so cheerful about that?" asked Naysmith. "It's awful. Sculpture just doesn't lend itself to abstraction as he seems to think."

Though the Brothers naturally tended to have similar tastes, environment could make a difference. Naysmith and Lampi plunged into a stiff-necked argument about modern art. It was going at a fine pace when they were interrupted.

The curtains of the booth had been drawn. They were twitched aside now and the waitress looked in. She was young and shapely, and the skimpy play suit might have been painted on. Beyond her, the bar room was a surge of people, a buzz and hum and rumble of voices. In spite of the laboring ventilators, there was a blue haze of smoke in the air.

"Would you like another round?" asked the girl.

"Not just yet, thanks," said Naysmith, turning his masked face toward her. He had dyed his yellow hair a mousey brown at the hideaway, and Lampi's was now black, but that didn't help much; there hadn't been much time to change the wiry texture. He sat stooped, so that she wouldn't see at a casual glance that he was as big as Lampi, and hoped she wasn't very observant.

"Want some company?" she asked. "I can fix it up."

"No thanks," said Naysmith. "We're waiting for the rocket."

"I mean later. Nice girls. You'll like them." She gave him a mechanically meretricious smile.

"Ummmm—well—" Naysmith swapped a glance with Lampi, who nodded. He arranged an assignation for an hour after the landing and slipped her a bill. She left them, swaying her hips.

Lampi chuckled. "It's hardly fair to a couple of hardworking girls," he said. "They will be expecting us."

"Yeah. Probably supporting aged grandmothers, too." Naysmith grinned and lifted the Scotch to the mouth-slit of his mask. "However, it's not the sort of arrangement two fugitives would make."

"What about the American Guardsmen?"

"Probably those burly characters lounging at the bar. Didn't you notice them as we came in? They'll have friends elsewhere who'll—"

"*Your attention, please. The first tender from the* Phobos *will be cradling in ten minutes, carrying half the passengers from Mars. The second will follow ten minutes later. Repeat, the first—*"

"Which one is Rosenberg on?" asked Lampi.

"How should I know?" Naysmith shrugged. "We'll just have to take our chance. Drink up."

He patted his shoulder-holstered gun and loosened the tunic over it. He and Lampi had obtained breastplates and half-boots at the hideaway; their masks were needle-proof, and arm or groin or thigh was hard to hit when a knee-length cloak flapped around the body. They should be fairly well immune to stet-guns if they worked fast. Not to bullets—but even the Guardsmen probably wouldn't care to use those in a crowd. The two men went out of the booth and mingled with the people swirling toward the passenger egress. They separated as they neared the gate and hung about on the fringe of the group. There were a couple of big hard-looking men in masks who had shouldered their way up next to the gate. One of them had been in the Moonjumper, Naysmith remembered.

He had no picture of Rosenberg, and Samsey's incoherent description had been of little value. The man was a nonentity who must have been off Earth for years. But presumably the Guardsmen knew what to look for. Which meant that—

There was a red and yellow glare high in the darkened heavens. The far thunder became a howling, bellowing, shaking roar that trembled in the bones and echoed in the skull. Nerves crawled with the nameless half terror of unheard subsonic vibrations. The tender grew to a slim spear-head, backing down with radio control on the landing cradle. Her chemical blasts splashed vividly off the concrete baffles. When she lay still and the rockets cut off, there was a ringing silence.

Endless ceremony—the mechanics wheeled up a stairway, the air-lock ground open, a steward emerged, a medical crew stood by to handle space sickness—Naysmith longed for a cigaret. He shifted on his feet and forced his nerves to a thuttering calm.

There came the passengers, half a dozen of them filing toward the gateway. They stopped one by one at the clearance booth to have their papers stamped. The two Guardsmen exchanged a masked glance.

A stocky Oriental came through first. Then there was a woman engineer in Spaceways uniform who held up the line as she gathered two waiting children into her arms. Then—

He was a small bandy-legged man with a hooked nose and a leathery brown skin, shabbily clad, lugging a battered valise. One of the Guardsmen tapped him politely on the arm. He looked up and Naysmith saw his lips moving, the face etched in a harsh white glare. He couldn't hear what was said over the babble of the crowd, but he could imagine it. "Why, yes, I'm Barney Rosenberg. What do you want?"

Some answer was given him; it didn't really matter what. With a look of mild surprise, the little fellow nodded. The other Guardsman pushed over to him, and he went out of the crowd between them. Naysmith drew his stet-gun, holding it under his cloak, and cat-footed after. The Guardsmen didn't escort Rosenberg into the shadows beyond the field, but walked over toward the Moonjumper. There was no reason for Rosenberg to suspect their motives, especially if they stood him a drink.

Naysmith lengthened his stride and fell in beside the right-hand man. He didn't waste time: his gun was ready, its muzzle against the victim's hip. He fired. The Guardsman strangled on a yell.

Lampi was already on the left, but he'd been a trifle slow. That enemy grabbed the Finn's gun wrist with a slashing movement. Naysmith leaned over the first guardsman, who clawed at him as he sagged to his knees, and brought the edge of his left palm down on the second one's neck, just at the base of the skull. The blow cracked numbingly into his own sinews.

"What the blazes—" Rosenberg opened his mouth to shout. There was no time to argue, and Lampi needled him. With a look of utter astonishment, the prospector wilted. Lampi caught him under the arms and hoisted him to one shoulder.

The kidnapping had been seen. People were turning around, staring. Somebody began to scream. Lampi stepped over the two toppled men and followed Naysmith.

Past the door of the bar, out to the street, hurry!

A whistle skirled behind them. They jumped over the slideway and dashed across the avenue. There was a transcontinental Diesel truck bearing down on them, its lights one great glare, the roar of its engine filling the world. Naysmith thought that it brushed him. But its huge bulk was a cover. They plunged over the slideway beyond, ignoring the stares of passersby, and into the shadows of a park.

A siren began to howl. When he had reached the sheltering gloom thrown by a tree, Naysmith looked behind him. Two policemen were coming, but they hadn't spotted the fugitives yet. Naysmith and Lampi ducked through a formal garden, jumping hedges and running down twisted paths. Gravel scrunched underfoot.

Quartering across the park, Naysmith led the way to his airboat. He fumbled the door open and slithered inside. Lampi climbed in with him, tossing Rosenberg into the back seat and slamming the door. The boat slid smoothly out into passing traffic. There were quite a few cars and boats abroad, and Naysmith mingled with them.

Lampi breathed heavily in the gloom. A giant neon sign threw a bloody light over his mask. "Now what?" he asked.

"Now we get the devil out of here," said Naysmith. "Those boys are smart. It won't take them long to alert traffic control and stop all nearby vehicles for search. We have to be in the air before that time."

They left the clustered shops and dwellings, and Naysmith punched the board for permission to take off southbound. The automatic signal flashed him a fourth-lane directive. He climbed to the indicated height and went obediently south on the beam. Passing traffic was a stream of moving stars around him.

The emergency announcement signal blinked an angry red. "Fast is right," said Lampi, swearing in four languages.

"Up we go," said Naysmith.

He climbed vertically, narrowly missing boats in the higher levels, until he was above all lanes. He kept climbing till his vehicle was in the lower stratosphere. Then he turned westward at top speed.

"We'll go out over the Pacific," he explained. "Then we find us a nice uninhabited islet with some trees and lie doggo till tomorrow night. Won't be any too comfortable, but it'll have to be done and I have some food along." He grinned beneath his mask. "I hope you like cold canned beans, Juho."

"And then—?"

"I know another island off the California coast," said Naysmith. "We'll disguise this boat at our first stop, of course, changing the number and recognition signal and so on. Then at the second place we'll refuel and I'll make an important call. You can bet your last mark the enemy knows who pulled this job and will have alerted all fuel station operators this time. But the man where we're going is an absentminded old codger who won't be hard to deceive." He scowled. "That'll take about the last of my cash money, too. Have to get more somehow, if we're to carry on in our present style."

"Where do we go from there?" said Lampi.

"North, I suppose. We have to hide Rosenberg somewhere, and you—" Naysmith shook his head, feeling a dull pain within him. That was the end of the masquerade. Jeanne Donner would know.

At first Barney Rosenberg didn't believe it. He was too shocked. The Guardsmen had simply told him they were representatives of some vaguely identified company which was thinking of developments on Mars and wanted to consult him. He'd been offered a hotel suite and had been told the fee would be nice. Now he looked at his kidnappers with bewildered eyes and challenged them to say who they were.

"Think we'd be fools enough to carry our real IDs around?" snorted Naysmith. "You'll just have to take our word for it that we're U.N. operatives—till later, anyway, when we can safely prove it. I tell you, the devil is loose on Earth and you need protection. Those fellows were after your knowledge, and once they got that you'd have been a corpse."

Rosenberg looked from one masked face to the other. His head felt blurred, the drug was still in him and he couldn't think straight. But those voices—

He thought he remembered the voices. Both of them. Only they were the same.

"I don't know anything," he said weakly. "I tell you, I'm just a prospector, home from Mars."

"You must have information—that's the only possibility," said

Lampi. "Something you learned on Mars which is important to them, perhaps to the whole world. What?"

Fieri in Drygulch, and the Pilgrim who had been so eager—

Rosenberg shook his head, trying to clear it. He looked at the two big cloaked figures hemming him in. There was darkness outside the hurtling airboat.

"Who are you?" he whispered.

"I told you we're friends. Un-men. Secret agents." Naysmith laid a hand on Rosenberg's shoulder. "We want to help you, that's all. We want to protect you and whatever it is you know."

Rosenberg looked at the hand—strong, sinewy, blunt-fingered, with fine gold hairs on the knuckles. But no, no, no! His heart began thumping till he thought it must shatter his ribs.

"Let me see your faces," he gasped.

"Well—why not?" Naysmith and Lampi took off their masks. The dull panel light gleamed off the same features; broad, strong-boned, blue-eyed. There was a deep wrinkle above each jutting triangle of nose. The left ear was faintly bigger than the right. Both men had a trick of cocking their head a trifle sideways when listening.

We'll tell him we're twin brothers, thought Naysmith and Lampi simultaneously.

Rosenberg shrank into the seat. There was a tiny whimper in his throat.

"Stef," he murmured. "Stefan Rostomily."

✳ X ✳

The newscasts told of crisis in the U.N. Étienne Fourre, backed by its President, was claiming that the Chinese government was pressing a fantastic charge to cover up designs of its own. A full-dress investigation was in order. Only—as Besser, Minister of International Finance, pointed out—when the official investigating service was itself under suspicion, who could be trusted to get at the facts?

In the United States, Security was after a dangerous spy and public enemy. Minute descriptions of Donner-Naysmith-Lampi were on all the screens. Theoretically, the American President could call off the hunt, but that would mean an uproar in the delicately balanced Congress; there'd have been a vote of confidence, and if the President lost that, he and his cabinet would have to resign—and who would be elected to succeed? But Naysmith and Lampi exchanged grins at the interview statement of the President, that he thought this much-hunted spy was in Chinese pay.

Officially, Canada was cooperating with the United States in chasing the fugitive. Actually, Naysmith was sure it was bluff, a sop to the anti-U.N. elements in the Dominion. Mexico was doing nothing—but that meant the Mexican border was being closely watched.

It couldn't go on. The situation was so unstable that it would have to end, one way or another, in the next several days. If Hessling's men dragged in a Brother—Whether or not Fourre's organization survived, it would have lost its greatest and most secret asset.

But the main thing, Naysmith reflected grimly, was to keep Fourre's own head above water. The whole purpose of this uproar was to discredit the man and his painfully built-up service, and to replace him and his key personnel with nationalist stooges. After that, the enemy would find the next stages of their work simple.

And what can I do?

Naysmith felt a surge of helplessness. Human society had grown too big, too complex and powerful. It was a machine running blind and wild, and he was a fly caught in the gears.

There was one frail governor on the machine, only one, and if it were broken the whole thing would shatter. What to do? What to do?

He shrugged off the despair and concentrated on the next moment. The first thing was to get Rosenberg's information to his own side.

The island was a low sandy swell in an immensity of ocean. There was harsh grass on it, and a few trees gnarled by the great winds, and a tiny village. Naysmith dropped Lampi on the farther side of the island to hide till they came back for him. Rosenberg took the Finn's mask, and the two jetted across to the fuel station. While their boat's tanks were being filled, they entered a public communibooth.

Peter Christian, in Mexico City—Naysmith dialed the number given him by Prior. That seemed the best bet. Wasn't the kid undergoing Synthesis training? His logic might be able to integrate this meaningless flux of data.

No doubt every call across either border was being monitored, illegally but thoroughly. However, the booth had a scrambler unit. Naysmith fed it a coin, but it didn't activate it immediately.

"Could I speak to Peter Christian?" he asked the servant whose face appeared in the screen. "Tell him it's his cousin Joe calling. And give him this message: 'The ragged scoundrel leers merrily, not peddling babies.'"

"*Señor?*" The brown face looked astonished.

"It's a private signal. Write it down, please, so you get it correct." Naysmith dictated slowly. "'The ragged scoundrel—'"

"Yes, understand. Wait, please, I will call the young gentleman."

Naysmith stood watching the screen for a moment. He could vaguely make out the room beyond, a solid and handsomely furnished place. Then he stabbed at the scrambler buttons. There were eight of them, which could be punched in any order to yield 40,320 possible combinations. The key letters, known to every Brother, were currently MNTSRPBL, and "the ragged scoundrel" had given Christian the order Naysmith was using. When Hessling's men got around to playing back their monitor tapes, the code sentence wouldn't help them unscramble without knowledge of the key. On the other hand, it wouldn't be proof that their quarry had been making the call; such privacy devices were not uncommon.

Naysmith blanked the booth's walls and removed his own and Rosenberg's masks. The little man was in a state of hypnosis, total recall of the Fieri manuscript he had read on Mars. He was already drawing structural formulas of molecules.

The random blur and noise on the screen clicked away as Peter Christian set the scrambler unit at that end. It was his own face grown younger which looked out at Naysmith—a husky blond sixteen-year-old, streaked with sweat and panting a little. He grinned at his Brother.

"Sorry to be so long," he said. "I was working out in the gym. Have a new mech-volley play to develop which looks promising." His English was fluent and Naysmith saw no reason to use a Spanish which, in his own case, had grown a little rusty.

"Who're you the adoptive son of?" asked the man. Privacy customs didn't mean much in the Brotherhood.

"Holger Christian—Danish career diplomat, currently ambassador to Mexico. They're good people, he and his wife."

Yes, thought Naysmith, they would be, if they let their foster child, even with his obvious brilliance, take Synthesis. The multi-ordinal integrating education was so new and untried, and its graduates would have to make their own jobs. But the need was desperate. The sciences had grown too big and complex, like everything else, and there was too much overlap between the specialties. Further progress required the fully trained synthesizing mentality.

And progress itself was no longer something justified only by Victorian prejudice. It was a matter of survival. Some means of creating a stable social and economic order in the face of continuous revolutionary change had to be found. More and more technological development was bitterly essential. Atomic-powered oil synthesis had come barely in time to save a fuel-starved Earth from industrial breakdown. Now new atomic energy fuels had to be evolved before the old ores were depleted. The rising incidence of neurosis and insanity among the intelligent and apathy among the insensitive had to be checked before other Years of Madness came. Heredity damaged by hard radiation had to be unscrambled, somehow, before dangerous recessive traits spread through the entire human population. Communications theory, basic to modern science and sociology, had to be perfected. There had to be. Why enumerate? Man had come too far and too fast. Now he was balanced on a knife edge over the red gulfs of hell.

When Peter Christian's education was complete, he would be one of Earth's most important men—whether he realized it himself or not. Of course, even his foster parents didn't know that one of his Synthesis instructors was an Un-man who was quietly teaching him the fine points of secret service. They most assuredly did not know that their so normal and healthy boy was already initiated into a group whose very existence was an unrecorded secret.

The first Brothers had been raised in families of Un-man technies and operators who had been in on the project from the start. This practice continued on a small scale, but most of the new children were put out for adoption through recognized agencies around the world—having first been provided with a carefully faked background history. Between sterility and the fear of mutation, there was no difficulty in placing a good-looking man child with a superior family. From babyhood, the Brother was under the influence—a family friend or a pediatrician or instructor or camp counselor or minister, anyone who could get an occasional chance to talk intimately with the boy, would be a sparetime employee of Fourre's and helped incline the growing personality the right way. It had been established that a Brother could accept the truth and keep his secret from the age of twelve, and that he never refused to turn Un-man. From then on, progress was quicker. The Brothers were precocious: Naysmith was only twenty-five, and he had been on his first mission at seventeen; Lampi was an authority in his field at twenty-three. There should be no hesitation in dumping this responsibility on Christian, even if there had been any choice in the matter.

"Listen," said Naysmith. "You know all hell has broken loose and that the American S-men are out to get us. Specifically, I'm the one they think they're hunting. But Lampi, a Finnish Brother, and I have put the snatch on one Barney Rosenberg from Mars. He has certain information the enemy wants." The man knew what the boy must be thinking—in a way, those were his own thoughts—and added swiftly: "No, we haven't let him in on the secret, though the fact that he was a close friend of Rostomily's makes it awkward. But it also makes him trust us. He read the report of a Fieri on Mars, concerning suspended animation techniques. He'll give it to you now. Stand by to record."

"Okay, *ja, si.*" Christian grinned and flipped a switch. He was still young enough to find this a glorious cloak-and-dagger adventure. Well, he'd learn, and the learning would be a little death within him.

Rosenberg began to talk, softly and very fast, holding up his structural formulas and chemical equations at the appropriate places. It took a little more than an hour. Christian would have been bored if he hadn't been so interested in the material; Naysmith fumed and sweated unhappily. Any moment there might come suspicion, discovery—The booth was hot.

"That's all, I guess," said Naysmith when the prospector had run down. "What do you make of it?"

"Why, it's sensational! It'll jump biology two decades!" Christian's eyes glowed. "Surgery—yes, that's obvious. Research techniques—*Gud Fader i himlen*, what a discovery!"

"And why do you think it's so important to the enemy?" snapped Naysmith.

"Isn't it plain? The military uses, man! You can use a light dose to immunize against terrific accelerations. Or you can pack a spaceship with men in frozen sleep, load 'em in almost like boxes, and have no supply worries enroute. Means you can take a good-sized army from planet to planet. And of course there's the research aspect. With what can be learned with the help of suspension techniques, biological warfare can be put on a wholly new plane."

"I thought as much." Naysmith nodded wearily. It was the same old story, the worn-out tale of hate and death and oppression. The logical end-product of scientific warfare was that *all* data became military secrets—a society without feedback or stability. That was what he fought against. "All right, what can you do about it?"

"I'll unscramble the record—no, better leave it scrambled—and get it to the right people. Hmmm—give me a small lab and I'll undertake to develop certain phases of this myself. In any case, we can't let the enemy have it."

"We've probably already given it to them. Chances are they have monitors on this line. But they can't get around to our recording and to trying all possible unscrambling combinations in less than a few days, especially if we keep them busy." Naysmith leaned forward, his haggard eyes probing into the screen. "Pete, as the son of a diplomat you must have a better than average notion of the overall politico-military picture. What can we do?"

Christian sat still for a moment. There was a curious withdrawn expression on the young face. His trained mind was assembling logic networks in a manner unknown to previous history. Finally he looked back at the man.

"There's about an eighty percent probability that Besser is the head of the gang," he said. "Chief of international finance, you know. That's an estimate of my own; I don't have Fourre's data, but I used a basis of Besser's past history and known character, his country's recent history, the necessary communications for a least-effort anti-U.N. setup on a planetary scale, the—never mind. You already know with high probability that Roger Wade is his chief for North America. I can't predict Besser's actions very closely, since in spite of his prominence he uses privacy as a cover-up for relevant psychological data. If we assume that he acts on a survival axiom, and logically apart from his inadequate grounding in modern socio-theory and his personal bias—hm."

"Besser, eh? I had my own suspicions, besides what I've been told. Financial integration has been proceeding rather slowly since he took office. Never mind. We have to strike at his organization. What to do?"

"I need more data. How many American Brothers are underground in the States and can be contacted?"

"How should I know? All that could would try to skip the country. I'm only here because I know enough of the overall situation to act usefully, I hope."

"Well, I can scare up a few in Mexico and South America, I think. We have our own communications. And I can use my 'father's' sealed diplomatic circuit to get in touch with Fourre. You have this Lampi with you, I suppose?" Christian sat in moody stillness for a while. Then:

"I can only suggest—and it's a pretty slim guess—that you two let yourselves be captured."

The man sighed. He had rather expected this.

Naysmith brought the boat whispering down just as the first cold light of sunrise crept skyward. He buzzed the narrow ledge where he had to land, swung back, and lowered the wheels. When they touched, it was a jarring, brutal contact that rattled his teeth together. He cut the motor and there was silence.

If Jeanne was alert, she'd have a gun on him now. He opened the door and called loudly: "The crocodiles grow green in Ireland." Then he stepped out and looked around him.

The mountains were a shadowy looming. Dawn lay like roses on their peaks. The air was fresh and chill, strong with the smell of pines, and there was dew underfoot and alarmed birds clamoring into the sky. Far below him, the river thundered and brawled.

Rosenberg climbed stiffly after him and leaned against the boat. Earth gravity dragged at his muscles, he was cold and hungry and cruelly tired, and these men who were ghosts of his youth would not tell him what the darkness was that lay over the world. Sharply he remembered the thin bitter sunup of Mars, a gaunt desert misting into life and a single crag etched against loneliness. Homesickness was an ache in him.

Only—he had not remembered Earth could be so lovely.

"Martin! Oh, Martin!" The woman came down the trail, running, slipping on the wet needles. Her raven hair was cloudy about the gallantly lifted head, and there was a light in her eyes which Rosenberg had almost forgotten. "Oh, my darling, you're back!"

Naysmith held her close, kissing her with hunger. One minute more, one little minute before Lampi emerged, was that too much?

He hadn't been able to leave the Finn anywhere behind. There was no safe hiding place in all America, not when the S-men were after him. There could be no reliable rendezvous later, and Lampi would be needed. He had to come along.

Of course, the Finn could have stayed masked and mute the entire while he was at the cabin. But Rosenberg would have to be left there, it was the best hideaway for him. The prospector might be trusted to keep secret the fact that two identical men had brought him here— or he might not. He was shrewd; Jeanne's conversation would lead him to some suspicion of the truth, and he might easily decide that she had been the victim of a shabby trick and should be given the facts. Then anything could happen.

Oh, with some precautions Naysmith could probably hide his real nature from the girl a while longer. Rosenberg might very well keep his mouth shut on request. But there was no longer any point in concealing the facts from her—she would not be captured by the gang before they had the Un-man himself. In any case, she must be told sooner or later. The man she thought was her husband was probably going to die, and it was as well that she think little of him and have no fears and sorrows on his account. One death was enough for her.

He laid his hands on the slim shoulders and stood back a bit, looking into her eyes. His own crinkled in the way she must know so well, and they were unnaturally bright in the dawn-glow. When he spoke, it was almost a whisper.

"Jeanne, honey, I've got some bad news for you."

He felt her stiffen beneath his hands, saw the face tighten and heard the little hiss of indrawn breath. There were dark rings about her eyes, she couldn't have slept very well while he was gone.

"This is a matter of absolute secrecy," he went on, tonelessly. "No one, repeat no one, is to have a word of it. But you have a right to the truth."

"Go ahead." There was an edge of harshness in her voice. "I can take it."

"I'm not Martin Donner," he said. "Your husband is dead."

She stood rigid for another heartbeat, and then she pulled wildly free. One hand went to her mouth. The other was half lifted as if to fend him off.

"I had to pretend it, to get you away without any fuss," he went on, looking at the ground. "The enemy would have—tortured you, maybe. Or killed you and Jimmy. I don't know."

Juho Lampi came up behind Naysmith. There was compassion on his face. Jeanne stepped backward, voiceless.

"You'll have to stay here," said Naysmith bleakly. "It's the only safe place. Here is Mr. Rosenberg, whom we're leaving with you. I assure you he's completely innocent of anything that has been done. I can't tell either of you more than this." He took a long step toward her. She stood her ground, unmoving. When he clasped her hands into his, they were cold. "Except that I love you," he whispered.

Then, swinging away, he faced Lampi. "We'll clean up and get some breakfast here," he said. "After that, we're off."

Jeanne did not follow them inside. Jimmy, awakened by their noise, was delighted to have his father back (Lampi had re-assumed a mask) but Naysmith gave him disappointingly little attention. He told Rosenberg that the three of them should stay put here as long as possible before striking out for the village, but that it was hoped to send a boat for them in a few days.

Jeanne's face was cold and bloodless as Naysmith and Lampi went back to the jet. When it was gone, she started to cry. Rosenberg wanted to leave and let her have it out by herself, but she clung to him blindly and he comforted her as well as he could.

✶XI✶

There was no difficulty about getting captured. Naysmith merely strolled into a public lavatory at Oregon Unit and took off his mask to wash his face; a man standing nearby went hurriedly out, and when Naysmith emerged he was knocked over by the stet-gun of a

Unit policeman. It was what came afterward that was tough. He woke up, stripped and handcuffed, in a cell, very shortly before a team of S-men arrived to lead him away. These took the added precaution of binding his ankles before stuffing him into a jet. He had to grin sourly at that, it was a compliment of sorts. Little was said until the jet came down on a secret headquarters which was also a Wyoming ranch.

There they gave him the works. He submitted meekly to every identification procedure he had ever heard of. Fluoroscopes showed nothing hidden within his body except the communicator, and there was some talk of operating it out; but they decided to wait for orders from higher up before attempting that. They questioned him and, since he had killed two or three of their fellows, used methods which cost him a couple of teeth and a sleepless night. He told them his name and address, but little else.

Orders came the following day. Naysmith was bundled into another jet and flown eastward. Near the destination, the jet was traded for an ordinary, inconspicuous airboat. They landed after dark on the grounds of a large new mansion in western Pennsylvania—Naysmith recalled that Roger Wade lived here—and he was led inside. There was a soundproofed room with a full battery of interrogation machines under the residential floors. The prisoner was put into a chair already equipped with straps, fastened down, and left for a while to ponder his situation.

He sighed and attempted to relax, leaning back against the metal of the chair. It was an uncomfortable seat, cold and stiff as it pressed into his naked skin. The room was long and low-ceilinged, barren in the white glare of high-powered fluoros, and the utter stillness of it muffled his breath and heartbeat. The air was cool, but somehow that absorbent quiet choked him. He faced the impassive dials of a lie detector and an electric neurovibrator, and the silence grew and grew.

His head ached, and he longed for a cigaret. His eyelids were sandy with sleeplessness and there was a foul taste in his mouth. Mostly, though, he thought of Jeanne Donner.

Presently, the door at the end of the room opened and a group of people walked slowly toward him. He recognized Wade's massive form in the van. Behind him trailed a bearded man with a lean, sallow face; a young chap thin as a rail, his skin dead white and his hands clenching and unclenching nervously; a gaunt homely woman; and a squat, burly subordinate whom he did not know but assumed to be an S-man in Wade's pay. The others were familiar to Service dossiers: Lewin, Wade's personal physician; Rodney Borrow, his chief secretary; Marta Jennings, Americanist organizer. There was death in their eyes.

Wade proceeded quietly up toward Naysmith. Borrow drew a chair for him and he sat down in it and took out a cigaret. Nobody spoke till he had it lighted. Then he blew the smoke in Naysmith's direction and said gently: "According to the official records, you really are Robert Naysmith of California. But tell me, is that only another false identity?"

Naysmith shrugged. "Identity is a philosophical basic," he answered. "Where does similarity leave off and identity begin?"

"Mmmmmm-hm." Wade nodded slowly. "We've killed you at least once, and I suspect more than once. But are you Martin Donner, or are you his twin? And in the latter case, how does it happen that you two, or you three, four, five, ten thousand—are *completely* identical?"

"Oh, not quite," said Naysmith.

"No-o-o. There are the little scars and peculiarities due to environment—and habits, language, accent, occupation. But for police purposes you and Donner are the same man. How was it done?"

Naysmith smiled. "How much am I offered for that information?" he parried. "As well as other information you know I have?"

"So." Wade's eyes narrowed. "You weren't captured—not really. You gave yourself up."

"Maybe. Have you caught anyone else yet?"

Wade traded a glance with the Security officer. Then, with an air of decision, he said briskly. "An hour ago, I was informed that a man answering your description had been picked up in Minnesota. He admitted to being one Juho Lampi of Finland, and I'm inclined to take his word for it though we haven't checked port-of-entry records yet. How many more of you can we expect to meet?"

"As many as you like," said Naysmith. "Maybe more than that."

"All right. You gave yourself up. You must know that we have no reason to spare your life—or lives. What do you hope to gain?"

"A compromise," answered Naysmith. "Which will, of course, involve our release."

"How much are you willing to tell us now?"

"As little as possible, naturally. We'll have to bargain."

Stall! Stall for time! The message from Rio has got to come soon. It's got to, or we're all dead men.

Borrow leaned over his master's shoulder. His voice was high and cracked, stuttering just a trifle: "How will we know you're telling the truth?"

"How will you know that even if you torture me?" shrugged Naysmith. "Your bird dogs must have reported that I've been immunized to drugs."

"There are still ways," said Lewin. His words fell dull in the muffling silence. "Prefrontal lobotomy is usually effective."

Yes, this is the enemy. These are the men of darkness. These are the men who in other days sent heretics to burning, or fed the furnaces of Belsen, or stuffed the rockets with radioactive death. Now they're opening skulls and slashing brains across. Argue with them! Let them kick and slug and whip you, but don't let them know—

"Our bargain might not be considered valid if you do that."

"The essential element of a bargain," said Wade pompously, "is the free will and desire of both parties. You're not free."

"But I am. You've killed one of me and captured two others. How do you know the number of me which is still running loose, out there in the night?"

Borrow and Jennings flickered uneasy eyes toward the smooth bare walls. The woman shuddered, ever so faintly.

"We needn't be clumsy about this," said Lewin. "There's the lie detector, first of all. Its value is limited, but this man is too old to have had Synthesis training, so he can't fool it much. Then there are instruments that make a man quite anxious to talk. I have a chlorine generator here, Naysmith. How would you like to breathe a few whiffs of chlorine?"

"Or just a vise—applied in the right place," snapped Jennings.

"Hold up a minute," ordered Wade. "Let's find out how much he wants to reveal without such persuasion."

"I said I'd trade information, not give it away," said Naysmith. He wished the sweat weren't running down his face and body for all of them to see. The reek of primitive, uncontrollable fear was sharp in his nostrils; not the fear of death, but of the anguish and mutilation which were worse than oblivion.

"What do *you* want to know?" snapped the Security officer contemptuously.

"Well," said Naysmith, "first off, I'd like to know your organization's purpose."

"What's that?" Wade's heavy face blinked at him, and an angry flush mottled his cheeks. "Let's not play crèche games. You know what we want."

"No, seriously, I'm puzzled." Naysmith forced mildness into his tones. "I realize you don't like the status quo and want to change it. But you're all well off now. What do you hope to gain?"

"What—That will do!" Wade gestured to the officer, and Naysmith's head rang with a buffet. "We haven't time to listen to your bad jokes."

Naysmith grinned viciously. If he could get them mad, play on those twisted emotions till the unreasoning thalamus controlled them—it would be hard on him, but it would delay their real aims. "Oh, I can guess," he said. "It's personal, isn't it? None of you really know what's driving you to this, except for the stupid jackals who're in with you merely because it pays better than any work they could get on their own merits. Like you, for instance." He glanced at the S-man and sneered deliberately.

"Shut up!" This time the blow was to his jaw. Blood ran out of his mouth, and he sagged a little against the straps that held him. But his voice lifted raggedly.

"Take Miss Jennings, for one. Not that I would, even if you paid me. You're all twisted up inside, aren't you? Too ugly to get a man, too scared of yourself to get a surgical remodeling. You're trying your clumsy damndest to sublimate it into patriotism—and what kind of symbol is a flagpole? I notice it was you who made that highly personal suggestion about torturing me."

She drew back, the rage of a whipped animal in her. The S-man took out a piece of hose, but Wade gestured him away. The leader's face had gone wooden.

"Or Lewin—another case of psychotic frustration." Naysmith smiled, a close-lipped and unpleasant smile of bruised lips, at the doctor. "I warrant you'd work for free if you hadn't been hired. A two-bit sadist has trouble finding outlets these days."

"Now we come to Rodney Borrow."

"Shut up!" cried the thin man. He edged forward. Wade swept him back with a heavy arm.

"Exogene!" Naysmith's smile grew warm, almost pitying. "It's too bad that human exogenesis was developed during the Years of Madness, when moral scruples went to hell and scientists were as fanatical as everyone else. They grew you in a tank, Borrow, and your pre-natal life, which every inherited instinct said should be warm and dark and sheltered, was one hell of study—bright lights, probes, microslides taken of your tissues. They learned a lot about the human fetus, but they should have killed you instead of letting such a pathetic quivering mass of engrammed psychoses walk around alive. If you could call it life, Exogene."

Borrow lunged past Wade. There was slaver running from his lips, and he clawed for Naysmith's eyes. The S-man pulled him back and suddenly he collapsed, weeping hysterically. Naysmith shuddered beneath his skin. *There but for the Grace of God—*

"And how about myself?" asked Wade. "These amateur analyses are most amusing. Please continue."

"Guilt drive. Overcompensation. The Service has investigated your childhood and adolescent background and—"

"And?"

"Come on Roger. It's fun. It won't hurt a bit."

The big man sat stiff as an iron bar. For a long moment there was nothing, no sound except Borrow's sobs; no movement. Wade's face turned gray.

When he spoke, it was as if he were strangling: "I think you'd better start that chlorine generator, Lewin."

"With pleasure!"

Naysmith shook his head. "And you people want to run things," he murmured. "We're supposed to turn over a world slowly recovering its sanity to the likes of you."

The generator began to hiss and bubble at his back. He could have turned his head to watch it, but that would have been a defeat. And he needed every scrap of pride remaining in this ultimate loneliness.

"Let me run the generator," whispered Borrow.

"No," said Lewin. "You might kill him too fast."

"Maybe we should wait till they bring this Lampi here," said Jennings. "Let him watch us working Naysmith over."

Wade shook his head. "Maybe later," he said.

"I notice that you still haven't tried to find out what I'm willing to tell you without compulsion," interjected Naysmith.

"Well, go ahead," said Wade in a flat voice. "We're listening."

A little time, just a little more time, if I can spin them a yarn—

"Étienne Fourre has more resources than you know," declared Naysmith. "A counter blow has been prepared which will cost you dearly. But since it would also put quite a strain on us, we're willing to discuss—if not a permanent compromise, for there can obviously be none, at least an armistice. That's why—"

A chime sounded. "Come in," said Wade loudly. His voice activated the door and a man entered.

"Urgent call for you, Mr. Wade," he reported. "Scrambled."

"All right." The leader got up. "Hold off on that chlorine till I get back, Lewin." He went out.

When the door had closed behind him, Lewin said calmly: "Well, he didn't tell us to refrain from other things, did he?"

They took turns using the hose. Naysmith's mind grew a little hazy with pain. But they dared not inflict real damage, and it didn't last long.

Wade came back. He ignored Lewin, who was hastily pocketing the truncheon, and said curtly: "We're going on a trip. All of us. Now."

The word had come. Naysmith sank back, breathing hard. Just at that moment, the relief from pain was too great for him to think of anything else. It took him several minutes to start worrying about whether Peter Christian's logic had been correct, and whether the Service could fulfill its part, and even whether the orders that came to Wade had been the right ones.

✸XII✸

It was late afternoon before Barney Rosenberg had a chance to talk with Jeanne Donner, and then it was she who sought him out.

He had wandered from the cabin after lunch, scrambling along the mountainside and strolling through the tall forest. But Earth gravity tired him, and he returned in a few hours. Even then, he didn't go back to the cabin, but found a log near the rim of the gorge and sat down to think.

So this was Earth.

It was a cool and lovely vision which opened before him. The cliffs tumbled in a sweep of gray and slate blue, down and down into the huge sounding canyon of the river. On the farther side the mountain lifted in a mist of dim purple up to its sun-blazing snow and the skyey vastness beyond. There were bushes growing on the slopes that fell riverward, green blurring the severe rock, here and there a cluster of fire-like berries. Behind Rosenberg and on either side were the trees, looming pine in a cavern of shadow, slim whispering beech, ash with the streaming, blinding, raining sunlight snared in its leaves. He had not remembered how much color there was on this planet.

And it was alive with sound. The trees murmured. Mosquitoes buzzed thinly around his ears. A bird was singing—he didn't know what kind of bird, but it had a wistful liquid trill that haunted his thoughts. Another answered in whistles, and somewhere a third was chattering and chirping its gossip. A squirrel darted past like a red comet, and he heard the tiny scrabble of its claws.

And the smells—the infinite living world of odors; pine and mould and wildflowers and the river mist! He had almost forgotten he owned a sense of smell, in the tanked sterility of Mars.

Oh, his muscles ached and he was lonely for the grim bare magnificence of the deserts and he wondered how he would ever fit into this savage world of men against men. But still—Earth was home, and a billion years of evolution could not be denied.

Someday Mars would be a full-grown planet and its people would be rich and free. Rosenberg shook his head, smiling a little. Poor Martians!

There was a light footstep behind him. He turned and saw Jeanne Donner approaching. She had on a light blouse-and-slack outfit which didn't hide the grace of her or the weariness, and the sun gleamed darkly in her hair. Rosenberg stood up with a feeling of awkwardness.

"Please sit down." Her voice was grave, somehow remote. "I'd like to join you for a little while, if I may."

"By all means." Rosenberg lowered himself again to the mossy trunk. It was cool and yielding, a little damp, under his hand. Jeanne sat beside him, elbows on knees. For a moment she was quiet, looking over the sun-flooded land. Then she took out a pack of cigarets and held them toward the man. "Smoke?" she asked.

"Uh—no, thanks. I got out of the habit on Mars. Oxygen's too scarce, usually. We chew instead, if we can afford tobacco at all."

"M-hm." She lit a cigaret for herself and drew hard on it, sucking in her cheeks. He saw how fine the underlying bony structure was. Well—Stef had always picked the best women, and gotten them.

"We'll rig a bed for you," she said. "Cut some spruce boughs and put them under a sleeping bag. Makes a good doss."

"Thanks." They sat without talking for a while. The cigaret smoke blew away in ragged streamers. Rosenberg could hear the wind whistling and piping far up the canyon.

"I'd like to ask you some questions," she said at last, turning her face to him. "If they get too personal, just say so."

"I've nothing to hide—worse luck." He tried to smile. "Anyway, we don't have those privacy notions on Mars. They'd be too hard to maintain under our living conditions."

"They're a recent phenomenon on Earth, anyway," she said. "Go back to the Years of Madness, when there was so much eccentricity of all kinds, a lot of it illegal. Oh, hell!" She threw the cigaret to the ground and stamped it savagely out with one heel. "I'm going to forget my own conditioning too. Ask me anything you think is relevant. We've got to get to the truth of this matter."

"If we can. I'd say it was a well-guarded secret."

"Listen," she said between her teeth. "My husband was Martin Donner. We were married three and a half years—and I mean married. He couldn't tell me much about this work. I knew he was really an Un-man and that his engineering work was only a blind, and that's about all he ever told me. Obviously, he never said a word about having—duplicates. But leaving that aside, we were in love and we got to know each other as well as two people can in that length of time. More than just physical appearance. It was also a matter of personality, reaction-patterns, facial expressions, word-configuration choices, manner of moving and working, the million little things which fit into one big pattern. An overall *gestalt*, understand?"

"Now this man—What did you say his name was?"

"Naysmith. Robert Naysmith. At least, that's what he told me. The other fellow was called Lampi."

"I'm supposed to believe that Martin died and that this— Naysmith—was substituted for him," she went on hurriedly. "They wanted to get me out of the house fast, couldn't stop to argue with me, so they sent in this ringer. Well, I saw him there in the house. He escaped with me and the boy. We had a long and uneasy flight together up here—you know how strain will bring out the most basic characteristics of a person. He stayed here overnight—" A slow flush crept up her cheeks and she looked away. Then, defiantly, she swung back on Rosenberg. "And he fooled me completely. Everything about him was Martin, *Everything!* Oh, I suppose there were minor variations, but they must have been very minor indeed. You can disguise a man these days, with surgery and cosmetics and whatnot, so that he duplicates almost every detail of physique. But can surgery give him the same funny slow way of smiling, the same choice of phrases, the same sense of humor, the same way of picking up his son and talking to him, the same habit of quoting Shakespeare, and way of taking out a cigaret and lighting it one-handed, and corner-cutting way of piloting an airboat—the same *soul*? Can they do that?"

"I don't know," whispered Rosenberg. "I shouldn't think so."

"I wouldn't really have believed it," she said. "I'd have thought he was trying to tell me a story for some unknown reason. Only there was that other man with him, and except for their hair being dyed I couldn't tell them apart—and you were along too, and seemed to accept the story," She clutched his arm. "Is it true? Is my husband really dead?"

"I don't know," he answered grayly. "I think they were telling the truth, but how can I know?"

"It's more than my own sanity," she said in a tired voice. "I've got to know what to tell Jimmy. I can't say anything now."

Rosenberg looked at the ground. His words came slowly and very soft: "I think your best bet is to sit tight for a while. This is something which is big, maybe the biggest secret in the universe. And it's either very good or very bad. I'd like to believe that it was good."

"But what do you know of it?" She held his eyes with her own, he couldn't look away, and her hand gripped his arm with a blind force. "What can you tell me? What do you think?"

He ran a thin, blue-veined hand through his grizzled hair and drew a breath. "Well," he said, "I think there probably are a lot of these identical Un-men. We know that there are—were—three, and I got the impression there must be more. Why not? That Lampi was a foreigner; he had an accent; so if they're found all over the world—"

"Un-man." She shivered a little, sitting there in the dappled shade and sunlight. "It's a hideous word. As if they weren't human."

"No," he said gently. "I think you're wrong there. They—well, I knew their prototype, and he was a *man*."

"Their—no!" Almost, she sprang to her feet. With an effort, she controlled herself and sat rigid. "*Who was that?*"

"His name was Stefan Rostomily. He was my best friend for fifteen years."

"I—don't know—never heard of him." Her tones were thick.

"You probably wouldn't have. He was off Earth the whole time. But his name is still a good one out on the planets. You may not know what a Rostomily valve is, but that was his invention. He tinkered it up one week for convenience, sold it for a good sum, and binged that away." Rosenberg chuckled dimly. "It made history, that binge. But the valve meant a lot to Martian colonists."

"Who was he?"

"He never said much about his background. I gathered he was a European, probably Czech or Austrian. He must have done heroic things in the underground and guerrilla fighting during the Third War. But it kind of spoiled him for a settled career. By the time things began to calm a little, he'd matured in chaos and it was too late to do any serious studying. He drifted around Earth for a while, took a hand in some of the fighting that still went on here and there—he was with the U.N. forces that suppressed the Great Jehad, I know. But he got sick of killing, too, as any sane man would. In spite of his background, Mrs. Donner, he was basically one of the sanest men I ever knew. So at last he bluffed his way onto a spaceship—didn't have a degree, but he learned engineering in a hell of a hurry, and he was good at it. I met him on Venus, when I was prospecting around; I may not look it, but I'm a geologist and mineralogist. We ended up on Mars. Helped build Sandy Landing, helped in some of the plantation development work, prospected, mapped and surveyed and explored—we must've tried everything. He died five years ago. A cave-in. I buried him there on Mars."

The trees about them whispered with wind.

"And these others are—his sons?" she murmured. She was trembling a little now.

Rosenberg shook his head. "Impossible. These men are *him*. Stef in every last feature, come alive and young again. No child could ever be that close to his father."

"No. No, I suppose not."

"Stef was a human being, through and through," said Rosenberg. "But he was also pretty close to being a superman. Think of his handicaps: childhood gone under the Second War and its aftermath, young manhood gone in the Third War, poor, self-educated, uprooted. And still he was balanced and sane, gentle except when violence was called for—then he was a hellcat, I tell you. Men and women loved him; he had that kind of personality. He'd picked up a dozen languages, and he read their literatures with more appreciation and understanding than most professors. He knew music and composed some good songs of his own—rowdy but good. They're still being sung out on Mars. He was an artist, did some fine murals for several buildings, painted the Martian landscape like no camera has ever shown it, though he was good with a camera too. I've already told you about his inventiveness, and he had clever hands that a machine liked. His physique stood up to anything—he was almost sixty when he died and could still match any boy of twenty. He—why go on? He was everything, and good at everything."

"I know," she answered. "Martin was the same way." Her brief smile was wistful. "Believe me, I had the devil's own time hooking him. Real competition there." After a moment she added thoughtfully: "There must be a few such supermen walking around in every generation. It's just a matter of a happy genetic accident, a preponderance of favorable characteristics appearing in the same zygote, a highly intelligent mesomorph. Some of them go down in history. Think of Michelangelo, Vespucci, Raleigh—men who worked at everything: science, politics, war, engineering, exploration, art, literature. Others weren't interested in prominence, or maybe they had bad luck. Like your friend."

"I don't know what the connection is with these Un-men," said Rosenberg. "Stef never said a word to me—but of course, he'd've been sworn to secrecy, or it might even have been done without his knowledge. Only what was done? Matter duplication? I don't think so. If the U.N. had matter duplication, it wouldn't be in the fix it is now. What was done—and *why*?"

Jeanne didn't answer. She was looking away now, across the ravine to the high clear beauty of mountains beyond. It was blurred in her eyes. Suddenly she got up and walked away.

✷XIII✷

There was a night of stars and streaming wind about the jet. The Moon was low, throwing a bridge of broken light across the heaving Atlantic immensity. Once, far off, Naysmith saw a single meteoric streak burning upward, a rocket bound for space. Otherwise he sat in darkness and alone.

He had been locked into a tiny compartment in the rear of the jet. Wade and his entourage, together with a pilot and a couple of guards, sat forward; the jet was comfortably furnished, and they were probably catching up on their sleep. Naysmith didn't want a nap, though the weakness of hunger and his injuries was on him. He sat staring out of the port, listening to the mighty rush of wind and trying to estimate where they were.

The middle Atlantic, he guessed, perhaps fifteen degrees north latitude. If Christian's prognosis of Besser's reactions was correct, they were bound for the secret world headquarters of the gang, but Wade and the others hadn't told him anything. They were over the high seas now, the great unrestful wilderness which ran across three-fourths of the planet's turning surface, the last home on Earth of mystery and solitude. Anything could be done out here, and when fish had eaten the bodies who would ever be the wiser?

Naysmith's gaze traveled to the Moon, riding cold above the sea. Up there was the dominion over Earth. Between the space-station observatories and the rocket bases of the Lunar Guard, there should be nothing which the forces of sanity could not smash. The Moon had not rained death since the Third War, but the very threat of that monstrous fist poised in the sky had done much to quell a crazed planet. If the Service could tell the Guard where to shoot—

Only it couldn't. It never could, because this rebellion was not the armed uprising of a nation with cities and factories and mines. It was a virus within the body of all humankind. You wouldn't get anywhere bombing China, except to turn four hundred million innocent victims who had been your friends against you—because it was a small key group in the Chinese government which was conspiring against sanity.

You can blast a sickness from outside, with drugs and antibiotics and radiation. But the darkness of the human mind can only be helped by a psychiatrist; the cure must come from within itself.

If the U.N. were not brought tumbling down, but slowly eaten away, mutilated and crippled and demoralized, what would there be to shoot at? Sooner or later, official orders would come disbanding its police and Lunar Guard. Or there were other ways to attack those Moon bases. If they didn't have the Secret Service to warn them, it would be no trick for an enemy to smuggle military equipment to the Moon surface itself and blow them apart from there.

And in the end—what? Complete and immediate collapse into the dog-eat-dog madness which had come so close once to ruining civilization? (*Man won't get another chance. We were luckier than we deserved the last time.*) Or a jerry-built world empire of oppression, the stamping out of that keen and critical science whose early dawn-light was just beginning to show man a new path, a thousand-year nightmare of humanity turned into an ant-hill? There was little choice between the two.

Naysmith sighed and shifted on the hard bare seat. They could have had the decency to give him some clothes and a cigaret. A sandwich at the very least. Only, of course, the idea was to break down his morale as far as possible.

He tried again, for the thousandth time, to evaluate the situation, but there were too many unknowns and intangibles. It would be stupid to insist that tonight was a crisis point in human history. It could be—then again, if this attempt of the Brotherhood ended in failure, if the Brothers themselves were hunted down, there might come some other chance, some compensating factor. *Might!* But passive reliance on luck was ruin.

And in any case, he thought bleakly, tonight would surely decide the fate of Robert Naysmith.

The jet slanted downward, slowing as it wailed out of the upper air. Naysmith leaned against the wall, gripping the edge of the port with manacled hands, and peered below. Moonlight washed a great rippling mass of darkness, and in the center of it something which rose like a metal cliff.

A sea station!

I should have guessed it, thought Naysmith wildly. His brain felt hollow and strange. *The most logical place; accessible, mobile, under the very nose of the world but hidden all the same. I imagine the Service has considered this possibility—only how could it check all the sea stations in existence? It isn't even known how many there are.*

This one lay amidst acres of floating weed. Probably one of the specially developed sea plants with which it was hoped to help feed an overcrowded planet; or maybe this place passed itself off as an experiment station working to improve the growth. In either case, ranch or laboratory, Naysmith was sure that its announced activities were really carried out, and there was a completely working staff with all equipment and impeccable dossiers. The gang's headquarters would be underneath, in the submerged bowels of the station.

An organization like this had to parallel its enemy in most respects. Complex and world-wide—no. System-wide, if it really included Pilgrim fanatics who wanted to take over Mars. It would have to keep extensive records, have some kind of communications center. *This is it! By Heaven, this is their brain!*

The shiver of excitement faded into a hard subsurface tingle. A dead man had no way of relaying his knowledge to Fourre.

There was a landing platform at one end of the great floating structure. The pilot brought his jet down to a skillful rest, cut the motors, and let silence fall. Naysmith heard the deep endless voice of the sea, rolling and washing against the walls. He wondered how far it was to the next humanity. Far indeed. Perhaps they were beyond the edge of death.

The door opened and light filtered into the compartment. "All right, Naysmith," said the guard. "Come along."

Obediently, the Un-man went out between his captors to stand on the platform. It was floodlit, cutting off the view of the ocean surging twenty or thirty feet under its rails. The station superstructure, gymbal-mounted and gyro-stabilized above its great caissons, wouldn't roll much even in the heaviest weather. There were two other jets standing nearby. No sign of armament, though Naysmith was sure that missile tubes were here in abundance and that each mechanic carried a gun.

The wind was chill on his body as he was led toward the main cabin. Wade strode ahead of him, cloak flapping wildly in the flowing, murmuring night. To one side, Naysmith saw Borrow's stiff white face and the sunken expressionlessness of Lewin. Perhaps those two would be allowed to work him over.

They entered a short hallway. At the farther end, Wade pressed his hand to a scanner. A panel slid back in front of an elevator cage. "In," grunted one of the S-men.

Naysmith stood quietly, hemmed into a corner by the wary bodies of his guards. He saw that Borrow and Jennings were shivering with nervous tension. A little humorless smile twisted his mouth. Whatever else happened, the Brotherhood had certainly given the enemy a jolt.

The elevator sighed to a halt. Naysmith was led out, down a long corridor lined with doors. One of them stood ajar, and he saw walls covered with micro-file cabinets. Yes, this must be their archive. A besmocked man went the other way, carrying a computer tape. Unaided human brains were no longer enough even for those who would overthrow society. Too big, too big.

At the end of the hall, Naysmith was ushered into a large room. It was almost as if he were back in Wade's torture chamber—the same bright lights, the same muffling walls, the same instruments of inquisition. His eyes swept its breadth until they rested on the three men who sat behind a rack of neuroanalyzers.

The Brothers could tell each other apart; there were enough subtle environmental differences for that. Naysmith recognized Lampi, who seemed undamaged except for a black eye; he must have been taken directly here on orders. There was also Carlos Martinez of

Guatemala, whom he had met before, and a third man whom he didn't recognize but who was probably South American.

They smiled at him, and he smiled back. Four pairs of blue eyes looked out of the same lean muscular faces, four blond heads nodded, four brains flashed the same intangible message: *You too, my Brother? Now we must endure.*

Naysmith was strapped in beside Martinez. He listened to Wade, speaking to Lucientes who had been suspected of being the Argentine sector chief of the rebels: "Besser hasn't come yet?"

"No, he is on the way. He should be very soon."

Besser is the real head, then, the organizing brain—and he is on his way! The four Brothers held themselves rigid, four identical faces staring uncannily ahead, not daring to move or exchange a glance. *Besser is coming!*

Wade took a restless turn about the room. "It's a weird business," he said thinly. "I'm not sure I like the idea of having all four together—in this very place."

"What can they do?" shrugged Lucientes. "My men captured Villareal here in Buenos Aires yesterday. He had been an artist, supposedly, and dropped out of sight when word first came about a fugitive Un-man answering that description. But he made a childish attempt to get back to his apartment and was arrested without difficulty. Martinez was obtained in Panama City with equal ease. If they are that incompetent—"

"But they aren't! They're anything but!" Wade glared at the prisoners. "This was done on purpose, I tell you. Why?"

"I already said—" Naysmith and Villareal spoke almost simultaneously. They stopped, and the Argentine grinned and closed his mouth. "I told you," Naysmith finished. "We wanted to bargain. There was no other quick and expedient way of making the sort of contact we needed."

"Were four of you needed?" snapped Wade. "Four valuable men?"

"Perhaps not so valuable," said Lewin quietly. "Not if there are any number of them still at large."

"They are not supernatural!" protested Lucientes. "They are flesh and blood. They can feel pain, and cannot break handcuffs. I know! Nor are they telepaths or anything equally absurd. They are—" His voice faltered.

"Yes?" challenged Wade. "They are what?"

Naysmith drew into himself. There was a moment of utter stillness. Only the heavy breathing of the captors, the captors half terrified by an unknown, and all the more vicious and deadly because of that, had voice.

The real reason was simple, thought Naysmith—so simple that it defeated those tortuous minds. It had seemed reasonable, and Christian's logic had confirmed the high probability, that one man identical with the agent who had been killed would be unsettling enough, and that four of them, from four different countries, would imply something so enormous that the chief conspirator would want them all together in his own strongest and most secret place, that he himself would want to be there at the questioning.

Only what happened next?

"They aren't human!" Borrow's voice was shrill and wavering. "They can't be. Not four or five or a thousand identical men. The U.N. has its own laboratories. Fourre could easily have had secret projects carried out."

"So?" Lewin's eyes blinked sardonically at the white face.

"So they're robots—androids, synthetic life—whatever you want to call it. Test-tube monsters!"

Lewin shook his head, grimly. "That's too big a stride forward," he said. "No human science will be able to do that for centuries to come. You don't appreciate the complexity of a living human being—and our best efforts haven't yet synthesized even one functioning cell. I admit these fellows have something—superhuman—about them. They've done incredible things. But they can't be robots. It isn't humanly possible."

"*Humanly!*" screamed Borrow. "Is man the only scientific race in the universe? How about creatures from the stars? Who's the real power behind the U.N.?"

"That will do," snapped Wade. "We'll find out pretty soon." His look fastened harsh on Naysmith. "Let's forget this stupid talk of bargaining. There can be no compromise until one or the other party is done for."

That's right. The same thought quivered in four living brains.

"I—" Wade stopped and swung toward the door. It opened for two men who entered.

One was Arnold Besser. He was a small man, fine-boned, dark-haired, still graceful at seventy years of age. There was a flame in him that burned past the drab plainness of his features, the eerie light of fanaticism deep within his narrow skull. He nodded curtly to the greetings and stepped briskly forward. His attendant came after, a big and powerful man in chauffeur's uniform, cat-quiet, his face rugged and expressionless.

Only—only—Naysmith's heart leap wildly within him. He looked away from the chauffeur-guard, up into the eyes of Arnold Besser.

"Now, then." The chief stood before his prisoners, hands on hips, staring impersonally at them but with a faint shiver running beneath his pale skin. "I want to know you people's real motive in giving yourselves up. I've studied your 'vised dossiers, such as they are, on the way here, so you needn't repeat the obvious. I want to know everything else."

"'The quality of mercy is not strained,'" murmured Lampi. Naysmith's mind continued the lovely words. He needed their comfort, for here was death.

"The issues are too large and urgent for sparring," said Besser. There was a chill in his voice as he turned to Lewin. "We have four of them here, and presumably each of them knows what the others know. So we can try four different approaches. Suggestions?"

"Lobotomy on one," answered the physician promptly. "We can remove that explosive detonator at the same time, of course. But it will take a few days before he can be questioned, even under the best conditions, and perhaps there has been some precaution taken so that the subject will die. We can try physical methods immediately on two of them, in the presence of each other. We had better save a fourth—just in case."

"Very well." Besser's gaze went a white-jacketed man behind the prisoners. "You are the surgeon here. Take one away and get to work on his brain."

The doctor nodded and began to wheel Martinez' chair out of the room. Lewin started a chlorine generator. The chauffeur-guard leaned against a table, watching with flat blank eyes.

The end? Goodnight, then, world, sun and moon and wind in the heavens. Goodnight, Jeanne.

A siren hooted. It shrilled up and down a saw-edged scale, ringing in metal and glass and human bones. Besser whirled toward a communicator. Wade stood heavy and paralyzed. Jennings screamed.

The room shivered, and they heard the dull crumping of an explosion. The door opened and a man stumbled in, shouting something. His words drowned in the rising whistle and bellow of rocket missiles.

Suddenly there was a magnum gun in the chauffeur's hand. It spewed a rain of slugs as he crouched, swinging it around the chamber. Naysmith saw Besser's head explode. Two of the guards had guns halfway out when the chauffeur cut them down.

The communicator chattered up on the wall, screaming something hysterical about an air attack. The chauffeur was already across to the door switch. He closed and locked the barrier, jumped over Wade's body, and grabbed for a surgical saw. It bit at the straps holding Naysmith, drawing a little blood. Lampi, Martinez, and Villareal were whooping aloud.

The chauffeur spoke in rapid Brazilo-Portuguese: "I'll get you free. Then take some weapons and be ready to fight. They may attack us in here, I don't know. But there will be paratroops landing as soon as our air strength has reduced their defenses. We should be able to hold out till then."

It had worked. The incredible, desperate, precarious plan had worked. Besser, in alarm and uncertainty, had gone personally to his secret headquarters. He had been piloted by his trusted gunman as usual. Only—Fourre's office would long have known about that pilot, studied him, prepared a surgically disguised duplicate from a Brazilian Un-man and held this agent in reserve. When Christian's message came, the chauffeur had been taken care of and the Un-man had replaced him—and had been able to slip a radio tracer into Besser's jet—a tracer which the Rio-based U.N. police had followed.

And now they had the base!

Naysmith flung himself out of the chair and snatched a gun off the floor. He exchanged a glance with his rescuer, a brief warm glance of kinship and comradeship and belongingness. Even under the disguise and the carefully learned mannerisms, there had been something intangible which he had known—or was it only the fact that the deliverer had moved with such swift and certain decision?

"Yes," said the Brazilian unnecessarily. "I too am a Brother."

✴XIV✴

There was one morning when Naysmith came out of his tent and walked down to the sea. This was in Northwest National Park, the new preserve which included a good stretch of Oregon's coast. He had come for rest and solitude, to do some thinking which seemed to lead nowhere, and had stayed longer than he intended. There was peace here, in the great rocky stretch of land, the sandy nooks between, the loneliness of ocean, and the forest and mountains behind. Not many people were in the park now, and he had pitched his tent remote from the camping grounds anyway.

It was over. The job was finished. With the records of Besser's headquarters for clues and proof, Fourre had been in a position to expose the whole conspiracy. Nobody had cared much about the technical illegality of his raid. Several governments fell—the Chinese had a spectacularly bloody end—and were replaced with men closer to sanity. Agents had been weeded out of every regime. In America, Hessling was in jail and there was talk of disbanding Security altogether. The U.N. had a renewed prestige and power, a firmer allegiance from the peoples of the world. Happy ending?

No. Because it was a job which never really ended. The enemy was old and strong and crafty, it took a million forms and it could never quite be slain. For it was man himself—the madness and sorrow of the human soul, the revolt of a primitive against the unnatural state called civilization and freedom. Somebody would try again. His methods would be different, he might not have the same avowed goal, but he would be the enemy and the watchers would have to break him. *And who shall watch the watchmen?*

Security was a meaningless dream. There was no stability except in death. Peace and happiness were not a reward to be earned, but a state to be maintained with toil and grief.

Naysmith's thinking at the moment concerned personal matters. But there didn't seem to be any answer except the one gray command: Endure.

He crossed the beach, slipping on rocks and swearing at the chill damp wind. His plunge into the water was an icy shock which only faded with violent swimming. But when he came out, he was tingling with wakefulness.

Romeo, he thought, toweling himself vigorously, *was an ass. Psychological troubles are no excuse for losing your appetite. In fact, they should heighten the old reliable pleasures. Mercutio was the real hero of that play.*

He picked his way toward the tent, thinking of bacon and eggs. As he mounted the steep, rocky bank, he paused, scowling. A small air-boat had landed next to his own. *Damn! I don't feel like being polite to anybody.* But when he saw the figure which stood beside it, he broke into a run.

Jeanne Donner waited for him, gravely as a child. When he stood before her, she met his gaze steadily, mute, and it was he who looked away.

"How did you find me?" he whispered at last. He thought the fury of his heartbeat must soon break his ribs. "I dropped out of sight pretty thoroughly."

"It wasn't easy," she answered, smiling a little. "After the U.N. pilot took us back to the States, I pestered the life out of everyone concerned. Finally one of them forgot privacy laws and told me—I suppose on the theory that you would take care of the nuisance. I've been landing at every isolated spot in the park for the last two days. I knew you'd want to be alone."

"Rosenberg—?"

"He agreed to accept hypno-conditioning for a nice payment—since he was sure he'd never learn the secret anyway. Now he's forgotten that there ever was another Stefan Rostomily. I refused, of course."

"Well—" His voice trailed off. Finally he looked at her again and said harshly: "Yes, I've played a filthy trick on you. The whole Service has, I guess. Only it's a secret which men have been killed for learning."

She smiled again, looking up at him with a lilting challenge in her eyes. "Go ahead," she invited.

His hands dropped. "No. You've got a right to know this. I should never have—oh, well, skip it. We aren't complete fanatics.

An organization which drew the line nowhere in reaching its aims wouldn't be worth having around!"

"Thank you," she breathed.

"Nothing to thank me for. You've probably guessed the basis of the secret already, if you know who Rostomily was."

"And what he was. Yes, I think I know. But tell me."

"They needed a lot of agents for the Service—agents who could meet specifications. Somebody got acquainted with Rostomily while he was still on Earth. He himself wasn't trained, or interested in doing such work, but his heredity was wanted—the pattern of genes and chromosomes. Fourre had organized his secret research laboratories. That wasn't hard to do, in the Years of Madness. Exogenesis of a fertilized ovum was already an accomplished fact. It was only one step further to take a few complete cells from Rostomily and use them as—as a chromosome source.

"We Brothers, all of us, we're completely human. Except that our hereditary pattern is derived entirely from one person instead of from two and, therefore, duplicates its prototype exactly. There are thousands of us by now, scattered around the Solar System. I'm one of the oldest. There are younger ones coming up to carry on."

"Exogenesis—" She couldn't repress a slight shudder.

"It has a bad name, yes. But that was only because of the known experiments which were performed, with their prenatal probing. Naturally that would produce psychotics. *Our* artificial wombs are safer and more serene even than the natural kind."

She nodded then, the dark wings of her hair falling past the ivory planes of her cheeks. "I understand. I see how it must be—you can tell me the details later. And I see why. Fourre needed supermen. The world was too chaotic and violent—it still is—for anything less than a brotherhood of supermen."

"Oh—look now!"

"No, I mean it. You aren't the entire Service, or even a majority of it. But you're the crack agents, the sword-hand." Suddenly she smiled, lighting up the whole universe, and gripped his arm. Her fingers were cool and slender against his flesh. "And how wonderful it is! Remember *King Henry the Fifth?*"

The words whispered from him:

"*And Crispin Crispian shall ne'er go by,*

From this day to the ending of the world,
But we in it shall be remembered,
We few, we happy few, we band of brothers—"

After a long moment, he added wryly: "But we can't look for fame. Not for a long time yet. The first requirement of a secret agent is secrecy, and if it were known that our kind exists half our usefulness would be gone."

"Oh, yes. I understand." She stood quiet for a while. The wind blew her dress and hair about her, fluttering them against the great clean expanse of sea and forest and sky.

"What are you going to do now?" she asked.

"I'm not sure. Naturally, we'll have to kill the story of a wanted murderer answering our description. That won't be hard. We'll announce his death resisting arrest, and after that—well, people forget. In a year or two the memory will be gone. But of course several of us, myself included, will need new identities, have to move to new homes. I've been thinking of New Zealand."

"And it will go on. Your work will go on. Aren't you ever lonely?"

He nodded, then tried to grin. "But let's not go on a crying jag. Come on and have breakfast with me. I'm a helluvva good egg frier."

"No, wait." She drew him back and made him face her. "Tell me— I want the truth now. You said, the last time, that you loved me. Was that true?"

"Yes," he said steadily. "But it doesn't matter. I was unusually vulnerable. I'd always been the cat who walks by himself, more so even than most of my Brothers. I'll get over it."

"Maybe I don't want you to get over it," she said.

He stood without motion for a thunderous century. A sea gull went crying overhead.

"You are Martin," she told him. "You aren't the same, not quite, but you're still Martin with another past. And Jimmy needs a father, and I need you."

He couldn't find words, but they weren't called for anyway.

THE BIG RAIN

✳ I ✳

The room was small and bare, nothing but a ventilator grill to relieve the drabness of its plastic walls, no furniture except a table and a couple of benches. It was hot, and the cold light of fluoros glistened off the sweat which covered the face of the man who sat there alone.

He was a big man, with hard bony features under close-cropped reddish-brown hair; his eyes were gray, with something chilly in them, and moved restlessly about the chamber to assess its crude homemade look. The coverall which draped his lean body was a bit too colorful. He had fumbled a cigarette out of his belt pouch and it smoldered between his fingers, now and then he took a heavy drag on it. But he sat quietly enough, waiting.

The door opened and another man came in. This one was smaller, with bleak features. He wore only shorts to whose waistband was pinned a star-shaped badge, and a needle-gun holstered at his side, but somehow he had a military look.

"Simon Hollister?" he asked unnecessarily.

"That's me," said the other, rising. He loomed over the newcomer, but he was unarmed; they had searched him thoroughly the minute he disembarked.

"I am Captain Karsov, Guardian Corps." The English was fluent, with only a trace of accent. "Sit down." He lowered himself to a bench. "I am only here to talk to you."

Hollister grimaced. "How about some lunch?" he complained. "I

265

haven't eaten for"—he paused a second—"thirteen hours, twenty-eight minutes."

His precision didn't get by Karsov, but the officer ignored it for the time being. "Presently," he said. "There isn't much time to lose, you know. The last ferry leaves in forty hours, and we have to find out before then if you are acceptable or must go back on it."

"Hell of a way to treat a guest," grumbled Hollister.

"We did not ask you to come," said Karsov coldly. "If you wish to stay on Venus, you had better conform to the regulations. Now, what do you think qualifies you?"

"To live here? I'm an engineer. Construction experience in the Amazon basin and on Luna. I've got papers to prove it, and letters of recommendation, if you'd let me get at my baggage."

"Eventually. What is your reason for emigrating?"

Hollister looked sullen. "I didn't like Earth."

"Be more specific. You are going to be narcoquizzed later, and the whole truth will come out. These questions are just to guide the interrogators, and the better you answer me now the quicker and easier the quiz will be for all of us."

Hollister bristled. "That's an invasion of privacy."

"Venus isn't Earth," said Karsov with an attempt at patience. "Before you were even allowed to land, you signed a waiver which puts you completely under our jurisdiction as long as you are on this planet. I could kill you, and the U.N. would not have a word to say. But we do need skilled men, and I would rather O.K. you for citizenship. Do not make it too hard for me."

"All right." Hollister shrugged heavy shoulders. "I got in a fight with a man. He died. I covered up the traces pretty well, but I could never be sure—sooner or later the police might get on to the truth, and I don't like the idea of corrective treatment. So I figured I'd better blow out whilst I was still unsuspected."

"Venus is no place for the rugged individualist, Hollister. Men have to work together, and be very tolerant of each other, if they are to survive at all."

"Yes, I know. This was a special case. The man had it coming." Hollister's face twisted. "I have a daughter—Never mind. I'd rather tell it under narco than consciously. But I just couldn't see letting a snake like that get 'corrected' and then walk around free again."

Defensively: "I've always been a rough sort, I suppose, but you've got to admit this was extreme provocation."

"That is all right," said Karsov, "if you are telling the truth. But if you have family ties back on Earth, it might lessen your usefulness here."

"None," said Hollister bitterly. "Not any more." The interview went on. Karsov extracted the facts skillfully: Hollister, Simon James; born Frisco Unit, U.S.A., of good stock; chronological age, thirty-eight Earth-years; physiological age, thanks to taking intelligent advantage of bio-medics, about twenty-five; Second-class education, major in civil engineering with emphasis on nuclear-powered construction machines; work record; psych rating at last checkup; et cetera, et cetera, et cetera. Somewhere a recorder took sound and visual impressions of every nuance for later analysis and filing.

At the end, the Guardian rose and stretched. "I think you will do," he said. "Come along now for the narcoquiz. It will take about three hours, and you will need another hour to recover, and then I will see that you get something to eat."

The city crouched on a mountainside in a blast of eternal wind. Overhead rolled the poisonous gray clouds; sometimes a sleet of paraformaldehyde hid the grim red slopes around, and always the scudding dust veiled men's eyes so they could not see the alkali desert below. Fantastically storm-gnawed crags loomed over the city, and often there was the nearby rumble of an avalanche, but the ledge on which it stood had been carefully checked for stability.

The city was one armored unit of metal and concrete, low and rounded as if it hunched its back against the shrieking steady gale. From its shell protruded the stacks of hundreds of outsize Hilsch tubes, swivel-mounted so that they always faced into the wind. It blew past filters which caught the flying dust and sand and tossed them down a series of chutes to the cement factory. The tubes grabbed the rushing air and separated fast and slow molecules; the cooler part went into a refrigeration system which kept the city at a temperature men could stand—outside, it hovered around the boiling point of water; the smaller volume of super-heated air was conducted to the maintenance plant where it helped run the city's pumps and generators. There were also nearly a thousand windmills, turning furiously and drinking the force of the storm.

None of this air was for breathing. It was thick with carbon dioxide; the rest was nitrogen, inert gases, formaldehyde vapor, a little methane and ammonia. The city devoted many hectares of space to hydroponic plants which renewed its oxygen and supplied some of the food, as well as to chemical purifiers, pumps and blowers. "Free as air" was a joke on Venus.

Near the shell was the spaceport where ferries from the satellite station and the big interplanetary ships landed. Pilots had to be good to bring down a vessel, or even take one up, under such conditions as prevailed here. Except for the landing cradles, the radio mast and the GCA shack in the main shell, everything was underground, as most of the city was.

Some twenty thousand colonists lived there. They were miners, engineers, laborers, technicians in the food and maintenance centers. There were three doctors, a scattering of teachers and librarians and similar personnel, a handful of police and administrators. Exactly fifteen people were employed in brewing, distilling, tavern-running, movie operation, and the other nonessential occupations which men required as they did food and air.

This was New America, chief city of Venus in 2051 A.D.

Hollister didn't enjoy his meal. He got it, cafeteria style, in one of the big plain messhalls, after a temporary ration book had been issued him. It consisted of a few vegetables, a lot of potato, a piece of the soggy yeast synthetic which was the closest to meat Venus offered—all liberally loaded with a tasteless basic food concentrate—a vitamin capsule, and a glass of flavored water. When he took out one of his remaining cigarettes, a score of eyes watched it hungrily. Not much tobacco here either. He inhaled savagely, feeling the obscure guilt of the have confronted with the have-not.

There were a number of people in the room with him, eating their own rations. Men and women were represented about equally. All wore coveralls or the standard shorts, and most looked young, but hard too, somehow—even the women. Hollister was used to female engineers and technicians at home, but here *everybody* worked.

For the time being, he stuck to his Earthside garments.

He sat alone at one end of a long table, wondering why nobody talked to him. You'd think they would be starved for a new face and word from Earth. Prejudice? Yes, a little of that, considering the political situation; but Hollister thought something more was involved.

Fear. They were all afraid of something.

When Karsov strolled in, the multilingual hum of conversation died, and Hollister guessed shrewdly at the fear. The Guardian made his way directly to the Earthling's place. He had a blocky, bearded man with a round smiling face in tow.

"Simon Hollister . . . Heinrich Gebhardt," the policeman introduced them. They shook hands, sizing each other up. Karsov sat down. "Get me the usual," he said, handing over his ration book.

Gebhardt nodded and went over to the automat. It scanned the books and punched them when he had dialed his orders. Then it gave him two trays, which he carried back.

Karsov didn't bother to thank him. "I have been looking for you," he told Hollister. "Where have you been?"

"Just wandering around," said the Earthling cautiously. Inside, he felt muscles tightening, and his mind seemed to tilt forward, as if sliding off the hypnotically imposed pseudo-personality which had been meant as camouflage in the narcoquiz. "It's quite a labyrinth here."

"You should have stayed in the barracks," said Karsov. There was no expression in his smooth-boned face; there never seemed to be. "Oh, well, I wanted to say you have been found acceptable."

"Good," said Hollister, striving for imperturbability.

"I will administer the oath after lunch," said Karsov. "Then you will be a full citizen of the Venusian Federation. We do not hold with formalities, you see—no time." He reached into a pocket and got out a booklet which he gave to Hollister. "But I advise you to study this carefully. It is a resume of the most important laws, insofar as they differ from Earth's. Punishment for infraction is severe."

Gebhardt looked apologetic. "It has to be," he added. His bass voice had a slight blur and hiss of German accent, but he was good at the English which was becoming the common language of Venus. "This planet vas made in hell. If ve do not all work together, ve all die."

"And then, of course, there is the trouble with Earth," said Karsov. His narrow eyes studied Hollister for a long moment. "Just how do people back there feel about our declaration of independence?"

"Well—" Hollister paused. Best to tell the unvarnished truth, he decided. "Some resentment, of course. After all the money we . . . they . . . put into developing the colonies—"

"And all the resources they took out," said Gebhardt. "Men vere planted on Venus back in the last century to mine fissionables, vich vere getting short efen then. The colonies vere made self-supporting because that vas cheaper than hauling supplies for them, vich vould haff been an impossible task anyvay. Some of the colonies vere penal, some vere manned by arbitrarily assigned personnel; the so-called democracies often relied on broken men, who could not find vork at home or who had been displaced by var. No, ve owe them notting."

Hollister shrugged. "I'm not arguing. But people do wonder why, if you wanted national status, you didn't at least stay with the U.N. That's what Mars is doing."

"Because we are . . . necessarily . . . developing a whole new civilization here, something altogether remote from anything Earth has ever seen," snapped Karsov. "We will still trade our fissionables for things we need, until the day we can make everything here ourselves, but we want as little to do with Earth as possible. Never mind, you will understand in time."

Hollister's mouth lifted in a crooked grin. There hadn't been much Earth could do about it; in the present stage of astronautics, a military expedition to suppress the nationalists would cost more than anyone could hope to gain even from the crudest imperialism. Also, as long as no clear danger was known to exist, it wouldn't have sat well with a planet sick of war; the dissension produced might well have torn the young world government, which still had only limited powers, apart.

But astronautics was going to progress, he thought grimly. Spaceships wouldn't have to improve much to carry, cheaply, loads of soldiers in cold sleep, ready to land when thermonuclear bombardment from the skies had smashed a world's civilization. And however peaceful Earth might be, she was still a shining temptation to the rest of the System, and it looked very much as if something was brewing here on Venus which could become ugly before the century was past.

Well—

"Your first assignment is already arranged," said Karsov. Hollister jerked out of his reverie and tried to keep his fists unclenched. "Gebhardt will be your boss. If you do well, you can look for speedy promotion. Meanwhile"—he flipped a voucher across—"here is the equivalent of the dollars you had along, in our currency."

Hollister stuck the sheet in his pouch. It was highway robbery, he knew, but he was in no position to complain and the Venusian government wanted the foreign exchange. And he could only buy trifles with it anyway; the essentials were issued without payment, the size of the ration depending on rank. Incentive bonuses were money, though, permitting you to amuse yourself but not to consume more of the scarce food or textiles or living space.

He reflected that the communist countries before World War Three had never gone this far. Here, everything was government property. The system didn't call itself communism, naturally, but it was, and probably there was no choice. Private enterprise demanded a fairly large economic surplus, which simply did not exist on Venus.

Well, it wasn't his business to criticize their internal arrangements. He had never been among the few fanatics left on Earth who still made a god of a particular economic set-up.

Gebhardt cleared his throat. "I am in charge of the atmosphere detail in this district," he said. "I am here on leafe, and vill be going back later today. Very glad to haff you, Hollister, ve are alvays short of men. Ve lost two in the last rock storm."

"Cheerful news," said the Earthman. His face resumed its hard woodenness. "Well, I didn't think Venus was going to be any bed of roses."

"It vill be," said Gebhardt. Dedication glowed on the hairy face. "Some day it vill be."

The oath was pretty drastic: in effect, Hollister put himself completely at the mercy of the Technic Board, which for all practical purposes was the city government. Each colony, he gathered, had such a body, and there was a federal board in this town which decided policy for the entire planet.

Anyone who wished to enter the government had to pass a series of rigid tests, after which there were years of apprenticeship and study, gradual promotion on the recommendation of seniors. The study was an exhausting course of history, psychotechnics, and physical science: in principle, thought Hollister, remembering some of the blubberheads who still got themselves elected at home, a good idea. The governing boards combined legislative, executive, and judicial functions, and totaled only a couple of thousand people for the whole world. It didn't seem like much for a nation of nearly two million, and the minimal paperwork surprised him—he had expected an omnipresent bureaucracy.

But of course they had the machines to serve them, recording everything in electronic files whose computers could find and correlate any data and were always checking up. And he was told pridefully that the schools were inculcating the rising generation with a tight ethic of obedience.

Hollister had supper, and returned to the Casual barracks to sleep. There were only a few men in there with him, most of them here on business from some other town. He was awakened by the alarm, whose photocells singled him out and shot forth a supersonic beam; it was a carrier wave for the harsh ringing in his head which brought him to his feet.

Gebhardt met him at an agreed-on locker room. There was a wiry, tough-looking Mongoloid with him who was introduced as Henry Yamashita. "Stow your fancy clothes, boy," boomed the chief, "and get on some TBI's." He handed over a drab, close-fitting coverall.

Hollister checked his own garments and donned the new suit wordlessly. After that there was a heavy plasticord outfit which, with boots and gloves, decked his whole body. Yamashita helped him strap on the oxygen bottles and plug in the Hilsch cooler. The helmet came last, its shoulderpiece buckled to the airsuit, but all of them kept theirs hinged back to leave their heads free.

"If somet'ing happens to our tank," said Gebhardt, "you slap that helmet down fast. Or maybe you like being embalmed. Haw!" His cheerfulness was more evident when Karsov wasn't around.

Hollister checked the valves with the caution taught him on Luna—his engineering experience was not faked. Gebhardt grunted approvingly. Then they slipped on the packs containing toilet kits, change of clothes, and emergency rations; clipped ropes, batteries, and canteens to their belts—the latter with the standard sucker tubes by which a man could drink directly even in his suit; and clumped out of the room.

A descending ramp brought them to a garage where the tanks were stored. These looked not unlike the sandcats of Mars, but were built lower and heavier, with a refrigerating tube above and a grapple in the nose. A mechanic gestured at one dragging a covered steel wagon full of supplies, and the three men squeezed into the tiny transparent cab.

Gebhardt gunned the engine, nodding as it roared. "O.K.," he said. "On ve go."

"What's the power source?" asked Hollister above the racket.

"Alcohol," answered Yamashita. "We get it from the formaldehyde. Bottled oxygen. A compressor and cooling system to keep the oxy tanks from blowing up on us—not that they don't once in a while. Some of the newer models use a peroxide system."

"And I suppose you save the water vapor and CO_2 to get the oxygen back," ventured Hollister.

"Just the water. There's always plenty of carbon dioxide." Yamashita looked out, and his face set in tight lines.

The tank waddled through the great air lock and up a long tunnel toward the surface. When they emerged, the wind was like a blow in the face. Hollister felt the machine shudder, and the demon howl drowned out the engine. He accepted the earplugs Yamashita handed him with a grateful smile.

There was dust and sand scudding by them, making it hard to see the mountainside down which they crawled. Hollister caught glimpses of naked fanglike peaks, raw slashes of ocher and blue where minerals veined the land, the steady march of dunes across the lower ledges. Overhead, the sky was an unholy tide of ragged, flying clouds, black and gray and sulfurous yellow. He could not see the sun, but the light around him was a weird hard brass color, like the light on Earth just before a thunderstorm.

The wind hooted and screamed, banging on the tank walls, yelling and rattling and groaning. Now and then a dull quiver ran through the land and trembled in Hollister's bones, somewhere an avalanche was ripping out a mountain's flanks. Briefly, a veil of dust fell so thick around them that they were blind, grinding through an elemental night with hell and the furies loose outside. The control board's lights were wan on Gebhardt's intent face, most of the time he was steering by instruments.

Once the tank lurched into a gully. Hollister, watching the pilot's lips, thought he muttered: "Damn! That vasn't here before!" He extended the grapple, clutching rock and pulling the tank and its load upward.

Yamashita clipped two small disks to his larynx and gestured at the same equipment hanging on Hollister's suit. His voice came thin but fairly clear: "Put on your talkie unit if you want to say anything." Hollister obeyed, guessing that the earplugs had a transistor arrangement powered by a piece of radioactive isotope which reproduced the vibrations in the throat. It took concentration to understand the language as they distorted it, but he supposed he'd catch on, fast enough.

"How many hours till nightfall?" he asked.

"About twenty." Yamashita pointed to the clock on the board, it was calibrated to Venus' seventy-two-hour day. "It's around one hundred thirty kilometers to the camp, so we should just about make it by sunset."

"That isn't very fast," said Hollister. "Why not fly, or at least build roads?"

"The aircraft are all needed for speed travel and impassable terrain, and the roads will come later," said Yamashita. "These tanks can go it all right—most of the time."

"But why have the camp so far from the city?"

"It's the best location from a supply standpoint. We get most of our food from Little Moscow, and water from Hellfire, and chemicals from New America and Roger's Landing. The cities more or less specialize, you know. They have to: there isn't enough iron ore and whatnot handy to any one spot to build a city big enough to do everything by itself. So the air camps are set up at points which minimize the total distance over which supplies have to be hauled."

"You mean action distance, don't you? The product of the energy and time required for hauling."

Yamashita nodded, with a new respect in his eyes. "You'll do," he said.

The wind roared about them. It was more than just the slow rotation of the planet and its nearness to the sun which created such an incessant storm; if that had been all, there would never have been any chance of making it habitable. It was the high carbon dioxide content of the air, and its greenhouse effect; and in the long night, naked arid rock cooled off considerably. With plenty of water and vegetation, and an atmosphere similar to Earth's, Venus would have a warm but rather gentle climate on the whole, the hurricanes moderated to trade winds; indeed, with the lower Coriolis force, the destructive cyclones of Earth would be unknown.

Such, at least, was the dream of the Venusians. But looking out, Hollister realized that a fraction of the time and effort they were expending would have made the Sahara desert bloom. They had been sent here once as miners, but there was no longer any compulsion on them to stay; if they asked to come back to Earth, their appeal could not be denied however expensive it would be to ship them all home.

Then why didn't they?

Well, why go back to a rotten civilization like—Hollister caught himself. Sometimes his pseudomemories were real enough in him to drown out the genuine ones, rage and grief could nearly overwhelm him till he recalled that the sorrow was for people who had never existed. The anger had had to be planted deep, to get by a narcoquiz, but he wondered if it might not interfere with his mission, come the day.

He grinned sardonically at himself. One man, caught on a planet at the gates of the Inferno, watched by a powerful and ruthless government embracing that entire world, and he was setting himself against it.

Most likely he would die here, and the economical Venusians would process his body for its chemicals as they did other corpses, and that would be the end of it as far as he was concerned.

Well, he quoted to himself, *a man might try.*

Gebhardt's camp was a small shell, a radio mast, and a shed sticking out of a rolling landscape of rock and sand; the rest was underground. The sun was down on a ragged horizon, dimly visible as a huge blood-red disk, when he arrived. Yamashita and Hollister had taken their turns piloting; the Earthman found it exhausting work, and his head rang with the noise when he finally stepped out into the subterranean garage.

Yamashita led him to the barracks. "We're about fifty here," he explained. "All men." He grinned. "That makes a system of minor rewards and punishments based on leaves to a city *very* effective."

The barracks was a long room with triple rows of bunks and a few tables and chairs; only Gebhardt rated a chamber of his own, though curtains on the bunks did permit some privacy. An effort had been made to brighten the place up with murals, some of which weren't bad at all, and the men sat about reading, writing letters, talking, playing games. They were the usual conglomerate of races and nationalities, with some interesting half-breeds; hard work and a parsimonious diet had made them smaller than the average American or European, but they looked healthy enough.

"Simon Hollister, our new sub-engineer," called Yamashita as they entered. "Just got in from Earth. Now you know as much as I do." He flopped onto a bunk while the others drifted over. "Go ahead. Tell all. Birth, education, hobbies, religion, sex life, interests, prejudices—they'll find it out anyway, and God knows we could use a little variety around here."

A stocky blond man paused suspiciously. "From Earth?" he asked slowly. "We've had no new people from Earth for thirty years. What did you want to come here for?"

"I felt like it," snapped Hollister. "That's enough!"

"So, a jetheading snob, huh? We're too good for you, I guess."

"Take it easy, Sam," said someone else.

"Yeah," a Negro grinned, "he might be bossin' you, you know."

"That's just it," said the blond man. "I was born here. I've been studying, and I've been on air detail for twenty years, and this bull walks right in and takes my promotion the first day."

Part of Hollister checked off the fact that the Venusians used the terms "year" and "day" to mean those periods for their own world, one shorter and one longer than Earth's. The rest of him tightened up for trouble, but others intervened. He found a vacant bunk and sat down on it, swinging his legs and trying to make friendly conversation. It wasn't easy. He felt terribly alone.

Presently someone got out a steel and plastic guitar and strummed it, and soon they were all singing. Hollister listened with half an ear.

* * *

"When the Big Rain comes, all the air will be good,
and the rivers all flow with beer,
with the cigarets bloomin' by the beefsteak bush,
and the ice-cream-bergs right here.
When the Big Rain comes, we will all be a-swillin'
of champagne, while the violin tree
plays love songs because all the gals will be willin',
and we'll all have a Big Rain spree!"

Paradise, he thought. *They can joke about it, but it's still the Paradise they work for and know they'll never see. Then why* do *they work for it? What is it that's driving them?*

After a meal, a sleep, and another meal, Hollister was given a set of blueprints to study. He bent his mind to the task, using all the powers which an arduous training had given it, and in a few hours reported to Gebhardt. "I know them," he said.

"Already?" The chief's small eyes narrowed. "It iss not vort' vile trying to bluff here, boy. Venus alvays callss it."

"I'm not bluffing," said Hollister angrily. "If you want me to lounge around for another day, O.K., but I know those specs by heart."

The bearded man stood up. There was muscle under his plumpness. "O.K., by damn," he said. "You go out vit me next trip."

That was only a few hours off. Gebhardt took a third man, a quiet grizzled fellow they called Johnny, and let Hollister drive. The tank hauled the usual wagonload of equipment, and the rough ground made piloting a harsh task. Hollister had used multiple transmissions before, and while the navigating instruments were complicated, he caught on to them quickly enough; it was the strain and muscular effort that wore him out.

Venus' night was not the pitchy gloom one might have expected. The clouds diffused sunlight around the planet, and there was also a steady flicker of aurora even in these middle latitudes. The headlamps were needed only when they went into a deep ravine. Wind growled around them, but Hollister was getting used to that.

The first airmaker on their tour was only a dozen kilometers from the camp. It was a dark, crouching bulk on a stony ridge, its intake funnel like the rearing neck of some archaic monster. They pulled up beside it, slapped down their helmets, and went one by one through the air lock. It was a standard midget type, barely large enough to hold one man, which meant little air to be pumped out and hence greater speed in getting through. Gebhardt had told Hollister to face the exit leeward; now the three roped themselves together and stepped around the tank, out of its shelter.

Hollister lost his footing, crashed to the ground, and went spinning away in the gale. Gebhardt and Johnny dug their cleated heels in and brought the rope up short. When they had the new man back on his feet, Hollister saw them grinning behind their faceplates. Thereafter he paid attention to his balance, leaning against the wind.

Inspection and servicing of the unit was a slow task, and it was hard to see the finer parts even in the headlights' glare. One by one, the various sections were uncovered and checked, adjustments made, full gas bottles removed and empty ones substituted.

It was no wonder Gebhardt had doubted Hollister's claim. The airmaker was one of the most complicated machines in existence. A thing meant to transform the atmosphere of a planet had to be.

The intake scooped up the wind and drove it, with the help of wind-powered compressors, through a series of chambers; some of them held catalysts, some electric arcs or heating coils maintaining temperature—the continuous storm ran a good-sized generator— and some led back into others in a maze of interconnections. The actual chemistry was simple enough. Paraformaldehyde was broken down and yielded its binding water molecules; the formaldehyde, together with that taken directly from the air, reacted with ammonia and methane—or with itself—to produce a whole series of hydrocarbons, carbohydrates, and more complex compounds for food, fuel and fertilizer; such carbon dioxide as did not enter other reactions was broken down by sheer brute force in an arc to oxygen and soot. The oxygen was bottled for industrial use; the remaining substances were partly separated by distillation—again using wind power, this time to refrigerate—and collected. Further processing would take place at the appropriate cities.

Huge as the unit loomed, it seemed pathetically small when you thought of the fantastic tonnage which was the total planetary atmosphere. But more of its kind were being built every day and scattered around the surface of the world; over a million already existed, seven million was the goal, and that number should theoretically be able to do the job in another twenty Earth-years.

That was theory, as Gebhardt explained over the helmet radio. Other considerations entered, such as the law of diminishing returns; as the effect of the machines became noticeable, the percentage of the air they could deal with would necessarily drop; then there was stratospheric gas, some of which apparently never got down to the surface; and the chemistry of a changing atmosphere had to be taken into account. The basic time estimate for this work had to be revised upward another decade.

There was oxygen everywhere, locked into rocks and ores, enough for the needs of man if it could be gotten out. Specially mutated bacteria were doing that job, living off carbon and silicon, releasing more gas than their own metabolisms took up; their basic energy source was the sun. Some of the oxygen recombined, of course, but not enough to matter, especially since it could only act on or near the surface and most of the bacterial gnawing went on far down. Already there was a barely detectable percentage of the element in the atmosphere. By the time the airmakers were finished, the bacteria would also be.

Meanwhile giant pulverizers were reducing barren stone and sand to fine particles which would be mixed with fertilizers to yield soil; and the genetic engineers were evolving still other strains of life which could provide a balanced ecology; and the water units were under construction.

These would be the key to the whole operation. There was plenty of water on Venus, trapped down in the body of the planet, and the volcanoes brought it up as they had done long ago on Earth. Here it was quickly snatched by the polymerizing formaldehyde, except in spots like Hellfire where machinery had been built to extract it from magma and hydrated minerals. But there was less formaldehyde in the air every day.

At the right time, hydrogen bombs were to be touched off in places the geologists had already selected, and the volcanoes would all wake up. They would spume forth plenty of carbon dioxide—though by that time the amount of the free gas would be so low that this would be welcomed—but there would be water too, unthinkable tons of water. And simultaneously aircraft would be sowing platinum catalyst in the skies, and with its help Venus' own lightning would attack the remaining poisons in the air. They would come down as carbohydrates and other compounds, washed out by the rain and leached from the sterile ground.

That would be the Big Rain. It would last an estimated ten Earth-years, and at the end there would be rivers and lakes and seas on a planet which had never known them. And the soil would be spread, the bacteria and plants and small animal life released. Venus would still be mostly desert, the rains would slacken off but remain heavy for centuries, but men could walk unclothed on this world and they could piece by piece make the desert green.

A hundred years after the airmen had finished their work, the reclaimed sections might be close to Earth conditions. In five hundred years, all of Venus might be Paradise.

To Hollister it seemed like a long time to wait.

✷ III ✷

He didn't need many days to catch on to the operations and be made boss of a construction gang. Then he took out twenty men and a train of supplies and machinery, to erect still another airmaker.

It was blowing hard then, too hard to set up the seal-tents which ordinarily provided a measure of comfort. Men rested in the tanks, side by side, dozing uneasily and smelling each other's sweat. They griped loudly, but endured. It was a lengthy trip to their site; eventually the whole camp was to be broken up and re-established in a better location, but meanwhile they had to accept the monotony of travel.

Hollister noticed that his men had evolved an Asian ability just to sit, without thinking, hour after hour. Their conversation and humour also suggested Asia: acrid, often brutal, though maintaining a careful surface politeness most of the time. It was probably more characteristic of this particular job than of the whole planet, though, and maybe they sloughed it off again when their hitches on air detail had expired and they got more congenial assignments.

As boss, he had the privilege of sharing his tank with only one man; he chose the wizened Johnny, whom he rather liked. Steering through a yelling sandstorm, he was now able to carry on a conversation—and it was about time, he reflected, that he got on with his real job.

"Ever thought of going back to Earth?" he asked casually.

"Back?" Johnny looked surprised. "I was born here."

"Well . . . going to Earth, then."

"What'd I use for passage money?"

"Distress clause of the Space Navigation Act. They'd have to give you a berth if you applied. Not that you couldn't repay your passage, with interest, in a while. With your experience here, you could get a fine post in one of the reclamation projects on Earth."

"Look," said Johnny in a flustered voice, "I'm a good Venusian. I'm needed here and I know it."

"Forget the Guardians," snapped Hollister, irritated. "I'm not going to report you. Why you people put up with a secret police anyway is more than I can understand."

"You've got to keep people in line," said Johnny. "We all got to work together to make a go of it."

"But haven't you ever thought it'd be nice to decide your own future and not have somebody to tell you what to do next?"

"It ain't just 'somebody.' It's the Board. They know how you and me fit in best. Sure, I suppose there are subversives, but I'm not one of them."

"Why don't the malcontents just run away, if they don't dare apply for passage to Earth? They could steal materials and make their own village. Venus is a big place."

"It ain't that easy. And supposin' they could and did, what'd they do then? Just sit and wait for the Big Rain? We don't want any free-loaders on Venus, mister."

Hollister shrugged. There was something about the psychology that baffled him. "I'm not preaching revolution," he said carefully. "I came here of my own free will, remember, I'm just trying to understand the set-up."

Johnny's faded eyes were shrewd on him. "You've always had it easy compared to us, I guess. It may look hard to you here. But

remember, we ain't never had it different, except that things are gettin' better little by little. The food ration gets upped every so often,
and we're allowed a dress suit now as well as utility clothes, and
before long there's goin' to be broadcast shows to the outposts—and
some day the Big Rain is comin'. Then we can all afford to take it free
and easy." He paused. "That's why we broke with Earth. Why should
we slave our guts out to make a good life for our grandchildren, if a
bunch of freeloaders are gonna come from Earth and fill up the planet then? It's *ours*. It's gonna be the richest planet men ever saw, and
it belongs to us what developed it."

Official propaganda line, thought Hollister. It sounded plausible
enough till you stopped to analyze. For one thing, each country still
had the right to set its own immigration policies. Furthermore, at the
rate Earth was progressing, with reclamation, population control,
and new resources from the oceans, by the time Venus was ripe there
wouldn't be any motive to leave home—an emigration which would
be too long and expensive anyway. For their own reasons, which he
still had to discover, the rulers of Venus had not mentioned all the
facts and had instead built up a paranoid attitude in their people.

The new airmaker site was the top of a ridge thrusting from a
boulder-strewn plain. An eerie copper-colored light seemed to tinge
the horizon with blood. A pair of bulldozers had already gone ahead
and scooped out a walled hollow in which seal-tents could be erected; Hollister's gang swarmed from the tanks and got at that job. Then
the real work began—blasting and carving a foundation, sinking
piers, assembling the unit on top.

On the fourth day the rock storm came. It had dawned with an
angry glow like sulfur, and as it progressed the wind strengthened
and a dirty rack of clouds whipped low overhead. On the third shift,
the gale was strong enough to lean against, and the sheet steel which
made the unit's armour fought the men as if it lived.

The blond man, Sam Robbins, who had never liked Hollister,
made his way up to the chief. His voice came over the helmet radio,
dim beneath static and the drumming wind: "I don't like this. Better
we take cover fast."

Hollister was not unwilling, but the delicate arc electrodes were
being set up and he couldn't take them down again; nor could he

leave them unprotected to the scouring drift of sand. "As soon as we get the shielding up," he said.

"I tell you, there's no time to shield 'em!"

"Yes, there is." Hollister turned his back. Robbins snarled something and returned to his labor.

A black wall, rust-red on the edges, was lifting to the east, the heaviest sandstorm Hollister had yet seen. He hunched his shoulders and struggled through the sleetlike dust to the unit. Tuning up his radio: "Everybody come help on this. The sooner it gets done, the sooner we can quit."

The helmeted figures swarmed around him, battling the thunderously flapping metal sheets, holding them down by main force while they were welded to the frame. Hollister saw lightning livid across the sky. Once a bolt flamed at the rod which protected the site. Thunder rolled and banged after it.

The wind slapped at them, and a sheet tore loose and went sailing down the hill. It struck a crag and wrapped itself around. "Robbins, Lewis, go get that!" cried Hollister, and returned attention to the piece he was clutching. An end ripped loose from his hands and tried to slash his suit.

The wind was so deafening that he couldn't hear it rise still higher, and in the murk of sand whirling about him he was nearly blind. But he caught the first glimpse of gale-borne gravel whipping past, and heard the terror in his earphones: "Rock storm!"

The voice shut up; orders were strict that the channel be kept clear. But the gasping men labored still more frantically, while struck metal rang and boomed.

Hollister peered through the darkness. "That's enough!" he decided. "Take cover!"

Nobody dropped his tools, but they all turned fast and groped down toward the camp. The way led past the crag, where Robbins and Lewis had just quit wrestling with the stubborn plate.

Hollister didn't see Lewis killed, but he did see him die. Suddenly his airsuit was flayed open, and there was a spurt of blood, and he toppled. The wind took his body, rolling it out of sight in the dust. *A piece of rock,* thought Hollister wildly. *It tore his suit, and he's already embalmed—*

The storm hooted and squealed about him as he climbed the sand wall. Even the blown dust was audible, hissing against his helmet. He fumbled through utter blackness, fell over the top and into the comparative shelter of the camp ground. On hands and knees, he crawled toward the biggest of the self-sealing tents.

There was no time for niceties. They sacrificed the atmosphere within, letting the air lock stand open while they pushed inside. Had everybody made it to some tent or other? Hollister wasn't sure, but sand was coming in, filling the shelter. He went over and closed the lock. Somebody else started the pump, using bottled nitrogen to maintain air pressure and flush out the poisons. It seemed like a long time before the oxygen containers could be opened.

Hollister took off his helmet and looked around. The tent was half filled by seven white-faced men standing in the dust. The single fluorotube threw a cold light on their sweating bodies and barred the place with shadows. Outside, the wind bellowed.

"Might as well be comfortable," said Johnny in a small voice, and began shucking his airsuit. "If the tent goes, we're all done for anyhow." He sat down on the ground and checked his equipment methodically. Then he took a curved stone and spat on it and began scouring his faceplate to remove the accumulated scratches in its hard plastic. One by one the others imitated him.

"You there!"

Hollister looked up from his own suit. Sam Robbins stood before him. The man's eyes were red and his mouth worked.

"You killed Jim Lewis."

There was murder here. Hollister raised himself till he looked down at the Venusian. "I'm sorry he's dead," he replied, trying for quietness. "He was a good man. But these things will happen."

Robbins shuddered. "You sent him down there where the gravel got him. I was there, too. Was it meant for me?"

"Nobody could tell where that chunk was going to hit," said Hollister mildly. "I could just as easily have been killed."

"I *told* you to quit half an hour before the things started."

"We couldn't quit then without ruining all our work. Sit down, Robbins. You're overtired and scared."

The men were very still sitting and watching in the thick damp heat of the tent. Thunder crashed outside.

"You rotten Earthling—" Robbins' fist lashed out. It caught

Hollister on the cheekbone and he stumbled back, shaking a dazed head. Robbins advanced grinning.

Hollister felt a cold viciousness of rage. It was his pseudo-personality, he realized dimly, but no time to think of that now. As Robbins closed in, he crouched and punched for the stomach.

Hard muscle met him. Robbins clipped him on the jaw. Hollister tried an uppercut, but it was skillfully blocked. This man knew how to fight.

Hollister gave him another fusillade in the belly. Robbins grunted and rabbit-punched. Hollister caught it on his shoulder, reached up, grabbed an arm, and whirled his enemy over his head. Robbins hit a bunkframe that buckled under him.

He came back, dizzy but game. Hollister was well trained in combat. But it took him a good ten minutes to stretch his man bleeding on the ground.

Panting, he looked about him. There was no expression on the faces that ringed him in. "Anybody else?" he asked hoarsely.

"No, boss," said Johnny. "You're right, o' course. I don't think nobody else here wants twenty lashes back at base."

"Who said—" Hollister straightened, blinking. "Lashes?"

"Why, sure. This was mutiny, you know. It's gotta be punished."

Hollister shook his head. "Too barbaric. Correction—"

"Look, boss," said Johnny, "you're a good engineer but you don't seem to understand much about Venus yet. We ain't got the time or the manpower or the materials to spend on them there corrective jails. A bull what don't keep his nose clean gets the whip or the sweatbox, and then back to the job. The really hard cases go to the uranium mines at Lucifer." He shivered, even in the dense heat.

Hollister frowned. "Not a bad system," he said, to stay in character. "But I think Robbins here has had enough. I'm not going to report him if he behaves himself from now on, and I'll trust the rest of you to cooperate."

They mumbled assent. He wasn't sure whether they respected him for it or not, but the boss was boss. Privately, he suspected that the Boards must frame a lot of men, or at least sentence them arbitrarily for minor crimes, to keep the mines going; there didn't seem to be enough rebellion in the Venusian character to supply them otherwise.

Chalk up another point for the government. The score to settle was getting rather big.

✳ IV ✳

Time was hard to estimate on Venus; it wasn't only that they had their own calendar here, but one day was so much like another. Insensibly and despite himself, Hollister began sliding into the intellectual lethargy of the camp. He had read the few books—and with his trained memory, he could only read a book once—and he knew every man there inside out, and he had no family in one of the cities to write to and think about. The job itself presented a daily challenge, no two situations were ever quite the same and occasionally he came near death, but outside of it there was a tendency to stagnate.

The other two engineers, Gebhardt and Yamashita, were pleasant company. The first was from Hörselberg, which had been a German settlement and still retained some character of its own, and he had interesting stories to tell of it; the second, though of old Venus-American stock, was mentally agile for a colonist, had read more than most and had a lively interest in the larger world of the Solar System. But even the stimulation they offered wore a little thin in six months or so.

The region spun through a "winter" that was hardly different from summer except in having longer nights, and the sterile spring returned, and the work went on. Hollister's time sense ticked off days with an accuracy falling within a few seconds, and he wondered how long he would be kept here and when he would get a chance to report to his home office. That would be in letters ostensibly to friends, which one of the spaceships would carry back; he knew censors would read them first, but his code was keyed to an obscure eighteenth-century book he was certain no one on Venus had ever heard of.

Already he knew more about this planet than anyone on Earth. It had always been too expensive to send correspondents here, and the last couple of U.N. representatives hadn't found much to tell. The secretiveness toward Earthmen might be an old habit, going back to the ultra-nationalistic days of the last century. Colony A and Colony B, of two countries which at home might not be on speaking terms, were not supposed to give aid and comfort to each other; but on Venus such artificial barriers had to go if anyone was to survive. Yamashita told with relish how prospectors from Little Moscow and Trollen had worked together and divided up their finds. But of course, you couldn't let your nominal rulers know—

Hollister was beginning to realize that the essential ethos of Venus was, indeed, different from anything which existed on Earth. It had to be, the landscape had made it so. Man was necessarily a more collective creature than at home. That helped explain the evolution of the peculiar governmental forms and the patience of the citizenry toward the most outrageous demands. Even the dullest laborer seemed to live in the future.

Our children and grandchildren will build the temples, read the books, write the music. Ours is only to lay the foundation.

And was that why they stuck here, instead of shipping back and turning the whole job over to automatic machinery and a few paid volunteers? They had been the lonely, the rejected, the dwellers in outer darkness, for a long time; now they could not let go of their fierce and angry pride, even when there was no more need for it. Hollister thought about Ireland. Man is not a logical animal.

Still, there were features of Venusian society that struck him as unnecessary and menacing. Something would have to be done about them, though as yet he wasn't sure what it would be.

He worked, and he gathered impressions and filed them away, and he waited. And at last the orders came through. This camp had served its purpose, it was to be broken up and replanted elsewhere, but first its personnel were to report to New America and get a furlough. Hollister swung almost gaily into the work of dismantling everything portable and loading it in the wagons. Maybe he finally was going to get somewhere.

He reported at the Air Control office with Gebhardt and Yamashita, to get his pay and quarters assignment. The official handed him a small card. "You've been raised to chief engineer's rank," he said. "You'll probably get a camp of your own next time."

Gebhardt pounded him on the back. "Ach, *sehr gut!* I recommended you, boy, you did fine, but I am going to miss you."

"Oh . . . we'll both be around for a while, won't we?" asked Hollister uncomfortably.

"Not I! I haff vife and kids, I hop the next rocket to Hʾrselberg."

Yamashita had his own family in town, and Hollister didn't want to intrude too much on them. He wandered off, feeling rather lonesome.

His new rating entitled him to private quarters, a tiny room with minimal furniture, though he still had to wash and eat publicly like everyone else except the very top. He sat down in it and began composing the planned letters.

There was a knock at the door. He fumbled briefly, being used to scanners at home and not used to doors on Venus, and finally said: "Come in."

A woman entered. She was young, quite good-looking, with a supple tread and spectacularly red hair. Cool green eyes swept up and down his height. "My name is Barbara Brandon," she said. "Administrative assistant in Air Control."

"Oh . . . hello." He offered her the chair. "You're here on business?"

Amusement tinged her impersonal voice. "In a way. I'm going to marry you."

Hollister's jaw did not drop, but it tried. "Come again?" he asked weakly.

She sat down. "It's simple enough. I'm thirty-seven years old, which is almost the maximum permissible age of celibacy except in special cases." With a brief, unexpectedly feminine touch: "That's Venus years, of course! I've seen you around, and looked at your record; good heredity there, I think. Pops O.K.'d it genetically— that's Population Control—and the Guardians cleared it, too."

"Um-m-m . . . look here." Hollister wished there were room to pace. He settled for sitting on the table and swinging his legs. "Don't I get any say in the matter?"

"You can file any objections, of course, and probably they'd be heeded; but you'll have to have children by someone pretty soon. We need them. Frankly, I think a match between us would be ideal. You'll be out in the field so much that we won't get in each other's hair, and we'd probably get along well enough while we are together."

Hollister scowled. It wasn't the morality of it—much. He was a bachelor on Earth, secret service Un-men really had no business getting married; and in any case the law would wink at what he had done on Venus if he ever got home. But something about the whole approach annoyed him.

"I can't see where you need rules to make people breed," he said coldly. "They'll do that anyway. You don't realize what a struggle it is on Earth to bring the population back down toward a sensible figure."

"Things are different here," answered Barbara Brandon in a dry tone. "We're going to need plenty of people for a long time to come, and they have to be of the right stock. The congenitally handicapped can't produce enough to justify their own existence; there's been a program of euthanasia there, as you may know. But the new people are also needed in the right places. This town, for instance, can only accommodate so much population increase per year. We can't send surplus children off to a special creche because there aren't enough teachers or doctors—or anything, so the mothers have to take care of all their own kids; or the fathers, if they happen to have a job in town and the mother is a field worker. The whole process has *got* to be regulated."

"Regulations!" Hollister threw up his hands. "Behold the bold frontiersman!"

The girl looked worried. "Careful what you say." She smiled at him with a touch of wistfulness. "It needn't be such a hindrance to you. Things are . . . pretty free except where the production of children is involved."

"I—this is kind of sudden." Hollister tried to smile back. "Don't think I don't appreciate the compliment. But I need time to think, adjust myself—Look, are you busy right now?"

"No, I'm off."

"All right. Put on your party clothes and we'll go out and have some drinks and talk the matter over."

She glanced shyly at the thin, colored coverall she wore. "These are my party clothes," she said.

Hollister's present rank let him visit another bar than the long, crowded room where plain laborers caroused. This one had private tables, decorations, music in the dim dusky air. It was quiet, the engineer aristocracy had their own code of manners. A few couples danced on a small floor.

He found an unoccupied table by the curving wall, sat down, and dialed for drinks and cigarettes. Neither were good enough to justify their fantastic cost but it had been a long time since he had enjoyed any luxuries at all. He felt more relaxed with them. The girl looked quite beautiful in the muted light.

"You were born here, weren't you, Barbara?" he asked after a while.

"Of course," she said. "You're the first immigrant in a long time. Used to be some deportees coming in every once in a while, but—"

"I know. 'Sentence suspended on condition you leave Earth.' That was before all countries had adopted the new penal code. Never mind. I was just wondering if you wouldn't like to see Earth—sometime."

"Maybe. But I'm needed here, not there. And I like it." There was a hint of defiance in the last remark.

He didn't press her. The luminous murals showed a soft unreal landscape of lakes and forests, artificial stars twinkled gently in the ceiling. "Is this what you expect Venus to become?" he asked.

"Something like this. Probably not the stars, it'll always be cloudy here but they'll be honest rain clouds. We should live to see the beginning of it."

"Barbara," he asked, "do you believe in God?"

"Why, no. Some of the men are priests and rabbis and whatnot in their spare time, but—no, not I. What about it?"

"You're wrong," he said. "Venus is your god. This is a religious movement you have here, with a slide rule in its hand."

"So—?" She seemed less assured, he had her off balance and the green eyes were wide and a little frightened.

"An Old Testament god," he pursued, "merciless, all-powerful, all-demanding. Get hold of a Bible if you can, and read Job and Ecclesiastes. You'll see what I mean. When is the New Testament coming . . . or even the prophet Micah?"

"You're a funny one," she said uncertainly. Frowning, trying to answer him on his own terms: "After the Big Rain, things will be easier. It'll be—" She struggled through vague memories. "It'll be the Promised Land."

"You've only got this one life," he said. "Is there any sound reason for spending it locked in these iron boxes, with death outside, when you could lie on a beach on Earth and everything you're fighting for is already there?"

She grabbed his hand where it lay on the table. Her fingers were cold, and she breathed fast. "No! Don't say such things! You're here too. You came here—"

Get thee behind me, Satan.

"Sorry." He lifted his glass. "Here's freefalling."

She clinked with him smiling shakily.

"There isn't any retirement on Venus, is there?" he asked.

"Not exactly. Old people get lighter work, of course. When you get too old to do anything . . . well, wouldn't you want euthanasia?"

He nodded, quite sincerely, though his exact meaning had gone by her. "I was just thinking of . . . shall we say us . . . rose-covered cottages, sunset of life. Darby and Joan stuff."

She smiled, and reached over to stroke his cheek lightly. "Thanks," she murmured. "Maybe there will be rose-covered cottages by the time we're that old."

Hollister turned suddenly, aware with his peripheral senses of the man who approached. Or maybe it was the sudden choking off of low-voiced conversation in the bar. The man walked very softly up to their table and stood looking down on them. Then he pulled out the extra chair for himself.

"Hello, Karsov," said Hollister dully.

The Guardian nodded. There was a ghostly smile playing about his lips. "How are you?" he asked, with an air of not expecting a reply. "I am glad you did so well out there. Your chief recommended you very highly."

"Thanks," said Hollister, not hiding the chill in his voice. He didn't like the tension he could see in Barbara.

"I just happened by and thought you would like to know you will have a crew of your own next trip," said the policeman. "That is, the Air Control office has made a recommendation to me." He glanced archly at Barbara. "Did you by any chance have something to do with that, Miss Brandon? Could be!" Then his eyes fell to the cigarettes, and he regarded them pointedly till Barbara offered him one.

"Pardon me." Hollister held his temper with an effort and kept his voice urbane. "I'm still new here, lot of things I don't know. Why does your office have to pass on such a matter?"

"My office has to pass on everything," said Karsov.

"Seems like a purely technical business as long as my own record is clean."

Karsov shook his sleek head. "You do not understand. We cannot have someone in a responsible position who is not entirely trustworthy. It is more than a matter of abstaining from criminal acts. You have to be with us all the way. No reservations. That is what Psych Control and the Guardians exist for."

He blew smoke through his nose and went on in a casual tone: "I must say your attitude has not been entirely pleasing. You have made some remarks which could be . . . misconstrued. I am ready to allow for your not being used to Venusian conditions, but you know the law about sedition."

For a moment, Hollister savored the thought of Karsov's throat between his fingers. "I'm sorry," he said.

"Remember, there are recorders everywhere, and we make spot checks directly on people, too. You could be narcoquizzed again any time I ordered it. But I do not think that will be necessary just yet. A certain amount of grumbling is only natural, and if you have any genuine complaints you can file them with your local Technic Board."

Hollister weighed the factors in his mind. Karsov packed a gun, and—But too sudden a meekness could be no less suspicious. "I don't quite understand why you have to have a political police," he ventured. "It seems like an ordinary force should be enough. After all . . . where would an insurrectionist go?"

He heard Barbara's tiny gasp, but Karsov merely looked patient. "There are many factors involved," said the Guardian. "For instance, some of the colonies were not quite happy with the idea of being incorporated into the Venusian Federation. They preferred to stay with their mother countries, or even to be independent. Some fighting ensued, and they must still be watched. Then, too, it is best to keep Venusian society healthy while it is new and vulnerable to subversive radical ideas. And finally, the Guardian Corps is the nucleus of our future army and space navy."

Hollister wondered if he should ask why Venus needed military forces, but decided against it. The answer would only be some stock phrase about terrestrial imperialists, if he got any answer at all. He'd gone about far enough already.

"I see," he said. "Thanks for telling me."

"Would you like a drink, sir?" asked Barbara timidly.

"No," said Karsov. "I only stopped in on my way elsewhere. Work, always work." He got up. "I think you are making a pretty good adjustment, Hollister. Just watch your tongue . . . and your mind. Oh, by the way. Under the circumstances, it would be as well if you did not write any letters home for a while. That could be misunderstood. You may use one of the standard messages. They are much cheaper, too." He nodded and left.

Hollister's eyes followed him out. *How much does he know?*

"Come on," said Barbara. There was a little catch in her voice. "Let's dance."

Gradually they relaxed, easing into the rhythm of the music. Hollister dismissed the problem of Karsov for the time being, and bent mind and senses to his companion. She was lithe and slim in his arms, and he felt the stirrings of an old hunger in him.

The next Venus day he called on Yamashita. They had a pleasant time together, and arranged a party for later; Hollister would bring Barbara. But as he was leaving, the Venusian drew him aside.

"Be careful, Si," he whispered. "They were here a few hours after I got back, asking me up and down about you. I had to tell the truth, they know how to ask questions and if I'd hesitated too much it would have been narco. I don't think you're in any trouble, but be careful!"

Barbara had arranged her vacation to coincide with his—efficient girl! They were together most of the time. It wasn't many days before they were married. That was rushing things, but Hollister would soon be back in the field for a long stretch and—well—they had fallen in love. Under the circumstances, it was inevitable. Curious how it broke down the girl's cool self-possession, but that only made her more human and desirable.

He felt a thorough skunk, but maybe she was right. *Carpe diem.* If he ever pulled out of this mess, he'd just have to pull her out with him; meanwhile, he accepted the additional complication of his assignment. It looked as if that would drag on for years, anyhow; maybe a lifetime.

They blew themselves to a short honeymoon at a high-class—and expensive—resort by Thunder Gorge, one of Venus' few natural beauty spots. The atmosphere at the lodge was relaxed, not a Guardian in sight and more privacy than elsewhere on the planet. Psych Control was shrewd enough to realize that people needed an occasional surcease from all duty, some flight from the real world of sand and stone and steel. It helped keep them sane.

Even so, there was a rather high proportion of mental disease. It was a taboo subject, but Hollister got a doctor drunk and wormed the facts out of him. The psychotic were not sent back to Earth, as they could have been at no charge; they might talk too much. Nor were there facilities for proper treatment on Venus. If the most drastic procedures didn't restore a patient to some degree of usefulness in a short time—they had even revived the barbarism of prefrontal lobotomy!—he was quietly gassed.

"But it'll all be diff'rent af'er uh Big Rain," said the doctor. "My son ull have uh real clinic, he will."

More and more, Hollister doubted it.

A few sweet crazy days, and vacation's end was there and they took the rocket back to New America. It was the first time Hollister had seen Barbara cry.

He left her sitting forlornly in the little two-room apartment they now rated, gathering herself to arrange the small heap of their personal possessions, and reported to Air Control. The assistant super gave him a thick, bound sheaf of papers.

"Here are the orders and specs," he said. "You can have two days to study them." Hollister, who could memorize the lot in a few hours, felt a leap of gladness at the thought of so much free time. The official leaned back in his chair. He was a gnarled old man, retired to a desk after a lifetime of field duty. One cheek was puckered with the scars of an operation for the prevalent HR cancer; Venus had no germs, but prepared her own special death traps. "Relax for a minute and I'll give you the general idea."

He pointed to a large map on the wall. It was not very complete or highly accurate: surveying on this planet was a job to break a man's heart, and little had been done. "We're establishing your new camp out by Last Chance. You'll note that Little Moscow, Trollen, and Roger's Landing cluster around it at an average distance of two hundred kilometers, so that's where you'll be getting your supplies, sending men on leave, and so forth. I doubt if you'll have any occasion to report back here till you break camp completely in a couple of years."

And Barbara will be here alone, Barbara and our child whom I won't even see—

"You'll take your wagon train more or less along this route," went on the super, indicating a dotted line that ran from New America. "It's been gone over and is safe. Notice the eastward jog to Lucifer at the halfway point. That's to refuel and take on fresh food stores."

Hollister frowned, striving for concentration on the job. "I can't see that. Why not take a few extra wagons and omit the detour?"

"Orders," said the super.

Whose orders? Karsov's? I'll bet my air helmet!—but why?

"Your crew will be . . . kind of tough," said the old man. "They're mostly from Ciudad Alcazar, which is on the other side of the world. It was one of the stubborn colonies when we declared independence, had to be put down by force, and it's still full of sedition. These spigs are all hard cases who've been assigned to this hemisphere so they won't stir up trouble at home. I saw in your dossier that you speak Spanish, among other languages, which is one reason you're being given this bunch. You'll have to treat them rough, remember. Keep them in line."

I think there was more than one reason behind this.

"The details are all in your assignment book," said the super. "Report back here in two days, this time. O.K.—have fun!" He smiled, suddenly friendly now that his business was completed.

❋ V ❋

Darkness and a whirl of poison sleet turned the buildings into crouching black monsters, hardly to be told from the ragged snarl of crags which ringed them in. Hollister brought his tank to a grinding halt before a tower which fixed him with a dazzling floodlight eye. "Sit tight, Diego," he said, and slapped his helmet down.

His chief assistant, Fernandez, nodded a sullen dark head. He was competent enough, and had helped keep the unruly crew behaving itself, but remained cold toward his boss. There was always a secret scorn in his eyes.

Hollister wriggled through the airlock and dropped to the ground. A man in a reinforced, armorlike suit held a tommy-gun on him, but dropped the muzzle as he advanced. The blast of white light showed a stupid face set in lines of habitual brutality.

"You the airman come for supplies?" he asked.

"Yes. Can I see your chief?"

The guard turned wordlessly and led the way. Beyond the lock of the main shell was a room where men sat with rifles. Hollister was escorted to an inner office, where a middle-aged, rather mild-looking fellow in Guardian uniform greeted him. "How do you do? We had word you were coming. The supplies were brought to our warehouse and you can load them when you wish."

Hollister accepted a chair. "I'm Captain Thomas," the other continued. "Nice to have you. We don't see many new faces at Lucifer—not men you can talk to, anyway. How are things in New America?"

He gossiped politely for a while. "It's quite a remarkable installation we have here," he ended. "Would you like to see it?"

Hollister grimaced. "No, thanks."

"Oh, I really must insist. You and your chief assistant and one or two of the foremen. They'll all be interested, and can tell the rest of your gang how it is. There's so little to talk about in camp."

Hollister debated refusing outright and forcing Thomas to show his hand. But why bother? Karsov had given orders, and Thomas would conduct him around at gun point if necessary. "O.K., thanks," he said coldly. "Let me get my men bunked down first, though."

"Of course. We have a spare barracks for transients. I'll expect you in two hours . . . with three of your men, remember."

Diego Fernandez only nodded when Hollister gave him the news. The chief skinned his teeth in a bleak sort of grin. "Don't forget to 'oh' and 'ah,'" he said. "Our genial host will be disappointed if you don't, and he's a man I'd hate to disappoint."

The smoldering eyes watched him with a quizzical expression that faded back into blankness. "I shall get Gomez and San Rafael," said Fernandez. "They have strong stomachs."

Thomas received them almost unctuously and started walking down a series of compartments. "As engineers, you will be most interested in the mine itself," he said. "I'll show you a little of it. This is the biggest uranium deposit known in the Solar System."

He led them to the great cell block, where a guard with a shock gun fell in behind them. "Have to be careful," said Thomas. "We've got some pretty desperate characters here, who don't feel they have much to lose."

"All lifers, eh?" asked Hollister.

Thomas looked surprised. "Of course! We couldn't let them go back after what the radiation does to their germ plasm."

A man rattled the bars of his door as they passed. "I'm from New America!" His harsh scream bounded between steel walls. "Do you know my wife? Is Martha Riley all right?"

"Shut up!" snapped the guard, and fed him a shock beam. He lurched back into the darkness of his cell. His mate, whose face was disfigured by a cancer, eased him to his bunk.

Someone else yelled, far down the long white-lit rows. A guard came running from that end. The voice pleaded: "It's a nightmare. It's just a nightmare. The stuff's got intuh muh brain and I'm always dreamin' nightmares—"

"They get twitchy after a while," said Thomas. "Stuff *will* seep through the suits and lodge in their bodies. Then they're not much good for anything but pick-and-shovel work. Don't be afraid, gentlemen, we have reinforced suits for the visitors and guards."

These were donned at the end of the cell block. Beyond the double door, a catwalk climbed steeply, till they were on the edge of an excavation which stretched farther than they could see in the gloom.

"It's rich enough yet for open-pit mining," said Thomas, "though we're driving tunnels, too." He pointed to a giant scooper. Tiny shapes of convicts scurried about it. "Four-hour shifts because of the radiation down there. Don't believe those rumors that we aren't careful with our boys. Some of them live for thirty years."

Hollister's throat felt cottony. It would be so easy to rip off

Thomas' air hose and kick him down into the pit! "What about women prisoners?" he asked slowly. "You must get some."

"Oh, yes. Right down there with the men. We believe in equality on Venus."

There was a strangled sound in the earphones, but Hollister wasn't sure which of his men had made it.

"Very essential work here," said Thomas proudly. "We refine the ore right on the spot too, you know. It not only supplies such nuclear power as Venus needs, but exported to Earth it buys the things we still have to have from them."

"Why operate it with convict labor?" asked Hollister absently. His imagination was wistfully concentrated on the image of himself branding his initials on Thomas' anatomy. "You could use free men, taking proper precautions, and it would be a lot more efficient and economical of manpower."

"You don't understand." Thomas seemed a bit shocked. "These are enemies of the state."

I've read that line in the history books. Some state, if it makes itself that many enemies!

"The refinery won't interest you so much," said Thomas. "Standard procedure, and it's operated by nonpolitical prisoners under shielding. They get skilled, and become too valuable to lose. But no matter who a man is, how clever he is, if he's been convicted of treason he goes to the mine."

So this was a warning—or was it a provocation?

When they were back in the office, Thomas smiled genially. "I hope you gentlemen have enjoyed the tour," he said. "Do stop in and see me again sometime." He held out his hand. Hollister turned on his heel, ignoring the gesture, and walked out.

Even in the line of duty, a man can only do so much.

Somewhat surprisingly Hollister found himself getting a little more popular with his crew after the visit to Lucifer. The three who were with him must have seen his disgust and told about it. He exerted himself to win more of their friendship, without being too obtrusive about it: addressing them politely, lending a hand himself in the task of setting up camp, listening carefully to complaints about not feeling well instead of dismissing them all as malingering. That led to some trouble. One laborer who was obviously faking a stomach-ache was ordered back to the job and made an insulting crack. Hollister knocked him to the floor with a single blow. Looking around at the others present, he said slowly: "There will be no whippings in this camp, because I do not believe men should be treated thus. But I intend to remain chief and to get this business done." Nudging the fallen man with his foot: "Well, go on back to your work. This is forgotten also in the records I am supposed to keep."

He didn't feel proud of himself—the man had been smaller and weaker than he. But he had to have discipline, and the Venusians all seemed brutalized to a point where the only unanswerable argument was force. It was an inevitable consequence of their type of government, and boded ill for the future.

Somewhat later, his radio-electronics technie, Valdez—a soft-spoken little fellow who did not seem to have any friends in camp—found occasion to speak with him. "It seems that you have unusual ideas about running this operation, señor," he remarked.

"I'm supposed to get the airmakers installed," said Hollister. "That part of it is right on schedule."

"I mean with regard to your treatment of the men, señor. You are the mildest chief they have had. I wish to say that it is appreciated, but some of them are puzzled. If I may give you some advice, which is doubtless not needed, it would be best if they knew exactly what to expect."

Hollister felt bemused. "Fairness, as long as they do their work. What is so strange about that?"

"But some of us . . . them . . . have unorthodox ideas about politics."

"That is their affair, Señor Valdez." Hollister decided to make himself a little more human in the technie's eyes. "I have a few ideas of my own, too."

"Ah, so. Then you will permit free discussion in the barracks?"

"Of course."

"I have hidden the recorder in there very well. Do you wish to hear the tapes daily, or shall I just make a summary?"

"I don't want to hear any tapes," stated Hollister. "That machine will not be operated."

"But they might plan treason!"

Hollister laughed and swept his hand around the wall. "In the middle of *that*? Much good their plans do them!" Gently: "All of you may say what you will among yourselves. I am an engineer, not a secret policeman."

"I see, señor. You are very generous. Believe me, it is appreciated."

Three days later, Valdez was dead.

Hollister had sent him out with a crew to run some performance tests on the first of the new airmakers. The men came back agitatedly, to report that a short, sudden rock storm had killed the technie. Hollister frowned, to cover his pity for the poor lonely little guy. "Where is the body?" he asked.

"Out there, señor—where else?"

Hollister knew it was the usual practice to leave men who died in the field where they fell; after Venusian conditions had done their work, it wasn't worthwhile salvaging the corpse for its chemicals. But—"Have I not announced my policy?" he snapped. "I thought that you people, of all, would be glad of it. Dead men will be kept here, so we can haul them into town and have them properly buried. Does not your religion demand that?"

"But Valdez, señor—"

"Never mind! Back you go, at once, and this time bring him in." Hollister turned his attention to the problem of filling the vacancy. Control wasn't going to like him asking for another so soon; probably he couldn't get one anyway. Well, he could train Fernandez to handle the routine parts, and do the more exacting things himself.

He was sitting in his room that night, feeling acutely the isolation of a commander—too tired to add another page to his letter to Barbara, not tired enough to go to sleep. There was a knock on the door. His start told him how thin his nerves were worn. "Come in!"

Diego Fernandez entered. The chill white fluorolight showed fear in his eyes and along his mouth. "Good evening, Simon," he said tonelessly. They had gotten to the stage of first names, though they still addressed each other with the formal pronoun.

"Good evening, Diego. What is it?"

The other bit his lip and looked at the floor. Hollister did not try to hurry him. Outside, the wind was running and great jags of lightning sizzled across an angry sky, but this room was buried deep and very quiet.

Fernandez's eyes rose at last. "There is something you ought to know, Simon. Perhaps you already know it."

"And perhaps not, Diego. Say what you will. There are no recorders here."

"Well, then, Valdez was not accidentally killed. He was murdered."

Hollister sat utterly still.

"You did not look at the body very closely, did you?" went on Fernandez, word by careful word. "I have seen suits torn open by flying rocks. This was not such a one. Some instrument did it . . . a compressed-air drill, I think."

"And do you know why it was done?"

"Yes." Fernandez's face twisted. "I cannot say it was not a good deed. Valdez was a spy for the government."

Hollister felt a knot in his stomach. "How do you know this?"

"One can be sure of such things. After the . . . the Venusians had taken Alcazar, Valdez worked eagerly with their police. He had always believed in confederation and planetary independence. Then he went away, to some engineering assignment it was said. But he had a brother who was proud of the old hidalgo blood, and this brother sought to clear the shame of his family by warning that Valdez had taken a position with the Guardians. He told it secretly, for he was not supposed to, but most of Alcazar got to know it. The men who had fought against the invaders were sent here, to the other side of the world, and it is not often we get leave to go home even for a short while. But we remembered, and we knew Valdez when he appeared on this job. So when those men with him had a chance to revenge themselves, they took it."

Hollister fixed the brown eyes with his own. "Why do you tell me this?" he asked.

"I do not—quite know. Except that you have been a good chief. It would be best for us if we could keep you, and this may mean trouble for you."

I'll say! First I practically told Valdez how I feel about the government, then he must have transmitted it with the last radio report, and now he's dead. Hollister chose his words cautiously: "Have you thought that the best way I can save myself is to denounce those men?"

"They would go to Lucifer, Simon."

"I know." He weighed the factors, surprised at his own detached calm. On the one hand there were Barbara and himself, and his own mission; on the other hand were half a dozen men who would prove most valuable come the day—for it was becoming more and more clear that the sovereign state of Venus would have to be knocked down, the sooner the better.

Beyond a small ache, he did not consider the personal element; Un-man training was too strong in him for that. A melody skipped through his head. "*Here's a how-de-do—*" It was more than a few men, he decided; this whole crew, all fifty or so, had possibilities. A calculated risk was in order.

"I did not hear anything you said," he spoke aloud. "Nor did you ever have any suspicions. It is obvious that Valdez died accidentally— too obvious to question."

Fernandez's smile flashed through the sweat that covered his face. "Thank you, Simon!"

"Thanks to *you*, Diego." Hollister gave him a drink—the boss was allowed a few bottles—and sent him on his way.

The boss was also allowed a .45 magnum automatic, the only gun in camp. Hollister took it out and checked it carefully. What was that classic verdict of a coroner's jury, a century or more ago in the States? "An act of God under very suspicious circumstances." He grinned to himself. It was not a pleasant expression.

✶VI✶

The rocket landed three days later. Hollister, who had been told by radio to expect it but not told why, was waiting outside. A landing space had been smoothed off and marked, and he had his men standing by and the tanks and bulldozers parked close at hand. Ostensibly that was to give any help which might be needed; actually, he hoped they would mix in on his side if trouble started. Power-driven sand blasts and arc welders were potentially nasty weapons, and tanks and 'dozers could substitute for armored vehicles in a pinch. The gun hung at his waist.

There was a mild breeze, for Venus, but it drove a steady scud of sand across the broken plain. The angry storm-colored light was diffused by airborne dust till it seemed to pervade the land, and even through his helmet and earphones Hollister was aware of the windyammer and the remote banging of thunder.

A new racket grew in heaven, stabbing jets and then the downward hurtle of sleek metal. The rocket's glider wings were fully extended, braking her against the updraft, and the pilot shot brief blasts to control his yawing vessel and bring her down on the markings. Wheels struck the hard-packed sand, throwing up a wave of it; landing flaps strained, a short burst from the nose jet arched its back against the flier's momentum, and then the machine lay still.

Hollister walked up to it. Even with the small quick-type air lock, he had to wait a couple of minutes before two suited figures emerged. One was obviously the pilot; the other—

"Barbara!"

Her face had grown thin, he saw through the helmet plate, and the red hair was disordered. He pulled her to him, and felt his faceplate clank on hers. "Barbara! What brings you here? Is everything all right?"

She tried to smile. "Not so public. Let's get inside."

The pilot stayed, to direct the unloading of what little equipment had been packed along; a trip was never wasted. Fernandez could do the honors afterward. Hollister led his wife to his own room, and no words were said for a while.

Her lips and hands felt cold.

"What is it, Barbara?" he asked when he finally came up for air. "How do we rate this?"

She didn't quite meet his eyes. "Simple enough. We're not going to have a baby after all. Since you'll be in the field for a long time, and I'm required to be a mother soon, it . . . it wasn't so hard to arrange a leave for me. I'll be here for ten days."

That was almost an Earth month. The luxury was unheard-of. Hollister sat down on his bunk and began to think.

"What's the matter?" She rumpled his hair. "Aren't you glad to see me? Maybe you have a girl lined up in Trollen?"

Her tone wasn't quite right, somehow. In many ways she was still a stranger to him, but he knew she wouldn't banter him with just that inflection. Or did she really think— "I'd no such intention," he said.

"Of course not, you jethead! I trust you." Barbara stretched herself luxuriously. "Isn't this wonderful?"

Yeah . . . too wonderful. "Why do we get it?"

"I told you." She looked surprised. "We've got to have a child."

He said grimly, "I can't see that it's so all-fired urgent. If it were, it'd be easier, and right in line with the Board's way of thinking, to use artificial insemination." He stood up and gripped her shoulders and looked straight at her. "Barbara, why are you really here?"

She began to cry, and that wasn't like her either. He patted her and mumbled awkward phrases, feeling himself a louse. But something was very definitely wrong, and he had to find out what.

He almost lost his resolution as the day went on. He had to be outside most of that time, supervising and helping; he noticed that several of the men had again become frigid with him. Was that Karsov's idea—to drive a wedge between him and his crew by giving him an unheard-of privilege? Well, maybe partly, but it could not be the whole answer. When he came back, Barbara had unpacked and somehow, with a few small touches, turned his bleak little bedroom-office into a home. She was altogether gay and charming and full of hope.

The rocket had left, the camp slept, they had killed a bottle to celebrate and now they were alone in darkness. In such a moment of wonder, it was hard to keep a guard up.

"Maybe you appreciate the Board a little more," she sighed. "They aren't machines. They're human, and know that we are too."

"'Human' is a pretty broad term," he murmured, almost automatically. "The guards at Lucifer are human, I suppose."

Her hand stole out to stroke his cheek. "Things aren't perfect on Venus," she said. "Nobody claims they are. But after the Big Rain—"

"Yeah. The carrot in front and the stick behind, and on the burro trots. He doesn't stop to ask where the road is leading. I could show it by psycho-dynamic equations, but even an elementary reading of history is enough once a group gets power, it *never* gives it up freely."

"There was Kemal Atatürk, back around 1920, wasn't there?"

"Uh-huh. A very exceptional case: the hard-boiled, practical man who was still an idealist, and built his structure so well that his successors—who'd grown up under him—neither could nor wanted to continue dictatorship. It's an example which the U.N. Inspectorate on Earth has studied closely and tried to adapt, so that its own power won't some day be abused.

"The government of Venus just isn't that sort. Their tactics prove it. Venus has to be collective till the Big Rain, I suppose, but that doesn't give anyone the right to collectivize the minds of men. By the time this hell-hole is fit for human life, the government will be unshakably in the saddle. Basic principle of psychobiology: survival with least effort. In human society, one of the easiest ways to survive and grow fat is to rule your fellow men.

"It's significant that you've learned about Ataturk. How much have they told you about the Soviet Union? The state was supposed to wither away there, too."

"Would you actually . . . conspire to revolt?" she asked.

He slammed the brakes so hard that his body jerked. *Danger! Danger! Danger! How did I get into this? What am I saying? Why is she asking me?* With a single bound, he was out of bed and had snapped on the light.

Its glare hurt his eyes, and Barbara covered her face. He drew her hands away, gently but using his strength against her resistance. The face that looked up at him was queerly distorted; the lines were still there, but they had become something not quite human.

"Who put you up to this?" he demanded.

"No one . . . what are you talking about, what's wrong?"

"The perfect spy," he said bitterly. "A man's own wife."

"What do you mean?" She sat up, staring wildly through her tousled hair. "Have you gone crazy?"

"*Could* you be a spy?"

"I'm not," she gasped. "I swear I'm not."

"I didn't ask if you were. What I want to know is could you be a spy?"

"I'm not. It's impossible. I'm not—"She was screaming now, but the thick walls would muffle that.

"Karsov is going to send me to Lucifer," he flung at her. "Isn't he?"

"I'm not, I'm not, I'm not—"

He stabbed the questions at her, one after another, slapping when she got hysterical. The first two times she fainted, he brought her around again and continued; the third time, he called it off and stood looking down on her.

There was no fear or rage left in him, not even pity. He felt strangely empty. There seemed to be a hollowness inside his skull, the hollow man went through the motions of life and his brain still clicked rustily, but there was nothing inside, he was a machine.

The perfect spy, he thought. *Except that Karsov didn't realize Unmen have advanced psych training. 1 know such a state as hers when I see it.*

The work had been cleverly done, using the same drugs and machines and conditioning techniques which had given him his own personality mask. (No—not quite the same. The Venusians didn't know that a mind could be so deeply verbal-conditioned as to get by a narcoquiz; that was a guarded secret of the Inspectorate. But the principles were there.) Barbara did not remember being taken to the laboratories and given the treatment. She did not know she had been conditioned; consciously, she believed everything she had said, and it had been anguish when the man she loved turned on her.

But the command had been planted, to draw his real thoughts out of him. Almost, she had succeeded. And when she went back, a quiz would get her observations out of her in detail.

It would have worked, too, on an ordinary conspirator. Even if he had come to suspect the truth, an untrained man wouldn't have known just how to throw her conscious and subconscious minds into conflict, wouldn't have recognized her symptomatic reactions for what they were.

This tears it, thought Hollister. *This rips it wide open.* He didn't have the specialized equipment to mask Barbara's mind and send her back with a lie that could get past the Guardian psychotechnies. Already she knew enough to give strong confirmation to Karsov's suspicions. After he had her account, Hollister would be arrested and they'd try to wring his secrets out of him. That might or might not be possible, but there wouldn't be anything left of Hollister.

Not sending her back at all? No, it would be every bit as much of a giveaway, and sacrifice her own life to boot. Not that she might not go to Lucifer anyhow.

Well—

The first thing was to remove her conditioning. He could do that in a couple of days by simple hypnotherapy. The medicine chest held some drugs which would be useful. After that—

First things first. Diego can take charge for me while I'm doing it. Let the men think what they want. They're going to have plenty to think about soon.

He became aware of his surroundings again and of the slim form beneath his eyes. She had curled up in a fetal position, trying to escape. Emotions came back to him, and the first was an enormous compassion for her. He would have wept, but there wasn't time.

Barbara sat up in bed, leaning against his breast. "Yes," she said tonelessly. "I remember it all now."

"There was a child coming, wasn't there?"

"Of course. They . . . removed it." Her hand sought his. "You might have suspected something otherwise. I'm all right, though. We can have another one sometime, if we live that long."

"And did Karsov tell you what he thought about me?"

"He mentioned suspecting you were an Un-man, but not being sure. The Technic Board wouldn't let him have you unless he had good evidence. That—No, I don't remember any more. It's fuzzy in my mind, everything which happened in that room."

Hollister wondered how he had betrayed himself. Probably he hadn't; his grumblings had fitted in with his assumed personality, and there had been no overt acts. But still, it was Karsov's job to suspect everybody, and the death of Valdez must have decided him on drastic action.

"Do you feel all right, sweetheart?" asked Hollister.

She nodded, and turned around to give him a tiny smile. "Yes. Fine. A little weak, maybe, but otherwise fine. Only I'm scared."

"You have a right to be," he said bleakly. "We're in a devil of a fix."

"You *are* an Un-man, aren't you?"

"Yes. I was sent to study the Venusian situation. My chiefs were worried about it. Seems they were justified, too. I've never seen a nastier mess."

"I suppose you're right," she sighed. "Only what else could we do? Do you want to bring Venus back under Earth?"

"That's a lot of comet gas, and you'd know it if the nationalist gang hadn't been censoring the books and spewing their lies out since before you were born. This whole independence movement was obviously their work from the beginning, and I must say they've done a competent job; good psychotechnies among them. It's their way to power. Not that all of them are so cynical about it—a lot must have rationalizations of one sort of another—but that's what it amounts to.

"There's no such thing as Venus being 'under' Earth. If ready for independence—and I agree she is—she'd be made a state in her own right with full U.N. membership. It's written into the charter that she could make her own internal policy. The only restrictions on a nation concern a few matters of trade, giving up military forces and the right to make war, guaranteeing certain basic liberties, submitting to inspection, and paying her share of U.N. expenses—which are smaller than the cost of even the smallest army. That's all. Your nationalists have distorted the truth as their breed always does."

She rubbed her forehead in a puzzled way. He could sympathize: a lifetime of propaganda wasn't thrown off overnight. But as long as she was with his cause, the rest would come of itself.

"There's no excuse whatsoever for this tyranny you live under," he continued. "It's got to go."

"What would you have us do?" she asked. "This isn't Earth. We do things efficiently here, or we die."

"True. But even men under the worst conditions can afford the slight inefficiency of freedom. It's not my business to write a constitution for Venus, but you might look at how Mars operates. They also have to have requirements of professional competence for public schools—deadwood gets flunked out fast enough—and the graduates have to stand for election if they want policy-making posts. Periodic elections do not necessarily pick better men than an appointive system, but they keep power from concentrating in the leaders. The Martians also have to ration a lot of things, and forbid certain actions that would endanger a whole city, but they're free to choose their own residences, and families, and ways of thinking, and jobs. They're also trying to reclaim the whole planet, but they don't assign men to that work, they hire them for it."

"Why doesn't everyone just stay at home and do nothing?" she asked innocently.

"No work, no pay; no pay, nothing to eat. It's as simple as that. And when jobs are open in the field, and all the jobs in town are filled, men will take work in the field—as free men, free to quit if they wish. Not many do, because the bosses aren't little commissars.

"Don't you see, it's the *mass* that society has to regulate; a government has to set things up so that the statistics come out right. There's no reason to regulate individuals."

"What's the difference?" she inquired.

"A hell of a difference. Some day you'll see it. Meanwhile, though, something has to be done about the government of Venus—not only on principle, but because it's going to be a menace to Earth before long. Once Venus is strong, a peaceful, nearly unarmed Earth is going to be just too tempting for your dictators. The World Wars had this much value, they hammered it into our heads and left permanent memorials of destruction to keep reminding us that the time to cut out a cancer is when it first appears. Wars start for a variety of reasons, but unlimited national sovereignty is always the necessary and sufficient condition. I wish our agents had been on the ball with respect to Venus ten years ago; a lot of good men are going to die because they weren't."

"You might not have come here then," she said shyly.

"Thanks, darling." He kissed her. His mind whirred on, scuttling through a maze that seemed to lead only to his silent, pointless death.

"If I could just get a report back to Earth! That would settle the matter. We'd have spaceships landing U.N. troops within two years. An expensive operation, of doubtful legality perhaps, a tough campaign so far from home, especially since we wouldn't want to destroy any cities—but there'd be no doubt of the outcome, and it would surely be carried through; because it would be a matter of survival for us. Of course, the rebellious cities would be helpful, a deal could be made there—and so simple a thing as seizing the food-producing towns would soon force a surrender. You see, it's not only the warning I've got to get home, it's the utterly priceless military intelligence I've got in my head. If I fail, the Guardians will be on the alert, they may very well succeed in spotting and duping every agent sent after me and flinging up something for Earth's consumption. Venus is a long ways off—"

He felt her body tighten in his arms. "So you do want to take over Venus."

"Forget that hogwash, will you? What'd we want with this forsaken desert? Nothing but a trustworthy government for it. Anyway—" His exasperation became a flat hardness: "If you and I are to stay alive much longer, it has to be done."

She said nothing to that.

His mind clicked off astronomical data and the slide rule whizzed through his fingers. "The freighters come regularly on Hohmann 'A' orbits," he said. "That means the next one is due in eight Venus days. They've only got four-man crews, they come loaded with stuff and go back with uranium and thorium ingots which don't take up much room. In short, they could carry quite a few passengers in an emergency, if those had extra food supplies."

"And the ferries land at New America," she pointed out.

"Exactly. My dear, I think our only chance is to take over the whole city!"

It was hot in the barracks room, and rank with sweat. Hollister thought he could almost smell the fear, as if he were a dog. He stood on a table at one end, Barbara next to him, and looked over his assembled crew. Small, thin, swarthy, unarmed and drably clad, eyes wide with frightened waiting, they didn't look like much of an army. But they were all he had.

"Señores," he began at last, speaking very quietly, "I have called you all together to warn you of peril to your lives. I think, if you stand with me, we can escape, but it will take courage and energy. You have shown me you possess these qualities, and I hope you will use them now."

He paused, then went on: "I know many of you have been angry with me because I have had my wife here. You thought me another of these bootlickers to a rotten government"—that brought them to full awareness!—"who was being rewarded for some Judas act. It is not true. We all owe our lives to this gallant woman. It was I who was suspected of being hostile to the rulers, and she was sent to spy on me for them. Instead, she told me the truth, and now I am telling it to you.

"You must know that I am an agent from Earth. No, no, I am not an Imperialist. As a matter of fact, the Central American countries were worried about their joint colony, Ciudad Alcazar, your city. It was suspected she had not freely joined this confederation. There are other countries, too, which are worried. I came to investigate for them; what I have seen convinces me they were right."

He went on, quickly, and not very truthfully. He had to deal with their anti-U.N. conditioning, appeal to the nationalism he despised. (At that, it wouldn't make any practical difference if some countries on Earth retained nominal ownership of certain tracts on Venus; a democratic confederation would reabsorb those within a generation, quite peacefully.) He had to convince them that the whole gang was scheduled to go to Lucifer; all were suspected, and the death of Valdez confirmed the suspicion, and there was always a labor short-age in the mines. His psych training stood him in good stead; before long he had them rising and shouting. *I shoulda been a politician,* he thought sardonically.

". . . And are we going to take this outrage? Are we going to rot alive in that hell, and let our wives and children suffer forever? Or shall we strike back, to save our own lives and liberate Venus?"

When the uproar had subsided a little, he sketched his plan: a march on Lucifer itself, to seize weapons and gain some recruits, then an attack on New America. If it was timed right, they could grab the city just before the ferries landed, and hold it while all of them were embarked on the freighter—then off to Earth, and in a year or two a triumphant return with the army of liberation!

"If anyone does not wish to come with us, let him stay here. I shall compel no man. I can only use those who will be brave, and will obey orders like soldiers, and will set lives which are already forfeit at haz-ard for the freedom of their homes. Are you with me? Let those who will follow me stand up and shout 'Yes!'"

Not a man stayed in his seat; the timid ones, if any, dared not do so while their comrades were rising and whooping about the table. The din roared and rolled, bunk frames rattled, eyes gleamed murder from a whirlpool of faces. The first stage of Hollister's gamble had paid off well indeed, he thought; now for the rough part.

He appointed Fernandez his second in command and organized the men into a rough corps; engineering discipline was valuable here. It was late before he and Barbara and Fernandez could get away to discuss concrete plans.

"We will leave two men here," said Hollister. "They will send the usual radio reports, which I shall write in advance for them, so no one will suspect; they will also take care of the rocket when it comes for Barbara, and I *hope* the police will assume it crashed. We will send for them when we hold New America. I think we can take Lucifer by surprise, but we can't count on the second place not being warned by the time we get there."

Fernandez looked steadily at him. "And will all of us leave with the spaceship?" he asked.

"Of course. It would be death to stay. And Earth will need their knowledge of Venus."

"Simon, you know the ship cannot carry fifty men—or a hundred, if we pick up some others at Lucifer."

Hollister's face was wintry. "I do not think fifty will survive," he said.

Fernandez crossed himself, then nodded gravely. "I see. Well, about the supply problem—"

When he had gone, Barbara faced her husband and he saw a vague fright in her eyes. "You weren't very truthful out there, were you?" she asked. "I don't know much Spanish, but I got the drift, and—"

"All right!" he snapped wearily. "There wasn't time to use sweet reasonableness. I had to whip them up fast."

"They aren't scheduled for Lucifer at all. They have no personal reason to fight."

"They're committed now," he said in a harsh tone. "It's fifty or a hundred lives today against maybe a hundred million in the future. That's an attitude which was drilled into me at the Academy, and I'll never get rid of it. If you want to live with me, you'll have to accept that."

"I'll . . . try," she said.

✶VII✶

The towers bulked black through a whirl of dust, under a sky the color of clotted blood. Hollister steered his tank close, speaking into its radio: "Hello, Lucifer. Hello, Lucifer. Come in."

"Lucifer," said a voice in his earphones. "Who are you and what do you want?"

"Emergency. We need help. Get me your captain."

Hollister ground between two high gun towers. They had been built and manned against the remote possibility that a convict outbreak might succeed in grabbing some tanks; he was hoping their personnel had grown lazy with uneventful years. Edging around the main shell of the prison, he lumbered toward the landing field and the nearby radio mast. One by one, the twenty tanks of his command rolled into the compound and scattered themselves about it.

Barbara sat next to him, muffled in airsuit and closed helmet. Her gauntleted hand squeezed his shoulder, he could just barely feel the pressure. Glancing around to her stiffened face, he essayed a smile.

"Hello, there! Captain Thomas speaking. What are you doing?"

"This is Hollister, from the Last Chance air camp. Remember me? We're in trouble and need help. Landslip damn near wiped our place out." The Earthman drove his machine onto the field.

"Well, what are you horsing around like that for? Assemble your tanks in front of the main lock."

"All right, all right, gimme a chance to give some orders. The boys don't seem to know where to roost."

Now! Hollister slapped down the drive switch and his tank surged forward. "Hang on!" he yelled. "Thomas, this thing has gone out of control—Help!"

It might have gained him the extra minute he needed. He wasn't sure what was happening behind him. The tank smashed into the radio mast and he was hurled forward against his safety webbing. His hands flew—extend the grapple, snatch that buckling strut, drag it aside, and *push!*

The frame wobbled crazily. The tank stalled. Hollister yanked off his harness, picked up the cutting torch, whose fuel containers were already on his back, and went through the air lock without stopping to conserve atmosphere. Blue flame stabbed before him, he slid down the darkened extra faceplate and concentrated on his job. Get this beast down before it sent a call for help!

Barbara got the bull-like machine going again and urged it ahead, straining at the weakened skeleton. The mast had been built for flexibility in the high winds, not for impact strength. Hollister's torch roared, slicing a main support. A piece of steel clanged within a meter of him.

He dropped the torch and dove under the tank, just as the whole structure caved in.

"Barbara!" He picked himself out of the wreckage, looking wildly into the hurricane that blew around him. "Barbara, are you all right?"

She crawled from the battered tank and into his arms. "Our car won't go any more," she said shakily. The engine hood was split open by a falling beam and oil hissed from the cracked block.

"No matter. Let's see how the boys are doing—"

He led a run across the field, staggering in the wind. A chunk of concrete whizzed by his head and he dropped as one of the guard towers went by. Good boys! They'd gone out and dynamited it!

Ignoring the ramp leading down to the garage, Fernandez had brought his tank up to the shell's main air lock for humans. It was sturdily built, but his snorting monster walked through it. Breathable air gasped out. It sleeted a little as formaldehyde took up water vapor and became solid.

No time to check on the rest of the battle outside, you could only hope the men assigned to that task were doing their job properly. Hollister saw one of his tanks go up under a direct hit. All the towers weren't disabled yet. But he had to get into the shell.

"Stay here, Barbara!" he ordered. Men were swarming from their vehicles. He led the way inside. A group of uniformed corpses waited for him, drying and shriveling even as he watched. He snatched the carbines from them and handed them out to the nearest of his followers. The rest would have to make do with their tools till more weapons could be recovered.

Automatic bulkheads had sealed off the rest of the shell. Hollister blasted through the first one. A hail of bullets from the smoking hole told him that the guards within had had time to put on their suits.

He waved an arm. "Bring up Maria Larga!"

It took a while, and he fumed and fretted. Six partisans trundled the weapon forth. It was a standard man-drawn cart for semiportable field equipment, and Long Mary squatted on it: a motor-driven blower connected with six meters of hose, an air blast. This one had had an oxygen bottle and a good-sized fuel tank hastily attached to make a super flame thrower. Fernandez got behind the steel plate which had been welded in front as armor, and guided it into the hole. The man behind whooped savagely and turned a handle. Fire blew forth, and the compartment was flushed out.

There were other quarters around the cell block, which came next, but Hollister ignored them for the time being. The air lock in this bulkhead had to be opened the regular way, only two men could go through at a time, and there might be guards on the other side. He squeezed in with San Rafael and waited until the pump cleaned out the chamber. Then he opened the inner door a crack, tossed a home-made shrapnel grenade, and came through firing.

He stumbled over two dead men beyond. San Rafael choked and fell as a gun spat farther down the corridor. Hollister's .45 bucked in his hand. Picking himself up, he looked warily down the cruelly bright length of the block. No one else. The convicts were yammering like wild animals.

He went back, telling off a few men to cut the prisoners out of their cells, issue airsuits from the lockers, and explain the situation. Then he returned to the job of cleaning out the rest of the place.

It was a dirty and bloody business. He lost ten men in all. There were no wounded: if a missile tore open a suit, that was the end of the one inside. A small hole would have given time to slap on an emergency patch, but the guards were using magnum slugs.

Fernandez sought him out to report that an attempt to get away by rocket had been stopped, but that an indeterminate number of holdouts were in the refinery, which was a separate building. Hollister walked across the field, dust whirling about smashed machines, and stood before the smaller shell.

Thomas' voice crackled in his earphones: "You there! What is the meaning of this?"

That was too much. Hollister began to laugh. He laughed so long he thought perhaps he was going crazy.

Sobering, he replied in a chill tone: "We're taking over. You're trapped in there with nothing but small arms. We can blast you out if we must, but you'd do better to surrender."

Thomas, threateningly: "This place is full of radioactivity, you know. If you break in, you'll smash down the shielding—or we'll do it for you—and scatter the stuff everywhere. You won't live a week."

It might be a bluff—"All right," said Hollister with a cheerful note, "you're sealed in without food or water. We can wait. But I thought you'd rather save your own lives."

"You're insane! You'll be wiped out—"

"That's our affair. Any time you want out, pick up the phone and call the office. You'll be locked in the cells with supplies enough for a while when we leave." Hollister turned and walked away.

He spent the next few hours reorganizing; he had to whip the convicts into line, though when their first exuberance had faded they were for the most part ready to join him. Suddenly his army had swelled to more than two hundred. The barracks were patched up and made habitable, munitions were found and passed about, the transport and supply inventoried. Then word came that Thomas' handful were ready to surrender. Hollister marched them into the cell block and assigned some convicts to stand watch.

He had had every intention of abiding by his agreement, but when he was later wakened from sleep with the news that his guards had literally torn the prisoners apart, he didn't have the heart to give them more than a dressing down.

"Now," he said to his council of war, "we'd better get rolling again. Apparently we were lucky enough so that no word of this has leaked out, but it's a long way yet to New America."

"We have not transportation for more than a hundred," said Fernandez.

"I know. We'll take the best of the convicts; the rest will just have to stay behind. They *may* be able to pull the same trick on the next supply train that our boys in Last Chance have ready for the rocket— or they may not. In any event, I don't really hope they can last out, or that we'll be able to take the next objective unawares—but don't tell anyone that."

"I suppose not," said Fernandez somberly, "but it is a dirty business."

"War is always a dirty business," said Hollister.

He lost a whole day organizing his new force. Few if any of the men knew how to shoot, but the guns were mostly recoilless and automatic so he hoped some damage could be done; doctrine was to revert to construction equipment, which they did know how to use, in any emergency. His forty Latins were a cadre of sorts, distributed among the sixty convicts in a relationship equivalent to that between sergeant and private. The whole unit was enough to make any military man break out in a cold sweat, but it was all he had.

Supply wagons were reloaded and machine guns mounted on a few of the tanks. He had four Venusian days to get to New America and take over—and if the rebels arrived too soon, police reinforcements would pry them out again, and if the radio-control systems were ruined in the fighting, the ferries couldn't land.

It was not exactly a pleasant situation.

The first rocket was sighted on the fifth day of the campaign. It ripped over, crossing from horizon to horizon in a couple of minutes, but there was little doubt that it had spotted them. Hollister led his caravan off the plain, into broken country which offered more cover but would slow them considerably. Well, they'd just have to keep going day and night.

The next day it was an armored, atomic-powered monster which lumbered overhead, supplied with enough energy to go slowly and even to hover for a while. In an atmosphere without oxygen and always riven by storms, the aircraft of Earth weren't possible—no helicopters, no leisurely airboats; but a few things like this one had been built as emergency substitutes. Hollister tuned in his radio, sure it was calling to them.

"Identify yourselves! This is the Guardian Corps." Hollister adapted his earlier lie, not expecting belief—but every minute he stalled, his tank lurched forward another hundred meters or so.

The voice was sarcastic: "And of course, you had nothing to do with the attack on Lucifer?"

"What attack?"

"That will do! Go out on the plain and set up camp till we can check on you."

"Of course," said Hollister meekly. "Signing off." From now on, it was strict radio silence in his army. He'd gained a good hour, though, since the watchers wouldn't be sure till then that he was disobeying— and a lovely dust storm was blowing up.

Following plan, the tanks scattered in pairs, each couple for itself till they converged on New America at the agreed time. Some would break down, some would be destroyed en route, some would come late—a few might even arrive disastrously early—but there was no choice. Hollister was reasonably sure none would desert him; they were all committed past that point.

He looked at Barbara. Her face was tired and drawn, the red hair hung lusterless and tangled to her shoulders, dust and sweat streaked her face, but he thought she was very beautiful. "I'm sorry to have dragged you into this," he said.

"It's all right, dear. Of course I'm scared, but I'm still glad."

He kissed her for a long while and then slapped his helmet down with a savage gesture.

The first bombs fell toward sunset. Hollister saw them as flashes through the dust, and felt their concussion rumble in the frame of his tank. He steered into a narrow, overhung gulch, his companion vehicle nosing close behind. There were two convicts in it—Johnson and Waskowicz—pretty good men, he thought, considering all they had been through.

Dust and sand were his friends, hiding him even from the infrared 'scopes above which made nothing of mere darkness. The rough country would help a lot, too. It was simply a matter of driving day and night, sticking close to bluffs and gullies, hiding under attack and then driving some more. He was going to lose a number of his units, but thought the harassing would remain aerial till they got close to New America. The Guardians wouldn't risk their heavy stuff unnecessarily at any great distance from home.

✳VIII✳

The tank growled around a high pinnacle and faced him without warning. It was a military vehicle, and cannons swiveled to cover his approach.

Hollister gunned his machine and drove directly up the pitted road at the enemy. A shell burst alongside him, steel splinters rang on armor. Coldly, he noted for possible future reference the relatively primitive type of Venusian war equipment: no tracker shells, no Rovers. He had already planned out what to do in an encounter like this, and told his men the idea—now it had happened to him.

The Guardian tank backed, snarling. It was not as fast or as maneuverable as his, it was meant for work close to cities where ground had been cleared. A blast of high-caliber machine-gun bullets ripped through the cab, just over his head. Then he struck. The shock jammed him forward even as his grapple closed jaws on the enemy's nearest tread.

"Out!" he yelled. Barbara snatched open the air lock and fell to the stones below. Hollister was after her. He flung a glance behind. His other tank was an exploded ruin, canted to one side, but a single figure was crawling from it, rising, zigzagging toward him. There was a sheaf of dynamite sticks in one hand. The man flopped as the machine gun sought him and wormed the last few meters. Waskowicz. "They got Sam," he reported, huddling against the steel giant with his companions. "Shall we blast her?"

Hollister reflected briefly. The adversary was immobilized by the transport vehicle that clutched it bulldog fashion. He himself was perfectly safe this instant, just beneath the guns. "I've got a better notion. Gimme a boost."

He crawled up on top, to the turret lock. "O.K., hand me that torch. I'm going to cut my way in!"

The flame roared, biting into metal. Hollister saw the lock's outer door move. So—just as he had expected—the lads inside wanted out! He paused. A suited arm emerged with a grenade. Hollister's torch slashed down. Barbara made a grab for the tumbling missile and failed. Waskowicz tackled her, landing on top. The thing went off.

Was she still alive—? Hollister crouched so that the antenna of his suit radio pocked into the lock. "Come out if you want to live. Otherwise I'll burn you out."

Sullenly, the remaining three men appeared, hands in the air. Hollister watched them slide to the ground, covering them with his pistol. His heart leaped within him when he saw Barbara standing erect. Waskowicz was putting an adhesive patch on his suit where a splinter had ripped it.

"You O.K.?" asked Hollister.

"Yeah," grunted the convict. "Pure dumb luck. Now what?"

"Now we got us one of their own tanks. Somebody get inside and find some wire or something to tie up the Terrible Three here. And toss out the fourth."

"That's murder!" cried one of the police. "We've only got enough oxy for four hours in these suits—"

"Then you'll have to hope the battle is over by then," said Hollister unsympathetically. He went over and disentangled the two machines.

The controls of the captured tank were enough like those of the ordinary sort for Barbara to handle. Hollister gave Waskowicz a short lecture on the care and feeding of machine guns, and sat up by the 40 mm. cannon himself; perforce, they ignored the 20. They closed the lock but didn't bother to replenish the air inside; however, as Hollister drove up the mountainside, Waskowicz recharged their oxygen bottles from the stores inside the vehicle.

The battle was already popping when they nosed up onto the ledge and saw the great sweep of the city. Drifting dust limited his vision, but Hollister saw his own machines and the enemy's. Doctrine was to ram and grapple the military tank, get out and use dynamite or torches, and then worm toward the colony's main air lock. It might have to be blown open, but bulkheads should protect the civilians within.

An engineer tank made a pass at Hollister's. He turned aside, realizing that his new scheme had its own drawbacks. Another police machine came out of the dust; its guns spoke, the engineers went up in a flash and a bang, and then it had been hit from behind. Hollister set his teeth and went on. It was the first time he had seen anything like war; he had an almost holy sense of his mission to prevent this from striking Earth again.

The whole operation depended on his guess that there wouldn't be many of the enemy. There were only a few Guardians in each town, who wouldn't have had time or reserves enough to bring in a lot of reinforcements; and tanks couldn't be flown in. But against their perhaps lesser number was the fact that they would fight with tenacity and skill. Disciplined as engineers and convicts were, they simply did not have the training—even the psychological part of it which turns frightened individuals into a single selfless unit. They would tend to make wild attacks and to panic when the going got rough—which it was already.

He went on past the combat, towards the main air lock. Dim

shapes began to appear through scudding dust. Half a dozen mobile cannon were drawn up in a semicircle to defend the gate. That meant—all the enemy tanks, not more than another six or seven, out on the ledge fighting the attackers.

"All right," Hollister's voice vibrated in their earphones. "We'll shoot from here. Barbara, move her in a zigzag at 10 kph, keeping about this distance; let out a yell if you think you have to take other evasive action. Otherwise I might hit the city."

He jammed his faceplate into the rubberite viewscope and his hands and feet sought the gun controls. Crosshairs—range—*fire one!* The nearest cannon blew up.

Fire two! Fire three! His 40 reloaded itself. Second gun broken, third a clean miss—*Fire four! Gotcha!*

A rank of infantry appeared, their suits marked with the Guardian symbol. They must have been flown here. Waskowicz blazed at them and they broke, falling like rag dolls, reforming to crawl in. They were good soldiers. Now the other three enemy mobiles were swiveling about, shooting through the dust. "Get us out of here, Barbara!"

The racket became deafening as they backed into the concealing murk. Another enemy tank loomed before them. Hollister fed it two shells almost point blank.

If he could divert the enemy artillery long enough for his men to storm the gate—

He saw a police tank locked with an attacker, broken and dead. Hollister doubted if there were any left in action now. He saw none of his own vehicles moving, though he passed by the remnants of several. And where were his men?

Shock threw him against his webbing. The echoes rolled and banged and shivered for a long time. His head swam. The motors still turned, but—

"I think they crippled us," said Barbara in a small voice.

"O.K. Let's get out of here." Hollister sighed; it had been a nice try, and had really paid off better than he'd had a right to expect. He scrambled to the lock, gave Barbara a hand, and they slid to the ground as the three fieldpieces rolled into view on their self-powered carts.

The stalled tank's cannon spoke, and one of the police guns suddenly slumped. "Waskowicz!" Barbara's voice was shrill in the earphones. "He stayed in there—"

"We can't save him. And if he can fight our tank long enough— Build a monument to him some day. Now come on!" Hollister led the way into curtaining gloom. The wind hooted and clawed at him.

As he neared the main lock, a spatter of rifle fire sent him to his belly. He couldn't make out. who was there, but it had been a ragged volley—take a chance on their being police and nailing him—"Just us chickens, boss!" he shouted. Somewhere in a corner of his mind he realized that there was no reason for shouting over a radio system. His schooled self-control must be slipping a bit.

"Is that you, Simon?" Fernandez's voice chattered in his ears. "Come quickly now, we're at the lock but I think they will attack soon."

Hollister wiped the dust from his faceplate and tried to count how many there were. Latins and convicts, perhaps twenty— "Are there more?" he inquired. "Are you the last?"

"I do not know, Simon," said Fernandez. "I had gathered this many, we were barricaded behind two smashed cars, and when I saw their artillery pull away I led a rush here. Maybe there are some partisans left besides us, but I doubt it."

Hollister tackled the emergency control box which opened the gate from outside. It would be nice if he didn't have to blast—Yes, by Heaven! It hadn't been locked! He jammed the whole score into the chamber, closed the outer door and started the pumps.

"They can get in, too," said Fernandez dubiously.

"I know. Either here or by ten other entrances. But I have an idea. All of you stick by me."

The anteroom was empty. The town's civilians must be huddled in the inner compartments, and all the cops must be outside fighting. Hollister threw back his helmet, filling his lungs with air that seemed marvelously sweet, and led a quick but cautious trot down the long halls.

"The spaceship is supposed to have arrived by now," he said. "What we must do is take and hold the radio shack. Since the police don't know exactly what our plans are, they will hesitate to destroy it just to get at us. It will seem easier merely to starve us out."

"Or use sleepy gas," said Fernandez. "Our suits' oxygen supply isn't good for more than another couple of hours."

"Yes . . . I suppose that is what they'll do. That ship had better be up there!"

The chances were that she was. Hollister knew that several days of ferrying were involved, and had timed his attack for hours after she was scheduled to arrive. For all he knew, the ferries had already come down once or twice.

He didn't know if he or anyone in his band would live to be taken out. He rather doubted it; the battle had gone worse than expected, he had not captured the city as he hoped—but the main thing was to get some kind of report back to Earth.

A startled pair of technies met the invaders as they entered. One of them began an indignant protest, but Fernandez waved a rifle to shut him up. Hollister glanced about the gleaming controls and meters. He could call the ship himself, but he didn't have the training to guide a boat down. Well—

He pulled off his gloves and sat himself at the panel. Keys clattered beneath his fingers. When were the cops coming? Any minute.

"Hello, freighter. Hello, up there. Spaceship, this is New America calling. Come in."

Static buzzed and crackled in his earphones.

"Come in, spaceship. This is New America. Come in, damn it!"

Lights flashed on the board, the computer clicked, guiding the beam upward. It tore past the ionosphere and straggled weakly into the nearest of the tiny, equally spaced robot relay stations which circled the planet. Obedient to the keying signal, the robot amplified the beam and shot it to the next station, which kicked it farther along. The relayer closest to the spaceship's present position in her orbit focused the beam on her.

Or was the orbit empty?

". . . Hello, New America." The voice wavered, faint and distorted. "*Evening Star* calling New America. What's going on down there? We asked for a ferry signal three hours ago."

"Emergency," snapped Hollister. "Get me the captain—fast! Meanwhile, record this."

"But—"

"Fast, I said! And record. This is crash priority, condition red." Hollister felt sweat trickling inside his suit.

"Recording. Sending for the captain now."

"Good!" Hollister leaned over the mike. "For Main Office, Earth, United Nations Inspectorate. Repeat: Main Office, U.N. Inspectorate. Urgent, confidential. This is Agent A-431-240. Repeat, Agent A-431-240. Code Watchbird. Code Watchbird. Reporting on Venusian situation as follows—" He began a swift sketch of conditions.

"I think I hear voices down the hall," whispered Barbara to Fernandez.

The Latin nodded. He had already dragged a couple of desks into the corridor to make a sort of barricade; now he motioned his men to take positions; a few outside, the rest standing by, crowded together in the room. Hollister saw what was going on and swung his gun to cover the two technies. They were scared, and looked pathetically young, but he had no time for mercy.

A voice in his earphones, bursting through static: "This is Captain Brackney. What d'you want?"

"U.N.I. business, Captain. I'm besieged in the GCA shack here with a few men. We're to be gotten out at all costs if it's humanly possible."

He could almost hear the man's mouth fall open. "God in space—is that the truth?"

Hollister praised the foresight of his office. "You have a sealed tape aboard among your official records. All spaceships, all first-class public conveyances, do. It's changed by an Un-man every year or so. O.K., that's an ID code, secret recognition signal. It proves my right to commandeer everything you've got."

"I know that much. What's on the tape?"

"This year it will be, ''Twas brillig and the slithy toves give me liberty or give me pigeons on the grass alas.' Have your radioman check that at once."

Pause. Then: "O.K. I'll take your word for it till he does. What do you want?"

"Bring two ferries down, one about fifty kilometers behind the other. No arms on board, I suppose? . . . No. Well, have just the pilots aboard, because you may have to take twenty or so back. How long will this take you? . . . Two hours? That long? . . . Yes, I realize you have to let your ship get into the right orbital position and—All right, if you can't do it in less time. Be prepared to embark anyone waiting out there and lift immediately. Meanwhile stand by for further instructions. . . . Hell, yes, you can do it!"

Guns cracked outside.

"O.K. I'll start recording again in a minute. Get moving, Captain!" Hollister turned back to the others.

"I have to tell Earth what I know, in case I don't make it," he said. "Also, somebody has to see that these technies get the boats down right. Diego, I'll want a few men to defend this place. The rest of you retreat down the hall and pick up some extra oxy bottles for yourselves and all the concentrated food you can carry; because that ship won't have rations enough for all of us. Barbara will show you where it is."

"And how will you get out?" she cried when he had put it into English.

"I'll come to that. You've got to go with them, dear, because you live here and know where they can get the supplies. Leave a couple of suits here for the technies, pick up others somewhere along the way. When you get outside, hide close to the dome. When the ferry lands, some of you make a rush to the shack here. It's right against the outer wall. I see you're still carrying some dynamite, Garcia. Blow a hole to let us through. . . . Yes, it's risky, but what have we got to lose?"

She bent to kiss him. There wasn't time to do it properly. A tommy gun was chattering in the corridor.

Hollister stood up and directed his two prisoners to don the extra suits. "I've no grudge against you boys," he said, "and in fact, if you're scared of what the cops might do to you, you can come along to Earth—but if those boats don't land safely, I'll shoot you both down."

Fernandez, Barbara, and a dozen others slipped out past the covering fire at the barricade and disappeared. Hollister hoped they'd make it. They'd better! Otherwise, even if a few escaped, they might well starve to death on the trip home.

The food concentrate would be enough. It was manufactured by the ton at Little Moscow—tasteless, but pure nourishment and bulk, normally added to the rest of the diet on Venus. It wouldn't be very palatable, but it would keep men alive for a long time.

The technies were at the board, working hard. The six remaining rebels slipped back into the room; two others lay dead behind the chewed-up barricade. Hollister picked up an auxiliary communication mike and started rattling off everything about Venus he could think of.

A Guardian stuck his head around the door. Three guns barked, and the head was withdrawn. A little later, a white cloth on a rifle barrel was wavered past the edge.

Hollister laid down his mike. "I'll talk," he said. "I'll come out, with my arms. You'll have just one man in sight, unarmed." To his men he gave an order to drag the dead into the shack while the truce lasted.

Karsov met him in the hall. He stood warily, but there was no fear on the smooth face. "What are you trying to do?" he asked in a calm voice.

"To stay out of your mines," said Hollister. It would help if he could keep up the impression this was an ordinary revolt.

"You have called that ship up there, I suppose?"

"Yes. They're sending down a ferry."

"The ferry could have an accident. We would apologize profusely, explain that a shell went wild while we were fighting you gangsters, and even pay for the boat. I tell you this so that you can see there is no hope. You had better give up."

"No hope if we do that either," said Hollister. "I'd rather take my chances back on Earth; they can't do worse there than treat my mind."

"Are you still keeping up that farce?" inquired Karsov. But he wasn't sure of himself, that was plain. He couldn't understand how an Un-man could have gotten past his quiz. Hollister had no intention of enlightening him.

"What have you got to lose by letting us go?" asked the Earthman. "So we tell a horror story back home. People there already know you rule with a rough hand."

"I am not going to release you," said Karsov. "You are finished. That second party of yours will not last long, even if they make it outside as I suppose they intend—they will suffocate. I am going to call the spaceship captain on the emergency circuit and explain there is a fight going on and he had better recall his boat. That should settle the matter; if not, the boat will be shot down. As for your group, there will be sleep gas before long."

"I'll blow my brains out before I let you take me," said Hollister sullenly.

"That might save a lot of trouble," said Karsov. He turned and walked away. Hollister was tempted to kill him, but decided to save that pleasure for a while. No use goading the police into a possible use of high explosives.

He went back to the shack and called the *Evening Star* again. "Hello, Captain Brackney? U.N.I. speaking. The bosses down here are going to radio you with a pack of lies. Pretend to believe them and say you'll recall your ferry. Remember, they think just one is coming down. Then—" He continued his orders.

"That's murder!" said the captain. "Pilot One won't have a chance—"

"Yes, he will. Call him now, use spacer code; I don't think any of these birds know it, if they should overhear you. Tell him to have his spacesuit on and be ready for a crash landing, followed by a dash to the second boat."

"It's still a long chance."

"What do you think I'm taking? These are U.N.I. orders, Captain. I'm boss till we get back to earth, if I live so long. All right, got everything? Then I'll continue recording."

After a while he caught the first whiff and said into the mike: "The gas is coming now. I'll have to close my helmet. Hollister signing off."

His men and the technies slapped down their cover. It would be peaceful here for a little time, with this sector sealed off while gas poured through its ventilators. Hollister tried to grin reassuringly, but it didn't come off.

"Last round," he said. "Half of us, the smallest ones, are going to go to sleep now. The rest will use their oxygen, and carry them outside when we go."

Someone protested. Hollister roared him down. "Not another word! This is the only chance for all of us. No man has oxygen for much more than an hour; we have at least an hour and a half to wait. How else can we do it?"

They submitted unwillingly, and struggled against the anaesthetic as long as they could. Hollister took one of the dead men's bottles to replace the first of his that gave out. His band was now composed of three sleeping men and three conscious but exhausted.

He was hoping the cops wouldn't assault them quickly. Probably not; they would be rallying outside, preparing to meet the ferry with a mobile cannon if it should decide to land after all. The rebels trapped in here would keep.

The minutes dragged by. A man at the point of death was supposed to review his whole life, but Hollister didn't feel up to it. He was too tired. He sat watching the telescreen which showed the space field. Dust and wind and the skeleton cradles, emptiness, and a roiling gloom beyond.

One of the wakeful men, a convict, spoke into the helmet circuit: "So you are U.N.I. Has all this been just to get you back to Earth?"

"To get my report back," said Hollister.

"There are many dead," said one of the Latins, in English. "You have sacrificed us, played us like pawns, no? What of those two we left back at Last Chance?"

"I'm afraid they're doomed," said Hollister tonelessly, and the guilt which is always inherent in leadership was heavy on him.

"It was worth it," said the convict. "If you can smash this rotten system, it was well worth it." His eyes were haunted. They would always be haunted.

"Better not talk," said Hollister. "Save your oxygen."

One hour. The pips on the radarscopes were high and strong now. The spaceboats weren't bothering with atmospheric braking, they were spending fuel to come almost straight down.

One hour and ten minutes. Was Barbara still alive?

One hour and twenty minutes.

One hour and thirty minutes. Any instant—

"There, señor! There!"

Hollister jumped to his feet. Up in a corner of the screen, a white wash of fire—here she came!

The ferry jetted slowly groundward, throwing up a blast of dust as her fierce blasts tore at the field. Now and then she wobbled, caught by the high wind, but she had been built for just these conditions. Close, close—were they going to let her land after all? Yes, now she was entering the cradle, now the rockets were still.

A shellburst struck her hull amidships and burst it open. The police were cautious, they hadn't risked spilling her nuclear engine and its radioactivity on the field. She rocked in the cradle. Hollister hoped the crash-braced pilot had survived. And he hoped the second man was skillful and had been told exactly what to do.

That ferry lanced out of the clouds, descending fast. She wasn't very maneuverable, but the pilot rode her like a horseman, urging, pleading, whipping and spurring when he had to. She slewed around and fell into a shaky curve out of screen range.

If the gods were good, her blast had incinerated the murderers of the first boat.

She came back into sight, fighting for control. Hollister howled. "Guide her into a cradle!" He waved his gun at the seated technics. "Guide her safely in if you want to live!"

She was down.

Tiny figures were running toward her heedless of earth still smoking underfoot. Three of them veered and approached the radio shack. "O.K.!" rapped Hollister. "Back into the corridor!" He dragged one of the unconscious men himself; stooping, he sealed the fellow's suit against the poison gases outside. There would be enough air within it to last a sleeper a few minutes.

Concussion smashed at him. He saw shards of glass and wire flying out the door and ricocheting nastily about his head. Then the yell of Venus' wind came to him. He bent and picked up his man. "Let's go!"

They scrambled through the broken wall and out onto the field. The wind was at their backs, helping them for once. One of the dynamiters moved up alongside Hollister. He saw Barbara's face, dim behind the helmet.

When he reached the ferry, the others were loading the last boxes of food. A figure in space armor was clumping unsteadily toward them from the wrecked boat. Maybe their luck had turned. Sweeping the field with his eyes, Hollister saw only ruin. There were still surviving police, but they were inside the city and it would take minutes for them to get out again.

He counted the men with him and estimated the number of food boxes. Fifteen all told, including his two erstwhile captives—Barbara's party must have met opposition—but *she* still lived, God be praised! There were supplies enough, it would be a hungry trip home but they'd make it.

Fernandez peered out of the air lock. "Ready," he announced. "Come aboard. We have no seats, so we must rise at low acceleration, but the pilot says there is fuel to spare."

Hollister helped Barbara up the ladder and into the boat. "I hope you'll like Earth," he said awkwardly.

"I know I will—with you there," she told him.

Hollister looked through the closing air lock at the desolation which was Venus. Some day it would bloom, but—

"We'll come back," he said.

AFTER DOOMSDAY

✳ I ✳

For man also knoweth not his time: as the fishes that
are taken in an evil net, and as the birds that are
caught in the snare; so are the sons of men snared in
an evil time, when it falleth suddenly upon them.
—*Ecclesiastes, ix, 12*

"Earth is dead. They murdered our Earth!"

Carl Donnan didn't answer at once. He remained standing by the
viewport, his back to the others. Dimly he was aware of Goldspring's
voice as it rose toward a scream, broke off, and turned into the hoarse
belly-deep sobs of a man not used to tears. He heard Goldspring
stumble across the deck before he said, flat and empty:

"Who are 'they'?"

But the footfalls had already gone out the door. Once or twice in
the passageway beyond, Goldspring evidently hit a bulkhead,
rebounded and lurched on. Eventually he would reach the stern,
Donnan thought, and what then? Where then could he run to?

No one else made a sound. The ship hummed and whispered, air
renewers, ventilators, thermostats, electric generators, weight
maintainers, the instruments that were her senses and the nuclear
converter that was her heart. But the noise was no louder in
Donnan's ears than his own pulse. Nor any more meaningful, now.
The universe is mostly silence.

There was noise aplenty on Earth, he thought. Rumble and bellow
as the crust shook, as mountains broke open and newborn volcanoes

331

spat fire at the sky. Seethe and hiss as the oceans cooled back down from boiling. Shriek and skirl as winds went scouring across black stone continents which had lately run molten, as ash and smoke and acid rain flew beneath sulfurous clouds. Crack and boom as lightning split heaven and turned the night briefly vivid, so that every upthrust crag was etched against the horizon. But there was no one to hear. The cities were engulfed, the ships were sunk, the human race dissolved in lava.

And so were the trees, he thought, staring at that crescent which hung gray and black and visibly roiling against the stars; so were grass in summer and a shout of holly berries in snow, deer in the uplands of his boyhood, a whale he once saw splendidly broaching in a South Pacific dawn, and the beanflower's boon, and the blackbird's tune, and May, and June. He turned back to the others.

Bowman, the executive officer, had laid himself on the deck, drawn up his knees and covered his face. Kunz the astronomer and Easterling the planetographer were still hunched over their instruments, as if they would find some misfunction that would give the lie to what they could see with unaided eyes. Captain Strathey had not yet looked away from the ruin of Earth. He stood with more-than-Annapolis straightness and the long handsome countenance was as drained of expression as it was of color.

"Captain," Donnan made himself say. "Captain, sir—" He waited. The silence returned. Strathey had not moved.

"Judas in hell!" Donnan exploded. "Your eyeballs gone into orbit around that thing out there?" He made three strides across the bridge, clapped a hand on Strathey's shoulder and spun him around. "Cut that out!"

Strathey's gaze drifted back toward the viewscreen. Donnan slapped him, a pistol noise at which Kunz started and began to weep.

"Look here," Donnan said between his teeth, "men in the observatory satellites, in the Moon bases, in clear space, wouldn't'a been touched. We've got to raise them. Find out what happened and—and begin again, God damn us." His tone wobbled. He swore at himself for it. "Bowman! Get on the radio!"

Strathey stirred. His lips went rigid, and he said in almost his old manner, "I am still the master of this ship, Mr. Donnan."

"Good. I thought that'd fetch you." Donnan let him go and fumbled after pipe and tobacco. His hands began to shake so badly that he couldn't get the stuff out of his pockets.

"I—" Strathey squeezed his eyes shut and knuckled his forehead. "A radio signal might attract . . . whoever is responsible." The tall blue-jacketed body straightened again. "We may have to risk it later. But for the present we'll maintain strict radio silence. Mr. Kunz, kindly make a telescopic search for Earth satellites and have a look at the Moon. Mr. Bowman—*Bowman!*—prepare to move ship. Until we know better what's afoot, I don't want to stay in an obvious orbit." He blinked with sudden awareness. "You, Mr. Donnan. You're not supposed to be here."

"I was close by, fetching some stuff," the engineer explained. "I overheard you as you checked the date." He paused. "I'm afraid everybody knows by now. Best order the men to emergency stations. If I may make a suggestion, that is. And if you'll authorize me to take whatever measures may be needed to restore order, I'll see to that for you."

Strathey stared at him for a while. "Very good," he said, with a jerky sort of nod. "Carry on."

Donnan left the bridge. Something to do, he thought, someone to browbeat, anything so as to get over these shakes. Relax, son, he told himself. The game's not necessarily over.

Is it worth playing further, though?

By God, yes. As long as one man is alive and prepared to kick back, it is. He hurried down the passageway with the slightly rolling gait that remained to him of his years at sea: a stocky, square-shouldered man of medium height in his mid-thirties, sandy-haired, gray-eyed, his face broad and blunt and weathered. He wore the blue zip-suit chosen for comfort as well as practicality by most of the *Franklin's* crew, but a battered old R.A.F. beret slanted athwart his brow.

Other men appeared here and there in the corridor, and now he could hear the buzz of them, like an upset beehive, up and down the ship's length—three hundred men, three years gone, who had come back to find the Earth murdered.

Not just their own homes, or their cities, or the United States of America. *Earth.* Donnan checked himself from dwelling on the distinction. Too much else to do. He entered his cabin, loaded his gun and holstered it. The worn butt fitted his palm comfortably; he had found use for this Mauser in a lot of places. But today it was only a badge, of course. He could not shoot perhaps one three-hundredth of the human species. He opened a drawer, regarded the contents thoughtfully, and took out a little cylinder of iron. Clasped in his fist, it would add power to a blow, without giving too much. He dropped it in a pocket. In his days on the bum, when he worked for this or that cheap restaurant and expected trouble, the stunt had been to grab a roll of nickels.

He went out again. A man came past, one of the civilian scientists. His mouth gaped as he walked. Donnan stepped in front of him. "Where are you going, Wright?" he asked mildly. "Didn't you hear the hooter?"

"Earth," Wright cried from jaws stretched open. "The Earth's been destroyed. I saw. In a viewscreen. All black and smoking. Dead as the Moon!"

"Which does not change the fact that your emergency station is back that-a-way. Come on, now, march. We can talk this over later on."

"You don't understand! I had a wife and three children there. I've got to know—Let me by, you bastard!"

Donnan put him on the deck with a standard devil's handshake, helped him up, and dusted him off. "Be some use to what's left of the human race, Wright. It was your family's race too." The scientist moved away, quaking but headed in the proper direction.

A younger man had stopped to watch. He spat on the deck. "What human race?" he said. "Three hundred males?"

The siren cut loose again, insanely.

"Maybe not," Donnan answered. "We don't know yet. There were women in space as well as men. Get on with your job, son."

He made his way aft, arguing, cajoling, once or twice striking. Strathey told him over the intercom that the other decks were under control. Not that there had been much trouble. Most personnel had gone to their posts as directed . . . the way Donnan had seen cattle go down a stockyard chute. A working minority still put some snap into their movements. He might have been astonished, in some cases, at what people fitted which category—big Yule, for instance, who had saved three men's lives when the storm broke loose on Ubal, or whatever the heathenish name of that planet had been, now uselessly wailing, and mild little Murdoch the linguist locating someone else to man Yule's torpedo tube—but Donnan had knocked around too much in his day to be surprised at anything people did.

When he felt the quiver and heard the low roar as the U.S.S. *Benjamin Franklin* got under way, he hesitated. His own official post was with his instruments, at the No. 4 locker. But—

There was little sense of motion. The paragravitic drive maintained identical pseudo-weight inboard, whether the ship was in free fall or under ten gravities' acceleration . . . or riding the standing waves of space at superlight quasi-speed, for that matter. Everything seemed in order. Too much so, even. Donnan preferred more flexibility in a crew. With sudden decision, he turned on his heel and went down the nearest companionway.

Ramri of Monwaing's Katkinu rated a suite in officer country, though much of this was devoted to storage of the special foods which he required and which he preferred to cook for himself. Donnan tried the door. It opened. He stepped through, closed and latched it behind him, and said, "You bloody fool."

The being who sat in a spidery aluminum framework rose with habitual gracefulness. Puzzlement blurred, for a moment, the distress in the great golden eyes. "What is the complaint, Carl-my-friend?" he trilled. His accent was indescribable, but made English a sound of beauty.

"Blind luck some hysterical type didn't decide your people attacked Earth, bust in and shoot you," Donnan told him.

The man felt collected enough now to stuff and light a pipe. Through the smoke veil, he considered the Monwaingi. Yeh, he thought, they're for sure prettier than humans, but you have to see them to realize it. In words, they sound like cartoon figures. About five feet tall, the short avian body was balanced on two stout yellow legs. (The clawed toes could deal a murderous kick, Donnan had observed; the Monwaingi were perhaps more civilized than man, but there was nothing Aunt Nelly about them.) The arms, thinner and weaker than human, ended in hands whose three fingers, four-jointed and mutually opposed, were surprisingly dextrous. The head, atop a long thick neck, was large and round, with a hooked beak. A throat pouch produced a whole orchestra of sounds, even labials. There was a serene grace in Ramri's form and stance; the Greeks would have liked to sculpture him. (Athens went down into a pit of fire.) But all you could really convey in words was the intense blueness of the feathers, the white plumage of tail and crest. Ramri didn't wear anything but a pouch hung from the neck, nor did he need clothes.

He plucked at the thong, miserable, looked toward Donnan and away. "I heard somewhat," he began. His tone died out in a sigh like violins. "I am so grieved." He leaned an arm on the bulkhead and his forehead on the arm, as a man might. "What can I say? I cannot even comprehend it."

Donnan started to pace, back and forth, back and forth. "You got no idea, then, what might have happened?"

"No. Certainly not. I swear—"

"Never mind, I believe you. What usually causes this sort of thing?"

Ramri pulled his face around to give Donnan a blank look. "Causes it? I do not snatch your meaning."

"How do other planets get destroyed?" Donnan barked.

"They don't."

"Huh?" Donnan stopped short. "You mean . . . no. In all the war and politicking and general hooraw throughout the galaxy—it's got to happen sometimes."

"No. Never to my knowledge. Perhaps occasionally. Who can know everything that occurs? But never in our purview of history. Did you imagine—Carl-my-friend, did you imagine my Society, any Society of Monwaing, would have introduced a planet to such a hazard? A . . . *sumdau thaungwa*—a world?" Ramri cried. "An intelligent species? An entire destiny?"

He staggered back to his framework and collapsed. A low keening began in his throat and rose, while he rocked in the seat, until the cabin rang. Even through the alien tone scale, Donnan sensed such mourning that his flesh crawled. "Stop that!" he said, but Ramri didn't seem to hear.

Was this the Monwaingi form of tears? He didn't know. There was so bloody much the human race didn't know.

And never would, probably.

Donnan beat one fist against the bulkhead. It was coming home to him too, forcing its way past every barrier he could erect, the full understanding of what had been done. Maybe so far he'd been saved from shivering into pieces by the habit of years, tight situations, violence, and death from New Mexico to New Guinea, Morocco to the Moon—and beyond—but habit was now crumpling in him too and presently he'd ram the pistol barrel up his mouth.

Or maybe, a remote part of him thought, he'd had less to lose than men like Goldspring and Wright. No wife waiting in a house they'd once painted together, no small tangletops asking for a story, not even a dog any more. There'd been girls here and there, of course. And Alison. But she'd quit and gone to Reno, and looking back long afterward he'd understood the blame was mostly his fiddlefooted own . . . and, returning from three years among strange suns, he had daydreamed of finding someone else and making a really honest try with her. But as the barriers came down, he saw there would be no second chance, not ever again, and he started to break as other men on the ship had broken.

Until suddenly he realized he was feeling sorry for himself. His father had taught him that was the lowest emotion a man could have. If nothing else, the impoverished rancher had given this to his son. (No, much more: horses and keen sunlight, sagebrush and blue distances and a Navajo cowboy who showed him how to stalk antelope—but all those things were vapors, adrift above growling emptiness.) The pipestem broke between Donnan's teeth. He knocked the bowl out most carefully and said:

"*Someone* did the job, I reckon. Not too long ago, either. Assuming only the superficial rocks were melted and the oceans didn't boil clear down to the bottom, it shouldn't take more than several months to cool as far as our bolometers indicate. Eh? So what's been going on in this neck of the galaxy while we were away? Guess, Ramri. You'd be more at home with interstellar politics than any human. Could the Kandemir-Vorlak war have reached this far?"

The Monwaingi cut off his dirge as if with a knife. "I do not know," he said in a thin voice, like a hurt child. (Oh, God-who-doesn't-give-a-hoot, the children never knew, did they? The end came too fast for them to feel, didn't it?) "I do not believe so. And in any event . . . would even Kandemir have been so . . . *pagaung* . . . and why? What could anyone gain? Planets have sometimes been bombarded into submission, but never—" He sprang to his feet. "We did not know, we of Monwaing!" he stammered. "When we discovered Earth, twenty years ago—when we began trading and you began learning and, and, and—we never dreamed this could happen!"

"Sure," said Donnan softly. He went over and took the avian in his arms. The beaked, crested head rested on the man's breast and the body shuddered. Donnan felt the panic of total horror recede in himself. *Someone aboard this bolt-bucket has to keep off his beam ends for a while yet,* he thought. *I reckon I can. Try, anyway.*

"Hell, Ramri," he murmured, "men have lived with more or less this possibility since they touched off their first atomic bomb, *and* that was—when? Forty-five, fifty years ago? Something like that. Since before I was born. So finally it's happened. But thanks to you, we had spaceships when it did. A few. There must be a few other Earth ships knocking around in the galaxy. Russian, Chinese . . . they say at least one of those was coeducational. The Europeans were building two when the *Franklin* left. There was talk of crewing one with women. Damnation, chum, maybe we'd all be finished, in one of our home-grown wars, if your people hadn't showed up. Maybe you've given us a chance yet. Anyhow, you Monwaingi weren't the only ones in space. Somebody from Kandemir or Vorlak or some other planet would have dropped in on Sol within a few years if you hadn't. Galactic civilization was spreading into this spiral arm, that's all. Now come on, wipe your eyes or blow your nose or twiddle your fingers or whatever your people do. We've got work ahead of us."

He felt the warmth—the Monwaingi had a higher body temperature than his—steal into him, as if he drew strength from this being. Ramri was viviparous, but had been nursed on food regurgitated by his parents; he breathed oxygen, but the proteins of his body were dextrorotatory where Donnan's were levorotatory; he could live in a terrestroid ecology, but only after he had been immunized against dozens of different allergens; he came from a technologically advanced planet, but the concepts of his civilization could hardly be put into human terms. And yet, Donnan thought, we aren't so different in what matters.

Or are we?

He didn't let himself stiffen, outwardly, but he stood for a while weighing the possibility in a mind turned cold. And then the siren blew again, and Strathey's voice filled the ship: "Battle stations!

Prepare for combat! Three unidentified objects approaching, six o'clock low. They seem to be nuclear missiles. Stand by for evasive action and combat!"

✳ II ✳

It is the business of the future to be dangerous.
—*Whitehead*

Ramri was out the door before the announcement was repeated. Though human space pilots were competent enough, there were as yet none who had grown up with ships, like him and his fathers through the past century and a half. The thousand subtleties of tradition were lacking. In an emergency, Ramri took the control board.

Donnan stared after him, wrestled with temptation, and lost. He, a plain and civilian mechanical engineer, had no right to be on the bridge. But what he'd lately seen there made him doubt if anyone else did either. Not that he figured himself for a savior; he just wanted to be dealt in. With a shrug, he started after the Monwaingi.

They didn't notice him, where he stopped by the door. Ramri had taken over the main pilot chair, a convertible one adjusted to his build. Captain Strathey and Goldspring, the detector officer—apparently recovered from the initial shock—flanked him. Bowman stood near the middle of the room, prepared to go where needed. A good bunch of boys, Donnan thought. A threat to their lives was the best therapy for this moment anyone could have offered them.

His eyes searched the ports. Earth had already shrunk to view, the horror was not visible, but the cool blue-green color he remembered from three years ago was now grayish white, sunlight reflected off stormclouds. Luna hung near, a pearl, unchanged and unchangeable. Off to one side, its radiance stopped down by the screen, the sun disc burned within outspread wings of zodiacal light. And beyond and around lay space, totally black, totally immense, bestrewn with a million wintry stars. He realized with a shudder how little difference Ragnarok had made. ·

But where were the missiles? Goldspring, hunched over his instruments, was sensing them by radar and nuclear emission and the paragravitic pulses of their engines. They should have approached faster than this. The lumbering *Franklin* could not possibly out-accelerate a boat whose only payload was a hydrogen warhead.

"Yes, three, I make it," Goldspring said tonelessly. "When can we go into superlight?"

"Not soon," Ramri answered. "The nearest interference fringe must be several A.U. from here." He didn't need to calculate with the long formulas involved; a glance at Sol, an estimate of fluctuation periods, and he knew. "I suggest we—yes—"

"Don't suggest," said Strathey tightly. "Order."

"Very well, friend." The Monwaingi voice sang a string of figures. Three-fingered hands danced over the keyboard. A set of specialized computers flashed the numbers he asked for. He threw a strong vector on the ship's path and, at the proper instant, released a torpedo broadside with the proper velocities.

Donnan sensed nothing except the shift in star views, until a small, brilliant spark flared and died sternward. "By the Lord Harry, we got one!" Goldspring exclaimed.

We shouldn't have, Donnan thought. Space missiles should be able to dodge better than that.

The ship thrummed. "I believe our chance of hitting the other two will improve if we let them come nearer," Ramri said. "They are now on a course only five degrees off our own; relative acceleration is low."

"How did they detect us, anyway?" Bowman asked.

"The same way we detected them," Goldspring answered. "Kept instruments wide open. Only *they* are set to home on any ship they spot."

"Sure, sure. I just wondered . . . I was off the bridge for a while. . . . Was radio silence broken? Or—" Bowman wiped his brow. It glittered with sweat, under the cold fluorescent panels.

"Certainly not!" Strathey clipped.

An idea nudged Donnan. He cleared his throat and stepped forward. The exec gaped at him, but left Strathey to roar: "What are you doing here? I'll have you in irons for this!"

"Had a notion, sir," Donnan told him. "Here we got a chance to learn something. And at no extra risk, since we've already been spotted."

The captain's face writhed. Red and white chased each other across his cheeks. Then something seemed to drain from him. He slumped in his chair and muttered, "What is it?"

"Throw 'em a radio signal and see if they respond."

"They're not boats with crews aboard," Goldspring protested. "Our receivers have been kept open. Boats would have called us."

"Sure, sure. I was just wondering if those critters were set to home on radio as well as mass and engine radiation."

Goldspring looked hard at Donnan. The detector officer was a tall man, barely on the plump side, with bearded fleshy features that had been good-humored. Now his eyes stared from black circles. He had had a family too, on Earth.

Suddenly, decisively, he touched the transmitter controls. The blips on his radar screen, the needles on other detection instruments, and the three-dimensional graph in the data summary box, all wavered before firming again. Donnan, who had come close to watch, nodded. "Yep," he said. "Thought so."

Given the additional stimulus of a radio signal, the blind idiot brains guiding the missiles had reacted. So powerful were the engines driving those weapons that the reaction had showed as a detectable slight change of path, even at these velocities. Then the missile computers decided that the radio source was identical with the object which they were attacking, and resumed pursuit.

"Yes," Ramri said gravely, "they are programmed to destroy communicators as well as ships. In a word, anything and everything in this neighborhood that does not give them a certain signal. . . . Stand by! Fire Nine, Eight, Seven on countdown." He rattled off coordinates and accelerations. Elsewhere in the ship, the torpedo-men adjusted their weapons, a task too intricate to be handled directly from the bridge. "Five, four, three, two, one, zero!"

The torps sprang forth. At once Ramri hauled back on his controls. Even a paragrav craft could not maneuver like an airplane, but he did his best, cramming force into an orthogonal vector until Donnan heard an abused framework groan. Flame bloomed, not a hundred miles away. The screens went temporarily black at that monstrous overload. As they returned to life, the third missile passed within yards.

There was time for men to glimpse the lean shape, time even for Strathey to press a camera button. Then it had vanished. Donnan exhaled in a gust. That had been too close for comfort.

He stared at the dispersing gas cloud where the torpedoes had nailed the second missile. The incandescent wisp was quickly gulped by surrounding darkness. Goldspring nodded at his instruments. "Number Three'll be back shortly, when it's braked the speed it's got."

"I'm surprised it didn't come closer," Donnan remarked. Keep this impersonal, he thought, keep it a problem in ballistics, don't imagine the consequences if that thing zeroes in on us. No use thinking about those consequences, anyway. You'd never feel them.

"I am also," Ramri declared. "I was not overly hopeful of our escaping. This ship is not designed for combat. Whoever programmed those missiles did a poor job."

"Did a good enough job on Earth," Bowman grated.

"Shut up!" Strathey's voice was very quiet.

"Stand by." Ramri's orders trilled forth. A final time, nuclei burst in space . . . so close that Donnan felt the gases buffet the *Franklin*, like a shock through his feet and into his bones, a clang and rattle that slowly toned itself away.

"Whew!" He shook his head, trying to clear it.

"How much radiation did we get that time?" Strathey asked.

"Does that matter?" Bowman replied, high-pitched and with a giggle. "We're none of us married."

Goldspring jerked in his seat. His eyes closed and he gripped the chair arms till his knuckles whitened. The viewscreen crowned his head with stars.

"Be quiet." Strathey's nostrils twitched. "Be quiet or I'll kill you."

"I'm s-sorry," Bowman stuttered. "I only—I mean—"

"Be quiet, I said!"

Goldspring relaxed like a sack of meal. "Forget it," he mumbled. "Not enough radiation to matter. The force screens can block a lot more than that." He went to work resetting his detectors.

Ramri extended one thin hand. "Let me see the pictures you took, if your pleasure be so," he requested. Strathey didn't seem to hear.

Donnan brought the self-developing film out. One frame was pretty clear, even showing details of the missile's drive coils.

Ramri stared at it a long while. The stillness grew and grew.

"Recognize the make?" Donnan inquired at last.

"Yes," Ramri breathed. "I believe so." He mumbled something in his own language. "Even of them," he added, "I hate to believe this."

"Kandemir?"

"Yes. A Kandemirian Mark IV Quester. I have inspected some that were obtained by the Monwaingi intelligence service. They are standard anti-ship missiles."

"Kandemir," Strathey whispered. "My God—"

"Wait a bit, skipper," Donnan urged. "Let's not jump to conclusions."

"But—"

"Look, sir, everything I've read and heard suggests to me that those missiles ought to have wiped us out. They should've dodged everything we could throw at them and hit us broadside on. We aren't a warship; our armament was for swank, and because the Pentagon insisted a ship headed into unknown parts of the galaxy should have some weapons. Ramri, you were puzzled too, weren't you, by our escape?"

"What is your meaning, Carl-my-friend?" The troubled golden eyes searched Donnan's whole posture.

The engineer shrugged. "Damn if I know. But I would expect a Kandemirian to do a better job of adjustment on his own machines. Mainly, though, I'd like to forestall any notion you guys may have gotten about heading straight for Kandemir and doing a kamikaze dive onto their main city."

"They don't have a main city." Bowman giggled again.

Goldspring glanced about. "I've just spotted several more objects approaching," he said. "They're still at the limits of detection, so I can't positively identify their type. But what else would they be except missiles?"

Donnan nodded. "The whole Solar System must be lousy with missiles in orbit."

"We cannot linger here, then," Ramri said. "To a certain extent, only a fortunate concatenation of initial vectors allowed us to stand off the first three, poorly self-guided though they were. The second attack, or the third, will surely destroy us." He considered the instrument readings. "However, we should certainly be able to reach the nearest interference fringe ahead of that flock. Once we go superlight, we will be safe."

From everything except ourselves, Donnan thought.

"Get going, then," Strathey rapped.

Ramri busied himself with computation and thereafter with piloting. The humans eased a trifle, lit cigarets, worked arms and legs to get some of the tension out. They were all shockingly haggard, Donnan observed; he wondered if he looked as corpse-like. But they were able to talk rationally.

"Did Kunz find what happened to our artificial Earth satellites?" he asked. "The observatories and moon relays and so on?"

"Gone," Strathey said. He gagged. "Also the Moon bases. A new crater where each base had been."

"Yeh, I reckon we had to expect that." Donnan sighed. McGee, assistant powerman at U.S.A.-Tycho, had been a particular friend of his. He remembered one evening when they got drunk and composed *The Ballad of Superintendent Ball*, whose scurrilous verses were presently being sung throughout the space service. And now McGee and Ball were both dead, and Donnan was signed on the Flying Dutchman. Well-a-day.

"Kunz and I tried to detect any trace of life," Goldspring said. "Not human . . . no such hope . . . but a ship or a base or anything of the enemy's—" His words faded out.

"No luck, eh? Wouldn't've expected it, myself," Donnan said. "Whoever murdered Earth had no reason to hang around. He'll let his missiles destroy anyone who comes snooping. Later on, at his leisure, he can come back here himself and do whatever he figures on."

Ramri turned around long enough to say harshly, "He would not wish his identity known. I tell you, no one has committed such an atrocity before. The whole galaxy will rise to crush Kandemir."

"If Kandemir is guilty," Donnan said. His shoulders slumped. "Anyhow, the whole galaxy will do no such thing. The whole galaxy will never hear about this incident. A few dozen planets in our local spiral arm may be shocked—but I wonder if they'll take action. What's Earth to them?"

"If nothing else," Ramri said, "they will wish to prevent any such thing being done to their own selves."

"How was it done, do you think?" Bowman asked wearily.

"Several multi-gigaton disruption bombs, fired simultaneously, would serve." Ramri's tone was the bleakest sound Donnan had ever heard. "The operation would require a small task force—each bomb is the size of a respectable asteroid—but still, the undertaking was not too big to be clandestine. The energy of the bombs would be released primarily as shock waves in crust and mantle, which in turn would become heat. There would be little residual radioactivity. . . . No, I beg you, I cannot talk further of this at present." As he faced back to the pilot board, he began keening, very low.

After a while Captain Strathey said, "We had better proceed to some habitable planet of a nearby star, such as Tau Ceti II. Any other surviving ships can join us there."

"How'd they know where to look?" Donnan asked. "There are hundreds of possibilities within easy range. And besides, for all they know, we'll've hightailed it to the opposite end of the galaxy."

"True. I thought at first we could pick some definite star to go to and place a radio transmitter, broadcasting a recording of our whereabouts, in orbit around Earth. Now that's obviously ruled out. Even if we could stop to make such a satellite, the missiles would destroy it."

"They'll also endanger any ship which returns here," Goldspring pointed out. "Our escape was indeed partly luck. The next people might not be so fortunate. We've got to do more than get word to the others where to find us. We've got to warn them not to return to the Solar System in the first place."

"Are there any others?" Bowman cried. "Maybe they've all come back and been wiped out. Maybe we're the last humans alive—" He clamped his jaws. His fingers twisted together.

"Maybe," said Donnan. "However, don't forget that several expeditions were a-planning at the time we left. We and the Russians had completed our big ships first, but China and the British Commonwealth had almost finished theirs and the Europeans expected to do so within another year. Of course, we don't know where any of 'em went. The Russkies and Chinese wouldn't say a meaningful word; the British and Europeans still hadn't made up their minds; and then some other countries like India might have gone ahead and started spacing too, that weren't figuring on it three years back. Sure, perhaps everybody else made short hops and got home before us and died with Earth. But I sort of doubt that. Humans had already visited a good deal of the local territory, as passengers on other planets' ships. There'd be small glory in repeating such a trip. Better go someplace new."

Like us, he thought, running headlong toward Sagittarius and the star clouds at galactic center. Doubtless we weren't the first. Among the millions of spacefaring races, we can't have been the first to look at the galaxy's heart, and curve up to look at the entire beautiful sight, and gather enough data to keep our scientists happy for the next hundred years. But none of our neighbor peoples had done so, even though they had spaceships before we did. They aren't that kind. They accepted space travel when it came to them, and traded and discovered and had adventures, and in the course of time they'd have gotten around to stunts like ours. But man had to go look first of all for God. And fail, naturally. Man is a nut from way back. The galaxy will miss a lot of fun, now he's gone.

He is not. I say he is not.

"Assume other Terrestrial ships are kicking around, then," Goldspring said with a humorless chuckle. "Assume, even, that they come home like us and escape again like *us*. Have *we* any idea where *they* will go?"

"Local, habitable planets," Strathey said. "That makes sense."

"Uh-uh." Donnan shook his head. "How do you know the enemy isn't there too? Or, at least, won't come hunting there for just such remnants as us?"

The idea rammed home and they stared at each other. Donnan went on: "Anyhow, we know already, from information given us by nonhumans and from expeditions of our own on chartered foreign ships . . . we know that the nearest terrestroid planets are pretty miserable places. At best you'll find yourself in a jungle, with gibbering stone-age natives for company. We aren't set up for that. Three hundred men would be so busy surviving they wouldn't have time to think."

"What do you propose instead?" None thought it strange that Strathey should ask the question.

"Well, I'd say go beyond this immediate vicinity, on to someplace civilized. Someplace with decent climate. Most especially, someplace where facilities are available. Why be second-rate Robinson Crusoes when we are first-rate technicians . . . and can get good jobs on the strength of that? Also, well be in a better position to hear any news of other ships like ours."

"Y-yes. Quite correct. I do think we should stop at Tau Ceti, perhaps one or two other local stars, and leave radio satellites. I admit the sheer number of such stars makes it improbable that any other survivors will come upon our message, but the time and effort we lose making the attempt will not be great. Thereafter, though . . . yes, I agree. One of the clusters of civilization, where numerous planets practice space travel."

"Which one?" Goldspring asked. "I've seen the estimate that there are a million such in the entire galaxy."

"Our own, of course," Ramri said over his shoulder. "The cluster of Monwaing and its colonies, Vorlak, Yann, Xo—"

"And Kandemir and its empire," Strathey reminded.

"Not to Kandemir, certainly," Ramri said. "But you must go to a Monwaingi world. Where else? You will be made welcome in any of our cultures. My own Tanthai on Katkinu in particular—but Monwaing itself would also—"

"No," Bowman interrupted.

"What?" Ramri blinked at him. The throat pouch quivered.

"No," repeated Bowman. "Not Monwaing or its colonies. Not till we know Monwaing isn't the one that destroyed Earth!"

✷ III ✷

> The horror of the human condition—any human condition—is that one soon grows used to it.
> —*Sanders*

Tau Ceti II was no place for a stroll. Safe enough, but there was nothing to see except a few thornplants straggling across rusty dunes, under a glaring reddish sun. The air was hot and dry and so charged with carbon dioxide that it felt perpetually stuffy. This was in the subarctic Camp Jeffers region, of course, explored by Australians in a chartered Vorlakka ship ten years ago. The rest of the planet was worse.

Nevertheless, after forty-eight hours in camp, Donnan had to get away or go *crazy*. He and Arnold Goldspring loaded their pack-boards and started off. No use asking the captain's permission. Strathey was disintegrating as fast as his crew, and it was becoming a rabble.

"Makes no sense to land in the first place," Donnan had grumbled. "They talk about a rest after being cooped in the ship. Hell, they'll be more cooped in a bunch of tents down there, and a lot less comfortable. All we want to do is make an orbital satellite and leave a radio note in it . . . once we've decided where we want to go from here."

"I said as much to the crew's committee," the captain answered. He wouldn't meet the engineer's eyes. "They insisted. I can't risk mutiny."

"Huh? You're the skipper, aren't you?"

"I'm a Navy man, Mr. Donnan. The personnel aboard are seventy-five percent civilians."

"What's that got to do with anything?"

"That's enough!" Strathey said, raw-voiced. "Get out of here."

Donnan got. But from then on he carried his gun in a shoulder holster beneath his coverall.

Endless, hysterical debate reached no decision on what to say in the recording. Should the *Franklin* find some primitive world, a safe hiding place . . . safe, also, from discovery by any other humans that might still be alive and looking for their kindred? Go to a planet in this nucleus of civilization? If so, which planet—when any might be the secret enemy? (Ramri now had two marines as a permanent guard. They had already had to discourage a few men who said no filthy alien was fit to live. But they were his jailers as well; everyone understood that, even if no one came right out and said so.) Or ought the *Franklin* to go across thousands of light-years to an altogether different group of spacefaring peoples? That wouldn't be too long a trip for her. But the sheer number of such clusters and the thinness of contact between them would make it unlikely that other humans searching at random would ever come upon word of the Americans.

As the shrillness mounted, Donnan finally said to hell with it and left camp.

Goldspring would once have been a cheerful companion. He had been, throughout the past three years, on scores of worlds. (Including a certain uncharted one, lonely and beautiful, almost another Earth, which they had excitedly discussed as a future colony. But that was before they came home.) Now he was sunk in moodiness. He spent his abundant free time among books and papers, making esoteric calculations. The work was an escape for him, Donnan knew; the Goldsprings had been a close-knit family. But when he began shaking so badly that he spilled half his food at mess, Donnan decided something else was indicated. He persuaded Goldspring to come along on the hike.

Eventually, one night under two hurtling moons, Goldspring cracked open. What he said was mostly reminiscence, and no one else's business. Donnan helped him through the spell as best he could. Thereafter Goldspring felt better. They started walking back.

It was good to have someone to talk with again. "What's this project of yours, Arn?" Donnan asked conversationally. "All the figuring you've been doing?"

"A theoretical notion." Like most of the ship's personnel, Goldspring was a scientist rather than a career spaceman. His specialty was field physics, and his doubling in brass as detector officer was incidental.

He tilted back his hat to mop his forehead. The nearby sun glowered on them, two specks in a rolling red immensity. Puffs of dust marked every step they made. The air shimmered. Nothing else moved.

"Yeh?" Donnan hitched his pack to a more comfortable position. "Can you put it in words a plain M.E. can understand?"

"I don't know. How familiar are you, really, with the concept the superlight drive is based on? The mathematical depiction of space as having a structure equivalent to a set of standing waves in an n-dimensional continuum."

"Well, I've read some of the popular accounts. Let's see if I remember. Where these waves interfere, you can slip from one to another. Out between the stars, where there isn't much gravitational distortion, the interference fringes come so close together that instead of taking the entire straight-line distance, as light does, you can skip most of it. The whole business is the other side of the galactic-recession phenomenon. Galaxies recede from each other because space is generated between them. A ship in super-light brings the stars closer, in effect, by using those zones where space is being cancelled out. Have I got it straight?"

Goldspring winced. "Never mind. I'm sorry I asked." For a time there was only the scrunch of their boots in sand. Then he shrugged. "Let's just say the possibility occurred to me of inverting the effect. Instead of passing a material object through the fringes, keep the object still and make it generate fringes artificially. Oh, not on anything like the cosmic scale. We haven't the mass or energy to affect more than a few thousand kilometers of radius. However, the result should be measurable. So far, developing the idea, I haven't seen any holes in my reasoning. I'd like to make an experimental test as soon as possible."

"Don't bother," Donnan said. "Look up the results in some scientific journal. Surely, in the thousands of years that there's been space travel, somebody else thought of this."

"No doubt," said Goldspring. "But not any local scientists. And by local I don't mean just this immediate civilization cluster, but everything within ten thousand light-years. I've studied a lot of nonhuman texts, both in translation and—in Tantha and Uru, anyhow—in the original. M.I.T. had quite a file of such books and journals. Nowhere have I seen mention of any such phenomenon.

"Besides," he added, "the applications would be so revolutionary that if the effect were known (assuming it really exists, of course!), we'd be using a lot different machines for a lot different purposes."

"Whoa! Wait a minute," Donnan objected. "That doesn't make sense. The Monwaingi discovered Earth only twenty years ago. Three years back, the first Earth-built spaceships were finally completed. Monwaing itself was discovered something like a hundred and fifty years ago. And the ships that started up modern civilization there were from a planet that'd been exploring space for God knows how many centuries. D'you mean to tell me a bunch of newcomers like us can show the galaxy something it hasn't known since our ancestors were hunting mammoths?"

"I do," said Goldspring. "Don't confuse science with technology. Most intelligent species that man's encountered to date don't think along identical lines with man. Why should they? Different biology, different home environment, different culture and history. Look what happened on Earth whenever two societies met. The more backward one would try to modernize, but it never quite became a carbon copy of the other. Compare the different versions of Christianity that evolved as Christianity spread through Europe; think of the ingenious new wrinkles in science and industry that the Japanese developed after they decided to industrialize. And that involved strictly human beings. The tendency toward parallel development is still weaker between wholly distinct species. Do you think we could ever . . . could ever have borrowed the Monwaingi concept of the nation as a mere framework for radically different civilizations to grow in? Or that we'd ever have had any reason, economic or otherwise, to develop pure biotechnics as far as them?"

"Okay, Arn, okay. But still—"

"No, let me finish. On Earth we seemed rather slow to assimilate the technology of galactic civilization. That's highly understandable. We had to find ways of attracting outworld traders, develop stuff they wanted, so that we in exchange could buy books and machines, get scholarships for our bright young men, rent spaceships for our own initial ventures. Our being divided into rival nations didn't help us, either. And the sheer job of tooling up required time. I'll give you an analogy. Suppose some imaginary time traveler from around the year you were born had gone back to . . . oh, say 1930 . . . and told the General Electric researchers of that time about transistors. It'd have taken those boys years to develop the necessary auxiliary machines, and develop the necessary skills, to use the information. They'd have to make up a quarter century of progress in a dozen allied arts. And—there wouldn't have been any initial demand for transistors. No apparatus in use in 1930 demanded such miniature electronic valves. The very need—the market—would have had to be slowly created."

"Shucks, I know that. I am an engineer, they tell me."

"But my point is," Goldspring said, "There would not have been any corresponding difficulty in assimilating the theory of the transistor. Any good physicist could have learned everything about solid-state phenomena in a few months. All he'd need would be the texts and a few instruments.

"Likewise, when the Monwaingi came, Terrestrial science leap-frogged a thousand years or more, almost overnight. Terrestrial technology was what lagged. And not by much, at that. Ramri often remarked to me how astonished he was at our rate of modernization."

"Okay, then, I concede," Donnan said. "I'll assume you brought a fresh viewpoint to this interference fringe subject and really have stumbled onto something that none of our neighbors ever thought of. But you can't make me believe that in the entire galaxy, throughout its history, you are unique."

"Oh, no, certainly not. My discovery (if, I repeat, it is a discovery and not a blind alley) must have been duplicated hundreds of times. It just didn't happen to have been duplicated locally. And the knowledge hasn't spread into our part of the galaxy. That's not surprising either. Who could keep up with a fraction of the intellectual activity on several million civilized planets? Why, I'll bet there are a billion professional journals—or equivalent thereof—published every day."

"Yeah." Donnan smiled rather sadly. "I know," he remarked, "when I was a kid in my teens, just before the Monwaingi came, I went on a science fiction kick. I must've read hundreds of stories where there were races traveling between the stars while humans had barely reached the nearer planets of their own system. But I can't recall one that ever guessed the truth—the bloody simple obvious truth of the case. Always, if the Galactics noticed us, they were benevolent secret guardians; or not-so-benevolent keepers; or kept strictly hands off. In some stories they did land openly, as the Monwaingi and the rest actually did. But as near as I remember, in the stories this was always a prelude to inviting Earth into the Galactic Federation.

"Hell, why should there be a Federation? Why should anyone give a hoot about us? Couldn't those writers see how *big* the universe is?"

—Big indeed. The diameter of this one galaxy is some hundred thousand light-years, the maximum width about ten thousand. It includes on the order of a hundred billion stars, at least half of which have at least one life-bearing planet. A goodly percentage of these latter also sustain intelligent life.

Sol lies approximately thirty thousand light-years from galactic center, where the stars begin to thin out toward emptiness; a frontier region, which the most rapidly expanding civilization of space travelers would still be slow to reach. And no such civilization could expand rapidly anyhow. There are too many stars.

At some unknown time in some unknown place, someone created the first superlight spaceship. Or perhaps it was created independently, many times and places. No one knows. Probably no one will ever know; there are too many archives in too many languages to search. But in any event, the explorers went forth. They visited, studied, mapped, traded. Most of the races they found were primitive—or, if civilized, were not interested in space travel for themselves. Some few had the proper degree of industrialization and the proper attitude of outwardness. They learned from the explorers. Why should they not? The explorers had nothing to fear from these strangers, who paid them well for instruction. There is plenty of room in space. Besides, a complete planet is self-sufficient, both economically and politically.

From these newly awakened worlds, then, a second generation of explorers went forth. They had to go further than the first; planets of interest to them lay far, far away, lost in a wilderness of suns whose worlds were barren, or savage, or too foreign for intercourse. But eventually someone, at an enormous distance from their home, learned space technology in turn from them.

Thus the knowledge radiated, through millennia: but not like a wave of light from a single candle. Rather it spread like dandelion seeds, blown at random, each seed which takes root begetting a cluster of offspring. A newly civilized planet (by that time, "civilization" was equated in the minds of spacefarers with the ability to travel through space) would occupy itself with its nearer neighbors. Occasionally there was contact with one of the other loose astro-politico-economic clumps. But the contact was sporadic. There was no economic force to maintain it; and culturally, these clusters soon diverged too much.

And once in a while, some daring armada—traders looking for a profit, explorers looking for knowledge, refugees looking for a home, or persons with motives less comprehensible to a human—would make the big jump and start yet another nucleus of civilization.

Within each such nucleus, a certain unity prevailed. There was trading; for, while no planet had to supply another with necessities, the materials of comfort, luxury, amusement, and research were in demand. There was tourism. There was a degree of interchange in science, art, religion, fashion. Sometimes there was war.

But beyond the nucleus, the cluster, there was little or nothing. No mind could possibly deal with all the planets in space. The number was so huge. A spacefaring people must needs confine serious attention to their own vicinity, with infrequent small ventures beyond. Anything more would have been impossible. The civilization-clusters were never hostile to each other. There was nothing to be hostile about. Conflicts occurred among neighbors, not among strangers who saw each other once a year, a decade, or a century.

Higgledy-piggledy, helter-skelter, civilization spread out among the stars. A million clusters, comprising one to a hundred planets each, furnished the only pattern there was. Between the clusters as wholes, no pattern whatsoever existed. A spaceship could cross the galaxy in months; but a news item, if sensational enough to make the journey at all, might take a hundred years.

There was little enough pattern within any given cluster. It was no more than a set of planets, not too widely separated, which maintained some degree of fairly regular contact with each other. These planets might have their own colonies, dependencies, or newly discovered spheres of influence, as Earth had been for Monwaing. But there was no question of a single culture for the whole cluster, or any sort of overall government. And never forget: any planet is a world, as complex and mysterious in its own right, as full of its own patterns and contradictions and histories, as ever Earth was.

No wonder the speculative writers had misunderstood their own assumptions. The universe was too big for them—

Donnan shook himself and forced his mind back to practicalities. "Think we might find some use for this prospective gadget of yours?" he asked.

"For a whole series of gadgets, you mean," Goldspring said. "Sure. That was why I tackled the math so hard after . . . after we came back and saw. If we aren't simply to become a bunch of hirelings, we'll need something special to sell." He paused. One hand went to his beard and tugged until the physical pain outweighed what was within. "Also," he said, "one day we'll know who killed five billion human beings. I don't think whoever that was should go unpunished."

"You'll vote, then, to stay in this local cluster? The guilty party must belong to it. Nobody from another cluster would mount a naval operation like that. Too far; no reason to."

"That's obvious." Goldspring nodded jerkily. "And out of the planets that even knew Earth existed, there are really only three possible suspects. Kandemir, Vorlak, and the Monwaing complex. The last two don't make sense either." He bit his lip. "But what does, in this universe?"

"I'll buck for sticking around myself," Donnan agreed, "though I got a kind of different reason. You see—Hullo, there's the end of our stroll."

They had mounted a high dune overlooking the sheltered valley in which the men had pitched camp. Even from this distance, the tents around the upright spears of the auxiliary boats looked slovenly. A dust cloud hung in the air above. A lot of movement, to raise that much. . . . Donnan broke out his field glasses. He stared for so long that Goldspring began to fidget. When he lowered them, the physicist snatched them while Donnan's mouth formed a soundless whistle.

"I don't understand," Goldspring said. "Looks like an assembly. Everyone seems to be gathered near Boat One. But—"

"But they're boiling around like ants whose nest was just stove in," Donnan snapped. "Seems as if we got back barely in time. Come on!"

His stocky form broke into a jogtrot. Goldspring braced himself and followed. For the next few miles they made no sound but footfalls and harshening breath.

The camp was near riot when they arrived. Three hundred men surged and yelled around the lead boat. Its passenger lock, high in the bows, stood open. The gangladder had been partially extended to form a rostrum, where Lieutenant Howard, the second mate, jittered among a squad of marines. Now and then he fumbled at a microphone. But the P.A. only amplified his stutters and the growling and shouting on the ground soon overwhelmed him. The marines stood alert, rifles ready. Under the overshadowing battle helmets, their faces looked white and very young.

Men clamored. Men talked to their fellows, argued, shouted, stamped off in a rage or struck blows which drew blood. Here and there a man who happened to have a gun stood as a sullen shield for a few of the timid. Two corpses sprawled near a tent. One had been shot. The other was too badly trampled for Donnan to be sure what had happened. Occasionally, above the hubbub, a pistol cracked. Warning shots only, Donnan hoped.

"What's going on?" Goldspring groaned. "What's happened, Carl—in God's name—"

Donnan stopped before a clump of peaceful men. He recognized them as scientists and technicians, mostly, huddled together, eyes glassy with shock. Their guardian was the planetographer Easterling, who had found an automatic rifle somewhere. He poked the muzzle in Donnan's direction. "Move along," he rapped. "We don't want any trouble."

"Nor me, Sam." Donnan kept hands well away from his own pistol. "I just returned. Been away the better part of a week, me and Arnold here. What the hell broke loose?"

Easterling lowered his weapon. He was a big young Negro; an ancient fear had doubled his bitterness at this violence which seethed toward explosion. But Donnan's manner eased his hostility. He had to raise his voice as a fresh babble of shouts—"Kill the swine! Kill the swine!"—broke loose from a score of men gathered some yards off. But his tone became steadier:

"Huh! No wonder you look so bug-eyed. Hell's the right word, man. All hell let out for noon. Half of 'em want to hang Yule and half of 'em want to give him a medal . . . and they're split apart on the question of where to go and what to do anyway, so this has turned arguments into fights. We had one riot a few hours back. It sputtered out when the marines beat off an attack on the boat. But now another attack's building up. When they've got enough nerve together, they'll try again to lynch Yule. Then the pro-Yules'll hit the lynchers from behind, I s'pose. Those who want to go to Monwaing and those who want to hide in some other cluster are close to blows on that difference too. Me, I hope we here can stay out of harm's way till the rest have knocked some sense back into each other. Come join us, we need sober men."

"I never thought—" Goldspring covered his eyes. "The best men the whole United States could find . . . they said . . . men come to this!"

Donnan spat. "With Earth gone, and a commander whose nerve went to pieces, I'm not surprised. What touched this mob action off, Sam? Where is the captain, anyway?"

"Dead," Easterling answered flatly. "We did get the whole story this morning, before the situation went completely to pot. Seems Bowman, the exec, made a pass at Yule. Or so Yule claims. Yule tried to kill him, barehanded. Bowman had a gun, but Yule got it away from him. Captain Strathey came running to stop the fight. The gun went off. An accident, probably . . . only then Yule proceeded to shoot Bowman too, with no doubt about malice aforethought. A couple of marines jumped him—too late. He's confined in Boat One now for court-martial. Lieutenant Howard assumed command. But as the day wore on, most of the camp stopped listening to him."

"I was afraid of something like this," Donnan breathed. "Yule wasn't scared of Bowman, I'll bet; he could've said no and let the matter rest. He was scared of himself. So are a lot of those guys milling around there."

"I wish we'd all died with Earth," Goldspring choked.

"To hell with that noise," Donnan said. "Those are good men. Good, you hear? Nothing wrong with 'em except they've had the underpinnings, and props and keystones and kingposts, knocked out from their lives. Strathey was the one who failed. He should have provided something new, immediately, to take up the slack and give the wound a chance to heal. Howard's failing 'em still worse. Why the blue blazes does he stand there gibbering? Why don't he take charge?"

"How?" Easterling's teeth flashed in a wolf grin.

"By not quacking at everybody but addressing himself directly to the ones like you, that he can see have got more self-control than average," Donnan said. "Organize them into an anti-riot guard. Issue clubs and tear gas bombs. Break a few heads, maybe, if he has to; but restore order before this thing gets completely out of hand. And then, stop asking them what they think we ought to do. Tell them what we're going to do."

"I think," said a man behind Easterling, very softly, "that Howard planned to get married when he came home."

"That's no excuse," Donnan replied. "Or if it is, we need somebody who doesn't make excuses."

Goldspring watched him for a long moment; and bit by bit, all their eyes swung to him. No one spoke.

Me? Donnan thought wildly. Me?

But I'm nobody. Ranch kid, tramp, merchant seaman, then an engineering degree and a bunch of jobs around the world. A few investments got me a bit of money that's now gone in smoke, and I made friends with a Senator who's now ash in the lava. I wanted badly enough to get on the *Franklin*—as what man didn't who had any salt in his blood?—that I lobbied for myself for six months. So I got an assignment, to study any interesting outplanet mechanical techniques we might happen upon. I did, on a dozen planets in four separate civilization-clusters; but anyone in my profession could have done as well. It wasn't important anyway. The *Franklin*'s real purpose was to get a sketch of a beginning of a ghost of an idea of the galaxy, its layout and characteristics, beyond what we'd learned from Monwaing. And to develop American spacefaring techniques. Both of which purposes became meaningless when America sank.

Me take over? I'd only get killed trying.

Donnan wet his lips. For a moment his heartbeat drowned the mob noise. He brought the pulse under control, but he must still husk a few times before he could say, "Okay, let's get started."

✶ IV ✶

O western wind, when wilt thou blow.
That the small rain down can rain?
Christ, if my love were in my arms
And I in my bed again!
      —*Anon.* (16th century)

As the *Europa* matched vectors, the missile became visible to unaided eyes. Sigrid Holmen looked from her pilot board and saw the shark form, still kilometers away but magnified by the screen, etched against blackness and thronged stars. Her finger poised on the emergency thrust button. Something would go wrong, she told herself wildly, it would, and no human muscles could close the engine circuit fast enough for the ship to escape. To travel so far and then return to be killed!

But did that matter? herself answered in uprushing anguish. When Earth was an ember, when hills and forests were vanished, when every trace of her folk from the time they entered the land to hunt elk as the glaciers melted to the hour when Father and Mother bade her good-bye in their old red-roofed house . . . when everything was gone? One senseless kick of some cosmic boot, and the whole long story came to an end and had all, all been for nothing.

Hatred of the murderers crowded out fear and grief alike. Hatred focused so sharply on the thing which pursued her ship that it seemed the steel must melt.

Steadily, then, her finger rested. She watched the missile drift across her view as it checked acceleration to change course. She watched it begin to overhaul again. Still the *Europa* plodded away from dead Earth at a stolid five gravities; and still Chief Gunnery Officer Vukovic crouched immobile over her instruments, adjusting her controls. Time stretched until Sigrid felt time must rip across.

"*Bien,*" Alexandra Vukovic said, and punched a button of her own. The slugs that hosed from No. One turret were not visible, but she leaned back and reached into her shapeless uniform tunic. She even grinned a little. The pack of cigarets was not yet out of her pocket when the slugs struck. From end to end they smote the missile. Thermite plus oxidizer seamed it with white fire. Sigrid watched the thin plates torn open, curling as if in agony. Good! she exulted. The missile dropped from view. She cut paragrav thrust and asked the radar officer, Katrina Tenbroek, for a reading. The Dutch girl forced herself out of a white-faced daze and reported the missile had ceased acceleration.

"We killed its brain, then," Alexandra Vukovic said. "As I hoped. I know we did not simply kill its engines. I took care not to strike that far aft. So the warhead is now disarmed. Well and good, we can approach."

She spoke the French that was the common language of the expedition with a strong Serbian accent, but fluently. Her wiry frame relaxed easy as a cat in the chair, and no further expression showed on her scarred face. She's tough, Sigird thought, not for the first time. Had to be, I suppose, to fight the Russians in the "Balkan incident" of 1980 as she did. But when the whole Earth has died . . . no, it isn't human to stay that cool!

Then she noticed how raggedly Alexandra inhaled her cigaret, and how fingernails had drawn blood from the gunner's palm.

Captain Edith Poussin's voice rapped over the intercom: "Oh, no, you don't, my dears. We aren't coming near that thing. It may be booby trapped."

"But Madame!" Sigrid Holmen sat straight in astonishment. "You agreed—when we decided there was a chance to capture it for examination—I mean, what's the use, if now we won't take a look?"

"We will," said Captain Poussin. "Yes, indeed. And perhaps find out whose it is, no?" Sigrid envisaged her in the central control chamber, plump, gray, reminding one more of some Dordogne housewife than an anthropologist and xenologist with an astronautical degree from the University of Oao on Unya. But her tone was like winter, and suddenly the pilot remembered those grandmothers who had sat knitting beneath the guillotine.

"Let us not be fools," Edith Poussin continued. "Two missiles we destroyed, one we have disabled; but does that not argue they orbit in trios? I think we can expect more to come along at any moment, as they happen within detection range of us. Fortunately, we have not such a great heavy ship as the Americans or Russians do. However, speed and maneuverability will not save us from a mass onslaught. No, our first duty is to escape." Clipped: "I want three volunteers to make us fast to that missile and examine it while we proceed toward the nearest interference fringe. Respectively a navigation officer, weapons expert, and electronician."

Sigrid rose. She was a tall young Swede, eyes blue and Italian-cut hair yellow, her features regular without being exceptional but her form handsomer than most. On that account she chose to wear less clothing than most of the *Europa*'s hundred women. But vanity had departed with Earth and hope. She was only conscious of an adrenalin tingle as she said, "That's us right here."

"Aye," said Alexandra. Katrina Tenbroek shook her head. "No," she stammered. "Please."

"Are you afraid?" scoffed the Yugoslav.

"None of that, Vukovic," the captain's voice interjected. "Apologize at once."

"Afraid?" Katrina shook her head. "What is there to be afraid of, after today? B—b—but I have to cry . . . for a while. . . . I'm sorry."

Alexandra stared at the deck. The scar on her cheek stood lividly forth. "I'm sorry too," she mumbled. "It is only that I don't dare cry." She turned on her heel.

"Wait!" Sigrid was surprised to hear herself call. "Wait till we're relieved."

Alexandra stopped. "Of course. Stupid of me. I—oh—" She smashed the butt of her cigaret and took another. Sigrid almost reminded her that there would be no more tobacco when the ship's supply was gone, not ever again, but checked the words in time.

Father, she thought. Mother. Nils. Olaf. Stockholm Castle, and sailboats among the islands, and that funny friendly little man in Lapland the year we took our vacation there. The whole Earth—I should not have studied space piloting. I should not have gone on practice cruises. That was time I could have spent with them. I should not have taken this berth. I sold my right to die with them. Oh, no, no, no, I am having a nightmare, I am insane, this cannot be. Or else God himself has gone senile and crazy. Why is the sun still shining? How does it dare?

Her relief, Herta Eisner, entered with Yael Blum and Marina Alberghetti. All three looked unnaturally relaxed. Sigrid knew why when the German girl extended a box of pills.

"No," Sigrid said. "I don't want to hide behind any damned chemistry."

"Take that tranquilizer," Captain Poussin called. "Everyone. That's an order. We can't afford emotions yet."

Sigrid gulped and obeyed. As she and Alexandra proceeded down the starboard corridor, she felt the drug take hold: an inward numbness, but a tautening and swiftening of the logical mind, so that ideas fairly flew across the surface. Red-haired Engineer Gertrud Hedtke of Switzerland met them at the suit locker. She pushed a paragrav barrow loaded with the tools and coiled cable they would need. Wordless, they helped each other into their spacesuits and went out the airlock.

Space gloomed and glittered around them. The sun was a fire too fierce to look at, the Milky Way an infinitely cold cataract, stars and stars filled the sky—through which, in free fall, they went endlessly tumbling. Away from the ship's background sounds, silence pressed inward till one's own breath became a noise like an elemental force. The noise of the quern Grotte, Sigrid thought remotely, which the giantesses Fenja and Menja turn beneath the sea, which grinds forth salt and cattle and treasure, broad lands and rich harvests and springtime dawns; which grinds forth war, bloody spears, death and burning and Fimbul Winter.

She turned her back on Grotte, scornfully, and gave her attention to the job.

The *Europa*, a slim tapered cylinder, as beautiful to see as she was to handle, had matched velocities with the missile at some four kilometers' remove. That should be safe, even if the hydrogen warhead did go off; empty space won't transmit concussion, and at that distance the screens could ward off radiant energy sufficiently well. Flitting about on paragrav units, the girls attached twin cables to the king-brace amidships and paid them out on their way to the prize. Modern galactic technology was marvelous, thought Sigrid; these metal cords which could withstand fifty thousand tons of pull were no thicker than her little finger and massed no more than a hundred kilos per kilometer. But I'd rather weave a bast rope with bleeding hands, to use on a green Earth, it cried within her.

The drug suppressed the wish. She approached the missile with no fear of an explosion. Her death would be meaningless, even welcome, when Earth's children and men were dead. Quickly she helped patch the cables on, then she and Alexandra left Gertrud to make a proper weld while they both ducked into a hole burned through the shell.

Darkness inside was total. As Sigrid groped for the flash button on her wrist, Captain Poussin's voice sounded in her helmet receiver: "Other objects detected approaching. We can outrun them at one-point-five gravities, I think. Stand by." She braced herself against the surge of weight.

Undiffused, the flashbeams were puddles of illumination which picked crowded enigmatic machinery out of night. Sigrid squirmed after Alexandra until they reached a central passageway big enough to stand in. The missile was being towed with its main axis transverse to the acceleration, so that they could walk down its length.

Gauges and switches threw back the light from a tangle of wires. A faceless troll shape in her armor, Alexandra asked low, "Do you recognize any of this?"

"Kandemirian?" Sigrid hesitated. "I think so. I don't know their languages or . . . or anything . . . but once I saw their principal alphabet in a dictionary. I believe the letters and numbers looked like this." One clumsy gauntlet pointed to a meter dial.

"Give me some light and I'll photograph a sample. The Old Lady will know." Alexandra unslung the camera from her waist. "But I can tell you for certain, this missile is Kandemirian built. They taught us what little was known about outworld military equipment, at the officers' academy in Belgrade. I've seen pictures of just this type. The corridor we're in is for workmen to move around, making repairs, and for technicians to go to program the brain. Those vermin," she added colorlessly.

"Kandemir. The nomad planet. But why would they—"

"Imperialists. They've already overrun a dozen worlds."

"But that's hundreds of light-years from here!"

"We've been gone for more than two years, Sigrid. Much could have happened." Alexandra laughed; the sound echoed in her helmet. "Much did happen. Come, let's look at the brain. That'll be toward the bow."

At the end of the passage they found the controls, what the thermite shells had left of them. Sigrid swung her light around, searching for any trace of—of what? A scrawl on the bulkhead caught her eye.

She leaned closer. "What's this?" she asked. "See here. Something scribbled in some kind of grease pencil."

"Notes to refer to, as the writer worked at programming the brain," Alexandra guessed. "Ummm . . . *sacre bleu*, I swear there are two distinct symbologies. Perhaps one is a non-Kandemirian alphabet? I'll photograph them for Madame." She busied herself. Sigrid gazed into blackness.

Gertrud came fumbling and clumping along. "Finish quickly, please," she said. "I just got a message from the ship. Still more missiles are on their way. We shall have to cast loose the tow and go at high acceleration to escape them."

"Well, I think we've gotten everything from this beast we need," Alexandra said.

Sigrid followed the others numbly. She did not begin to come to herself until they were back in the *Europa*.

The ship throbbed with gathering speed, outward bound, soon to go superlight and return to the stars. Earth's corpse and the hounds that guarded it receded sternward. As their tranquilizers wore off, most of the crew wept. Hysterics had been forestalled; they simply wept in quiet hopelessness.

After some hours, Captain Poussin summoned the missile party to her cabin. Walking down the corridor, Sigrid felt her eyes hot and puffed. But *I am over the worst,* she decided. *I will mourn you forever, Earth, Father and Mother, but I am no longer willing to die. For while we live, there is the hope of revenge; and infinitely more, the hope of homes and children on some new Earth where you shall never be forgotten.*

The captain's cabin was a small, comfortable, book-lined room. She sat beneath pictures of her husband, many years dead, and her sons and grandsons who must now also be dead. Her face showed little sign of tears and she had set forth a bottle of good wine. "Come in, do," she said. "Be seated. Let's discuss our situation." But when she poured the wine, she spilled some on the tablecloth.

"Has the captain examined the pictures we took?" Alexandra began.

Edith Poussin nodded. Her mouth grew tight. "Unquestionably that was a Kandemirian missile," she stated. "But one thing puzzles me. Those symbols written on the bulkhead near the pilot computer." As if to keep from looking at the pictures above her, she grabbed a sheet of paper. "Here, let me reproduce the lines. I won't copy them exactly. You'd have too much trouble distinguishing signs all of which are new to you. I'll substitute letters of our own alphabet. For this wiggly thing in the middle of most of the lines, I'll use a colon. Now see—" She wrote rapidly.

A B C D E F G H I J K A L
M N O P Q M R
B A : N Q
A B I J : M O Q M P
J E H C : N M Q P P O

She continued similarly until everything had been transferred, then threw her penstyl down. "There! Can you make anything of that?"

"No," said Alexandra. "But weren't some of those symbols actually Kandemirian numbers?"

"Yes. I've represented those by the letters A through L. The others I've rendered as M through R. I don't know what signs they are, what language or—Anyhow, you'll notice that they are always separated from the Kandemirian numerals."

"I think," Sigrid ventured, "this must be a conversion table."

"That's obvious, I would say," the captain agreed. "But conversion into what? And why?" She paused. "And who?"

Alexandra struck a fist on her knee. "Let us not play games, Madame. The Kandemirian imperialists have subjugated many different language groups on a dozen or more planets. This must have been a notation made by some workman belonging to an enslaved race."

"May have been," Edith Poussin corrected. "We don't know. We dare not leap to conclusions. Especially when we have been out of touch with local events for more than two years."

Two years, Sigrid thought. Two magnificent years. Not just the glory of the galaxy, new suns, new folk, new knowledge as the *Europa* circumnavigated the great Catherine's wheel of stars, though that was enough splendor for a lifetime. But the final proof to a continent still skeptical of international cooperation and complete sexual equality, that many nations together could do this thing and that it could be done by women.

The years were bitter in her mouth.

She squared her shoulders. "What does Madame plan to do?" she asked.

The captain sipped for a while without answer. "I am holding private conferences like this with the most sensible officers," she admitted. "I am open to suggestions."

"Let me, then, propose we go to . . . Monwaing, or one of its colonies," Alexandra said. "We can find out there what happened. And they will help us."

Gertrud shuddered. "If they don't cut our throats," she said. "Are you so sure they did not do this? Yes, yes, those traders and teachers who lived on Earth for years at a time, they were polite and gentle, yes. But they were not human!"

"In any event," Edith Poussin said bleakly, "no planet acts as a whole. The kindliest ordinary citizens might have fiends for leaders."

She frowned at her wine. "I wish we had followed the American and British example, and taken a nonhuman pilot along, even though we were bound for regions equally strange to everyone in this cluster. We might have gotten a little insight—No, I feel myself it is too risky to seek out anyone who might have had any interest, one way or another, in Earth's fate."

"What do we risk?" Alexandra murmured.

Sigrid raised her head. "There were other ships from Earth. They may still be out there."

"If the missiles haven't gotten them," Gertrud said. She snatched her glass and drank deeply.

"The all-male European expedition can't have gotten home," Sigrid declared. "They planned on at least three years in the Magellanic Clouds. No one knows where the Russians went, or the Chinese. And the Chinese crew included both sexes. And the Russians might have completed their own female ship and gotten her into space before—Maybe several other countries launched ships too. They were talking of it when we left. They were going to purchase ships, at least, now that they had the financial means." She clenched her jaw. "We'll meet someone again, someday."

"How?" Captain Poussin raised her brows. "The difficulties . . . well, I've threshed those out with the first and second mates already. There is no interstellar radio. If we go outside the local civilization-cluster, there is hardly any interstellar travel. How can two or three or a dozen dustmotes of ships, blundering blind in the galaxy, come upon each other before we die of old age?"

Sigrid stared at the deck, crossed and uncrossed her long legs, sent a warmth of wine down her throat and listened to silence. There must be an answer, she told herself desperately. Her father, the shrewd and gentle ship's chandler who became a rich man by his own efforts, had taught her to believe there was little men couldn't do if they really wanted to. And women, he had added with his big laugh which she would not hear again. When a woman set out to be an irresistible force, he said, any immovable objects in the neighborhood had better get out of the way.

"We don't want to cower on some empty planet where no one will ever come," Alexandra declared. "We should go to a civilization. Our skills will be useful; we can earn our keep."

Sigrid nodded, recalling cities and ships where folk had been mightily impressed. Not that humans were so outstanding in themselves, but they carried the arts of their own cluster, which were not identical with those of other places. A blue-faced reptile had given her an energy gun in exchange for one of her paintings; she had delighted a six-limbed shipyard master by explaining to him certain refinements in the pilot board which a British engineer had added to the Monwaingi design. And this was in spite of their having picked up only a few words of each other's languages, in the brief time the *Europa* stayed. Surely a hundred highly skilled Terrestrials could make themselves valuable somewhere.

"To another civilization-cluster, then," Gertrud said, almost eagerly. "That will be safest. No one there will have any interest in . . . in hurting us. We will come as total strangers."

"I believe so," the captain said. "You echo my own thoughts. However, the problem remains, if we go that far afield, how shall we inform any other surviving humans of our whereabouts? Of our existence, even?"

It was as if her father's laugh sounded in Sigrid's head. She sprang to her feet. Her glass tipped and crashed to the deck. No one noticed. "I have an idea, Madame!"

In this world a man must be either anvil or hammer.
— *Longfellow*

The hall was built with massive dark timbers, the beam ends chiseled into the gaping heads of sea monsters. Exquisitely carved screens from a former era emphasized rather than hid that brutal vigor which the single long room embodied. Fluorescent globes threw their light off polished cups, shields, crowns, guns, booty from a dozen planets, and off the bronze wall plaques that displayed the emblems of Vorlak's warlords. At one end of the hall, flames roared and whirled up the chimney. The statue of the Overmaster at the other end was in shadow.

And that was symbolic, Donnan reflected. Eight thousand years of planetary unification had ended when the first space visitors came to Vorlak, two centuries ago. Now the Imperium was a ghost, continuing its ghostly rituals in the High Palace at Aalstath. The reality of power was the Dragar class, masters of warships and warriors, touchy, greedy, recklessly brave—beings such as these, who sat their thrones down the length of the hall and stared over their golden goblets at the human.

Hlott Luurs, the Draga of Tolbek, leaned forward. The wooden serpents which trellised his seat cast gloom on the jeweled, many-colored luster of his robes; but the muzzled, furry face was thrust plainly into the light. "Aye," he said, "as nearly as we know, Earth perished less than one of her own years agone. Otherwise the matter *is* a mystery."

The volume of his voice seemed to stir the battle banners hung from dimly seen rafters. Through open doors came a noise of surf and shrill night-birds; a saurian spouted and roared beyond the reef. The air filled Donnan's nostrils with cold unearthly smells.

He gauged his reply with care, according to what he knew about these folk. If he insulted them, he would be killed as soon as he left the sacred precincts of the council hall, and the orbiting *Franklin* would be blown to subatoms. On the other hand, a Draga was not insulted by the assumption he might be merciless.

"We came to Vorlak, my captain," he said, "because we did not really believe your people had done the deed. We thought to offer you our services in your war against Kandemir. But you will understand that first we've got to be certain you are not our enemy."

They both spoke in Uru, a modified form of the language used by the first interstellar visitors to this region. Some such *lingua franca* was necessary throughout a cluster; every spaceman mastered it as part of his training. Uru was flexible, grammatically streamlined, and included standardized units of measurement. Any oxygen breather could pronounce its phonemes, or at least write its alphabet, well enough to be understood. In fact, several other clusters, their own civilizations first seeded by explorers of that ancient race, had adopted the same auxiliary speech.

"You have my word we never harmed Earth," Hlott Luurs declared. "And I have been president of the Dragar Council for the past four years. I would have known."

He might not remain president, Donnan knew. The ever-shifting coalitions of these baronial admirals might overthrow him any day. But at the moment he dominated them, and therefore ruled his entire species.

To question his word of honor would be a mortal insult. And most likely he was telling the truth. Nevertheless—Donnan exchanged a glance with Ramri, whom he had taken along to this meeting. You'll know better how to be tactful, old chap, he appealed.

The shining blue Monwaingi form trod forward. "My captain, may I beg your indulgence," Ramri fluted. "The situation among the Terrestrial crew is precarious. You can understand what a shock the destruction of their planet was to them. Disorder culminated in near mutiny. Carl Donnan took the lead in restoring discipline, and was therefore elected chief. But as yet his authority is not firm. You must recall that modern humans have no tradition of absolute loyalty to one's captain. Many men questioned his decision to come here. Some are ignorant of Vorlakka customs. They would not realize that the word of Hlott Luurs is more than sufficient. Suspicious, they would cause trouble."

"Kill them," advised a Draga from the row of thrones.

"No," said Donnan harshly. "With almost the whole human race gone, I can't destroy any others for any reason."

"And yet," said Hlott, "you bring your ship here and offer to fight on our side."

"That's what we call a calculated risk." Donnan shifted on his feet. More and more, the situation began to look hopeless. They hadn't even given him a chair. That meant he was an inferior, a poor relation at best, fair game at worst.

His eyes flickered along the ranked captains. They were supposed to be humanoid, he reminded himself. Biped, about as tall as he was, with powerful arms ending in regular five-fingered hands, they were placental mammals and biochemically very similar to men. (That had been one reason for coming here. Humans could eat the local food, which they could not on any Monwaingi planet.) But the torso was shorter and thicker, the legs longer and heavier, the feet webbed. The head was flattened, low-browed, the brain case bulging out behind. The small external ears could fold to keep out water, the eyes had a nictitating membrane. The face was bluntly doglike, black-nosed, with carnivore teeth. Sleek brown fur covered the entire body. This race was adapted to a planet whose land mass was mostly islands, which the tides of the nearby moon made into brackish swamps. Their history had eventuated in a maritime world empire, whose hereditary skippers and merchants had now—since the breakdown of the empire—become the Dragar, warlords and traders through an immense volume of space.

Silence waxed in the hall. It was broken by one who sat on Hlott's left. His plain black robe was conspicuous amidst that color and metal. "Honorable Captain Donnan," he said, as softly as a Vorlakka throat could manage, "this unworthy person believes he has an indication that may serve as convincing evidence. Formerly it was a state secret, but the never-to-be-sufficiently-regretted destruction of your beautiful home has rendered such secrecy pointless. My captains know whereof I speak. If I may be allowed to use the archives?"

Stillness descended again. Even the fire and surf seemed to hush themselves. Odd, Donnan thought. Ger Nenna sat in this council as representative of the Overmaster, who was the merest figurehead. The imperial scholar-bureaucracy to which Ger belonged had even less reason for continued existence. And yet, grudgingly, the Dragar deferred to him. Hlott rubbed a chinless jaw for two or three minutes, pondering. But in the end he said, "As the honorable minister will."

One refreshing aspect of feudalism was, to Donnan, the ease with which such decisions could be made. Ger Nenna rose, bowed, and walked across to a replicom unit. He stood punching buttons while the Dragar drank and servants hurried to refill their golden goblets. Ramri whispered in English: "Do you see any hope for our plans, Carl-my-friend?"

"Dunno," the man answered as softly.

"If we fail here—you will understand, will you not, how I can at once hope for your success and your failure?—surely then you will come to my home. I am positive we can offer still better proof of innocence than any which these beings may possess."

Donnan tried to smile into the wistful beaked face. "You know *I* know you didn't do it," he said.

After getting the captaincy on Tau Ceti II, he had managed some change in Ramri's status. The avian was no longer in danger from the human crew. They accepted Donnan's making him unofficial first mate of the ship, though he was careful never to give any direct orders. There was no longer a guard on him. But if Donnan had sent Ramri home, the crew would not have liked it. They didn't accuse Monwaing of slaying Earth. They didn't know. The fact remained, however, that the Monwaingi planets had had the most to do with Earth and might thus most easily have found some reason to eliminate it. Until more facts were available, Ramri was a hostage of sorts. He accepted his status without complaint.

He reached quickly to give Donnan's arm a grateful squeeze. The replicom extruded a reel, duplicating material in the archives at Aalstath. Ger Nenna brought it over to Donnan.

"Naturally the honorable captain reads Russian," he said.

"A little," Donnan answered. "We got men aboard who're good at it."

"Then here is a treaty made between this Council and the Soviet Union, almost three years ago. The Russian exploratory ship which departed about the same time as your own, captain, carried officials empowered to deal with outworld governments. They concluded this agreement, which had been under secret negotiation for some time previously. The Soviet Union was to produce for us a large amount of arms in certain categories, at a favorable price; and numerous of their military personnel were to serve us as auxiliaries, thereby gaining experience in modern warfare. The Russian vessel then proceeded into far space, and we have no subsequent knowledge of it. But several armament cargoes were delivered to our ships—secretly, at a rendezvous on Venus. Here are copies of the manifests. And this correspondence shows that the first contingent of Soviet officers was due to depart for Vorlak very soon. Then the sorrow came that Earth was destroyed."

Donnan bent his attention to the reel. Yes, here were parallel Russian and Vorlakka texts. He could read enough of the former to get the drift. "—common cause of the peace-loving peoples against imperialist aggressors . . . unity in the great patriotic struggle—" He didn't think any nonhuman could have done the phrasing that exactly. Plus all this other documentation. The Vorlakka would not have known the *Franklin* would arrive to ask for an accounting. They would hardly have prepared this file against an improbable contingency; the more so since they were openly contemptuous of the *Franklin*'s power. Besides, the Dragar were not cloak-and-dagger types. If they had blown up Earth, they wouldn't have hidden the fact; not so elaborately, anyhow.

And the evidence fitted Terrestrial facts also. The Communists never had given up their ambitions, even when the fluid situation after the Monwaingi arrived forced them to pull in their horns while they reassessed matters. The secrecy of this agreement with Vorlak was not just to protect Earth against Kandemirian reprisal. It was so the Soviets could quietly get ahead of every other country in the development of a really up-to-date war machine. Here again, Donnan didn't believe that the Vorlakkar, who had never had any extensive contact with Earth, could have faked so precise a picture.

He was convinced.

He looked up. The lines from nose to mouth stretched and deepened in his face as he said: "Yes, my captains, proof aplenty. And further evidence against Kandemir. If their spies found out what was going on—" He couldn't continue.

"Quiet likely," Hlott nodded. He seemed to have reached a decision while the human read. "Since you have come as our guests, begging sanctuary, and there is no feud between us, honor demands that we grant your wish. A place will be prepared for you. Your skills can earn you good pay in my own factories . . . unless, as I suspect, my honorable colleagues want a share of you. Return now to your boat, and see my chief aide tomorrow."

Donnan rallied his nerve. "Thanks, my captain," he said. "But we can't take that."

"What?" Hlott dropped a hand to the light ax at his waist. The Dragar leaned forward in their chairs. A hiss of indrawn breath went down their rank.

"We came as free people, freely offering our services," Donnan said. "We didn't come to be domesticated. Give us what we need and we'll fight for you. Otherwise, goodbye."

Hlott gnawed his lip. "You dare—" began a noble. Hlott shushed him and shrugged elaborately. "Goodbye," he said.

"My captain." Ger Nenna bowed low. "Unworthy, I pray your indulgence. Grant these folk their wish."

"Give them warships? Our painfully gathered intelligence of the enemy? These novices that never saw a space battle?" Hlott snorted an obscenity.

"My captain," said Ger, "these novices, as you call them, were not content to read texts and hear third-hand accounts of the galaxy. They set out for themselves. They have been to farther and stranger places than any Vorlakka skipper. They are no novices.

"Furthermore, their planet was in constant upheaval for nigh a century. My captain will recall that the Russians told us about guerrilla operations, border clashes, crafty international maneuverings. They understand war, these males who are your guests. They need only a little technical instruction. Thereafter . . . My captains hazard a ship or two. The Earthmen hazard not only their own lives, which of course are nothing, but conceivably the last life of their race. What Vorlakka would dare do likewise, with the spirits of his ancestors watching?"

Taken aback, Hlott said, "Well . . . even so—"

"A slime worm like myself may not remind my captains of their duty," Ger said. "And yet, does not the honor of a Draga require him to grant each person his own inalienable right? Food and protection to the groundling, justice and leadership to the crew member, respect to the colleague, deference to the Overmaster.

"These folk, who are freeborn, have come to be revenged on Kandemir, which murdered their planet—a murder so enormous that the hardest Draga must stand aghast. Vengeance is a right as well as a duty. Can the Dragar deny them their right?"

The fire roared on the hearth.

After a long while, Hlott nodded. "This is so. You shall have your right, Carl Donnan." With sudden, gusty good humor: "Who knows, you may deal Kandemir a strong blow. Bring him a chair, you scuts! Fill him a goblet. We'll drink to that!"

Some time later, not altogether steady on his feet, Donnan left to return to his spaceboat. Ger Nenna accompanied him and Ramri. The hall's noise and brightness fell behind them as they walked downhill. The coppery shield of the moon, two degrees wide, was dropping swiftly horizonward, but the island was still flooded by its light, icy, unreal, as if frost lay on the jungle behind and the beach in front, as if the docked submarines and seaplanes floated in a bath of mercury. Surf flamed white on the reef. The ocean churned and glowed beyond. Overhead the sky was strange. Nearly two hundred light-years from Earth, in the direction of Scorpio, the stars drew enigmatic pictures across the dark. Brightest among them, Antares burned blood red.

The wind, wet and pungent in his face, sobered Donnan. "I didn't have a chance to thank you before, Ger Nenna," he said. "Pardon me, but why did you help us? Your own class, the scholars, don't believe in revenge, do they?"

"No," said the black-robed one. "But we believe in justice. And . . . I think the galaxy has need of your race."

"Thanks," Donnan mumbled. He began to understand why the Overmaster's representatives were respected. Partly, to be sure, they symbolized the golden age, the Eternal Peace which Vorlak remembered so wistfully. But partly, too, they embodied wisdom. And the Dragar were at least wise enough collectively to feel the lack of wisdom in themselves.

"You jumped to conclusions, though," Donnan said. "I'm not entirely convinced Kandemir is guilty."

"Why, then, did you come here to fight against them, if I may presume to ask?"

"Well, we need employment, and I don't have any special compunctions about helping to stop them."

"You could have found safer employment, however, for your remnants. A factory job, such as was offered you."

"Yeh. Nice, humble obscurity." Donnan tamped his pipe, struck a light and fumed into the wind. "I don't believe we're the last survivors of our species. If we are, then *our* getting killed won't matter anyway; but I refuse to believe we are. I think a few other human ships must be scattered through the galaxy. If they haven't yet returned to the Solar System, they should be warned against doing so, or the missiles there may clobber them. If they have already come back, and escaped, as we did, obviously they haven't gone to some planet in this cluster. We'd hear about that. So, they could be anywhere among a couple hundred billion stars. How can we get word to them?

"I figure one way is to make such a hooraw that the tale will go from end to end of the galaxy. There's some intercluster travel, after all. Not much, but some. Doubtless the news that a whole planet has been wiped out is already circulating. But over so much space and time and ignorance, people'll soon forget which one, or even where it is.

"What I'd like to do is produce a sensation they won't forget and won't garble too much. I don't know exactly what. Something about a footloose crew of bipeds who got their planet kicked out from under them and are raising the roof about it in this specific cluster. I hope that eventually the other human ships will hear the yarn and understand."

He laughed, a short metallic bark in the wind and moonlight. "A war is a good chance to make a splash," he finished. "And here we got a war ready-made."

✳ VI ✳

Hell from beneath is moved for thee to meet thee at thy coming.
—*Isaiah, xiv, 9*

The hot F6 dwarf that was Kandemir's sun lay about 175 light-years from Vorlak, northward and clockwise. Although its third planet was somewhat heavier than Earth, the intense irradiation had thinned and dried the atmosphere. Even so, a man who took precautions against ultraviolet could live on Kandemir and eat most of the food.

History there had taken an unusual course. Vast fertile plains fostered the growth on one continent of a nomadic society which conquered the sedentary peoples. This was not like cases on Earth when barbaric wanderers overran a civilization. On Kandemir, the nomads were the higher culture, those who invented animal domestication, writing, super-tribal government, and machine technology. The cities became mere appendages where helots labored at the tasks such as mining which could not move with the seasons. When the nomads learned how to cross Kandemir's small, shallow oceans, their way of life soon dominated the world. Warfare and economic competition between their hordes spurred the advent of an industrial revolution. But gunpowder, steam engines, and mass production shifted the balance. Nomad society could not readily assimilate them; it developed strains. A century ago, Kandemir had become as chaotic as the last years of Earth. Then explorers from T'sjuda came upon it and began to trade.

Numerous Kandemirians went to space as students, workers, and mercenary soldiers—for T'sjuda, like Xo and some other powers, was not above occasional imperialism on backward planets. The Kandemirians returned home with new ideas for revitalizing their old culture. Under Ashchiza the Great, the Erzhuat Horde forced unification on Kandemir and launched a feverish program of modernization; but one adapted to nomadism. The cybernetic machine replaced the helot, the spaceship replaced the wagon, the clans became the crews of distinct fleets. Soon Kandemirian merchants and adventurers swarmed through space. Yet their tradition bound them to the mother world, where they returned for those seasonal rites of kinship that corresponded in them to a religion. Thus the Grand Lord remained able to command their allegiance.

As time passed, their habits (which others interpreted as cruelty, arrogance, and greed) brought them ever more often into conflict with primitive races. These were easy prey. But this, increasingly, caused trouble with advanced worlds such as T'sjuda, who had staked out claims of their own. Action and reaction spiraled into open battle on the space frontiers. Defeated at first, Kandemir rallied so violently that its enemies asked for terms. The peace settlement was harsh; in effect, the one-time teachers of the nomads became their vassals.

The little empire which thus more or less happened in the time of Ashchiza's son, began to grow more rapidly under his grandson Ferzhakan. Decentralized and flexible, nomadic overlordship was well suited to the needs of interstellar government; the empire worked. For glory, wealth, and protection—most especially to gain the elbow room which Kandemirian civilization required in ever greater quantities, for space traffic as well as for the gigantic planetary estates of its chieftains—the empire must expand. Ferzhakan dreamed of ultimate hegemony over this entire spiral arm.

His policy soon brought an opposing coalition into existence. This was dominated by the Vorlakka Dragar, who also had far-flung interests. The nomad fleet was stopped at the Battle of Gresh. But that fight was a draw. Neither side could make further headway. The war settled down to years of raids, advances and retreats, flareups and stalemates, throughout the space between the two planets. Well off to one side, Monwaing and her daughters maintained what was officially an armed neutrality, in practice an assistance and encouragement of Vorlak. The other independent, space-traveling races in the cluster were too weak to make much difference.

The nearest strong Kandemirian base to Vorlak was forty light-years off, at a star the Vorlakkar called Mayast. As his borrowed destroyer slipped from the last interference fringe and accelerated inward on paragrav, Donnan saw it burn blue-white in the forward viewscreen. Like a fire balloon to starboard, the biggest planet of the system glowed among specks that were moons. Howard, now chief navigator, swung his scopes and poised fingers over the calculator keyboard. "No," said Ramri, "the declination is eleven point four two degrees—" He broke off. "You are right. I was wrong. Forgive me."

Even in that moment, Donnan grinned. Despite his wide experience, Ramri could still get number systems confused. It was more than the different planets using different symbols; the mathematics varied intrinsically. The Monwaingi based their arithmetic on six. But this was a Vorlakka ship, whose ten-fingered builders used a decimal system like Earth's.

Howard ignored the avian, but Olak Faarer, the Draga observer, scowled and recomputed the fix for himself. He made no bones about doubting the competence of the fifty Terrestrials who had taken over the *Hrunna*. They had demonstrated their skill after a month of lessons, as well as on the days of their voyage hither. But the Vorlakka aristocrat remained scornful of them.

As far as that goes, Donnan reflected, the rest of the boys, waiting back on the *Franklin* in orbit around Vorlak, didn't look any too confident in us. Does seem like a hare-brained stunt at that. One lone destroyer, to punch through these defenses, approach so close to the enemy base that they can't stop our missile barrage, and then get away unsigned! When the Vorlakkar have been trying for a decade. . . .

He looked at Goldspring. "Anything registered yet?" he asked. Foolish question, he realized at once. He'd be told the moment that haywired instrument over which the physicist was crouched gave a wiggle. But damn it, you could talk as big as you pleased: when you sailed to battle your heart still banged and you wanted a beer in the worst way. Silliness was excusable.

"N-no. I'm not sure. Wait. Wait a minute." In one minute, at forty gravities' acceleration, the *Hrunna* added better than fourteen miles per second to an already tremendous velocity. Goldspring nodded. "Yes. Two moving sources over in that direction." He read off the coordinates. Donnan tapped a few pilot keys, spinning the ship about and applying full thrust orthogonally to her path. After three or four minutes, Goldspring nodded. "Okay," he said. "We're beyond range."

Howard studied the integrated data on his meters and punched out a new set of vectors on the control board. The ship had never actually departed from her sunward plunge—so high a velocity was not soon killed—but she began a modification of path, correcting for the previous force, so as to rendezvous with Mayast II according to plan.

Olak Faarer glided across the bridge and gazed at the steady oscilloscope trace on Goldspring's instrument. "What were they, those objects you detected?" he asked. "Ships, unmanned patrol missiles, or what?"

"I don't know," Goldspring said. "My gizmo isn't that good . . . yet. I only know they were sources of modulated paragravitic force, at such-and-such a distance, velocity, and acceleration. In other words, they were something running under power." He added dryly, "We may assume that anything under power in this system is dangerous."

"So is anything in free fall," Olak grumbled.

"Oh, Lord," Donnan groaned. "How often must I tell you—um-m-m—that is, surely my honorable colleague understands that at such speed as we've got, nothing which doesn't have a velocity comparable in both magnitude and direction is likely to be able to do much about us."

"Yes, yes," Olak said stiffly. "I have had your device explained to me often enough. A paragrav detector with unprecedented sensitivity. I admit it is a good instrument."

"Only the first of a long series of instruments," Goldspring promised. "And weapons. My staff and I have barely begun to explore the possibilities opened by our new theory of space-time-energy relationships. The workers on the *Franklin* may already have a surprise for us when we get home."

"Perhaps," Olak said with impatience. "Nonetheless! I did not say anything hitherto, lest I be thought a coward. But now that we are irrevocably committed, I tell you frankly that this trusting our lives to a single handmade prototype of a single minor invention is utter foolishness."

Donnan sighed. "I've argued this out a thousand times with a hundred Dragar," he said. "I thought you were listening. Okay, then, I'll explain again.

"Arn's gadget there doesn't merely respond to paragrav waves like the ordinary detector. It generates microwaves of its own, and thus it can use interferometric principles. The result is, it can spot other ships twice as far and three times as accurately as the best conventional instrument.

"Well, if we're aware of the enemy long before they can detect us, we can take evasive action and stay beyond their own instrumental range. Your previous raids here failed because the system is so thick with patrol ships and orbital missiles. Your squadrons were homed on before they got near the base planet. But by the time we today get so close they can't help spotting us, we'll also be traveling too fast to intercept. So will the torps we launch. We'll zip right through their inner defenses, wipe out their fort, and reach the opposite interference fringe before they've had time to sneeze."

Olak had bristled with increasing indignation as Donnan's insulting résumé of what everyone knew proceeded. The Dragar flashed teeth. "I am not a cub, colleague," he growled. "I have heard this many times before."

"Then may I beg my honored colleague to act as if he had?" Donnan murmured.

Olak clapped a hand to his sidearm. Donnan locked eyes with him. After a few seconds that quivered, the Draga gave way. He stamped over to the port screen and glared out at the stars.

Donnan permitted himself a moment of untensing. That had been a near thing. These otter-faced samurai had tempers like mercury fulminate. But he had to get the moral jump on them.

Eventually they must become *his* allies—or the tale of the last Earthmen would not be colorful enough to cross the galaxy. And the best means of putting them down, however dangerous, seemed to be to outpride them.

"Hold it!" Goldspring rattled off a series of figures. Donnan and Howard modified course again.

"That one's up ahead, right?" Donnan asked.

"Yes." Goldspring tugged his beard. "May have been looking for us."

"I thought I picked up a trace a few minutes ago," said Wells at the radar. "I didn't mention it, because it was gone again right way. Could have been an automatic spy station . . . which could have alerted yonder ship."

Donnan nodded. Everybody had realized nothing could be done about that. Black-painted, solar-powered, of negligible mass, a detector station in orbit could not be avoided by the *Hrunna.* Any ship which passed close would be spotted by its instruments and a warning would be beamcast to the nearest patrol unit. Spaceships would then go looking for the stranger. However, Donnan expected to detect those searchers in ample time to elude their own instruments.

Still, he wished a station had not blabbed so early in the game. Perhaps the Kandemirians were even more thorough about their defenses than Vorlakka intelligence had indicated.

He got out his pipe and reached for his pouch. But no. Better not. Almost out of tobacco. Ration yourself, son, till you can locate a substitute somewhere. . . . The thought led him to wine, and horses, and Alison, and every beloved thing that would not exist again. He chewed savagely on the cold pipe.

The destroyer flung herself onward. Men swapped a few words, attempted jokes, shifted at their posts and stared at their weapons. On the gun deck Yule, whom Donnan had pardoned for the murder of Bowman but whom no one quite trusted any longer, huddled against his torpedo tube as if the launching coils were his mother. Up on the bridge, Ramri and the standby navigator played chess. Slowly the blue sun swelled in the screens. Ever more often, the ship moved crabwise to evade being detected.

Until:

"That vessel registering now is running very nearly parallel to us, at about the same speed and acceleration," Goldspring computed. "We'll enter the effective range of his instruments before long."

"Can't avoid him, eh?" Donnan said.

"No. The enemy craft have gotten too thick. See, if we dodge this way we'll run smack into this cluster of boats—" Goldspring pointed to a chart he was maintaining—"and if we deviate very far in the other direction, we'll be spied by that large craft yonder. And he could loose quite a barrage, I'm sure. We'll do our best to hold our present vector and take our chances with the ship I just mentioned."

"Hm, I dunno. If his own vectors are so similar to ours—"

"Not similar enough. He'd have to accelerate at thirty gees to get really near us. And he's a cruiser, at least, judging from the power of his emission. A cruiser can't do thirty."

"A cruiser's torpedoes can do a hundred or more."

"I know. He probably will fire at us. But according to my data, with our improved detection capability, we'll have sighting information at least ten seconds in advance of his. So our broadside will intercept his completely—nothing will get through—at a distance of half a kilomile."

"Well," Donnan sighed, "I'll take your word for it. This was bound to happen sooner or later."

Olak's eyes filmed and his nostrils flared. "I had begun to fear we would see no combat on this mission," he said.

"That would'a suited me fine," Donnan answered. "Space war's too hard on my nerves. A bare-knuckle brawl is kinda fun, but this sitting and watching while a bunch of robots do your fighting for you feels too damned helpless. . . Steady as she goes, then."

They weren't very far from the planet, he told himself. In another hour they could discharge their missiles. But that hour might get a bit rough.

Gunnery was out of his department. His officers' orders barked in his awareness, but he paid little attention. Hands loose on the pilot board, he thought mostly about Earth. There had been a girl once, not Alison, though Alison's lips had also been sweet. . . . Sparks flared and died among the stars. "One, two, three, four," Goldspring counted. "Five, six!"

"No more?" Ramri asked from the chessboard.

"No. Nothing more registers. We intercepted his whole barrage.

And we've three torps left over that are still moving. They just might
zero in on that fellow."

"Excellent," said Ramri. He tapped the sweating man who sat
across the board from him. "Your move, Lieutenant. . . . Lieutenant!
Do you feel all right?"

Wells yelled. Donnan didn't stop to look. He crammed on a full
sideways vector. Engines roared. Too late! For a bare instant, the
sternward screen showed him the heavy, clumsy object that darted
from low larboard. Then the deck rolled beneath him. He saw it split
open. A broken girder drove upward and sheared the head off
Ramri's chess partner.

Blood geysered. The crash of explosion struck like a fist in the
skull. Donnan was hurled against his safety web. Olak Faarer, who
had not been seated, cartwheeled past him, smashed into the panel
and bounced back, grotesquely flopping. Paragrav was gone; weightlessness became an endless tumble, through smoke and screams,
thunderous echoes, the hiss of escaping atmosphere. Blood drops
danced in the air, impossibly red.

The screens went blank. The lights went out. Too weak to be felt
as such, the pseudogravity of the ship's lunatic spin sent wreckage
crawling within the smashed hull. End over end, the ruin whirled on
a hyperbolic orbit toward the blue sun.

✸VII✸

> Then endure for a while, and live for a happier day.
> *—Virgil*

Prisoner!

He had been one twice before, on a vag rap in some Arkansas tank
town and then, years afterward, when a bunch of Chinese "volunteers" overran the Burmese valley where he was building a dam. But
Donnan didn't care to think about either occasion, now. At their
worst, those jails had stood on a green and peopled Earth.

The sky overhead was like incandescent brass. He couldn't look
near the sun. Squinting against its lightning-colored glare, he saw the

horizon waver with mirage. A furnace wind sucked moisture from skin and nose; he heard its monotonous roar as background to the crunch of bootsoles on gravel. And yet this was not a desert. Clusters of serpentine branches with leathery brown fringes rose thickly on every side, tossing and snapping in the blast. Overhead glided a kite-shaped animal whose skin glittered as if strewn with mica. The same glint was on the scales of the natives, who otherwise looked more like giant four-legged spiders with quadruple eyes and tentacular arms than anything else. No doubt they found this environment pleasant, as did the Kandemirian platoon to whom they kowtowed.

Donnan had rarely felt so alone. Failure, the death of ten men who trusted him and the captivity of forty others, had been horrible in him since the moment the enemy frigate laid alongside and the boarding party entered. There wasn't much the humans could have done except surrender, of course. Their ship was a hulk, only space-suits kept them alive, few even had a sidearm. They shambled to the other craft and waited apathetically in irons while they were ferried to Mayast II.

And now some big cheese wants to interrogate me himself, Donnan thought dully. How can I breathe the same air as Earth's murderers?

The beehive native huts which straggled around the fortifications were left behind as the platoon passed a steel gate and entered a mountainous concrete dome. The warren inside was unimportant, Donnan knew, frosting on the cake. The real base was buried deep in the planet's crust. Even so, his barrage could have wrecked it; if—

Activity hummed around him, tall Kandemirian forms striding with tools and weapons and papers down rubbery-floored corridors, offices where they squatted before legless desks under the arching leaves of uzhurun plants. They did not speak unnecessarily. The stillness was uncanny after the booming wind outside. Their odor overwhelmed him, acrid and animal.

He must concede they were handsome. A seven-foot humanoid with exaggerated breadth of shoulders and slenderness of waist looked idealized rather than grotesque. So did the nearly perfect ovoid of the head, its curve hardly broken by wide greenish-blue eyes with slit pupils, tiny nose, the peculiarly human and sensitive lips. Behind the large, pointed ears, a great ruff of hair framed the face.

Otherwise the skin was glabrous, silken smooth; the mobile twin tendrils on the upper lip were scent organs. The hands were also
humanoid, in spite of having six fingers and jet-black nails. The dig-
nified appearance was enhanced by austere form-fitting clothes in
subdued colors. Against this, the blazons of rank and birth stood
startlingly forth.

Donnan felt dumpy in their presence. He straightened his shoulders. So what, by God!

A door, above which was painted a giant eye, flew open. The
guard platoon halted, not stiffly and with clattering heels as Earth's
soldiers had been wont, but gliding to a partial crouch. Each touched
to his head the stubby barrel of his cyclic rifle. Someone whistled
within. The leader nudged Donnan forward. The door closed again
behind the man.

One guard stood in a corner, watchful. Otherwise the room's only
occupant was a middle-aged officer whose clan badge carried the
pentacle of supreme nobility. He belonged to that Kandemirian race
whose skin was pale gold and whose ruff was red. A scar seamed one
cheek. Still squatting, he smiled up at Donnan. "Greeting, shipmaster," he said in fluent Uru. "I bid you welcome." He arched naked
brows with a most human sardonicism. "If you choose to accept my
sentiments."

Donnan nodded curtly and lowered himself tailor fashion to the
floor. The Kandemirian touched a button on his desk. "You see
Tarkamat of Askunzhol, who speaks for the Baikush Clan and for the
field command of the Grand Fleet," he said without pretentiousness.

Almost, Donnan himself whistled. The high admiral in person,
director of combat operations along the whole Vorlakka front! "I had
no idea . . . we'd be of this much interest," he managed to say. "Uh—"

A silver plate in the desktop slid back and a tray emerged with two
cups of some hot liquid. "What records about your species I could find
in the files of this base," Tarkamat said, "mention that indak will not
hurt you. In fact, many of you find—found the beverage pleasant."

Automatically, Donnan reached for a cup. *No!* He yanked his
hand back as if it had been scalded.

Tarkamat made a purring noise that might correspond to laughter. "Believe me, if I wished you drugged, I would order that done.
What I offer you with the indak is the status of . . . no, not quite a

guest, but more than a captive. Drink."

Donnan began to shake. He needed a while before he could stammer, "I, I, I'll be damned if I'll . . . take anything . . . from you! From any murdering sneak . . . of a Kandemirian."

The soldier tilted his rifle and growled. Tarkamat hushed him with a soft trill. For a moment the admiral studied his prisoner, scarred countenance enigmatic. Then, very quietly, he said: "Do you believe my folk annihilated yours? But you are wrong. We had no part in that deed."

"Who did, then?" Donnan shouted. He started to rise, fists knotted, but sank down again and struggled for breath.

The red-ruffed head wove back and forth. "I do not know, shipmaster. Our intelligence service has made some effort to learn who is responsible, but thus far has failed. Vorlak seems the likeliest possibility."

"No." Donnan gulped toward a degree of self-possession. "I was there. They showed me proof they were innocent."

"What proof?"

"A treaty—" Donnan stopped.

"Ah, so. Between themselves and some Terrestrial nation? Yes, we knew about that, from various sources." Tarkamat made a negligent gesture. "We feel quite sure that none of the minor independent powers, such as Xo, struck at Earth. They lack both resources and motive."

"Who's left but Kandemir, then?" Donnan's voice was jagged and strange in his own ears. "Earth—one nation of Earth, at least—was helping your enemies; that's motive. And the Solar System is patrolled by your robot missiles. I took photographs."

"So did we," Tarkamat answered imperturbably. "We sent an expedition there to look about when we heard the news. It was also attacked. But the Mark IV Quester is, frankly, not the best weapon of its type. Hundreds have been captured by foreign powers, enemy and neutral, through being disabled or having their computers jammed or simply because their warheads were duds. Someone who wished to blacken our name—and has, in fact, succeeded, because few people believe our denials—such a party could have accumulated those missiles for the purpose. Please note, too, that the Mark IV is not ordinarily as slow and awkward as those encountered in the Solar

System. Does that not suggest they were deliberately throttled down, to make sure that there would be escapees to carry the tale?"

"Or to give your propaganda exactly the argument you've just given me," Donnan growled. "You can't sweep under the rug that the treaty between Russia and Vorlak gave you reason to destroy Earth."

"Then why have we not made a similar attempt on Monwaing?" Tarkamat countered. "They, in their alleged neutrality, have been more useful to the Vorlakka cause for a much longer time than one country on Earth supplying a few shiploads of small arms." He lifted his head, superciliously. "We have refrained, not from squeamishness, but because the effort would be out of proportion to the result. Especially since a living planet is far more valuable to us in the long run. We could not colonize a Monwaingi world without sterilizing it first; but despite the cooler sun, we could have planted ourselves firmly on Earth . . . if we chose . . . when we got around to it. The biochemistries are enough alike."

His tone hardened: "Do not imagine your world, or any country on it, amounted to anything militarily. Had that one nation, that Ro-si-ya or whatever it was called, had it proven a serious annoyance, do you know what we would have done? If simple threats would not make them desist, we would have used the tried and true process which has gained Kandemir easy domination over five other backward planets. We would have sent a mission to the Terrestrial rivals of Ro-si-ya, pointed out how strong she was becoming in relation to them, and made them our cat's paws. Why expend good Kandemirian lives to conquer Earth when the Earthlings themselves would have done half the work for us?"

Donnan bit his lip. He hated to admit how the argument struck home. What he remembered of human history told him how often a foreign invader had entered as the ally of one local faction. Romans in Greece, Saxons in Britain, English in Ireland and India, Spaniards in Mexico—*If I forget thee, O Jerusalem!*

"Very clever," he said. "Have you any actual proof?"

Tarkamat smiled. "Who is interrogating whom, shipmaster? Accept my word or not, as you choose. Frankly, the clans care little what others think of them. However," he added more seriously, "we are not fiends. Look about you with unprejudiced eyes. Our overlordship may seem harsh at times. And it is in fact, when our interests so require. But our proconsuls are not meddlesome. They respect ancient usage. The subject peoples gain protection and share in the prosperity of an ever-widening free trade sphere. We do not drain their wealth. If anything, they live better than the average Kandemirian."

Harking back over what he had learned, Donnan must needs nod. The Spartan virtues of the nomads did include governmental honesty. "You forget one thing," he said. "They aren't free any longer."

"So your culture would claim," Tarkamat replied with sudden brutality. "But your culture is dead. What use can sentimentality be to you? Make the best of your situation."

"I'm sentimental enough not to collaborate with whoever killed my people," Donnan snapped.

"I told you Kandemir did not. Your opinion is of insufficient importance to me for me to belabor that subject further. A handful of rootless mercenaries like yourselves hardly seem worth keeping prisoner, even. Except . . . for the astonishingly deep penetration you made of our defenses. I want to know how that was done."

"Luck. You got us in the end, after all."

"By using a new device we had been reserving for the next major battle."

"I can guess what that was," Donnan said, hoping to postpone the real unpleasantness. (Why? he wondered. What did it matter? What did anything matter?) "Missiles, like ships, operate on paragrav these days, to get the range and acceleration that it offers. So countermissiles are equipped with paragrav detectors. They home on the engines of a target object. Only if the engine is switched off do they use radar, infrared, and other shorter-range equipment. Well, you used a big paragrav job to match vectors with our ship. We spotted it easily. But it didn't try to zero on us. It ran parallel instead, and released a flight—not of regular torps, but of rockets. We weren't on the lookout for anything so outmoded. Over that short distance, an atomic-powered ion drive could rendezvous with us. We didn't know it was there till too late to dodge."

"Actually, you were hit by only one rocket out of several," Tarkamat confessed. "But one suffices. You would have been blown to gas, had our anxiety to know your secret not made us preset the warheads for minimal blast."

"There is no secret." Donnan felt sweat gather in his armpits and trickle down his ribs. Before him wavered the image of Goldspring, half stunned, bleeding in the face, elbowing aside the wreckage and the dead that bobbed around him, by flashbeam light ripping and hammering the detector into shapelessness while the enemy frigate closed in.

"There most certainly is," Tarkamat stated flatly. "Statistical analysis of what course data we have for you strongly suggests you were able to detect us at unprecedented distances. Our own best paragrav instruments are crowding the theoretical limit of sensitivity. Therefore you employed some new principle. This in turn may conceivably lead to entire new classes of weapons. I do not intend to play games, shipmaster. I presume you have no great emotional attachment to Vorlak, but some of your crew. One crewman per day will be executed before your eyes until you agree to collaborate. The method of execution I have in mind takes several hours."

I expected something like this, Donnan thought. Coldness and grayness drowned his spirit. As if from immensely far away, he heard Tarkamat continue:

"If you cooperate, you can expect good treatment. You will be settled on a congenial planet. Any other humans who may be found can join you there. An able species like yours can surely fit itself into the framework set by the imperium. But I warn you against treachery. You will be allowed to build and demonstrate your devices, but under the close supervision of our own physicists, to whom the principles involved must be explained beforehand. Since I presume you left people behind at Vorlak, who will also be working along these lines, delays shall not be tolerated. Very well, shipmaster, give me your answer."

Why keep on? the mind sighed in Donnan. Why not surrender? Maybe they really did not bomb Earth. Maybe the best thing is to become their serfs. Oh, Jesus, but I'm tired.

I was tired in that Burma prison camp too, he thought drearily. I didn't believe we'd ever get sprung, me and the others. Barbed wire, jungle, sloppy-looking guards with almighty quick guns, miserable villagers who didn't dare help us—But that was on Earth. There was still a future then. We could plan on . . . on sunrise, and moonrise, and rain and wind and light; on the game continuing after we ourselves stopped playing. So, we didn't stop. We cooked up a hundred plans for crashing out. One of 'em, at least, was pretty good. Might have worked, if the diplomats hadn't arranged our release about that time. If it had not worked, well, we'd have been decently dead, shoveled down into an earth that still lived.

That's why I've gone so gutless, he thought. Now there's nothing in space or time except my own piddling self.

The hell there isn't!

The knowledge burst within him. He sat straight with an oath.

Tarkamat regarded him over a steaming cup. "Well, shipmaster?" he murmured.

"We'll do what you want," Donnan said. "Of course."

✳VIII✳

Mit shout and crash and sabre flash,
And vild husaren shout
De Dootchmen boorst de keller in,
Und rolled de lager out;
Und in the coorlin' powder shmoke,
Vhile shtill de pullets sung,
Dere shtood der Breitmann, axe in hand,
A knockin' out de boong.
Gling, glang, gloria!
Victoria! Encoria!
De shpicket beats de boong.

—*Leland*

From their window high in that tower known as i-Chula—the Clouded—Sigrid Holmen and Alexandra Vukovic could easily see aro-Kito, One Who Awaits. That spire lifted shimmering walls and patinaed bronze roof above most of its neighbors; otherwise its corkscrew ramps and twisted buttresses were typical Eyzka architecture. The operations within, however, resembled none which had yet been seen on Zatlokopa, or in this entire civilization-cluster. Terran Traders, Inc., had leased the whole building.

As yet the company was not big enough to fill every room. There was no reason why the *Europa* crew should not live there, and a number of the women did. But some, like Sigrid and Alexandra, had to get away from their work physically or explode. They took lodgings throughout the city.

Occasionally, though, as the company's growth continued, work sought them out. This evening Alexandra was bringing an important potential client home for dinner. The sha-Eyzka were very human in that respect; they settled more deals over dessert and liqueurs than over desks and disto-scribes. If Terran Traders could please Taltla of the sha-Oktzu, and land that house's account, a big step forward would have been taken.

Sigrid looked at her watch. By now she was used to the time units, eight-based number system, and revolving clock faces employed here. Damn! The others would arrive in ten minutes, and she hadn't perfumed yet.

A moment she lingered, savoring the fresh air that blew across her skin. Zatlokopa was not only terrestroid, but midway through an interglacial period, climatically a paradise for humans. The women had quickly adopted a version of native dress, little more than shorts and sandals, with the former only for the sake of pockets. The sun slanted long rays across the towers, a goldenness that seemed to fill the atmosphere. How quiet it was!

Too quiet, she thought. A winged snake cruised above the many-steepled skyline, but nothing else moved, no groundcars, no fliers, not a walker in the grassy lanes between buildings or a boat on the sunset-yellow canals. The city had subways, elevated tunnel-streets that looped like vines from tower to tower, halls and shaftways in the houses themselves. This was not Earth, she knew, it never had been, never could be. Nothing could ever again be Earth.

A spaceship lifted silent on paragravity, kilometers distant and yet so big that she saw sunlight burn along its flanks. The Holdar liner, she thought; we have a consignment aboard. That reminded her. She had no time for self-pity. Closing the window, she hurried into the kitchen and checked the autochef. Everything seemed under control. Thank God for the high development of robotics in this cluster. No human cook had the sense of taste and smell to prepare a meal that an Eyzka would think fit to eat.

Sigrid returned to the living room, where Earth-type furniture looked homely and lost amidst intricate vaulting and miniature fountains. The perfume cabinet slid open for her. She consulted a chart. Formality on Zatlokopa paid no attention to clothes, but made a ritual of odors. For entertaining a guest of Taltla's rank, you used a blend of Class Five aerosols. . . . She wrinkled her nose. Everything in Class Five smelled alike to her—rather like ripe silage. Well, she could drench herself with . . . let's see, the sha-Eyzka usually enjoyed cologne, and there was some left from the ship. . . . Her hand closed on the little cut-glass bottle.

The door said: "Two desire admittance."

Had Alexandra brought the fellow here early? She'd been *told* not to. "Let them in," Sigrid said without looking at the scanner. The door opened.

Blank metal met her eyes. Not sun-browned human skin or the green and gold fur of an Eyzka, but polished alloy. The robots were approximately humanoid, a sheer two and a half meters tall. She stared up, and up, to faceless heads and photoelectric slits. Those glowed dull red, as if furnaces burned behind.

"*Kors i Herrans namn!*" she exclaimed. "What's this?"

One glided past her, cat-silent. The other extended an arm and closed metal fingers on her shoulder, not hard, but chilling. She tried indignantly to step back. The grip tightened. She sucked in a gasp.

The other robot came back. It must have checked if she was alone. The first said: "Come. You need not be harmed, but make no trouble." It spoke Uru, which was also the interstellar auxiliary language in this cluster as in several others.

"What the blazes do you mean?" Anger drove out fear.

Hearing her speak in Eyzka, the robot shifted to that language, fluent though accented. It laid its free hand on her head. The fingers nearly encircled her skull. "Come, before I squeeze," it ordered.

That grip could crush her temples like an almond shell. "Make no outcry," the second robot warned. Its accent was even thicker.

Numbly, she accompanied them out. The corridor was a tube from nowhere to nowhere; doors were locked and blind; only the ventilators, gusting a vegetable smell in her face, made any noise. Her skin turned cold and wet, her lips tingled. They picked the right hour for a kidnapping she thought in hollowness. Nearly everyone is still at work, or else inside preparing for the worker's return. You won't find casuals moving about, as you would in a human city. This is not Earth. Earth is a cinder, ten thousand light-years distant.

She grew aware of a pain in one hand. With a dull astonishment, she saw that she still gripped the cologne bottle. The faceted glass had gouged red marks into her palm.

Suddenly she lifted the thing, unscrewed the atomizer nose and poured the contents over her head.

Steel fingers snatched it from her. They took a good deal of skin along too. Sigrid tried not to whimper with pain. She sucked her hand while the twin giants bent their incandescent gaze on the bottle. The throbbing eased. No bones seemed broken. . . .

The robots conferred in a language she didn't know. Then to her, in sharp Eyzka: "Attempted suicide?"

"The liquid isn't corrosive," the other machine observed.

You noseless idiot! Sigrid thought wildly. She jammed her bleeding hand into one pocket and let them hustle her along.

Footfalls were inaudible. Nothing lived, nothing stirred, save themselves. They went down a dropshaft to a tunnel. A public gravsled halted at an arm signal. They boarded and it accelerated smoothly along its route.

They aren't independent robots, Sigrid decided. She was becoming able to think more coolly now. They're remote-control mechanisms. I've never seen their type before. But then, there are thousands of kinds of automaton in this galactic region, and I've been here less than a year. Yes, they're just body-waldos.

But whose? Why?

Not natives. The sha-Eyzka had received the humans kindly, in their fashion: given them the freedom of Zatlokopa, taught them language and customs, heard their story. After that the newcomers were on their own, in the raw capitalism which dominated this whole cluster. But a small syndicate of native investors had been willing to take a flyer and help them get started. There wasn't much question of commercial rivalry yet. The women's operations were too radically unlike anything seen before. Carriers and brokers existed in plenty throughout this cluster, but not on the scale which Terran Traders contemplated—nor with such razzle-dazzle innovations as profit sharing, systems analysis, and motivational research among outworld cultures. So the kidnappers were not likely to be Eyzka competitors.

The accent with which the robots spoke, and the failure of their operators to guess what was in the cologne bottle, also suggested—

The sled halted for a native passenger. He bounded on gracefully, beautiful as a hawk or a salmon had been beautiful on Earth. Steel fingers clenched about Sigrid's wrist till she felt her bones creak. She didn't cry out, though. "Not one sign to him," the robot murmured in Uru.

"If you'll let me go, I won't," she managed.

The pressure slackened. She leaned weakly back on the bench. The Eyzka gave her a startled glance, took out a perfumed handkerchief, and moved pointedly as far from her as he could.

Presently she was taken off the sled. Down another ramp, through another passage, twist, turn, a last downward spiral, a dark dingy tunnel with a hundred identical doors, and one that opened for her. She stepped through between the robots. The door closed again at her back.

A dozen creatures sat at a table. They were squat and leathery, with flat countenances. Two more were at a waldo panel in the rear of the room. Those had obviously been guiding the robots. They also turned to face her, and the machines flanking Sigrid became statues. The room was redly lit, shadowy and cold. A record player emitted a continuous thin wailing.

Forsi, Sigrid realized. The second most powerful race in this cluster. She might have guessed.

One goblin leaned toward her. His skin rustled as he moved. "There is no reason to waste time," he clipped. "We have already learned that you stand high among the sha-Terra. The highest ranking one, in fact, whom it was practicable for us to capture. You will cooperate or suffer the consequences. Understand, to Forsi commercial operations are not merely for private gain, as here on Zatlokopa, but are part of a larger design. You, Terran Traders corporation have upset the economic balance of this cluster. We extrapolate that the upsetting will grow exponentially if not checked. In order to counteract your operations, we must have detailed information about their rationale and the fundamental psychology behind it. You have shrewdly exploited the fact that no two species think entirely alike and that you yourselves, coming from an altogether foreign civilization-complex, are doubly unpredictable. We shall take you home with us and make studies."

Despite herself, Sigrid's knees wobbled. She struggled not to faint.

"If you cooperate fully, the research may not damage you too much," said the Forsi. "At least, the work will not be made unnecessarily painful. We bear you no ill will. Indeed, we admire your enterprise and only wish you had chosen our planet instead of Zatlokopa." He shrugged. "But I daresay climate influenced you."

"And society." Despite herself, her voice was husky with fear. "A decent culture to live in."

He was not insulted. Another asked curiously, "Did you search long before picking this culture?"

"We were lucky," Sigrid admitted. Anything to gain time! "We had . . . this sort of goal . . . in mind—a free enterprise economy at a stage of pioneering and expansion—but there are so many clusters. . . . After visiting only two, though, we heard rumors about yours." A measure of strength returned. She straightened. The Forsi were apparently even more dull-nosed than humans, which gave some hope. "Do you think you can get away with this crime?" she blustered. "Let me go at once and I'll make no complaint against you."

The goblins chuckled.

"Best we start with you at once," the leader told her. "If we can reach the spaceport before the evening rush, so you are not noticed by anyone, our ship can ask immediate clearance and lift within an hour. Otherwise we may have to wait for the same time tomorrow."

Sigrid shivered in the bitter air.

"What harm have we done?" she protested. "We sha-Terra don't threaten anybody. We're alone, planetless, we can't have children or—"

The chief signalled his waldo operators, who returned to their control boards.

"We hope to leave within a few years," Sigrid pleaded. "Can't you realize our situation? We've made no secret of it. Our planet is dead. A few ships with our own kind—males—are scattered we know not where in the galaxy. We fled this far to be safe from Earth's unknown enemy. Not to become powerful here, not even to make our home here, but to be safe. Then we had to make a living—"

"Which you have done with an effectiveness that has already overthrown many calculations," said a Forsi dryly.

"But, but, but listen! Certainly we're trying to become rich. As rich as possible. But not as an end in itself. Only as a means. When we have enough wealth, we can hire enough ships . . . to scour the galaxy for other humans. That's all, I swear!"

"A most ingenious scheme," the chief nodded. "It might well succeed, given time."

"And then . . . we wouldn't stay here. We wouldn't want to. This isn't our civilization. We'd go back, get revenge for Earth, establish ourselves among familiar planets. Or else we'd make a clean break, go far beyond every frontier, colonize a wholly new world. We are not your competitors. Not in the long run. Can't you understand?"

"Even the short run is proving unpleasant for us," the chief said. "And as for long-range consequences, you may depart, but the corporate structure you will have built up—still more important, the methods and ideas you introduce—those will remain. Forsi cannot cope with them. So, you will now go with us through the rear exit. A private gravsled is waiting to bring us to the spaceport."

The waldo operators put arms and legs into the transmission sheaths, heads into the control hoods. A robot reached out for Sigrid.

She dodged. It lumbered after her. She fled across the room. No use yelling. Every apartment in this city was soundproofed. The second robot closed in from the other side. They herded her toward a corner.

"Behave yourself!" The chief rose and rapped on the table. "There are punishments—"

She didn't hear the rest. Backed against a wall, she saw the gap between the machines and moved as if to go through it. The robots glided together. Sigrid spun on her heel and went to the right. An arm scooped after her. It brushed her hair, then she was past.

The robots whirled and ran in pursuit. She snatched up a stool and threw it. The thing bounced off metal. Useless, useless. She scuttled toward the door. A robot got there first. She ran back. A Forsi left his seat and intercepted her.

Cold arms closed about her waist. She snarled and brought her knee sharply up. Vulnerable as a man, the creature yammered and let go. She sprang by him. The stool lay in her path. She seized it and brought it down on a bald head at the table. The *thonk!* was loud above their voices.

Up onto the table top she jumped. The chief grabbed at her ankles. She kicked him in one bulging eye. As he sagged, cursing his pain, she stepped on his shoulder and leaped down behind.

Running faster than human, the robots were on either side of her. She dropped to the floor and rolled beneath the table. The Forsi shouted and scrambled. For a minute or more they milled around, interfered with the robots. She saw their thick gray legs churn and stamp.

Someone bawled an order. The Forsi moved out of the way. One robot lifted the table. Sigrid rose as it did. The other approached her. She balanced, waiting. As it grabbed, she threw herself forward. The hands clashed together above her head. She went on her knees before its legs. There was just room to squeeze between. She twisted clear, bounced to her feet, and pelted toward the rear exit.

No doubt it wouldn't open for her—How long had she dodged and ducked? How long could she? The breath was raw in her gullet.

The front door spoke. "Open!" Sigrid yelled, before anyone could shout a negative. And it was not set to obey only a few beings. It flung wide.

Four sha-Eyzka stood there. And Alexandra, Alexandra. She had the only gun. It flew to her hand.

The robots wheeled and pounced. A bullet ricocheted off one breastplate with a horrible bee-buzz. Alexandra's face twisted in a grin. She held her ground as the giants neared, aimed past them, and fired twice. The operators slumped. The robots went dead.

The Forsi leader howled a command. Recklessly, his followers attacked. Two more were shot. Then they were upon Alexandra and her companions in a wave.

Sigrid ran around the mêlée. To the control panels! She yanked one body from its seat. The sheaths and masks didn't fit her very well, and she wasn't used to waldo operation in any event. However, skill wasn't needed. Strength sufficed. The robot had enough of that. She began plucking gray forms off her rescuers and disabling them. The fight was soon over.

An Eyzka called the police corporation while the others secured the surviving Forsi. "There's going to be one all-time diplomatic explosion about this, my dear," Alexandra panted. "Which . . . I think . . . Terran Traders, Inc., can turn to advantage."

Sigrid grinned feebly. "What a ravening capitalist you have become," she said.

"I have no choice, have I? You were the one who first proposed that we turn merchants." The Yugoslav girl hefted her gun. "But if violence is to be a regular thing, *I* will make a suggestion or two. Not that you did badly in that department, either. When you weren't home, and Taltla said the hallway reeked of cologne, I knew something was amiss. Whoo, what a dose you gave yourself! A week's baths won't clean it all off. These lads I got together to help me could even follow where you'd gone by sled, you left such a scent." She looked at the sullen prisoners. Her head shook, her tongue clicked. "So they thought to get tough with us? Poor little devils!"

✳IX✳

> Waken, all of King Volmer's men!
> Buckle on rusted swords again,
> Fetch in the churches the dust-covered shield.
> Blazoned by trolls and the beasts of the field,
> Waken your horses, which graze in the mould,
> Set in their bellies the rowels of gold,
> Leap toward Gurre town,
> Now that the sun is down!
>
> —*Jacobsen*

Rain came from the north on a wind that bounced it smoking off roofs and flattened the snake trees on runneling mud. Lightning glared above, stark white and then a blink of darkness; thunder banged through all howls and gurgles. The Loho crawled into their beehive huts and wallowed together, each heap a family. Not even the Tall Masters could demand they work in such weather! Only Dzhugach Base, domes and towers and sky-pointing ships, held firm in the landscape.

During the past few weeks, Donnan had come to know the Kandemirians well enough that he suspected a certain symbolism when Koshcha of the Zhanbulak told him over the intercom that the paragrav detector would receive a free-space test as scheduled. He saluted and switched off the speaker. "They're on their way, boys," he said. "Twitter-tweet— "he meant one of the natives that did menial work around the place; a few spoke Uru—"remarked to me that it's raining cats and dogs, which on this planet means tigers and wolverines. But our chums aren't going to let that stop them."

He saw how the forty men grew taut. Howard moistened his lips, O'Banion crossed himself, Wright whispered something to Rogers, Yule in his loneliness on the fringe clamped fists together till the knuckles stood white. "Calm down, there," Donnan said. "We don't want to give the show away yet. Maybe no one here savvies English or can read a human expression, but they aren't fools."

Goldspring wheeled forward the detector, haywired ugliness on a lab cart. The biggest chunk of luck so far in this caper, Donnan thought, had been Koshcha's agreement to let them have one model here in their living quarters to tinker with when Goldspring and his assistants were not actually in the base workshop. To be sure, the human request was reasonable. In the present state of the art, an interferometric detector was not a standardized jigsaw puzzle but a cranky monster made to work by cut and try. So the more time Goldspring had to fool around with such gadgets, the sooner he would get at least one of the lot functioning. This was the more true as the detectors being built here were much scaled up from the one he had used aboard the *Hrunna*.

As for the rest of the men, especially those not qualified to help in the workshop, they also benefited. Without something like this, to think about and discuss, they might have gone stir crazy. No hazard was involved to the Kandemirians, no fantasy about the prisoners turning a micro-ultra-filtmeter into a Von Krockmeier hyperspace lever and escaping. Koshcha's physics team knew precisely what each electronic component was and for what mathematical reason it was there. No Earthling touched any equipment until Goldspring's lectures had convinced some very sharp minds that his theory was sound and his circuit diagrams valid. Furthermore, the prison suite was bugged.

Nevertheless, Koshcha might well have refused Donnan's request for parts to build a detector in the living quarters. If so, Donnan's plan for crashing out would not have been completely invalidated, but the escape of the entire human crew would have been impossible.

Not that it looked very probable yet.

Goldspring's face glistened with sweat. "Ready to go, then . . . I think," he said. The few trained men who were supposed to accompany him into space today gathered close around, apart from the rest. Donnan joined their circle. His grin at them was the merest rictus. His own mouth was dry and he couldn't smell their sweat, he stank so much himself. His awareness thrummed.

But he functioned with an efficiency that a distant part of him admired. The technicians around the cart shielded it from the telecom eye. Goldspring unbolted a cover on the awkward machine. Donnan plunged his hands into its guts.

A minute later he nodded and stepped back. Goldspring returned the cover. Ramri joined Donnan, taking the man's arm and standing close to hide the bulge under the coat.

"Do you truly believe we shall succeed?" the Monwaingi fluted in English.

"Ask me again in an hour," Donnan said. Idiotically, since they had discussed this often before: "You sure you can operate such a boat, now? I mean, not just that it's built for another species than yours, but the whole layout'll be new. The manuals will be in a foreign language. Even the instruments, the meters—Kandemirian numbers are based on twelve, aren't they?—I mean—"

"I believe *we* can do it," Ramri said gently. "Spaceships from similar planets do not differ that much from each other. They cannot. As for navigation tables and the like, I do have some familiarity with the Erzhuat language." His feathers rose, so that blueness rippled along them. "Carl-my-friend, you must not be frightened. This is a moment for glory."

"Tell me that, too, later on." Donnan tried to laugh. He failed.

"No, can you not understand? Had there been no such hope as this, I would have ended my own life weeks ago. So nothing can be lost today. In all the years I spent on Earth as an agent of the Tanthai traders, I never grasped why the onset of hope should terrify you humans more than despair does."

"Well, we, uh, we just aren't Monwaingi, I reckon."

"No. Which is best. What a splendid facet of reality was darkened when Earth came to an end! I do not think there can ever have been a nobler concept than your own country's constitutional law. And chess, and Beethoven's last quartets, and—" Ramri squeezed the arm he held. "No, forgive me, my friend, your facet is not gone. It shall shine again . . . on New Earth."

They said no more. A thick stillness descended on the room.

After some fraction of eternity, the main door opened. Four soldiers glided in and posted themselves, two on either side, guns covering the men. Koshcha and half a dozen associates followed. The chief physicist gestured imperiously. "Come along, you," he snapped in Uru. "Goldspring's party. The rest get back there."

Donnan and Ramri advanced. The Kandemirians seemed endlessly tall. They've only got thirteen or fourteen inches on you, Donnan told himself under the noise in his head. That don't signify. The hell it doesn't. Longest fourteen inches I ever looked up. He cleared his throat. "I'd like to come too," he said. "In fact, I'd like to take our full complement along."

"What nonsense is this?" Koshcha stiffened.

Donnan came near enough to buttonhole the scientist, if a buttonhole had been there. "We're all technically trained," he argued. "We're used to working as a team. We've all fiddled around with the detector you let us build in here, talked about it, made suggestions. You'd find our whole bunch useful."

"Crammed into a laboratory flitter with my own personnel?" Koshcha scoffed. "Don't be a clown, Donnan."

"But damn it, we're going off our trolleys in here. The agreement was we'd switch sides and work for your planet. Well, we've done so. We've produced several detectors in your workshops and one in here. Their ground tests have been satisfactory. So when are you going to start treating us like allies instead of prisoners?"

"Later. I tell you, no arrangements—"

Donnan pulled the gun from beneath his coat and jammed it into Koshcha's belly. "Not a move!" he said in a near whisper. "Don't so much as twitch a tendril. Anybody."

The unhuman eyes grew black with pupil dilation. One soldier tried to swing his rifle around from its inward aim. Ramri kicked;

three talons struck with bone-breaking force. The weapon clattered down as the soldier doubled in anguish.

Donnan could only hope that his men, crowding near, screened this tableau from the telecom eye with their backs—and that the Kandemirians in the warden's office were too confident by now to watch the spy screen continuously. "Drop your guns or Koshcha dies," he said.

Like most nomadic units, this one was organized by clans; the technicians and their bodyguards were blood relatives. And the leader of the group was also a senior Zhanbulak. Furthermore, Donnan had plainly thumbed his rifle to continuous-fire explosive. Before he could be shot, he would have chewed up several Kandemirians. The three soldiers who still covered his men with their own guns might have threatened to shoot them. But the soldiers were too shaken. Donnan heard their rifles fall. "About face," he commanded. "To the hangar . . . march!"

The Kandemirians stumbled out the door, looking stunned, and down a long, bare, coldly lit corridor. Donnan paced them at the rear, his gun in the crook of an arm. His crew surged after.

Koshcha's mind must be churning below that red ruff. How had the Terrestrials gotten a weapon? By what treachery, through what rebellious Loho or (oh, unthinkable!) what bribed clansman? Maybe in another minute or two someone would guess the answer. But that would be too late. Four men behind Donnan had guns now, dropped by the guards.

Four real guns.

Hand-make a new type of device. Complicate your problem by building it on a larger scale than before. Your circuits will remain essentially the same, and understandable. Your captors will issue you precisely those conductors, resistors, amplifiers and other components that you can prove you need. But who pays attention to the chassis? It is only a framework, supporting and enclosing the instrument's vitals. You may have to adjust this or that electronic part to compensate for its properties, but not by much. The chassis is negligible.

So if anyone asks why you are turning out a slim hollow cylinder on lathe and drill beam, explain casually that it is to strengthen the frame and hold a sheaf of wires. If your angle braces have odd shapes, this must be dictated by the geometry of the layout. If a hole in the cabinet, accidentally burnt through, is repaired by bolting a scrap of metal over it, who will notice the outline of that scrap? And so on and so on.

Come the moment of untruth, you quickly remove those certain parts from the chassis, fit them together, and have quite a good imitation of a cyclic rifle.

If the scheme had failed, Donnan wasn't sure what he would have done. Probably have yielded completely and let Kandemir have his soul. As matters had developed, though, he was committed. If his plan went up the spout now, his best bet was to try and get himself killed.

Fair enough, he thought.

They started down a ramp. Two noncoms going the other way saluted. They couldn't hide their surprise at the human crowd in the officers' wake. "Let 'em have it, boys," Donnan said. "Quiet, though."

A gun burped. The noncoms fell like big loose-jointed puppets. Their blood was darker red than a man's. Donnan wondered momentarily if they had wives and kids at home.

"No, you murderer!" Koshcha stopped, half turning around. Donnan jerked the fake gun at him.

"March!"

They hustled on. There was little occasion, especially today, for anyone to use the flitter hangar. But on arrival—

Two sentries outside the gate slanted their rifles forward. "Halt! By what authority—" A blast from behind Donnan smashed them to fragments, smeared across the steel panels.

A Kandemirian prisoner roared, wheeled, and sprang at him. He gave the fellow his gun butt in the mouth. The Kandemirian went to one knee, reached forward and caught Donnan's ankle. They rolled over, grappling for the throat. Rifles coughed above them. An alarm began to whistle.

"The door's locked!" Ramri shouted. "Here, give me a weapon, I shall try to blast the lock."

The Kandemirian's smashed mouth grinned hatred at Donnan. The giant had gotten on top of him, twelve fingers around the windpipe. Donnan felt his brain spin toward blackness. He set his own wrists between the enemy's and heaved outward with all the force in his shoulders. The black nails left bloody tracks as they were pulled free. Donnan slugged below the chest. Nothing happened. The Kandemirians didn't keep a solar plexus there. He climbed to a sitting position by means of the clansman's tunic. The unfairly long arms warded him off. Thumbs sought his eyeballs. He ducked his head and pummeled the enemy's back.

Ramri left the sprung door in a single jump. One kick by a spurred foot opened the Kandemirian's rib cage. Donnan crawled from beneath. The alarm skirled over his heartbeats and his gulps for air.

"Hurry!" Howard shouted. "I hear 'em coming!"

The men poured through, into the cavernous hangar. Rank upon rank of small spacecraft gleamed almost as far as you could see. One was aimed roofward in its cradle. The airlock stood open. A fight ramped around there, as the humans attacked its crew.

"I must have a few moments aboard to study the controls," Ramri said to Donnan, who lurched along on Goldspring's arm. "I know that one alone can manage a flitter in an emergency, but I am not certain how, in this case."

"We'll oblige you," Lieutenant Howard said. He called out orders. A good man, Donnan thought remotely; a damn good second-rank officer. His trouble had been trying to be skipper. Well, I'm not showing up any too brilliantly in that post either, am I?

A flying wedge of humans formed behind Howard, He had a gun. The rest had mass and desperation. They charged over the gang ramp and through the lock. The Kandemirians gave way—no choice—and tried to follow. The remaining Terrestrials fell on them afresh. Bullets raved.

"Let's get you aboard also, captain," Goldspring said. "Get everybody aboard. We haven't much time."

"Haven't any time," said Yule. "Here comes the garrison."

A few giants loomed at the sagging door. Slugs hailed around them. One fell, the other two ran from sight. "They'll be back," Donnan mumbled. "And there are more entrances than this. We need a few men to hunker down—the boats and cradles'll provide cover—and stand 'em off till we can lift. Gimme a gun, somebody. Volunteers?"

"Here," said Yule. A curious, peaceful look descended on his face. He snatched away the rifle which O'Banion had handed Donnan.

"Gimme that," Donnan choked.

"Get him aboard, Mr. Goldspring," Yule ordered. "He'll be needed later on."

Donnan clung to the physicist, too dizzy and beaten to protest. Goldspring regarded Yule for a second or two. "Whoever stays behind will probably be killed," he said slowly.

Yule spat. "I know. So what? Not that I'm any goddam hero. But I'm a man."

"I'll design a weapon in your name," Goldspring said. "I thought of several while we were here."

"Good." Yule shoved him toward the lock. Three other men joined the rearguard. They posted themselves wherever they could find shelter. Presently they were alone, except for the dead.

Then, from several directions, the Kandemirians poured in. Explosions echoed under the roof. Thermite blazed and ate. Goldspring risked his life to appear in the airlock and wave: *We can go now.*

"You know damn well my squad 'ud never make it," Yule shouted at him. "Shut that door, you idiot, and let us get back to work!" He wasn't sure if Goldspring could hear through the racket or see through the smoke and reek. But after a few seconds the lock closed. The flitter sprang from its cradle. Automatic doors opened above. Rain poured in, blindingly, for the moment that the flitter needed to depart.

—"We are safe," Ramri sighed.

"From everything but missiles and half the Grand Fleet, trying to head us off before we make an interference fringe," Donnan said grimly.

"What can they do but annihilate us?"

"Uh . . . yes. I see what you mean. Safe."

Ramri peered into the viewscreen. Lightning had given way to the stars. "My friend," he said, and hesitated.

"Yes?" Donnan asked.

"I think—" The troubled voice faded. "I think we had best change course again." The Monwaingi touched controls. They were depending on random vectors to elude pursuit. After all, space was big and the Kandemirian defenses had been designed to halt things that moved planetward, not starward.

"That isn't what you were getting at," Donnan said.

"No." Decision came. Ramri straightened until his profile jutted across the constellations. "Carl-my-friend, I offer apology. But many years have passed since I saw my own people. I am the only one here who can read enough Erzhuat to pilot this vessel. I shall take us to Katkinu."

"Shucks, pal," Donnan said. "I expected that. Go right ahead." His tone roughened. "I'd like a few words with your leaders anyway."

A nation, to be successful, should change its tactics every ten years.
—*Napoleon*

For a moment, when his gaze happened to dwell on the horizon, Donnan thought he was home again. Snowpeaks afloat in serene blue, purple masses and distances that shaded into a thousand greens as the valley floor rolled nearer, the light of a yellow sun and the way cloud shadows raced across the world, wind blustering in sky and trees, woke him from a nightmare in which Earth had become a cinder. He thought confusedly that he was a boy, foot-loose in the Appalachians; he had slept in a hayloft and this dawn the farmer's daughter kissed him goodbye at the mailbox, which was overgrown with morning glory . . . A night that stung descended on his eyes.

Ramri glanced at him, once, and then concentrated on steering the groundrunner. After his years on Earth and in space, the avian found it a little disconcerting to ride on the chairlike humps of a twenty-foot, eight-legged mammaloid and control it by touching spots that were nerve endings. Such vehicles had been obsolescent on Katkinu even when he left. The paragrav boats that flitted overhead were more to Tanthai liking. But today he and Donnan were bound from his home to the Resident, who was of the Laothaung Society. Paying a formal call on a high official from *that* culture, and arriving in dead machinery, would have been an insult.

After a while, Donnan mastered himself. He fumbled with his

pipe. The devil take tobacco rationing . . . just now . . . especially since Ramri assured him that the creation of an almost identical leaf would be simple for any genetic engineer on any Monwaingi planet. When he had it lit, he paid close attention to nearby details. Katkinu was not Earth, absolutely not, and he'd better fix that squarely in his head.

Even to the naked eye, the similarities of grass and foliage and flowers were superficial. Biochemical analysis showed how violently those life forms differed from himself. He had needed anti-allergen shots before he could even leave the space flitter and step on Katkinuan soil. The odors blown down the wind were spicy, mostly pleasant, but like nothing he had ever known at home. Along this road (paved, if that was the word, with a thick mossy growth, intensely green) walked blue parrot-faced creatures carrying odd-shaped tools and bundles. Houses, widely scattered, each surrounded by trees and a brilliant garden, were themselves vegetable: giant growths shaped like barrel cacti, whose hollow interiors formed rooms of nacreous beauty. A grain-field was being cultivated by shambling octopids, mutated and bred for one purpose—like the thing on which he rode.

Yeh, he thought, I get the idea. These people aren't human. Even Ramri, who sings Mozart themes and has Justice Holmes for a hero—Ramri, about the most *simpá·tico* guy I ever met—he's not human. He came back to his wife and kids after eight years or whatever it was; and he might simply have stepped around the corner for a beer.

Of course, Donnan's mind rambled on, that's partly cultural. The Tanthai civilization puts a premium on individualism. The family isn't quite that loose in the other Monwaingi Societies, I reckon. But no human anywhere could have been that casual about a long separation, when obviously they're an affectionate couple. Ramri did say to me once, his species doesn't have a built-in sex drive like ours. When the opposite sex is out of sight, it really and truly is out of mind. Nevertheless—!

Or was I just missing the nuances? Did a few words and a hug accomplish as much for Ramri and his wife as Alison and I could've gotten across in a week?

If I'd ever given Alison the chance.

He said quickly: "You'd better put me straight on the situation here. I'm still vague on details. As I understand your system, each planet colonized by your people has a governor general from Monwaing, the mother world. Right?"

Ramri scratched his crest. "Well, no," he answered. "Or yes. A semantic question. And not one that can ever be resolved fully. After all, since Resident Wandwai is a Laothaungi, he speaks another language from mine, lives under different laws and customs, enjoys art forms strange to me. So what he understands by the term *Subo*—'Resident,' you say—is not identical with what a Tanthai like myself understands. Such differences are sometimes subtle, sometimes gross, but always present. He doesn't even use the same phonetic symbols."

"Huh? I never realized—I mean, I assumed you'd at least agree on an alphabet and number signs."

"Oh, no. Some Societies do, to be sure. But Laothaung, for instance, which makes calligraphy a major art, finds our Tanthai characters hideous. All Monwaingi writing does go from left to right, like English or Erzhuat, and not from right to left like Japanese or Vorlakka. But otherwise there is considerable variation from Society to Society. Likewise with mathematical ideograms. . . . Naturally, any cultured person tries to become familiar with the language and traditions of the more important foreign Societies. Wandwai speaks fluent Tanthai. But I fear I am quite ignorant of Laothaungi. My interests were directed elsewhere than the arts. In that, I am typical of this planet Katkinu. We Tanthai have taken far more interest in physical science and technology than most other Monwaingi civilizations. Some, in fact, have found such innovations extremely repugnant. But physics proved welcome to the Tanthai world-view."

"Hey," Donnan objected, "your people must have had some physics even before the galactics discovered Monwaing. Otherwise you could never have developed these systematic plant and animal mutations, let alone build spaceships yourselves."

"Yes, yes. There was considerable theoretical physics on Monwaing when the Uru explorers arrived. And it found a certain amount of practical application. The emphasis lay elsewhere, though. Your recent development on Earth was almost a mirror image of Monwaing two centuries past. You knew far more biological theory than you had yet put into engineering practice, because your intellectual and economic investments were already heaviest in physical, inanimate matter. Our situation was the reverse."

"This is getting too deep for me," Donnan said. "I'll never comprehend your setup. Especially as it was before you got space travel. I can see your different civilizations these days, scattering out to new planets where they aren't bothered by unlike neighbors. But how did totally different cultures ever coexist in the same geographic area?"

"They still do, on Monwaing," Ramri said. "For that matter, several other Societies have planted colonies of their own here on Katkinu. Tantha merely has a majority." He pointed out a cluster of buildings, tall garishly colored cylinders erected in steel and plastic, half a mile off the road. The avians walking between them wore embroidered jackets over their feathers. "That is a Kodau village, for example. I suppose you could best describe them as religious communists. They don't bother us and we don't bother them. I admit, such peace was slowly and painfully learned. If we never had major wars on Monwaing, we had far more local flareups than you humans. But eventually methods were developed for arbitrating disputes. That is what a nation was, with us—a set of public technical services, jointly maintained. And peacekeeping is only another technology, no more mysterious than agronomy or therapeutics. Once that idea caught on, a planetary government was soon organized."

He cocked an eye at Donnan, decided the man still needed to be soothed, and continued reciting the banal and obvious:

"To be sure, as proximity and mutual influence grew, the various cultures were losing their identities. Space travel came as a savior. Now we have elbow room again. We can experiment without upsetting the balance between ourselves and our intermingled neighbor Societies. And fresh, new influences have come from space to invigorate us.

"Really, Carl-my-friend, despite our many talks in the past, I do not believe you know what an impact Terrestrial ideas have had on the Monwaingi. You benefitted us not simply by selling us raw materials and machine parts and so on—your engineers, in effect, working cheaper than ours for the sake of learning modern techniques—but you presented us with your entire philosophy. Tantha in particular had looked upon itself as rather reactionary and anti-scientific.

You made us realize that technology *per se* did not conflict with our world-view, only biological technology. The inherent callousness of manipulating life." His gesture at the beast they rode was eloquent, like a man's grimace.

"That ruthlessness was spreading into the psychotechnical field too," he went on. "In other Societies, talk was being heard of adjusting the personality to suit—like the genes of any domestic animal! Such concepts alarmed us. Yet if we Tanthai failed to keep pace with innovation, we would dwindle, impotent. . . . Then, suddenly, on Earth and especially in America, we found a socio-economic system based on physics rather than biology. It was less subtle, perhaps, than the traditional Monwaingi approach; but potentially it was of far greater power . . . and humaneness. We were eager to adopt what we had seen. Do you know, even I am astounded at how far change has progressed on Katkinu in my absence. Why, in my own house, fluorescent panels. When I left, glowfly globes were still the only artificial light. And that is a trivial example. I tell you, your species has inspired my Society."

"Thanks," Donnan grunted.

Humans couldn't have had such a history, he thought. Maybe the vilayet system of the Ottoman Empire had approximated it, but not very closely. No human culture had ever experimented with radical social change and not paid a heavy emotional price. Think how many psychiatrists had been practicing in the U.S.A., or walk down any American street and count on one hand the people who actually looked as if they enjoyed life. To a Monwaingi, though, change came natural. They didn't need roots the way men did. Possibly their quasi-instinctive rituals of music and dance, universal and timeless, gave the individual that sense of security and meaningfulness which a human got from social traditions.

No help here for the last Earthmen, Donnan thought wearily. We've got to find our own planet and start up our own way of life again. If we can have kids who'll get some benefit from our trouble. Otherwise, to hell with it. Too much like work.

Ramri made an embarrassed, piping noise. "Er . . . we seem to have wandered over half the galaxy in this discussion," he said. "You started asking what Resident Wandwai and his staff do. Well, he represents the mother world, and thus the whole coalition of our planets and Societies. He administers the arbitration service. And, these days, he is a military liaison officer. You know that the Kandemirian menace requires each Society to maintain spatial defense forces. The central government on Monwaing coordinates their activities as needed, through the Resident on each colonial world."

Also, Donnan reflected, the central government on Monwaing operates some damned efficient cold-war type diplomacy, espionage, and general intriguing. Yes, I do think we had to come to one of these planets and talk with one of their big wheels.

"I know each Society has spokesmen on Monwaing," be said, "but does each one have an equal voice in policy?"

"A shrewd question," Ramri approved. "No, certainly not. How could the primitivistic Maudwai or the ultra-pacifistic Bodantha find ways to keep Kandemir from gobbling up our scattered planets? The handling of foreign affairs and defense gravitates naturally toward members of the most powerful cultures, notably Laothaung and Thesa. We Tanthai are not unrepresented; still, we tend to be explorers and traders rather than admirals and ambassadors. . . . You needn't worry about etiquette or protocol today. Resident Wandwai won't expect you to know such fine points. Talk as plainly as you wish. He was so quick to grant your request for an interview that I am sure he is also anxious for it."

Donnan nodded and puffed his pipe in silence. He couldn't think of anything else to say, and by now, like his whole crew, had learned patience. If they must zigzag clear into the Libra region, a hundred light-years closer to Earth than Vorlak was, and then cool their heels for days or weeks in the Monwaingi sector of space, why quibble over the extra hour this beastie took to carry him where he was going? The time wasn't really wasted, even. At least, Goldspring and his helpers were drafting some gadgets with awesome potentialities.

Sooner or later, if he didn't get killed first, Donnan would find who had murdered Earth and exact a punishment. But no hurry about that. He smoked, watched the landscape go by, and thought his own thoughts. Now and then, as on this ride today, he had some bad moments; but in general, he had begun to be able to remember Earth with more love than pain.

The trill jarred him to alertness. "We approach."

He stared about. The groundrunner was passing through an avenue of grotesquely pollarded trees, whose shapes kept altering as the wind tossed and roared in them. On either side lay terraced gardens whose forms and hues were like some he recognized from dreams. Directly ahead rose an outsize building . . . no, a grove of house-trees, vines, hedges, cascading from a matted-together roof to a fluidly stirring portico. The music that wailed in an alien scale seemed to originate within those live walls. He had seen nothing like this on Katkinu. But naturally, if the Resident belonged to a different culture from the Tanthai—

A dwarfish being took charge of the groundrunner. The being's eyes were vacant and it could only respond to Ramri's simplest commands. Another organic machine; but Donnan was shocked at its obviously Monwaingi descent. Planned devolution went rather further than chattel slavery had ever done on Earth. No wonder the Tanthai wanted to get away from biotechnology.

He climbed down the vehicle's extended foreleg and followed Ramri into the portico. Three soldiers stood on guard, armed with tommy guns adapted from a Terrestrial pattern as well as with fungus grenades. Ramri and they exchanged intricate courtesies. One of them conducted the visitors along a rustling archway, where sunlight came and went in quick golden flecks, and so to an office.

That room was more familiar, its walls the mother-of-pearl grain of dukaung wood, the desk and sitting-frame like any furniture in Ramri's home. But Donnan could not recognize the calligraphic symbols burned into the ceiling. Resident Wandwai of Laothaung made a stately gesture which sent Ramri into a virtual dance. Donnan stood aside, watching his host. Wandwai belonged to a different race as well as another civilization. His feathers were almost black, eyes green, beak less strongly curved and body stockier than Ramri's. Besides the usual purse at the neck, he wore golden bands twining up his shanks.

Formalities past, the Resident offered Ramri a cigar and lit one for himself. He invited Donnan to sit on top of the desk while he and the space pilot relaxed in frames. "I wish I could give you refreshment, captain," he said in fluent Uru. "But poisoning you would be poor hospitality."

"Thanks anyway," Donnan said.

"Since the first news of your arrival here, I have been eager to see you," Wandwai continued. "However, custom forced me to wait until you requested this meeting. My custom, I mean; it would have been impolite for a Tanthai not to issue an invitation. In the absence of knowledge about your own preferences, I decided to abide by Laothaungi usage."

"I should think military business would take precedence over company manners," Donnan said.

"Military? Why so? Earth never gained any intrinsic military importance."

Donnan swallowed hurt and anger. A Tanthai wouldn't have spoken so cruelly. Doubtless Wandwai didn't realize—yes, the Laothaungi having a biotechnical orientation, they would indeed be more hardboiled than average—"We escaped from Kandemir's main advance base," the human pointed out. "Didn't you expect we'd have information?" He paused, hoping for an impressive effect. "Like the fact that Earth *was* getting a bit involved in the war."

"I presume you refer to the pact between Vorlak and that one Terrestrial nation. Really, captain, we knew about that before the papers were even signed. Momwaingi agents were everywhere on your planet, remember." Wandwai stopped and considered his words. Donnan wished he could read expressions or interpret shadings of tone. "We did not like that treaty," the Resident admitted. "The eventual Kandemirian response to such provocation could be ominous to us, whose scattered planets have an Earthward flank with no defense or buffer in between. We withdrew as many of our people from Earth as we could."

"I heard about that withdrawal from some of Ramri's friends, the other day," Donnan said rather grimly.

"Not that we expected immediate trouble in that area," Wandwai said. "But it seemed well to play safe . . . especially since the coming upset of the uneasy power balance among Terrestrial nations might bring on a general internecine war. I regret that so few Tanthai listened to the central government's warnings and came home before Earth perished. Other cultures had fewer but wiser people there."

You arrogant bastard! Donnan flared in himself.

Wandwai disarmed him by letting the cigar droop in his delicate fingers and saying at once, low and like a threnody: "Forgive any unintentional offense on my part, captain. I know, to a very small degree, what a sorrow you have suffered. Can we Monwaingi in any way offer help or consolation, call on us as your first and best friends. The news that Earth had been sterilized sent a wave of horror through us. No one believed the Kandemirian denial of guilt. The Monwaingi coalition has, ever since, been aiding Vorlak far more heavily than before. Independent planets such as Unya and Yann tremble on the brink of declaring war; one hopeful sign that Kandemir can be defeated will decide them. Vassal worlds like T'sjuda have seen local revolts, which can probably be developed into full-scale insurrections. You know what a threat Kandemir is. By thus stirring the whole cluster to action, Earth has not died in vain."

Something in the phrasing drew Donnan's attention. Slowly he focused his mind. He felt muscles tighten; a chill went tingling over his scalp.

"You don't, yourself, believe the nomads did it," he breathed.

"No," said Wandwai. "Of course, once Earth was gone, they seized the opportunity to interdict the Solar System by planting orbital missiles whose control code is known only to them. Who else could those weapons belong to?"

"Why'd they do that, if they didn't kill Earth in the first place?"

"When the planet has cooled, a few years hence, it will still have water, oxygen, an equable temperature. The biosphere can be rebuilt. I feel sure Kandemir plans to colonize Earth sometime in the future. But certain very recent evidence has come to our attention on Monwaing which strongly indicates they are merely seizing an opportunity which was presented to them; that they did not commit the actual murder. Frankly, we have not released the information, since general anti-Kandemirian sentiment is desirable. But you, as a human, have the right to know."

Donnan slid off the desk. He stood with legs apart, shoulders hunched, fists doubled, braced for the blow. "Have you got any notion . . . who did it?"

Ramri came to stand beside him and stare in bewilderment at the Resident. Wandwai nodded. "Yes," he said. "I do."

✳ XI ✳

Kine die, kinfolk die,
And so at last yourself.
This I know that never dies:
How dead men's deeds are deemed.
                              —*Elder Edda*

"Okay," Donnan said hoarsely. "Spit it out."

Still the Resident watched him, eyes unblinking in that motionless black head. Until: "Are you strong enough?" Wandwai asked, almost inaudible. "I warn you, the shock will be great."

"By God, if you don't quit stalling—! Sorry, Please go ahead."

Wandwai beckoned a desk drawer to open. "Very well," he agreed. "But rather than state the case myself—I fear my own cultural habits strike you as tactless—let me present the evidence. Then you can reach your own conclusions. When I knew you were coming here, I took this item from the secret file." He extracted a filmspool. The click of his claws on the floor, the snap as he put the spool in a projector seemed unnaturally loud. "This records an interview on Monwaing itself, between Kaungtha of Thesa, interrogation expert of the naval intelligence staff attached to the central government, and a certain merchant from Xo, which you will recall is a spacefaring planet still neutral in the war."

"One moment, honored Resident," Ramri interrupted. "May I ask why—if the secret is important—you have a copy?"

"Knowing several Earth ships were absent at the time of the catastrophe, Monwaing anticipated that one or more would seek a planet of ours," Wandwai answered. "We are the only race whose friendship they could feel certain about. Not knowing which planet, however, or exactly how the crews would react to their situation, the government provided this evidence for every office. Otherwise, refusing to believe a bald statement, the Terrestrials might have departed for an altogether different civilization-cluster." He sighed. "Perhaps you will do so anyway, captain. The choice is yours. But at least you have been given what data we had."

Ramri inhaled on his cigar, raggedly. A whiff sent Donnan spluttering to one side but he never took his eyes off the projector. With a whirr, a cube of light sprang into existence. After a moment, quarter size, a three-dimensional scene appeared within.

Through an open ogive window he saw a night sky aglitter with stars, two crescent moons, a rainbow arch that was the rings around Monwaing. Crystal globes in which a hundred luminous insects darted like meteors hung from the ceiling. Behind a desk sat an avian whose feathers were bluish green and who wore a golden trident on his breast. He ruffled papers in his hands, impatiently, though he never consulted them.

The being who stood before the desk was a Xoan. Donnan recognized that from pictures only; few had ever visited Earth, which lay beyond their normal sphere of enterprise. The form was centauroid, which is to say there was a quadrupedal body as big as a Shetland pony and an upright torso with arms. But iridescent skin, erectile comb on the head, face dominated by a small proboscis, removed any further resemblance to anything Earthly. The Xoan seemed nervous, shuffling his feet and twitching his trunk.

A disembodied voice sang some phrases in a Monwaingi language. Ramri whispered: "That's Thesai. 'Interview between Interrogator Kaungtha and Hordelin-Barjat, chairman of the navigation committee of the spaceship *Zeyan 12* from the planet generally known as Xo: catalogue number—' Never mind. The date is—let me translate—about six months ago."

Kaungtha's replica emitted a trill or two. Then, in Uru, his voice said from the light cube: "Be at ease, Navigator. We wish you no harm. This interview is only to put on official record certain statements previously made by you."

"Under duress!" The Xoan had a ridiculous squeaky voice. "I protest the illegal detention of my ship and personnel on this planet, the grilling I have undergone, the mental distress—"

"At ease, Navigator, I beg you. Your detention was perfectly in accord with ordinary interstellar practice as well as Monwaingi law. If contamination is suspected, what can we do but impose quarantine?"

"You know perfectly well that—" Hordelin-Barjat subsided. "I understand. If I cooperate, you will give us a clean bill of health and allow us to depart. So . . . I am cooperating." Anxiously: "But this will remain secret? You do promise that. If my superiors ever learn—"

Kaungtha rustled his papers. "Yes, yes, you have our assurance. Believe me, Monwaing is as interested in discretion as Xo. You fear repercussions because of your planet's part in the affair. We much prefer to spare Xo any unfortunate consequences to reputation and livelihood, and let the blame continue to rest where it does. However, for our own guidance, we do want accurate information."

Hordelin-Barjat: "But how did you ever come to suspect that we—"

Kaungtha (mildly): "The source of the original hints we got deserves the same protection as you. Not so? Let us commence, then. Your vessel belongs to the Xoan merchant fleet, correct?"

Hordelin-Barjat: "Yes. Our specialty, as a crew, is to establish first contact with promising new markets and to conduct preliminary negotiations. We—that is—the planets where Xo has been trading for the last several generations . . . they are becoming glutted, or else so civilized they no longer import the . . . uh . . . specialized items manufactured on our world. We need fresh markets. Earth—"

Kaungtha: "Just so. After studying all the information available to you about Earth, you went there, secretly, in the *Zeyan 12*. That was approximately two years ago, correct?" (A sudden bark) "Why secretly?"

Hordelin Barjat (shaken): "Well . . . that is . . . no wish to offend others—Monwaing already had interests on Earth—"

Kaungtha: "Nonsense! No treaty forbade competition in the Terrestrial market. The Monwaingi confederation as a whole undertakes no obligation to protect the commercial interests of those member Societies that engage in trade. No, the secrecy was required by your tentative purpose. Explain in your own words what you had in mind."

Hordelin-Barjat: "I—that is—I mean—All those ridiculous nations and tribes there—hold overs from the Stone Age, and still unable to agree . . . in the face of galactic culture . . . agree on unity and global peace—"

Kaungtha: "You hoped, then, to sell one or two of those countries a highly advanced weapon that would overthrow the delicate balance of power existing on Earth. If this became known in advance to the rival nations, either preventive war would break out at once or an agreement would be reached to ban such devices. In either case, Xo would make no sale. Hence the secrecy."

Hordelin-Barjat: "I wouldn't put it just that way, officer. We had no intention—we never foresaw—I tell you, they were mad. The whole race was mad. Best they did die, before their lunacy threatened everyone else."

Kaungtha (sighing): "Spare me the rationalizations."

Hordelin-Barjat: "But, but, but you must understand—We are not murderers! Insofar as a psychology so alien could be predicted, we felt that . . . well, believe me, we had even read some of their own theoretical works, analyses of their own situation. A weapon like this had been discussed by Terrestrial thinkers in various books and journals. They felt—that is, the ultimate deterrent to aggressions, a guaranteed peace—Well, if the Earthlings themselves believed such a device would have this effect, how should we know otherwise?"

Kaungtha: "Some of them did. Most did not. In two decades of dealing with Terrestrials, we Monwaingi have gotten some insight into their thought processes. They are—were—they had more individual variability than Xoans; more than any two members of one given Monwaingi Society." (Leaning forward, harsh tone, machine-gun rattle of papers). "You gathered those data which pleased you and ignored the rest."

Hordelin-Barjat: "I—we—"

Kaungtha: "Proceed. Which country did you sell this weapon to?"

Hordelin-Barjat: "Well, actually . . . two. Not two countries exactly. Two alliances. Power blocs. Whatever they were called. We avoided the major powers. Among other reasons, they—uh—"

Kaungtha: "They had too many extraterrestrial contacts. Word of your project might easily have leaked out to civilized planets, which might well have forbidden it. Also, being strong to begin with, the large nations would feel less menaced from every side; less persecuted; less petulant. In a word, less ready to buy your wares. Proceed."

Hordelin-Barjat: "I strongly object to your, er, cynical interpretation of our motives."

Kaungtha: "Proceed, I told you."

Hordelin-Barjat: "Uh—uh—well, our clients had to be countries that did possess some military force—space missiles and so on—and thereby might well expect to be attacked with missiles in the early stages of a war. We approached the Arabian-North African alliance for one. It felt itself being encircled as relations between Israel and the more southerly African states grew increasingly close. And then there was the Balkan alliance, under Yugoslavian leadership—suspicious of the Western countries, still more suspicious of Russia, from whose influence they had barely broken free—and sure to be a battleground if outright war ever did break out between East and West."

Kaungtha: "Let us positively identify the areas in question. You do not pronounce them very reliably, Navigator." (Projecting a political globe of Earth) "Here, here, here, here. Have I indicated the correct regions?"

Hordelin-Barjat: "Yes." (Hastily) "You realize these were second- and third-rate powers. They needed defense, not means of aggrandizement. What we sold them—"

Kaungtha: "Describe that briefly, please."

Hordelin-Barjat: "A set of disruption bombs. Buried deep in the planetary crust . . . and beneath the ocean beds . . . strategic locations—You are familiar with the technology. They—the bombs belonging to a given alliance—they would go off automatically. If more than three nuclear explosions above a certain magnitude occurred within the borders of any single member country . . . all those bombs would explode. At once."

Kaungtha (softly): "And would wipe the planet clean. In seconds."

Hordelin-Barjat: "Yes, humane, quick, yes. Of course, that was not the intention. Not anyone's intention. These small powers—they planned to go, oh, very discreetly, in deepest secrecy—they would approach the other governments and say, 'In the event of general war, we are doomed anyway. But now you will die with us. Therefore you must refrain from making war, ever again.' I assure you, the idea was to promulgate peace."

Kaungtha: "Did you witness the actual installation?"

Hordelin-Barjat: "No. My ship only conducted, uh, preliminary negotiations. Others came later, technicians and, so on. I was informed . . . once . . . verbally . . . that the task had been completed and payment made. But I never saw—" (Shriller than before) "I give you assurance I was as shocked as anyone to hear—not long afterward—my superiors, too—Who could have known that the whole Terrestrial species was insane?"

Kaungtha: "Have you any idea what might have happened, exactly?"

Hordelin-Barjat: "No. Perhaps . . . oh, I can't say. . . . No doubt a war did break out—regardless. If they were already on edge, those governments, then the increased tension . . . feeling this was a bluff that should be called—Or even an accident. I don't know, I tell you! Let me alone!"

Kaungtha: "That appears sufficient, Navigator. End interview."

The cube of light blanked out.

Donnan heard himself speaking in a voice not his own, "I don't believe it! I won't! Take back your lies, you—"

Ramri pushed him against the wall and held him till he stopped struggling. Wandwai gazed at the symbols burned into the ceiling as if to find some obscure comfort.

"Not murder, then," the Resident said at last. "Suicide."

"*They wouldn't!*"

"You may reject this evidence," said the gentle, surgical voice. "Admittedly it is not conclusive. The Xoan might have lied. Or, even if he told the truth, the Kandemirians might still have launched an attack. Especially if they, somehow, learned about those bombs. For then the destruction of Earth would be absurdly simple. A few medium-power nuclear missiles, landing within a fair-sized geographical area, would touch off the supreme explosion. But Earth herself would nevertheless have provided the means."

Donnan covered his face and sagged.

When he looked at them again, Wandwai had put the projector and spool away. "For the sake of surviving humans, captain, as well as Monwaingi policy," the Resident murmured, "I trust you will hold this confidential. Now come, shall we discuss your further plans? Despite the ecological problems, I am sure a home can be made for you within our hegemony—"

"No," said Donnan.

"What?" This time Wandwai did blink.

"No. We're heading back to Vorlak. Our ship, the rest of our people—"

"Oh, they can come here. Monwaing will arrange everything with the Dragar."

"I said no. We got a war to finish."

"Even after Kandemir is proven probably innocent?"

"I don't accept your proof. Y-y-you'll have to trot out something more solid than a reel of film. I'm going to keep on looking . . . on my own account. . . . Anyway, Kandemir did kill some of my crew. And ought to be stopped on general principles. And there's still the idea we had of making a galaxy-wide splash. I'm going. Thanks for your . . . your hospitality, guv'nor. So long."

Donnan lurched from the room.

Ramri stared after him a minute, then started in pursuit. Wandwai, who had remained still except for slow puffs on his cigar, called: "Do you think it best we stop him?"

"No, honored Resident," Ramri answered. "It is necessary for him to depart. I am leaving too."

"Indeed? After so long an absence from home?"

"He may need me," Ramri said, and left.

✳ XII ✳

Who going through the vale of misery use it for a well:
   and the pools are filled with water.
They will go from strength to strength.
           —*The Book of Common Prayer*

Black and mountainous, the ancestral castle of Hlott Luurs covered the atoll on which it was built and burrowed deep into the rock. Sheer walls of fused stone ended in watchtowers overlooking the fishers' huts on two neighboring islets, and in missile turrets commanding the sky above. Today, as often at every latitude on Vorlak, that sky hung low. Smoky clouds tinged with bronze by the hidden sun flew on a wind that whipped the sea to a grey-green restlessness. When he stood up, Carl Donnan got a faceful of spindrift. The air was warm, but the wind whistled and the surf boomed with a singularly cold noise.

He braced his feet against roll and lurch as Ger Nenna changed course. "We must go in by the west gate," the scholar called. "None but Dragar and the Overmaster may use the north approach." His fur gleamed with salt water; he had removed his robes to keep them dry when the boat started off from Port Caalhova. Donnan stuck to his shabby coverall and a slicker.

Pretty overbearing type, that Hlott, the man thought. Oh, sure, he's entitled to be ceremonious—president of the Council and all that. And in times like these you can't blame him for not allowing any fliers but his into this area. And his refusal to talk with me after I got back is within his rights. But when you add everything together, he's treating us humans like doormats and it has got to stop. He put arms akimbo. The old Mauser would have been comforting on his hip today. But naturally, he wasn't allowed to bear weapons here. He couldn't even have gotten this interview had it not been for Ger Nenna's repeated petitions.

They passed a few fisher craft, off which commoners dove like seals to herd schools detected by sonar beams into giant scoops.

A patrol boat set down on the water and the pilot bawled a challenge. Ger identified himself and was waved on. A clifflike wall loomed dead ahead. The portcullis was raised as Ger steered toward the entrance. Within, several boats lay docked in a basin. Ger made fast.

"Have you reconsidered your plan, captain, as I requested?" he asked.

"Uh-huh," Donnan nodded. "But I'll stick with it."

"Have you fully understood how dangerous it is? A Draga, any Draga, is supreme within his own demesne. Hlott could kill you here and there would be no lawful redress, no matter how small and poor an aristocrat he was."

"But he is not small and poor," Donnan pointed out. "He's the boss of this planet. And there lies my chance." He shrugged. The bitterness that Ger had noticed and wondered about, ever since the *Hrunna* survivors returned from Katkinu, whetted his tone. "We're the ones who're poor, we humans. Nothing to lose. And that fact can also be turned into an asset."

Ger toweled himself more or less dry and slipped the plain black robe over his head. "In the Seven Classics of Voyen," he said anxiously, "one may read, 'Many desperations do not equal one hope.' Captain, you know I favor your cause. Not from charity, but on the dim chance that you may indeed bring this wretched war to an end. Only when the interstellar situation has become stable will there be any possibility of restoring—no, not the Eternal Peace; that is gone forever—but the true Vorlakka civilization. You must never believe these swaggering Dragar represent our inherent nature as a species."

"Lord, no." Donnan shucked his slicker and helped Ger tie an embroidered honorific sash. "In fact, pal, if the breakdown of your old universal state had *not* thrown up a warlord class, you'd be a pretty sorry lot. Ready? Let's go, then. Yonder guard is beginning to give us a fishy look."

They debarked and were frisked. Ger was searched nominally and with a ritual apology, Donnan like a criminal arrested for malicious hoodblinkery and aggravated conspiculation. He submitted without paying much heed. He was too busy rehearsing what—No, by God! A set speech was exactly the wrong approach. Marshal his facts, sure; but otherwise play it by ear. Keeping cool was the main thing. He was about to walk a tightrope over a pit full of razor blades.

A servant ushered them down wet, ringing corridors, up ramps worn smooth by warlike generations, and so at last to a relatively small room. It had a transparent domed roof, the walls were brightly colored, and furniture stood about. A solarium, Donnan guessed. The guide bowed low and went out. The door shut behind him, thick and heavy.

Hlott Luurs was sprawled nude on a couch. The light from above rippled along his mahogany fur. He raised himself to one elbow and regarded them with chill eyes. No one else was present, but a web-footed, long-fanged animal, tiger size, lay at his feet. A borren, Donnan recognized. It rumbled at him until Hlott clicked his tongue for silence.

Ger Nenna advanced and bent his head. "My captain," he greeted, "dare this worm express thanks for your graciousness in heeding his prayer, or should he accept it in silence as the winter earth accepts vernal sunshine?"

"If the honorable steersman truly wants to show gratitude," said Hlott dryly, "he can spare me any future time-wastings as silly as this."

"I beg leave to assure the President that the Terrestrial captain brings news of great import."

"Yes, he does." Hlott's gaze smoldered on Donnan. Briefly, teeth flashed white in his blunt muzzle. "But I've already heard that news, you see. A good destroyer thrown away at Mayast, together with Draga Olak Faarer's life, my kinsman. Kandemir handed the secret of the new paragrav detector, as the price for sparing the flotsam lives of a few Earthlings. That is the news. And now this creature not only has the insolence to return to Vorlak—he demands we put him in charge of still more operations! Be grateful to Ger Nenna, you. I'd have blasted every last wretch of your gang before now, had he not persuaded me otherwise."

Donnan sketched an obeisance. "My captain," he said, "you agreed yourself to let us try that raid, and you were told that success wasn't guaranteed. Trying to shift the whole blame on us would be a sneaking trick."

"What?" Hlott's hackles rose. He sat straight. The borren sensed his mood and got up too, tail lashing, throat like thunder.

Donnan didn't stop to be afraid. He dared not. He kept his words loud and metallic: "Thanks for finally agreeing to hear our side of the fiasco. If you really plan to listen to me. And you'd better. This affair hasn't weakened us as you think. We're stronger than before. By 'we' I mean the *Franklin*'s men; but we'll include Vorlak if you want."

The borren started toward him. Hlott called it back with a curt order. *I gauged him right, then,* Donnan thought, beneath his own pulsebeat and sweat. *He's not so stuck on himself that he won't stop to look at facts shoved under his nose. He's not stupid at all, really; just raised in a stupid milieu.*

He won't kill me simply because he gets peeved. No. He'll have excellent logical reasons.

The Draga shivered with self-restraint. "Speak, then," he said in a strangled voice. "Explain how Kandemir's possessing the new detector strengthens anyone except Tarkamat."

"Those detectors are prototypes, my captain," said Donnan, moderating his tone. "At best, a few enemy ships may now have handmade copies. It'll take months to get them into real production. So unless we let the stalemate drag on, we haven't lost much on that account.

"The Kandemirians also have a glimpse of the theory behind the detectors. But a very partial glimpse. And they'll need time to digest their knowledge, time to see the implications and develop the possibilities. We—Arnold Goldspring and his helpers—have been thinking about this subject, off and on, for close to three years while we cruised around exploring. We've given it really concentrated attention since we returned to this cluster.

"When Goldspring and I arrived back at Vorlak from Katkinu, we found that his associates who'd stayed behind in the *Franklin* had not been idle. Thanks to Ger Nenna, who arranged access to computers and other high-powered research tools, they'd gone a long ways toward developing half a dozen new applications. It's a case of genuine scientific breakthrough. Inventions based on Goldspring's principle are going to come thick and fast for a while. And we've got the jump on everybody else."

"I have been told about theoretical designs and laboratory tests," Hlott said disgustedly. "How long will it take to produce something that really works?"

"Not long, my captain," Donnan said. "That is, if a massive scientific-technological effort can be mounted. If the best Vorlakka and allied minds can work together. And that's the real technique we Earthlings have got that you don't. A feudal society like yours, or a nomadic culture like Kandemir, or a coalition of fragments like Monwaing, isn't set up to innovate on purpose. We can tell you how to organize a development project. In less than a year, we can load you for . . . for borren . . . and break the deadlock."

"So you say," Hlott growled. "Your record to date hardly justifies belief."

"Most honored captain," Ger begged, "I have inspected the work of these people. My feeble powers were insufficient to grasp their concepts. I could only gape in awe at what was demonstrated. But scholars in the physical sciences, who have studied more deeply, assure me—"

"I don't give a curse in nonexistence what they assure you, honorable steersman," Hlott answered. "If it pleases them to tinker with a new idea, let them. Something worthwhile may or may not come from it. But I am responsible for the survival of Vorlak as an independent world—and I am not going to gamble half our resources on as crazy an effort as this, masterminded by a mouthful of planetless lunatics. Go!"

Ger wrung his hands. "Noble master—"

Hlott rose to his feet. "Go," he shouted. "Before I chop you both in pieces!"

The borren snarled and crouched.

"But the noble President of Council does not realize—"

Donnan waved Ger back. "Never mind, pal," he said. "I know you hate to come right out and say this. But it's got to be done."

He planted himself solidly before the Draga and stated: "You must know I've got the backing of several Councillors. They liked what we showed them."

"Yes." Hlott relaxed enough to snort a laugh. "I have heard. Praalan, Seva, Urlant. The weakest and most impressionable members of the entire Draga class. What does that mean?"

"Exactly this, my captain." Donnan's lips bent into a sort of smile. He ticked the points off on his fingers. "One: they agree with me that if the stalemate drags on much longer, Kandemir is going to win for sure. The nomad empire has more resources in the long run. Two: once equipped with the new detectors, and the prospect of still fancier gadgets—remember, Kandemir's vassals include sedentary industrial cultures that do know how to organize weapons development—Tarkamat is going to come out looking for a showdown. So we haven't got very much time in any case. Three: if we prepare for it, we, the anti-Kandemirian alliance, can force the showdown ourselves, with a pretty fair chance of winning. Four: this is so important that Praalan and Company can't continue to support a President of the Council too bullheaded to realize the simple facts."

Muscles bunched and knotted along the warlord's body. Almost, the borren went for Donnan's throat. Hlott seized its neck and expended enough temper restraining that huge mass to retort, slit-eyed but self-possessed:

"Ah, you have gone behind my back, then, and awakened intrigues against me, eh? That shall certainly be repaid you."

"I couldn't help going behind your back," Donnan snapped. "You kept it turned on me, in spite of my loudest hollering."

"Praalan, Seva, and Urlant! What can they accomplish? Let them try to force an election. Just let them dare."

"Oh, they won't by themselves, my lord. I talked 'em out of that. Persuaded them they don't, none of them, have the following—or the brains and toughness—to boss these roughneck admirals. They wouldn't last a week. However . . . they do have *some* resources. In cahoots, their power is not negligible. So if they were to join forces with Yenta Saeter, who is very nearly as strong as you—"

"What!"

"Got the idea? My three chums will support Yenta because I've talked them into the idea that it's more important what weapons Vorlak can get than what master Vorlak has. Yenta doesn't think too much of me and my schemes, but he's agreed to organize my project once he gets the Presidency, in return for the help of my three Dragar."

Hlott cursed and struck. Donnan sidestepped the blow. The borren glided forward. Donnan closed with Hlott. He didn't try to hurt the noble, but he went into a clinch. The unhuman body struggled to break loose. Cable-strong arms threw Donnan from side to side. Teeth sought his shoulder.

"Easy, friend. Easy!" Donnan gasped. As the borren lunged, the man forced Hlott around as a shield. The great jaws nearly closed on the Draga's leg. The borren roared and drew back.

"Let's not fight, my captain," the Terrestrial said. His teeth rattled with being shaken. He bit his tongue and choked on an oath. "If . . . wait, call off your pet, will you?—if I meant you any harm, would I . . . have come here . . . and told you?"

Momentarily balked, the borren turned on Ger, who scuttled around a couch. "*Farlak!*" Hlott yelled. The beast flattened its ears and snarled. Hlott shouted again. It lay down stiff and reluctant.

Donnan let go, staggered to a couch, sat down and panted. "My . . . my captain . . . is strong as a devil," he wheezed, rather more noisily than he had to. "I couldn't . . . have held out . . . another minute."

A flicker of smugness softened the wrath on the lutrine face. Hlott said frigidly, "Your presumption deserves a very slow death."

"Pardon me, my captain," Donnan said. "You know I'm not up on your customs. Back home, in my country, one person was pretty much equal to another. I can't remember what's good manners in a society as different as this."

He rose again. "I didn't come to threaten you or any such thing," he continued, feeling how big a liar he was. "Let's say I just wanted to warn you . . . let you know what the sentiments of your colleagues are. I'd hate to see our side lose a leader as brilliant as yourself. If you'd only consider this one question of policy, you could swing back Seva, Urlant, and Praalan to your side. And—uh—" he laid a finger alongside his nose and winked—"if this move were made precisely right, the honorable Yenta could be enticed out on a nice breezy limb . . . and suddenly discover he was alone there, and you stood behind him with a bucksaw."

Hlott poised in silence. Donnan could almost watch the fury drain from him and the calculation rise. Muscle by muscle, the human allowed himself to relax. He'd probably won his case.

Practical politics was another art which had been more highly developed on Earth than it was here.

✳ XIII ✳

THE BATTLE OF BRANDOBAR
Annotated English version

To the literary historian, this ballad is notable as the first important work of art (as opposed to factual records, scientific treatises, or translations from planetary languages) composed in Uru. However, the student of military technics can best explain various passages which, couched in epical terms, convey the general sense but not the details.

The naval engagement in question was fought near the Brandobar Cluster, an otherwise undistinguished group of stars between Vorlak and Mayast. On the one side was the alliance of Vorlak, Monwaing, and several lesser races. Secret demonstrations of new weapons, combined with indignation at the ruin of Earth, had induced a number of hitherto neutral planets to declare war on Kandemir. Opposed to them was the Grand Fleet of the nomads, which included not only their clan units but various auxiliaries recruited from non-Kandemirian subjects of their empire. Their force was numerically much stronger than the attackers.

✳ ✳ ✳

Three kings rode out on the way of war
(The stars burn bitterly clear):
Three in league against Tarkamat,
Master of Kandemir.

And the proudest king, the Vorlak lord,
(The stormwinds clamor their grief)
Had been made the servant in all but name
Of a planetless wanderer chief.

And the secondmost king was a wingless bird
(A bugle: the gods defied!)
Who leagued at last with the Vorlak lord
When the exiles were allied.

And the foremost king in all but name
(New centuries scream in birth)
Was the captain of one lonely ship
That had fled from murdered Earth.

For the world called Earth was horribly slain
(The stars burn bitterly clear)
By one unknown; but the corpse's guards
Were built on Kandemir.

The Earthlings fled—to seek revenge
(The stormwinds clamor their grief)
For ashen homes and sundered hopes
First seen in unbelief.

And haughty Vorlak spoke to them
(A bugle: the gods defied!):
"Kandemir prowls beyond our gates.
Can ye, then, stay the tide?"

And the Monwaing wisemen spoke to them
(New centuries scream in birth):
"Can ye arm us well, we will league with you,

Exiles from shattered Earth."

And the wanderer captain told the kings
(The stars burn bitterly clear):
"I have harnessed and broken to my will
Space and Force and Fear."

Tarkamat, Master of Kandemir,
(The stormwinds clamor their grief)
Laughed aloud: "I will hurl them down
Like a gale-blown autumn leaf."

And he gathered his ships to meet the three
(A bugle: the gods defied!)
As an archer rattles his arrow sheaf
And shakes his bow in pride.

Forth from their lairs, by torchlight suns,
(New centuries scream in birth)
The nomad ships came eager to eat
The wanderers from Earth.

And hard by a cluster of youthful suns
(The stars burn bitterly clear)
Known by the name of Brandobar,
They saw the enemy near.

And the three great kings beheld their foe
(The stormwinds clamor their grief)
With half again the ships they had,
Like arrows in a sheaf.

"Now hurl your vessels, my nomad lords,
(A bugle: the gods defied!)
One single shattering time, and then
Their worlds we shall bestride."

"Sleep ye or wake ye, wanderer chief,

(New centuries scream in birth)
That ye stir no hand while they seek our throats,
Yon murderers of Earth?"

Militechnicians can see from the phrasing alone, without consulting records, that the allied fleet must have proceeded at a high uniform velocity—free fall—in close formation. This offered the most tempting of targets to the Kandemirians, whose ships had carefully avoided building up much intrinsic speed and thus were more maneuverable. Tarkamat moved to englobe the allies and fire on them from all sides.

"Have done, have done, my comrades twain.
(The stars burn bitterly clear)
Mine eyes have tallied each splinter and nail
In yonder burning spear.

"Let them come who slew my folk.
(The stormwinds clamor their grief)
We wait for them as waits in a sea
The steel-sharp, hidden reef."

The reference here is, of course, to the highly developed interferometric paragravity detectors with which the whole allied fleet was equipped, and which presented to the main computer in their flagship a continuous picture of the enemy dispositions. The nomads had some too, but fewer and of a less efficient model.

Now Kandemir did spurt so close
(A bugle: the gods defied!)
They saw his guns and missiles plain
Go raking for their side.

The exile captain smiled a smile
(New centuries scream in birth)
And woke the first of the wizardries
Born from the death of Earth.

Then Space arose like a wind-blown wave

(The stars burn bitterly clear)
That thunders and smokes and tosses ships
Helpless to sail or steer.

And the angry bees from the nomad hive
(The stormwinds clamor their grief)
Were whirled away past Brandobar
Like a gale-blown autumn leaf.

This was the first combat use of the space distorter. The artificial production of interference phenomena enabled the allied craft to create powerful repulsion fields about themselves, or change the curvature of the world lines of outside matter—two equivalent verbalizations of Goldspring's famous fourth equation. In effect, the oncoming enemy missiles were suddenly pushed to an immense distance, as if equipped with faster-than-light engines of their own.

Tarkamat recoiled. That is, he allowed the two fleets to interpenetrate and pass each other. The allies decelerated and re-approached him. He acted similarly. For, in the hours that this required, his scientists had pondered what they observed. Already possessing some knowledge of the physical principles which underlay this new defense, they assured Tarkamat that it must obey the conservation-of-energy law. A ship's power plant could accelerate a missile away, but not another ship of comparable size. Nor could electromagnetic phenomena be much affected.

Tarkamat accordingly decided to match velocities and slug it out at short range with his clumsy but immensely destructive blaster cannon. He would suffer heavy losses, but the greater numbers at his command made victory seem inevitable.

Tarkamat, Master of Kandemir,
(A bugle: the gods defied!)
Rallied his heart. "Close in with them!
Smite them with fire!" he cried.

The nomad vessels hurtled near
(New centuries scream in birth)

And the second wizardry awoke,
Born from the death of Earth.

Then Force flew clear of its iron sheath.
(The stars burn bitterly clear)
Remorseless lightnings cracked and crashed
In the ships of Kandemir.

And some exploded like bursting suns
(The stormwinds clamor their grief)
And some were broken in twain, and some
Fled shrieking unbelief.

Over small distances, such allied vessels as there had been time to
equip with it could use the awkward, still largely experimental, but
altogether deadly space-interference fusion inductor. The principle
here was the production of a non-space band so narrow that particles
within the nucleus itself were brought into contiguity. Atoms with
positive packing fractions were thus caused to explode. Only a very
low proportion of any ship's mass was disintegrated, but that usually served to destroy the vessel. More than half the Kandemirian fleet
perished in a few nova-like minutes.

Tarkamat, unquestionably one of the greatest naval geniuses in
galactic history, managed to withdraw the rest and re-form beyond
range of the allied weapon. He saw that—as yet—it was too restricted in distance to be effective against a fortified planet, and ordered a
retreat to Mayast II.

Tarkamat, Master of Kandemir,
(A bugle: the gods defied!)
Told his folk, "We have lost this day,
But the next we may abide.

"Hearten yourselves, good nomad lords.
(New centuries scream in birth)
Retreat with me to our own stronghold.
Show now what ye are worth!"

The third of those wizardries awoke
(The stars burn bitterly clear)
Born from the death of Earth. It spoke,
And the name of it was Fear.

For sudden as death by thunderbolt,
(The stormwinds clamor their grief)
Ringing within the nomad ships
Came the voice of the exile chief.

Tarkamat, Master of Kandemir,
(New centuries scream in birth)
Heard with the least of his men the words
Spoken from cindered Earth.

On the relatively coarse molecular level, the space-interference inductor was both reliable and long-range. Carl Donnan simply caused the enemy hulls to vibrate slightly, modulated this with his voice through a microphone, and filled each Kandemirian ship with his message.

"We have broken ye here by Brandobar.
(The stars burn bitterly clear)
If ye will not yield, we shall follow you
Even to Kandemir.

"But our wish is not for ashen homes,
(The stormwinds clamor their grief)
But to make you freemen once again
And not a nomad fief.

"If ye fight, we will hurl the sky on your heads.
(A bugle: the gods defied!)
If ye yield, we will bring to your homes and hearts
Freedom to be your bride.

"Have done, have done; make an end of war
(New centuries sing in birth)

And an end of woe and of tyrant rule—
In the name of living Earth!"

Tarkamat reached a cosmic interference fringe and went into faster-than-light retreat. The allies, though now numerically superior, did not pursue. They doubted their ability to capture Mayast II. Instead, they proceeded against lesser Kandemirian outposts, taking these one by one without great difficulty. Mayast could thus be isolated and nullified.

The effect of Donnan's words was considerable. Not only did this shockingly unexpected voice from nowhere strike at the cracked Kandemirian morale; it offered their vassals a way out. If these would help throw off the nomad yoke, they would not be taken over by the winning side, but given independence, even assistance. There was no immediate overt response; but the opening wedge had been driven. Soon allied agents were being smuggled onto those planets, to disseminate propaganda and organize underground movements along lines familiar to Earth's history.

Thus far the militechnic commentator. But the literary scholar sees more in the ballad. Superficially it appears to be a crude, spontaneous production. Close study reveals it is nothing of the sort. The simple fact that there had been no previous Uru poetry worth noticing would indicate as much. But the structure is also suggestive. The archaic imagery and exaggerated, often banal descriptions appeal, not to the sophisticated mind, but to emotions so primitive they are common to every spacefaring race. The song could be enjoyed by any rough-and-ready spacehand, human, Vorlakka, Monwaingi, Xoan, Yannth, or whatever—including members of any other civilization-cluster where Uru was known. And, while inter-cluster traffic was not large nor steady, it did take place. A few ships a year did venture that far.

Moreover, while the form of this ballad derives from ancient European models, it is far more intricate than the present English translation can suggest. The words and concepts are simple; the meter, rhyme, assonance, and alliteration are not. They are, indeed, a jigsaw puzzle, no part of which can be distorted without affecting the whole.

Thus the song would pass rapidly from mouth to mouth, and be very little changed in the process. A spacehand who had never heard of Kandemir or Earth would still get their names correct when he sang what to him was just a lively drinking song. Only those precise vocables would sound right.

So, while the author is unknown, *The Battle of Brandobar* was obviously not composed by some folkish minstrel. It was commissioned, and the poet worked along lines carefully laid down for him. This was, in fact, the *Benjamin Franklin*'s message to humans throughout the galaxy.

✳ **XIV** ✳

Then I saw there was a way to Hell, even from the gates of Heaven.
—Bunyan

No, Sigrid Holmen told herself. Stop shivering, you fool. What is there to be afraid of?

Is it that . . . after five years . . . this is the first time I have been alone with a man? Oh, God, how cold those years were!

He wouldn't do anything. Not him, with the weather-beaten face that crinkled when he smiled, and his hair just the least bit grizzled, and that funny slow voice. Or even if he did—The thought of being grasped against a warm and muscular body made her heart miss a beat. They weren't going to wait much longer, the crews of *Europa* and *Franklin*. The half religious reverence of the first few days was already waning, companionships had begun to take shape, marriages would not delay. To be sure, even after the casualties the Americans had suffered in the Kandemirian war, they outnumbered the women. The sex ratio would get still more lopsided if—no, when!—more ships came in from wherever they were now scattered. A girl could pick and choose.

Nevertheless, murmured Sigrid's awareness, I had better choose mine before another sets her cap for him. And he wanted to see me today, all by myself. . . .

The warmth faded in her. She couldn't be mistaken about the way Carl Donnan's eyes had followed each motion she made. But something else had been present as well, or why should his tone have gone so bleak? She had sat there in the ship with the ranking officers of both expeditions, exchanging data, and described how she boarded the Kandemirian missile, and had seen his face turn stiff. Afterward he drew her aside; low-voiced, almost furtive, he asked her to visit him confidentially next day.

But why should I be afraid? she demanded of herself again, angrily. We are together, the two halves of the human race. We know now that man will live; there will be children and hearthfires on another Earth—in the end, on a thousand or a million other Earths.

Kandemir is beaten. They have not yet admitted it, but their conquests have been stripped from them, their provinces are in revolt, they themselves requested the cease-fire which now prevails. Tarkamat spars at the conference table as bravely and skillfully as ever he did in battle, but the whole cluster knows his hope is forlorn. He will salvage what he can for his people, but Kandemir as an imperial power is finished.

Whereas we, the last few Homines sapientes, sit in the councils of the victors. Vorlak and Monwaing command ships by the thousands and troops by the millions, but they listen to Carl Donnan with deepest respect. Nor is his influence only moral. The newly freed planets, knowing that singly they can have little to say about galactic affairs, have been deftly guided into a coalition—loose indeed, but as close-knit as any such league can be among entire worlds. Collectively, they are already a great power, whose star is in the ascendant. And . . . their deliberative assembly is presided over by a human.

Why am I afraid?

She thrust the question away (but could not make herself unaware of dry mouth and fluttering pulse) as she guided her aircar onto the landing strip. Long, shingle-roofed log buildings formed a square nearby. Trees, their leaves restless in a strong wind, surrounded three sides. The fourth looked down the ridge where Donnan's headquarters stood, across the greennesses of a valley, a river that gleamed like metal and the blue upward surge of hills on the other horizon. This was not Earth, this world called Varg, and the area Donnan occupied—like other sections lent the humans by grateful furry natives off whom the nomad overlordship had been lifted—the area was too small to make a home. But until men agreed on what planet to colonize, Varg was near enough like Earth to ease an old pain. When Sigrid stepped out, the wind flung odors of springtime at her.

Donnan hurried from the portico. Sigrid started running to meet him, checked herself, and waited with head thrown back. He had remarked blonde hair was his favorite, and in this spilling sunlight— he extended a hand, shyly. She caught it between her own, felt her cheeks turn hot but didn't let go at once.

"Thanks for coming, Miss Holmen," he mumbled.

"Vas nothing. A pleasure." Since his French was even rustier than her English, they used the latter. Neither one considered a nonhuman language. She liked his drawl.

"I hope . . . the houses we turned over to you ladies . . . they're comfortable?"

"Oh, *ja, ja.*" She laughed. "Every time ve see a man, he asks us the same."

"Uh . . . no trouble? I mean, you know, some of the boys are kind of impetuous. They don't mean any harm, but—"

"Ve have impetuous vuns too." They released each other. She turned in confusion from his gray gaze and looked across the valley. "How beautiful a view," she said. "Reminds me about Dalarna, v'en I vas a girl—do you live here?"

"I bunk here when I'm on Varg, if that's what you mean, Miss Holmen. The other buildings are for my immediate staff and any visiting firemen. Yeh, the view is nice. But . . . uh . . . didn't you like that planet—Zatlokopa, you call it?—the one you lived on, in the other cluster. Captain Poussin told me the climate was fine."

"Vell, I say nothing against it. But thank God, ve vere too busy to feel often how lonely it vas for us."

"I, uh, I understand you were doing quite well."

"Yes. Vuns ve had learned, v'at you say, the ropes, ve got rich fast. In a few more years, Terran Traders, Inc., vould have been the greatest economic power in that galactic region. Ve could have sent a thousand ships out looking for other survivors." She shrugged. "I am not bragging. Ve had advantages. Such as necessity."

"Uh-huh. What a notion!" He shook his head admiringly. "We both had the same problem, how to contact other humans and warn them about the situation. Judas priest, though, how much more elegant your solution was!"

"But slow," she said. "Ve vere not expecting to be able to do much about it for years. The day Yael Blum came back from Yotl's Nest and told v'at she had heard, a song being sung by a spaceman from another cluster—and ve knew other humans vere alive and ve could safely return here to them—no, there can only be two such days in my lifetime."

"What's the other one?"

She didn't look at him, but surprised herself by how quietly she said, "V'en my first-born is laid in my arms."

For a while only the wind blew, loud in the trees. "Yeah," Donnan said at last, indistinctly, "I told you I bunked here. But it's not a home. Couldn't be, before now."

As if trying to escape from too much revelation, she blurted, "Our problems are not ended. Vat vill the men do that don't get . . . get married?"

"That's been thought about," he answered, unwilling. "We, uh, we should pass on as many chromosomes as possible. That is, uh, well, seems like—"

Her face burned and she held her eyes firmly on the blue hills. But she was able to say for him: "Best that in this first generation, each voman have children by several different men?"

"Uh—

"Ve discussed this too, Carl, v'ile the *Europa* vas bound here. Some among us, like . . . oh . . . my friend Alexandra, for vun . . . some are villing to live with any number of men. Polyandry, is that the vord? So that solves part of the problem. Others, like me—vell, ve shall do v'at seems our duty to the race, but ve only vant a single real husband. He . . . he vill have to understand more than husbands needed to understand on Earth."

Donnan caught her arm. The pressure became painful, but she wouldn't have asked him to let go had it been worse.

Until, suddenly, he did. He almost flung her aside. She turned in astonishment and saw he had faced away. His head was hunched between his shoulders and his fists were knotted so the knuckles stood white.

"Carl," she exclaimed. Carl, *min käre,* v'at is wrong?"

"We're assuming," he said as if strangled, "that the human race ought to be continued."

She stood mute. When he turned around again, his features were drawn into rigid lines and he regarded her as if she were an enemy. His tone stayed low, but shaken: "I asked you here for a talk . . . because of something you said yesterday. I see now I played a lousy trick on you. You better go back."

She took a step from him. Courage came. She stiffened her spine. "The first thing you must come to understand, you men," she said with a bite in it, "is that a voman is not a doll. Or a child. I can stand as much as you."

He stared at his boots. "I suppose so," he muttered. "Considering what you've already stood. But for three years, now, I've lived alone with something. Most times I could pretend it wasn't there. But sometimes, lying awake at night—Why should I wish it onto anyone else?"

Her eyes overflowed. She went to him and put her arms about his neck and drew his head down on her shoulder. "Carl, you big brave clever fool, stop trying to carry the universe. I vant to help. That's v'at I am for, you silly!"

After a while he released her and fumbled for his pipe. "Thanks," he said. "Thanks more than I can tell."

She attempted a smile. "Th-th-the best thanks you can give is to be honest vith me. I'm curious, you know."

"Well—" He filled the pipe, ignited the tobacco surrogate and fumed forth clouds. Hands jammed in pockets, he started toward the house. "After all, the item you mentioned gave me hope my nightmare might in fact be wrong. Maybe you won't end up sharing a burden with me. You might lift it off altogether." He paused. "If not, we'll decide between us what to do. Whether to tell the others, ever, or let the knowledge die with us."

She accompanied him inside. A long, airy room, paneled in light wood, carelessly jammed with odd souvenirs and male impedimenta, served him for a private office. She noticed the bunk in one corner and felt the blood mount in head and breast. Then the lustrous blue form of a Monwaingi arose and fluted politely at her. She didn't know whether to be grateful or to swear.

"Miss Holmen, meet Ramri of Tantha," Donnan said. "He's been my sidekick since we first left Earth, and my right hand and right eye since we got back. I figured he'd better sit in on our discussion. He probably knows more about this civilization-cluster than any other single being."

The delicate fingers felt cool within her own. "Welcome," said the avian in excellent English. "I cannot express what joy your ship's arrival has given me. For the sake of my friends, and your race, and the entire cosmos."

"*Takkar så mycket,*" she whispered, too moved to use any but her father's language.

Donnan gave her a chair and sat down behind the desk. Ramri went back to his sitting-frame. The man puffed hard for a moment before he said roughly: "The question we have to answer somewhere along the line, or we'll never know where we stand or what to expect, is this. Who destroyed Earth?"

"V'y . . . Kandemir," Sigrid replied, startled. "Is there any doubt?"

"Kandemir has denied it repeatedly. We've ransacked captured archives and interrogated prisoners for a good two years now, ever since Brandobar, without finding any conclusive proof against them. Well, naturally, you say, that don't signify. Knowing how such an act would inflame public opinion against them, they'd take elaborate security precautions. Probably keep no written records whatsoever about the operation, and use hand-picked personnel who'd remain silent unto death. You know how strong clan loyalty is in their upper-echelon families. So Kandemir might or might not be guilty, as far as that goes."

"But the Solar System vas guarded by their missiles!" she protested.

"Yeah," Donnan said. "And isn't that a hell of a clumsy way to preserve the secret? Especially when those missiles were so programmed as to be less than maximum efficient. This is not mere guesswork, based on the chance that the *Europa* and the *Franklin* both managed to escape. Three months ago, I sent an expedition to the Solar System equipped with our new protective gizmos. Arn Goldspring was in charge, and what he can't make a piece of apparatus do isn't worth the trouble. His gang disarmed and captured several missiles, and dissected them down to the last setscrew. They were standard Kandemirian jobs. No doubt about that. But every one had been clumsily programmed. Doesn't that suggest somebody was framing Kandemir?"

"Framing?" Sigrid blinked. "Vat . . . oh, yes. I see. Somevun vant-ed to make Kandemir seem guilty." She frowned. "Yes, possible. Though v'at ve found v'en ve boarded that vun missile suggests—" She ran out of words.

"That's what I wanted to talk about," said Donnan. "What you found, by a lucky chance, was unique. No such clue turned up in any that Goldspring examined. Did you bring your notes along as I asked?"

She handed them to him. He stared at them while silence stretched. Ramri walked around and looked over his shoulder.

"What d'you make of this?" Donnan asked at length.

"One set of symbols are Kandemirian numerals, of course," Ramri said. "The other . . . I do not know. I may or may not have seen them before. They look almost as if once, long ago, I did. But even in a single cluster, there are so many languages, so many alphabets—" His musings trailed off. Very lightly, he stroked a hand across Donnan's forehead. "Do not let this fret you, Carl-my-friend," he murmured. "Over and over I have told you, what you learned on Katkinu is not the end of all faith. A mistake only. Anyone, any whole race, let alone a few bewildered members of a race, anyone can err. When will you listen to me, and forget what you saw?"

Donnan brushed him away and looked hard at Sigrid. "What did you think of this clue, you ladies?" he asked. "You had three years to mull it over."

"Ve did not think much," she admitted. "There vas so much else to consider, everything ve had lost and everything ve must do to regain our hopes. Ve recognized the numerals. Ve thought maybe the other symbols vere letters. You know, in some obscure Kandemirian alphabet, different from the usual Erzhuat. Just as Europe, Russia, Greece, Israel, China used different languages and alphabets but the same Arabic numerals. Ve guessed probably these vere notes scribbled for his own guidance by some vorkman helping adjust the missile, who vas not too familiar vith the mechanism."

"There are only six distinct unknown symbols," Donnan grunted. "Not much of an alphabet, if you ask me." He frowned again at the paper.

"They might then be numbers," Ramri offered. "The workman may not have been Kandemirian at all. He could have belonged to a subject race. If the Kandemirians used vassals for the job who were never told what their task was, never even knew what planetary system they were in, that would increase secrecy."

"But the missiles themselves, you dolt!" Donnan snarled. "*They* were the giveaway. What use these fancy precautions if anyone who saw a Mark IV Quester barreling toward him, and got away, could tell the galaxy it was Kandemirian?"

Ramri left the desk, stared at the floor, and said with sorrow, "Well, you force me, Carl. This was explained to you on Katkinu."

Sigrid watched the paper on the desk as if she could almost read something in those scrawls that it was forbidden to read. "Ve didn't think much about this," she said helplessly. "For vun thing, none of us knew much about Kandemir anyvay, not even Captain Poussin. And vith so much else—Our notes lay forgotten in the ship. Until now."

Realization stabbed home. She gasped, summoned her strength and said harshly, "All right. You have fiddled around plenty long. Vat did they show you on Katkinu?"

Donnan met her gaze blindly. "One more question," he said without tone. "Seems I heard . . . yeah, you've got a Yugoslav and an Israeli aboard, haven't you? Either of them know anything about plans to emigrate from Earth? Were either the Balkan or the Arab countries—the Israelis would be bound to have some idea what the Arabs were up to—either alliance building more ships? Recruiting colonists of any sort?"

"No," Sigrid said.

"You positive?"

"Yes. Surely. Remember, I vas concerned in the pan-European project. I saw shipyards myself, read the journals, heard the gossip. Maybe some very small ships vas being made secretly, but something big enough to take many people to another planet, no. Not at the time ve left. And I don't think there vas time aftervard to build much, before the end came."

"No. There wasn't." Donnan shook himself. "Okay," he said quickly, "that's clue number two you've given me. However fine it would be to have more people alive, I admit I was hoping for the answer you gave. How I was hoping!

"You see, on Katkinu I was shown a film made by the Monwaingi intelligence service. An interview with a trader from Xo, who admitted his combine had sold the Balkan and the Arab alliances something that military theorists once labeled a doomsday weapon. The ultimate deterrent." His voice grew saw-edged. "A set of disruption bombs, able to sterilize the planet. Armed to go off automatically in the event of an attack on the countries possessing same. Got the idea? The Monwaingi believe Earth was not murdered. They think Earth committed suicide."

Sigrid sagged in her chair. A dry little sound came from her, nothing else was possible. Donnan slammed the desk with his fist. "You see?" he almost shouted. "That's what I didn't want to share. Monwaing was willing to keep the secret. Why shouldn't I? Why let my friends wonder too what race of monsters they belong to? Wonder what's the use of keeping alive, then force themselves to go through the motions anyway—you see?"

He checked himself and went on more quietly: "I've tried to investigate further. Couldn't get any positive information one way or the other from Xo, in spite of some very expensive espionage. Well, naturally, they'd burn their own records of such a transaction. If you sold someone a gun and he turned out to be a homicidal maniac, even if you hadn't known he was, you wouldn't want to admit your part. Would you? Who'd ever come to your gunshop again?

"How do we explain those Kandemirian missiles? Well, Monwaing thinks Kandemir did plant those, but only after the deed was done. To stake a claim. The Solar System is strategically located: outflanks the Monwaingi stars. And when Earth has cooled, it'll be colonized with less difficulty than many other planets would give. As for why the missiles are so inefficient, they are intended as a warning rather than an absolute death trap.

"Please note that Kandemir has never denied doing this much. Nor affirmed it, to be sure. But they did announce in their arrogant way that come the proper time, they would exercise rights of salvage; and meanwhile they wouldn't be responsible for accidents to anyone entering the Solar System."

Donnan rose. His chair clattered to the floor. He ignored it, strode around to Sigrid, hunkered down before her and took her hands. "Okay," he said, suddenly gentle. "You know the worst. I think we three, here and now, have got all the clues anyone will ever have for certain. Maybe we can figure out who the enemy is. Or was. Buck up, kid. We've got to try."

✳ XV ✳

I tell you naught for your comfort,
Yea, naught for your desire,
Save that the sky grows darker yet
And the sea rises higher.
—Chesterton

As if thrusting away an attacker, she sprang to her feet. Donnan went over on his rear. "Oh," she exclaimed. "I'm so sorry." She bent to help him rise. He didn't require her assistance but used it anyway. Their faces came close. He saw her lips stir. Suddenly his own quirked upward.

"We needed some comic relief," he said. His arm slid down to her waist, lingered there a moment; she laid her head on his shoulder as fleetingly; they separated, but he continued to feel where they had touched. Not quite steadily, he went back to his desk, took his pipe and rekindled it.

"I think now I can stand any answer we may find," he said low.

Color came and went beneath her skin. But she spoke crisply: "Let us list the possibilities. Ve have Kandemir and Earth herself as suspects. But who else? Vorlak? I do not vant to slander an ally, but could . . . v'at you call him . . . Draga Hlott, for some reason—"

"No," Donnan said. He explained about the treaty with Russia. "Besides," he added, "as the war developed, I got more and more pipelines into the Vorlakka government. Ger Nenna, one of their scholar-administrator class, was particularly helpful. They, the Dragar, aren't any good at double-dealing. Not only had they no reason to attack Earth—contrariwise—but if they ever did, they wouldn't have operated under cover. And if by some chance they had pulled a sneak assault, they wouldn't have been able to maintain the secret. No, I cleared them long ago."

"Similar considerations apply to the lesser spacefaring worlds, like Yann and Unya," Ramri said. "They all feared Kandemir. While the Soviet-Vorlakka agreement was not publicized, everyone knew Earth was as natural a prey for the nomads as any other planet and, if the war lasted, would inevitably become involved on the allied side to some degree. Even were they able, no one would have eliminated a potential helper."

"I checked them out pretty thoroughly with espionage just the same," Donnan said bluntly. "They're clean. The only alternatives are Kandemir and suicide."

Sigrid twisted her hands together. "But suicide does not make sense," she objected. "It is not only that I do not vant to believe it. In some vays it vould be more comfortable to."

"Huh?" Both Donnan and Ramri stared.

"*Ja,* v'y not? Then ve vould know Earth's killers are dead and cannot threaten us any more."

Donnan raised his shoulders and spread his hands. "I'd forgotten women are the cold-blooded, practical sex," he muttered.

"No, but look, Carl. Let us suppose the doomsday veapon vas actually installed. Then v'y did no country try to plant some people off Earth? Even if, let us say, vuns she had this last resort . . . even if Yugoslavia expected no vun vould dare attack her—still, Yugoslavia vould have been in a better bargaining position yet vith people on other planets. For then they could say, v'atever happened, a part of them would survive. And any other government notified about the veapon vould have tried to take out similar insurance. Insurance against accident, if nothing else. Or against . . . oh . . . blackmail, in case Yugoslavia ever got a nihilist dictator like Hitler vas in his day. So there vould have been *some* emigration from Earth. But ve know for sure there vas not. Even if the emigrants left this cluster, spacemen like Monvaingi vould have noticed it and you vould have heard them talk about it."

Donnan yanked his attention from her to her words. They made sense. He'd speculated along some such lines himself, but had been too shaken emotionally to put his ideas in her cool terms, and too busy making war to straighten out those private horrors that inhibited his reasoning about the subject.

"One possibility," he said. "If Kandemir got wind of the doomsday weapon, Kandemir might'a seized the opportunity, since the destruction of Earth would then be like shooting fish in a barrel. Yugoslavia and the rest might never have had time to organize colonization schemes."

The fair head shook. "I think not," she answered. "Maybe they vere angry men governing Earth's nations, but they vere shrewd too. They had to be. Countries, especially little countries, did not last long in this century if they had stupid leaders. The Balkan and Arab politicians vould have foreseen just the chance of attack you mention. Not only Kandemir, but any planet—any pirate fleet, even, if somebody got vun—anybody could blackmail Earth. No? So I do not think they vould have bought a doomsday veapon unless lots of spaceships vere included in the package."

An eerie tingle moved up Donnan's spine. He smote one fist into the other palm, soundlessly, again and again. "By God, yes," he whispered. "You've hit the point that Monwaing and I both missed. The Monwaingi couldn't be expected to know our psychology that well, I reckon, but I should have seen it. The whole concept of the weapon was lunacy. But lunatics are at least logical thinkers."

Sigrid threw back her shoulders. The lilting voice lifted till it filled the room: "Carl, I do not believe there ever vas any such veapon sold. It just does not figure. Most 'specially not in galactic terms. See, yes, there still vere countries that did not like each other. But those old grudges vere becoming less and less important all the time. There vas still some fighting, but the big atomic var never happened, in spite of almost every country having means to fight it. Does that not show the situation vas stable? That there never vould have been a var? At least, not the var everybody vas vorrying about.

"Earth vas turning outvard. The old issues vere stopping to matter. Vat vas the use of a doomsday veapon? It vould have been a Chinese vall, built against an enemy that no more existed. For the same price, buying spaceships, buying modern education for the young people, a country could have gained ten times the power . . . and achievement . . . and safety. I tell you, the suicide story is not true."

For a moment neither of the others spoke. They couldn't. Ramri's feathers rose. He swelled his throat pouch and expostulated, "But we know! Our intelligence made that Xoan admit—"

"He lied," Sigrid interrupted. "Is your intelligence alvays correct?"

"Why? Why?" Ramri paced, not as a man does, but in great leaps back and forth between the walls. "What could Xo gain from such a lie? No conceivable advantage! Even the individual who finally confessed, he got nothing but clearance for his ship to leave Monwaing. Absurd!"

Donnan gazed long at his friend before he said, "I think you'd better own up, Ramri: your general staff was had. Let's go on from there."

The end of his nightmare had not eased the wire tautness in him. He bent over the sheet of paper on his desk as if it were an oracular wall. The unhuman symbols seemed to intertwine like snakes before his eyes. He focused, instead, on the Roman analogues which had been written in parallel columns.

A B C D E F G H I J K AL
M N O P Q MR
BA : NQ
ABIJ : MOQMP

Transliteration of some Delphic language—No, no, don't be silly. A through AL simply stands for the first twelve numbers of the duodecimal Kandemirian system, with L the sign for zero. So—

It was like a knife stab. For an instant his heartbeat ceased. He felt a sense of falling. The pulse resumed, crazily, with a roaring in his ears.

As if over immense distances, he heard Ramri say, making an effort at calm:

"By elimination, then, Kandemir does seem to be the murderer planet. Possibly they engineered this Xoan matter as a red herring. And yet I have never felt their guilt was very plausible. That is one reason why I was so quick, however unwilling, to suppose Earth had indeed committed suicide."

"Vell," said the girl, "I am not so familiar vith local situations, but I understand the Kandemirians are—or vere, before you broke their power—merciless conquerors. Earth vas still another planet to conquer. And then the Russians actively helped Vorlak."

"Yes, but Tarkamat himself denied to Carl—contemptuously—that the Soviet assistance was significant. Which does sound reasonable. What indeed could a few shiploads of small arms and a handful of student officers amount to, on the scale of interstellar war? If necessary, Kandemir could have lodged a protest with the Soviet government, and made it stick by a threat of punitive action. The Russians would have backed down for certain. Because even a mild raid from

Kandemir would have left them so brutally beaten that they would be helpless in the face of their Western rivals. In fact, Tarkamat proved very knowledgeable about Terrestrial politics. He remarked to Carl that if and when he decided to overrun Earth, he would have used native allies more than his own troops. *Divide et impera,* you know. Yet for all the strength and information he had, Tarkamat never even bothered to announce that he knew about the Soviet action.

"Why should he lay Earth waste? Its biochemistry was similar to that of Kandemir. Which made the living planet a far more valuable prize than the present lump of rock, which can only be reseeded with life at great difficulty and expense, over a period of God knows how long. The nomads are ruthless, but not stupid. Their sole conceivable motive for sterilizing Earth would have been as a terrible object lesson to their enemies. And then they would have boasted of what they did, not denied it."

Donnan forced himself to take the paper in his hand and punch some keys on his desk calculator. He had never done harder work in his life.

"Yes, yes, you speak sensible," Sigrid was agreeing. "Also, as ve have said, if they vere going to interdict the Solar System, they could have done the job better than vith obsolescent missiles badly programmed. For that matter, Mr. Ramri, v'y should they patrol the System at all? They could have taken it over as part of the general settlement after they von the var, as they expected to vin. Until then, just an occasional visit to make sure nobody vas using it against them vould have been enough."

The calculator chattered. Donnan's brain felt like a lump of ice.

"Do you imply that Kandemir never even placed those missiles there?" Ramri asked. "But who did?"

Numbers appeared on the calculator dial. The equation balanced.

Donnan turned around. His voice was flat and empty. "I know who."

"What? *Hvad?*" They stepped closer, saw his expression, and grew still.

An immense, emotionless steadiness descended on the man. He pointed. "These notes scribbled inside that one missile," he said. "What they were should have been obvious all along. The women failed to see it because they had too much else to think about. They dismissed the whole question as unimportant. But I should have realized the moment I looked. You too, Ramri. I suppose we didn't want to realize."

The golden eyes were level upon him. "Yes? What are those symbols, then, Carl?"

"A conversion table. Jotted down by some technician used to thinking in terms of one number system, who had to adjust instruments and controls calibrated in another system.

"The Kandemirians use a twelve-based arithmetic. These other numerals are based on six."

The girl bit her lip and frowned, puzzled why Donnan was so white. Ramri stood as if carved until, slowly, he spread out his two three-fingered hands.

"It checks," Donnan said. "The initial notation alone, giving the numbers from one to six in parallel rows, is a giveaway. But here are the conversions of some other figures, to which I reckon this or that dial had to be set. The squiggle in between, that Sigrid represented by a colon, has to be an equality sign. BA is 25 in Kandemirian; so is NQ in the other system. ABIJ and MOQMP both represent 2134. And so on. No doubt about it."

Ramri made a croaking noise. "A subject race," he managed to articulate. "I, I, I think the Lenyar of Druon . . . the nomads conquered them a long time ago . . . they did formerly employ—"

Donnan shook his head. "Nope," he told them. "Won't do. You yourself just listed the reasons for calling Kandemir innocent of this particular crime."

Understanding came upon Sigrid. She edged away from Ramri, lifting her hands to fend him off. "Monvaing?" she breathed.

"Yes," said Donnan.

"No!" Ramri yelled. "I give you my soul in pawn, it is not true!"

"I never said you were party to the deed yourself," Donnan answered. A dim part of him wanted to take Ramri in his arms, as he had done the day they first saw murdered Earth. But his feet seemed nailed to the floor.

His voice proceeded, oddly echoing within his skull: "Once we grant Monwaing did this, the pieces fall into place. The only objections I can see are that Monwaing wouldn't destroy a good market and a potential ally, and in any event would be too decent to do such a thing.

"But Ramri, Monwaing isn't a single civilization. You didn't recognize these numerals here. Nobody on your planet uses them. However, there are Monwaingi planets you've never seen. And some of the civilizations developed by your race are very hardboiled. The biotechnic orientation. If it's okay to manipulate life in any way convenient, then it's okay to destroy life on any scale convenient. Tantha wouldn't do so; but Laothaung, say, might. And the central government is dominated by Laothaung and similarly minded Societies.

"Those cultures aren't traders, either. Earth as a market meant little to them. What did concern them was Earth as a keg of dynamite. Remember, Resident Wandwai admitted we were too poor and backward as yet to be of military help; and he admitted knowing about that provocative treaty between Russia and Vorlak. Laothaung might well have feared that Kandemir would seize the excuse to invade Earth—thereby spreading the war to Monwaing's most vulnerable flank.

"Oh, they didn't hate humans. I'm sure we survivors would have been well treated, had we stayed in their sectors. But neither did they love us. We, like any living creatures, were just phenomena, to be dealt with as suited their own ends. If they destroyed Earth, they could pin the blame on Kandemir by such methods as planting captured Kandemirian missiles in orbit . . . but not making the missiles too damned effective. That was quite a sound calculation, too. Anger against Kandemir helped out the war effort no end.

"To play safe, they prepared a second-line cover story. I don't know whether the Xoan was bribed or forced to tell that whopper about the doomsday weapon. I do know the story was well concocted, with a lot of detail such as only an alien race that has close acquaintance with Earth could have gotten straight. However, wasn't it a little too pat, that Wandwai had a copy of a top-secret film right in his own regional office? That struck me as odd at the time.

"What else might Monwaing gain by blasting Earth? The planet itself, in due course. They figured on winning the war, as belligerents generally do figure. Because of the ecological differences, Monwaing could only colonize Earth if it was sterile first. Your setup of many different cultures, each wanting at least one world to itself, makes you actually a good deal more imperialistic than Kandemir ever was. You simply aren't so blunt about it.

"Yeh. I've no doubt left in my mind. Monwaing killed our planet. A real slick job. The only thing they overlooked was what a helpless, fugitive shipload of surviving humans might end up doing. You can't blame them for not foreseeing that. I wouldn't have myself."

Donnan stopped talking.

"You have no proof," Ramri keened.

"No courtroom proof," Donnan replied. "Now that we know where to search, though, I don't doubt we can find it."

"What . . . do you plan . . . to do, Carl?"

"I don't know," Donnan admitted heavily. "Sit on the lid till the Kandemirian business is finished, I reckon. Meanwhile we can gather evidence and make ready to act."

"Å, nej," Sigrid cried out. "Not another var, so soon!"

Ramri shuddered. And then the beaked head lifted. Sunlight came in a window and blazed along his feathers. He said with death in his tone: "That will not be necessary. Not for you."

The frozenness began to break in Donnan. He took an uneven step toward the being who had been his friend. "I never thought *you*—" he stammered. "Only the smallest handful of your race—"

Ramri avoided him. "Of course," he said. "The majority of us shall restore our honor. But this may not be done easily. More than a few individuals must suffer. More, even, than one or two Societies. You need not concern yourselves in this affair, humans. You must not. It is ours.

"I hope the settlement and cleansing need annihilate no more than our mother planet."

He stroke jerkily toward the door. "I shall organize the search for positive evidence myself," he said, like a machine, never looking back at them. "When the case is prepared, it shall be put before the proper representatives of each Society. Then the groundwork of action must be quietly laid. I expect our civil war will begin in about one year."

"Ramri, no! Why, your people are the leaders of this whole cluster—"

"You must succeed us."

The Monwaingi went out. Donnan realized he had never known him.

Sigrid came to give the man what comfort she was able. Presently they heard an aircar take off. It hit the sky so fast that it trailed a continuous thunderbolt, as if new armadas were already bound for battle.

They looked at each other. "What have we done?"

EPILOGUE

✳ I ✳

His name was a set of radio pulses. Converted into equivalent sound waves, it would have been an ugly squawk; so because he, like any consciousness, was the center of his own coordinate system, let him be called Zero.

He was out hunting that day. Energy reserves were low in the cave. That other who may be called One—being the most important dweller in Zero's universe—had not complained. But there was no need to. He also felt a dwindling potential. Accumulators grew abundantly in their neighborhood, but an undue amount of such cells must be processed to recharge One while she was creating. Motiles had more concentrated energy. And, of course, they were more highly organized. Entire parts could be taken from the body of a motile, needing little or no reshaping for One to use. Zero himself, though the demands on his functioning were much less, wanted a more easily assimilated charge than the accumulators provided.

In short, they both needed a change of diet.

Game did not come near the cave any more. The past hundred years had taught that it was unsafe. Eventually, Zero knew, he would have to move. But the thought of helping One through mile upon mile, steep, overgrown, and dangerous, made him delay. Surely he could still find large motiles within a few days' radius of his present home. With One's help he fastened a carrier rack on his shoulders, took weapons in hand, and set forth.

That was near sunset. The sky was still light when he came on

453

spoor: broken earthcrystals not yet healed, slabs cut from several boles, a trace of lubricant. Tuning his receptors to the highest sensitivity, he checked all the bands commonly made noisy by motiles. He caught a low-amplitude conversation between two persons a hundred miles distant, borne this far by some freak of atmospherics; closer by he sensed the impulses of small scuttering things, not worth chasing; a flier jetted overhead and filled his perception briefly with static. But no vibration of the big one. It must have passed this way days ago and now be out of receptor-shot.

Well, he could follow the trail, and catch up with the clumsy sawyer in time. It was undoubtedly a sawyer—he knew these signs—and therefore worth a protracted hunt. He ran a quick check on himself. Every part seemed in good order. He set into motion, a long stride which must eventually overhaul anything on treads.

Twilight ended. A nearly full moon rose over the hills like a tiny cold lens. Night vapors glowed in masses and streamers against a purple-black sky where stars glittered in the optical spectrum and which hummed and sang in the radio range. The forest sheened with alloy, flashed with icy speckles of silicate. A wind blew through the radiation-absorber plates overhead, setting them to ringing against each other; a burrower whirred, a grubber crunched through lacy crystals, a river brawled chill and loud down a ravine toward the valley below.

As he proceeded, weaving among trunks and girders and jointed rods with the ease of long practice, Zero paid most attention to his radio receptors. There was something strange in the upper communication frequencies tonight, an occasional brief note . . . set of notes, voice, drone, like nothing he had heard before or heard tell of. . . . But the world was a mystery. No one had been past the ocean to the west or the mountains to the east. Finally Zero stopped listening and concentrated on tracking his prey. That was difficult, with his optical sensors largely nullified by the darkness, and he moved slowly. Once he tapped lubricant from a cylinder growth and once he thinned his acids with a drink of water. Several times he felt polarization in his energy cells and stopped for a while to let it clear away: he rested.

Dawn paled the sky over distant snowpeaks, and gradually turned red. Vapors rolled up the slopes from the valley, tasting of damp and sulfide. Zero could see the trail again, and began to move eagerly.

Then the strangeness returned—louder.

Zero slid to a crouch. His lattice swiveled upward. Yes, the pulses did come from above. They continued to strengthen. Soon he could identify them as akin to the radio noise associated with the functioning of a motile. But they did not sense like any type he knew. And there was something else, a harsh flickering overtone, as if he also caught leakage from the edge of a modulated short-wave beam—

The sound struck him.

At first it was the thinnest of whistles, high and cold above the dawn clouds. But within seconds it grew to a roar that shook the earth, reverberated from the mountains, and belled absorber plates until the whole forest rang. Zero's head became an echo chamber; the racket seemed to slam his brain from side to side. He turned dazzled, horrified sensors heavenward. And he saw the thing descending.

For a moment, crazily, he thought it was a flier. It had the long spindle-shaped body and the airfins. But no flier had ever come down on a tail of multicolored flame. No flier blocked off such a monstrous portion of sky. When the thing must be two miles away!

He felt the destruction as it landed, shattered frames, melted earthcrystals, a little burrower crushed in its den, like a wave of anguish through the forest. He hurled himself flat on the ground and hung on to sanity with all four hands. The silence which followed, when the monster had settled in place, was like a final thunderclap.

Slowly Zero raised his head. His perceptions cleared. An arc of sun peered over the sierra. It was somehow outrageous that the sun should rise as if nothing had happened. The forest remained still, hardly so much as a radio hum to be sensed. The last echoes flew fading between the hills.

A measure of resolution: this was no time to be careful of his own existence. Zero poured full current into his transmitter. "*Alarm, alarm! All persons receiving, prepare to relay. Alarm!*"

Forty miles thence, the person who may as well be called Two answered, increasing output intensity the whole time: "Is that you, Zero? I noticed something peculiar in the direction of your establishment. What is the matter?"

Zero did not reply at once. Others were coming in, a surge of voices in his head, from mountaintops and hills and lowlands, huts and tents and caves, hunters, miners, growers, searakers, quarriers, toolmakers, suddenly become a unity. But he was flashing at his own home: "Stay inside, One. Conserve energy. I am unharmed, I will be cautious, keep hidden and stand by for my return."

"Silence!" called a stridency which all recognized as coming from Hundred. He was the oldest of them, he had probably gone through a total of half a dozen bodies. Irreversible polarization had slowed his thinking a little, taken the edge off, but the wisdom of his age remained and he presided over their councils. "Zero, report what you have observed."

The hunter hesitated. "That is not easy. I am at—" He described the location. ("Ah, yes," murmured Fifty-Six, "near that large galena lick.") "The thing somewhat resembles a flier, but enormous, a hundred feet long or more. It came down about two miles north of here on an incandescent jet and is now quiet. I thought I overheard a beamed signal. If so, the cry was like nothing any motile ever made."

"In these parts," Hundred added shrewdly. "But the thing must have come from far away. Does it look dangerous?"

"Its jet is destructive," Zero said, "but nothing that size, with such relatively narrow fins, could glide about. Which makes me doubt it is a predator."

"Lure accumulators," said Eight.

"Eh? What about them?" asked Hundred.

"Well, if lure accumulators can emit signals powerful enough to take control of any small motile which comes near and make it enter their grinders, perhaps this thing has a similar ability. Then, judging from its size, its lure must have tremendous range and close up could overpower large motiles. Including even persons?"

Something like a shiver moved along the communication band.

"It is probably just a grazer," said Three. "If so—" His overt signal trailed off, but the thought continued in all their partly linked minds: *A motile that big! Megawatt-hours in its energy cells. Hundreds or thousands of usable parts. Tons of metal. Hundred, did your great-grandcreator recall any such game, fabulous millennia ago?*

No.

If it is dangerous, it must be destroyed or driven off. If not, it must be divided among us. In either case: attacked!

Hundred rapped the decision forth. "All male persons take weapons and proceed to rendezvous at Broken Glade above the

Coppertaste River. Zero, stalk as close as seems feasible, observe what you can, but keep silence unless something quite unforeseeable occurs. When we are gathered, you can describe details on which we may base a specific plan. Hasten!"

The voices toned away in Zero's receptor circuits. He was alone again.

The sun cleared the peaks and slanted long rays between the forest frames. Accumulators turned the black faces of their absorber plates toward it and drank thirstily of radiation. The mists dissipated, leaving boles and girders ashine with moisture. A breeze tinkled the silicate growths underfoot. For a moment Zero was astonishingly conscious of beauty. The wish that One could be here beside him, and the thought that soon he might be fused metal under the monster's breath, sharpened the morning's brightness.

Purpose congealed in him. Further down was a turmoil of frank greed. In all the decades since his activation there had been no such feast as this quarry should provide. Swiftly, he prepared himself. First he considered his ordinary weapons. The wire noose would never hold the monster, nor did he think the iron hammer would smash delicate moving parts (it did not seem to have any), or the steel bolts from his crossbow pierce a thin plate to short out a crucial circuit. But the clawed, spearheaded pry bar might be of use. He kept it in one hand while two others unfastened the fourth and laid it with his extra armament in the carrier rack. Thereupon they deftly hooked his cutting torch in its place. No one used this artificial device except for necessary work, or to finish off a big motile whose cells could replace the tremendous energy expended by the flame, or in cases of dire need. But if the monster attacked him, that would surely constitute dire need. His only immediate intention was to spy on it.

Rising, he stalked among shadows and sun reflections, his camouflage-painted body nearly invisible. Such motiles as sensed him fled or grew very still. Not even the great slasher was as feared a predator as a hunting person. So it had been since that ancient day when some forgotten savage genius made the first crude spark gap and electricity was tamed.

Zero was about halfway to his goal, moving slower and more carefully with each step, when he perceived the newcomers.

He stopped dead. Wind clanked the branches above him, drown-

ing out any other sound. But his electronic sensors told him of . . .
two . . . three moving shapes, headed from the monster. And their
emission was as alien as its own.

In a different way. Zero stood for a long time straining to sense
and to understand what he sensed. The energy output of the three
was small, hardly detectable even this close; a burrower or skitterer
used more power to move itself. The output felt peculiar, too, not
really like a motile's: too simple, as if a mere one or two circuits oscil-
lated. Flat, cold, activityless. But the signal output, on the other
hand—it must be signal, that radio chatter—why, that was a shout.
The things made such an uproar that receptors tuned at minimum
could pick them up five miles away. As if they did not know about
game, predators, enemies.

Or as if they did not care.

A while more Zero paused. The eeriness of this advent sent a tingle through him. It might be said he was gathering courage. In the
end he gripped his pry bar more tightly and struck off after the three.

They were soon plain to his optical and radar senses among the
tall growths. He went stock-still behind a frame and watched.
Amazement shocked his very mind into silence. He had assumed,
from their energy level, that the things were small. But they stood
more than half as big as he did! And yet each of them had only one
motor, operating at a level barely sufficient to move a person's arm.
That could not be their power source. But what was?

Thought returned to him. He studied their outlandishness in
some detail. They were shaped not altogether unlike himself, though
two-armed, hunchbacked, and featureless. Totally unlike the monster, but unquestionably associated with it. No doubt it had sent
them forth as spy eyes, like those employed by a boxroller. Certain
persons had been trying for the last century or so to develop, from
domesticated motiles, similar assistants for hunting persons. Yes, a
thing as big and awkward as the monster might well need auxiliaries.

Was the monster then indeed a predator? Or even—the idea went
like a lightning flash through Zero's entire circuitry—a thinker? Like
a person? He struggled to make sense of the modulated signals
between the three bipeds. No, he could not. But—

Wait!

Zero's lattice swung frantically back and forth. He could not shake off the truth. That last signal had come from the monster, hidden by a mile of forest. From the monster to the bipeds. And were they answering?

The bipeds were headed south. At the rate they were going, they might easily come upon traces of habitation, and follow those traces to the cave where One was, long before Hundred's males had gathered at Broken Glade.

The monster would know about One.

Decision came. Zero opened his transmitter to full output, but broadcast rather than beamed in any degree. He would give no clue where those were whom he called. "*Attention, attention!* Tune in on me: direct sensory linkage. I am about to attempt capture of these motiles."

Hundred looked through his optics, listened with his receptors, and exclaimed, "No, wait, you must not betray our existence before we are ready to act."

""The monster will soon learn of our existence in any event," Zero answered. "The forest is full of old campsites, broken tools, traps, chipped stones, slag heaps. At present I should have the advantage of surprise. If I fail and am destroyed, that ought still to provide you with considerable data. Stand alert!"

He plunged from behind the girders.

The three had gone past. They sensed him and spun about. He heard a jagged modulation of their signal output. A reply barked back, lower in frequency. The voice of the monster? There was no time to wonder about that. Slow and clumsy though they were, the bipeds had gotten into motion. The central one snatched a tube slung across its back. Pounding toward them, through shattering crystals and clangorous branches, Zero thought, *I have not yet made any overtly hostile move, but—* The tube flashed and roared.

An impact sent Zero staggering aside. He went to one knee. Ripped circuits overwhelmed him with destruction signals. As the pain throbbed toward extinction, his head cleared enough to see that half his upper left arm was blown off.

The tube was held steady on him. He rose. The knowledge of his danger flared in him. A second biped had its arms around the third, which was tugging a smaller object from a sheath.

Zero discharged full power through his effectors. Blurred to view by speed, he flung himself to one side while his remaining left hand threw the pry bar. It went meteorlike across a shaft of sunlight and struck the tube. The tube was pulled from the biped's grasp, slammed to the ground and buckled. Instantly Zero was upon the three of them. He had already identified their communication system, a transmitter and antenna actually outside the skin! His one right hand smashed across a biped's back, tearing the radio set loose. His torch spat with precision. Fused, the communicator of a second biped went dead.

The third one tried to escape. Zero caught it in four strides, plucked off its antenna, and carried it wildly kicking under one arm while he chased the other two. When he had caught the second, the first stood its ground and battered forlornly at him with its hands. He lashed them all together with his wire rope. As a precaution, he emptied the carrier rack of the one which had shot him. Those thin objects might be dangerous even with the tube that had launched them broken. He stuffed the bipeds into his own carrier.

For a moment, then, he lingered. The forest held little sonic noise except the wind in the accumulators. But the radio spectrum clamored. The monster howled; Zero's own broadcast rolled between sky and mountainside, from person to person and so relayed across the land.

"No more talk now," he finished his report. "I do not want the monster to track me. I have prevented these auxiliaries from communicating with it. Now I shall take them to my cave for study. I hope to present some useful data at the rendezvous."

"This may frighten the monster off," Seventy-Two said.

"So much the better," Hundred answered.

"In that case," Zero said, "I will at least have brought back something from my hunt."

He snapped off his transmission and faded into the forest shadows.

✳ II ✳

The boat had departed from the spaceship on a mere whisper of jets. Machinery inboard hummed, clicked, murmured, sucked in exhausted air and blew out renewed; busied itself with matters of warmth and light, computation and propulsion. But it made no more than a foundation for silence.

Hugh Darkington stared out the forward port. As the boat curved away from the mother ship's orbit, the great hull gleamed across his sky—fell astern and rapidly dwindled until lost to view. The stars which it had hidden sprang forth, icy-sharp points of glitter against an overwhelming blackness.

They didn't seem different to him. They were, of course. From Earth's surface the constellations would be wholly alien. But in space so many stars were visible that they made one chaos, at least to Darkington's eyes. Captain Thurshaw had pointed out to him, from the ship's bridge, that the Milky Way had a new shape, this bend was missing and that bay had not been there three billion years ago. To Darkington it remained words. He was a biologist and had never paid much attention to astronomy. In the first numbness of loss and isolation, he could think of nothing which mattered less than the exact form of the Milky Way.

Still the boat spiraled inward. Now the moon drifted across his view. In those eons since the *Traveler* left home, Luna had retreated from Earth: not as far as might have been predicted, because (they said) Bering Straits had vanished with every other remembered place; but nonetheless, now it was only a tarnished farthing. Through the ship's telescopes it had looked like itself. Some new mountains, craters, and maria, some thermal erosion of old features, but Thurshaw could identify much of what he once knew. It was grotesque that the moon should endure when everything else had changed.

Even the sun. Observed through a dimmer screen, the solar disc was bloated and glaring. Not so much in absolute terms, perhaps. Earth had moved a little closer, as the friction of interplanetary dust and gas took a millennial toll. The sun itself had grown a little bigger and hotter, as nuclear reactions intensified. In three billion years such things became noticeable even on the cosmic scale. To a living organism they totaled doomsday.

Darkington cursed under his breath and clenched a fist till the skin stretched taut. He was a thin man, long-faced, sharp-featured, his brown hair prematurely sprinkled with gray. His memories included beautiful spires above an Oxford quad, wonder seen through a microscope, a sailboat beating into the wind off Nantucket, which blew spray and a sound of gulls and church bells at him, comradeship bent over a chessboard or hoisting beer steins, forests hazy and ablaze with Indian summer: and all these things were dead. The shock had worn off, the hundred men and women aboard the *Traveler* could function again, but home had been amputated from their lives and the stump hurt.

Frederika Ruys laid her own hand on his and squeezed a little. Muscle by muscle he untensed himself, until he could twitch a smile in response to hers. "After all," she said, "we knew we'd be gone a long time. That we might well never come back."

"But we'd have been on a living planet," he mumbled.

"So we can still find us one," declared Sam Kuroki from his seat at the pilot console. "There're no less than six G-type stars within fifty light-years."

"It won't be the same," Darkington protested.

"No," said Frederika. "In a way, though, won't it be more? We, the last humans in the universe, starting the race over again?"

There was no coyness in her manner. She wasn't much to look at, plump, plain, with straight yellow hair and too wide a mouth. But such details had ceased to matter since the ship ended time acceleration. Frederika Ruys was a brave soul and a skilled engineer. Darkington felt incredibly lucky that she had picked him.

"Maybe we aren't the last, anyhow," Kuroki said. His flat features broke in one of his frequent grins; he faced immensity with a sparrow's cockiness. "Ought to've been other colonies than ours planted, oughtn't there? Of course, by now their descendants 'ud be bald-headed dwarfs who sit around thinking in calculus."

"I doubt that," Darkington sighed. "If humans had survived anywhere else in the galaxy, don't you think they would at least have come back and . . . and reseeded this with life? The mother planet?" He drew a shaken breath. They had threshed this out a hundred times or more while the *Traveler* orbited about unrecognizable Earth, but they could not keep from saying the obvious again and again, as a man must keep touching a wound on his body. "No, I think the war really did begin soon after we left. The world situation was all set to explode."

That was why the *Traveler* had been built, and even more why it had departed in such haste, his mind went on. Fifty couples scrambling off to settle on Tau Ceti II before the missiles were unleashed. Oh, yes, officially they were a scientific team, and one of the big foundations had paid for the enterprise. But in fact, as everyone knew, the hope was to insure that a fragment of civilization would be saved, and someday return to help rebuild. (Even Panasia admitted that a total war would throw history back a hundred years; Western governments were less optimistic.) Tension had mounted so horribly fast in the final months that no time was taken for a really careful check of the field drive. So new and little understood an engine ought to have had scores of test flights before starting out under full power. But . . . well . . . next year might be too late. And exploratory ships *had* visited the nearer stars, moving just under the speed of light, their crews experiencing only a few weeks of transit time. Why not the *Traveler*?

"The absolute war?" Frederika said, as she had done so often already. "Fought until the whole world was sterile? No. I won't believe it."

"Not in that simple and clean-cut a way," Darkington conceded. "Probably the war did end with a nominal victor: but he was more depopulated and devastated than anyone had dared expect. Too impoverished to reconstruct, or even to maintain what little physical plant survived. A downward spiral into the Dark Ages."

"M-m-m, I dunno," Kuroki argued. "There were a lot of machines around. Automation, especially. Like those self-reproducing, sun-powered, mineral-collecting sea rafts. And a lot of other self-maintaining gadgets. I don't see why industry couldn't be revived on such a base."

"Radioactivity would have been everywhere," Darkington pointed out. "Its long-range effect on ecology . . . Oh, yes, the process may have taken centuries, as first one species changed or died, and then another dependent on it, and then more. But how could the human survivors recreate technology when biology was disintegrating around them?" He shook himself and stiffened his back, ashamed of his self-pity a minute ago, looking horror flatly in the face. "That's my guess. I could be wrong, but it seems to fit the facts. We'll never know for certain, I suppose."

Earth rolled into sight. The planetary disc was still edged with blueness darkening toward black. Clouds still trailed fleecy above shining oceans; they gleamed upon the darkness near the terminator as they caught the first light before sunrise. Earth was forever fair.

But the continental shapes were new, speckled with hard points of reflection upon black and ocher where once they had been softly green and brown. There were no polar caps; sea level temperatures ranged from eighty to two hundred degrees Fahrenheit. No free oxygen remained: the atmosphere was nitrogen, its oxides, ammonia, hydrogen sulfide, sulfur dioxide, carbon dioxide, and steam. Spectroscopes had found no trace of chlorophyll or any other complex organic compound. The ground cover, dimly glimpsed through clouds, was metallic.

This was no longer Earth. There was no good reason why the *Traveler* should send a boat and three highly unexpendable humans down to look at its lifelessness. But no one had suggested leaving the Solar System without such a final visit. Darkington remembered being taken to see his grandmother when she was dead. He was twelve years old and had loved her. It was not her in the box, that strange unmeaningful mask, but where then was she?

"Well, whatever happened seems to be three billion years in the past," Kuroki said, a little too loudly. "Forget it. We got troubles of our own."

Frederika's eyes had not left the planet. "We can't ever forget, Sam," she said. "We'll always wonder and hope—they, the children at least—hope that it didn't happen to them too cruelly." Darkington started in surprise as she went on murmuring, very low, oblivious of the men:

*"to tell you of the ending of the day.
And you will see her tallness with surprise,
and looking into gentle, shadowed eyes
protest: it's not that late; you have to stay
awake a minute more, just one, to play
with yonder ball. But nonetheless you rise
so they won't hear her say, 'A baby cries,
but you are big. Put all your toys away.'*

"She lets you have a shabby bear in bed,
though frankly doubting that you two can go
through dream-shared living rooms or wingless flight.
She tucks the blankets close beneath your head
and smooths your hair and kisses you, and so
goes out, turns off the light. 'Good night. Sleep tight.'"

Kuroki glanced around at her. The plaid shirt wrinkled across his wide shoulders. "Poems yet," he said. "Who wrote that?"

"Hugh," said Frederika. "Didn't you know he published poetry? Quite a bit. I admired his work long before I met him."

Darkington flushed. Her interest was flattering, but he regarded *Then Death Will Come* as a juvenile effort.

However, his embarrassment pulled him out of sadness. (On the surface. Down beneath, it would always be there, in every one of them. He hoped they would not pass too much of it on to their children. Let us not weep eternally for Zion.) Leaning forward, he looked at the planet with an interest that mounted as the approach curve took them around the globe. He hoped for a few answers to a hell of a lot of questions.

For one thing, why, in three billion years, had life not reevolved? Radioactivity must have disappeared in a few centuries at most. The conditions of primordial Earth would have returned. Or would they? What had been lacking this time around?

He woke from his brown study with a jerk as Kuroki said, "Well, I reckon we can steepen our trajectory a bit." A surprising interval had passed. The pilot touched controls and the mild acceleration increased. The terrestrial disc, already enormous, swelled with terrifying velocity, as if tumbling down upon them.

Then, subtly, it was no longer to one side or above, but was beneath; and it was no longer a thing among the stars but the convex floor of bowl-shaped creation. The jets blasted more strongly. Kuroki's jaws clenched till knots of muscle stood forth. His hands danced like a pianist's.

He was less the master of the boat, Darkington knew, than its helper. So many tons, coming down through atmospheric turbulence at such a velocity, groping with radar for a safe landing spot, could not be handled by organic brain and nerves. The boat's central director—

essentially a computer whose input came from the instruments and whose efferent impulses went directly to the controls—performed the basic operations. Its task was fantastically complex: very nearly as difficult as the job of guiding the muscles when a man walks. Kuroki's fingers told the boat, "Go that way," but the director could overrule him.

"I think we'll settle among those hills." The pilot had to shout now, as the jets blasted stronger. "Want to come down just east of the sunrise line, so we'll have a full day ahead of us, and yonder's the most promising spot in this region. The lowlands look too boggy."

Darkington nodded and glanced at Frederika. She smiled and made a thumbs-up sign. He leaned over, straining against his safety harness, and brushed his lips across hers. She colored with a pleasure that he found oddly moving.

Someday, on another planet—that possibly hadn't been born when they left Earth—

He had voiced his fears to her, that the engine would go awry again when they started into deep space, and once more propel them through time, uncontrollably until fuel was exhausted. A full charge in the tanks was equivalent to three billion years, plus or minus several million; or so the physicists aboard had estimated. In six billion A.D. might not the sun be so swollen as to engulf them when they emerged?

She had rapped him across the knuckles with her slide rule and said no, you damned biologist, but you'll have to take my word for it because you haven't got the math. I've studied it as far as differential equations, he said. She grinned and answered that then he'd never had a math course. It seemed, she said, that time acceleration was readily explained by the same theory which underlay the field drive. In fact, the effect had been demonstrated in laboratory experiments. Oh, yes, I know about that, he said; reactive thrust is rotated through a fourth dimension and gets applied along the temporal rather than a spatial axis. You do not know a thing about it, she said, as your own words have just proved. But never mind. What happened to us was that a faulty manifold generated the t-acceleration effect in our engine. Now we've torn everything down and rebuilt from scratch. We know it'll work right. The tanks are recharged. The ship's ecosystem is in good order. Any time we want, we can take off for a younger sun, and travel fifty light-years without growing more than a few months older. After which, seeing no one else was around, she sought his arms; and that was more comforting than her words.

A last good-by to Grandmother Earth, he thought. *Then we can start the life over again that we got from her.*

The thrust upon him mounted. Toward the end he lay in his chair, now become a couch, and concentrated on breathing.

They reached ground.

Silence rang in their ears for a long while. Kuroki was the first to move. He unstrapped his short body and snapped his chair back upright. One hand unhooked the radio microphone, another punched buttons. "Boat calling *Traveler,*" he intoned. "We're okay so far. Come in, *Traveler.* Hello, hello." Darkington freed himself, stiffly, his flesh athrob, and helped Frederika rise.

She leaned on him a minute. "Earth," she said. Gulping: "Will you look out the port first, dearest? I find I'm not brave enough."

He realized with a shock that none of them had yet glanced at the landscape. Convulsively, he made the gesture. He stood motionless for so long that finally she raised her head and stared for herself.

✳ III ✳

They did not realize the full strangeness before they donned spacesuits and went outside. Then, saying very little, they wandered about looking and feeling. Their brains were slow to develop the gestalts which would allow them really to see what surrounded them. A confused mass of detail could not be held in the memory, the underlying form could not be abstracted from raw sense impressions. A tree is a tree, anywhere and anywhen, no matter how intricate its branching or how oddly shaped its leaves and blossoms. But what is a—

—thick shaft of gray metal, planted in the sand, central to a labyrinthine skeleton of straight and curved girders, between which run still more enigmatic structures embodying helices and toruses and Mˆbius strips and less familiar geometrical elements; the entire thing some fifty feet tall; flaunting at the top several hundred thin metal plates whose black sides are turned toward the sun?

When you have reached the point of being able to describe it even this crudely, then you *have* apprehended it.

Eventually Darkington saw that the basic structure was repeated, with infinite variation of size and shape, as far as he could see. Some specimens tall and slender, some low and broad, they dominated the hillside. The deeper reaches were made gloomy by their overhang, but sun speckles flew piercingly bright within those shadows as the wind shook the mirror faces of the plates. That same wind made a noise of clanking and clashing and far-off deep booming, mile after metal mile.

There was no soil, only sand, rusty red and yellow. But outside the circle which had been devastated by the boat's jets, Darkington found the earth carpeted with prismatic growths, a few inches high, seemingly rooted in the ground. He broke one off for closer examination and saw tiny crystals, endlessly repeated, in some transparent siliceous material: like snowflakes and spiderwebs of glass. It sparkled so brightly, making so many rainbows, that he couldn't well study the interior. He could barely make out at the center a dark clump of . . . wires, coils, transistors? *No,* he told himself, *don't be silly.* He gave it to Frederika, who exclaimed at its beauty.

He himself walked across an open stretch, hoping for a view even vaguely familiar. Where the hillside dropped too sharply to support anything but the crystals—they made it one dazzle of diamonds—he saw eroded contours, the remote white sword of a waterfall, strewn boulders and a few crags like worn-out obelisks. The land rolled away into blue distances; a snowcapped mountain range guarded the eastern horizon. The sky overhead was darker than in his day, faintly greenish blue, full of clouds. He couldn't look near the fierce big sun.

Kuroki joined him. "What d'you think, Hugh?" the pilot asked.

"I hardly dare say. You?"

"Hell, I can't think with that bloody boiler factory clattering at me." Kuroki grimaced behind his faceplate. "Turn off your sonic mike and let's talk by radio."

Darkington agreed. Without amplification, the noise reached him through his insulated helmet as a far-off tolling. "We can take it for granted," he said, "that none of this is accidental. No minerals could simply crystallize out like this."

"Don't look manufactured to me, though."

"Well," said Darkington, "you wouldn't expect them to turn out their products in anything like a human machine shop."

"Them?"

"Whoever . . . whatever . . . made this. For whatever purpose."

Kuroki whistled. "I was afraid you'd say something like that. But we didn't see a trace of—cities, roads, anything—from orbit. I know the cloudiness made seeing pretty bad, but we couldn't have missed the signs of a civilization able to produce stuff on this scale."

"Why not? If the civilization isn't remotely like anything we've ever imagined?"

Frederika approached, leaving a cartful of instruments behind. "The low and medium frequency radio spectrum is crawling," she reported. "You never heard so many assorted hoots, buzzes, whirrs, squeals, and whines in your life."

"We picked up an occasional bit of radio racket while in orbit," Kuroki nodded. "Didn't think much about it, then."

"Just noise," Frederika said hastily. "Not varied enough to be any kind of, of communication. But I wonder what's doing it?"

"Oscillators," Darkington said. "Incidental radiation from a variety of—oh, hell, I'll speak plainly—machines."

"But—" Her hand stole toward his. Glove grasped glove. She wet her lips. "No, Hugh, this is absurd. How could any one be capable of making . . . what we see . . . and not have detected us in orbit and—and done something about us?"

Darkington shrugged. The gesture was lost in his armor. "Maybe they're biding their time. Maybe they aren't here at the moment. The whole planet could be an automated factory, you know. Like those ocean mineral harvesters we had in our time"—it hurt to say that—"which Sam mentioned on the way down. Somebody may come around periodically and collect the production."

"Where do they come from?" asked Kuroki in a rough tone.

"I don't know, I tell you. Let's stop making wild guesses and start gathering data."

Silence grew between them. The skeleton towers belled. Finally Kuroki nodded. "Yeah. What say we take a little stroll? We may come on something."

Nobody mentioned fear. They dared not.

Re-entering the boat, they made the needful arrangements. The *Traveler* would be above the horizon for several hours yet. Captain Thurshaw gave his reluctant consent to an exploration on foot. The idea conflicted with his training, but what did survey doctrine mean under these conditions? The boat's director could keep a radio beam locked on the ship and thus relay communication between Earth and orbit. While Kuroki talked, Darkington and Frederika prepared supplies. Not much was needed. The capacitor pack in each suit held charge enough to power thermostat and air renewer for a hundred hours, and they only planned to be gone for three or four. They loaded two packboards with food, water, and the "buckets" used for such natural functions as eating, but that was only in case their return should be delayed. The assorted scientific instruments they took were more to the point. Darkington holstered a pistol. When he had finished talking, Kuroki put the long tube of a rocket gun and a rackful of shells on his own back. They closed their helmets anew and stepped out.

"Which way?" Frederika asked.

"Due south," Darkington said after studying the terrain. "We'll be following this long ridge, you see. Harder to get lost." There was little danger of that, with the boat emitting a continuous directional signal. Nonetheless they all had compasses on their wrists and took note of landmarks as they went.

The boat was soon lost to view. They walked among surrealistic rods and frames and spirals, under ringing sheet metal. The crystals crunched beneath their tread and broke sunlight into hot shards of color. But not many rays pushed through the tangle overhead; shadows were dense and restless. Darkington began to recognize unrelated types of structure. They included long, black, seemingly telescopic rods, fringed with thin plates; glassy spheres attached to intricate grids; cables that looped from girder to girder. Frequently a collapsed object was seen crumbling on the ground.

Frederika looked at several disintegrated specimens, examined others in good shape, and said: "I'd guess the most important material, the commonest, is an aluminum alloy. Though—see here—these fine threads embedded in the core must be copper. And this here is probably manganese steel with a protective coating of . . . um . . . something more inert."

Darkington peered at the end of a broken strut through a magnifying glass. "Porous," he said. "Good Lord, are these actually capillaries to transport water?"

"I thought a capillary was a hairy bug with lots of legs that turned into a butterfly," said Kuroki. He ducked an imaginary fist. "Okay, okay, somebody's got to keep up morale."

The boat's radio relayed a groan from the monitor aboard the ship. Frederika said patiently, "No, Sam, the legs don't turn into a butterfly—" but then she remembered there would never again be bravely colored small wings on Earth and banged a hand against her faceplate as if she had been about to knuckle her eyes.

Darkington was still absorbed in the specimen he held. "I never heard of a machine this finely constructed," he declared. "I thought nothing but a biological system could—"

"Stop! Freeze!"

Kuroki's voice rapped in their earphones. Darkington laid a hand on his pistol butt. Otherwise only his head moved, turning inside the helmet. After a moment he saw the thing too.

It stirred among shadows, behind a squat cylinder topped with the usual black-and-mirror plates. Perhaps three feet long, six or eight inches high . . . It came out into plain view. Darkington glimpsed a slim body and six short legs of articulated dull metal. A latticework swiveled at the front end like a miniature radio-radar beamcaster. Something glinted beadily beneath, twin lenses? Two thin tentacles held a metal sliver off one of the great stationary structures. They fed it into an orifice, and sparks shot back upward—

"Holy Moses," Kuroki whispered.

The thing stopped in its tracks. The front-end lattice swung toward the humans. Then the thing was off, unbelievably fast. In half a second there was nothing to see.

Nobody moved for almost a minute. Finally Frederika clutched Darkington's arm with a little cry. The rigidness left him and he babbled of experimental robot turtles in the early days of cybernetic research. Very simple gadgets. A motor drove a wheeled platform, steered by a photoelectric unit that approached light sources by which the batteries might be recharged and, when this was done, became negatively phototropic and sought darkness. An elementary feedback circuit. But the turtles had shown astonishing tenacity, had gone over obstacles or even around. . . .

"That beast there was a good deal more complicated," she interrupted.

"Certainly, certainly," Darkington said. "But—"

"I'll bet it heard Sam talk on the radio, spotted us with radar—or maybe eyes, if those socketed glass things were eyes—and took off."

"Very possibly, if you must use anthropomorphic language. However—"

"It was eating that strut." Frederika walked over to the piece of metal which the runner had dropped. She picked it up and came stiffly back with it. "See, the end has been ground away by a set of coarse emery wheels or something. You couldn't very well eat alloy with teeth like ours. You have to grind it."

"Hey!" Kuroki objected. "Let's not go completely off the deep end."

"What the hell's happened down there?" called the man aboard the *Traveler*.

They resumed walking, in a dreamlike fashion, as they recounted what they had seen. Frederika concluded: "This . . . this arrangement might conceivably be some kind of automated factory—chemosynthetic or something—if taken by itself. But not with beasts like that one running loose."

"Now wait," Darkington said. "They could be maintenance robots, you know. Clear away rubbish and wreckage."

"A science advanced enough to build what we see wouldn't use such a clumsy system of maintenance," she answered. "Get off your professional caution, Hugh, and admit what's obvious."

Before he could reply, his earphones woke with a harsh jabber. He stopped and tried to tune in—it kept fading out, he heard it only in bursts—but the bandwidth was too great. What he did hear sounded like an electronic orchestra gone berserk. Sweat prickled his skin.

When the sound had stopped: "Okay," breathed Kuroki, "you tell me."

"Could have been a language, I suppose," said Frederika, dry-throated. "It wasn't just a few simple oscillations like that stuff on the other frequencies."

Captain Thurshaw himself spoke from the orbiting ship. "You better get back to the boat and sit prepared for quick blastoff."

Darkington found his nerve. "No, sir. If you please. I mean, uh, if there are intelligences . . . if we really do want to contact them . . . now's the time. Let's at least make an effort."

"Well—"

"We'll take you back first, of course, Freddie."

"Nuts," said the girl. "I stay right here."

Somehow they found themselves pushing on. Once, crossing an open spot where only the crystals stood, they spied something in the air. Through binoculars, it turned out to be a metallic object shaped vaguely like an elongated manta. Apparently it was mostly hollow, upborne by air currents around the fins and propelled at low speed by a gas jet. "Oh, sure," Frederika muttered. "Birds."

They re-entered the area of tall structures. The sonic amplifiers in their helmets were again tuned high, and the clash of plates in the wind was deafening. Like a suit of armor, Darkington thought idiotically. Could be a poem in that. Empty armor on a wild horse, rattling and tossing as it was galloped down an inexplicably deserted city street—symbol of—

The radio impulses that might be communication barked again in their earphones. "I don't like this," Thurshaw said from the sky. "You're dealing with too many unknowns at once. Return to the boat and we'll discuss further plans."

They continued walking in the same direction, mechanically. *We don't seem out of place here ourselves, in this stiff cold forest,* Darkington thought. *My God, let's turn around. Let's assert our dignity as organic beings. We aren't mounted on rails!*

"That's an order," Thurshaw stated.

"Very well, sir," Kuroki said. "And, uh, thanks."

The sound of running halted them. They whirled. Frederika screamed.

"What's the matter?" Thurshaw shouted. "What's the matter?" The unknown language ripped across his angry helplessness.

Kuroki yanked his rocket gun loose and put the weapon to his shoulder. "Wait!" Darkington yelled. But he grabbed at his own pistol. The oncomer rushed in a shower of crystal splinters, whipping rods and loops aside. Its gigantic weight shuddered in the ground.

Time slowed for Darkington, he had minutes or hours to tug at his gun, hear Frederika call his name, see Kuroki take aim and fire. The shape was mountainous before him. Nine feet tall, he estimated in a far-off portion of his rocking brain, three yards of biped four-armed monstrosity, head horned with radio lattice, eyes that threw back sunlight in a blank glitter, grinder orifice and— The rocket exploded. The thing lurched and half fell. One arm was in ruins.

"Ha!" Kuroki slipped a fresh shell into his gun. "Stay where you are, you!"

Frederika, wildly embracing Darkington, found time to gasp, "Sam, maybe it wasn't going to do any harm," and Kuroki snapped, "Maybe it was. Too goddam big to take chances with." Then everything smashed.

Suddenly the gun was knocked spinning by a hurled iron bar they hadn't even noticed. And the giant was among them. A swat across Kuroki's back shattered his radio and dashed him to earth. Flame spat and Frederika's voice was cut short in Darkington's receivers.

He pelted off, his pistol uselessly barking. "Run, Freddie!" he bawled into his sonic microphone. "I'll try and—" The machine picked him up. The pistol fell from his grasp. A moment later, Thurshaw's horrified oaths were gone: Darkington's radio antenna had been plucked out by the roots. Frederika tried to escape, but she was snatched up just as effortlessly. Kuroki, back on his feet, stood where he was and struck with ludicrous fists. It didn't take long to secure him either. Hog-tied, stuffed into a rack on the shoulders of the giant, the three humans were borne off southward.

✳ IV ✳

At first Zero almost ran. The monster must have known where its auxiliaries were and something of what had happened to them. Now that contact was broken, it might send forth others to look for them, better armed. Or it might even come itself, roaring and burning through the forest. Zero fled.

Only the monster's voice, raggedly calling for its lost members, pursued him. After a few miles he crouched in a rod clump and

strained his receptors. Nothing was visible but thickly growing accumulators and bare sky. The monster had ceased to shout. Though it
still emitted an unmodulated signal, distance had dwindled this until
the surrounding soft radio noise had almost obliterated that hum.

The units Zero had captured were making considerable sound-
wave radiation. If not simply the result of malfunction in their damaged mechanism, it must be produced by some auxiliary system
which they had switched on through interior controls. Zero's sound
receptors were not sensitive enough to tell him whether the emission
was modulated. Nor did he care. Certain low forms of motile were
known to have well-developed sonic parts, but anything so limited in
range was useless to him except as a warning of occurrences immediately at hand. A person needed many square miles to support himself. How could there be a community of persons without the effort-
less ability to talk across trans-horizon distances?

Irrelevantly, for the first time in his century and a half of existence, Zero realized how few persons he had ever observed with his
own direct optics. How few he had touched. Now and then, for this
or that purpose, several might get together. A bride's male kin assist-
ed her on her journey to the groom's dwelling. Individuals met to
exchange the products of their labor. But still—this rally of all functional males at Broken Glade, to hunt the monster, would be the
greatest assemblage in tradition. Yet not even Hundred had grasped
its uniqueness.

For persons were always communicating. Not only practical
questions were discussed. In fact, now that Zero thought about it,
such problems were the least part of discourse. The major part was
ritual, or friendly conversation, or art. Zero had seldom met Seven as
a physical entity, but the decades in which they criticized each other's
poetry had made them intimate. The abstract tone constructions of
Ninety-six, the narratives of Eighty, the speculations about space and
time of Fifty-nine—such things belonged to all.

Direct sensory linkage, when the entire output of the body was
used to modulate the communication band, reduced still further the
need for physical contact. Zero had never stood on the seashore himself. But he had shared consciousness with Fourteen, who lived there.
He had perceived the slow inward movement of waves, their
susurrus, the salt in the air; he had experienced the smearing of

grease over his skin to protect it from corrosion, drawing an aquamotile from a net and feasting. For those hours, he and the searaker had been one. Afterward he had shown Fourteen the upland forest. . . .

What am I waiting for? Consciousness of his here-and-now jarred back into Zero. The monster had not pursued. The units on his back had grown quiescent. But he was still a long way from home. He rose and started off again, less rapidly but with more care to obliterate his traces.

As the hours passed, his interior sensors warned him increasingly of a need for replenishment. About midday he stopped and unloaded his three prizes. They were feebly squirming and one of them had worked an arm loose. Rather than lash them tight again, he released their limbs and secured them by passing the rope in successive loops around their middles and a tall stump, then welding everything fast with his torch.

That energy drain left him ravenous. He scouted the forest in a jittery spiral until he found some accumulators of the calathiform sort. A quick slash with his pry bar exposed their spongy interiors, rich with energy storage cells and mineral salts. They were not very satisfying eaten unprocessed, but he was too empty to care. With urgency blunted, he could search more slowly and thoroughly. Thus he found the traces of a burrow, dug into the sand, and came upon a female digger. She was heavy with a half-completed new specimen and he caught her easily. This too would have been better if treated with heat and acid, but even raw the materials tasted good in his grinder.

Now to get something for One. Though she, better than he, could slow down her functioning when nourishment was scarce, a state of coma while the monster was abroad could be dangerous. After hunting for another hour, Zero had the good luck to start a rotor. It crashed off among the rods and crystals, faster than he could run, but he put a crossbow bolt through its hub. Dismembered and packed into his carrier, it made an immensely cheering burden.

He returned to his prizes. Moving quietly in comparison to the windy clatter of the forest, he came upon them unobserved. They had quit attempting to escape—he saw the wire was shiny where they had tried to saw it on a sharp rock—and were busy with other tasks. One of them had removed a box-like object from its back and inserted its head(?) and arms through gasketed holes. A second was just removing a similar box from its lower section. The third had plugged a flexible tube from a bottle into its face.

Zero approached. "Let me inspect those," he said, before thinking how ridiculous it was to address them. They shrank away from him. He caught the one with the bottle and unplugged the tube. Some liquid ran out. Zero extended his chemical sensor and tasted cautiously. Water. Very pure. He did not recall ever having encountered water so free of dissolved minerals.

Thoughtfully, he released the unit. It stoppered the tube. So, Zero reflected, they required water like him, and carried a supply with them. That was natural; they (or, rather, the monster they served) could not know where the local springs and streams were. But why did they suck through a tube? Did they lack a proper liquid-ingestion orifice? Evidently. The small hole in the head, into which the tube had fitted, had automatically closed as the nipple was withdrawn.

The other two had removed their boxes. Zero studied these and their contents. There were fragments of mushy material in both, vaguely similar to normal body sludge. Nourishment or waste? Why such a clumsy system? It was as if the interior mechanism must be absolutely protected from contact with the environment.

He gave the boxes back and looked more thoroughly at their users. They were not quite so awkward as they seemed at first. The humps on their backs were detachable carriers like his. Some of the objects dangling at their waists or strapped to their arms must also be tools. (Not weapons or means of escape, else they would have used them before now. Specialized artificial attachments, then, analogous to a torch or a surgical ratchet.) The basic bipedal shape was smoother than his own, nearly featureless except for limb joints. The head was somewhat more complicated, though less so than a person's. Upon the cylindrical foundation grew various parts, including the sound-wave generators which babbled as he stood there watching. The face was a glassy plate, behind which moved . . . what? Some kind of jointed, partly flexible mechanism.

There was no longer any possibility of radio communication with—or through—them. Zero made a few experimental gestures, but the units merely stirred about. Two of them embraced. The third waved its arms and made sonic yelps. All at once it squatted and drew geometrical shapes in the sand, very much like the courtship figures drawn by a male dune-runner.

So . . . they not only had mechanical autonomy, like the spy eyes of a boxroller, but were capable of some independent behavior. They were more than simple remote-control limbs and sensors of the monster. Most probably they were domesticated motiles.

But if so, then the monster race had modified their type even more profoundly than the person race had modified the type of its own tamed motiles down in the lowlands. These bipeds were comically weak in proportion to size; they lacked grinders and liquid-ingestion orifices; they used sonics to a degree that argued their radio abilities were primitive; they required ancillary apparatus; in short, they were not functional by themselves. Only the care and shelter furnished by their masters allowed them to remain long in existence.

But what are the masters? Even the monster may well be only another motile. Certainly it appeared to lack limbs. The masters may be persons like us, come from beyond the sea or the mountains with skills and powers transcending our own.

But then what do they want? Why have they not tried to communicate with us? Have they come to take our land away?

The question was jolting. Zero got hastily into motion. With his rack loaded, he had no room for his prizes. Besides, being crammed into it for hours was doubtless harmful to them; they moved a good deal more strongly now, after a rest, than when he first took them out. He simply left them tied together, cut the wire loose from the stump, and kept that end in one hand. Since he continued to exercise due caution about leaving a trail, he did not move too fast for them to keep up. From time to time they would stagger and lean on each other for support—apparently their energy cells polarized more quickly than his—but he found they could continue if he let them pause a while, lie down, use their curious artifacts.

The day passed. At this time of year, not long past the vernal equinox, the sun was up for about twenty hours. After dark, Zero's captives began stumbling and groping. He confirmed by direct sense perception that they had no radar. If they ever did, that part had been wrecked with their communicators. After some thought, he fashioned a rough seat from a toppled bole and nudged them to sit upon it. Thus he carried them in two hands. They made no attempt to escape, emitted few sounds, obviously they were exhausted. But to his surprise, they began to stir about and radiate sonics when he finally reached home and set them down. He welded the end of their rope to an iron block he kept for emergencies.

Part of him reflected that their mechanism must be very strange indeed, maybe so strange that they would not prove ingestible. Obviously their cells went to such extremes of polarization that they became comatose, which a person only did in emergencies. To them, such deactivation appeared to be normal, and they roused spontaneously.

He dismissed speculation. One's anxious voice had been rushing over him while he worked. "What has happened? You are hurt! Come closer, let me see, oh, your poor arm! Oh, my dear!"

"Nothing serious," he reassured her. "I shot a rotor. Prepare yourself a meal before troubling about me."

He lowered himself to the cave floor beside her great beautiful bulk. The glow globes, cultivated on the rough stone walls, shed luster on her skin and on the graceful tool tendrils that curled forth to embrace him. His chemical sensor brought him a hint of solvents and lubricants, an essence of femaleness. The cave mouth was black with night, save where one star gleamed bright and somehow sinister above the hills. The forest groaned and tolled. But here he had light and her touch upon his body. He was home.

She unshipped the rack from his shoulders but made no motion toward the food-processing cauldron. Most of her tools and all her attention were on his damaged arm. "We must replace everything below the elbow," she decided; and, as a modulation: "Zero, you brave clever adored fool, why did you hazard yourself like that? Do you not understand, even yet, without you my world would be rust?"

"I am sorry . . . to take so much from the new one," he apologized,

"No matter. Feed me some more nice large rotors like this and I will soon replace the loss, and finish all the rest too." Her mirth fluttered toward shyness. "I want the new one activated soon myself, you know, so we can start another."

The memory of that moment last year, when his body pattern flowed in currents and magnetic fields through hers, when the two patterns heterodyned and deep within her the first crystallization took place, glowed in him. Sensory linkage was a wan thing by comparison.

What they did together now had a kindred intimacy. When she had removed the ruined forearm and he had thrust the stump into her repair orifice, a thousand fine interior tendrils enfolded it, scanning, relaying, and controlling. Once again, more subtly than in reproduction, the electro-chemical-mechanical systems of One and Zero unified. The process was not consciously controllable; it was a female function; One was at this moment no different from the most primitive motile joined to her damaged mate in a lightless burrow.

It took time. The new person which her body was creating within itself was, of course, full size and, as it happened, not far from completion. (Had the case been otherwise, Zero would have had to wait until the new one did in fact possess a well-developed arm.) But it was not yet activated; its most delicate and critical synaptic pathways were still only half-finished, gradually crystallizing out of solution. A part could not lightly nor roughly be removed.

But in the end, One's functions performed the task. Slowly, almost reluctantly, Zero withdrew his new hand. His mind and hers remained intertwined a while longer. At last, with a shaky little overtone of humor, she exclaimed, "Well, how do your fingers wiggle? Is everything good? Then let us eat. I am famished!"

Zero helped her prepare the rotor for consumption. They threw the damaged forearm into the cauldron too. While they processed and shared the meal, he recounted his experiences. She had shown no curiosity about the three bipeds. Like most females, she lacked any great interest in the world beyond her home, and had merely assumed they were some new kind of wild motile. As he talked, the happiness died in her. "Oh, no," she said, "you are not going out to fight the lightning breather, are you?"

"Yes, we must." He knew what image terrified her, himself smashed beyond hope of reconstruction, and added in haste: "If we leave it free, no tradition or instinct knows what it may do. But surely, at the very least, so large a thing will cause extensive damage. Even if it is only a grazer, its appetite will destroy untold acres of accumulators; and it may be a predator. On the other hand, if we destroy it, what a hoard of nourishment! Your share and mine will enable us to produce a dozen new persons. The energy will let me range for hundreds of miles, thus gaining still more food and goods for us."

"If the thing can be assimilated," she said doubtfully. "It could be full of hydrofluoric acid or something, like a touch-me-not."

"Yes, yes. For that matter, the flier may be the property of intelligent beings: which does not necessarily mean we will not destroy and consume it. I intend to find out about that aspect right now. If the monster's auxiliaries are ingestible, the monster itself is almost sure to be."

"But if not—Zero, be careful!"

"I will. For your sake also." He stroked her and felt an answering vibration. It would have been pleasant to sit thus all night, but he must soon be on his way to rendezvous. And first he must dissect at least one specimen. He took up his pry bar and approached the three units.

✳V✳

Darkington awoke from a nightmare-ridden half-sleep when he was dumped on the cave floor. He reached for Frederika and she came to him. For a space there was nothing but their murmuring.

Eventually they crouched on the sand and looked about. The giant that captured them had welded the free end of the wire rope to an immovable chunk of raw iron. Darkington was attached at that side, then the girl, and Kuroki on the outer end. They had about four feet of slack from one to the next. Nothing in the kit remaining to them would cut those strands.

"Limestone cave, I guess," Kuroki croaked. Behind the faceplate he was gaunt, bristly, and sunken-eyed. Frederika didn't look much better. They might not have survived the trip here if the robot hadn't carried them the last few hours. Nonetheless an odd, dry clarity possessed Darkington's brain. He could observe and think as well as if he had been safe on shipboard. His body was one enormous ache, but he ignored that and focused on comprehending what had happened.

Here near the entrance, the cave was about twenty feet high and rather more wide. A hundred feet deeper inward, it narrowed and ended. That area was used for storage: a junk shop of mechanical and electronic parts, together with roughly fashioned metal and stone tools that looked almost homelike. The walls were overgrown with thin wires that sprouted scores of small crystalline globes. These gave off a cool white light that made the darkness outside appear the more elemental.

"Yes, a cave in a sheer hillside," said Frederika. "I saw that much. I kept more or less conscious all the way here, trying to keep track of our route. Not that that's likely to do us much good, is it?" She hugged her knees. "I've got to sleep soon—oh, but I have to sleep!"

"We got to get in touch." Kuroki's voice rose. (Thank heaven and some ages-dead engineer that sound mikes and earphones could be switched on by shoving your chin against the right button! With talk cut off, no recourse would have remained but to slip quietly into madness.) "God damn it, I tried to show that tin nightmare we're intelligent. I drew diagrams and—" He checked himself. "Well, probably its builders don't monitor it. We'll have another go when they show up."

"Let's admit the plain facts, Sam," Frederika said tonelessly. "There aren't any builders. There never were any."

"Oh, no." The pilot gave Darkington a beggar's look. "You're the biologist, Hugh. Do you believe that?"

Darkington bit his lip. "I'm afraid she's right."

Frederika's laugh barked at them. "Do you know what that big machine is, there in the middle of the cave? The one the robot is fooling around with? I'll tell you. His wife!" She broke off. Laughter echoed too horribly in their helmets.

Darkington gazed in that direction. The second object had little in common with the biped shape, being low and wide—twice the bulk—and mounted on eight short legs which must lend very little speed or agility. A radio lattice, optical lenses, and arms (two, not four) were similar to the biped's. But numerous additional limbs were long goosenecks terminating in specialized appendages. Sleek blued metal covered most of the body.

And yet, the way those two moved—

"I think you may be right about that also," Darkington said at last.

Kuroki beat the ground with his fist and swore. "Sorry, Freddie," he gulped. "But won't you, for God's sake, explain what you're getting at? This mess wouldn't be so bad if it made some sense."

"We can only guess," Darkington said.

"Well, guess, then!"

"Robot evolution," Frederika said. "After man was gone, the machines that were left began to evolve."

"No," said Kuroki, "that's nuts. Impossible!"

"I think what we've seen would be impossible any other way," Darkington said. "Metallic life couldn't arise spontaneously. Only carbon atoms make the long hookups needed for the chemical storage of biological information. But electronic storage is equally feasible. And . . . before the *Traveler* departed . . . self-reproducing machines were already in existence."

"I think the sea rafts must have been the important ones." Frederika spoke like someone in dream. Her eyes were fixed wide and unblinking on the two robots. "Remember? They were essentially motorized floating boxes, containing metallurgic processing plants and powered by solar batteries. They took dissolved minerals out of sea water, magnesium, uranium, whatever a particular raft was designed for. When it had a full cargo, it went to a point on shore where a depot received its load. Once empty, it returned to open waters for more. It had an inertial navigation device, as well as electronic sensors and various homeostatic systems, so it could cope with the normal vicissitudes of its environment.

"And it had electronic templates which bore full information on its own design. They controlled mechanisms aboard, which made any spare part that might be needed. Those same mechanisms also kept producing and assembling complete duplicate rafts. The first such outfit cost hundreds of millions of dollars to manufacture, let alone the preliminary research and development. But once made, it needed no further investment. Production and expansion didn't cost anyone a cent.

"And after man was gone from Earth . . . all life had vanished . . . the sea rafts were still there, patiently bringing their cargoes to crumbling docks on barren shores, year after year after meaningless year—"

She shook herself. The motion was violent enough to be seen in armor. "Go on, Hugh," she said, her tone turned harsh. "If you can."

"I don't know any details," he began cautiously. "You should tell me how mutation was possible to a machine. But if the templates were actually magnetic recordings on wire or tape, I expect that hard radiation would affect them, as it affects an organic gene. And for a while there was certainly plenty of hard radiation around. The rafts started making imperfect duplicates. Most were badly designed and, uh, foundered. Some, though, had advantages. For instance, they stopped going to shore and hanging about for decades waiting to be unloaded. Eventually some raft was made which had the first primitive ability to get metal from a richer source than the ocean: namely, from other rafts. Through hundreds of millions of years, an ecology developed. We might as well call it an ecology. The land was reconquered. Wholly new *types* of machine proliferated. Until today, well, what we've seen."

"But where's the energy come from?" Kuroki demanded.

"The sun, I suppose. By now, the original solar battery must be immensely refined. I'd make a guess at dielectric storage on the molecular level, in specialized units—call them cells—which may even be of microscopic size. Of course, productivity per acre must be a good deal lower than it was in our day. Alloys aren't as labile as amino acids. But that's offset to a large extent by their greater durability. And, as you can see in this cave, by interchangeability."

"Huh?"

"Sure. Look at those spare parts stacked in the rear. Some will no doubt be processed, analogously to our eating and digesting food. But others are probably being kept for use as such. Suppose you could take whole organs from animals you killed and install them in yourself to replace whatever was wearing out. I rather imagine that's common on today's Earth. The 'black box' principle was designed into most machines in our own century. It would be inherited."

"Where's the metal come from in the first place?"

"From lower types of machine. Ultimately from sessile types that break down ores, manufacture the basic alloys, and concentrate more dielectric energy than they use. Analogous to vegetation. I daresay the, uh, metabolism involves powerful reagents. Sulfuric and nitric acids in glass-lined compartments must be the least of them. I doubt if there are any equivalent of microbes, but the ecology seems to manage quite well without. It's a grosser form of existence than ours. But it works. It works."

"Even sex." Frederika giggled a little crazily.

Darkington squeezed her gauntleted hand until she grew calmer.

"Well," he said, "quite probably in the more complex machines, reproduction has become the specialty of one form while the other specializes in strength and agility. I daresay there are corresponding psychological differences."

"Psychological?" Kuroki bridled. "Wait a minute! I know there is—was—a lot of loose talk about computers being electronic brains and such rot, but—"

"Call the phenomenon what you like," Darkington shrugged. "But that robot uses tools which are made, not grown. The problem is how to convince it that *we* think."

"Can't it see?" Frederika exclaimed. "We use tools too. Sam drew mathematical pictures. What more does it want?"

"I don't know enough about this world to even guess," Darkington said tiredly. "But I suppose . . . well . . . we might once have seen a trained ape doing all sorts of elaborate things, without ever assuming it was more than an ape. No matter how odd it looked."

"Or maybe the robot just doesn't give a damn," Kuroki said. "There were people who wouldn't have."

"If Hugh's guess about the 'black box' is right," Frederika added slowly, "then the robot race must have evolved as hunters, instead of hunting being invented rather late in their evolution. As if men had descended from tigers instead of simians. How much psychological difference would that make?"

No one replied. She leaned forlornly against Darkington. Kuroki turned his eyes from them, perhaps less out of tact than loneliness. His girl was several thousand miles away, straight up, with no means for him to call her and say good-by.

Thurshaw had warned the insistent volunteers for this expedition that there would be no rescue. He had incurred sufficient guilt in letting three people—three percent of the human race—risk themselves. If anything untoward happened, the *Traveler* would linger a while in hopes the boat could somehow return. But in the end the *Traveler* would head for the stars. Kuroki's girl would have to get another father for the boy she might name Sam.

I wish to hell Freddie were up there with her, Darkington thought. *Or do I? Isn't that simply what I'm supposed to wish?*

God! Cut that out. Start planning!

His brain spun like wheels in winter mud. What to do, what to do, what to do? His pistol was gone, so were Kuroki's rockets, nothing remained but a few tools and instruments. At the back of the cave there were probably stored some weapons with which a man could put up a moment's fight. (Only a moment, against iron and lightning; but that would end the present, ultimate horror, of sitting in your own fear-stink until the monster approached or the air-renewal batteries grew exhausted and you strangled.) The noose welded around his waist, ending in a ton of iron, choked off any such dreams. They must communicate, somehow, anyhow, plead, threaten, promise, wheedle. But the monster hadn't cared about the Pythagorean theorem diagrammed in sand. What next, then? How did you say "I am alive" to something that was not alive?

Though what was aliveness? Were proteins inherently and unescapably part of any living creature? If the ancient sea rafts had been nothing except complicated machines, at what point of further complication had their descendants come to life? *Now stop that, you're a biologist, you know perfectly well that any such question is empirically empty, and anyhow it has nothing to do with preserving the continuity of certain protein chemistries which are irrationally much loved.*

"I think it talks by radio." Kuroki's slow voice sounded oddly through the thudding in Darkington's head. "It probably hasn't got any notion that sound waves might carry talk. Maybe it's even deaf. Ears wouldn't be any too useful in that rattletrap jungle. And our own radios are busted." He began to fumble in the girl's pack. "I'm not feeling you up, Freddie. Your spacesuit isn't exactly my type. But I think I could cobble together one working set from the pieces of our three, if I can borrow some small tools and instruments. Once we make systematic noises on its talk band, the robot might get interested in trying to savvy us."

"Sam," she said faintly, "for that idea you can feel me up all you want."

"I'll take a rain check." He could actually chuckle, Darkington heard. "I'm sweaty enough in this damn suit to pass for a rainstorm just by myself."

He began to lay out the job. Darkington, unable to help, ashamed that he had not thought of anything, turned attention back to the robots. They were coupled together, ignoring him.

Frederika dozed off. How slowly the night went. But Earth was old, rotating as wearily as . . . as himself. . . . He slept.

A gasp awoke him.

The monster stood above them. Tall, tall, higher than the sky, it bestrode their awareness and looked down with blank eyes upon Kuroki's pitiful, barely begun work. One hand was still a torch and another hand had been replaced; it was invulnerable and soulless as a god. For an instant Darkington's half-aroused self groveled before it.

Then the torch spat, slashed the wire rope across, and Kuroki was pulled free.

Frederika cried out. "Sam!"

"Not . . . so eager . . . pal," the pilot choked in the robot's arms. "I'm glad you like me, but . . . ugh . . . careful!"

With a free hand, the robot twisted experimentally at Kuroki's left leg. The suit joints turned, Kuroki shrieked. Darkington thought he heard the leg bones leave their sockets.

"No! You filthy machine!" He plunged forward. The rope stopped him cold. Frederika covered her faceplate and begged Kuroki to be dead.

He wasn't, yet. He wasn't even unconscious. He kept on screaming as the robot used a prying tool to drag the leg off his armor. Leakseal compound flowed from between the fabric layers and preserved the air in the rest of his suit.

The robot dropped him and sprang back, frantically fanning itself. A whiff of oxygen, Darkington realized amidst the red and black disintegration of his sanity. Oxygen was nearly as reactive as fluorine, and there had been no free oxygen on Earth since— Kuroki's agony jerked toward silence.

The robot reapproached with care, squatted above him, poked at the exposed flesh, tore loose a chunk for examination and flung it aside. The metal off a joint seemed better approved.

Darkington realized vaguely that Frederika lay on the ground close to Kuroki and wept. The biologist himself was even nearer. He could have touched the robot as well as the body. Instead, though, he retreated, mumbling and mewing.

The robot had clearly learned a lesson from the gas, but was just as clearly determined to go on with the investigation. It stood up, moved a cautious distance away, and jetted a thin, intensely blue flame from its torch hand. Kuroki's corpse was divided across the middle.

Darkington's universe roared and exploded. He lunged again. The rope between him and Frederika was pulled across the firebeam. The strands parted like smoke.

The robot pounced at him, ran into the oxygen gushing from Kuroki's armor, and lurched back. Darkington grabbed the section of rope that joined him to the block. The torch was too bright to look at. If he touched its flame, that was the end of him too. But there was no chance to think about such matters. Blindly and animally, he pulled his leash across the cutting jet.

He was free.

"Get out, Freddie!" he coughed, and ran straight toward the robot. No use trying to run from a thing that could overtake him in three strides. The torch had stopped spitting fire, but the giant moved in a wobbly, uncertain fashion, still dazed by the oxygen. By pain? Savagely, in the last spark of awareness, Darkington hoped so. "*Get out, Freddie!*"

The robot staggered in pursuit of him. He dodged around the other machine, the big one that they had called female. To the back of the cave. A weapon to fight with, gaining a moment where Frederika might escape. An extra pry bar lay on the floor. He snatched it and whirled. The huge painted shape was almost upon him.

He dodged. Hands clashed together just above his helmet. He pelted back to the middle of the cave. The female machine was edging into a corner. But slow, awkward—

Darkington scrambled on top of it.

An arm reached from below to pluck him off. He snarled and struck with the pry bar. The noise rang in the cave. The arm sagged, dented. This octopod had nothing like the biped's strength. Its tool tendrils, even more frail, curled away from him.

The male robot loomed close. Darkington smashed his weapon down on the radio lattice at his feet. It crumpled. He brandished the bar and howled senselessly, "Stand back, there! One step more and I'll give her the works! I'll kill her!"

The robot stopped. Monstrous it bulked, an engine that could tear apart a man and his armor, and raised its torch hand.

"Oh, no," Darkington rasped. He opened a bleeder valve on his suit, kneeling so the oxygen would flow across the front end of the thing on which he rode. Sensors ought to be more vulnerable than skin. He couldn't hear if the she-robot screamed as Kuroki had done. That would be on the radio band. But when he gestured the male back, it obeyed.

"Get the idea?" he panted, not as communication but as hatred. "You can split my suit open with your flame gun, but my air will pour all over this contraption here. Maybe you could knock me off her by throwing something, but at the first sign of any such move on your part, I'll open my bleeder valve again. She'll at least get a heavy dose of oxy. And meanwhile I'll punch the sharp end of this rod through one of those lenses. Understand? Well, then, stay where you are, machine!"

The robot froze.

Frederika came near. She had slipped the loop of cable joining her to Kuroki off what was left of his torso. The light shimmered on her faceplate so Darkington couldn't see through, and her voice was strained out of recognition. "Hugh, oh, Hugh!"

"Head back to the boat," he ordered. Rationality was returning to him.

"Without you? No."

"Listen, this is not the place for grandstand heroics. Your first duty is to become a mother. But what I hope for, personally, is that you can return in the boat and fetch me. You're no pilot, but they can instruct you by radio from the ship if she's above the horizon. The general director does most of the work in any event. You land here, and I can probably negotiate a retreat for myself."

"But—but—the robot needed something like twenty hours to bring us here. And it knew the way better than I do. I'll have to go by compass and guess, mostly. Of course, I won't stop as often as it did. No more than I have to. But still—say twenty hours for me—you can't hold out that long!"

"I can damn well try," he said. "You got any better ideas?"

"All right, then. Good-by, Hugh. No, I mean so long. I love you."

He grunted some kind of answer, but didn't see her go. He had to keep watching the robot.

✳ VI ✳

"Zero!" his female called, just once, when the unit sprang upon her back. She clawed at it. The pry bar smashed across her arm. He felt the pain-surge within her sensors, broadcast through her communicator, like a crossbow bolt in his body.

Wildly, he charged. The enemy unit crashed the bar down on One's lattice. She shrilled in anguish. Affected by the damage that crippled her radar, her communicator tone grew suddenly, hideously different. Zero slammed himself to a halt.

Her sobbing, his own name blindly repeated, overwhelmed the burning in him where the corrosive gas had flowed. He focused his torch to narrow beam and took careful aim.

The unit knelt, fumbling with its free hand. One screamed again, louder. Her tendrils flailed about. Numbly, Zero let his torch arm droop. The unit rose and poised its weapon above her lenses. A single strong thrust downward through the glass could reach her brain. The unit gestured him back. He obeyed.

"Help," One cried. Zero could not look at the wreckage of her face. There was no escaping her distorted voice. "Help, Zero. It hurts so much."

"Hold fast," he called in his uselessness. "I cannot do anything. Not now. The thing is full of poison. That is what you received." He managed to examine his own interior perceptions. "The pain will abate in a minute . . . from such a small amount. But if you got a large dose—I do not know. It might prove totally destructive. Or the biped might do ultimate mechanical damage before I could prevent it. Hold fast, One mine. Until I think of something."

"I am afraid," she rattled. "For the new one."

"Hold fast," he implored. "If that unit does you any further harm, I will destroy it slowly. I expect it realizes as much."

The other functional biped came near. It exchanged a few ululations with the first, turned and went quickly from the cave. "It must be going back to the flying monster," said One. The words dragged from her, now and then she whimpered as her perceptions of damage intensified, but she could reason again. "Will it bring the monster here?"

"I cannot give chase," said Zero unnecessarily. "But—" He gathered his energy. A shout blasted from his communicator. "*Alarm, alarm! All persons receiving, prepare to relay. Alarm!*"

Voices flashed in his head, near and far, and it was as if they poured strength into him. He and One were not alone in a night cave, a scuttling horror on her back and the taste of poison only slowly fading. Their whole community was here.

He reported the situation in a few phrases. "You have been rash," Hundred said, shaken. "May there be no further penalties for your actions."

"What else would you have had him do?" defended Seven. "We cannot deal randomly with a thing as powerful as the monster. Zero took upon himself the hazards of gathering information. Which he has succeeded in, too."

"Proving the danger is greater than we imagined," shuddered Sixteen.

"Well, that is a valuable datum."

"The problem now is, what shall we do?" Hundred interrupted. "Slow though you say it is, I expect the auxiliary that escaped can find the monster long before we can rendezvous and get up into the hills."

"Until it does, though, it cannot communicate, its radio being disabled," Zero said. "So the monster will presumably remain where it is, ignorant of events. I suggest that those persons who are anywhere near this neighborhood strike out directly toward that area. They can try to head off the biped."

"You can certainly capture it in a few minutes," Hundred said.

"I cannot leave this place."

"Yes, you can. The thing that has seized your female will not logically do anything more to her, unprovoked, lest she lose her present hostage value."

"How do you know?" Zero retorted. "In fact, I believe if I captured its companion, this unit would immediately attack One. What hope does it have except in the escape of the other, that may bring rescue?"

"Hope is a curious word to use in connection with an elaborated spy eye," Seven said.

"If it is," Zero said. "Their actions suggest to me that these bipeds are more than unthinking domesticated motiles."

"Let be!" Hundred said. "There is scant time to waste. We may not risk the entire community for the sake of a single member. Zero, go fetch back that biped."

Unmodulated radio buzzed in the night. Finally Zero said, "No." One's undamaged hand reached toward him, but she was too far away for them to touch each other. Nor could she caress him with radar.

"We will soon have you whole again," he murmured to her. She did not answer, with the community listening.

Hundred surrendered, having existed long enough to recognize unbendable negation. "Those who are sufficiently near the monster to reach it before dawn, report," he directed. When they had finished—about thirty all told—he said, "Very well, proceed there. Wherever feasible, direct your course to intercept the probable path of the escaped unit. If you capture it, inform us at once. The rest of us will rendezvous as planned."

One by one the voices died out in the night, until only Hundred, who was responsible, and Seven, who was a friend, were in contact with Zero. "How are you now, One?" Seven asked gently.

"I function somewhat," she said in a tired, uneven tone. "It is strange to be radar blind. I keep thinking that heavy objects are about to crash into me. When I turn my optics that way, there isn't anything." She paused. "The new one stirred a little bit just now. A motor impulse pathway must have been completed. Be careful, Zero," she begged. "We have already taken an arm tonight."

"I cannot understand your description of the bipeds' interior," Hundred said practically. "Soft, porous material soaked in sticky red liquid; acrid vapors—How do they *work*? Where is the mechanism?"

"They are perhaps not functional at all," Seven proposed. "They may be purely artificial devices, powered by chemical action."

"Yet they act intelligently," Zero argued. "If the monster—or the monster's masters—do not have them under direct control—and certainly there is no radio involved—"

"There may be other means than radio to monitor an auxiliary," Seven said. "We know so little, we persons."

"In that case," Zero answered, "the monster has known about this cave all the time. It is watching me at this moment, through the optics of that thing on One's back."

"We must assume otherwise," Hundred said.

"I do," Zero said. "I act in the belief that these bipeds are out of contact with the flier. But if nevertheless they perform as they have been doing, then they certainly have independent function, including at least a degree of intelligence." A thought crashed through him, so stunning that he could not declare it at once. Finally: "They may be the monster's masters! It may be the auxiliary, they the persons!"

"No, no, that is impossible," Hundred groaned. Seven's temporary acceptance was quicker; he had always been able to leap from side to side of a discussion. He flashed:

"Let us assume that in some unheard-of fashion, these small entities are indeed the domesticators, or even the builders, of that flying thing. Can we negotiate with them?"

"Not after what has happened," Zero said bleakly. He was thinking less about what he had done to them than what they had done to One.

Seven continued: "I doubt it myself, on philosophical grounds. They are too alien. Their very functioning is deadly: the destruction wrought by their flier, the poison under their skins. Eventually, a degree of mutual comprehension may be achieved. But that will be a slow and painful process. Our first responsibility is to our own form of existence. Therefore we must unmistakably get the upper hand, before we even try to talk with them." In quick excitement, he added, "And I think we can."

Zero and Hundred meshed their intellects with his. The scheme grew like precipitation in a supersaturated pond. Slow and feeble, the strangers were only formidable by virtue of highly developed artifacts (or, possibly, domesticated motiles of radically modified type): the flier, the tube which had blown off Zero's arm, and other hypothetical weapons. But armament unused is no threat. If the flier could be immobilized—

Of course, presumably there were other dwarf bipeds inside it. Their voices had been heard yesterday. But Zero's trip here had proven that they lacked adequate nighttime senses. Well, grant them radar when in an undamaged condition. Radar can be confused, if one knows how.

Hundred's orders sprang forth across miles to the mountaineers now converging on the flier: "Cut the heaviest accumulator strands you can find in the forest. Twist them into cables. Under cover of darkness, radar window, and distraction objects, surround the monster. We believe now that it may not be sentient, only a flier. Weld your cables fast to deeply founded boles. Then, swiftly, loop them around the base of the flier. Tie it down!"

"No," said Twenty-nine, aghast. "We cannot weld the cables to its skin. It would annihilate us with one jetblast. We would have to make nooses first and—"

"So make the nooses," Zero said. "The monster is not a perfectly tapered spindle. The jets bulge out at the base. Slip the nooses around the body just above the jets. I hardly think it can rise then, without tearing its own tubes out."

"Easy for you to say, Zero, safe in your cave."

"If you knew what I would give to have matters otherwise—"

Abashed, the hunters yielded. Their mission was not really so dangerous. The nooses—two should be ample if the cable was heavy—could be laid in a broad circle around the area which the jets had flattened and devastated. They could be drawn tight from afar, and would probably slip upward by themselves, coming to rest just above the tubes, where the body of the flier was narrowest. If a cable did get stuck on something, someone would have to dash close and free it. A snort of jetfire during those few seconds would destroy him. But quite probably the flier, or its masters, could be kept from noticing him.

"And when we do have the monster leashed, what then?" asked Twenty-nine.

"We will do what seems indicated," Hundred said. "If the aliens do not seem to be reaching a satisfactory understanding with us—if we begin to entertain any doubts—we can erect trebuchets and batter the flier to pieces."

"That might be best," said Zero, with a revengeful look at One's rider.

"Proceed as ordered," said Hundred.

"But what about us?" Zero asked. "One and myself?"

"I shall come to you," Seven said. "If nothing else, we can stand watch and watch. You mentioned that the aliens polarize more easily than we do. We can wait until it drops from exhaustion."

"Good," said Zero. Hope lifted in him as if breaking through a shell. "Did you hear, One? We need only wait."

"Pain," she whispered. Then, resolutely: "I can minimize energy consumption. Comatose, I will not sense anything. . . ." He felt how she fought down terror, and guessed what frightened her: the idea that she might never be roused.

"I will be guarding you all the time," he said. "You and the new one."

"I wish I could touch you, Zero—" Her radiation dimmed, second by second. Once or twice consciousness returned, kicked upward by fear; static gasped in Zero's perception; but she slipped again into blackness.

When she was quite inert, he stood staring at the unit on her. No, the entity. Somewhere behind that glass and horrible tissue, a brain peered back at him. He ventured to move an arm. The thing jerked its weapon aloft. It seemed indeed to have guessed that the optics were her most vulnerable spot. With immense care, Zero let his arm fall again. The entity jittered about, incapable of his own repose. Good. Let it drain its energy the faster.

He settled into his own thoughts. Hours wore away. The alien paced on One's broad back, sat down, sprang up again, slapped first one hand and then another against its body, made long noises that might possibly be intended to fight off coma. Sometimes it plugged the water tube into its face. Frequently Zero saw what looked like a good chance to catch it off guard—with a sudden rush and a flailing blow, or an object snatched off the floor and thrown, or even a snap shot with his torch—but he decided not to take the hazard. Time was his ally.

Besides, now that his initial rage had abated, he began to hope he might capture the entity undamaged. Much more could be learned from a functional specimen than from the thing which lay dismembered near the iron block. Faugh, the gases it was giving off! Zero's chemical sensor retracted in disgust.

The first dawnlight grayed the cave mouth.

"We have the flier!" Twenty-nine's exuberant word made Zero leap where he stood. The alien scrambled into motion. When Zero came no closer, it sagged again. "We drew two cables around its body. No trouble whatsoever. It never stirred. Only made the same radio hum. It still has not moved."

"I thought—" someone else in his party ventured. "Not long ago . . . was there not a gibberish signal from above?"

"There might well be other fliers above the clouds," agreed Hundred from the valley. "Have a care. Disperse yourselves. Remain under cover. The rest of us will have rendezvoused by early afternoon. At that time we will confer afresh. Meanwhile, report if anything happens. And . . . good work, hunters."

Twenty-nine offered a brief sensory linkage. Thus Zero saw the place: the cindered blast area, and the upright spindle shining in the first long sunlight, and the cables that ran from its waist to a pair of old and mighty accumulator boles. Yes, the thing was captured for certain. Wind blew over the snowpeaks, set forest to chiming and scattered the little sunrise clouds. He had rarely known his land so beautiful.

The perception faded. He was in his cave again. Seven called: "I am getting close now, Zero. Shall I enter?"

"No, best not. You might alarm the alien into violence. I have watched its movements the whole night. They grow more slow and irregular each hour. It must be near collapse. Suppose you wait just outside. When I believe it to be comatose, I will have you enter. If it does not react to the sight of you, we will know it has lost consciousness."

"If it is conscious," mused Seven. "Despite our previous discussion, I cannot bring myself to believe quite seriously that these are anything but motiles or artifacts. Very ingenious and complex, to be sure . . . but *aware*, like a person?"

The unit made a long series of sonic noises. They were much weaker than hitherto. Zero allowed satisfaction to wax in him. Nevertheless, he would not have experienced this past night again for any profit.

Several hours later, a general alarm yanked his attention back outward. "The escaped auxiliary has returned! It has entered the flier!"

"What? You did not stop it?" Hundred demanded.

Twenty-nine gave the full report. "Naturally, after the change of plan, we were too busy weaving cables and otherwise preparing ourselves to beat the forest for the dwarf. After the flier was captured, we dispersed ourselves broadly as ordered. We made nothing like a tight circle around the blasted region. Moreover, our attention was directed at the flier, in case it tried to escape, and at the sky in case there should be more fliers. Various wild motiles were about, which we ignored, and the wind has gotten very loud in the accumulators.

Under such circumstances, you will realize that probability actually favored the biped unit passing between us and reaching the open area unobserved.

"When it was first noticed, no person was close enough to reach the flier before it did. It slid a plate aside in one of the jacks which support the flier and pulled a switch. A portal opened in the body above and a ladder was extruded. By that time, a number of us had entered the clearing. The unit scrambled up the ladder. We hesitated, fearing a jetblast. None came. But how could we have predicted that? When at last we did approach, the ladder had been retracted and the portal was closed. I pulled the switch myself but nothing happened. I suppose the biped, once inside, deactivated that control by means of a master switch."

"Well, at least we know where it is," Hundred said. "Disperse again, if you have not already done so. The biped may try to escape, and you do not want to get caught in the jetblast. Are you certain the flier cannot break your cables?"

"Quite certain. Closely observed, the monster—the flier seems to have only a thin skin of light alloy. Nor would I expect it to be strong against the unnatural kind of stresses imposed by our tethers. If it tries to rise, it will pull itself in two."

"Unless," said Fourteen, as he hastened through valley mists toward Broken Glade, "some biped emerges with a torch and cuts the cables."

"Just let it dare!" said Twenty-nine, anxious to redeem his crew's failure.

"It may bring strong weapons," Zero warned.

"Ten crossbows are cocked and aimed at that portal. If a biped shows itself, we will fill it with whetted steel."

"I think that will suffice," Zero said. He looked at the drooping shape upon One. "They are not very powerful, these things. Ugly, cunning, but weak."

Almost as if it knew it was being talked about, the unit reeled to its feet and shook the pry bar at him. Even Zero could detect the dullness in its noises. *Another hour,* he thought, *and One will be free.*

Half that time had gone by when Seven remarked from outside, "I wonder why the builders . . . whoever the ultimate intelligences are behind these manifestations . . . why have they come?"

"Since they made no attempt to communicate with us," Zero said in renewed grimness, "we must assume their purpose is hostile."

"And?"

"Teach them to beware of us."

He felt already the pride of victory. But then the monster spoke.

Up over the mountains rolled the voice, driven by the power which hurled those hundreds of tons through the sky. Roaring and raging through the radio spectrum, louder than lightning, enormous enough to shake down moon and stars, blasted that shout. Twenty-nine and his hunters yelled as the volume smote their receptors. Their cry was lost, drowned, engulfed by the tide which seethed off the mountainsides. Here and there, where some accumulator happened to resonate, blue arcs of flame danced in the forest. Thirty miles distant, Zero and Seven still perceived the noise as a clamor in their heads. Hundred and his followers in the valley stared uneasily toward the ranges. On the seashore, females called, "What is that? What is that?" and aquamotiles dashed themselves about in the surf.

Seven forgot all caution. He ran into the cave. The enemy thing hardly moved. But neither Zero nor Seven observed that. Both returned to the entrance and gazed outward with terror.

The sky was empty. The forest rang in the breeze. Only that radio roar from beyond the horizon told of anything amiss. "I did not believe—" stammered Seven. "I did not expect—a tone that loud—"

Zero, who had One to think about, mustered decisiveness. "It is not hurting us," he said. "I am glad not to be as close as the hunters are, but even they should be able to endure it for a while. We shall see. Come, let us two go back inside. Once we have secured our prisoner—"

The monster began to talk.

No mere outrageous cry this time, but speech. Not words, except occasionally. A few images. But such occurrences were coincidental. The monster spoke in its own language, which was madness.

Seized along every radio receptor channel there was in him, total sensory and mental linkage, Zero became the monster.

DITditditdit DAH dit-nulnulnulnul-ditditDAHdah & the vector sum: infinitesimals infinitelyadded from nul-to-INFINITY, dit—dit-dit-DAH-ditditditnul (gammacolored chaos, *bang* goes a universe scattering stars&planets&bursts-of-fire BLOCK THAT NEUTRON BLOCK THAT NEUTRON BLOCK THAT NEUTRON BLOCK THAT BLOCK THAT BLOCK THAT NEUTRON NEUTRON) oneone***nononul—DATTA—ditditchitterchitterchitter burning suns & moons, burning stars & brains, burn ingburningburning. Burning DahditDahditDahdit give mefifty million logarithms this very microsecond or you will Burn ditditditdit—DAYAD-HVAM—DAMYATA

and one long wild logarithmic spiral down spacetime energy continuum of potentialgradient Xproduct i,j,k but multiply Time by the velocity of light in nothingness and the square root of minus one (two, three, four, five, six CHANGE for duodecimal computation zzzzzzzzzzz)

integral over sigma of del cross H d sigma equals one over c times integral over sigma partial of E with respect to t dot d sigma but correct for nonsphericalshapentropicoordinatetransformation top&quantumelectrodynamichargelectricalephaselagradientemper ature rising to burning Burning BURNING

dit-dit-chitterchitterchitter from eyrie to blind gnawer and back again O help the trunk is burningburningburning THEREFORE ANNUL in the name of the seven thunders

Everything-that-has-been, break up the roots of existence and strike flat the thick rotundity o' the world RRRIP space-time across and throw it on the upleaping primordial energy for now all that was & will be, the very fact that it once *did* exist, is canceled and torn to pieces and

Burning

Burning

Burning

Burning

AND the bindng energy of a lambda hyperon by a sigma—minus exploding

As the sun fell down the bowl of sky, and the sky cracked open, and the mountains ran like rivers forming faces that gaped and jeered, and the moon rose in the west and spat the grisliness of what he had done at him, Zero ran. Seven did not; could not; lay by the cave entrance, which was the gate of all horrors and corruptions, as if turned to salt. And when God descended, still shouting in His tongue which was madness, His fiery tail melted Seven to a pool.

Fifty million years later the star called Wormwood ascended to heaven; and a great silence fell upon the land.

Eventually Zero returned home. He was not surprised to find that the biped was gone. Of course it had been reclaimed by its Master. But when he saw that One was not touched, he stood mute for a long while indeed.

After he roused her, she—who had been unawake when the world was broken and refashioned—could not understand why he led her outside to pray that they be granted mercy, now and in the hour of their dissolution.

✷ VII ✷

Darkington did not regain full consciousness until the boat was in space. Then he pulled himself into the seat beside Frederika. "How did you do it?" he breathed.

Her attention remained focused on piloting. Even with the help of the director and radio instructions from the ship, it was no easy task for a novice. Absently, she answered, "I scared the robots away. They'd made the boat fast, you see. With cables too thick to pull apart. I had to go back out and cut them with a torch. But I'd barely gotten inside ahead of the pack. I didn't expect they would let me emerge. So I scared them off. After that, I went out, burned off the cables, and flew to get you."

"Barely in time," he shuddered. "I was about to pass out. I did keel over once I was aboard." A time went by with only the soft rushing noise of brake jets. "Okay," he said, "I give up. I admit you're beautiful, a marvel of resourcefulness, and I can't guess how you shooed away the enemy. So tell me."

The director shut off the engine. They floated free. She turned her face, haggard, sweaty, begrimed, and dear, toward him and said diffidently, "I didn't have any inspiration. Just a guess and nothing to lose. We knew for pretty sure that the robots communicated by radio. I turned the boat's 'caster on full blast, hoping the sheer volume would be too much for them. Then something else occurred to me. If you have a radio transceiver in your head, hooked directly into your nervous system, wouldn't that be sort of like telepathy? I mean, it seems more direct somehow than routing everything we say through a larynx. Maybe I could confuse them by emitting unfamiliar signals. Not any old signals, of course. They'd be used to natural radio noise. But—well—the boat's general director includes a pretty complicated computer, carrying out millions of operations per second. Information is conveyed, not noise; but at the same time, it didn't seem to me like information that a bunch of semisavages could handle.

"Anyhow, there was no harm in trying. I hooked the broadcaster in parallel with the effector circuits, so the computer's output not only controlled the boat as usual but also modulated the radio emission. Then I assigned the computer a good tough problem in celestial navigation, put my armor back on, summoned every ounce of nerve I had, and went outside. Nothing happened. I cut the cables without seeing any trace of the robots. I kept the computer 'talking' while I jockeyed the boat over in search of the cave. It must have been working frantically to compensate for my clumsiness; I hate to imagine what its output 'sounded' like. Felt like? Well, when I'd landed, I opened the airlock and, and you came inside, and—" Her fists doubled. "Oh, God, Hugh! How can we tell Sam's girl?"

He didn't answer.

With a final soft impulse, the boat nudged against the ship. As grapnels made fast, the altered spin of the vessels put Earth back in view. Darkington looked at the planet for minutes before he said:

"Good-by. Good luck."

Frederika wiped her eyes with hands that left streaks of dirt in the tears. "Do you think we'll ever come back?" she wondered.

"No," he said. "It isn't ours any more."